Saving Madeline

Saving Madeline

A Novel by

RACHEL ANN NUNES

SHADOW
MOUNTAIN

This is a work of fiction. Characters and events in this book are products of the author's imagination or are represented fictitiously.

Visit us at ShadowMountain.com

Library of Congress Cataloging-in-Publication Data
Nunes, Rachel Ann, 1966–
    Saving Madeline / Rachel Ann Nunes.
        p.   cm.
    Summary: Public defender Caitlin McLoughlin must defend a father who has kidnapped his daughter Madeline in order to keep her from his drug-addicted ex-wife.
    ISBN 978-1-60641-049-3 (paperbound)
    1. Public defenders—Fiction.   2. Parental kidnapping—Fiction.   I. Title.
PS3564.U468S28 2009
813'.6—dc22
                                                                          2009026230

Printed in the United States of America
Edwards Brothers Incorporated, Ann Arbor, MI

10   9   8   7   6   5   4   3   2   1

For Madeline Evans and her wonderful parents, David and Sharilyn. You have always been an example to me, and I loved the years we spent as your next-door neighbors!

And to the many young children in the world who don't have anyone to fight for them. I hope this book can be your voice.

Acknowledgments

Thank you to all the great people at Shadow Mountain for their work on this novel. They always do such a fabulous job.

Thanks also to JoAnn Jolley for her kind and thorough editing. It was fun working again with the editor who championed my very first book.

CHAPTER

1

C aitlin McLoughlin's client was guilty. In a vicious and premeditated attack, Chet Belstead had pushed his former girlfriend down in the new grass of April and raped her. There were five deep stab wounds, with jagged lines connecting them across the woman's back like a contorted dot-to-dot picture. It was a miracle she'd survived.

He had worn a mask, and unfortunately there was little physical evidence to connect him with the crime. Nothing except the lack of an alibi and the fact that he'd threatened her with violence after she began dating another man. That he'd been seen loitering near the grocery store where she worked on the night of the attack wasn't exactly solid proof.

Enough evidence for a trial but never for a conviction. Caitlin had known Belstead would walk away free—until she had made sure he wouldn't.

"We've tested the knife found in a trash can at an abandoned house two blocks north of the defendant's apartment," announced deputy district attorney Mace Keeley, speaking for the prosecuting team. "The knife has traces of the victim's blood." Mace paused dramatically as he always did before going in for the kill, a flair Caitlin both hated and admired. That he was drop-dead gorgeous didn't help matters—at least for her client. "The knife also contains two of the defendant's fingerprints."

Caitlin didn't meet her client's gaze as the state prosecutor's words hung heavily in the courthouse. After the first shock of silence, murmurs burst like a wave from the spectators. The faces of the victim's family showed terrible triumph. Caitlin kept her own face stoic, not feigning surprise, as some might have done in her position.

Months ago Caitlin had hoped Belstead was innocent. It happened now and again, in her work as a legal defender, that her client was wrongly accused or simply in the wrong place at the wrong time. But those cases were few and far between these days, or at least they were assigned to attorneys who weren't as experienced or as good as Caitlin. She almost always got the dirty ones.

In this case she had known her client was guilty from the moment she'd walked into the room at the jail where they'd met for the first time. He'd been far too slow to bring his hazel eyes to meet hers, his lazy, annoyingly confident smile covering his plain face. She understood at once that underneath his apparent normalcy was a monster that existed only for himself.

She'd started their business immediately, willing her cheeks not to flush with annoyance. Her pale, freckled skin she'd acquired from her Irish father, along with her copper-colored hair, but from her English mother she'd inherited a stiff backbone and the famous English aplomb that served her well as a defense attorney.

At first Belstead had faked innocence. They all did. But she wasn't fooled. He was easier than most to figure out. She'd once made the mistake of taking off her jacket in his presence, when the heat of the holding cell had been unbearable. Though her thick blouse was more than modest, his stare made her feel dirty. That was when he'd mentioned the knife, wrapped in his thin jacket and thrown away in an unused trash can. Perhaps he'd thought the danger the knife represented would make him seem more attractive.

After another few days of subtle prodding, she learned the route he'd taken home from the park that night, and that information allowed her to determine the most obvious place he might have deposited the knife. He'd believed she would never manage to connect the bits of information he'd given her—and even if she did, so what? She was bound by ethics as his legal counsel to keep her mouth shut and let him go free. In his mind there was no possible way he could be convicted.

That's where he'd been wrong. A simple anonymous phone call to the police hadn't been all that hard to instigate.

Beneath her outward calm, Caitlin allowed herself to feel the slightest bit of satisfaction.

"In light of this new evidence," Judge Harper said, inclining his gray head, "I'm going to give the defense time to consider options before we continue on . . ." He paused and consulted briefly with his clerk. "Apparently both the prosecutor and the defense are scheduled for a separate trial tomorrow, so we'll continue the next day—Friday—as originally scheduled. But I want any new motions, if any, on my desk by close tomorrow. I'm also granting the prosecutor's request to revoke bail. Defendant is remanded to custody. Court is now adjourned."

Caitlin stood with the others as the judge rose and left the room. She could tell by the rigid lines of the judge's weathered face that Belstead was as good as on his way to prison. *Chalk one up for the good guys.*

Yet as much as Belstead deserved to rot in prison for the full length of time the crime required, her training now demanded that she try to arrange a plea deal for him. Hopefully he'd be too stubborn to accept, or the prosecutors too sure of their evidence to offer anything worthwhile.

Belstead leapt to his feet, pushing close to her, ignoring the bailiff who stood ready to escort him to a cell. "I thought you said I was getting off!" he growled, his hazel eyes level with hers. "You said they didn't have enough proof!"

Caitlin faced him, taking in the desperate, wild look that no longer matched the closely cropped sandy hair and shaved face. He was pleasant-looking in an ordinary way, but there was nothing to set him apart from dozens of other ordinary middle-aged men. Except perhaps his clothes. These had obviously been chosen with great care, as though he was trying to impress someone. Women, most likely. Girls. A wolf in sheep's clothing.

"It seems," Caitlin said deliberately, "this new information changes things. Don't get upset. I'll look at the evidence and how they got it and see what we can do." Normally she hated it when the prosecutors managed to sneak in something like this at the end of a trial, but today she felt only triumph.

"How they got it? *How they got it?*" Belstead's voice rose to a scream. "You know how they got it!" Abruptly his voice became a deadly whisper. "You told him! You must have. No one else knew." He swore viciously, making a move toward her. The bailiff grabbed his arms and pulled him back.

"You're not helping your case." Caitlin made her voice icy hard. "Word of this tantrum will get back to the judge. Now calm down! Obviously, someone was rooting through the trash and found this so-called evidence. Or there was a witness who led them to it. I'll find out and see what we can do to negate the effects."

Her words had the desired calming effect, and his narrow shoulders slumped. "See that you do," he muttered. "Or else."

"Or else what?" She lifted her chin as she met his gaze.

"Nothin'." His eyes were full of hatred as the bailiff took him from the room. The threat was probably just talk, but she was glad she would be able to sleep that night, knowing there was no chance he would be anywhere near her house. That was a relief after the past few months of such close contact. She suspected he'd want another attorney, but unfortunately for her he didn't have the money to hire one on his own. Working full time at a local hamburger joint didn't exactly add up to high-class attorney wages, and any cash that hadn't been eaten by his rent had probably gone toward clothing. She could, of course, recuse herself from the case, but that would be giving in to her fear.

Caitlin swallowed with difficulty and closed her burning eyes.

"So, your client's guilty," said a voice beside her.

Caitlin opened her eyes to see Mace Keeley approaching, followed by several of his coworkers. "Big surprise," she muttered, her stomach tightening as it always did in the presence of the deputy district attorney.

He laughed. "Public defending is the worst, isn't it?" Though in his late thirties, he was a posterchild for a surfer—blond hair, blue eyes, and a build that made women drool. Most women, anyway, though Caitlin tried not to be one of them. The aloof manner she strove for at work protected her most days, but sometimes a little scene of the two of them alone on a beach somewhere stole into her daydreams.

"Well, there is a good side to your losing," said Wyman Russell, the deputy DA originally assigned to prosecute the case.

"And what's that?" Caitlin forced herself to respond politely to the shorter man. Though he was reasonably handsome and his voice pleasant, she didn't like Wyman. Not because of his thinning brown hair and flabby body or even because two years ago he'd been chosen for the job that should have been hers but because of the calculating way he looked at her. The feeling had been bad enough when he and his wife were living together, but now that they were separated he seemed to find altogether too many opportunities to unnerve Caitlin. Either he had the hots for her, was jealous of her success, or was just particularly weird. She was leaning toward the latter.

Wyman grinned. "Chet Belstead is going to jail for a long time. That's worth any loss."

He won't be going away for long enough, Caitlin thought as the two men chuckled.

The truth was that Wyman Russell had simply been lucky. He was a terrible prosecutor, and in the past she'd defended against him successfully in several cases he should have won— cases she'd hoped he'd win, given her clients' obvious guilt. Perhaps that was why Mace had been called in to help with this case, to be sure Wyman didn't mess up again. The family of the victim was working the media hard, and a loss by the DA's office would not be taken lightly. Mace or no Mace, she would have won—if she hadn't helped things along.

"It's not over yet," she forced herself to say. Mechanically, she began picking up her papers and storing them in her brown leather briefcase, too aware of Mace and the fact that he was still watching her. Her nerves tingled.

Wyman stepped around Mace, coming uncomfortably close. "You still think you're going to get him off? How? His fingerprints were found on the weapon, and the victim is ready to swear it was his voice she heard in the park that night. They dated for six months. She should know."

The arrogance in his voice stung her into replying. "I'm sorry, but I cannot discuss my client with anyone, especially with you. You'd better get back to examining the knife and the jacket and hope you have enough evidence to convince him to cut a deal."

Mace laughed. "She has a point, Wyman. I for one am interested to see what she comes up with." He smiled at Caitlin and she grinned, swaying toward him slightly before she pulled herself back. Apparently it had been far too long since she'd been in a relationship with a man as attractive as Mace. Or any man for that matter. "See you later, Caitlin," he said with another smile.

She watched him walk away for several long seconds before she realized Wyman hadn't followed him. "How did you know there was a jacket with the knife?" he asked.

Caitlin froze. Hadn't Mace mentioned it during the trial? She went over the scene in her mind. No, he hadn't. They must have been withholding the information, hoping to find the source of the anonymous phone call. Anonymous was nowhere near as good as a live witness.

"He told you, didn't he? That idiot told you what he did!" A sort of mad glee lit Wyman's eyes.

"What my client tells me is privileged information. I shouldn't have to remind you." Though she spoke calmly, a tremor of fear shuddered up Caitlin's spine. What if they found the boy who had made the anonymous call and traced him back to her? If anyone accused her of a breach of ethics and they found evidence, she could be disbarred.

The courtroom was clear now except for the two of them and Jodi Rivers, a paralegal from the Legal Defenders Association who was standing near the door waiting for Caitlin. Wyman reached out and briefly touched Caitlin's arm. "We have more in common than you think, Caitlin." The arrogance was gone from his voice.

"What are you saying?"

"We both want the bad guys to go to prison."

She studied his face. "Maybe so, but my *job* is to get as many clients through the system as quickly as possible—period. Even if they get off. You're the one who's supposed to send them to prison." She didn't add that he wasn't very good at it, but she didn't have to. His record spoke for itself.

"We could be on the same team," he said lightly. "Think about it."

"I tried to join the DA, but you took my spot. Remember?"

"You holding a grudge? Besides, sometimes you can accomplish more working outside the DA's office."

Wyman left her then, but she knew it wasn't over. Two days ago, she wouldn't have hesitated to slam his slightly veiled suggestion of cooperation back in his face as a blatant breach of ethics. But doing so now might make him more eager to open an investigation into the anonymous caller, and the caller would eventually lead to Kenny Pratt, a local private detective she sometimes used. Kenny would never volunteer the information that he'd been making inquiries on her behalf, but she employed him often enough for the DA's office to make a connection. At least she hadn't told Kenny her true reason for sending him to the street where the knife had been found.

"I found a teenager," he had said, calling her from his cell phone. "Says he saw a guy run by, looking real nervous. There's a streetlight right outside, and he claims the man was covered in blood. A bit later the kid heard a bang at the abandoned house next door. Maybe a garbage can lid. I checked out the house, and it still looks abandoned. The garbage can is about half full. I didn't go through it. Anyway, it wasn't on the night you were asking about. It was two days before."

Two days before the date she'd given Kenny, but two days landed the event squarely on the night of Belstead's attack. She'd known Kenny Pratt would report anything he discovered—anything near the date in question. She forced her voice to be calm. "Not something I can use, but you might encourage the boy to call the police. Whatever the man dumped might still be there. Maybe it connects to something else they're working on. That's a scary neighborhood down there."

"I'll do that. You want me to keep poking around? I covered the whole block, but I might have missed someone."

"No. I think it's a dead end."

"It's your call."

"Send me a bill."

He laughed. "I always do."

The police had taken a day to find the knife and another two to connect it to the rape. That was fast, considering the months that had passed since the crime.

Simple. Not really any connection to her at all.

I shouldn't have done it. Despite all her rationalization, she'd been wrong to go that far. She had put herself at risk—and that meant putting Amy at risk.

The thought of Amy made her sit down hard on the first row of benches. Amy would be waiting for her even now, playing with dolls or coloring a picture. Sweet Amy, who knew only the world of a child and would never have to make the decisions Caitlin did.

"Caitlin? Are you okay?"

She looked around at Jodi, surprised to see the younger woman still waiting for her. "Yeah, I'm fine."

"Too bad about the knife."

She sighed. Jodi Rivers was a good paralegal, so good that in some cases Caitlin met with her clients only once before a hearing or trial. That left her free to spend her time on the most difficult or disturbing cases. Like Chet Belstead's. In fact, if she had still been working misdemeanor cases as she had at the beginning of her career, she'd only see her clients at the trial itself, never actually talking to them alone, relying instead on Jodi to take care of the legwork.

Yet for all her experience, Jodi was still young and too idealistic to understand that because of Caitlin, many really bad guys walked free to harm others again. Jodi still believed in second chances; Caitlin had seen repeated offenders too often to subscribe to that useless vein of thought.

Jodi sat down, her long, dark hair falling over her shoulders nearly to her slender waist. Caitlin envied that waist, not to mention the hair and flawless complexion. Of course, anything was preferable to her own red hair and freckles. Jodi tapped a French-manicured finger on the file she held. "I saw him staring at you. I think he likes you."

Caitlin sat up straighter. "You do?"

"Yes, and he's cute. I mean, he could be a little taller, but he's taller than you, at least. I hear he and his wife are getting a divorce."

Wife? Mace Keeley didn't have a wife. He was rumored to be in a long-distance romance with an attorney in California, though if they didn't love each other enough to be together, Caitlin didn't hold out much hope for the relationship.

That could only mean Jodi wasn't talking about Mace. "Uh," she groaned. "If you're talking about Wyman Russell, then eewww." The dragged-out word said it all.

Jodi shrugged. "He's not bad looking."

"He's a terrible prosecutor! You saw how he brought Mace Keeley in to help this case." Though now, since there was so much damning evidence, Wyman would probably try to resume the case on his own. He'd want the glory of the win for himself.

Jodi grinned. "I see your point. A woman can overlook a lot of things in a man but not stinking at his job. But speaking of Mace Keeley, what I wouldn't give to get a date with him!"

"You and most of the other women around here."

Jodi shrugged. "Lucky for him, I guess." She clapped her hands on her knees, just visible beneath her tight skirt, and leaned forward. "Well, I'm heading back to the office. Can I help you with anything this afternoon?"

"I wish. But it's stuff I have to deal with. After I make sure the DA sends me everything on this new evidence, I have to go chat with another client so we're ready for trial tomorrow morning." A typical busy Wednesday for her.

"You mean the arsonist?"

"That's the one." The defendant had killed an old man in the fire, so Wyman had gone after him with a murder one charge, but there was enough doubt in Caitlin's mind about the defendant's intention that she was giving the case her full attention. Since she was up against Wyman again, she would probably save her client from life imprisonment. Unfortunately.

Nodding, Jodi arose. "Well, give me a holler if you need some help with visual aids for the arson trial."

"I thought you had a brief to write for Sampson."

"I do, but it's boring." Jodi laughed and started down the aisle.

"In that case, I'll take you up on the visual aids. There's a file on my desk that has them outlined. Top one. Red folder, I think. And, Jodi, thanks."

"No problem."

Caitlin scraped through the rest of her day, finally heading through the snow-lined streets to her home in West Valley City. A stack of files she would work on later filled her briefcase. Though it was only six-thirty, her eyes ached and her head screamed for sleep. All she wanted was to crash in bed and never wake up. Instead, she made the usual detour two streets from her house to pick up Amy at the sitter's. Caitlin had looked for several months to find a woman who could handle Amy, and the white-haired Sarah Burnside, a sixty-eight-year-old Mormon grandmother of thirty, had been a real find.

Sarah's husband, Kyle, let her in, and Caitlin found Amy sitting on a stool in the kitchen with Sarah, kneading saltwater dough on the countertop. "I'm helping." Amy's short red hair, a shade darker than Caitlin's, framed her round, grinning face. Any time flour and water were involved, Amy was content.

"I see," Caitlin said. "That's very nice."

At the sink, Sarah rinsed a final dish before drying her hands. "You can take that home, Amy."

"Oh, thank you! You're so nice, Sarah." Amy began rolling the dough in a ball with plump fingers. "Can I have a sack?"

"Of course, dear." Sarah moved her bulky form to a drawer and drew out a plastic zip bag.

Leaving Sarah to store the dough, Amy slid off her stool and hugged Caitlin, nearly overpowering her with exuberance. Amy didn't realize how strong she was, which was why it was important that her sitter be sturdy. "I missed you so much. Did you miss me?"

Caitlin looked up into her younger sister's eyes, as green as her own were blue. "I did miss you." And it was true. With Amy things were always simpler. She was twenty-seven, but intellectually she would always remain five or six. Their parents had married late, having Caitlin when their mother was forty-three, and Amy surprised them five years later. There wasn't a time when Caitlin hadn't been involved in taking care of her sister, and now that their parents were gone, the burdens and the joys rested solely on her shoulders.

Amy didn't look any different from other women her age, and sometimes that was the most difficult thing for Caitlin. Sometimes she almost forgot that she could never share her life with Amy the way most sisters could. Amy would never be able to counsel her about a boyfriend, or buy her that sweater she had her eye on. Or even fix dinner on the nights Caitlin was too exhausted to stand. But these were selfish thoughts, and for the most part Caitlin was happy that her little sister would never know all the pain the world carried.

On the drive home Amy began her usual babble about the day's events. Caitlin only half-listened, nodding at all the appropriate times. Most of it would be a repeat of the day before. In fact, Amy often got events from past weeks mixed up. It didn't really matter. But suddenly her words grabbed Caitlin's attention.

"Caitlin, will you ever have a baby?"

Caitlin glanced over at the passenger seat to see Amy looking at her earnestly. "Why do you ask that?"

"I think you should. If you had a baby, I could watch it. I would be a good baby-sitter."

"I'm sure you would, but having a baby is kind of

complicated." She didn't know how to explain reproduction to her sister, much less falling in love and making a permanent commitment. "Remember our gerbils and how they won't have any more babies since they don't have a husband?"

"That's because we gave all the husbands away. I liked having the babies. They were cute."

"We couldn't keep so many in the cage. They wouldn't be happy."

"We wouldn't have tons of babies. Just one." Amy tilted her head in a pleading gesture. "Please, Caitlin. Sarah's daughter had a baby, and I got to hold him today. I was very careful. He smiled at me."

"I bet that was a lot of fun."

"So will you have a baby? Please?"

Caitlin stifled a sigh. "I don't even have time to meet a man, much less marry one. Besides, I don't know that we want a guy hanging around all the time. I sort of like having you all to myself."

Amy giggled. "Me too."

They pulled into the driveway of their modest home. The garage could hold two cars, though they didn't need the space. Amy would never drive. While Amy ran to play with the gerbils they kept in a corner of their small kitchen, Caitlin rummaged in the freezer for a bagged pasta meal she'd bought at Costco. Amy loved the curly noodles and the meat, and usually even ate a carrot or two, though she wouldn't touch the broccoli. The calories in the meal were outrageous—probably one of the reasons Caitlin had put on a few pounds lately, but at least it cooked quickly and tasted good.

Amy talked to the gerbils, repeating everything she'd already told Caitlin about her day, her big hands gentle with the creatures. She'd had twenty-seven years to learn to be five.

"Why don't you go wash up?" Caitlin suggested. "It's almost ready."

From her seated position by the gerbil cage, Amy's face lifted toward Caitlin, her childlike sweetness shining through. "Can we have ice cream after?"

"Why not?" There was really no point in denying Amy the treat. It wasn't as if she would have to fit into a prom dress any time soon. Sorrow came with the thought, but it was erased by Amy's gleeful cheer.

"I love you so much, Caitlin. You're the best sister ever!" She jumped up and gave Caitlin a hug.

Forty minutes later, Caitlin was washing their dinner dishes when her cell phone rang. "I'll get it!" Amy left her bowl of Neapolitan ice cream and raced over to Caitlin's purse on the counter, delivering the cell phone to Caitlin's damp hand.

"Hello?"

"Caitlin, it's Wyman."

Her heart thudded in her chest. "Hi, Wyman. What's up?"

"It's about the Belstead trial."

She sighed. "You know we can't discuss it."

"I thought it wouldn't hurt to stop by."

"You're at my house?" If she had to have a visitor, why couldn't it have been Mace? *If only I could be so lucky,* she thought.

"I wanted to make sure you were home before I knocked."

Caitlin strode to the front door, pulling it open. Sure enough, Wyman was climbing from a sleek gray car, careful not to put his feet in the mound of snow the plow had left next to the curb. She shut her phone and watched him walk up the drive. The house had been built on a postage stamp-sized lot, like all the other houses in the subdivision, so it didn't take him long to reach her. "We can't talk about the trial," she warned.

"Either of them. If you have a plea deal, I want it in writing during normal work hours."

"Okay. Then how about dinner this weekend?"

"I'm sorry, I can't."

"It's just dinner, Caitlin. I promise, no shop talk."

"I'm busy."

His light blue eyes narrowed, reminding her of ice. "Look, it's only fair that you know. This afternoon we tracked down the teenager who made the anonymous call about your client's knife. He said a man came around asking about anything odd happening in the area, and apparently that's the only reason he came forward in the first place. The man was probably a private detective, and some in the DA's office find it strange that a private detective would just happen to be snooping around in that area."

"What does that have to do with me?" Caitlin said coldly.

"That's what I want to find out."

"And you'll find nothing. The way I see it, you should be grateful for any break in the case. You and I both know I was about to win."

Wyman studied her, an unperturbed smile on his face. Caitlin felt ill.

"Caitlin? Who is it?" Amy peered around her at Wyman, pushing Caitlin to the side in her enthusiasm. Ice cream smeared her chin, signaling that she'd been licking her bowl clean.

"A man from work," Caitlin said, automatically shifting to the softer voice she reserved for Amy.

"Hi." Amy grinned and lifted a hand in greeting. "I'm Caitlin's sister."

Wyman looked back and forth between them, apparently

noting the similarities—the freckles, the hair, even the build, though Amy was heavier and taller than Caitlin.

Amy wiped her chin on her sleeve. "Caitlin, I like my new ice cream better than the kind with those yucky nuts. Can we always buy this kind?"

"Yes. Now why don't you go get your pajamas on?"

Amy clapped her hands. "I'll get the book!" She glanced at Wyman. "'Bye!"

Realization came over Wyman's face, followed by a fleeting expression of what Caitlin was sure was revulsion. Then Wyman smiled. "I didn't know you supported a sister."

Caitlin didn't respond.

"Well, think about what I said." With a wink, he turned and sauntered down her drive.

Caitlin thought fast. If she went out with him maybe he'd get off the trail. After all, her client would go to prison and Wyman would get credit for his conviction. What did it matter how it came about? Going out with Wyman a time or two might stall him long enough that the point would be moot.

But what if it wasn't enough? She shivered. He might be handsome in Jodi's eyes, but right now everything about him repulsed her. The idea of going out with him wasn't her idea of fun, no matter that it'd been two years since she'd dated anyone seriously.

"Okay," she called, raising her voice to be heard. "Dinner."

He stopped and turned, a slow smile coming over his face. "I'm glad you changed your mind. We'll make plans tomorrow then, after the arson trial."

Caitlin nodded, already wishing she hadn't agreed. But for Amy's sake she had to protect her career, and for now that meant playing along with Wyman's little game.

2

P arker Hathaway walked slowly, almost casually, to the front door of the house in South Salt Lake, not crouching or darting, yet keeping to the shadows made by the huge walnut tree in the front yard. The back door would have been a better choice for staying out of view, but it was too close to the neighbor's dog kennel. If the child's mother awoke, she'd call the police.

Or maybe not. Given her current circumstances, Dakota Allen was more likely to call the hulking, balding boyfriend who'd been hanging around almost constantly during the past week, though Parker had made sure his battered car wasn't in the driveway tonight. Of course, Dakota might still be awake. He didn't know anything about her sleeping habits these days. Did she drop off the moment her head touched the pillow? Or maybe she lay awake nights like he did, thinking of how he had to do something—anything—to prevent the disaster he knew was imminent.

It didn't matter. He hadn't come for her. When he was through here, she'd hate him with a murderous passion that might just barely begin to approach the feelings he harbored for her.

He shivered in the cold, and thoughts of the small whisky jar he'd once kept in the cab of his truck made him ache with longing. But that was a place he would never go again. He forced his thoughts back to the task at hand. Two more minutes, maybe three tops, if all went well. He slipped the credit card into the crack between the door frame and the faceplate of the lock mechanism. Good, the dead bolt hadn't been used. He'd hoped for that. Maybe she'd been too tired. Or maybe she simply didn't care. Women like Dakota didn't. Not about the things that most people considered important. They were too busy using others to expect to be victims themselves.

Even if she'd thrown the dead bolt, he'd come prepared with the glass cutter in the truck, but this was better, cleaner. Less evidence that he'd been inside the house. What he planned to do there could land him behind bars. Deep behind bars.

Far more easily than Parker had dared hope, the card released the latch. He eased the door open, and only as he went inside did he allow his gaze to scan the neighborhood. Not furtively but carelessly, as though he belonged. Indeed, he had belonged to a neighborhood exactly like this one for as long as he'd been able to bear it. A neighborhood like this and all it entailed was what had driven him too near the edge of sanity.

No one was in sight, and even if someone was looking out a window at that moment, they might assume he was the husband coming home after a midnight shift. They were used to having people come in at all hours here. Three o'clock, the time he'd chosen, was when they had the least traffic. He'd watched for three nights to be sure, eating up tankfuls of gasoline in the car he'd borrowed for the purpose.

He took a step inside, shut the door quietly, and then took another step as his eyes strained to be sure the tiny living room was empty. The furnishings were plain, with a tattered brown couch, a blue love seat, and a coffee table that had seen better days. The floor was clean. This surprised him, and he felt his first tremor of doubt.

No. Doubts were fatal. He had no choice but to continue.

Desperation drove Parker onward. Another step and the floorboards creaked. He froze, listened for a full minute, and then continued when only silence met his ears. Moonlight filtered in from the kitchen window between sheer curtains that even in the dim light appeared tired and desolate. The counters were clear, though dishes were piled high in the sink, some with globs of food stuck to them. Turning his head, he slid down the dark hallway, a step at a time, stopping to listen between each movement.

Two rooms were at the end, both doors closed. What mother closed her bedroom door in the middle of the night with a helpless child sleeping nearby? How would she hear its cry? He took the left door, the front bedroom. He'd seen Madeline in the window and knew it was hers. Carefully, he twisted the doorknob and pushed open the door. There was the faintest of creaks but not loud enough for alarm. The bedroom was not as plain as the living room. There were colorful posters on the wall, stuffed animals, an easel for drawing, and newer furniture that matched.

His breath caught in his throat as he saw Madeline lying in her bed beneath the window, a smile curving the edges of her button lips. Moonlight spilled onto her outstretched hand, a hand that beckoned to him. His heart constricted as it always did at seeing her face.

No doubts here. They belonged together. *I'm coming, sweetheart.* In three steps he was kneeling at her bed, his hands reaching toward her.

A sound made his hands jerk to a stop—a soft murmur that came not from the bed but from the crib against the wall. Curious, he stood and peeked inside. There was another child, a boy, by the length of his hair. Not more than a year old. He hadn't realized this child would be here tonight. Scrubbing a hand over the week-old growth on his face, he considered the boy. He wished he could take them both.

Better to stick to the plan. Where he was going with Madeline, he couldn't take the boy. He would only be a liability. Jaw clenched, he turned his back on the crib, kneeling again near the bed. He pulled down her blanket, scooting one hand under her warm body. She wore a thin nightgown, completely inappropriate for the November night, even in a heated house. With his other hand he grabbed the princess lap blanket folded at the bottom of the bed and pulled it up to her neck, tucking the furry warmth around her body as he drew her toward him.

She stirred as Parker rose to his feet, folding her tightly against his chest. He rocked her until she buried her face in his shirt and was still. *It'll all be over soon,* he promised. Turning, he tripped over the jumble of stuffed animals on the floor, but he caught himself in time. The dresser was open, and clothes peeked out this way and that. She wouldn't need them.

He was nearing the bedroom door when footsteps made him freeze. There was no time to hide before the other bedroom door was flung open. Dakota, most likely. He stood motionless in the darkness as she stumbled to the bathroom down the hall, not shutting the door behind her. The sound of urination filled the quiet of the house.

Parker swore under his breath. The closet—he should hide there. But if she were to check on the children, the missing girl would be noticed immediately. Then he'd have to do something to prevent the mother from calling anyone.

Or he could put Madeline back in her bed.

Swiftly, he crossed the room and laid the child down, pulling the larger blanket over her to hide the furry one. Then he sprinted to the closet.

He needn't have worried. The woman didn't come in the children's bedroom, yet she didn't shut her door, either. He waited for her to fall asleep again, though he knew every minute put him closer to discovery.

After fifteen minutes, he could wait no longer. Again Parker knelt by the bed and scooped up the little girl. This time she didn't react but slept on like an angel. Down the dark hallway he went, shuffling slowly to be sure he didn't trip over anything. Then he was at the front door, shutting it behind him and stepping quietly over crunchy mounds of snow. The truck was parked between this house and the neighbor's. He climbed inside and, still holding the child, started the engine.

The cab was cold—he hadn't planned for the wait inside the house—but he'd brought blankets. Headlights appeared ahead, and he stiffened until a car passed, the lights fading behind him. He should have borrowed his friend's car again instead of using his own truck, but that hadn't been possible tonight, and he couldn't afford to wait. The cost might be too high.

Two blocks away, he stopped and settled Madeline on the seat next to him, tucking blankets around her to help her feel secure. The faint red lights from the dashboard barely illuminated her baby face, but he could see that her eyes had opened, small slits in her chubby roundness. "Daddy? Is that you?"

The light made it difficult for her to really see much of anything, and her apparent trust made the ache in his chest intensify. Parker swallowed, the dryness hurting his throat. "It's okay, sweetheart," he murmured. "Sleep, now. That's my girl."

Obediently, she shut her eyes and was lost again in her dreams.

He drove to I-15, heading south. What he wouldn't give for a drink. Just a sip to burn a little warmth down his throat. He knew it was a battle he'd fight for the rest of his life, but no way would he let that vice steal what he had worked so hard to achieve. His entire life and future were tied up in that little girl lying there so peacefully on the seat. He must arrive at his destination. Then he could decide what to do next.

• • •

Parker reached Mt. Pleasant in two hours. Normally, he could have shaved off twenty minutes or more of the journey, but he didn't want to attract any unwanted attention. Not that there were too many policemen out at this time. He was, however, starting to pass people driving north or south to their jobs in bigger neighboring towns. There wasn't much to do by way of work in Mt. Pleasant, unless you happened to work at the gas station or grocery store.

He passed the family-owned Kathy's Herb Shoppe on Main Street and turned the corner to his mother's house, pulling up in the driveway and jumping out to punch in the code on the side of the garage. Normally, he'd park outside if he came so early, but today he didn't want to risk his truck being seen. The stop was necessary in his mind, though, because he needed to talk to his mother, to prepare her for what was going to happen. He was all Norma Hathaway had left.

She was waiting by the kitchen door when he entered with his key. In one hand she held the telephone, in the other a can of pepper spray. When she saw him, the anxious look on her tired face vanished, and she stepped toward the door, rapidly punching in the code for the alarm he had installed last year when there had been a rash of burglaries in the neighborhood. Petty things like small TVs and thin gold bands had gone missing, but worse was the violation people had felt. They didn't have a lot in this town, and Parker had wondered why anyone would target them—until a gang of teenagers had been arrested. Biggest news of the city in the past decade. At least before today. By evening, his mother would be the recipient of many meals and desserts from the neighbors, outpourings of their love and sympathy over her loss.

"Have you been drinking?" she asked, studying him carefully.

He shook his head, irritated but not angry. "No."

She had a right to suspect him, though he hadn't let her down in a long time. She would probably always wonder if he would fail, and her constant worry and fear alone were enough to keep him sober—even if he hadn't already decided that he would never return to his old ways.

One thing both of them would agree upon: his actions of this night were not a failure. Though his mother hadn't known of his plan, she would be happy he'd succeeded. She knew what was at stake every bit as much as he did.

"Look," Parker said, speaking urgently. "I'm only here for a few minutes. Have to work this morning." He was employed at a construction site in Manti, a good half hour's drive from Mt. Pleasant.

"Why are you here?" Her hands were on her sturdy hips, and her brown eyes that matched the shoulder-length hair were intense.

In answer, Parker took her hand and led her out to the garage. She hesitated when one of her slippers fell off, and he impatiently waited for her to put it back on. "People are going to be coming around asking questions," he said. "I didn't want you to worry."

They stood on the passenger side of his truck now, and he gestured toward the window. His mother was short and had to stand on tiptoe to see inside. It always amused people that Norma could be so short while Parker and his brother had been such tall, strapping boys. Like their father. But he didn't want to think about his father or his brother. There had been no love lost between them during his growing up years, and he still paid the price for that every day of his life.

"Madeline," Norma breathed. She stepped back, flung open the door, and reached for the child.

"No." Parker held her back. "Don't wake her. I've got to get her to Manti before I go to work."

"But who'll watch her?"

"I have someone."

Norma's brow wrinkled. "Someone she knows?"

Parker shook his head. "She's used to strangers."

"Let me come with you." Her brown eyes were ringed in small wrinkles, really the only place that showed her fifty-seven years. Wrinkles born of great suffering.

"I don't want you involved. People are going to be asking questions. I only came here so you'd know she's okay when the questions come. But I can't tell you where I'm taking her, and you can't admit to anyone that I was even here."

"You're going away. I'll never see you again." Panic laced Norma's voice.

"No." He shook his head. "If it comes to that, we'll go together."

"It will come to that. Dakota won't let it rest."

"Maybe she will."

"Then the law won't."

"I can't let Madeline get hurt!" Desperation tightened his chest. "I have to protect her."

"I know." His mother's arms went around him, as comforting as they had been when he was a child. "I'll get my stuff taken care of," she whispered. "Don't you worry. I'll sell the house, cash out everything. We'll disappear."

He knew how much it cost her to say that. This was her home. She'd come here as a young bride, raised two sons, and become a widow. She was offering to leave all her friends and extended family.

"It might not be necessary."

"It will. You can't hide."

"Maybe I can—for long enough. Maybe the authorities will find out about Dakota."

"Maybe."

Parker drew back and shut the truck door.

"You call and let me know where she is."

He shook his head. "I'll be here sometime during the weekend, same as always. This time without Madeline." That was a given because his daughter would have to remain in hiding, but he wanted his mother prepared. She lived for Madeline's visits.

"I love you, Parker. Don't you forget that."

"I love you, too, Mom."

"Grandma?" Madeline was sitting up and rubbing her eyes.

This wasn't going at all as Parker had planned. He shouldn't have stopped. Now if the authorities caught him, Madeline would remember that she'd seen her grandmother.

Norma opened the truck door and gathered the little girl into a hug. "Oh, baby. It's so good to see you. But you have to lie down now and go back to sleep. You and your daddy are taking a little trip."

Madeline grinned. "I like trips with Daddy." She yawned. "Is it my birthday again?" For her fourth birthday two months ago, he had taken her to Disneyland.

"Not yet," Parker told her. "And we're not going to Disneyland, but we'll have fun anyway."

"That's right." Norma patted the seat. "You're tired, sweetie. Lay your head right there and take a little nap."

Madeline yawned again. "Okay, Grandma."

Parker exchanged a meaningful look with his mother. "I'd better get going."

"Yes. You'd better."

He hugged Norma and whispered in her ear, "I'm sorry. Sorry for all of this. I'm sorry it's going to be so awful for you." Answering questions, lying for him and Madeline—who knew what she might be forced to do? He knew her well enough to understand that a little part of her would die every time she took a step closer to the wrong side of the law. That he felt the same showed he'd come a long way.

"I'm stronger than you think," she said. "I'll manage. You just keep her safe."

He drove to Manti, not to the small apartment he shared with two guys from work but to a small, run-down house on the edge of town that he'd rented fully furnished for less than he'd expected. There was still time to change Madeline's hair color and her clothes before the local girl he'd hired came to baby-sit, a girl who barely spoke English, and whose family had reasons of their own not to contact authorities. Then he'd drive his truck back to his apartment and climb in his window in time to "wake up" with the other guys.

He'd tried to think of everything, but what if he'd missed something important? His heart banged in his chest with a fierceness he hadn't felt since that first time Dakota had left him and taken Madeline, and he'd realized he had no way to protect his daughter.

For now, at least, Madeline was safe.

As he carried her inside, her arms went up around his neck. "I'm glad you came and got me, Daddy. I missed you."

Tears gathered in his eyes. "We're together now. And I'm not ever letting you go again if I can help it."

CHAPTER

3

C aitlin met police detective Sally Crumb at the Judge Café on Broadway that served only breakfast and lunch until three in the afternoon. They both enjoyed the food and the ambience—along with dozens of other downtown workers, many of them attorneys—so it was a frequent choice for their weekly lunches together. That it was within walking distance of the courthouse made it an extra plus for Caitlin. She detested fighting the busy traffic.

When Caitlin arrived, her cheeks tingling with cold from her brisk walk, Sally was already waiting in one of the many niches the restaurant owners had carved out when remodeling the historic building. Pictures of old Salt Lake stretched over the dark wood of the bar, and the architectural features of the walls were accented by the paint's subdued yellow tone.

"How is the arson trial going?" Sally asked as Caitlin set down her briefcase and shrugged off her full-length gray wool coat.

"Horrendous. I mean, we're not contesting the fact that my client started the fire, so why bring in all that evidence? We would have finished already if not for all of that." She rubbed her fingers to warm them. "They won't be able to convict him of first degree murder, though."

"But he intentionally lit the fire that caused a death, so it should still be murder one." Sally tucked the strands of her short bleached hair behind her ears, making it look even shorter. She was tall for a woman, and if the weight she carried had been on a man's frame, she would have still been considered on the slender side, but on her, the wide shoulders and hips lent an impressive air of solid authority. Yet Sally was all woman, and a pretty one at that, from her size eleven shoes to her expressive, wide-set brown eyes.

Caitlin sighed. "He didn't intend to burn the building down exactly. At least so he claims, and he seems to have a lot of friends who support that claim." .

"Seems?" Sally arched a thin brow.

"After the testimony today, the DA offered a plea deal. Arson and manslaughter. I'm urging my client to take it."

"Even though he might not be as guilty as the DA thinks?"

"Oh, he's guilty. I just don't know exactly how guilty." Caitlin propped her elbow unabashedly on the table and let her chin drop in her hands. "I'm tired, Sally. I'm tired of defending these people. Sometimes I want to lock them all up."

Sally chuckled. "I know how you feel. But someone's got to do it."

"Maybe it's time I got out."

"What, and make it so the guys don't have anything to rib me about down at the precinct?" Sally's colleagues held no love for the Legal Defenders Association, and their mistrust of Sally's friendship with Caitlin was nothing new. But Sally and Caitlin had been friends from the minute they'd met during a DUI case that had turned out to be caused by prescription medication rather than alcohol. It was one of the few good cases Caitlin could remember in the past three years.

"Ah, here comes the food," Sally added. "I ordered you a grilled nectarine and chicken salad. Dressing on the side. Hope that's okay."

"Whatever you got is fine." They were always in such a hurry at lunch that their standing rule was for the first to arrive to order for both. Only once had Caitlin been held up long enough to make Sally take the extra lunch home for her dinner. Never had she been forced to eat something she absolutely detested.

"So how's Amy?" Sally asked as the waitress set down her plate. She was having the Judge's Favorite, a healthy serving of hearty meat loaf with mashed potatoes, gravy, summer squash, and mushrooms.

"The same. She never really changes."

One side of Sally's mouth lifted in a lopsided smile. "Some mothers would love their children to never grow up."

Caitlin considered the statement as she moved her chicken and nectarines around on their bed of romaine lettuce. She'd never held any hope of Amy growing up, except in disjointed dreams that didn't make any sense. "Maybe they wouldn't mind so much if they knew the alternative."

"Probably. Still, sometimes I'd give anything to have Randi younger again. Fifth grade is tough."

"Is she doing better at the new school?"

"Yes. She's finally found some friends."

"Good." Unlike Randi, Amy had a lot of friends because she loved everyone and never took offense. Unfortunately, she could never play without supervision because she was often too rough on her younger playmates.

As though reading her thoughts, Sally stopped eating and reached into the inner pocket of her suit coat, bringing out a folded paper. "There are much worse things in life." She opened the paper to reveal a photocopied picture of a little girl. The child stared up at them, her eyes bright, her round face grinning. Her hair was so blonde that it looked almost as white as the page, framing her face like a halo.

"She went missing last night from her bedroom," Sally said. "The mother has no idea when it might have happened. The girl was there at ten or so when she put the children to bed, and then when the little brother started crying in the morning about nine, the mother discovered she was missing. We're working on an Amber Alert now."

"Poor thing." Caitlin set down her fork and took the picture. The child was beautiful and so young. "Who could have taken her?"

"So far we have no leads. We're talking to the relatives now. The father was at work in Manti when we called, but the mother had already called him before she contacted us, so we didn't have the element of surprise. I'm going down there after I leave here to see if I can find any leads."

"I take it he and the mother are divorced?"

"About a year now."

"He's a suspect?"

"Everyone's a suspect. A high percentage of children are taken by family members, but there are still far too many stranger abductions. It'd be a lot easier for us if the mother could pinpoint the time of disappearance a little better. Apparently she got up to use the bathroom in the night and walked right past the room, but she didn't go in."

"I always check on Amy if I wake up." Caitlin set down the picture, but the little girl's trusting eyes still danced before her.

"You'd think she'd have checked on them since her kids are so young, but the mother claims she'd taken a sleep aid and wasn't thinking well."

"Claims?" Caitlin said through a mouthful of red peppers and cucumbers.

Sally snorted. "In this business I don't trust anyone. The mother has a history of drug arrests but no convictions on her adult record, and nothing within the past three years, so she's either cleaned up or—"

"Hasn't been caught." Caitlin sipped her glass of water. "It's a sad world when a child can't sleep safely in her own bed."

"Sad indeed."

They were silent a moment as they both took another bite of their food, Caitlin washing hers down with water, and Sally with her usual soft drink.

"I heard about the knife they found," Sally said. "Tough luck for your client."

Caitlin shrugged. "They've tacked on attempted murder to the charges, but the DA offered a plea deal this morning. Twenty years. Apparently they fear I'll drag the case on for weeks, which I refuse to do because it absolutely won't change the outcome. My client has until three o'clock this afternoon to agree. Or his trial will resume tomorrow as originally scheduled." Against her gut feeling, she'd advised Belstead to take the deal.

"And if he doesn't take it?"

"He'll serve twenty-five to life instead. If convicted, of course. Which he will be."

"I know what you hope he'll do." Sally gave her another lopsided smile.

"Either way, the trial will be over tomorrow. Then that stress at least will be gone. And I'll never have to see that creep again. Well, except at the sentencing." Caitlin massaged her temple where she had the beginnings of a terrible headache.

"You know what you need? A man. Preferably one with a little muscle. Dating does wonders for stress."

Caitlin choked on her water, sending it spraying over the table. "You'd know." Sally's husband, Tony, was a building contractor who had more muscles in one arm than most men possessed in their entire bodies. His animal magnetism was palpable.

"Oh, yeah, I know." Sally grinned. "So, anyone interesting on the horizon?" She looked around the restaurant, as though scoping out potential dates. Her voice lowered. "What about the infamous deputy DA with the girlfriend in California? Any news on that front?"

Caitlin groaned. "I can't believe I told you about Mace."

"We all have weak moments. And he's worth having one over. I got a glimpse of him this week when he came to the precinct. He is something else. Hot."

"And as untouchable as ever," Caitlin said. "But I do have a date for Saturday." Better to change the subject before anyone in the restaurant overheard Mace's name. It was bound to get back to the circles she traveled in if she wasn't careful.

"Who?" Sally leaned toward her. "Tell me right now, or I'm going to arrest you."

Caitlin laughed and held out her wrists. "Take me away. I need a break."

"I know you're overworked if sitting in jail with a bunch of drunks and druggies sounds restful."

"Really, it's nothing. Just another deputy DA." After the arson trial dismissed for lunch, she and Wyman had agreed on

Saturday night. He'd wanted Friday, but Caitlin liked to keep Friday night clear so she didn't spend the entire day away from Amy. She worked late far too many nights as it was.

"Good-looking?" Sally prompted. She scooped up a fork of mashed potatoes, eating them with undisguised relish.

Caitlin rolled her eyes. "Look, this guy is handsome, sort of, but it's not like that between us." She didn't want to admit she suspected Wyman's motive was blackmail. That would get Sally's investigative nose going overtime, and Sally was one woman she didn't want on the case. "He's separated from his wife, maybe even divorced already, but I don't plan to get involved until I make sure where he stands. It's more of a business dinner than anything." Actually, she didn't plan on getting involved at all, but she didn't want Sally digging around or feeling sorry for her.

"Let me know if you need me to order a background check."

"What?" Another laugh burst from Caitlin. "I can't believe you just said that."

"Hey, it's for a good cause." Sally shoveled in a few more bites as they waited for their check. "I'd better get on my way to Manti. I'll drop you somewhere if you'd like."

"The courthouse. I have a meeting with a judge before I talk to my arson client about the plea deal."

"No problem."

A few minutes later, Sally pulled to the curb to let Caitlin out at the tall white building with its six tall pillars and many windows that reflected the weak afternoon sun. "See you next week," Caitlin told her. "Good luck finding that little girl."

"If she's still alive." Sally's reply was grim, and Caitlin knew she was thinking about another little girl who'd gone missing in Salt Lake two weeks before. The seven-year-old had been raped and killed within an hour of leaving her home, her body found days later in the basement of a neighboring apartment. Vicious, violent crimes that targeted the most helpless were what they dealt with on a regular basis. Most people had no idea.

Sally lifted her chin. "I'll find the guy who did this, and when I do, you'd better not get him off."

"Wouldn't dream of it." Caitlin watched her drive away, feeling a sense of something she couldn't put her finger on.

Across the street stood the county building, looking old and picturesque, peeking behind the bare trees. She liked the view better in the summer when green leaves filled the trees and the blue sky overhead held nothing but warmth.

"Caitlin!"

She lowered her gaze from the building and saw Mace Keeley coming across the street toward her. He smiled and motioned her to wait, and she checked her watch surreptitiously before nodding, pleased to see she had plenty of time for a chat.

"Needed some records," he said casually, tossing his head in the direction of the county building.

"Convenient, isn't it?" She herself had gone across the street more times than she could count to confer with one county employee or another.

"I heard you gave Wyman a run for his money this morning."

She grinned. "He offered a deal. Arson and manslaughter."

Mace whistled. "Your client is lucky."

"There wasn't a lot of proof."

"He going to take it?"

"If I have any say. I'll find out within the hour."

"Good. One more client through the system."

"Yep." They stood silently for brief seconds, their breath making white puffs in the cold air. Caitlin's heart was thudding so furiously, she thought it a miracle he couldn't hear the barrage.

Be calm, she told herself. She angled toward the courthouse and he turned with her. Together they started up the stairs, joining the half-dozen other people who were heading inside. Mace held the door open for her, and she passed close enough to feel the warmth emanating from him and to smell the faint aroma of his aftershave.

In the building, he touched her arm, guiding her to the side so they wouldn't be overheard by the passersby. His skin felt hot to the touch. "I was wondering if you'd like to have dinner with me sometime."

Caitlin tried not to show shock, grateful she'd inherited a poker face from her English mother. Usually at work the proper English part of her was more prominent than the Irish. At least so far. Yet inside she was shouting, *Yes, yes! I'll go out to dinner with you. Kiss me now!*

"Well, that depends," she said casually.

"Depends on what?" He gave her a lazy smile, completely confident of his charms. Her insides responded with a rush of warmth.

Concentrate, she told herself. "Well, rumor has it that you might be moving to California. It's very hard to have dinner from so far away."

"Ah, I see." He regarded her quietly a moment, his blue eyes glinting with amusement. "Well, I'm sorry to have to quell that particular rumor, but between you and me, I never did plan on moving there."

Caitlin hoped he meant what she thought he did. At the

very least, she'd let him know she was going into their dinner with open eyes. "In that case, dinner sounds fun."

"What about Saturday? I'd say Friday, but I have a case that's going to keep me late."

She opened her mouth to agree but then remembered her plans with Wyman. "Oh, I can't Saturday." She let a hint of disappointment tinge her voice. "I have plans already." She wished she'd told Wyman to shove off.

"Maybe another time."

"If you get off early Friday, call me. I'll be working late myself." *Did I just say that?* she thought. She hoped it sounded natural. Only thirty-two years old, and she'd been out of the game too long.

"I'll do that." He seemed sincere enough that she wondered fleetingly how she would explain it to Amy if he followed through. Maybe Sally would agree to let her go over for the evening to play with Randi.

With a nod and another breathtaking smile, Mace started away from her, and though she needed to go that same way, she busied herself by walking in the opposite direction to give him a head start. No sense in starting the rumors flying already. She'd worked hard to keep her professional life separate from her personal, and just because Mace made her pulse race was no reason to give that up now. She might be secretly wishing she had a man in her life, but chasing off all the womanizing young attorneys who thought nothing of working their way through any and all willing females was not on her list of things she most wanted to do. Better that they think her a hard woman with no interest in a relationship.

Reaching the end of the hall, she checked her watch once again and headed toward the judge's office.

"Hey, Caitlin."

She'd been so intent on her thoughts that she hadn't noticed Wyman before she nearly ran into him. "Oh, hi."

"Talk to your arsonist about the deal?"

"In a bit. I've got a meeting first with one of the judges."

"Well, I'll let you go then." He reached out and touched her arm in a gesture that seemed too intimate. "I'm really looking forward to Saturday night. I think you'll find we have a lot in common."

Inwardly, Caitlin shuddered. "I'm sure it'll be interesting." She glanced at her watch pointedly. "Oops, gotta run. Don't want to keep the judge waiting." She moved around him and continued on, aware of his eyes following her down the hall.

CHAPTER

4

Parker Hathaway had been tense all morning, even
before Dakota called in tears about Madeline. Her tears
hadn't moved him, though his ex-wife apparently
thought he'd drop everything and go running up to Salt Lake.
Instead, he'd told her to call the police. This was part of the
plan, that she'd call the police and they would find evidence to
convict her.

He didn't receive a call from the police until two hours
later, and that told him Dakota had cleaned up the house
before reporting Madeline's absence, or at least made sure there
was nothing lying around that would reflect badly upon her.
The house had been searched top to bottom. Nothing. Officers
were beginning to comb the neighborhoods, and volunteers
were gathering to form search parties. Since Parker hadn't
deigned to show up, the detective was coming to him. He'd
have to explain himself somehow; he hoped it would be

enough because he wasn't leaving town. Not unless they made him.

The detective came to the building site at three, wearing an ordinary suit on her large frame and driving an unmarked car. She was alone, which he thought odd, but perhaps that meant they didn't really consider him a suspect.

One could hope.

She stopped and talked to the foreman, who pointed him out. Parker ignored them and kept working, using his crane to lift timbers to the men up on the scaffolding. The office space they were building was making good headway, even in the cold, though they needed to get the roof on before the next snowfall.

"Mr. Hathaway?" she called up to him over the roar of the engine.

He held up his finger, finished positioning his load, and then cut the motor. "I'm Parker Hathaway," he said, climbing down from the cab.

"I'm Sally Crumb. We spoke on the phone this morning."

"You find my daughter? Is she okay?" He felt his heart rate speeding up, as though she could see into his lie.

"No. I'm sorry. I do need to ask you some questions, and I think it's only fair to tell you we have a squad car at your apartment right now. The building manager let them in."

He shrugged. "I have nothing to hide. But you're barking up the wrong tree. Madeline was with her mother last night, and I was at my apartment. My roommates can attest to that. I went to bed when they did and one of them was still there when I got up this morning."

"Yes, we know." She gave him a flat smile that did little to lighten the somber expression on her attractive face. She had blonde hair much like Madeline's had been before this morning, though the locks were shorter and probably dyed.

He followed her to the trailer the foreman used as his office, abandoned now for their use. "I don't understand," he said, unzipping his coat. "Shouldn't you be out there searching for my daughter? I mean, if she really is missing?"

"Oh, she's missing all right." Her eyes narrowed.

Parker scratched his unshaved face. "Her mother has problems with drugs. I've been worried for years that something would happen to Madeline."

"And you did nothing?"

"Except for right after Dakota left me and I didn't know where she was staying, I've kept every single visit with my daughter since the divorce. I call her every day. Check the phone records. What more could I do when the law says my daughter has to live with her mother?"

Detective Crumb tilted her head to study him, her pen tapping on the notebook in her lap. "Our records show that your wife was the one who filed for divorce."

"We'd be married if she hadn't."

"You still love her?"

Likely the detective thought love was a motive for kidnapping, and she was right. But it hadn't been for love of Dakota.

"Dakota and I didn't have a marriage since before Madeline was born, and the only reason I stayed at all was for Madeline. That's the truth." Parker stood. "Look, if you're going to charge me with something, then do it. Otherwise, I'm going back to work."

"You're not joining the search for your daughter?" Surprise registered in the detective's eyes.

He stared at her, knowing he had to make this good. "Madeline isn't lost. Dakota's stashed her somewhere—

probably to punish me for not giving her even more money than I already do. She disappeared with her once before, you know. For months I didn't know where my daughter was. Dakota's the one who needs to be investigated. Find her friends, and I'll bet one of them has Madeline. Meanwhile, I have to work to make sure that when you do find my daughter, she'll have food to put in her stomach and a roof over her head."

"Then give me a list of Dakota's friends." She arose, extending her notebook and pen to him.

He strode to the desk, leaning over it, and began scribbling names. "These are the friends she used to have when I knew her. Like I said, even when we were together, we had separate lives." His script was large and deep and angry, but he'd let her draw what conclusions she wanted from that.

The detective stood mutely near him as he wrote, and when he was finished and returned the notebook, she asked quietly, "What happened between you? If you don't mind my asking."

Parker did mind, but this was also part of the plan. "I was tired of living that life. I want what every other normal man wants—the American Dream. But Dakota wasn't ready to grow up. I don't think she ever will be. Look, Detective, when I went to pick up my daughter last week, I saw a plastic bag of drugs sitting in plain view on the television set. If my daughter had gotten hold of that . . ." He shook his head. "That's what I'm up against."

"Why didn't you call the police?"

"I don't know. I was too stunned, I guess. She'd promised me she wasn't using anymore. I've cursed myself every day since then for not calling." The reality was far worse than the words. Every night he awoke in a sweat, fearing that day would be the one he'd get the call telling him that his precious daughter had paid the price for his past.

Detective Crumb nodded, something akin to pity crossing her broad face. "Thank you, Mr. Hathaway. We'll keep in touch."

He nodded and watched her leave the trailer. If he'd played his cards right, she wouldn't suspect him for not jumping into his truck and driving to Salt Lake.

Or maybe she could see right through him.

He sat back down in one of the chairs near the desk, feeling as though he hadn't slept in weeks. Leaning forward, he propped his elbows on his knees and let his head fall into his hands.

"Everything all right?" Bob Jenkins, the sturdy, muscled foreman, entered the trailer.

Parker shook his head. "My daughter's missing."

Bob's jaw dropped. "You're kidding. That's terrible!" He looked over his shoulder and only then did Parker notice that Jason Rosen, the thin, gray-haired contractor who employed them both, had come in after Bob. Like Bob and many of the guys at the site, Rosen was a Mormon, and Parker had a lot of respect for the way he ran his business.

Rosen took a few steps toward Parker. "When did it happen?"

"Last night. They're not sure."

"Geez, I don't know what to say," muttered Bob. Parker wondered if he was thinking about his own five daughters, all of them under ten years old.

"We can help search the area," Rosen said. "Pull in hundreds of people within the hour."

Parker felt a stab of guilt, though he wasn't surprised at the offer. From what he'd observed all his life, the Mormons were always ready to help. "I don't know what the police want. They don't seem to think she just wandered off."

"I'll follow up with them," Rosen said, and Parker admired how sure he was.

There was an uncomfortable silence and then Rosen spoke again. "I know this is a bad time, but actually I came to offer you a job as a foreman on a new office complex we're building in Salt Lake."

Salt Lake now meant leaving Madeline. He shook his head. "I appreciate the offer, I really do, but I can't take it on right now. I wouldn't want to do any less than my best."

"I understand." The look in Rosen's eyes told him he respected Parker for rejecting the offer on those grounds. Parker felt ill at the deception.

"Do you need time off?" Bob asked.

"No. The police are doing everything they can. I have to believe that's enough. In fact, I really believe she's not missing at all, that this is just one more trick up my ex-wife's sleeve."

The men alternately nodded and shook their heads. Parker didn't think either really understood. They had never seen their wives strung out on meth. They probably thought he was a negligent father for not running up to Salt Lake. He should have thought this through better.

"I would like a few minutes to stop by my mother's," he said. "She's got to be worried." The detective would probably visit her, too, and Parker hoped she was up to it.

"Sure, knock off early today," Bob said. "The guys can handle it."

"And let us know if we can help," Rosen added.

Parker nodded, though neither of the men could hold his gaze for long. No doubt they were remembering the child who had been found murdered only weeks ago in a Salt Lake neighborhood.

Madeline wouldn't be a statistic. He'd made sure of that. Now if only he could manage to keep her safe until enough evidence was found to make sure she'd be safe forever.

•   •   •

Sally Crumb drove away from the construction site, all her nerves humming with warning. Parker Hathaway was lying. For a man to hold on to a loveless marriage for years to protect a young child was believable but to think that same man would remain at work while his daughter was missing wasn't. The situation reeked of deception.

Still, there was something inherently endearing about the man, and she had the feeling he might be a person one would be lucky to call a friend. Loyal to the extreme. Of course that didn't mean he wasn't responsible for his daughter's disappearance. In fact, it could mean he was very much involved.

The accusations about his ex-wife would have to be checked out. He seemed sincere on that account and so certain the child's mother was responsible for Madeline's disappearance. His story seemed to explain why Dakota Allen had waited hours to report Madeline's disappearance. Of course she could have been calling friends and driving around the neighborhood.

Maybe.

Sally shook her head and called the team who was at Parker's apartment with the local authorities. "Find anything?"

"Nothing. No sign of the little girl or anything belonging to her. Just a few pictures. We've been very thorough. Roommates say they've only seen the child once a few months ago."

That was odd. Hathaway said he never missed a weekend. Was that part of the lie? "Talk to the neighbors," she said, "and then head on back. The locals can take it from there."

So had he meant by weekends that he'd gone to see Madeline, or that she actually spent time with him elsewhere? Had he taken her to a hotel in Salt Lake? To his mother's? The more she thought about it, the more likely this last idea seemed. A responsible man would want his daughter to spend time with her grandmother, and a normal home environment would be a better choice than an apartment with single men whose lives might not be conducive to the needs of a small child.

Pulling over to the side of the road, Sally thumbed through the file she'd begun gathering on the kidnapping. It was less than half an inch thick so far, but that would quadruple before the day was over and all the feelers she had out came in. There it was. Norma Hathaway's address in Mt. Pleasant. She'd called the woman this morning, but no one answered. Someone from the local police had been by to chat with her earlier this afternoon, but Sally hadn't seen a report. Certainly wouldn't hurt to stop by since it was directly on her way home.

As she drove, Sally entertained herself with visions of miraculously finding Madeline at her grandmother's. Maybe the whole thing was a mistake. Maybe tonight she could go to sleep without nightmares of the scene Salt Lake police had found two weeks ago: a strangled seven-year-old whose body showed obvious signs of sexual violation.

Yet the very intuition that made her a good detective also made it impossible for her to believe in this fantasy. Something was wrong. Everything in her gut screamed it. From her negative impression of the child's mother to the certainty that Parker Hathaway was lying. Where did Madeline fit into all this?

Maybe the grandmother would be the key to unraveling the puzzle.

Norma Hathaway turned out to be a short, sturdy, neatly dressed woman with stylish brown hair. She looked at Sally's badge with brown eyes that were red from crying, her expression solemn and unsurprised.

"I'm Detective Crumb," Sally said. "Your son might have called to let you know I was in town. Could I come in for a few minutes?"

Neither confirming nor denying the phone call, Norma opened the screen door to let her in. "I've already talked to the police." She led the way to the living room, seating herself in an armchair while indicating that Sally should take the couch.

"I know you've talked to local authorities, but I have a few more questions. I just came from talking to your son."

"He hasn't done anything wrong. He's a good dad."

"As opposed to Madeline's mother?"

Norma lifted her shoulders. "Dakota's always been self-centered. I know she's using drugs, and that means she's not good for Madeline."

"Apparently the custody judge didn't agree."

Norma opened her mouth as though to protest, then changed her mind. "Look, shouldn't you be out there trying to find my granddaughter?"

"We have a great many people working on that. But in every kidnapping case, talking to relatives is vital. Most children are taken by relatives or someone familiar to them."

Norma nodded. "What do you want to know?"

"Do you see your granddaughter a lot?"

"Every other weekend. She's the light of my life." For the first time, a faint smile touched her lips. "Parker and I tried to make things good for her when she was here, so she could see what a regular life is like."

Sally felt some satisfaction knowing her hunch had been correct.

"At her mother's, everything is always fluid," Norma continued. "Dakota doesn't have a steady job, and Madeline's shuffled around a lot to neighbors and friends. Parker volunteers to take her, but Dakota's afraid she'll lose child support if she lets him take her too much. Dakota has another child, too. A little boy. He spends most of his time with his dad's relatives."

"You obviously have no love for your ex-daughter-in-law."

"Not one bit. She was a horrible wife. She nearly destroyed my son."

"Can you think of anyone who would take Madeline?"

There was a flash of something in Norma's eyes, but she shook her head, her lips pursed tightly, and Sally knew she wouldn't be able to get anything more from the woman. Yet Sally could tell Norma felt deeply guilty about something, and that told her far more than the woman herself would.

"I would like your permission to send a team here to your house."

"My house? Why?"

"Since Madeline stayed here so much, there might be clues."

"She was taken from her mother's, not from here."

"We've been through Ms. Allen's house very thoroughly, I assure you. But you wouldn't want us to overlook anything. Would it be all right?"

"Yes. I have nothing to hide."

Sally wasn't so sure about that, but she kept her peace. "Thank you, Mrs. Hathaway," she said, rising. At the door, Sally turned to her. "I have just one more question. Do you know where your granddaughter is?"

Norma blinked in surprise at her question, but there was a ring of sincerity when she responded. "I don't know where my granddaughter is right now, but I can say with all truthfulness that even if she was home with her mother, she'd still be in terrible danger. Dakota's the one you need to look into, Detective Crumb."

"That may be so, Mrs. Hathaway. Let's just hope Madeline is safe, or all the looking in the world won't make a difference." Turning on her heel, Sally stalked to her unmarked squad car.

She didn't leave right away but grabbed her cell phone. "I want a team to go over Norma Hathaway's house," she barked. "No warrant necessary. She's agreed to let us in. And I've changed my mind about sending you home. I want surveillance on both Parker and Norma Hathaway. I'll coordinate things with the local authorities. Call it a gut feeling, or whatever, but I think the Hathaways are hiding something."

Clicking the phone shut, she looked up at the small, well-kept rambler for several minutes before driving away. Though she wished she could follow up on her feelings herself, there was more information she needed to sift through first. And once in a while, even she was wrong.

CHAPTER

5

For two days now, Parker Hathaway had been forced to sneak out of his own apartment through a window under the cover of darkness and use a fire escape to get to the ground. Then he'd had to jog five miles to the rented house on the edge of town. He didn't know why the police had staked out his truck and apartment, but he couldn't take the risk of leading them to Madeline.

When he arrived on Friday night, Madeline was waiting for him in the front room of the house. He could see her framed in the light from the window as she watched for him. "Daddy," she called through the window. Faster than he could climb the four cement steps framed by a wobbling wrought iron railing, she was out the door and climbing into his arms.

"Careful, babe. I'm a little sweaty."

"Why?"

"'Cuz I just ran all the way here." He'd showered off all the

51

dirt from the construction site at the apartment, but now he'd have to shower again.

"Did your truck break?" she asked with concern.

"Something like that. Is Carla here?"

"She's making dinner."

"Did you have fun with her today?"

Madeline nodded eagerly, her now-brown locks flowing in stray wisps around her face. "We played hide and seek, and she helped me build a tent, and she was teaching me Spanish. I can say table and chair and a whole bunch of other stuff." She demonstrated as they walked inside, and Parker was impressed.

"That's great! Just so you don't forget how to speak English. I don't know Spanish."

Madeline giggled. "That would be funny if I was saying stuff and if you didn't know what I was saying. And then I would have to tell you and you would say, 'Oh, that's what Madeline is saying.'" Parker laughed. Madeline always made up imaginary scenarios that amused both of them.

Carla had paused in the kitchen as they came in. She smiled. "I feeneesh deener for Madeleen. Then I go."

"Thank you," he said, marveling at how quickly she was learning the language. He'd been in Mexico once for a week and hadn't understood a thing. Apparently Carla was more adaptable. He'd felt from first meeting her that she was intelligent, and it was one of the reasons he'd hired her. That and he knew she wasn't likely to run to the police. "Is there anything I should know about? Did everything go okay?"

Carla nodded. "Ees fine. She ees a good geerl."

"I'm glad. You can always call me if you need something." The owner of the house had agreed to leave in a phone under his name—long distance blocked—so Carla and Madeline had access to a phone. He'd given her the number of the new cell phone he'd recently bought, the one that didn't use his real name. It was possible the police had some way of hearing or tracing his conversations on his official cell phone.

Carla nodded, but Parker suspected that her limited English would prevent her from ever calling. He'd have to teach Madeline how to dial tonight in case she needed him. He went into the bathroom and removed his shirt.

"Are you going to take a bath?" Madeline asked, watching him from the doorway with interest. He could tell she was disappointed.

"Nope. Just cleaning up a bit." He leaned over the sink, splashing water on his face, over his head, neck, and under his arms. Then he rubbed himself dry with a towel, pulling on a new shirt from the duffle bag he'd carried through the streets. After Madeline was in bed, he'd shower properly and leave the dirty clothes here for a spare, since Carla had agreed to do the laundry. That beat jogging over here carrying an extra set of clothes.

He hadn't found time to shave in nearly a week, and he stared into the mirror at a face he barely recognized. How long would he be able to keep up this duplicity? Though tomorrow was Saturday, he still had to work, and that meant another five-mile jog back to his apartment in the morning after Carla arrived, and another five miles after a grueling day at work. Yet he couldn't afford to quit working. Two months earlier he'd opened his apartment to roommates to lower the costs he'd known were pending, but he still had his child care payments to Dakota, the apartment rent, the truck payment, the rent on the house for Dakota and Madeline, and few savings to tide him over.

How long before he made a serious mistake? How long before the police figured out what he'd done? They would have followed him here already if Donald, one of his roommates, hadn't recognized the officers in the unmarked car parked in front of their apartment. Fortunately for Parker they'd been the same men who'd interviewed Donald earlier, and he had noticed them shortly before Parker had come home from work.

Worry bit at Parker's mind. What if the police couldn't find anything on Dakota? What if they didn't even try? What if they stayed on his tail for a month? A year? More? How could he give Madeline any semblance of a normal life?

"Daddy?"

Parker was startled from his thoughts by Madeline's voice. He took his unseeing gaze from the mirror. "All finished, honey. Let's go get some dinner, and then we'll play. I missed you so much today."

"Can we go outside?" Madeline asked. "Carla said no."

Parker smiled past his exhaustion. "If we bundle you up really well, we can go outside for a bit. But Carla was right about not going outside during the day."

"Why?"

"It's not safe here unless I'm home."

She nodded solemnly, easily accepting his explanation. "Can we make a snowman? A really big one?"

"The snow's too old and crunchy to pack, but as soon as it snows again, we'll make the biggest and bestest snowman ever."

Madeline hugged him. "Yay!"

He lifted her into his arms and started for the door.

"Daddy?" she asked. "When am I going back to Mommy's?"

"Do you miss her?"

She shook her head. "Not yet. I been here only one, two days." She held up two fingers as she counted them. "I don't want to go away yet."

"Okay. Then you can stay."

She put her arms around his neck, squeezing him tightly and bringing tears to his eyes. "I wish Reese was here," she whispered in her ear. "He would like to have fun with you, too."

Reese, the little boy who'd been in the crib—Madeline's half brother—was now in as much danger as Madeline had been. "He'll be fine," Parker said, despite the pit of cold settling in his stomach. "He has a daddy, too." From what Madeline had told him, Reese spent a lot of time with his father. With luck, maybe Dakota would allow the man to take custody while the police investigated Madeline's disappearance.

"Come on," he said, moving Madeline around to his back. "I'll give you a horsey ride to the kitchen."

Madeline's laughter filled the tiny house.

•   •   •

At eight o'clock on Friday night, Caitlin was lying in bed in her pajamas watching TV, Amy sprawled next to her. There were dolls and stuffed animals and an array of picture books as well, since Amy always liked to stave off boredom.

The day had been long and torturous. Chet Belstead had refused the plea deal and they had continued the trial. Contrary to Caitlin's expectation, Wyman hadn't retaken his case. In fact, he hadn't even shown up. Only Mace Keeley was there, as smooth-talking and flamboyant as ever. And as gorgeous. The jury loved him. After final arguments, the jury was out less than an hour before Belstead was found guilty. He went crazy at the verdict, cursing the jurors and judge, and finally lunging for Caitlin, but the bailiff, Mace, and several other men in the courtroom had managed to drag him out before there was any damage. Caitlin knew his final sentence would likely be a lot stiffer for his stupidity.

She hadn't seen Mace after he'd left with the bailiff and her client, not that she had expected to, though that fact didn't stop her hopes from rising as her cell phone rang. Her exhaustion vanished when she saw it was Mace. "Hello?" She hoped she didn't sound as eager and breathless as she felt.

"Hi, Caitlin. It's Mace. I think I'm going to be finished a bit early after all. You still up for dinner in, say, an hour?"

An hour gave her thirty-five minutes to change, throw on a bit of makeup, and find a sitter for Amy, and then twenty-five more minutes to make the restaurant and find parking. In attorney time, that was eons. "Sure. But I've got a few things to wrap up myself. Can we meet somewhere?"

"How about at Caffe Molise?" He obviously assumed she was still at her office. "They're open at least until ten, I believe."

"I'll be there." Caffe Molise was a popular Italian restaurant, and to get a reservation this quickly in the winter when there wasn't outdoor dining was no small feat. Mace must know someone to have organized this date so quickly—unless he'd anticipated that he would be able to get free and had made reservations earlier, just in case. Or maybe working late had been a lie all along, and instead he'd had a date that evening who'd canceled on him, leaving Caitlin his second choice.

Sometimes she hated being so analytical.

"I'm looking forward to seeing you." His voice was casual, but she sensed innuendo beneath the words, and her thoughts scattered. Who cared how she ended up at dinner with Mace Keeley? Just so she did.

"Me too." Caitlin hung up the phoned and kicked into high gear. She began dialing a telephone number as she shrugged off her pajamas and stared into her closet, wondering what to wear. Something attractive but that wouldn't show too much bare skin, as it was cold outside and she was supposedly coming from work. She chose a sheer red top with her fitted black suit coat and skirt. After she lost the jacket, the top would be dressy and the skirt just tight enough and short enough to emphasize her legs, which she had always considered her best feature.

Sally wasn't answering her home or cell phone, and neither were either of Caitlin's next-door neighbors or Amy's baby-sitter. Caitlin put a dab of perfume behind her ears and on her neck, beginning to feel a touch of despair. Her demanding job hadn't left her time for many friends, and that meant she didn't have a lot of people she could call on for help. Wait, she did have a cousin who lived in Salt Lake. Where was the number? She found it at last, only to learn the number had been disconnected.

"Now who?" she muttered, glancing at Amy, who was still sprawled on the bed, thumbing through her picture books. If only their parents were alive. If only Amy was normal. Sighing in disgust at her own thoughts, Caitlin slumped on the bed.

"Are you okay?" Amy asked. "You look mad. Did I do something?"

"No, sweetie. You didn't do anything."

Caitlin searched through the phone numbers on her cell phone again. Jodi. Maybe she would be willing. At least she knew about Amy.

"Hello?"

"Hi, Jodi. It's Caitlin. Look, are you busy right now? I've had something really important come up, and I need someone to stay with my sister."

"I'm just heading to a movie," Jodi said. "I'd volunteer to

take her with me, but"—her voice lowered—"I'm with this really hot guy I met in court yesterday. Sorry."

"That's okay. Thanks anyway."

Caitlin spied Sally's husband on her list of contacts. He'd at least know where she was.

"Hello?" Tony answered on the second ring.

"Hi, it's Caitlin. I'm looking for Sally."

"She's on a stakeout. She should be home, but she's got some hunch about this kidnapping, and she's pulling overtime. I decided to take Randi to visit my parents."

"You're clear up in Logan?"

"Yep. I thought I might as well drive up, since Sally's down in Manti."

"I see."

"You can call her on her cell."

"She's not answering."

"I'm sorry. Was it very important?"

Only an entire future with Mace Keeley. "Nothing that can't wait," she said aloud.

When Caitlin hung up the phone, she saw that all of her minutes were gone. *So much for eons of time,* she thought with despair.

Could she take Amy on her date? She let herself hope for a few minutes longer. Amy might behave. She might actually eat the food she was given without complaint. Maybe she would be too tired to talk incessantly. She might not ask Mace to father Caitlin's children.

No. Taking Amy would be a disaster. Especially when Mace was only expecting her. And how romantic would it be anyway, with Amy watching their every move? Caitlin had no choice but to call Mace back and cancel.

"Hi," he said, sounding happy to hear from her.

She took a deep breath. "Hi, Mace. Look, I'm sorry, but I'm going to have to cancel. I thought I had everything taken care of, but there's something else I have to do. I'm really sorry. How about a rain check?"

"If you want I could stop by with some take-out." His voice sounded strangely compelling.

"I can't. I won't be alone. I was looking forward to it, but—"

"No problem," he said quickly. "I know how it is. We'll do something another day."

Caitlin stared at the phone in her hand for long minutes after their conversation. She knew she might never have another opportunity with him. She wished she didn't care so much.

Amy's arms went around her. "Caitlin, why are you sad?"

Caitlin returned Amy's hug, blinking back unbidden tears. They settled back on her pillows before Caitlin answered. "Well, there's a guy I kind of like, and I was going to go see him tonight, but it didn't work out."

"Because of me." Amy frowned. "I could stay by myself."

"No, you can't."

"If I was smarter, I could."

Her tone made Caitlin feel worse. Though Amy had enough intelligence to understand that something was different about her, they didn't usually discuss it.

"Oh, Amy." Caitlin pulled her sister closer, gazing into her eyes. "I love you exactly the way you are."

Amy's lip curved in her sweet smile. "I love you, too, Caitlin. More than anyone." She laid her head on Caitlin's shoulder.

They were quiet a long moment as Caitlin pondered her life. Any man she became involved with would have to know about and accept Amy. Because no matter what, she would never, ever leave Amy behind.

"Is he cute?" Amy asked suddenly.

Caitlin laughed. "Very cute."

"Would he make good babies?"

"I'm sure he'd make incredible babies." Though the picture of Mace as a husband was not something Caitlin was going to torture herself with tonight.

"Good." Amy was quiet for a moment and then abruptly her eyes closed. Like many young children, for Amy the difference between wakefulness and sleep was a matter of seconds.

Caitlin eased her arm out from under her sister and went to change back into her pajamas. She was reaching for the remote and getting ready to numb her brain into thoughtlessness by watching whatever was on TV when Sally called.

"Hi," Sally asked. "Need something?"

"You're on a stakeout?"

"I'm keeping an eye on the father of that kidnapped girl I told you about. I was chatting with some of his neighbors when you called before."

"I saw the Amber Alert."

"Hopefully it'll bring in more tips."

"So you think the father did it?"

"I don't know, but he's lying about something. But it's odd. He's my most likely suspect, but I kind of like him."

"Why?"

"I don't know. Maybe I'm partial to men in construction."

"Ah. Does he look like Tony?"

"Not at all. But he's not bad. If I weren't married . . ."

Caitlin ignored that. Both of them knew Sally was wildly crazy about Tony.

"So why did you call?" Sally asked into the silence.

"I wanted to see if I could drop Amy at your place for the night. I had the chance to go out to dinner with Mace Keeley."

"Ah, the handsome deputy DA."

"The one and only."

"Apparently all that drooling over him this past year hasn't been in vain. Miracles do happen."

"I have not been drooling over him!"

"Yes, you have."

"Well, so what?"

"I think it's fabulous, Caitlin. Why didn't you tell me before? I could have assigned this evening to someone else."

"It wasn't planned. He was working late and managed to get off earlier. When he called, we decided to do dinner. But I couldn't take Amy, so I had to cancel."

"Next time, give me some notice. Randi would love to have Amy over."

"I'm not so sure there'll be a next time."

Sally was quiet a long moment. "You're selling yourself short, you know. You're the hottest lawyer babe I know. And don't compare yourself with that toothpick, white-faced paralegal you work with, either. You're a woman, not a little girl."

Caitlin sighed. She knew Sally meant well, but she wasn't helping.

"Well, at least you have tomorrow night," Sally added.

Caitlin made a face but managed not to groan. With the excitement and subsequent disappointment of Mace's invitation, she'd forgotten all about her date with Wyman. What if he tried to blackmail her into giving him more information on other cases? Or used his knowledge to try to force her into a dating relationship?

He doesn't have proof.

Yet.

"Oh, yes. Can't forget tomorrow," Caitlin said with false gaiety. "And I guess I'd better let you go get the bad guys."

"I'm not so sure he is the bad guy, but I'm doing everything I can to bring that little girl home to her mother—whether the woman deserves it or not."

Caitlin hung up and watched TV until she fell asleep. Instead of dreaming about Mace Keeley, she dreamed of Wyman Russell running after her with the bloody knife he carried wrapped in a dark blue jacket.

CHAPTER

6

Parker heard pans clanging in the kitchen and came to consciousness with a start. From the angle of the light spilling in from the gauzy green curtains, he was late. His head felt full of sand, and his muscles protested the slightest move. Apparently working construction used different muscles than jogging and playing half the night with a four-year-old.

There was something heavy on his chest, and he looked down to see Madeline's head there, her feet splayed toward the side of the bed. Seeing her cleared the fog from his brain and sent him into action. This innocent, precious child was the reason he was going to such great effort, the reason he had to make it all work. Gently, he eased out from under Madeline, leaning over to place a kiss on the small mole on her right cheek.

Hopefully, she'd sleep a good portion of the day so she wouldn't have as much time to get bored. He should probably think about finding her a preschool eventually. He doubted Carla would be able to teach her to read English.

Quickly, he changed from his pajama bottoms into his extra pair of jeans, having tossed the other pair into the dirty laundry the night before. He'd showered last night and his shirt was still fairly clean, so he was good to go.

Carla was in the kitchen, and her pretty brown face lit up at seeing him. "Good morning," she said. Her long hair was secured in the back with a clip the way Dakota had sometimes worn hers. For some reason it made him feel sad.

"Good morning." He ran a hand through his hair. "I'm late, so I have to get going. She stayed up pretty late. It's probably best to let her sleep."

Carla nodded. "She sleep. I bring book to read."

"Okay. Thanks."

"Want to eat?" Carla said, motioning to the stove where she was already cooking something he thought might be Madeline's lunch. Their deal was that she'd buy food and make all the meals for Madeline, and enough dinner for him as well. "I make eggs, eef you like."

"No, thanks. I'll get something later. I'm really late." He pulled his sweatshirt over his head, wishing it wasn't so cold outside and that he didn't have five miles to run before he could get his truck.

"Daddy?" Madeline was in the doorway, rubbing her eyes. "Are you leaving?" Her lips drew into a pout.

"I have to work. But remember we'll spend the whole day together tomorrow."

"Can we see Grandma?"

He thought about it. "Maybe. I'll try to make it work." He bent down and held out his arms, and Madeline ran into them. "Be a good girl for Carla today, okay? If you need me, call the phone like I showed you last night. But only if it's really important, okay? Otherwise, I'll call you at lunchtime again."

"Okay, Daddy, but it's kind of boring here."

"I'll bring you some games."

"Can I watch TV?"

"Yes." He hadn't figured on her being bored. Usually when they were together, they had so much planned they couldn't squeeze all the activities into the two short days they had been allotted for his visitation. "I'll be back soon, sweetie. I love you."

She squeezed his neck with mock ferociousness. "I love you too, Daddy. You're my bestest, bestest daddy ever."

"And you're my bestest girl."

After cautioning her to stay inside, he left for the long run to his apartment. The cold morning air seared the inside of his nose and throat as he ran. Since he worked outside most days, he had learned to deal with the cold, but he still hated it with a passion. When it was hot he could dunk his head and gulp down water to chase away the heat from inside. The cold was another story. It seeped between the layers of clothing, crawled into his pores and mouth and nose, lodging in his bones and making him feel stiff and old. Maybe he should take that job as a foreman. He'd worked hard for the opportunity and it wasn't really a surprise to have it offered. Of course, even if he could move Madeline, it was already too late for that opportunity.

As he ran, the weight of what he was trying to do threatened to crush him. The police were following him, not checking out Dakota as he'd hoped. For all he knew, Dakota was playing the poster mother for all lost children. Dakota, who'd thought nothing of letting her daughter live in a meth house, or who had locked Madeline in her room so she could be alone with her friends to do a little recreational crack.

65

He made it back to his apartment and in through the window, changing quickly into a long-sleeved work shirt and his heavy coat. The unmarked car was still outside the apartment, and he stifled the urge to wave to the officers. No use letting them know he knew they were there. They might make their surveillance more subtle and track him to Madeline.

Driving to work, the realization hit him. *I can't keep this up.* The police weren't going to stop any time soon, and hiding inside all day was no life for a child—or for him. His mother was right. They would have to disappear.

· · ·

As Caitlin readied for her date Saturday night, Amy was more excited than Caitlin was. In fact, she dreaded the evening with Wyman. He was picking her up at six—a time she insisted on so they wouldn't be too late getting home. Gloria, her neighbor on the left, had agreed to watch Amy, but Caitlin had promised to pick her up before ten. Nine preferably. Or maybe eight? Would Wyman believe that?

She grimaced into the mirror. Oddly enough, she looked really good, even if she did say so herself. Her unruly copper hair often waved or curled out of control, usually in a half-and-half mixture that looked rather uneven and that almost always prompted Caitlin to pin up her hair for work, but today the hair was being remarkably well-behaved. A little gel had helped even out the waves and curls, and the air drying helped tamed the frizz. Her makeup had gone on well, and the fitted blue blouse she'd chosen to wear over black slacks made her eyes even bluer. She'd chosen these clothes because she didn't know where they were going and didn't really care about making an impression, but even she had to admit that she looked, well, hot.

"You look so beautiful," Amy said with a sigh. "Like a princess." She whirled around the bathroom, looking rather incongruous and awkward given her height and bulk.

Caitlin hugged her. "Thank you, Amy."

"I know you don't like him a real lot, but I think he's nice." Amy obviously hadn't noticed the revulsion Wyman had shown for her, and Caitlin was glad. There were distinct advantages to being one of the pure and innocent.

Her mind churned over what Wyman might say or do this evening. As always, her thoughts fell into the same pattern. Did he think she would start feeding him information about her cases?

He can't prove anything, she told herself for the hundredth time in the past few days. But she knew there were ways. Now that they'd tracked down the boy, they'd work on Kenny, and though Kenny had always been reliable, he might accidentally let something slip. Would there be enough to prove misconduct? If so, would that set Chet Belstead free?

The thought made her sick. But what else could she have done? Watch him walk away free, only to meet up with him again when he was arrested for a similar crime? When another victim and her family sat on the benches with devastation in their eyes?

The nauseated feeling increased. She knew she had made her choice, and now she had to do what she could to keep Chet Belstead in jail and to protect her job and Amy.

"Come on," Caitlin said, pushing away the dark thoughts. "Let's get you over to Gloria's."

"Yippee!" Amy loved Gloria, who worked at the Hostess outlet and always brought home their products. At least once a week they would find donuts or some other treat in a plastic sack on their doorknob.

Before they left the bathroom the doorbell rang, and Amy ran to open it. Caitlin followed more slowly in her black high-heeled boots. "It's that one guy!" Amy called. "He has some flowers and they're so pretty. Hurry, Caitlin!"

Caitlin came into view, pulling on her dressy leather jacket. She met Wyman's eyes and was satisfied to see his admiration, though why she'd care for his admiration was beyond her. "Hi," she said pleasantly, her eyes dropping to the bouquet of roses in his hands. She hadn't expected flowers.

"You ready?"

"I need to walk Amy next door."

"I can do it myself." Amy edged past Wyman and out onto the porch.

"Wait," Wyman said. "Here." He gave the flowers to Amy. Her mouth dropped open and her eyes went wide. Caitlin hadn't seen her so surprised since two years ago when Caitlin had redone her room in a princess motif for her twenty-fifth birthday.

"Me?" Amy asked. "Aren't they for Caitlin?"

"They're for you. Go ahead, take them."

Amy took the flowers and bounced up and down. "They're so pretty. So pretty! I never had flowers before, did I, Caitlin? I love them!" She hugged them to her chest, plastic and all.

Caitlin was laughing, feeling grateful to Wyman despite her distaste for him. "Careful of the thorns. Come on, bring them into the kitchen. Let's get you a vase to take to Gloria's. She can help you arrange them in water."

"Okay." Amy lumbered past Wyman.

"Come in," Caitlin invited. "It'll just be a moment."

Amy had already found a vase, though they were on the

top shelf. There was one advantage to her being so tall. "Is this one good?"

Caitlin shook her head. "It's very pretty, but I don't think it'll hold all those flowers. Is there a bigger one?"

Amy reached for it. "I got it." She did a little dance. "I can't wait to show Gloria. And can I show them to Sarah? Will they still be alive when I go there again?"

"I'm sure they'll still be good by Monday."

Amy breezed into the living room and out the front door. By the time Caitlin and Wyman were off the front porch she was already at Gloria's. The tall, dark-haired woman waved to them before taking Amy inside and shutting the door.

"Thanks for that," Caitlin said as they walked to Wyman's gray car—a Lexus, she noted.

He shrugged. "I didn't think you'd mind sharing your flowers."

She stifled a retort that she hadn't expected flowers at all.

"Truthfully, I've never seen a woman so excited about flowers before," he said as he opened her door.

"Well, Amy's not exactly a woman."

"I know."

She studied him as she walked around the car. He was different this evening, though she couldn't tell exactly why. He wore a blue plaid sport jacket and solid blue pants that were more attractive than his typical dark work suit, but his hair was still thinning and his handsome face a bit on the fleshy side. So what exactly was different about him?

He'd been nice to Amy. That had to be it. Despite the revulsion she'd clearly seen on his face earlier in the week, he'd been kind to her. Why? Was it a trick, a ploy to make her relax? She couldn't afford to relax. Wyman was her enemy both in and out of court, and she couldn't let her guard down even for a moment.

"Where are we going?" she asked.

"You'll see."

She arched a brow. "A surprise?"

"Hopefully." He smiled, ignoring the coolness of her tone.

Opera was playing in the car, and though Caitlin had developed a taste for the music since passing the bar, she didn't want to enjoy herself. She held her body stiff and her lips together as she stared out the window in silence. She didn't want to be here with him, and there was no use pretending.

He drove to the Avenues in Salt Lake City, pulling up in the last open parking place before a squat, two-story stucco building that looked as if it might contain three or four offices. She couldn't tell if the stucco was tan or gray, it was so nondescript.

"There's a restaurant here?" she asked.

He pointed to a sign over one of the double doors. "Cafe Shambala. It's Tibetan food. I hope you like it."

She'd tasted some once and hadn't hated it, so she shrugged. "Yeah. It's fine." *I'm really only here to find out what you want.*

Inside, large colorful posters and flags lined the walls, and there were several prominent pictures of an older man with dark hair. "The Dalai Lama," Wyman explained. Besides the posters, the decorations were sparse. The clientele seemed varied, though most were relatively young. "Don't let the place fool you," Wyman told her. "They serve really good food."

There seemed to be only one server, but he came to their table before Caitlin had time to completely remove her leather jacket.

"The chicken curry is excellent," Wyman suggested as the

server hovered over them with a pad and pencil. "Or the chicken and broccoli, if you like broccoli."

"Okay, I'll have the chicken and broccoli."

"I'll have the curry," Wyman said. "And we'd like this mo-mo appetizer." He lifted his eyes to Caitlin. "They don't have a liquor license here, but they have a sort of yogurt shake called a lassi that's nice."

Caitlin had tried lassi at another restaurant and hadn't been impressed, but she agreed anyway to get the evening over with as soon as possible. "I'll have that, then. And some water, please." The server hurried away with their order.

The kitchen was open to the restaurant, and they could see workers preparing the meals. Caitlin wondered if it gave customers comfort when they chose some of the stranger meals. "This is really cozy," she said, settling back in her chair. "Nice." Relaxing was actually a better word since the earlier tension in her body was gone.

"You sound surprised."

She shrugged. She *was* surprised, but she wasn't going to admit it. She'd expected a bigger show, something along the lines of Mace's restaurant choice, but not this little place, with its sparse decorations and intimate atmosphere. If the food tasted as good as it smelled, she would at least derive some enjoyment from this forced expedition.

"Something funny?" Wyman asked.

She shook her head. "Not really. I'm just wondering why you asked me here."

"Ah. Business first. I get it." His eyes narrowed. "Okay, I want to know if you're involved with how we found the evidence against your client."

Caitlin considered him a moment. There had been a slight hesitation before he'd spoken. She wouldn't be as good an attorney as she was if she hadn't recognized it. "Are you sure that's it? A few days ago you said something about working together." She fixed an unwavering stare on him.

He dropped his gaze first, and she had the distinct feeling he was hiding something. "You applied for my job two years ago," he said. "There may be another opening soon. You could come and work for the good guys for a change."

He couldn't possibly know how wonderful that sounded. "Strange," she said, her voice flat, "I thought you were trying to blackmail me into giving you privileged client-attorney information." Keeping the emotion from her words was the way to unnerve creeps. It worked every day with the hardened criminals she worked with, as well as the young attorneys, who seemed to spend at least half their time trying to find dates.

"Then why are you here?"

"Maybe to gain evidence against *you*." Going on the attack was not a new ploy but one he apparently recognized.

He smiled. "I haven't done anything wrong."

"Neither have I." Her voice trembled ever so slightly, making her furious with herself.

His gaze shifted to the kitchen and then back to her. There were still a few empty tables in the restaurant, and they were relatively isolated, but more customers were coming in. They would soon risk being overheard. "Look, let's drop this for now and enjoy dinner. For what it's worth, I'm betting you're not involved in anything that could get you disbarred."

"I didn't get that impression a few days ago," she retorted icily.

He was silent for several seconds. "Look, you need to be careful of Mace."

"Mace?" This surprised her. "What does he have to do with

this?" Had Wyman somehow heard of her almost date with him yesterday? She'd have to be more careful.

"I know everyone thinks Mace Keeley is God's gift to the DA's office. But I work with the guy, and I think a little caution in is order."

"He seems nice enough." Not to mention gorgeous, hot, and the focus of more than a few of her dreams, though Wyman didn't need to hear that from her.

"He is. Right up until he stabs you in the back."

"His record for winning cases is unparalleled."

"Whereas mine is at the bottom?" Wyman smirked. "Interesting. Makes you wonder how the cases are assigned."

Caitlin pondered his words. This vein of conversation was completely unexpected. She'd thought Wyman might present some evidence of her breach of ethics, not act like a jealous suitor. Could it be possible that Wyman was attracted to her on more than a casual what-will-you-do-so-I'll-keep-quiet level? The thought stunned her into complete and utter silence.

"Ah, here comes our food." Wyman's sarcasm was gone. "You're in for a treat."

They ended up sharing the meals, dishing from the serving plates to other plates the server had brought them. Caitlin, who had never really enjoyed curry because it was too hot, loved the curry chicken so much that she forgot herself and ate seconds.

They talked about the courthouse and people they knew, keeping the conversation away from current cases or anything serious. When they finally finished dinner, Caitlin was surprised to see that two hours had slipped away.

Wyman saw her looking at her watch. "It's about time, huh? You need to get back to Amy?"

"Yes." Caitlin grabbed at the excuse, not because she wasn't enjoying herself but because she was. She still hadn't decided if Wyman was out to get her disbarred or into a romance. Either way, he wasn't a good candidate for Amy's husband and baby scenario, and Caitlin had worked too hard to let a mediocre attorney get in the way of her career.

They talked only occasionally on the way home, but the drive was comfortable. Wyman walked her to the door when they arrived at her house. The automatic light went on, and she bent to open the door with her key.

Wyman didn't take the hint. "I had a cousin like Amy," he said, his breath turning white as it hit the cold air. "When we were young, I didn't really notice any difference, but around nine or ten I started hating it. My mom and my aunt always wanted me to take him with me when I hung out with the guys. I thought it was embarrassing, so we used to play a lot of jokes on him." He shook his head, not looking at her now. "I feel guilty every time I think of it. He never, ever caught on. He practically worshiped me."

"Did something happen to him?" Caitlin was visualizing a prank that went too far, something that might have scarred a younger Wyman.

He shook his head. "He's still alive, living with my aunt. I never see him. It's just . . . when I met your sister the other day . . . well, let's just say it wasn't what I expected. I had an entirely different concept of you. At work you're so . . . well, intent. You don't hold back any punches or seem to have any love for your clients. You're tough."

She knew what he wasn't saying. He'd thought she was the kind of woman who might not care about ethics. "You asked me out because of my sister?" That was a first. Usually guys headed toward the hills when they sensed that kind of responsibility. His right shoulder lifted in a half shrug. "I don't know how I feel about that," she said.

His face came closer, and she could tell he was going to kiss her. A part of her ached to be kissed, to be touched, but this was too much, too soon. She didn't understand anything about this man and wasn't sure if she even liked him. She stepped back, her hand reaching for the doorknob. "Last I heard, you had a wife. Unless you're divorced now."

He nodded, his expression contrite. "We're separated, but you're right. I'm sorry. It doesn't look good, but I really don't know where that's going yet. Until I know for sure—"

She took pity on him. "Wyman, I had a good time tonight. I really did. Well, all but that first bit at the restaurant." She smiled. "But I only went tonight because of our business relationship. You and I . . ." She shook her head. "It's not going anywhere."

He leaned over and kissed her cheek. "I meant what I said earlier about Mace. I know you think he's a paragon, but consider this. Have you ever wondered why you and I try so many cases together?"

Caitlin shook her head, not understanding his implication.

"Think about it. Look at Mace's cases."

When she didn't reply, he lifted his right shoulder, turned, and sprinted to his Lexus.

Caitlin watched him go, finding it difficult to reorder her previous impressions of Wyman. Was he what he appeared to be, or was he playing some game she didn't yet understand?

G randma!" Madeline shot from the doorway of the rental house and into Norma's arms. The two put their heads together and began chattering as though it was any normal Sunday at Norma's house in Mt. Pleasant.

Parker set down the boxes of clothes from his apartment and smiled. Madeline's joy was worth all the subterfuge of getting his mother here. He'd packed early this morning and had driven to her house, his faithful police escort following behind. Carrying his boxes, they had gone through Norma's back fence and over a few streets to the house of a family friend, who had loaned them a car. Then Parker had driven straight here.

He'd thought about blindfolding his mother so the secret would be safer, but he might need her to check on Madeline if their departure from the state was delayed. Besides, she wouldn't tell. She knew as well as he did the danger Madeline would be in if she was returned to her mother.

"I weel be going then," Carla said from the doorway of the kitchen. "Unteel tonight when you need me."

"Thanks, Carla. I appreciate your help." He'd given her Monday and Tuesday off in exchange for coming in this morning for two hours and for another two later that evening when he took his mother home and jogged back from his apartment. She had been only too happy to agree. He felt a momentary pang of guilt that when she returned on Wednesday, he and Madeline wouldn't be there. Well, he'd leave her as much severance as he could pay.

Carla looked at him. "Eef Madeleen asleep tonight when you leave, you need me still to stay?"

"Yes, I'll still need you." He was surprised at the question. Had Carla been raised in a home where it was okay to leave small children if they were sleeping? Or maybe she didn't understand the distance and time involved. He couldn't possibly explain his need for jogging back to the house. "She's too young to ever be alone."

"Okay." She smiled, nodded at him, and went out the back door.

Parker returned his attention to Madeline and his mother.

"I love your new hair," Norma was saying.

"It's like yours, Grandma." Madeline twirled around to show off her dark locks.

"Look what Grandma brought you." Norma took out bubblegum and two packs of cards from her purse. "Old Maid and Go Fish. Your favorites!"

"Goody!"

Parker felt grateful. Madeline could play these games forever, and that meant that he might just be able to take a little nap. With all the lack of sleep, the worry, and additional exercise, he was feeling decidedly exhausted. But Madeline was safe, and that was the most important thing.

He sat on the couch and was dozing before he knew it, dreaming of Dakota when they first met at a bar. She was young and pretty and flirty and had her sights on him. He'd drunk heavily in those days, and she was just as eager to drink. They'd gone through the next days in a whirl of partying and semi-consciousness. She'd wanted to get married, so they did after only two months, living hand to mouth, working only when absolutely necessary. Parker had thought he was happy, but more often than not tears had wet his pillow at night. He'd been lost. Adrift in a sea. Missing his family. Seeing no sense to the world or a reason for his existence. Until Madeline.

And then the terrible call that changed everything.

Parker jerked awake, sweating. Madeline and his mother were nowhere to be seen. His heart constricted with fear that left him tingling to his fingertips. Had the police found them and taken Madeline away? Why hadn't they taken him? He shook the thoughts away. *Be sensible.*

He found Madeline in the kitchen making cookies with ingredients Norma had brought from home. Parker watched his mother and daughter from the doorway, enjoying Madeline's enthusiasm. They interacted in a way that went beyond the casual, a way far beyond how Madeline interacted with her mother.

Norma came over to stand beside him as Madeline was pouring the chocolate chips, a few at a time, into the batter, stopping to eat a few or to make the chocolate pieces talk to one another. "I've liquidated one of my investments," she said calmly but in a painful way, as though she was barely holding everything together. "Here's my bank card if you need it. There's about ten thousand so far." She held up a hand when he looked as though he might protest. "No. I know you have a bit saved, and since I'm on your account, I'll take that when I join you. But it'd be better if you didn't take it all out now. If they're watching you, they've probably got a finger on your bank accounts."

Could they really do that? Parker decided they probably could but only if they had a warrant, and what proof would they have for one of those? Maybe it didn't matter in a kidnapping case. He took the card.

"I'll call you on this cell phone when we're settled," he said, handing her a new cell phone he'd bought for her yesterday on his lunch hour. As he'd done with his new phone, he'd made sure to use a false name and pay cash. It'd only work for a month, but that should be long enough. He'd also quit his job on Saturday night, saying he was heading up north to search for his daughter.

Her gaze rested on Madeline. "So we're really going to do this."

"Mom, you don't have to." Parker hated the idea of her selling her house and moving away from a lifetime of friends. It wasn't fair for her to have to start over and live on the run.

"Yes I do. You and Madeline are all the family I have, and you should know how important family is to me. Make no mistake; as soon as I've wrapped up everything here, I'm going to wherever you are." She glanced at the phone. "I'll be waiting for your call."

Parker's emotion bubbled up inside him, threatening to spill over. "I'm sorry I haven't been the son you deserve. I'd do anything to be him."

They both knew who he was talking about. Him. Vincent, the perfect older son, the one who'd been obedient to their demanding father, the one who'd studied diligently and worked for the future he would never have. Even in death, Parker felt envious of Vincent and his choices. He wished they'd been his.

"I don't want you to be Vincent," Norma said softly. Her face was solemn and her brown eyes unwavering. "I never have." She put an arm around his waist and leaned into him. "And neither did your father. He didn't understand how to let you be yourself, that you needed to find your own way. And you did."

Maybe. Or not really. His youthful decisions had caused so much pain, and by the time he'd finally gained the sense to put the past behind him and take responsibility for his life, it was too late to matter to either his brother or his father. The irony was that the responsibility had ultimately taken him from Dakota and her world.

But not from Madeline, the precious child who had been all his from the moment she'd taken her first breath. He wouldn't change her existence for anything, not even to recover those useless, mindless years he'd spent as Dakota's hostage. At least now the time when she could use Madeline as a weapon was over. He would take Madeline far away where she could have a normal life and keep her there until Dakota self-destructed, and they could come home again.

"All done!" Madeline announced, shoving one more chocolate chip into her mouth. Her lips and fingers were streaked with chocolate.

"Good job," Norma exclaimed with the sincere-sounding admiration Parker remembered from his own childhood. "Let's get these babies in the oven."

All too soon darkness replaced the day. Madeline fell asleep, a contented smile on her face from her full day of attention and love. When Carla showed up to watch Madeline, Parker drove his mother to her friend's house.

They returned the borrowed car without incident, and as they crossed several streets and yards on their way home, Parker went over his plans. Once his mother was safely home, he'd drive his truck to the apartment, stuff more clothes in garbage bags, and jog back with them to the house. Tomorrow he would take out a large sum of money, buy a car—maybe from a junkyard he knew where they weren't picky about records—and pack up everything he'd managed to bring over these past few days, including all of Madeline's new clothing. Then they would leave Utah. His mother would eventually sell his truck, and his apartment would be rented to others. Meanwhile, Norma would wrap up her own private affairs and follow when she could leave without being suspected. Maybe not for a year or more. Sadness at this thought filled him as they made their way through his mother's fence and up to the back door of her house.

A heartbeat later, pandemonium set in as two uniformed policemen stepped out of the dark bushes, guns drawn. "Police!" one shouted. "Keep your hands where we can see them."

Norma cried out and Parker stiffened. "What is this about?" he demanded.

Detective Sally Crumb emerged from the shadows, wearing a navy suit. "Why don't you tell me? Where have you been, Mr. Hathaway?"

"None of your business," Parker spat.

Norma put a hand on his arm to calm him. "My son and I were visiting friends. Is that a crime? Why are you on my property? Spying on us? We haven't done anything wrong!"

"No?" The detective tilted her head and folded her arms

over her ample chest. "Do you want to tell us exactly where you've been? What friends? Just so we can verify."

No answer.

"I thought not."

Parker struggled to control his fury but knew his mother was right. If they were to come out of this safely, they had to remain calm.

"This is ridiculous," Norma insisted. "Now put away those guns and tell us what you want in a civilized manner."

Hesitating only a few seconds, Detective Crumb nodded at her associates, who holstered their weapons. But Parker noticed that each left one hand ready to pull them out again if needed.

"We'd like to take Mr. Hathaway in for questioning."

"I've answered all your questions."

Detective Crumb stared at him without expression. "You either come with me or I'll arrest you."

"What?" Now that the anger was fading, he was too numb to even feel shock. "Why?"

"Your truck has been identified as being in Salt Lake near your ex-wife's house on the night Madeline went missing."

"There must be some mistake," Norma said.

Parker remembered the passing car. Whoever it was must have come forward. However, that didn't mean they could identify him or that they'd have enough proof to arrest him.

"There are hundreds of trucks that look like Parker's," Norma added. "Besides, he was here."

Parker looked at her in warning, but she blundered on. "You can ask my neighbor. He came to fix the leak in my sink before work on Thursday."

"We did talk to your neighbors," Detective Crumb said. "They did see his truck leave, but they didn't see what time he got here. Even if he'd been here all night, that doesn't preclude him from having been in Salt Lake in the middle of the night."

"That's ridiculous!" Norma's calm evaporated.

Making a quick decision, Parker took a step toward Detective Crumb. "Let's go in, then. This shouldn't take long."

"Actually, we'll need to take you and the truck to Salt Lake. You'll be in a lineup tonight. Might take a few hours. Or longer."

Parker exchanged glances with Norma. He hoped she remembered where Madeline was so she could take care of her. "I'll go with you, just let me tell my mother good-bye."

"Go ahead." Detective Crumb wasn't moving an inch.

Parker leaned down and hugged Norma. "Be careful," he whispered. "Don't lead them there."

Norma's arms tightened around him. "I love you, Parker. I'll get you out. You'll see."

Parker took out his keys and waved them in the air. "Do you want to drive, Detective? Or shall I?"

She took the keys and tossed them to one of the officers. "Neither."

"You'll need gas," Parker informed him. Since he'd planned to leave the truck in Utah when he left, there'd been no use in filling it.

"Come on, Mr. Hathaway."

With a last look at his mother, Parker fell in between Detective Crumb and the other officer as they marched to the front of the house. There were two more plainclothes policemen waiting near the unmarked police car. Detective Crumb chatted briefly with them before opening the back door for Parker and ushering him inside. Apparently only one of the plainclothes policemen was going with them. The other went to stand with a policeman in uniform who was still talking to Norma.

"Aren't they coming?" Parker asked.

Detective Crumb nodded at the wiry man in the driver's seat, giving him permission to pull out. "Not yet," she answered. "Your mother might need to get a few things before she joins us."

Pain shot through Parker's chest. "Join us," he managed.

Crumb smiled at him, her attractive face unmoving. "We're taking her in for questioning, too. We think she's covering for you."

Parker barely heard the words, but he understood them. No one would be around for Madeline. Only Carla, who was expecting him back very soon. What would she do when he didn't return? Would she stay? Would she take Madeline home with her? Would she call the police? Worse, would she just leave Madeline alone sleeping, expecting him to return?

No. She wouldn't do that. But he didn't really know her that well, or the members of her family, at least a few of whom were in the U.S. illegally. Carla wouldn't call the police. But that was the only thing he was sure of.

Madeline! he thought. What was he going to do now?

• • •

Sally Crumb could tell Parker Hathaway was anxious. He wasn't very good at hiding the emotion. He kept staring blankly out the window or looking at the time on his cell phone. She remembered the days when people wore wristwatches; now cell phones had taken their place. And a good thing, too—a watch couldn't make or receive a call, or let a detective know so clearly that a person was distressed.

Why was he so nervous? Did it mean he'd been in Salt Lake that night? Or was it for another reason?

If he had been in Salt Lake the night Madeline had gone missing, he was most certainly involved in the disappearance. But what had he done with the child? By all accounts, even the child's mother, Dakota Allen, who seemed to hate Parker as much as she disgusted him, was adamant that if he was involved he wouldn't harm her.

"I hope it was him," Dakota had told Sally that morning. "Because then I'd know she was okay."

Sally didn't like Dakota. From their first meeting, the blonde woman was evasive and uncooperative about giving out the names of her friends. Since talking to Parker that first day, Sally had done all the checks, but though Dakota had been arrested many times for possession or for being publicly drunk, she'd never been convicted. Sally was still looking for clues, not limiting herself to the past few months. Sometimes you had to go back a few years to find the evidence.

The little boy with Dakota—a son from another relationship—seemed happy enough and well cared for, but that didn't make Sally feel any better about Dakota. She had a feel for these things, and something didn't add up. Like with Parker.

She itched to get her hands on his cell phone. She'd managed to do some preliminary checking on him within the realm of her warrant, but his cell phone had supposedly been shut off. Now here he was with another one, and it might hold the answers. She'd be sure to get a warrant before morning.

Parker met her gaze as he slipped his phone back into his pocket. "I have to get to work tomorrow. How long is this going to be?"

"As long as it takes. At least we managed to arrange things

for tonight. Not easy on a Sunday. If you're cleared, you'll be free to go." He seemed more at ease then, so maybe he was only worried about his job. Sally narrowed her eyes as she studied him.

He met her stare without flinching. "I would never do anything to hurt my daughter."

She nodded. "I believe that. Not purposefully, anyway."

"Dakota lived in a meth house before I moved her to this other one. The only time I saw Madeline during those months was when she brought her to me. It was a living nightmare not knowing where she was and not seeing her regularly. When I found out what kind of place they were staying at, I rented the other house. I thought she'd change, but she hasn't."

"How do I know you're telling the truth?"

"She's doing drugs. Madeline isn't safe with her."

"So you keep saying, and I promise you I'm pursuing every lead I have in that respect. But I need to know—did you take your daughter to protect her?"

He looked out the window. "I haven't done anything wrong."

• • •

Sally stood with the witness, a man who worked the night shift at a frozen food company. Dale Stewart lived in Madeline's neighborhood, and on his way home each morning he almost never came across anyone.

"Could have been him," he said. "Can't tell you any better. It was dark, but I had my brights on. Didn't expect to see anyone. But it was definitely that truck I saw, or one exactly like it. I remember the dent in the front bumper and half of the license plate."

"Thank you, Mr. Stewart. We appreciate your coming in."

Stewart inclined his head in acknowledgment. "Anything, as long as it helps bring back that little girl."

An officer led him out, and Sally stared at the lineup for a short moment. "Okay, you can tell them to go." She turned to the chief of police standing beside her. "It's enough to hold him, I think."

"And to press initial charges. But there needs to be more proof for a conviction. You know that as well as I do." The chief was a tall, impressive man, if a little on the thin side. His suit hung on his lean frame, but his face was one you could trust. He could make hard decisions when necessary, but he was compassionate about it. Moreover, he trusted his employees to do their jobs without checking up on them constantly.

"I'll get proof." She was thinking of Hathaway's new cell phone. "As long as I have enough to legally hold him and to examine his belongings, I think I'll find exactly what I'm looking for."

"What about the mother?"

"Hasn't given us a thing."

"Maybe she doesn't know anything."

"Maybe. But I want to keep her in holding a bit longer. When we do let her go, we can tail her." Sally didn't think it'd be necessary, but it paid to be careful.

"Keep me informed. I'm heading back home."

"Thanks for coming in tonight."

"Hey, we're all rooting for this girl. We need to do what it takes to find her."

Sally nodded and strode from the room, feeling sure the answer was close at hand.

Parker was waiting for her in an empty questioning room.

He sat at a table, long legs sprawled, his hair mussed. "So, am I free to go? Or are you going to arrest me?"

"Your truck was positively identified as being near your daughter's house that night," Sally informed him without emotion, "so we do have reason to hold you while we investigate."

His shoulders sagged slightly. "How long?"

"Twenty-four hours unless we file charges. If you're arrested, it will be another day or so before you're arraigned."

He sat up and banged his fist on the table. "Even if my truck was there, couldn't I sometimes drive by my daughter's house to make sure everything's okay? Is that a crime? Don't you ever check on your children?"

"We'll need to see your cell phone, Mr. Hathaway. It wasn't with your other belongings."

Parker blinked. "They must have misplaced it."

Sally pursed her lips at this lie. She'd had the squad car checked as well as the garbage bins he might have had access to but without result. Yet there were many other places he could have stashed the phone—in a plant, under a cushion, in a box of miscellaneous items—and if it was turned off as she suspected, there would be no ringing from incoming calls to alert them.

"Okay," she said, switching tactics. "Tell me again why you were in Salt Lake that night."

"I didn't say I was. I said it was possible." He shook his head. "Look, you've already asked me a million questions tonight, and I've answered them. But I know the drill. Even if you have a reason to hold me here, I have the right to speak with a lawyer before I say anything more."

"Do you have one?"

"No. And I can't pay one, either. Not with all my child support and bills. Maybe my mother will help. Can I see her?"

"I'm sorry. We're questioning her now."

"Are you detaining her, too?"

"Unlike you, she is free to go any time she pleases."

"I bet you didn't tell her that, though, did you?" he growled.

"Where's your phone?"

"I don't know what you're talking about, but I already told you I'm not answering any more questions until I talk to a lawyer."

"Fine. Have it your way." Biting back frustration, Sally left the room. On her way down the hall, she took out her cell and phoned Tony. "Hi," she said.

"I was beginning to think you got lost."

"I wish."

"So, you coming home tonight?"

"Not yet. We found a suspect."

"Ah." He would know what that meant, but he was also familiar enough with the routine not to ask any questions.

"How's Randi?"

"Fine. Just got her to bed. Don't worry about it."

"I do worry. I hate working so much."

"It's not all the time. Just when it's important. She understands. She told me she hopes you find the little girl."

"I'm closer. We're going over all his old phone records again and the pictures we took at his apartment. There has to be something more. Everyone's pulling overtime on this."

"Try not to come home too late." There was a husky note in her husband's voice. "If I'm still awake, I'll give you a back rub."

"Mmm. Sounds heavenly. I'll do my best." She spied one of her colleagues coming toward her, waving a paper and looking excited. "I gotta go, hon. See you tonight. And if not I'll take a raincheck on that back rub."

"Deal."

Clapping the phone shut, she asked, "What you got, Jim?"

Jim smiled. "Remember that unknown number we were trying to trace from Hathaway's records? Finally got ahold of the guy, and guess what? He rented Hathaway a house on the edge of town, starting last week. Hathaway must have made that first call from his old cell."

Gotcha, Sally thought. To Jim she said, "Let's get local officers there now."

"Already on it."

* * *

Though Parker was trying to maintain a calm exterior, he was beginning to feel desperate at how long he'd been separated from Madeline. Too much time had gone by since Detective Crumb had told him his truck had been positively identified. He remembered the passing car that night. Why hadn't he parked on a different street?

Even if the detective came in here this minute and told him she changed her mind and he was free to leave, it would take him two hours to get back to Manti—more if he had to worry about losing a tail. How had his life deteriorated so quickly? It was like being back in a relationship with Dakota.

Meanwhile, he couldn't helping worrying that Carla might have left Madeline alone at the rental house. Maybe she had something important awaiting her attention and rationalized that he would only be gone a short time. They didn't really have a long-standing relationship, and he couldn't guess at her thought process or the culture in which she had been raised. *If she leaves Madeline, I'll fire her,* he vowed. Of course the idea was ludicrous because he'd planned to let her go anyway.

One option was to tell Detective Crumb the truth. Maybe she was looking into Dakota's drug use, and they could work together to make sure Madeline was safe. Or maybe Dakota would be more careful now that the authorities were aware of what was going on.

Or were they? They didn't seem to be good at getting to the truth. What if nothing changed and Madeline remained at risk? For all he knew the cops didn't take his accusations seriously, and telling the truth now might only mean that he wouldn't have another chance to save his daughter. Dakota obviously wasn't changing any time soon. That was something he should have counted on, since he knew from experience how enticing her lifestyle was and how hard it would be to break free. His daughter shouldn't have to deal with that, not at four or at any age.

At least he'd had the presence of mind to stash his new cell phone under the window blinds in the lobby earlier when they'd arrived, pretending to stumble into the wall. In the unmarked squad car, he'd seen Detective Crumb looking at it with interest and had realized the numbers in the memory or on the phone records would lead directly to the rental house. But those numbers were safe now, and with any luck, he and Madeline would be in Las Vegas before the phone was discovered.

If they let him make a phone call, maybe he could call Carla to make sure all was well. He would offer her triple the normal wage to stay until he was free. Yet what if he and his mother were arrested and held for days? And could he trust that his call wouldn't be traced? What would Carla do with Madeline if she didn't hear from him?

The agony of worry ate at him, crumbling his confidence. All he wanted was to protect his daughter, but speaking up or staying quiet both seemed to have serious consequences. Except, of course, that Dakota and drugs were assured, while Carla was an unknown.

Better to go with the unknown. He'd have to trust Carla for a little longer, regardless of how it ripped him apart. He'd never, ever forgive himself if any harm came to Madeline.

A new worry was beginning to edge into his mind. If they allowed his mother to go free tonight, they would likely follow her to the rental house in a way she couldn't detect. After all, they were trained at what they did and would be expecting her to try to get around them now. The last thing he wanted was to see his mother in jail. He had to prevent that along with everything else. He had to get them to let him see her.

Weight pushed down on his shoulders, threatening to crush out all hope. He was so exhausted that his brain no longer seemed to be functioning. But the clock was ever ticking. His only hope was to somehow get free so he could take Madeline away from Utah and the threat Dakota represented.

He laid his head down on the table, trying to clear it of a sudden dizziness. If they were keeping him overnight, as it appeared they would, where would he stay? In here? Or did they have a jail cell with a bed?

Some time later the door opened, and he tried to blink away the exhaustion. How long had she left him here? At least an hour, though he could be wrong. "Where's my lawyer?" he demanded. "And are you going to give me a bed, or is this part of the torture routine?"

The detective didn't smile. "We traced your phone records, and we found the man you rented a house from in Manti. Care to tell me why you rented a house there?"

Parker swallowed, his throat dry as though he'd been drinking sand. "A lot of people move," he said carefully.

Crumb folded her long arms across her chest. "The game is up, Parker. We found the house and your daughter's clothes. She's been there very recently."

"But she's not there now." He wondered if his statement betrayed the shock he felt.

"No," Crumb said. "She's not. The house is empty."

CHAPTER

8

Early Monday morning Caitlin McLoughlin sat at her desk, wishing she could have stayed home. Another plea deal and two more clients she would have to visit in jail. All of them guilty—that was obvious from the documentation. A robbery and an assault. Beautiful. More briefs to prepare and lies to hear.

When her phone rang, she grabbed it almost eagerly, though there was a high probability the call would mean more work. "Hello?"

"Hi, Caitlin."

"Sally?" Caitlin smiled. It was really too soon to discuss their weekly lunch date, their schedules being so unpredictable, but she was happy to hear from Sally anytime. "What's up? Nothing bad, I hope."

"No, everything's fine. Well, I was up half the night and not for one of Tony's back rubs."

"You find the girl?"

"Not yet." Frustration laced Sally's voice. "But I think I know who took her. Only things have gone wrong, and I don't know how to fix them. The guy won't trust me, and I really don't blame him."

"Who?"

"The father."

"Ah. Do you think he's hurt her?"

"Absolutely not. This guy loves his kid, and I think he took her to protect her from the mother. We found someone who identified him as being near the girl's home the night she went missing, so we brought him in. And also his mother. Neither would tell us anything useful. With a little research, though, we discovered he'd rented a house on the edge of town, and there were little girl's clothes there, and the local officers we sent out could have sworn the bed was still warm."

"She left right before you got there?"

"I think so. I mean, I could be wrong. Maybe she wasn't there at all, but it adds up because when the father had visiting rights, he always brought the daughter to the grand-mother's. The rental house had to be where he was hiding her."

"Did someone warn them?"

"No. Hathaway didn't call anyone. Neither did the grand-mother." Sally paused while Caitlin took the information in.

"So that means—what?"

"Either the little girl got up and wandered out into the night alone, or there's an accomplice who got scared and fled with the child. Either way, she's in danger. Hathaway is pacing in the holding cell as we speak. He hasn't slept much, and any-one can see he's worried."

"But he won't talk."

"No. I'm tempted to let him loose and follow him to find out what he knows, but the higher-ups won't let me. There's too much evidence against him. And part of me agrees because he's smart. He might shake the tail and flee with the girl. So, that's where you come in."

"Me?"

"He wants to see a lawyer."

"Ah." Now Caitlin understood.

"He'd probably be happy with any public defender," Sally said, "but despite everything, I really think this guy loves his daughter, and I don't want to see him in the hands of just any- one."

"But, Sally, if what you say is true, he kidnapped his own daughter out of her bed in the middle of the night."

"I know how it sounds, but I've met the mother, and of the two of them, I'd choose him."

"The law won't."

"I know." Sally sighed. "Look, will you come talk to him?"

"When?"

"As soon as possible. We need to find the child. Every minute that passes means more danger. We have no idea who the accomplice is, or if there even is one."

Caitlin looked at the files on her desk. She could get Jodi or one of the other paralegals to fill in for her for a few hours. It wasn't like she had court proceedings this morning. "Okay, I'll be there in a bit."

"Thanks. I owe you one."

Caitlin laughed. "No, this counts as two."

"I'll watch Amy for you while you go out with the hot DA. Hmm, wonder if he's any good at back rubs."

"If only I could be so lucky." Not that she would find out any time soon. She and Mace weren't anywhere near that level of intimacy. Besides, Caitlin wasn't into casual relationships. She wanted something permanent, something real. Something like Sally and Tony had. Disconnecting the line with a little sigh, she began dialing Jodi's extension.

• • •

Things had gone from bad to worse. Parker had spent the night pacing the small holding cell where they had kept him in isolation. He'd learned that his mother had been released, but he hadn't seen her, and she didn't know anything about Carla.

Where had Carla taken Madeline? In the best case scenario, he told himself that when he hadn't returned, she'd taken Madeline home to her own house because she'd had to watch her siblings or nephews. Madeline was safe and happy, sleeping like an angel, and would awake and begin playing with the other children. Other visions were not so nice—Carla kidnapping Madeline, selling her into slavery or something equally heinous.

He'd have to tell them everything he knew. Soon. There was simply no other option. Even if Carla planned to bring Madeline back, she'd only find the police there waiting for her. And if the worst became a reality, he had already given Carla a big head start.

There was a sound at the door, and a stocky officer he didn't recognize entered the room. They'd already come once to give him a breakfast he hadn't been able to eat, so this time surely there was news. Maybe they were letting him out.

"You have a visitor," the man said far too cheerfully for Parker's mood. "An LDA."

"A what?"

"Someone from the Legal Defenders Association—a public defender."

"Oh." Parker felt a little surge of hope.

"You want to clean up a little first?"

Parker was wearing the same jeans and T-shirt he'd been wearing when he'd been picked up. They had let him keep his coat, too, but his hair was uncombed, and he still hadn't found time to shave. But what he looked like didn't matter. Time was all important. "No. I'm fine," he said. "Take me to him."

"Her," the officer corrected. "And I must say, you're pretty lucky. Detective Crumb must have pulled a few strings to get her. They say she's the best."

Parker didn't hold out much hope of that. From what he'd heard in the circles he'd traveled with Dakota, public defenders were overworked and underpaid. The more experienced defenders often didn't even meet their clients until the day of the trial, sending aides to do all the footwork. So it was likely that Crumb had found the newest attorney on the list and sent her to him—provided she even was a real attorney.

The woman had her back to him as the officer led him into a new room he hadn't been in before, her eyes focused on the tiny, bar-covered window on the far wall several yards away. She wore a maroon suit on a figure that was a little on the full side, with curves in all the right places, though the suit seemed to do its best to hide that fact. Her bright, copper-colored hair was drawn severely into a knot at the nape of her neck, and when she faced him, the solemness of her pale features was broken only by the myriad of copper freckles scattered over her face. She was younger than he expected and beautiful in a slightly exotic way, though he couldn't figure out how red hair and freckles could possibly be exotic. In another setting—no, in another lifetime—he might have asked her out.

"Hello, Mr. Hathaway," she said, coming toward him, her hand outstretched. "I'm Caitlin McLoughlin, and I've been assigned to your case." She spoke perfect English, yet there was almost an Irish lilt to the tone. Like music. Her eyes were a startling blue, and her lips full and kissable despite the withdrawn formality of her expression and demeanor.

Parker suddenly felt worn and dirty. He wished he'd had time to shower and shave, though none of that was really important now. What he had to do was to concentrate on Madeline, and this woman might be the means of getting him out of here.

Her hand was small but firm in his grasp. "I've been briefed, Mr. Hathaway, but I'll need more information." She glanced at the officer who'd brought Parker. "Thank you. We'll be all right." He nodded and left the room, shutting the door behind him.

"I need to get out of here as soon as possible," Parker told her forcefully.

"Unfortunately, that's not going to happen." She sat on one of the chairs at the table and indicated that he should do the same. "At least not today. Given the circumstances, I anticipate that you will be arrested before the end of the day. I will be able to have you arraigned tomorrow, but depending on the evidence the prosecution has, we may or may not get you out on bail." She sat back in her chair, watching him.

"Then why are you even here?" he growled, remaining on his feet. "I need to get out now."

"Why?" She asked it simply, as though she had no idea what was at stake. Maybe she didn't. Maybe they hadn't told her the details.

"My daughter is missing. You know that much."

She lifted her chin slightly. "Yes, but only since last night, I believe."

So she knew more than she'd let on, and that meant the

police knew more as well. "They're never going to let me out, are they?"

"Not until you tell them what you know."

"No." He looked around the room, wondering if even now they were listening. "You don't understand."

"Why don't you tell me?"

"Because I'd be playing into their hands."

"Anything you say to me here stays here. I'm your counsel."

"They aren't listening?"

For the first time a smile curved those full lips. "Not a chance. That would be against the law."

He relaxed slightly. "I don't know where to begin."

"Begin with what happened."

"My ex-wife is doing drugs. I lived with Dakota for too long not to know that my daughter is in danger every second she's in her care. But I can't get anyone to listen to me."

"She doesn't have a record, but I do see some DUIs on yours."

"That was years ago."

"Are you still drinking?"

"I'm not an alcoholic, I'm a drunk. Alcoholics go to meetings." He'd seen that on a T-shirt once, and it would surely put her in her place.

She tilted her head. "Mr. Hathaway, this is no time to joke. You're the one who asked for legal counsel. Now either you start talking to me—with respect—or I'm leaving, and you can deal with another legal defender."

Shame washed through Parker. Swallowing with difficulty, he lowered himself onto the chair opposite her. "I'm sorry."

"That's okay. Now do you want my help, or do you want someone else?"

"Are you good?"

A twitch on one side of her mouth seemed to hint at a smile. "I'm the best at what I do." She hesitated before adding, "But while we're speaking candidly, I can also tell you that I dislike defending guilty men."

"Then why are you a public defender?"

A line appeared on her brow. "I assure you, I ask myself that question a hundred times a week, and the only answer I have besides the fact that it pays the bills is that every now and then, I actually help someone who's innocent."

There was passion in the words. This was a woman who believed in ideals and in defending the defenseless. Maybe she could understand about Dakota and Madeline. She seemed to be his best hope.

"Haven't you ever done anything you might have otherwise considered wrong to protect someone you care about?" he asked quietly.

She started shaking her head and then stopped, as though remembering something. "The end doesn't justify the means. Or so my father used to say."

Parker lifted a brow. "I believe that, or I used to. But drugs don't play fair, and my daughter's life is more important to me than my own." This woman couldn't possibly know how much it had cost him to go against the law, how every minute he'd been wracked with guilt, but he wouldn't be the one to enlighten her.

"You took her that night."

He nodded. "I thought I could keep her in Manti until the police found evidence against Dakota, but I realized on Saturday that it wouldn't work. Today we were going to disappear."

"Why didn't you run right from the beginning?"

"I should have. But I was working, and I wanted to be able to support my daughter."

"Who was helping you?"

"I acted alone."

"You left your four-year-old daughter all day in a house by herself?" There was a sharpness now to her tone, a subtle anger.

"I got a sitter. A Hispanic woman. Very smart, nice. I knew she had relatives who are in the country illegally, and she wouldn't want to contact the police even if she suspected Madeline was kidnapped."

"This woman was at the house last night with Madeline?"

"Yes." Then he rushed on with everything he'd been thinking. "But the police can't prove Madeline was there. She could have been there weeks ago."

"You've only had the house since last week."

"I could have only been preparing for her to go there."

"They found her fingerprints. Mr. Hathaway, I know you want to get out and see if you can find your daughter, but they're not going to let you, and I can't make them."

"What if I tell *you* where she is? Could you go get her?"

The attorney shook her head. "There are rules about endangering children, and I won't cross that line. Besides, they'd have me followed. But if you do cooperate with the police, things will go a lot more smoothly for you, and we'll have a much better case. That means you'll be around to see your daughter grow up."

He sighed and stared at the table. "I'm terrified that Carla has done something terrible, but if she hasn't, I don't want her mixed up in this."

"What if I can promise that?" Her hands were folded on the table, and he noticed she wore a ruby ring on her right hand but nothing on the left.

He lifted his gaze and saw those blue eyes locked onto his, almost like a touch. She was compelling, he'd give her that. No wonder she was supposedly so good at what she did. "Can you promise to save Madeline from her mother?"

"Not in so many words, but I know Detective Crumb personally, and I can tell you she'll do everything in her power and then some to get to the bottom of this. For some crazy, odd reason, she seems to be on your side."

This surprised him. "I thought she hated me."

"She just wants Madeline safe."

"So do I."

He agonized over the decision, while at the same time recognizing there was really no choice. "Okay. But I want assurances that Carla, if she didn't do anything, will be left out of this. And my mother."

"Was your mother involved?"

"No. I did tell her after I did it, though. She agrees with me. She's already lost too—" He broke off. That was none of Caitlin McLoughlin's business.

"Okay, Mr. Hathaway, I'll go have a chat with the detective. I'll be right back."

"Call me Parker."

She gave him a slow smile that made his stomach feel warm, completely shattering his former coolness toward her. What would those lips taste like? How would the softness of her feel if he gathered her into his arms? *Stop.* He had to keep his mind on his daughter. His social life had been neglected far too long to allow the desire for one to start weighing in on matters now.

"Okay," she said. "Parker it is. And you can call me Caitlin." He felt happy at the invitation, though he sensed she made the offer more in the hope of evoking trust than from a desire to be familiar. "Is there anything I can get you to make you more comfortable?" she added.

A bath and a week of sleep, he thought. He shook his head. "No, thanks. No one can give me what I need."

She regarded him silently for several seconds before nodding. "Maybe not yet. But sometimes we're forced to choose between the lesser of two evils."

"That's just it," he said. "I don't know which that is."

• • •

Caitlin left the room feeling shaken. When she had first caught sight of the unshaven man, she had classified him immediately as one more low-life scum who was nothing but a drain on the system. A father using his child for attention—or worse. Yet when she'd looked deeper, when she stared into his honest brown eyes and saw the concern etched on the sharp angles of his jaw, all her instincts told her Sally was right about him. There was an earnestness in Parker Hathaway that called to her sense of justice. He was a desperate man, that much was true, but he believed with his whole heart that he was acting in the best interests of his daughter.

She could do a lot with such a defense, especially if she could prove even part of his accusations against his ex-wife. Drugs were a hot topic these days, and far too many children had become innocent victims. Many of the judges were cracking down on convictions. Parker would be put on probation and likely have only supervised visits with Madeline for the foreseeable future, but she might be able to spare him jail time. Well, that is if she cleaned him up and if his record wasn't too spotty. For all she knew there was more on him that Sally hadn't yet dug up. The prosecutor wouldn't leave anything out.

Of course, everything would hinge on whether or not they actually found Madeline safe and sound. If Madeline turned up dead, jail time would be a given.

"Well?" Sally had been down the hall but was already halfway to Caitlin's side.

"First, I want to know something. How late is he on child support?"

"As far as I can tell, he's never missed a payment. The guy's been a saint for the past few years, but I found out he did quit his job last Saturday. I think he was getting ready to run."

"He should have run from the beginning."

Sally smirked. "Is that your advice as an attorney?"

Caitlin ignored the comment. "I think he'll tell you what you want to know, but he would like to see that the baby-sitter and his mother stay out of it. No legal repercussions."

"That depends. Are they accomplices or bystanders?"

"Well, provided the baby-sitter hasn't kidnapped the child a second time"—Caitlin gave her a wry glance—"she doesn't even know Madeline was kidnapped. As for Hathaway's mother, she had no foreknowledge and wasn't involved in anything that may have allegedly happened." Caitlin stopped. "We'll need to get the DA involved if we're going to be able to guarantee their immunity, and that means you'll have to charge my client."

"I'll start on the paperwork and get someone over from the DA's office."

"Thanks."

As Sally hurried down the hallway, Caitlin went back inside the room where Parker waited. "It's all in motion," she announced. "I'll have to talk to the DA and make sure they won't involve your mother, but for now, let's talk about what you do know, so I can advise you on exactly what to say."

"I have Carla's name and number memorized, and I know where she lives, more or less, since I went there to meet her a few weeks ago." He frowned. "Look, do you think they'd let me go with them? I don't want Madeline to be scared when she sees the police."

Caitlin felt an unexpected tenderness toward him at the request. "I'll ask." But she was sure he would be denied if the police had Carla's number and could trace it. So now was the time to make the decision—was she really going to fight for his rights? Or just do the minimum?

He smiled at her, a small smile but one full of hope. Hope that he might make his daughter feel easier at what would happen. Nothing for himself. "If we really want to go," Caitlin said, including herself in the deal, "we won't give them Carla's full name and number unless we need to. We'll just say you know where she lives. You think you can find it?"

"I can get us in the general area, and there's a big slatted barrel of flowers out in the front of the yard. I'll know it when I see it." His voice was full of what they didn't say—the possibility that Madeline was no longer there.

"Good. Someone from the DA's office should be here soon, so we'll have a chat with them. But I do all the talking. Understand?"

"Yes. Thank you."

She shrugged. His thanks made her feel uncomfortable.

"Is there a bathroom around here?" he asked. "Maybe a razor? I could do with a shave."

She nodded. "I'll see what I can do. But make it snappy."

"I'll be finished before the DA is here."

True to his word, the DA was nowhere in sight when an officer led Parker Hathaway back to the room where Caitlin and Sally were waiting. He was vastly different from the despondent, unkempt man she had met earlier. His brown, slightly wavy hair was neatly combed, reaching halfway past his ears in front, longer in back. Without the growth of beard, Caitlin could see the planes of his face, not sharp as she'd previously thought but strong and angular, his nose a little on the large side but well-suited for his handsome face. Someone had given him another T-shirt, a white one that was a bit snug for his muscular build and broad shoulders. He was nowhere near as large as Sally's Tony but on the same scale at least. Unbidden, Caitlin briefly had a vision of what those arms might feel like if they were around her.

Sally bumped her arm, giving her a look that told her she was staring. Caitlin felt herself color. *Shoot,* she thought. Parker Hathaway was her client and not something to be ogled. It really had been too long since she'd had a boyfriend. But a boyfriend ate up too much free time, something she had little of these days. What wasn't taken by her job was absorbed by Amy.

Parker regarded her quietly, a slight quirk of his left eyebrow telling her he'd noticed her stare. She prayed he couldn't guess exactly what she'd been thinking. "I'm ready," he said. "Where is the DA?"

"Here," Mace Keeley walked in behind him through the open door.

Caitlin felt both an excitement at seeing Mace and a little resentment. He had always brought out these feelings in her— the first because he was so gorgeous and made her knees weak, and the second she'd always chalked up to professional jealousy. Mace's case record was impeccable.

Mace smiled and walked toward her, ignoring everyone else in the room. "Caitlin," he said, his voice warm. "I didn't realize you were assigned to this case. I did ask who was for the defense, but they didn't know."

"I just found out myself an hour ago. It that a problem?"

"No." His voice lowered. "I was sorry about Friday."

A thrill raced up her back. "Me too."

With a private smile for her, Mace turned and sat at the table, opening a file. Caitlin felt eyes on her and glanced over to Parker. His expression was unreadable, but she felt sure he hadn't missed the exchange. No matter. She absolutely wouldn't allow her feelings for Mace enter the equation. She had to be at her best as she had promised Parker—and herself.

She sat across from Mace and motioned Parker to sit next to her. "In exchange for information as to the whereabouts of Madeline Hathaway, who was discovered missing from her home on Thursday morning, my client would like immunity for his mother and the baby-sitter he employed, neither of whom had anything to do with the abduction."

"The mother could be charged as an accessory after the fact," protested Mace, lifting a page that held the case summary Sally had faxed him.

"Who bloody cares!" Sally burst out. "A little girl's welfare is at stake here. We need to find her quickly. Prosecuting the grandmother who loves her is very much a losing proposition all around. No buts about it."

Mace regarded Caitlin. "Is that your assessment?"

"We need to find her now." Caitlin was glad she had managed to regain complete control over her face. "That is my client's price."

"Nothing for himself?"

Caitlin knew it was a trick question, and she didn't rise to the bait. There was no way they would give Parker Hathaway immunity for what he'd done. She felt Parker start to say something, but she lifted her hand and put it briefly on his to still the words.

His hand was surprisingly warm. She glanced over and saw him looking at their hands. His eyes lifted to hers and suddenly a connection sprang to life, one that didn't need words but hinted at a passion she had only dreamed about. Surprised, she withdrew her hand and forced herself to continue talking.

"Nothing for himself. We already have adequate defense in that regard. His mother's involvement is negligible anyway, but my client would feel better with a signed statement absolving her from prosecution."

Mace rested his chin on the palm of his hand, his long fingers on his cheek as he studied first Caitlin and then Parker. Caitlin found herself glad Parker had shaved.

"Okay," Mace said. "It's a deal."

"Good." Sally rose from the table, satisfaction in her voice. "Then let's just hope Madeline is still in Manti."

CHAPTER

9

Fifteen minutes after their discussion with the DA, Caitlin was sitting in the backseat of an unmarked squad car next to Parker Hathaway, with Sally and another officer in the front. Behind them drove a police car with two officers inside. Both cars drove at a high speed, using the police lights on top of the cars to speed up the journey.

"This drive always takes me two hours," Parker commented, the barest of smiles arcing his lips.

Sally grinned. "That's the advantage to working for the law. Time is important here."

Parker's gaze shifted to the window, and Caitlin was able to study him covertly. His face seemed relaxed, but there was a tautness in his body as if every muscle were straining, anxious. Just the way she'd feel if Amy were missing.

He was good-looking, and he probably had been even before shaving, if she could have gotten around the worn jeans, rumpled and stained shirt, and the uncombed hair. Or perhaps she had seen only what she'd expected to see.

His head turned and their eyes met, sending a delicious tingle to Caitlin's stomach. She flushed. What had happened to her straight-faced attorney skills? The Irish in her seemed to be taking over where this man was concerned.

He smiled and asked in a low voice, "What are you thinking?"

How his lips might feel against hers didn't seem an appropriate answer. She shrugged, not trusting her voice for speech.

He held her stare for long seconds more, and Caitlin couldn't look away. *I should recuse myself from this case,* she thought suddenly. But she knew she wouldn't. She didn't want to pass him off to someone else.

In the front, Sally laughed at something the other officer said, and the mood was broken. Yet every so often, Caitlin felt Parker's eyes contemplating her.

In Manti they were joined by two squad cars from local authorities. Caitlin thought it was overkill, knowing Parker even as little as she did, but then remembered the baby-sitter might not be what they hoped.

Sally was on the phone with the local authorities. "Still nothing new from the rental house," she informed them. Caitlin knew she'd been expecting Carla to show up there with Madeline.

"It's more toward the middle of town," Parker said to the officer who was driving. "Then west from there."

When they reached the right area, Parker had the man drive up and down each street. "There," he said finally. "The one with the barrel in front."

The white, two-story house with red doors and shutters was as old as most of the other houses in this section but not particularly run-down. The lawn sported patches of snow, and it looked as though someone had tried to build a fort at one time.

"You two stay here with Jim," Sally ordered.

"Please," Parker said. "Let me go."

Sally regarded him silently for a long moment. "Okay. No funny business." She patted the gun in her shoulder holster, just visible under her cream-colored jacket.

"I'm going, too," Caitlin said.

"This could be a kidnapping," Sally snapped.

"If it is, they're long gone."

Sighing, Sally nodded her consent. She made them wait by the car while she went to talk to the other officers. Two were going to the front door with them; the men from the local force would go around to cover the back.

The house had a long front porch, with cream-colored plastic chairs stained from the snow and rain. Freshly painted gingerbread trim swirled around the porch's solid-looking framework. Parker pushed the bell. Footsteps came almost immediately, and an older Hispanic woman answered the door. The smile that had begun on her round, weathered face faded as she saw the uniformed officers behind them.

"Is Carla here?" Parker asked. Caitlin sensed the urgency in his voice, and the woman must have as well because she tore her gaze from the officers.

"Are you father of Madeleen?" the woman asked.

"Yes."

"You are very late. Carla had to go."

"Is Madeline here?" asked Caitlin.

The woman nodded her graying head, opening the door so they could see the living room and a hallway. "Stay here." She went down the hall, calling something in Spanish. Before she was out of sight, two black-haired children tumbled into view, laughing and speaking rapidly. Caitlin had learned enough Spanish to follow slow conversations, but all she understood now was the bare gist of the children begging their grandmother to let their new friend stay.

The woman shook her head and said in English, "Her father ees here."

"Madeline!" called the children. "Your father! Your father is here. You have to go home."

Madeline appeared at the end of the hall, looking the same and yet different from the pictures on the television. Her hair was now brown, but her brown eyes and her smooth white face were exactly the same. "Daddy!" she screamed. Grinning widely, she hurtled down the hall and into her father's arms.

"I love Carla's house!" she bubbled. "Can I come again? I really want to come here and play when you're not home. I like these kids! I like you best, but they're so fun to play with."

Parker buried his face in his daughter's hair. Caitlin saw tears shimmering in his eyes. "I missed you so much, sweetheart. I'm glad you've been having fun." He glanced at Caitlin, and she could see the regret there, regret that he had agreed to show them where Carla lived. Here at least Madeline had been safe.

"She ees that girl in the TV," the grandmother said, nodding vigorously. "I tell Carla, but she no believe. I tell her to call police." She looked with mistrust at the officers. "But we have nothing to do with it. Nothing." She emphasized with her hands.

"We know," Sally said. "Look, my associates here will just ask you a few questions. Okay?" The old woman nodded.

Parker leaned over to catch her attention. "Thank you for taking care of my daughter. Tell Carla thank you. I will send her the money I owe her." Hugging Madeline to him, he backed away.

"Where are we going, Daddy?" Madeline asked. "Why are the policemen here? Did Carla do something wrong?"

"No. They just want to make sure you're safe. They want to take you back to your mom."

"Oh." The little girl's excitement dimmed at the prospect. "Will Mommy let me come here to play?"

"I don't know. We'll have to ask." Parker hugged her again.

Madeline leaned into her father, her arms curling tightly around his neck, her cheek on his shoulder with her face pointed in Caitlin's direction. Her smile faded and disappeared altogether, as though sucked away by an unseen force. "She won't let me come back. She never does." She spoke so softly Caitlin knew she was the only one who heard.

The drive back to Salt Lake went far too quickly. For part of that time, Caitlin was on the phone with Jodi, doing as much work as she could from a distance and reorganizing her afternoon, but for most of the time, she was listening to Madeline talk with her father. Caitlin had thought Amy talked a lot, but this four-year-old was incessant and would have bordered on annoying if she hadn't been so cute and precocious.

"Who are you anyway?" she asked Caitlin after she had described in detail her games with the two Hispanic children.

Caitlin wondered if Parker wanted her to know the truth, and when he gave a slight nod, she answered. "I'm your daddy's legal defender, which means I'm going to help him with some legal stuff."

Madeline scrunched up her eyes in mistrust. "Legal stuff?"

"It's when the law—the police—think you've done something wrong. I try to straighten everything out."

"Oh." The child turned to Parker. "Did you do something wrong?"

"No. But people think I did."

"What do they think?"

"They're mad 'cause I took you away from your mom."

"But I always come to see you."

"I know. This time it's a little different because your mom didn't know."

"You should have told her, Daddy. Now she is gonna be mad. Couldn't you just give her some money?"

Parker laughed. "I wish that would take care of it. Don't worry, sweetheart. Everything will be okay."

Madeline nodded confidently and turned back to Caitlin. "I'm glad you're going to help my dad. What's your name?"

"Caitlin McLoughlin."

"That's pretty. Do you have kids?"

She smiled and shook her head. "No, but I do have a sister just a little bit older than you who lives with me." That wasn't exactly true, but she didn't want to get into an explanation with Parker there. Besides, it wasn't as though Parker and Madeline would ever meet Amy.

"Can I play with her? Do you live near me? My mom might let me go to your house, if you could pick me up." Madeline's brown eyes were eager.

"I don't know," Caitlin stalled, feeling drawn toward the child but knowing that was unwise, given the circumstances.

Madeline turned to Parker. "You'll take me over there, won't you, Daddy?" She smiled at Caitlin. "He always takes me. We go lots of places. One day we went to a candy place with my preschool. It was fun. They make candy there. We got to eat some." Then she was off on another tangent, and Caitlin was glad the subject of playing with Amy had been left behind—at least for now.

At the police station, Madeline skipped ahead down the hall, stopping to peer in windows. Sally turned to Parker. "You'd better say good-bye. Your ex-wife is here. We have to turn Madeline over to her."

Parker stiffened. "Can't you put her in state custody?"

"I'm sorry. I don't have a legal reason."

"Please." His voice was an agonized whisper that matched the pain on his face. It was so acute and private that Caitlin had to momentarily look away.

Madeline was coming back to them now, singing a song Caitlin didn't recognize.

"Mr. Hathaway," Sally was saying, "I gave you my word that I would do everything I could to keep Madeline safe, and I mean it. But it will take time."

"Find out where her mother lived before the house they're in now. I know for sure it was a meth house. That's why I set them up in this house."

"I'll have a good talk with your ex-wife," Sally promised. "Threaten her if I have to. That should keep her clean. But for now, you need to say good-bye and go with Officer Clegg."

Parker knelt on the floor in front of Madeline. "Sweetheart, I have to go now. I'll see you as soon as I can."

With the sudden clarity that will sometimes affect small children, Madeline clung to her father. "I don't want you to go. Can't I stay with you? Please?"

"Hey, it's okay, sweetheart. You're going back to Mommy's like you always do. I'll see you soon." He hugged her, his entire face drawn tight.

Caitlin didn't have the heart to break in and tell them he

wouldn't likely have visiting rights for some time. Her own eyes watered.

Madeline was consoled, her trust all too apparent. "Okay."

"Now remember what I told you. Don't eat anything if you don't know what it is. Like if it's in the cupboard or something. Or on the TV in a bag. Only eat what Mommy gives you. Even if you find it in her purse, don't eat it." Parker glanced up at Caitlin and Sally in challenge, and neither woman objected, but Caitlin found it difficult to hide her shock. If Madeline's mother wasn't doing drugs, this kind of talk could be damaging. If she was, the cautions, however needed, were equally horrifying.

"I know," Madeline said in an aggrieved voice that she would likely perfect in her teen years. "You always tell me that."

Caitlin knew, as Parker must, that all the coaching in the world often fell apart. Studies had proven that even children rigorously taught not to handle guns did so when given the opportunity out of their parents' sight. Natural curiosity was too strong for such young children to show discipline. Which, of course, was why parents were needed to guide them through the hazards of life until they had the maturity to understand and control their actions. Caitlin still had to keep all cleaners and other hazardous items out of Amy's reach, and she'd been five for twenty-two years.

"It's time," Sally said gently. She gave Caitlin the wry smile that she used when she was emotionally engaged.

Parker kissed his daughter's forehead. "You go with Detective Crumb and Ms. McLoughlin."

"Her name is Caitlin, Daddy." Madeline reached up and took Caitlin's hand.

Surprised and a little touched, Caitlin squeezed it lightly.

Parker met Caitlin's gaze. "When will I be able to leave here?"

"Tomorrow. After the arraignment, we'll go over your case."

"Okay." He turned and went with the officer who had driven them to Manti.

Sally started down the hall. "Your mother is anxious to see you, Madeline. But after you give her a hug, I need to talk to her a bit by myself. Caitlin, you probably have to get back to the courthouse, so I'll find someone to stay with Madeline while I talk with her mother."

"I'll stay. They'll just think I'm taking an extra long lunch. Madeline and I will go see what's in the vending machine."

"There are donuts on my desk," Sally offered. "I'll have them brought in."

"I love donuts," Madeline chirped.

Caitlin laughed. "We all do. And trust me when I say you need to eat as many as possible while you're young."

"You can say that again." Sally stopped in front of an open door. "She's in there, Madeline." In a lower voice, she added to Caitlin, "Her name is Dakota Allen. Apparently she dropped the Hathaway after the divorce."

Caitlin walked into the room and saw a woman about her height pacing the room. But any further resemblance was nil. Dakota wore jeans with wavy script down one leg, the waistband so low and tight that though she wasn't a heavy woman, rolls of skin bunched over the top. Her chest spilled out of a tight tank top which she wore under a short camouflage jacket. Blonde hair with dark roots coming in and too much makeup completed the picture. Caitlin wondered, as she always did when she saw such women, how Dakota Allen could possibly think she looked anything but cheap and trashy.

Madeline did not, as Caitlin expected, pull away and race to her mother. Instead, it was Dakota Allen who sprang across the room and hugged her daughter, practically ripping her from Caitlin's grasp.

"Oh, Maddy, I've missed you so much! I was so scared!" She talked high and fast and had an odd, nervous laugh.

"I was just with Daddy." Madeline's voice was petulant.

"He has no right taking you like that! He's never going to again. I promise you. Never!"

Madeline had been returning her mother's hug, but now her arms dropped to her sides, and Caitlin could tell she was fighting tears. "Why are you mad at Daddy?"

"Because he stole you away! And look at your hair! He changed the color to hide you from me. What a mess!"

"He didn't steal me! I just saw him like I always do. And I like my hair. It's like Grandma's." Madeline began crying in earnest now. "I want my daddy!"

"I can't believe you're acting like this! I've been so worried, not knowing where you were. It's been horrible!" Dakota tried to pull Madeline to her, but Madeline resisted. Dakota continued to talk rapidly, trying to make Madeline understand, to come to her way of thinking.

Madeline put her hands over her ears. *"No entiendo,"* she said.

Caitlin caught Sally's eye and dipped her head slightly. *Do something.*

"Uh, can I talk to you for a moment, Ms. Allen?" Sally asked. "I know you're anxious to take Madeline home, but there are a few more things we need to take care of. Caitlin and Madeline can visit the vending machine while we talk."

Dakota stood, looking in confusion from Sally to Madeline. "Okay," she agreed. In a high, false voice, she said to Madeline, "Go with this nice lady for a minute, and then I'll take you home."

Even with her hands over her ears, Madeline heard and walked over to Caitlin, slipping her hand in hers. "Can I have a candy bar? Chocolate." Tears stood out on her pale cheeks.

Dakota smiled. "Say please, Maddy."

"Please?" Madeline repeated obediently, without glancing at her mother.

"Sure," Caitlin said. "As long as it's okay with your mom."

Dakota nodded. "It's fine. Thanks."

Madeline pulled Caitlin toward the door, and gladly Caitlin escaped. After meeting Dakota Allen, her sympathy with Parker had grown. She understood, perhaps even better than he did, what danger Madeline was in. Not necessarily from getting into a stash of drugs but of growing up to be like her mother—a spoiled, self-indulgent woman who lived off government aid and the largesse of others. A woman who didn't create a stable home for her children but who flitted from bad relationship to bad relationship as her hormones and opportunity allowed, her days seen only through the lens of alcohol and drugs. It was an affliction commonly passed from mother to daughter unless somewhere the cycle was broken.

Apparently Parker Hathaway had also been caught in that cycle, though his parents had not led him there. What had broken it for him? These were questions Caitlin would have to know the answer to before she could understand him well enough to defend his actions.

Or at least that's what she told herself.

Sally would have a lot of information on Parker, and as his attorney, she would have access to it all. Likely there would be more she'd have to track down. Maybe it was time to give Kenny a call. She'd been meaning to touch bases with him anyway, to see if Wyman Russell had been nosing around. With all the distractions today, she'd almost forgotten that little problem.

"Haven't you ever done anything you might have otherwise considered wrong to protect someone?" Parker had asked.

She believed, as she'd told him, that the end didn't justify the means, and yet she wouldn't change her own decision any more than he'd change his. Maybe her father hadn't understood all the implications of the motto. Sometimes the possible cost of the end was so great that the means, as long as they weren't too horrible, were justified.

"Isn't that the candy machine?" Madeline asked.

"Oh, yeah." They had been about to walk past it. "What do you want?"

"Can I have two?"

Caitlin laughed. "Yes, I think I have enough change. But only two."

Madeline grinned up at her. "You're really nice." She pointed out the candy bars she wanted before adding, "Will you ask my mom if I can play with your sister?"

"Boy, you're persistent."

Madeline giggled, her dimples showing. "Daddy says that's part of my name. But it's really not."

"I always say that about Amy, too."

"That means we'll be the bestest friends."

For a brief moment, Caitlin wished with her whole heart that such a thing could be possible.

● ● ●

"Please, sit down over here." Sally indicated a couch along the wall. "There are some important matters we need to discuss."

"What?" Dakota's eyes narrowed, and she held her arms stiffly to her sides as she sat.

"Well, to begin with, you should know that psychologists have counseled in kidnapping cases like this that it's probably best to play down the whole experience, and especially not to verbally attack the parent responsible."

"Parker kidnapped my daughter!"

"I know that, and you have every right to be upset. But in Madeline's eyes, she just went for a visit with her daddy, and she doesn't understand why you're so upset with him. When you voice your anger at Parker, Madeline feels she has to choose, and that's simply not a good place for a child of that age to be." Sally knew she was overstepping her bounds by talking this way to Dakota, but she felt she owed it to both Parker and Madeline.

"So I just ignore what happened?"

"I'm not saying that. I'm saying Madeline's going to feel a lot of guilt and resentment if she has to choose."

Dakota nodded. "I guess I see that." She shook her head. "I'm never letting him come near her again. How do I know he won't take her away?"

"You don't. That will all have to be worked out in a family court. Do you have a lawyer?"

"No. But I definitely want to press charges. I want him punished!"

"If you're willing to compromise, a plea bargain might be better. Faster. Less stressful for your daughter."

"I don't want him to get off. I want him to pay. He took my little girl who I love more than life!" Tears watered Dakota's eyes. "And that reminds me—I really want to thank you for finding her. Thank you so much."

"You're welcome." Sally inclined her head, trying to reconcile this sudden graciousness with the harsh woman who wanted Parker to rot in jail. "As for charges, I'm sure the DA's office will be in touch, and Family Services will likely want to talk with you as well." This last would be about the drug accusations, but Dakota would find that out soon enough.

"Family Services? Why? I haven't done anything wrong."

"Well, they like to cover all the bases, especially when the child involved is as young as Madeline."

"Oh." Dakota's gaze wandered to the door. "Is that all?"

"Well, as part of the case, we have to do a little background on you and Madeline. You've been at your house for only three months. Where were you before that?"

"At a friend's."

Sally didn't speak but nodded as though expecting more. This tactic often worked with suspects. Dakota wasn't an exception.

"Parker and I'd broken up sometime before that, and I didn't know where to go. Couldn't really afford the apartment where we'd been. So I moved in with a friend."

"A man?"

Dakota bristled. "He was just a friend."

Sally knew he'd been more than that. She saw it in the way Dakota held her body, in the way her eyes slid past hers. She knew it because of the lifestyle Dakota lived. Yes, occasionally friends were just friends, but that usually wasn't the case when people of the opposite sex lived together. "And what was his name?"

"Ron Hill."

"He lives in South Salt Lake?"

"Jordan. But he doesn't live there anymore."

"And where is he now?"

Dakota shook her head. "I don't know. And I don't see what this has to do with anything." She stood, rubbing her hands together. "I'd better go find Madeline."

Sally knew that was as far as she'd get, and legally she couldn't detain Dakota or force her to answer. She'd have to leave the questioning for Caitlin in court, if the case went that far.

Madeline's voice floated into the room from the open doorway, and seconds later Caitlin and Madeline came into sight, each eating a chocolate bar.

"That looks yummy!" Dakota cooed. "Are you ready to go?"

"I guess. Want a bite, Mommy?"

"No, thanks. I'm just anxious to get you home. Your brother's missed you so much."

"Where is Reese?" Madeline scanned the room, as though expecting to see him under a chair or perhaps sleeping on the couch.

"He's with his daddy."

"Oh." Madeline's smile had vanished again, and Sally felt her heart go out to the child.

Dakota took a step toward Caitlin. "Thank you so very much for everything. I'm very much indebted to you. Thank you for your help in bringing back my girl."

"You're welcome." Caitlin appeared as surprised as Sally had felt—not so much at the thanks but the graciousness of it.

Madeline tugged on Caitlin's hand. "You forgot to ask."

"Ask?" Caitlin lifted a brow.

"If I can play at your house with your sister. The one that's five."

Ah, Sally thought. Like most young children, Madeline seemed to have a good memory when it concerned fun.

Dakota blinked her surprise. "Well, uh, I'm sure this lady has a lot to do, Maddy. Maybe we can work something out another day."

Sally recognized that cop-out. She'd used it enough with

Randi. Given enough time, even children with good memories forgot.

Madeline stamped her foot. "But I want to play with her today."

"We'll see. Right now we have to get your brother. And I'm sure this lady is working."

Caitlin nodded, and the excuses seemed to mollify Madeline for the moment.

"She's helping Daddy," Madeline stated. "I don't remember what."

Dakota hesitated, her eyes meeting Caitlin's. "Don't you work here at the police station?"

"I thought you knew. I'm the appointed counsel for your ex-husband."

"You're his lawyer?" Dakota asked, aghast. Her eyes glittered darkly at Caitlin.

"Appointed by the court," Sally reiterated. "Parker doesn't have the means to get his own attorney right now." Then an idea occurred to her, something that might help in the short term. "Caitlin here is going to try to get him out working again as soon as possible so you can get child support."

Dakota's eyes opened wide. Apparently, in her vengeful mood, she hadn't thought about the money. "Well, I'd better go." Taking Madeline's hand, she marched from the room. Silently, Sally and Caitlin watched them walk down the hall. Only Madeline looked back at them and waved.

"I have this feeling she's not going to let Madeline play with Amy," Sally mused.

Caitlin snorted. "You think? If looks could kill, I'd be dead."

"She wants him prosecuted."

"I'd feel the same way in her shoes, but"—she shook her head—"I don't like that woman."

"Maybe that's because you like a certain client just a little too much?"

"That's completely uncalled for!"

Sally grinned, seeing she'd struck a nerve. "I don't think so. But for what it's worth, I agree with you, and that's why I'm going to give you copies of all my research on the case so far. The last place I want Parker Hathaway is in jail. Someone's got to keep an eye out for that child."

"Thank you. I appreciate it. I'm actually not too worried about jail time. It's the visiting rights that will be problematic. Unless I find something solid on Dakota Allen, they may never let him have unsupervised visiting rights again."

10

Tuesday morning, Parker walked out of the courtroom feeling more humiliated than he had felt since his fifth-grade teacher caught him cheating on a test and called his father in to "discuss" the matter. It had been a stupid thing to do because he'd never failed a test, even when he hadn't read the material. He'd done it just to prove he could. Or maybe to get his father's attention. Well, he'd gotten attention all right but only for one evening.

His arraignment had been held between the arraignments of other arrestees, whose alleged crimes ranged from unpaid parking tickets to drunken driving and on to robbery. He'd pleaded not guilty, though he was sure everyone knew he was lying; and though the slick DA fought against giving him reasonable bail, Caitlin had convinced the judge he was not a flight risk, and the bail was arranged.

He hadn't yet been offered the plea deal by the DA that Caitlin thought they might expect, and in fact the DA appeared completely ready to prosecute him to the full extent of the law. Worse, Dakota had taken out a restraining order that prevented him from coming within three hundred feet of her, the house, or Madeline. He'd felt sick at that, though Caitlin had warned him it was coming. She assured him that as long as they could convince a judge to allow him to see Madeline, they would waive the restraining order for supervised visits.

Supervised visits. The words left a horrible taste in his mouth.

With rare exceptions, he'd never been separated from Madeline by more than a few days since her birth. She was a large part of how he'd been able to pull his life together after the wild, uncaring months with Dakota. And now, at least temporarily, he was forbidden to see her at all.

Parker stretched his shoulders uncomfortably in the suit his mother had brought yesterday for the arraignment. It had set him apart from the other criminals, and for that he was glad, but he'd never been comfortable in dress clothes. You couldn't work or sweat or have fun in dress clothes—not like you could in a good pair of familiar, comfortable jeans.

He hadn't allowed his mother to attend the court proceedings. This was the day she usually got together with her women friends for brunch, and he had used that excuse to keep her away. The truth was he couldn't bear to have her see him standing before a judge. His father wouldn't have been surprised, perhaps, but his mother had always held out hope for his future.

A future that was now uncertain.

The DA had pulled Caitlin aside after the arraignment, and they were now chatting some feet away, heads close together. Parker didn't know if it was customary for the legal defender and the DA to be so chummy, but he didn't like Mace Keeley, who was as good-looking as he was smooth in the courtroom. Parker knew his type—a pretty boy who was good with people and desk work but was useless for anything truly physical. Not the kind of neighbor you'd ask to help you load a moving van or lay a bit of sod, but a guy who habitually attended the gym to make sure he didn't flab. He probably didn't even cut his own grass.

Yet Caitlin was interested in Keeley. He could tell by the way her face lit up as they talked, her smile turning her pale face beautiful. A few curling wisps of copper hair had escaped the pins at the back of her head, softening her freckled face. He felt an urge to punch Keeley.

Instead, he walked purposefully toward them. Caitlin smiled at him, but Keeley ignored his presence and said, "Saturday, then. I'll call you about the time."

"Sounds good." Caitlin's voice was light, and Parker had the feeling she was trying not to let Keeley's words be too important. Or maybe she really didn't care. Maybe she was a player like Keeley. The thought disturbed him.

"What now?" he asked.

"They'll be releasing your truck in an hour or so, and you can pick it up at the station. Meanwhile, we need to discuss your case."

"I need to see Madeline."

"You can't visit yet—not even with someone there."

He nodded. "I know." He wondered if she could see his anguish, if it was etched on his face as clearly as he felt it carved into his heart.

"You still might go to prison. I'll do everything I can to keep you out, but since Dakota has custody, the law is on her side."

"I know."

"I thought money might be a factor in our favor, that

maybe she'd get the DA to drop the charges, but apparently she's found another way of supporting herself, and she's out for blood."

Probably her new boyfriend, but Parker didn't feel the need to say it aloud. Caitlin knew what kind of woman she was. She dealt with people like Dakota every day.

With people like him.

No, I'm not like Dakota anymore.

"It won't last," he said confidently. "Her plans don't often pan out. In fact, never—at least not for very long." *Except for me,* he added silently. She'd caught him permanently, or for as long as she could hold Madeline hostage. "Has Detective Crumb found anything yet?"

Caitlin shrugged. "I haven't heard from her today, but I'm sure if you call her later, she'll have an update. Meanwhile, it's vital for your case that we get you working and established so if we really go to trial, we'll have a strong case to present to a jury."

"A jury?"

"It's your right, and I feel the best thing for our case. Many of them will have children and a healthy hatred of recreational drugs."

"How soon will we go to trial?"

"Not for a month at the very least. Could be a lot more, depending."

Parker felt the sudden urge to be sick. "But we can help Madeline before that, can't we?"

She didn't reply right away, gesturing for him to walk with her. "Look, Parker, I've been appointed to represent you in the criminal case, nothing more. I'm not experienced with family court. I suggest you find someone to help you there."

"Who?" He didn't even want to think about how he'd pay.

"I'll make some calls and give you a name by the end of the day. But for now, you need to decide about a job. Because whatever happens with visiting rights, that will be a big factor."

"The contractor I worked for offered me a job as a foreman here in Salt Lake. I'm sure that's not still available, but he might have another position."

"Is he the contractor for the job you dumped Saturday?"

Parker nodded, refusing to let her comment needle him. "He might not want me."

"Let's go see."

Parker blinked in surprise. "You'll take me?"

"Well, your truck isn't available yet. Besides, we have an appointment with him in fifteen minutes."

It was the first real inkling of hope he'd experienced that day. "You are good."

She shrugged. "I get up early. Now come on. I still have two briefs to work on before lunch."

He held the door open for her, and her arm brushed his chest as she passed, sending heat rushing through him. He had a strong and sudden urge to run his hand over her milky skin, to kiss her smooth neck.

Dream on, he thought. She would never look twice at a man like him. Pretty boy Keeley was her type.

She had come to a stop outside the door, waiting for him. Their eyes met and attraction shot through him again. What was wrong with him? She was completely off-limits.

It was all he could do to look away.

• • •

Parker met Jason Rosen at the temporary office of the new building project in West Valley. The gray-haired man stood and met Parker halfway across the room, offering his hand in greeting. After that, he waited for Parker to speak, and an awkwardness fell between them. Parker wished he could flee, and in his earlier days he would have, but now there was too much at stake. Construction jobs didn't abound in the winter as they often did in the summer.

"I suppose you've heard about what happened," he began.

Rosen shrugged his narrow shoulders. "I don't believe everything I hear. I do know that you quit down in Manti, and I figured it was related to your daughter."

This was where things could get tricky. Caitlin had advised him to stick to the basics. "My ex-wife is doing drugs. I removed my daughter because I feared she was in danger." He swallowed hard. "What I did was against the law, but she's back with her mother, and I'm working with authorities to make sure she remains safe. Because of that, I'd like to work near Salt Lake. I promise to work hard if you give me another chance."

Rosen tilted his head, his stern expression softening. "In this business, I work with a lot of men who come and go, men who have a variety of strengths and problems, and trials. Some are solid, some are even bright, some would sooner steal from me than give me a good day's work. But rarely do I see someone like you, who has the potential to excel in this business. You have worked for me an entire year, and never once have you not shown up or been lazy on the job. I can't give you the foreman job because I can't risk having your personal problems interfering with the overall construction, but I will gladly give you a job for as long as you're able to work. Even if it's just a week or two. We're actually shorthanded right now. When this is all behind you, we can discuss future projects."

"Thank you." Parker felt a rush of gratitude. "When do I start?"

Rosen eyed his suit. "Right now, if you have a change of clothes."

"I do. In the car."

"Then let's get to work."

• • •

Parker emerged from the trailer looking decidedly more happy than when he'd gone in. Caitlin climbed out of the car into the cold morning air as he approached. He wore the suit well, though she knew he took no pleasure in dressing up. Still, he looked good—as good as any attorney or executive she had dated. "I take it he said yes?"

"I start right now." He gestured toward the backseat, where the small suitcase his mother had brought him the night before lay on the seat. "I'll change inside."

She stepped away so he could open the back door and reach inside the car for his suitcase. "What about your truck?"

"I forgot about that. I'll have to get it later. Maybe after work? Do you know when they close?"

"I'll ask Sally."

"Thanks."

"You don't have a lunch."

He grinned. "Believe me, it won't be the first time I've worked all day without eating. Besides, the boss always has donuts or something around. And there're soft drinks available. I'll be fine."

Caitlin wanted to protest, but he was a grown man, and it really was none of her business. "Do you have a number where I can reach you?"

"Actually, my phone is still at the police station. I was hoping to pick it up when I got the truck. But don't worry—I'll catch a cab. I have a bit of money in my wallet. The police were kind enough to give that back this morning."

"We still need to talk strategy for your case."

"Any chance we could meet some evening?"

She could tell he was worried about messing up his chance at the new job, as well he should be. Not having a job would be a definite disadvantage to their case, especially if Dakota was pressuring Mace to go for blood. "Evening is fine—at least early evening. In fact, why don't I pick you up tonight, and we can get your truck and talk? I can't stay long, but I can at least outline what I think will be our best defense."

"Thank you. That's more than I expected."

And far more than she should have offered, but something about this man had her going out of her way to help him. *Because he's innocent,* she thought. Of course she had yet to prove that. Maybe Sally had uncovered more information.

Caitlin smiled. "I don't like to lose."

"Neither do I. But I've also got a feeling your pretty boy doesn't like to lose, either."

"Pretty boy?"

"That blond DA."

"He's brilliant." Caitlin wasn't sure why she felt the need to defend Mace.

Parker shrugged. "You would know, but I'm not sure how brilliant you have to be to prosecute a case like mine. After all, I'm guilty."

"Guilty of taking Madeline," she retorted, "but not of kidnapping."

"Apparently the law thinks it's the same thing."

"Not if I have anything to say about it."

"I hope you do." He grinned again, this time sending a fluttering of something to her stomach. "For what it's worth, I think you're better than pretty boy any day—and certainly better looking." His voice had grown husky on the last words, and Caitlin would have had to be blind and dumb not to know the message he was sending, whether intentionally or not. He was attracted to her. This was obvious in the way his eyes touched her face, lingering on her lips. She could feel his awareness of her, yet not in the distorted, perverse way she'd felt with many of her clients. This was . . . different.

"What time do you get off?" she asked, masking her confusion.

"Usually five, but I'll work until whatever time you get here."

She nodded. "See you then." She turned and reached for her door just as he tried to open it for her. Their hands collided and their faces were inches apart. She could almost taste the masculine aroma of him. Her heart thundered. Neither moved for what seemed like long seconds, and then she straightened and backed away, laughing with him as he finished opening the door. "Thank you," she said.

"You're welcome."

She drove away, feeling more than a little satisfaction that he didn't go inside but stood and watched her leave.

• • •

"Sally? It's Caitlin. I'm in my car on my way to the office, but I wanted to know if there's any news on the Hathaway case."

"Not exactly."

"What does that mean?" Caitlin snapped, slamming on her brakes as the brake lights of the car in front of her went on.

"Wow, who woke up on the wrong side of the bed this morning?"

"Hey, it's you I'm doing this favor for."

"It *was* me, but now you're doing it for him. Not that I blame you. If I were single, I'd take a second look at him myself."

"He's *so* not my type." But Caitlin's cheeks flamed, and she was glad Sally wasn't with her in the car to see her face. It was one thing to feel attracted to her client but quite another to act on it—which she had no intention of doing. She had enough going on in the romance field with Mace and Wyman hanging around.

"Whatever you want to tell yourself. But keep in mind he's not a criminal. Not like most of those others you've had to defend."

"Look, I'm just doing my job. Like you, I didn't get good vibes from the ex-wife. And Madeline doesn't deserve any of this."

"Kids with rotten parents never do."

"That's exactly why I'm so interested in the case. I'd like to make sure Parker doesn't do prison time for this—and make sure nothing happens to that little girl. I did some research on the Internet last night. Do you know how many children die because of drug use in their homes? And not just from abuse or neglect. One toddler sucked on a plastic sack full of drugs and died. Another baby died after his mother used cocaine while nursing him. Horrid, horrid stories. Hundreds it seems. If what Parker claims is true, Madeline and her little brother are in big danger."

"I've alerted Family Services, and they sent someone out, but they reported nothing out of the ordinary."

"Well, yeah, Dakota knew she'd be checked out."

"I talked to a lot of her friends. All druggy types." Sally clicked her tongue. "If you can be guilty by association, she's as guilty as sin."

"'By association' isn't going to get Parker off. What about that guy she said she lived with?"

"That's the 'not exactly' I was talking about. Ron Hill is nowhere to be found. Some of Dakota's friends remember hearing about a Ron but nothing of a Ron Hill. There are no public records at all for the man, and no police ones, either."

"Which means he probably doesn't exist."

"Right. He gave her a false name, or she gave us one. I hope it was her because that means she has something to hide."

Caitlin considered this. "We have to find out more."

"I know, but I've got a murder case and another missing person case that just came in today—a man. I'm up to my ears investigating leads. And I gotta tell you that now Madeline's back home safe, the brass aren't too excited to pursue anything more. I have Dakota's name and all the particulars tagged, though, so if anything regarding her comes up, the information will forward to me, but anything else I do on the case will be on my own time or squeezed in between official projects."

"I understand. You've been a big help so far. But maybe I'll talk to Kenny Pratt."

"He's good. Tell him if he needs info from us to call me. We've worked together before."

"Thanks, Sally."

"Good luck. And Caitlin? If the opportunity presents itself, I say go for it." She was talking about Parker again. "I know for a fact it's been years since you've even dated a man, much less been in a relationship. Maybe it's time to take a chance."

Caitlin was painfully aware of that fact. "I have Amy to think about. I have to be careful."

"That's an excuse, Caitlin. You're thirty-two years old— maybe it's time to make your opportunity and not wait for it."

"I'm going out with Mace on Saturday," she said abruptly.

"What? When did this happen, and how come you didn't tell me?"

"I'm telling you now. We talked after the arraignment this morning. He asked. I said yes."

"Good." Sally oozed satisfaction. "Talk about opportunity! Call me Sunday and tell me everything. I'll want to hear all the juicy details. And I mean juicy."

Caitlin groaned. "It's only a first date."

"You never know."

"I'm not looking for a casual relationship. Not everyone hits it off like you and Tony."

"You're right." Sally's voice had become serious. "Tony's the only one for me."

Caitlin laughed. "At least that leaves a guy or two for me to choose from."

"And one of those choices works in construction. Believe me, they're the best."

Another reminder about Parker that Caitlin decided to ignore. "Sally, I'm hanging up now. I've got to call Kenny."

"Yeah, and I've got to find this missing guy. Not a fun prospect. I've met his wife, and I suspect he wants to be wherever he is at the moment."

Caitlin clicked off the phone and dialed Kenny. He didn't answer, but she left a message. He was good at calling back. Sure enough, her phone was ringing before she'd reached her upstairs office.

"Hello?"

"Caitlin, girl, what's up?"

"I have a new case, and I need information to help my client."

"Help him? Does this mean you actually have an innocent one?"

"I think so. He was arrested for kidnapping his own child. Look, is there sometime we can meet to discuss the case? I know it's lunchtime, and I'm booked solid for the next three hours or so, but I'll have a little time, say, about three-thirty."

"Why don't I stop by your office around then," he said. "I'll be in the area anyway, and that way I can save you time."

"Great." Caitlin was relieved. After all the time she'd taken with Parker on Monday and this morning, she was running behind on her other cases. There was only so much she could delegate to the paralegals and secretaries.

"Besides," Kenny added, "there's another matter we need to discuss. Remember that job you had me do a couple weeks ago? Well, there's been someone from the DA's office snooping around about that. I'd like to be let in on the loop."

Caitlin closed her eyes for a moment. She'd forgotten all about that. "Okay, Kenny. We'll talk. See you at three-thirty."

• • •

Caitlin had fifteen minutes to spare until her appointment with Kenny Pratt. She took the opportunity to file some of her completed cases. As she did, she looked over other cases she'd completed throughout the year, remembering the details and who had prosecuted her clients. Mace Keeley had been the prosecutor in only one of her recent cases—a drug-using, hit-and-run perp who had exacted sympathy from no one, least of all Caitlin.

She had seen Mace in numerous cases in the courthouse,

but in the past year, she had gone up against him personally three times. On the other hand, Wyman seemed to represent a good fourth of her cases, while the other DAs had prosecuted a fairly even number. It wasn't unusual that Wyman should have so many. Because he was the newest of the district attorneys, he would likely have less choice in which cases he was assigned. Since she was considered tough, some of the attorneys might pass at going against her, especially if the case wasn't promising. Could that be why she remembered beating Wyman so often? But what didn't make sense was that Mace hadn't taken his fair share against her, and the cases he had prosecuted had been absolutely irrefutable, leaving him no chance of losing.

No, that had to be all in her mind.

Still . . .

She picked up the phone. "Jodi? Look, I know you're swamped, but when you get a moment, do you think you could do a little checking in our company files and find out which cases Mace Keeley prosecuted against our LDA attorneys?"

"Ah, so it's serious."

"Jodi!"

"I saw the way he was looking at you this morning in court, don't think I didn't. Lucky girl."

"It's nothing."

"Sure, whatever you say."

"Thank you, Jodi." Caitlin hung up, not liking what was happening. If Jodi had noticed her and Mace, it was only a matter of time until others did the same.

And what of it? asked a voice inside her head. *I deserve a chance at love as much as anyone else.* She sat back in her chair, thinking of her upcoming date with Mace, but oddly enough it was Parker's face she saw.

"Caitlin?" Kenny Pratt came into the room, startling her from her reverie. "I knocked but no one answered. The door was ajar."

Caitlin came to her feet, feeling rattled. "I left it open for you. Come on in." She indicated one of the chairs in front of the desk, taking the other for herself. She'd learned Kenny didn't take well to formal discussions, so she tried to keep things as casual as possible, and eliminating the desk between them went a long way toward that goal.

Kenny was small, dark-haired, and wiry, with an unassuming face that was easy to trust. His way with words caused most people to spill their darkest secrets or left them wishing they had secrets to spill. This latter group often found their neighbors' secrets almost as satisfying to share, which was fine by Kenny. Even Caitlin, knowing his profession, had to be careful she didn't get sucked in.

Before sitting, he shrugged off the thick black coat that made even his thin frame appear almost stocky. "So what's up?" His eyes, so dark they were almost black, glittered.

She sighed. "First we'd better talk about the DA."

Kenny sat back in his seat. "Why are they asking questions about that last case I worked for you? What did you do to tick them off?"

She was glad he didn't have an idea as to what she'd done, but she had little hope of keeping it that way. Better for him to know what she was up against. Not that she would share the whole story. He didn't have to know she'd hired him not to free her client but to convict him.

"I had a client charged with rape and assault with a deadly weapon. He claimed he was innocent."

"And was he?"

Caitlin smiled dryly. "Aren't they all?"

"So he was guilty as sin."

"He claimed he was elsewhere that night, and I sent you to see if there were any witnesses that could attest to his presence."

"And I found one."

"Yes. Only what he saw was detrimental to my client."

Kenny tented his hands in his lap. "You didn't let it die."

"A citizen has the duty to report unusual activity to the police, so that's what I told you to encourage the witness to do."

Kenny leaned forward quickly, the suddenness of his movement startling her once more. "I see now why the DA is snooping around. You were about to win the case, and they had an apple fall into their lap. Or a knife wrapped in a jacket, to be exact."

"You think they'd be grateful."

Kenny shook his head. "You're not telling me everything. My guess is that you knew the knife was there. Your client must have told you at some point, and you made sure the beans were spilled."

So much for not telling him the whole story. "You're wrong, Kenny," she said lightly. "I was simply trying to defend my client."

"If that was really true, you wouldn't have told me to tell the kid to call the police. If your participation in this comes to light, your client will claim a mistrial and the evidence might be thrown out."

"Without the evidence, he'd walk." Caitlin met his gaze, and to her surprise, he was the one who dropped his eyes first.

"I've done a lot of things in my life to get information," Kenny said, "but I've never risked as much as you did by sending me to that street. I understand why you did it, but this is a serious breach of attorney-client confidentiality."

Caitlin shrugged. "Morality is an interesting subject. Would you want a man like him freed to stalk your daughter?"

"If I had a daughter, no. Believe it or not, I admire you for what you've done. I just don't think it was a good career move."

Caitlin didn't know how much she valued Kenny's opinion until she felt relief flood through her. He supported her decision, however reluctantly. He even admired her for it. "What I don't get is why the DA is so interested," she mused.

He leaned back again and crossed his legs, the picture of relaxation. "They smell something wrong, and you know as well as I do that certain unscrupulous attorneys would enjoy the publicity they'd get from exposing this breach. Never underestimate the ambition of an attorney." He chuckled wryly. "Present company included."

Caitlin never thought of herself as hard and ambitious, but it didn't come as a surprise that others thought of her that way. Half of success was the front you showed to the world, and the other half was what you were willing to do to win.

"They traced the boy to me, but that's as far as it went," Kenny said. "And that's as far as it will go—unless I'm called to testify. I won't lie in court."

"It won't come to that. You're the only connection."

"I don't like being in that position."

She sighed. "I know, Kenny, and I'm sorry. Short of making an anonymous call myself, I didn't know what to do. I could have planted a story, but there wasn't enough time. As it was, he nearly walked."

Kenny ran his short, strong fingers through his thinning hair. "Just be careful for the next few months."

"I will." She hesitated a few seconds before asking. "The DA—was it Wyman Russell?"

"No. Actually, it was an aide from the DA's office. Didn't tell me who he was working for, so it could have been any of them." He grinned suddenly. "Sorry, I can't tell you who you're going to have to bribe to make this go away."

"Very funny." She made a face as she remembered her dinner with Wyman. To think she'd actually enjoyed her dinner with him! He was playing her, that much was apparent now.

"Well," she said, dismissing Wyman from her thoughts, "all unpleasantness aside, let's get down to new business." She picked up a manila folder from her desk where she had placed copies of all the information she'd gathered so far—much of it from Sally. She quickly outlined the case. "It's all here." She tapped the folder. "But in a nutshell, I need evidence against the ex-wife. Proof, if possible, that she's doing drugs and the child's in danger. Anything that reflects poorly upon her."

Kenny thumbed through the documents. "Is she really that bad?" There was disapproval in his voice, and Caitlin knew he didn't like the idea of getting between a mother and her child.

"After meeting the woman, I agree with my client. He may not have gone about it the right way, but something is wrong. If I were to go by the child's reaction alone, I'd have her removed from the home. But Family Services says they can't do anything if we don't have some kind of proof. Particularly, we want to find the man the woman used to live with. We believe he may be the link we need, but we aren't sure we have his correct name."

"Not going to be easy without a name." He came to his feet slowly.

"If it was going to be easy, I wouldn't need you."

He laughed. "Touché. I'll call you as soon as I have something."

"No need to tell you we're working on a deadline here." She walked with him to the door.

"You won't go to trial for a month at least."

"Well, there'll be a pretrial first, but the real issue is that little girl. I'll never forgive myself if something happens to her."

11

When the guys started heading home from the site, Parker borrowed Rosen's cell phone. He called Caitlin, but she didn't pick up, and then he placed a call to Dakota. There was a pit of helplessness in his stomach, an ache that no one but Madeline could fill. How could he be a responsible father if he wasn't allowed to see his girl?

"Hello?" Dakota's voice was bright and not upset, so she obviously wasn't expecting him.

"Hi, Dakota. It's me, Parker."

"You! How dare you call after what you did?" A string of shrill swear words followed her pronouncement, and he winced as he held the phone away from his ear. Apparently, he was more evil and vile than just about anything in the world. Great. Not a hopeful start. At least he'd had the presence of mind to go outside and away from everyone as he made this call.

"Look, Dakota, I'm sorry. I shouldn't have done it." He grimaced because what he really meant was that he shouldn't have done it the way he had. He should have taken Madeline far, far from Dakota's clutches. "Look, I'm calling to make sure Madeline is safe."

"Of course she's safe!" Dakota screamed. "You stupid man!"

"I know you're doing drugs again," he said over another tumult of words. "You promised me that once I got you the house, you'd stop. You said you'd keep it away from Madeline. For crying out loud, Dakota, I saw the bag of whatever it was on the TV the last time I picked her up." Why he hadn't called the police that day was something he'd have to live with for the rest of his life.

The jumble of words ceased for a moment. "Is this what you're telling the police? You realize it's your word against mine. The word of a *kidnapper*. How far's that going to go? Besides, if there were any drugs, and I'm not saying there were, they could have been yours. You could have planted them."

"What if Madeline had gotten hold of it? Did you think of that? You know nothing's out of her reach. She climbs like a little monkey."

"It was a bag of sugar, that's all. We were coloring it for cookies."

"Dakota, this is our daughter we're talking about!"

"*My* daughter, and you need to back off! I'd never let anything happen to her. I love her."

"I know you wouldn't hurt her purposefully, but accidents happen. Look, all I'm asking is to let her stay with my mom until you get on your feet."

"You just want custody. Well, I can tell you that's not going to happen. I don't need you, and I don't need your money. I have someone else to help me now. I'm on my feet, and for

147

once you don't have control over me because of the money. I'm so sick of you calling the shots. For all I care you can rot in prison!"

Gritting his teeth in frustration, he walked around the huge shell that would someday be a large building. It was good workmanship, he could see, and he was glad he worked for a man who didn't cut corners to gain additional profit. Cheated customers didn't come back for more.

"Dakota," he said, trying to remain calm. He'd learned the hard way that it never paid to meet her viciousness with anger—not when Madeline was in the middle. "Please. I've forgiven you a lot over the years, haven't I? Please forgive me for this. All I want is for Madeline to be happy. Please."

"We don't need you," Dakota repeated. Her voice was still hard but less vicious now.

"Can I at least talk to her? I don't want her to worry. She was stressed when I left her."

"And whose fault is that? No, you can't talk to her. You've had her all weekend. On *my* weekend, I might add. Look, I've got to go. Don't call me again. I'll contact you through the authorities—if you're going to be around to contact. Or should I call that cute little lawyer of yours? The way she was all over Madeline, you're probably sleeping with her."

"What are you talking about? I didn't even know her before yesterday!" How could Dakota possibly be jealous of Caitlin? Dakota was the one who'd slept around while they were married, not him. Even if he'd been so inclined, he'd been too busy working and watching Madeline. "Besides, what would you care if—"

She had already hung up. Parker sighed heavily. He'd only wanted to talk to his little girl, to make sure she was all right, but apparently Dakota was out to make his life as difficult as possible.

Slowly, he began walking back to the heated trailer where Rosen would be waiting for his phone. *I should have run,* he thought. If he had, Madeline would be safe right now. That was the second mistake he'd made.

It's not too late.

He contemplated this new thought. There was a court order preventing him from going near Dakota and Madeline, but that didn't have to stop him, not if it might mean saving Madeline's life. It would take planning and preparation if he was to pull it off, but he was good at that. He would have to be. There would be no third chance.

A car honked, and he looked to see Caitlin driving into the construction site. He pointed at the phone in his cold hand and made a motion toward the trailer. She nodded, her face smiling openly, less businesslike than that morning, making her seem relaxed and warm, and also somehow reminding him of what Dakota had said about Caitlin and Madeline. Maybe she really did care about Madeline's welfare to the extent that she'd do everything in her power to discover the proof he needed. Maybe giving her a few days wouldn't be a bad idea—provided he could get them to check regularly on Madeline. Dakota was likely to be on her best behavior right now.

After returning the phone to Rosen and collecting his suitcase, he jogged to the car and climbed into the front seat next to Caitlin. Her face was no longer smiling. A tiny crease had formed between her eyebrows.

"What's wrong?" he asked.

She shook her head and then nodded. "My sister, Amy. Just had a call from her sitter. She's missing."

"What?" He tried to remember what she'd told Madeline

about her sister, but nothing stood out in his mind. Just that she was young enough to want to play with Madeline.

"I called Sally—Detective Crumb. She says she'll send someone if I want, but I think I should check the neighborhood first. The sitter is an older lady, and she hasn't searched yet."

"Better hurry. It'll be dark soon, and colder. Where was she?"

"Here in West Valley. About ten minutes away. She wanders off sometimes, but usually only when it's warm."

"Let's go. I'll help search." He nodded toward the gearshift.

Hesitating, Caitlin blinked slowly, her lashes leaving delicate shadows under her eyes. "Your truck," she began.

"It's not going anywhere."

"I could call you a cab."

He waved the suggestion aside. "Your sister's only five, right?" he said, remembering at last what little she'd said on the trip from Manti. How horrible and terribly ironic that her sister had gone missing when she had been instrumental in making him turn over Madeline. What if Amy had been kidnapped?

"Well, sort of."

"You can tell me on the way."

She put the car into reverse and didn't speak again until they were at the stoplight on the main road. "Amy is only five or six—at least in her mind. On the outside, she's twenty-seven." She waited a moment for him to digest the information and then continued. "They don't know why it happened. Maybe the birth itself." She shook her head. "You can tell when she talks, but well, just looking at her you might not notice anything."

Which explained why Caitlin wasn't as worried about a possible kidnapping, though there was still a lot that could go wrong with a full-grown woman who was mentally handicapped.

He sensed a waiting about her, and unsure what she wanted or needed, he said, "We'll find her." She nodded, her lips pursed and her face tight with worry.

The baby-sitter was a sturdy older woman with white hair, who burst from the house as they pulled into the driveway. Both Caitlin and Parker jumped from the car and met her on the walkway.

"Oh, Caitlin, I'm so sorry! She heard me talking to you on the phone about being late, and she was pouting. You know how she gets. Neither Kyle nor I saw her leave. She was sneaky about it."

Caitlin patted the woman's shoulder. "It's not your fault, Sarah. I told you about last summer and how she used to disappear."

"But she hates being out in the cold. She took her coat, at least, thank goodness. And I called you the minute I knew she wasn't in the house."

"Then she couldn't have gone far." Caitlin scanned the street.

"I'll go that way," Parker said, motioning one way with his head. "You go the other. We'll knock on doors and ask people to search their own houses and yards. If we don't find her on this street, you'd better take Detective Crumb up on her offer. It's getting colder by the minute."

"Okay."

"I'll go inside and call everyone I know," the sitter added.

At the first two houses, Parker talked to the people living there. All were extremely helpful. "If you find her on your property, please let us know," he urged.

"We'll help you after we look here," he was told at each

house. Parker felt an odd lump in his throat at their concern. Caitlin had chosen a wonderful neighborhood to live in.

The next house was empty, but he searched the yard anyway. Dusk was quickly approaching; he'd have to find a flashlight soon. He could hear people shouting Amy's name as neighbors joined the hunt. In the backyard of the fourth house, which was also empty, he spied a playhouse complete with a balcony, slide, swing, and a sandbox underneath that would probably be attractive in the summer but now looked dark, deserted, and unfriendly. He realized he was thinking like an adult who knew the floors would be cold, the inside dark, and the furniture dirty. But Madeline wouldn't think such things. She'd be excited to have a little house all her own, and she would try to make it as comfortable as possible. Besides, though it was almost dark now, it hadn't been when Amy left the sitter's.

"Amy?" he called.

No response. It had been a long shot anyway. He was about to leave for the next house, but thoughts of Madeline stopped him. Madeline loved to play hide and seek; maybe Amy did, too. He'd take a peek inside and be on his way. Zipping his coat against the ever-increasing cold, he approached the little playhouse and climbed the stairs to the deck. One way led to the door of the house, the other to the slide. From his vantage point on the deck, he could see a glow coming from the house. "Amy? I'm a friend of your sister's, and we came to get you. Are you here?"

No response, but he heard a rustling inside the playhouse. "Amy?" He peeked in and saw a woman sitting on a blanket. Even in the dim light he could make out her red hair. She was bigger than Caitlin, in both height and weight, but there was an obvious family resemblance in the lines of her face. "There you are."

"I'm a bird and this is my nest," she said in a little girl voice.

He took a few steps inside, ducking his head so he wouldn't hit the ceiling. There was a second floor to the house, he saw, a loft really, and he was glad Amy hadn't climbed up there. There wasn't a safety rail and she might have fallen.

"A bird," he said conversationally. "What kind of a bird?"

"One that flies." Amy hesitated. "I'm not supposed to talk to strangers without Caitlin around."

Parker squatted down next to the woman, who regarded him with suspicion. "Then we'd better go find Caitlin. She's really worried about you."

"Good. She was late. Again." Amy stuck out her lower lip, the quintessential pouting child.

"I wasn't worried about you," Parker added.

Amy tilted her head. "You weren't?"

"Not if you can fly. If anything bad came, you'd just fly away."

She nodded vigorously. "That's right. I can fly. Are you a bird, too?"

"Sometimes. At least when my little girl wants me to be."

"You're a dad?"

"Yes."

"Oh." She sounded disappointed.

"Is that a bad thing?"

Amy shrugged. "I want a baby for Caitlin so I can play with it. And then maybe Caitlin wouldn't work so much. But if you're a dad, you have a family."

"Part of one anyway. But I'm not married right now." Parker wondered why he cared that she knew. "I'm divorced."

153

Amy's brow gathered. "Divorced? Is that where people decide they don't love each other anymore and go live in different houses?" When he nodded, she added, "That's sad."

"Sometimes it's necessary. But we never divorce our children. We keep on loving them and taking care of them forever and ever."

Amy laughed. "Of course."

"So, should we go find Caitlin?"

"Not until we have our tea." Amy reached over for a pretend pot and poured into a pretend cup. She did the same for him.

Parker sat on the wood floor Indian-style and reached for the make-believe cup, sipping rather noisily.

"No," Amy said. "You have to hold out your little finger like this." She demonstrated.

"I didn't know that. I'll have to tell my daughter."

"Caitlin taught me. We always do it like this."

Parker had a hard time imagining his proper attorney sitting down to make-believe tea, but he liked the picture. It reminded him of how soft she'd been around Madeline. How alive and passionate about her work. He felt his attraction for her grow at the thought, but he immediately squashed the idea of any romantic involvement. She lived in a completely different world. Besides, he wasn't ready for another relationship with a woman. Any woman.

"I didn't know birds could drink tea," he said.

"I have powers. Kind of like magic."

"That's very handy."

"Yes, I have hands and feathers."

"What else can you do?"

"I can fly, and I can . . ." She paused, considering. "Well, do other stuff I don't know yet."

"See through metal? Make people tell the truth?" Madeline had often used these ideas in her play.

"Yes," she agreed. "Would you like some more tea?"

"Sure. Hit me again. But then I really have to go find your sister."

"Would you like to have a baby with her?"

Parker smiled at her innocence. He'd already ruled out the notion of pursuing any kind of a romantic relationship with Caitlin, but maybe if they'd met under another circumstance, he might have acted on his attraction and asked her out. Maybe. Regardless, this situation was what it was, and he couldn't afford to alienate his court-appointed attorney. Besides, what could she possibly see in him? Over the past few years, he'd gained a respect for women like her. Women who kept their promises and who didn't use others.

Yet how did he know this about her? He didn't, not really, but the fact that she took her responsibility toward Amy seriously told him far more than she probably wanted him to know. She was a good person. He knew what it took to be a responsible parent, and it wasn't easy.

"I'm ready," Amy announced. She turned out her light and set it in an alcove. "Ooh, it's dark. Scary."

"It'll be a bit lighter outside," he said, coming to his feet. "I'll help you."

"Okay." Suddenly her hand was thrust into his, and she held on with a grip that was far stronger than Madeline's had ever been.

He led her to the door and outside, where the light had faded completely. "I've been gone all day," Amy said with wonder. "It's dark now."

"It gets dark fast in the winter. And cold. That's why you

should never leave without telling someone where you're going. You might get lost."

"No, I won't." But she stepped closer to him as they left the stairs. She still gripped his hand tightly. Parker felt odd walking around with this woman-child holding his hand. Yet he didn't let go or pull away. For all her twenty-seven years, Amy was still a child. He would want Caitlin to offer support to Madeline in the same way, if the situation had been reversed.

They were spotted almost immediately as they rounded the front yard of the house. "They found her!" a teen shouted and pulled out a cell phone to begin texting others the good news. He could still hear shouts of Amy's name in the distance, but gradually these ceased as the news spread. Parker and Amy were nearly back to the sitter's when Caitlin came running down the street as fast as her high heels allowed. She slowed as she reached them.

"Amy, where have you been?" Caitlin's eyes went to their linked hands, but Amy was already pulling away and launching herself at her sister.

"I was a bird in a nest, so I could have just flown away and not get hurt. And then we had tea." Amy pointed at him. "He drank two cups, and I had three. Then it got dark, but he saved me from monsters."

"His name is Parker," Caitlin said, hugging her sister. "And you can't leave like that. I was so scared!"

Amy looked appropriately chastened, though Parker thought he saw a mischievous smile touch her lips for the briefest of moments. "I'm sorry, Caitlin. I didn't want you to work late. I was missing you today."

"Well, I'm here now. But I still have to take Parker into Salt Lake to get his truck."

"Can I go?"

Caitlin sighed. "Yes." Her eyes met Parker's. "Thank you."

"I'm glad we found her."

"Oh, Caitlin, I just remembered something very, very important," Amy said, tugging on Caitlin's arm."

"What's that?"

"Parker isn't married anymore, so he can still have a baby with you."

Caitlin's eyes opened so wide that Parker had to grin. "Amy," she groaned. "Sorry about that," she added to Parker. "She's got a thing about babies lately."

"Well, technically, she's right," he had to say, wishing it wasn't so dark and cold so he could see if she was blushing. Her freckles did seem to be standing out a bit more prominently.

Her mouth opened, but nothing came out. She seemed both surprised and confused. The urge to pull her to him took him by surprise. What was he thinking? Teasing her was one thing, touching her was another. He might not be able to stop.

People were converging upon them now, everyone happy that Amy had been found. White clouds of warm breath filled the cold air.

"Thank you," Caitlin said at least a dozen times.

Parker backed to the edge of the small crowd and watched them talk and eventually disperse. Amy enjoyed the attention, while Caitlin seemed only to endure it, though he was sure that wouldn't be obvious to anyone there. She was complete grace.

Stop, he told himself. He turned and walked back to Caitlin's car. His hands and face felt numb from the cold, and for once he was glad of it. Numb made things hurt less. There was so much he couldn't have. Madeline, a normal life. He had to hope Caitlin could make it all possible for him. Maybe.

Caitlin and Amy caught up to him as he reached the door.

"I'll just call Sally," Caitlin said. "There's probably still time to get your truck."

He nodded and opened the front passenger door for Amy, who was at his elbow, looking up at him with a child's worship. She reminded him of Madeline. Where was his daughter now? Was Dakota taking care of her? Was she safe?

Helpless. He hated feeling that way. It made him desperate.

Caitlin was talking on the phone, and from the expression on her face, it wasn't good news. "Sorry," she said when she'd disconnected. "Sally says they're all closed up. We'll have to get it first thing in the morning. She can have someone get us in by seven."

That meant he was stuck without transportation, but at least he had his clothes and a bit of cash. "Is there a motel around here? Someplace with a restaurant close?"

"Oh, that's right. You didn't have lunch. You must be starving."

His stomach growled at even the mention of food, though he'd eaten four donuts that afternoon. "I could eat a horse."

"Look, the least I can do is feed you."

"It's okay. You've got to take care of Amy."

"We'll go to my house. Amy will love having you."

He was curious to see where she lived, to see her in her own private environment, but surely there were rules against consorting with your clients. Being with her was proving both difficult and tempting. "Okay, if it's no bother," he agreed, wondering if he would regret the decision later. Maybe if he hadn't been so tired he would have been able to protest more strongly, but he was both exhausted and ravenous. Not a good combination on any day.

"Good." She gave him a smile that made heat course

through his veins. He looked out the window to mask his reaction. Already he could tell this was a big mistake.

"I can show you my real tea set," Amy bubbled into the silence. "I have the princess ones. I have Belle and Sleeping Beauty, and Snow White. I don't have Ariel, and I like her best because she has red hair like me, but I have her on my bed. And I also have . . ."

Parker let the words rush over him, enjoying the babble that so reminded him of Madeline. His sore heart felt lighter.

When Caitlin pulled up at her small house a few streets over, their eyes locked briefly and his confusion was back. What was he beginning to feel for this woman? Was it because he hoped she could reunite him with Madeline? Because he was physically attracted to her? Or because he was fascinated with her laugh, the slight lilt in her voice, the soft look of her lips, or how her hair had escaped the mass gathered at the back of her head? The way she spoke to Amy? All of the above?

He was a mess. What he needed was a good night's sleep so he could think clearly. Be in control. He closed his eyes for a moment, but all that got him was a vision of Caitlin looking up at him.

CHAPTER

12

C aitlin was going against all her personal rules by inviting Parker to her house. She knew attorneys who
often helped their clients out with places to stay and
clothes to wear. Others actually had affairs or became close
friends with the people they represented. Caitlin had always
been careful to keep her professional life separate from her personal one—an excellent policy, seeing as she mostly represented people guilty of very nasty crimes. Like Chet Belstead,
who, thanks to her, was going to spend twenty-five years
behind bars, if society had any luck at all.

"Have a seat," she offered. "This shouldn't take too long."
She kept a frozen chicken casserole around for emergencies
when store-bought frozen food didn't seem appropriate; it was
her mother's special recipe, and she decided to use it now. The
casserole would only take ten minutes to mostly thaw in the
microwave and then another thirty in the oven. That would
give her time to make a salad. No, scratch that because she was

out of lettuce, but she had a bagged salad from Costco that had bits of blue cheese and dried cranberries. For a bagged salad, it tasted quite good.

Parker sat at the table, his dark eyes following her as she opened the freezer and cupboards. He had the air of a man who'd worked hard and was exhausted, both mentally and physically. She was glad she'd decided on the casserole instead of something less healthy and filling.

If the truth were told, she didn't invite many personal friends back to her place, either. Previously, male friends had thought it was because of Amy, and in part it was, but Caitlin also didn't like the idea of opening herself to someone by having him see her real life. It made things much easier at break-up if most of the relationship had taken place elsewhere.

"If there's someplace I can wash up," Parker said, "I'd be glad to help."

She noted there was a shadow on his face, though he'd shaven that morning, and his shirt was rumpled and probably dirty from the day's work. What he needed was a good shower, but that would have to wait until they found a motel. "I'm almost finished here," she said, "but the bathroom's down the hall."

"I'll show you." Amy jumped up from where she knelt by the hamster cage.

"You can show him but then let him have his privacy."

Amy sighed in exasperation. "He's just going to wash his hands."

"Amy," Caitlin warned.

Parker laughed. "Where is this bathroom, Amy? And just so you know, I am definitely closing the door."

Amy rolled her eyes. "Come on. It's down here." She clumped to the hall and Parker stood to follow.

161

He took his suitcase with him, Caitlin noted, and at the last moment she said, "You could take a shower if you want. There's time." He stopped and met her gaze with a look that sent a longing through her. Caitlin flushed. "I mean if you want."

"I do want. I really need a shower. I just didn't think you'd want . . . I could wait until the motel."

"No, go ahead. It's fine." It wasn't like it was her bathroom. The hall bathroom was Amy's, filled with her toys and mermaid towels. Not personal at all.

Caitlin busied herself getting the dishes from the cupboard until she was sure he was gone. Then she put her hands to her burning face. A man showering in her house. Not something that happened every day—or ever, now that she thought about it.

This is ridiculous, she thought. Not only was he her client, but he seemed to have no interest in her. He hadn't even made a pass yet, which most of her male clients did within the first half hour of meeting her.

And why not? Didn't he find her attractive?

She poured out the bagged salad, thinking of the connection she'd felt between them. *Imagined, more like,* she told herself. *It was nothing.*

She set the table, using her nicer dishes. For an added touch, she lit a candle. For the aroma, not for mood. After all, she wouldn't be turning off the light, and Amy would be right there with them.

She took the partially thawed casserole from the microwave and slipped it into the oven. Dumping rolls into a basket and covering them with a towel, she nodded. The only thing missing was a good dressing, and she might as well make one since she had time. As she mixed the vinegar with the spices, she began to hum under her breath, and the tension drained from her. She'd forgotten how much she enjoyed puttering around the kitchen. It brought back memories of cooking with her mother while her father played cards with Amy at the table, his Irish brogue thick and musical.

A noise at the doorway to the kitchen distracted her thoughts. Parker was there in a change of clothes and his hair combed. He looked more rested. "I'll have to find a place to stay up here—an apartment or something. Someplace preferably with access to a washer and dryer. I'm going to run out of clothes soon. My mother didn't pack for more than a few days."

"You can go home and get more," Caitlin told him.

"I will. If we manage to get my truck tomorrow." Grinning, he crossed the space between them.

"We will."

"You aren't going to change into something more comfortable?" he asked, looking at her languidly.

She glanced down at her suit. "I always dress like this."

"I don't think I could stand to be in a suit all the time."

"It's a matter of what you get used to. Couldn't you imagine a time when you might be wearing a suit all day?"

"There would have to be a big incentive." He was close now, too close.

"Now that you mention it, I think I will change." She was glad to have an excuse to escape. "No use in risking a dry-cleaning bill sooner than necessary." One moment she was wondering why he wasn't attracted to her, and the next she was running away. What did she really want?

Nothing, she thought. *From him I want nothing. I'm just helping his daughter.*

As she changed, she tried to think of Mace, tried to imagine his handsome face bending over hers, but all she saw was Parker. She chose her clothes almost without thinking: soft black knit pants that flattered her hips, and a fitted pink and black top, also made of thin knit, lying attractively over her curves but not at all revealing or uncomfortable.

She went to Amy's room to see what she was doing and found her sister curled up asleep on the floor by the dollhouse their father had made them when they were young. Her favorite Barbie was in one hand, and twin babies on the carpet next to her cheek. "Amy," Caitlin said softly. "Let's get you to bed."

"I want to sleep here," Amy muttered, not opening her eyes.

"Okay, but don't blame me if you end up with a cricked neck tomorrow." Caitlin retrieved Amy's pillow and her Ariel blanket, tucking her in as best she could. "You're sure you're not hungry?"

"I ate with Sarah."

She always did, but that usually didn't stop her from eating again with Caitlin. As a result, she and Sarah Burnside had worked out portion control to try to keep Amy's weight from becoming too much of a problem.

Caitlin smoothed her sister's red hair. "You sleep then. If you need me, call me."

Amy didn't answer, having already drifted off again.

That left Caitlin alone with Parker, and she had to admit that a part of her was just the tiniest bit excited at the prospect.

He was sitting at the table, his sock-clad feet stretched out before him, looking as though he belonged. Caitlin had left her own shoes at the door when they'd entered and had taken off her nylons when she'd changed. Being barefoot seemed suddenly intimate, and she wished she'd taken time to put on socks like Parker had done.

"You look nice," he said, his eyes traveling the length of her. "Tell me the truth—it's a lot more comfortable than a suit."

She laughed. "You're right."

"Where's Amy?"

"Sleeping. She was playing with her dolls and dropped off. I couldn't get her awake enough to get her to walk to her bed. She weighs more than I do." Caitlin opened the top cupboard where she kept the slab of gray speckled granite that matched her countertop. It was handy for hot pans from the oven, but rarely did she have the opportunity to use it. She had to reach up with both hands to support its weight.

He stood. "I can help if you want."

"Oh, she'll be fine. She'll wake up before too long to use the bathroom, and then I can get her into bed."

"I meant this." He reached from behind her and took the heavy slab with one hand, his chest brushing her back.

"Thanks." She turned slowly toward him. His arm slid against hers as he brought the slab to his side. Neither moved, and the tension between them was so thick Caitlin could hardly breathe. This close she could see the details of his face, the firm line of his jaw, the slightly prominent nose, the individual hairs that made up the brows framing his brown eyes.

Her heart thumped loudly in her ears. He was going to kiss her, she was sure of it. And she was going to let him. In fact, if he didn't she would shrivel up and die. His face came marginally closer. Their eyes were locked. It was all she could do not to grab him and hurry things along. Then suddenly he was turning away, stepping more gracefully than she would have thought, given his bulk and their awkward proximity. Disappointment throbbed through her.

"Don't you want . . . ?" she began.

He set the granite slab on the table. "Want what?"

Her face burned and she turned away, wishing she had never spoken. He walked to her and put a firm hand on her shoulder, turning her toward him. "Want what?" he repeated.

His pretense stung. How dare he play with her! "Nothing," she muttered. "I need to check the casserole." She pulled away and walked toward the oven.

"If I'd tried to kiss you, would you have let me?"

She swallowed hard, drawing her hand back from the oven door. "You wanted to kiss me?"

He let out a short laugh. "Want? Oh, Caitlin. I've been wanting to kiss you since the moment I first saw you."

She stiffened. He was making fun of her. "This isn't a game."

"I don't think it is. But look at it from my perspective. You're all the hope I have right now of saving my daughter. If I scare you away . . ."

"I don't scare easily."

"Oh?" His left brow rose. "I'm not sure I believe that. In court maybe not, but this is completely different."

"Well, then I guess it's good there's nothing between us. We can focus on your case."

"Are you saying there could be more?" He took the three steps that separated them.

She didn't know what she was saying. "I don't believe that's what either of us want."

"Speak for yourself."

The gruffness in his voice thrilled her. She gazed at him from beneath lowered lids. "What do you mean?"

"I'm saying I'm attracted to you."

"I don't believe you." He was probably saying it so she wouldn't dump his case.

He took another step. "I never lie." His arms went around

her, pulling her toward him. With his eyes watching her face, he lowered his lips to hers, kissing her with none of the initial tentativeness of her previous boyfriends, leaving her no doubt as to his intent.

His hand went to her hair, freeing it from the clip. "That's better," he murmured, combing his hand through her unruly hair. "You are so beautiful."

She felt beautiful. At that moment it didn't matter that she needed to lose ten pounds, or that she often felt awkward in social situations. All that mattered were his lips on hers and the way his hands felt in her hair. All the carefully constructed walls around her were tumbling down.

"Caitlin," he murmured against her lips.

"Caitlin?" came a loud echo. Amy's voice came from the doorway.

They broke apart self-consciously. Caitlin knew her face was redder than her hair. "Amy," she said faintly.

"What were you doing?" Amy asked, rubbing her sleep-filled eyes with one hand while the other still clutched a Barbie. "Why were you kissing?"

"I, um—"

"You told me never to let a boy kiss me."

"This is different," Caitlin said.

"Why?"

"Because I'm older and because I know Parker." Caitlin glanced at him. He was watching the interaction, an amused smile on his face. He was enjoying this!

Amy leaned forward and said in a loud whisper, "So do we get a baby now?"

"No." Caitlin felt her face flush again. Turning, she busied herself with the oven.

Amy was right. She had thrust aside all propriety, and for

what? For a man who was likely taking advantage of her weakness. She had never considered dating a client before, and Parker, for all his charm, was nothing more than a client, willing to do whatever it took to get him free of the charges against him. Even romancing his attorney, who hadn't had a decent boyfriend in two years.

Anger slowly replaced the attraction in her heart. Caitlin welcomed it, stoked it, glad for the strength it gave her. If she'd wanted casual kissing, she could have found that anywhere. But that wasn't her intention. She wanted a real relationship, and that meant looking elsewhere. "I thought you were sleeping, Amy. What woke you up?"

"Something," Amy said, shrugging. "I don't know. Maybe I'm hungry."

Or maybe she'd felt Caitlin's emotions clear from the bedroom. "Sit at the table then," Caitlin told her. "Dinner's ready."

Caitlin didn't look at Parker until they were safely eating. He didn't seem to have changed his attitude toward her or to be dwelling on their kiss. Instead, he concentrated on his food, wolfing it down with the air of a man who had gone a long time without a meal. She picked more slowly at her plate, her appetite gone. The food tasted like cardboard.

"Great salad," Parker commented. "I didn't think I'd like these red things."

"Cranberries."

"I like them better than raisins," Amy put in. She was wiggling a little in her seat, a sure sign she needed to use the bathroom.

"Great idea, putting them in a salad."

Caitlin didn't feel obligated to tell him it came from a bag.

Parker looked over at her, still eating. "This is really great. Thanks for having me."

"You're welcome." Caitlin looked quickly away from his unsettling eyes.

Amy yawned. "My Barbie wants to sleep."

She hadn't eaten anything except the cranberries from the salad. Caitlin sighed. "Go to the bathroom first and then put her to bed." Amy stumbled off, muttering something to her doll.

Parker set down his fork, though his plate was still half full with his second helping. "Sorry about that."

She knew he was referring to how Amy had walked in on them. "You enjoyed it!" Caitlin let annoyance color her voice.

"I was just thinking how I'd explain it to Madeline. You know, if she'd been the one to walk in." He took a long drink of milk before picking up his fork again.

Caitlin's annoyance melted away, taking with it most of the anger she'd wanted to hold against him. "I've tried to keep Amy protected, you know, from boys who'd take advantage of her. Once when my parents were still alive, a boy in our neighborhood in Chicago got her in a field all alone. I was sent out to look for her and found her—just in time. Thankfully, he ran off when he saw me. My father was furious." She gave him a wry grin. "You've never seen an angry man until you've see an Irish man angry."

Parker chewed his food thoughtfully. "I thought the Irish were fun-loving."

"They're as fiery as they are fun."

"Which is why you are so wicked in court, I bet. And now I know what I'm hearing in your voice. You sound a little Irish."

Caitlin laughed. "My father was a first-generation immigrant from Ireland. I was a big copycat when I was little. My mother hated it. She was born in England, and even after her family moved to the States she had a very proper English upbringing. But I loved to make my father laugh, so I learned the accent pretty well. I guess it still comes through a little."

"Did you ever visit Ireland?"

"A few times when I was small."

"I went to Ireland once."

That surprised her. He didn't seem the type. "You did?"

"Yeah. After high school, some friends and I went back-packing in Europe for a month. I was interested in construction even then, and I convinced myself it was a good chance to look at all sorts of buildings."

"And was it?"

He laughed. "Believe it or not, it wasn't nearly as fun as we expected, though it was certainly exciting. We ended up sleeping on the roadside a lot, and found ourselves in more than a few dangerous situations. I was extremely homesick after a few weeks. Looking back, I think we went more to give our parents grief than anything. We thought we were so mature."

"How long were you in Ireland?"

"Three or four days. We caught a boat or something over from England. What I remember most is green. It was beautiful. The girls, especially." He winked. "But it was different from what I expected—I guess because there seemed to be fewer extremists. You know, fighting in the streets or whatever. The quiet majority seemed to be just regular folks, caring more about daily life rather than worrying if you were Protestant or Catholic."

"That's true—unless you happen to stray into one of the more volatile neighborhoods—especially in my dad's era. That's why he left the country in the first place. He emigrated to Chicago and met my mom. Later, he actually convinced her to give Ireland a try—that was before I was born—but going back didn't work out, so they stayed in Chicago. Both taught history at the University of Chicago."

"How'd they end up in Utah?"

"My mom's family originally emigrated to Utah for religious purposes, so she spent a lot of time here as a child, and she always wanted to move back. She was offered a job at the University of Utah, and convinced my father to come with her—after all, she'd tried Ireland. Later my father began teaching at the university, too. They liked it here, especially the mountains. So they stayed."

"I love the mountains. Another place you shouldn't wear suits." He scooped up his last bite as Caitlin rolled her eyes.

"I can do anything in a suit."

"Impressive."

Caitlin took a breath. "Look, Parker, about what happened earlier. . ."

He slid his chair next to hers, reaching over to touch her hand. She rose, avoiding contact that might not allow her to think properly.

"What I'm saying is that we made a mistake." She began picking up dishes, avoiding his eyes.

"A mistake. But I thought—"

"We need to focus on your case right now. Distractions are the last thing we need. Besides, we both have responsibilities." Yet Caitlin knew the real reason was that she didn't want to be used and thrown away. She had a problem with commitment, but once she was committed, she wanted the relationship to last longer than the rinse cycle. Parker might not be like most of her clients, but he was still a man whose life didn't exactly match her own.

He frowned, his eyes narrowing. "Now you're the one playing games."

Caitlin recoiled. "I'm the one being professional. Look, Parker, if you want a casual relationship, you'll have to look elsewhere." She met his eyes now, her chin lifted firmly. Was that hurt in his expression? Before she could decide, the emotion was gone.

"Whatever you want." There was heat in his voice but carefully held in check. "Maybe you'd better take me to that motel now."

She nodded. "I can clean this up later."

But he was already gathering the rest of the dishes from the table. "I'll help you now. It's getting late."

They worked in frosty silence, each minute a torture. When they finally finished, Caitlin said, "I'll go wake up Amy. The motel's really close, but I can't leave her."

"Okay." He dried his hands on her dish towel.

She stared at those strong hands, the ones that had so tenderly combed through her hair. Abruptly, she felt weak with indecision. Maybe she should give him a chance.

No. She forced herself to leave the kitchen. When she returned with an extremely sleepy and cranky Amy, she found Parker sitting at the table, staring at a picture of Madeline in his wallet. "You're right," he said softly. "I can't ever let myself forget, not even for a moment, what I'm fighting for."

She nodded and moved away quickly before her heart could feel too much pity. If she stayed to offer him comfort, things could too easily escalate to more—much more. *Why did I let it happen?* She wished desperately that the moment in the kitchen hadn't occurred. Now her heart had been awakened to him. Now she wanted more.

When they reached the motel she pulled up outside the lobby, but he didn't get out immediately. "Caitlin." His voice came softly, sounding a bit gravelly.

She met his gaze as his hand reached out, touching her arm lightly and searing it through the cloth that separated them. "Yes?"

"I'm sorry."

She nodded. "Me, too."

He glanced at the backseat where Amy was sprawled, snoring soundly, and then back to her face. "I'm attracted to you. I want you to know that. And for the record, I haven't had a casual relationship since I met Dakota."

She didn't reply. It was all she could do not to lean over and put her arms around him, let him kiss her. But if she did that, tomorrow she'd regret it.

"Good night," she said firmly.

His hand slid from her arm, leaving it cold. "Good night."

Back at home inside her room she lay awake for a long time, staring at the ceiling.

CHAPTER

13

Parker spent an uncomfortable night on the hard motel
bed. Not that the mattress was uncomfortable but
rather his thoughts. His mind was full, not of Madeline
and the court case as they should have been, but of what had
happened between him and Caitlin.

Caitlin was happy they'd been interrupted, so he had to be
satisfied with that. He knew that on some level she was
attracted to him, despite their different economic and social circumstances. But attraction hardly made a difference if she
wasn't willing to admit to it.

He sighed as he shaved and dressed for work in the small
bathroom. Last night in Caitlin's car, he'd dared hope she was
reconsidering the possibility of a relationship, or that she might
admit the connection between them was as strong as he felt it
was, but she had made her intention to keep away from him
clear. At least she was still helping him with his case. Despite

his growing attraction to her, the only reasonable thing for him to do was to pull back or risk losing her help.

He was dressed and had eaten cold cereal from the break-fast alcove in the lobby when she arrived at the motel, wearing a gray suit that was snug at the waist, showing the outline of her figure to advantage. Her hair was swept up tightly, but that didn't detract from her beautiful blue eyes or those soft lips. Dragging his eyes away was more than difficult, and after a while he gave up trying.

"Sleep well?" she asked casually.

He gave her a lazy smile and said, "I couldn't sleep. I had, uh, other things on my mind." The way he said it while watching her so intently left little room to misconstrue his meaning, and he loved the way her face flushed. *Did she do that in court?* He wondered. No, because she didn't really care about those cases. Her heart wasn't in them as it was in his. Or was he just fooling himself?

"Well," she said, turning from him, her voice going cool, "maybe it was sleeping in a different place."

"I'll need to find an apartment. A guy at work said he knows of a place available on a week-to-week basis. Another guy says he knows some people in a house who are looking for another tenant."

Caitlin met his gaze again, but this time her emotions appeared completely under control. No telltale flush. "I hope they have a washing machine."

He wanted to jump up from the table and reach out to her, to kiss her again to see if there was still a reaction. But she was the one calling the shots, and if he wanted to protect Madeline, he had to follow her rules.

• • •

175

Detective Crumb was waiting for them at the precinct when they arrived, Parker's truck keys in hand. "I already authorized the release," she said to Parker. "Sorry it was too late yesterday. I hope you managed all right."

"We managed," Caitlin said shortly. "Thanks."

The detective looked at her closely. "What's wrong?"

"Nothing." Caitlin blinked at her innocently. "Everything's fine."

She seemed fine to Parker, but if Sally saw something different in Caitlin, maybe she was right. The two seemed to be close. "We had a late night," Parker volunteered.

"Oh?" Sally reminded him of a hawk, pouncing on its prey. "How is Amy after her little escapade?"

"Same as ever." Caitlin glanced at Parker as though daring him to add anything further. "Well, I'd better get to work. Parker, I'll call you if I have any news. We still need to go over a few things."

"Wait." He touched her arm, felt her stiffen and pull away. "I'll need to find my phone, give you the number."

Detective Crumb grinned. "Oh, that's right. The missing cell phone. Well, look what housekeeping turned up. You're lucky it wasn't stolen." Drawing her hand from the pocket of her slacks, she held out his thin black phone.

"Stolen from a police station?" Parker said. "Not likely. But thanks, Detective Crumb."

"Call me Sally. Seems we're going to be around each other a bit in the next month or so." As he nodded, she continued, "Good move hiding the phone—I guess. Though it made no difference in the end."

"What's the number?" Caitlin punched it into her own phone before turning away.

"You sure everything's okay?" Sally asked her. "You look

different." Sally's gaze shifted to Parker, examined him, and then back to Caitlin.

"I'm fine." Caitlin clicked her tongue in irritation. "I didn't sleep well, that's all."

So she'd been awake last night, too. Parker caught her gaze, and to his amusement, she flushed. He smiled gently. This was the Caitlin he was getting to know. The Irish part of her that burned fiery and emotional instead of the cold outer shell she normally showed the world.

"I'll call you," she said again. Turning on her heel, she strode down the hall.

Detective Crumb—no, Sally—watched her leave. "I'll call you about lunch!" she yelled after the retreating form. Caitlin waved a response but didn't turn.

"What did you do to her?" Sally asked Parker bluntly.

"Nothing."

"It better be nothing. I'm sure I don't have to remind you that I'm a police detective and Caitlin is my friend."

A none-too-subtle warning. "I get it." He jingled the keys in his hand. "Now where's my truck?"

"I'll show you."

Once in his truck, Parker checked his phone. One message looked like it came from Dakota's phone, though he had never given her this number. He punched in the code to retrieve his messages.

"Daddy, it's me. Where are you? Why is Mommy so mad at you? She was calling you bad words, but I plugged my ears. I miss you a lot. I wish I could go to Grandma's. Oh, Mommy's coming. Bye."

She'd left the message last night after ten. He smiled, feeling happier than he had since having to say good-bye. He had to see her somehow. Since he hadn't yet been convicted of anything, there must be a way to secure visiting rights. This was America, after all. Wasn't he supposed to be innocent until proven guilty?

Only he'd learned that sometimes it didn't always work that way, especially where custody issues were concerned, even if he knew he'd acted for Madeline's benefit. He'd wait until she called again, and she would call. Madeline was the most persistent child he knew. Well, really the only child he knew, unless you counted Amy. He knew Madeline would love Amy and vice versa.

His smile faded. Unless they never had a chance to meet. Even he might not be allowed that close to Caitlin's personal life again. The knowledge was hard to take, given that every time he closed his eyes he saw her face with her eyes half-closed, her lips lifting to meet his.

Then there was the more pressing problem of the drugs Dakota was using. He had to fight back, and that meant calling Family Services—calling them every day until they made an investigation. Someone had to protect Madeline, and if the authorities wouldn't do it, he would be forced to take other measures.

Opening his cell phone, he dialed information. "Hi, I need the number for Family Services in Salt Lake. No wait, I think it's called the Department of Child and Family Services. DCFS, or something. Thanks."

He spent the entire twenty-five minutes it took him to drive to work to be transferred and re-transferred to a Mrs. Turnball in CPS—which he assumed meant Child Protective Services. It took additional conversations during his breaks and his lunch to get her to agree, not to open a case against Dakota, but to a late meeting to discuss visitation. The terse Mrs. Turnball wasn't happy about the after-hours meeting, and the child advocate assigned to Madeline's case, a Mr. Reeve, seemed even more annoyed when Parker finally caught up with him. But Parker had learned that part of success in anything depended upon your ability to keep talking politely when every hope seemed lost. Finally they agreed to meet at six, and he was to bring representation if he had any.

He didn't—at least for visitation. Not yet. But maybe Caitlin would help this once. He was sure if Mrs. Turnball and Mr. Reeve met with him, he would be able to sway them to his side regarding visitation with Madeline. If they recommended him, surely no judge would deny his request.

Shortly before his last break ended, his phone rang and he answered without checking the caller ID. "Hello?"

"Daddy?"

"Madeline. Oh, sweetheart, it's so good to hear your voice."

"Are you coming to get me on Friday?"

"I'm trying to. I have a meeting with some people today to make it happen."

"Good, 'cause I'm bored. Mommy just sleeps or talks to Lyn. They keep kissing and kissing. It's gross."

"Are you eating well?"

"Lyn said he's gonna take us to eat. But Mommy's gonna take us to her friend's house instead."

Parker nearly growled in frustration. He would be more than willing to watch Madeline, and even the boy, Reese, but Dakota would never allow that now unless she was forced to. "I meant did you eat anything today."

"Cereal, pizza. And we had crackers and milk. You know, the brown ones."

"Graham crackers?"

"Yeah."

"Sounds good."

"Reese is here all the time now. His daddy went away to work."

"Is that good?"

"I like him here. We play, even though he's so little."

"Is Mommy acting funny?"

"No, but Reese fell asleep. I'm bored."

"What about your princess books? You could look at them. You could draw me a picture."

"Okay. You want purple or pink?"

"Surprise me."

"Okay."

Parker wanted to stay on the phone forever with his little girl, but he had to get back to work. The money would be what would get them to a new life if Caitlin wasn't successful.

"I love you, Madeline."

"I love you, too, Daddy."

CHAPTER

14

C aitlin regretted last night. But what she couldn't say for sure was if she regretted that the moment between her and Parker happened at all, or pushing him away after it had. She was still thinking about him when a knock came on her office door. "Come in," she called, looking up from the brief she was preparing—or pretending to prepare, since every few minutes she kept stopping to reread bits of Parker's file. She'd have to ask Jodi to go over the brief to make sure it was comprehensible.

Mace Keeley smiled at her from the doorway. "Hi. I was in the neighborhood and thought I'd stop by."

The Legal Defenders Association wasn't exactly on his normal beat, so Caitlin knew she should be flattered, but the truth was she'd forgotten all about Mace since she'd seen him last. When had that been anyway? It seemed she and Parker had been in a world completely their own. She shivered, not appreciating the analogy. Parker was a client who needed her help. End of story.

Mace sauntered forward as she stood. "So, today's the day."

"What?"

"Chet Belstead's sentencing."

"Oh, right." Knowing the outcome, she'd already put Belstead out of her mind, though she would have to appear one last time in court with him, an unpleasantness that couldn't be avoided.

"Funny how he almost got off." Mace curved his lips in that beautiful smile.

Caitlin walked around her desk to stand beside him. "Well, in the end he was guilty, so I guess it worked out. I couldn't get him to accept your plea deal."

"That's good for everyone else. Sorry you lost the case."

"But it's one more you won, right? I don't think you've lost a case in years." She still had the files by her desk to prove it. "At least not one I'm familiar with."

Mace shrugged, leaning against the desk. "A streak of good luck."

He was closer than casual conversation merited, but Caitlin didn't back away. "I guess," she said, and then because she was an attorney and accustomed to probing for more, she added, "Maybe it's your case assignments you've been lucky with."

He pushed away from the desk, standing at his full height. There was definitely a tension in him that hadn't been there before. But why? It didn't seem a big thing to be assigned cases that happened to be open and shut. Unless he'd engineered it.

Something in her mind clicked, but she rejected it almost immediately. What would be the purpose of wrangling for only easy cases? Half the satisfaction of being an attorney was matching wits with other competent counsel. Besides, such a thing didn't seem like the confident Mace Keeley.

"I've watched you in the courtroom," she added. "You do good work." She was honest in saying this, though she now understood the cases he'd prosecuted—at least those in connection with the LDA—had been relatively simple. Even Wyman might have been able do justice to most of them.

Mace relaxed, but that too was subtle. If she hadn't studied people as long as she had, she might not have noticed. But his next words showed her that he hadn't appreciated her comment. "What about you? Do you often lose your cases at the last moment? With condemning evidence showing up out of nowhere?"

Caitlin laughed. "My clients are almost always guilty. Believe me, that can happen anytime."

"Ah."

Her laughter had broken the tension between them, though there was still an odd look in his eyes. Caitlin didn't know him well enough to perceive what it might mean. His hands moved toward her, touching her arms lightly, pulling her closer.

Oh, that's what it means. Though she'd dreamed of this moment for months, her inner walls were rising fast. She'd spent the last years trying *not* to get involved with anyone she worked with or went up against in court on even a semi-regular basis, and old habits were hard to break—even if it was for someone as good-looking as Mace.

His lips touched hers, so briefly she wondered why he'd bothered. It hadn't lasted long enough for her to decide how she felt about it, or if she wanted to react. So different from the way she'd felt with Parker. "I'm looking forward to our date on Saturday," he said.

One more thing she'd forgotten. Why had last night with Parker erased everything she'd held dear? "Me, too."

"Talking about these people you represent," he said, his hands falling from her. "I don't know how you do it. I mean, like you said, they're often guilty. Don't you sometimes just want to do something to help lock them away?"

A chill rushed through Caitlin. "Well," she said dryly, "I did apply to the DA's office. Anyway, it makes no difference how I feel. I have a duty to protect my client, and that's what I do. It's only when a DA doesn't do a proper job that I have to set a criminal free."

He studied her face for a long moment. "I guess you're right."

She tilted her head. "So about the Hathaway case . . . will you be prosecuting?"

"The ex-wife wants us to go as far as we can. He is guilty. Is there any reason you feel we shouldn't prosecute?"

"He was trying to protect his daughter."

"If the police hadn't picked him up when they did, that mother might never have seen her little girl again."

That was also true. Caitlin felt weariness bow her shoulders. When she was with Parker, she believed in him completely, but he *had* taken Madeline. Mace obviously believed it was a case he'd easily win, and if she didn't find evidence soon, Mace was going to use his charm in the courtroom to try to lock Parker away. Or at least keep him from Madeline until she was too old to care.

Mace took a step toward the door. "I can't wait for Saturday. Is six-thirty okay?"

"Perfect."

"I'll pick you up at your house then. Wear something . . ." He paused. "Wear something dressy."

She nodded, lifting a hand in farewell. But he seemed to change his mind about leaving and came toward her again. His arms went around her and this time when he kissed her, she was left with no question about how he felt for her or about his expertise. While his touch didn't evoke the emotion that Parker's kiss had, it was promising, and there was a measure of comfort in knowing she was in control of her actions. He continued the kiss, and she allowed herself to respond.

Not bad at all. Too bad it had to follow last night's experience with Parker. That was hard to live up to. But Mace was more her type. She had to remember that.

Mace drew away, smiling. "Saturday," he said, leaving her no doubt as to his meaning. She watched him leave. A scene like this had been in her daydreams for months, and the reality was pleasant indeed. Yet at the same time his confidence irritated her.

She leaned on the edge of her desk, frowning at the door, pondering both her feelings for Mace and his involvement in Parker's case. Mace seemed so sure that he would win, and he hadn't been wrong or lost a case in a very long while. It would be so much easier if she were going up against Wyman.

Wyman. Her hand went to the phone. She had his number here somewhere, and maybe he could shed some insight on her recent discoveries. Within a few minutes she was connected.

"Wyman Russell."

"Wyman, it's Caitlin McLoughlin."

"Caitlin. Good to hear from you! Did your client decide to take the plea deal? It's too late, you know."

"I'm not calling about that. Look, it's about Mace." She walked across the room to the window. It had taken her two years to earn this office, but usually she was so busy she forgot to look outside. Snow still clung to the ground in some spots, though most had melted. There was no one in the parking lot except a man in a suit who was talking on a cell phone.

"Oh, and I was beginning to think you'd consider working with me."

Was he hinting again at her giving him privileged information? Since he hadn't approached her privately again this week, she'd begun to hope they'd left that behind. Well, she wouldn't take that crap. "Last I checked they don't have openings in the DA's office, so what do you mean by that? Just spit it out."

"Nothing nefarious, if that's what you're implying." He sounded surprised at her vehemence. "I'm leaving to start my own practice. Well, with an uncle of mine. I would have told you at our dinner the other night, but I hadn't turned in my resignation yet. I did that on Monday. I thought you might have heard."

"I hadn't." She struggled to wrap her mind around this new idea. Attorneys as bad as Wyman didn't simply start their own practices—unless they weren't really as bad as they seemed. Unless they'd been assigned all the difficult cases. She considered the implications. She'd prided herself on being a good attorney, but apparently she didn't know as much as she thought. "Uh, congratulations," she murmured, feeling completely stupid.

"We're looking for attorneys," Wyman added. "I'd love to have you work for us. Or you could always apply to the DA's office for my old job. I did mention Saturday night that there might be an opening soon. I just didn't say it was mine."

"Oh."

"So what was it you wanted to ask about Mace?"

Caitlin forced herself to regain her equilibrium. "I've looked at his cases, at least the ones he's prosecuted and we've defended. They were all obvious wins."

Silence. "And?" Apparently Wyman wasn't going to launch into an explanation as she'd hoped.

"I want to know if the other cases he's prosecuted, cases not with LDA, are the same."

Wyman chuckled without mirth. "Every single one. You can bet he didn't horn in on the Belstead case because I was losing. It was because we found the evidence to put the guy away."

"I see." She had assumed Mace was helping Wyman because he hadn't wanted him to mess up the important case, but again she'd been wrong. Unless Wyman was lying, which at this point she wasn't ruling out. "How can he get those assignments?"

"Who knows? He's got pull, or someone likes him. He's ambitious. Maybe all of the above. But that's all I'm going to say. I'm still here for two more weeks."

Caitlin nodded, though he couldn't see her. She let her mind run over the facts, sifting and sorting. If Wyman was leaving and wasn't trying to get her to betray her clients' confidences, then who had sent the aide to see Kenny?

"Wyman," she asked, "did you send anyone to talk to Kenny Pratt about the Belstead case? He's doing some work on a new case for me, and since he'd heard I was the LDA in the Belstead case, he mentioned someone had been to see him. He couldn't make sense of it, and frankly neither can I."

"You know this Kenny Pratt is the one who lost the case for you, right? He was the investigator who encouraged the witness to come forward."

"Isn't that what any good citizen would do?"

"Maybe. The most important question, though, is why he was there in the first place. Do you know what case he was on or who he was working for?"

Fear shot through her. "Are you on a witch hunt?"

There was a long pause before Wyman said. "Caitlin, I didn't send anyone to talk to Kenny, and I don't know who did. And all this about a witness and Kenny Pratt are frankly none of my concern anymore. But I'm going to tell you one thing. Don't waste your time with Mace. He isn't worth it."

Caitlin didn't respond, her brain still puzzling over which DA was behind the Kenny investigation. If Wyman wasn't, who was? She had a sinking feeling that she just might know.

"Thank you, Wyman," she said slowly.

"No problem. And I meant what I said about you joining me, Caitlin. I think you're the best attorney the LDA has. And last Saturday night obviously showed we'd work well together." There was something in his voice now that was familiar, but there was still his wife to think about—separated or not.

"I'll think about it."

"You do that."

Caitlin hung up. Her thoughts were racing in all directions, but she had to get this brief finished before she grabbed something to eat and headed over to the court for the Belstead sentencing hearing.

Her phone began ringing—her cell, not the office phone, and she dived for her purse to answer it. The number belonged to Kenny Pratt. "Hello?"

"Hi," he said without preamble. "I have news, but nothing I can prove yet."

"What do you mean?"

"It's that guy the ex-wife was supposed to be staying with at what your client thought was a meth house."

Caitlin checked her notes. "Ron Hill?"

"Yeah. The reason the cops can't find any record of this guy is probably because he doesn't exist, but as I chatted up her friends, the name Ron Briggs came up. It's possible he was the one Dakota was with."

"But that was what, four months ago?"

"Three," Kenny corrected, "and it's important because if we can talk with him we might be able to prove he had a meth lab and that Dakota Allen knew about it and exposed her kids to it."

Caitlin paced to the window. "Even if she isn't convicted, that would be enough for my case. Especially when I bring in statistics about how many children die in drug-related deaths caused directly or indirectly by their parents."

"Well, if the mother's on drugs, that child is in more danger now than of being hit by a car, even if she was sitting in the middle of the road."

"We need to find this Ron . . ."

"Briggs. I'm on it. But if you could talk to your detective buddy at the police department, she might be able to get the information faster. They might not have a file on him, but it's worth checking. I'd call myself, but I'm rather busy at the moment."

"I'll call her and let you know."

"Good. Meanwhile, I'll follow up a few leads I have on Dakota's current lifestyle. And I mean follow literally; she's in her car in front of me now. If she's doing drugs, she'll mess up soon."

"Is Madeline with her?"

"Yes, and the other child, too. Tiny thing."

"How do they seem?"

"All right. She's using a car seat for the younger one, not the girl, though. Must not know it's a law."

"Maybe we could have her pulled over for that. It would be a strike in our favor."

"Let me know. I can tell the cops where she is at any moment."

"Thanks."

"You're welcome. She's stopping. Gotta go." The phone went dead.

Caitlin was just about to dial Sally when a knock at the door stopped her. Before she could call to whoever it was to come in, the door burst open and Sally entered. "Good, you're here."

"I was just calling you." Caitlin shut her phone and crossed back to her desk, slipping the phone inside her purse.

Sally shrugged. "You were acting weird this morning. I don't have time to grab lunch later, and I know you have a full afternoon at court, so I thought I'd stop by."

Caitlin didn't hide her exasperation. "There's nothing wrong! But Kenny did come up with something we need you to check out. We think we discovered the real name of the guy Dakota Allen used to live with at the meth house." Caitlin leaned over and wrote on a card from her desk. "Any information you can give us would be nice, but it'd really help if we could talk to him. We could use his testimony about the danger Dakota put Madeline in. He might even know something about Dakota's current drug use. Here's his name—Ron Briggs. Not Hill."

"I'll look into it." Sally fingered the card, but her gaze never left Caitlin's face. "So are you going to tell me what happened last night?"

Caitlin sighed and sank into her chair. "We went back to my place for dinner after we found Amy. I knew he hadn't eaten all day, and dinner seemed the least I could do. He'd been so nice about Amy. But then Amy fell asleep, and we were alone . . ."

"And?" Sally but her hands on the desk, her brown eyes dark and eager.

Caitlin knew her face was burning a bright red. "Well, one thing led to another, and we kissed." She remembered the desire that had seemed to spring from nowhere.

"How was it?"

"Good," Caitlin admitted. "It was totally wrong, but it was good."

"Then what?"

"Nothing. Amy woke up. We ate dinner, and then I drove Parker to a motel."

Sally blinked in disgust. "That's all? No plans for a date?"

"He's a client." Caitlin stood, her energy too stoked to be confined to the chair. "Do you know how many clients want to go out with me?"

"All of them, I bet." Sally gave her a flat smile. "But he's not your typical client, is he?"

"No. Yes. He's a client. That's it."

Sally's eyes narrowed. "Something else is going on here, Caitlin. What aren't you telling me?"

That when he looks at me I feel alive. That I want him to kiss me so badly I'm afraid once it's over I won't be able to let go. But she couldn't say this to Sally or anyone. "I want a solid relationship, Sally. I don't play the field with just anyone. That's not who I am. You should know that by now."

"I'm only saying you won't ever know what you might be missing if you don't give it a chance. Who knows? Maybe he'll be the best thing that ever happened to you."

Or the worst. Too often in her line of business Caitlin had seen it work out that way. In the beginning her clients thought something was the best opportunity they'd ever encountered, but it ended up ruining their lives.

191

"I want what my parents had," she said quietly. "What you and Tony have."

"You aren't falling for this guy, are you?"

"No. I'm just . . . Amy's been talking a lot about babies lately. It reminded me that I'm not getting any younger."

"Ah, the biological clock. I hear you there. But that's exactly why you should give Parker a chance before you settle down. Frankly, construction workers are some of the steadiest guys around." She frowned. "And they've got muscles."

"Sally," Caitlin groaned. Normally she didn't mind having a friend who seemed to think large muscles were a necessary quality in a man, but today was an exception. "You aren't hearing me. Besides, Parker isn't my type."

"You must be holding out for that gorgeous DA. Now, *that* I can understand."

Caitlin took the path of least resistance. "He came by just a while ago."

"Lip action?"

"Yep."

"Good?"

"He certainly knows what he's doing."

Sally nodded. "What he lacks in muscle he probably makes up for in technique. Still, you may find out that a pretty face doesn't do it for you. It never did for me, though Tony is cute in his own way."

"Not only is Tony handsome but he's the only man alive who could keep up with you."

Sally laughed. "True." She lifted the card with Ron Briggs's name. "I'll get back to you on this, but don't forget what I told you. If you change your mind about Hathaway, I say go for it. He's cute." She grinned knowingly at Caitlin before escaping from the room.

Propping her elbows on her desk, Caitlin let her head drop into her hands. She suspected she hadn't fooled Sally at all. And what if Sally was right? Maybe if she let herself go out with Parker a few times, she could get him out of her system and move on to something more permanent. Maybe.

She groaned. Who was she fooling? What if she was the one who got caught and couldn't walk away? Sally was right that her biological clock had kicked in when she'd least expected it, and what she wanted now was a real relationship. Her parents had been happily married to someone in the same profession, and if she ever was going to have a family, that's what she wanted for herself—a meeting not just of minds but of lives. With all his problems, Parker obviously wasn't the man for the job.

Pushing these thoughts aside, she picked up the phone and dialed. "Jodi, I really need some help on this brief. I can't seem to concentrate this morning."

"No wonder, what with the Belstead sentencing. I'm really sorry about that, Caitlin."

"It's okay. He is guilty, after all."

"There is that. I bet you haven't had lunch yet. Leave the brief and the file on your desk and go get yourself something to eat. I'll take care of everything. You don't want to faint at the courthouse."

"Not going to happen. But thanks for taking care of the brief."

"No problem."

Caitlin was feeling better already. Seeing Chet Belstead sentenced would be the highlight of her day, and if she had to do it over again, she'd probably go through the same hoops to get him there. Some cases were worth losing big.

She'd barely arrived at the courthouse when she received a

text message from Parker: *I meet with Family Services at 6. Will u come?*

She wasn't technically representing him in a custody case, but when it came to social services, having her there would be better than no representation. Since she had never given him the name of anyone else to use, it was natural for him to turn to her. In between her cases that afternoon, she'd have to call in some favors and learn some fast tips from her attorney acquaintances. She was willing to do that. For Madeline, of course.

She typed out a brief response: *yes.*

CHAPTER

15

C het Belstead was sentenced to forty-one years in prison for rape and attempted murder. He'd serve a good portion of that, even if he became a model prisoner, and maybe when he came out he'd be a changed man. Caitlin always hoped for the best. Some of her clients did learn, though she didn't hold much hope for Belstead. If he ever came into the system again, she would refuse to represent him. Not that he'd want her since she had failed him this time. The whole case made her feel dirty, though the satisfaction on the faces of the victim's family had been some recompense for her breach of ethics.

When Sally called later that afternoon, Caitlin still had one client to represent before the judge, but there were three others ahead of them, so she had time to talk. She stepped out of the courtroom to answer.

"Bad news," Sally said. "Ron Briggs is dead. He was picked up three weeks ago and charged with producing meth. He

managed to suicide while he was out on bail. On a drug over-
dose, of all things."

Caitlin groaned. "Just my luck."

"Well, we're still checking his cohorts. We suspect one guy
was a partner, and although the house is closed down now, we
think he might be working elsewhere. These operations aren't
usually run by one person. I have some names, and I'll forward
them to your e-mail, if that's okay. Maybe your PI can make
some progress."

"That reminds me. Could I have Dakota pulled over for not
using a car seat?"

"Hey, that's a good idea."

"I'm hoping I can use it when we talk to Family Services in
a few hours. Parker wants to see Madeline."

"Of course he does."

"I'll call Kenny and have him text you her location.
Provided she's in the car."

"Okeydokey, I'll do my best. But keep in mind I'm pulling
favors for you on this one."

"Hey, you're the one who brought me in on the case. You
owe me."

"All right already. I'll drum up some uniforms to chase
down Dakota Allen. But someday you might thank me for getting you involved."

"What?"

"I got a hunch." Sally hung up before Caitlin could protest.

Caitlin found a relatively quiet corner and accessed her
e-mail with her phone, forwarding the names Sally had sent to
Kenny's cell phone. Then she called him to find out Dakota's
location.

"She's at home," Kenny said in a bored tone. "Must be
sleeping, 'cuz the house looks dead except for every now and

then the little girl looks out the window. It's freezing out here, so I wish something would happen. If I turn on the car too much, someone's bound to notice. Wait, someone just drove up in the driveway. A man. Big guy. Looks like a football jock who's gone to a bit of fat. Receding hairline, longish in back. Dopey look."

"Probably the new boyfriend."

"License plates don't match the notes you gave me. Car screams money."

"Can't be him, then. Supposedly, he drives a piece of junk."

"Maybe he's come into some dough."

"That would explain why Dakota doesn't need her ex all of a sudden. Well, let me know when she's on the move. And did you get those names I just sent?"

"I got 'em. Already forwarded them to a contact."

"Thanks."

"Caitlin, how much budget you got for this case anyway?"

Caitlin hesitated. Her budget at the LDA for outside services was extremely limited. Management went over expenses with a careful eye, and they didn't smile nicely on an attorney who went too far above and beyond in their defense of a client, especially an obviously guilty one. "Enough," she said. "As long as we prove something."

"And if we don't?"

"I have savings." She cringed as she said this, not wanting to hear Kenny's response.

He was quiet a moment. "It means that much to you?" His tone wasn't condemning or deriding but rather curious.

"I want to help Madeline."

"Okay. I'll be in touch."

Caitlin hung up the phone. Never before had she offered to spend her own money on a client. As a public attorney she didn't exactly have the highest pay scale, and because of Amy she guarded funds carefully. Her parents had left them a tiny trust fund and a small lump sum that she'd put down on their house, but many months she had to be careful in order to have enough for Amy's day care, her medicines, food, and the mortgage.

I'll make Parker pay me back. She smiled because somehow, though he had fewer resources at the moment than she did, she knew he would fulfill his obligations. According to the information Sally had found, he always did.

• • •

Caitlin arrived at the Department of Child and Family Services ten minutes early. She wasn't surprised to see Parker waiting in the cold outside the building, his shoulders hunched and his hands buried in his coat pockets for warmth. His face broke into a smile as she walked toward him.

"Thanks for coming."

Warmth spread through her. This man was beautiful. Not in the way that Mace Keeley was beautiful but in a way that made her nerves hum. Maybe she should take Sally's advice and see where the attraction took them.

His eyes passed briefly over her, communicating unmistakable approval. She wore only her gray business suit, but she flushed all the same. *Stupid Irish coloring,* she thought. Why was it so hard to maintain her poker face with him?

He smiled and said with a bit of amusement in his voice, "Miss me?"

"Desperately," she responded airily. "I always miss my most problematic clients."

His smile didn't change, but his eyes burned into hers.

Who was she fooling? Not him and not herself. "Well, thanks for coming."

"Look, I told you once before," she said as they headed inside, "I have no experience in child custody cases, so I don't know what to expect. But I really don't hold any hope of them letting you see Madeline until the case is over."

He held open the door. "I can't accept that. I have to try."

Caitlin stopped in the lobby, looking at him for a full minute without speaking. She remembered how his lips had felt on hers, and how close they'd been in her kitchen. She remembered his concern for his daughter and how careful he'd been with Amy.

She clenched her hands at her sides, steeling herself against the emotion in his face. "Okay, but here's what I don't get." She kept her voice low so the few people across the room couldn't hear. "You said you'd do anything to get custody of Madeline, yet there's no record of a court battle or anything like it. You gave up custody of your daughter without a fight, and what I want to know is why."

His face had drained of color, and for a moment she regretted the question, but she had to know.

"Madeline isn't my, uh, biological daughter," he said finally, his voice tense. "I mean, Dakota and I were married when she got pregnant, and I thought Madeline was mine, and I've loved her all these years like she was mine. But it turns out she isn't."

Caitlin's hands relaxed. That would explain a lot. If he wasn't the biological father, he would have little standing in court. "So how did you find out she wasn't yours?"

He toed the floor with a boot-clad foot that reminded her he'd come directly from work. She would have rather had him dress up for this meeting, but it was too late now.

"A few years after Madeline was born, Dakota told me she'd been with someone else and that he was the father."

The torture in his face was real, but Caitlin wasn't about to go easy on him. "And you believed her? You gave up without a fight? Without proof?"

He blinked several times. "What do you mean? You know how much I love Madeline, and how much I see her. I haven't given up anything."

"I'm saying you believed a woman whom you claim has used drugs in front of her own child. You said you were married at the time of Madeline's conception. So were you actually with her at the time? Were you living as husband and wife?"

"Of course."

"Then how do you know Madeline isn't yours?"

"I figured women know these things."

"And when did she tell you this? Not when things were good, I bet."

His head swung back and forth. "No. It was when Madeline was two, and I came home from work and found Dakota and some of her friends passed out on drugs and Madeline locked in the back bedroom, crying. I was going to leave with Madeline, but Dakota told me she'd never let me take Madeline because she wasn't mine."

"So you stayed."

"I stayed another year—and that's when she left. Went to live in that house where they were making meth. She had her son there, and I know for sure he isn't mine. Anyway, she let me see Madeline as long as I agreed to all her terms of the divorce. She'd bring Madeline to me then, and it was several months before I even found out where they were living. As soon as I found out where they were, I knew it wasn't a good situation, and I got her into the house they're in now."

"I hate to break this to you, Parker, but Dakota was probably lying to you about Madeline."

He groaned, rubbing a hand across his face. "I can't believe I let her do this. I should have called the police the day I saw the drugs on her TV, or when she was doing drugs with her friends, but because I didn't, Madeline's in danger every single day."

Caitlin's heart softened against her own will. It was hard to keep up indifference toward this man whose one look made her knees tremble. "Look, you're not the first man this has happened to. If we can prove she's lying, it only makes your case stronger."

"And if she's telling the truth?"

She knew what he meant. If the court ordered a paternity test and he wasn't the father, he wouldn't have much standing, despite his years of devotion. She shook her head.

"I can't risk it." The ache in his voice made her want to comfort him. "Madeline couldn't be any more mine no matter what genes she may have. I couldn't love her any more or be any more responsible."

"At least we can play our cards a little better now that you know it's possible she is lying. If she doesn't bring it up, then we can assume either she doesn't know for sure herself who the father is—or she knows it's you and doesn't want you to find out."

Parker gave her a half-smile. "That makes sense. If she was sure, she'd bring it out right away."

"Well, she could be reluctant because it makes her look bad."

He frowned. "Then I guess I still don't know."

"You said yourself it didn't matter."

"It doesn't, except in the legal sense." He glanced at his cell phone. "It's time. We should find Mrs. Turnball."

• • •

Parker shrugged off his coat as they sat in two of the three chairs in front of the desk. The woman facing them was unsmiling, her blonde hair cut close around her face, curling under in one long, tight curl that made Parker want to fluff up her hair to see if the curl changed shape. The style was unbecoming and decades out of date, and her reddish complexion did little to enhance the whole picture. Wrinkles gathered around her eyes, and laugh lines carved into her face. Parker had been prepared to hate this woman by the crisp, no-nonsense tone of her voice, but her face told him that if she had one fault it was caring too much. The sternness in her voice and the careful demeanor came from fighting for children, and he couldn't fault her for that, even if she was misguided in his case.

"Thank you for seeing me, Mrs. Turnball."

"You're welcome." Her tone hadn't changed, but he could see she was reevaluating him. He knew he was considered good-looking by women, and in his youth he'd used it to his advantage. But something told him if he tried to charm Mrs. Turnball, she'd see right through it. She was accustomed to people trying to fool her, much like Caitlin was in her line of work. Better to be sincere.

Caitlin opened her briefcase on her lap and took out a pen. "My client would like to see his daughter."

"Uh, if you don't mind," Mrs. Turnball said, "the child advocate should be here during our conversation. If you'll wait a moment, I think I hear him coming down the hall now."

A few seconds later a man appeared. He was round and short and sported a thick goatee. Not at all like Parker had envisioned his daughter's appointed advocate. "Sorry I'm late," he puffed, out of breath.

Parker stood and offered his hand. "Mr. Reeve?"

"Yes." Mr. Reeve nodded to Mrs. Turnball and Caitlin before taking the last seat with a slight sigh of relief.

"Okay, now that we're all here . . ." Mrs. Turnball nodded to Caitlin.

"My client," Caitlin began again, "is here for two primary reasons. One, he'd like to see his daughter. Two, he would like CPS to open an investigation into his ex-wife's drug use."

"We only promised to discuss visiting rights," Mrs. Turnball said quickly.

Caitlin looked thoughtful. "I understand that is a primary concern, but Mr. Hathaway has reason to believe Madeline is in immediate danger. He has personally seen drugs on the premises, and before he moved Dakota Allen and her daughter to the house where they now live, Dakota was living with a man who was picked up for having a meth lab on his premises."

"Are you sure she lived with this man? Will he swear to it?" asked Mrs. Turnball.

"He was out on bail when he committed suicide last week."

"I see." Mrs. Turnball made a note on the paper lying on her desk.

Mr. Reeve grunted. "Is there any solid connection? Witnesses and so forth who can attest to her being at that place?"

"Not names that I can give you," Parker said. "Dakota wouldn't even give the police his correct name."

Caitlin frowned at him, her eyes telling him to shut up, but

Parker couldn't stop. "The meth house is done and gone, so it's not really the issue here. What Dakota is doing now is the problem. A few weeks ago I saw a bag of drugs on the TV. That's why I did what I did. I can't risk my daughter, and Dakota obviously isn't ready to grow up and take responsibility."

"Look." Mr. Reeve crossed his legs, leaning back on his seat, plump hands folded on his stomach. "Given the circumstances, Mrs. Turnball can't open an investigation on just your word. You kidnapped your own daughter, Mr. Hathaway, and there are some who think you are inventing a drug problem for your ex-wife to protect yourself. If you had gone through channels—"

Parker leapt to his feet. "If I'd gone through channels, Madeline might be dead right now, another headliner in the newspaper! This is a child we're talking about. My child. How can you just sit there and do nothing?"

Caitlin was at his side, her hand on his arm. "Parker," she said in warning. "Please. Sit down."

He knew she meant sit down and shut up, but looking into her face he saw compassion and strength. This was her territory, and if he wanted to do Madeline any good, he had to trust her. Though it was the hardest thing he'd ever done, he clenched his jaw and sat. So much for his plan of getting his way with calm discussion.

"Please excuse my client," Caitlin said smoothly. "As you can tell, he's very emotional about his daughter. Keep in mind that we are certain Dakota Allen is a danger, and that will be a large part of his defense. In fact, my department has a private investigator looking into the matter now, and we are also cooperating with Detective Sally Crumb at the police department. We strongly feel it is only a matter of time until we are able to obtain solid evidence. However, that time is what we're worried about."

Mrs. Turnball shifted uncomfortably, her lips pursed in a near scowl. "There isn't much we can do about that."

"We just want someone to have a chat with Dakota Allen so she's aware there is suspicion. Maybe make a home visit to see things personally."

Mrs. Turnball nodded. "Actually, I have talked several times with Ms. Allen, and we did visit her home. We found nothing to cause suspicion."

"We heard that someone from this office visited her. But was it a surprise visit?"

"No."

Caitlin nodded solemnly as if having proven a great point, though Parker couldn't tell if the others were impressed. They should be. She was incredibly confident, and her words made it seem as if the police were inches away from charging Dakota with drug use.

Regret once again filled him. If only he'd called the police that day when he'd seen the drugs! But growing up as he had, the police had always been someone you ran from, not called willingly. How little he'd understood then how his actions would affect his future. Madeline's future. He vowed to make it right, if it was the last thing he did.

"I'll take this under advisement," Mrs. Turnball said. "But until the police are able to give us what we need . . ." She lifted her shoulders and hands in a delicate shrug.

Caitlin inclined her head regally. "We appreciate any attention you give this matter. You should be aware, if you already aren't, that there is a paternal grandmother who is ready and willing to look after Madeline until things are cleared up."

"We are aware of that," said Mrs. Turnball.

"As for visitation—" Caitlin began.

"The judge has denied all contact for the time being," Mr. Reeve interrupted.

Parker had heard that at the arraignment, but it hit him just as hard the second time. His hands tightened on the armrests, and he had to swallow several times to rid himself of the sudden lump in his throat. He blinked hard to prevent tears.

Caitlin's hand was on his arm again, and slowly he was able to relax. "We do understand the reasoning behind this order," Caitlin said, "but my client has not been found guilty. He is worried about his daughter and would at least like to see her to make sure she's all right."

"I met with Madeline before I came here," Mr. Reeve said, giving them a smile that was small despite the large size of his mouth. "That's why I was late. Apparently Ms. Allen was pulled over for not using a child seat on the way to our appointment, so we got a late start. Madeline does miss you a great deal, Mr. Hathaway, and I personally believe it would be in her best interest to continue seeing you." He glanced over at Parker and then away again, as if embarrassed to see his emotion. "If you can manage to get the case before another judge, I would be willing to recommend supervised visits." He raised a hand as though to ward off another of Parker's rants, though Parker had no intention of losing control again. "That's the best I can do. I don't know any judge who would give any more, no matter how strongly anyone urged it. And in good conscience, I couldn't request more anyway. Your daughter needs security at the moment, and for better or worse, her mother's house gives that to her."

Parker wanted to break the man's head, but Caitlin was nodding. "We would very much appreciate your recommendation."

"We're finished here, then." Mrs. Turnball stood. "We'll keep in touch."

That was it? Parker felt numb. Did these people even see Madeline as a person? "Please," he said, his voice sounding gruff even to his own ears. "Please help my little girl."

"We'll do everything we can, I assure you." Mrs. Turnball led the way to the door, ushering them out. Mr. Reeve stayed behind, and Parker felt their eyes on him and Caitlin as they moved down the hallway.

"What a waste of time," he murmured as they rounded a corner and the eyes fell away.

"On the contrary," Caitlin said, slowing to a stop. "With Mr. Reeve's promise, we'll be able to see a different judge and get you temporary visitation. That's something. Then there was the car seat incident. Not a good thing in their sight, I'm sure. I hoped Sally would get to it in time."

"That was your doing?"

Caitlin shrugged. "The law in Utah says that even four-year-olds need to be in some kind of a seat. Dakota wasn't using one and got pulled over. Anyway, I think you impressed Mrs. Turnball."

"Me?" He wanted to gape at her. "I lost control."

Caitlin's hand went to his face, her fingers sliding across his cheek and up to his eye. Her fingers came away wet. "I think it's apparent you love your daughter, that's all."

His skin burned where she had touched him. "She called me today. She's all right. So far."

Caitlin smiled. "I'm glad."

"Thanks for what you did in there."

"You're welcome."

"Look, I know you've already worked late, but would you like to have dinner? My treat."

She hesitated, and he took that as willingness. "There are a few things we need to discuss," she said, "but I have to get back to Amy. Especially after last night."

"Oh, I meant her, too. Of course. I like Amy. She reminds me a lot of Madeline. In how they think and act, I mean."

Caitlin's eyes met his, her top teeth coming down on her bottom lip. He followed the gesture, remembering how soft her lips were.

"Okay," she said finally. "But I'd better choose the place. Amy can be interesting to take out. We can't go to any restaurants with play areas for children because she's too tall for the height requirement. She gets really upset when the employees kick her off the equipment." She took out her cell phone to check the time. "Looks like I'd better pick her up now."

"I'll follow you," he said, motioning toward his truck.

"What about a place to stay?" She asked this with a hint of reluctance, as if afraid he might want to spend the night at her place. But that was far from his plans. He wasn't into frustration; he already had enough problems to keep him up at night.

"I rented a room today in an apartment, sight unseen. I paid for a week, and I can stay on a weekly basis if I want to continue. There's no lease or strings, which is great given my situation. Like a motel, only cheaper. The apartment's in West Valley. Not too far from you. Close to the construction site. Supposed to be furnished and have laundry service once a week."

"Sounds perfect. That way if you don't like it you can take your time to find something better."

"I'll probably need a different place for Madeline when she stays with me." The words came with difficulty, because having Madeline with him seemed almost impossible at the moment. He was glad Caitlin didn't remind him just how impossible.

Darkness had fallen while they'd been in the building, and the moonlight reminded him of last night when they'd been alone in the darkness of her house. "Caitlin," he said.

"Yes?"

He wanted to kiss her. He wanted to take her in his arms and hold her. But he couldn't make her feel the same for him. "Nothing." With effort he turned and strode toward his truck.

16

Y ou're going to *what?*" Sally asked, practically yelling the words.

Caitlin had to hold the phone away from her ear because the sound threatened to break her eardrum. "Stop screeching!"

"Well, you can't be serious about taking Amy with you to dinner. You complain all the time about how she gets when she's tired, and you sound as if you're about to drop yourself."

"It's been a long day," Caitlin admitted. "Maybe I should just go home."

"No, you deserve a dinner out, and you said yourself you had things you had to discuss with Parker."

"Nothing that can't wait. Keep in mind that usually I don't even see my clients more than once before trial."

"Parker's not just anyone."

"I know."

"Ah," Sally said, her voice rife with meaning.

"I didn't mean—"

"I'm picking up Amy, and I'll take her home to play with Randi. It's been too long since they've been together. And Tony loves Amy, you know that."

"It's not necessary, Sally. I'm really worried about setting her off again."

"Nonsense. She loves coming to my house. She'd *live* there if you'd let her. Now stop worrying and go out and have a nice, quiet dinner. And if something interesting presents itself, go for it." Sally hung up.

Something interesting? Sally's suggestion was altogether too close to Caitlin's private thoughts for comfort. She glanced in her rearview mirror where she could see Parker's truck following her. She turned on her blinker and pulled out of traffic. As Parker followed her to the side of the road, she dialed his phone.

"Hello?"

"Change of plans. Sally butted in and is taking Amy to play with her daughter. So we don't have to pick her up."

"Are you still all right with having dinner?"

She should say no. "Sure."

"Great. You know what? My new apartment is just down the street and around the corner. Why don't we lose one of these vehicles at the apartment complex and go together?"

"All right." Then in case she sounded too eager, she added, "We can talk about your case on the way."

A few minutes later, they pulled into the parking lot of an apartment complex at the edge of town. It wasn't top-of-the-line, but it didn't look seedy, either. "Want to come with me in the truck?" Parker asked.

"I'd rather take my car." That gave her some power, at least.

He quirked an eyebrow. "Fine."

"Aren't you going to peek inside your apartment?" She was curious, she had to admit. What about roommates? He hadn't mentioned those. "You might need something they don't have—sheets or whatever. I can lend you some until you can get down to your mother's to get your things."

"Leave it to a woman to think of that. Remind me again after dinner, and I'll run inside before you leave."

Caitlin planned to make sure she also went inside to check out the place. She told herself her interest was as his attorney—she had to make sure everything looked good when they went to court—but she was honest enough to admit to herself that it wasn't her only interest.

"Well?" he asked as she drove from the parking lot. "Where are we heading?"

Caitlin shrugged. "I was thinking of Golden Corral, mostly because of Amy. It's one of her favorites, but if she's not with us, how about Marie Callender's? The food's decent, and I really love their pecan pie." It was also more reasonably priced than the really excellent restaurants, and if Parker insisted on paying, she didn't want to stick him with a huge bill. He'd likely need every asset he could gather to fight for his daughter.

"Fine. Anything sounds good to me, as long as it's edible."

She laughed. "You wouldn't say that if you'd eaten at as many restaurants as I do."

"Hot dates?" He gave her a crooked smile.

"A lot of working lunches. It's part of the game."

He tilted his head and as the oncoming cars passed, illuminating his face, she could tell that he was considering her words. "Do you enjoy being a lawyer?"

Her first idea was to spout off the same platitudes she told everyone when this question came up—that she loved her work but the hours were sometimes a challenge. And then

whip into some funny story about one of her past cases that
would make them laugh and forget they'd ever tried to ask her
such a personal question.

"I'm good at being an attorney," she said instead. "I don't
know what else I would do."

"That wasn't the question."

"I know, but that's too hard to answer."

"Why?" He seemed honestly curious.

"Because some days I love it so much I want to sing." She
smiled. "There's absolutely no better high than doing a great
job and seeing the law work as it's supposed to. But then there
are the other times, far too many of them, when you wish you
never had to see another criminal again."

"I suppose it's worse being a legal defender."

"You see a lot of evil everywhere, but it does seem lately
that I've been given more than my share of the really bad guys."
She thought of Belstead and shivered. "I should be flattered,
though, because the harder and more serious the case, the
more they trust you. It might even end up reflected in my pay
someday." She'd reached the restaurant now and pulled into the
parking lot. Parker was silent as she searched for an empty
spot. "There," she said, turning the wheel and coming to a stop.
She set the emergency brake and glanced at him.

"I'm sorry," he said quietly.

His stare made her feel uncomfortable. "For what?"

"For being one of those criminals."

"What are you talking about?" She made no effort to hide
her surprise. "You're one of the innocent, Parker. The ones I set
out to protect way back when I was in law school."

He grinned. "Well, I'm glad I've convinced you of that."

"You don't have to worry. All I need is a little evidence, and
we'll not only get you free of these charges, we'll bring

Madeline home." She meant his home, of course, but the way it came out seemed as if she was referring to a home they shared. Suddenly feeling self-conscious, she busied herself collecting her keys and purse.

"So do you like your work?" she asked as they walked into the restaurant.

"Actually, I do. I like working with my hands and building things, and it's not bad pay if you work your way up. I'll be taking out my contractor's license soon, after I'm sure I have a feel for everything." He held the door open for her. "Then I'll be doing my own projects."

"Did you always like to build things? I mean, I was always pretending to go to court as a child. Poor Amy was accused of more wrongdoings by the time she was five than most people are in ten lifetimes."

He laughed. "I bet. I can just see you."

"Of course I always got her off."

"What about now? Do you always get them off? The innocent ones, I mean."

Their hands brushed, sending a jolt of electricity through her veins. She swallowed hard. "Always. So far."

"Good."

Yet she'd always known there would come a time in her career when she might not win the case that should be won at all costs. It was assumed that such a thing would eventually happen in every career. She and other students had held endless debates about such an event in their college days, but so far she'd been able to win any case where she honestly believed the client to be innocent. Of course, in her line of work that might not be saying much, since she mostly defended the guilty.

Mostly.

She hoped her time to fail hadn't come with Parker. She didn't know if she could live with herself if he ended up behind bars. *Stop it,* she told herself. *I'll find what I need to prove he was acting in Madeline's best interest. Or at least that he thought he was.*

"I built a lot of things when I was young," Parker said. "Though sometimes my family didn't appreciate it when I borrowed their belongings to use in construction."

"Something tells me there's a story or two behind that statement."

"My brother wasn't too happy when I used his bike to build my two-level go-cart. Or go-bus as my friends and I called it."

"Go-bus." She had to smile at that.

"Yeah, it fit all three of my close friends, too. You should have seen us cruising around town."

"What'd your brother do?"

"He didn't talk to me for two weeks." He winked. "That was actually a blessing. Because when he did talk he was always trying to get me to do something I didn't want to do."

"Like what?"

"Like my chores, my homework."

"Ah, I see."

They fell silent as they were taken to a table, and then Parker spoke again. "I had to pay for the bike. I didn't know it then, but my father was teaching me responsibility." The words came out low and thoughtful, and Caitlin had the impression that something in the memory had made him sad.

Before she could decide how to respond, Parker picked up their former conversation. "What I like best about my job is that I have a lot of time to think."

"I wish I did. Sometimes the legal field is way too hectic."

His eyebrow quirked. "Sometimes?"

She laughed. "Okay, all the time."

215

"I go camping in the summers. There's this bit of land my family owns out in the middle of this small valley near Mt. Pleasant. I've always dreamed of buying up all the rest of the land and building a house there. Room to walk. No neighbors too close. You know, where you can go out in your backyard and no one's around for miles."

She had the feeling he'd shared something he didn't normally talk about. "Sounds beautiful."

"Well, building the house isn't the most important thing to me anymore. Not since Madeline."

"I can understand that." She'd once had dreams that hadn't involved mothering Amy—not that she would give Amy up for all the dreams in the world. Her sister was everything to her.

The waitress appeared before them, a big-boned, twenty-something brunette with heavy lipstick and a ponytail. "May I take your order?"

Parker ordered turkey with mashed potatoes and cranberries with no gravy, while she ordered the chili and cornbread. Cornbread was one of her favorites, but she didn't have it often.

"So," Parker said. "What do you dream about?"

She looked at him from beneath her eyelashes, wondering that he'd thought to ask. "I want to go back to Chicago where I was born, maybe for a year or two, or longer if I could make it work, to look up old family friends, visit a few of my father's favorite Irish pubs. You know. There are a lot of Irish people there who would have known my parents."

"So why haven't you gone?"

"I decided it'd be too difficult with Amy, especially on my own. She's settled here. We're settled. If my parents were alive, it might be a different story." Or if she had someone to help— but that wasn't a thing to say to a man whose presence made it difficult for her to remember what food she'd ordered. She shrugged. "I really haven't thought about it much in the past few years. I'm too busy." Not quite true. Sometimes she still thought about it, even while understanding that it wasn't likely to happen. To imagine herself walking down the roads she might have walked with her father as a child, to perhaps meet a few people who still spoke with the Irish accent that filled her soul with music.

"What happened to your parents?"

"My mother got really sick. It went on for months, and the doctors didn't know what it was. When she died, my father took it really hard. He followed her the next year. It was a blessing, really, for him to go. He wasn't himself without her. I've never known a man who loved a woman so much. In fact, there was never another person for either of them from the day they met."

There was comfortable silence as Parker considered her words. "He was a lucky man."

It was exactly the right answer. "They were both lucky. They found each other late in life, but it was enough. They were happy." If she found only half her parents' contentment, she'd be fortunate, though so far her luck in love had run to short relationships that had ended without fanfare. Probably because she wasn't willing to settle for half of the happiness she'd seen in her parents. Deep down, she wanted it all.

"You could still go to Chicago," Parker said, his eyes glittering in the dim light. "Amy would probably love it. I think living in an Irish community would be enjoyable. Especially if all the women look like you."

Caitlin knew it was a compliment, and she did feel beautiful at that moment. "Thank you."

"It's true." He held her gaze for a long moment and had

opened his mouth to say something more when the waitress came back with their food.

What had he been going to say?

They ate, though it seemed that neither of them was really hungry. Or at least not for food. They exchanged stories until their plates were empty and it was time to leave. Caitlin felt light and happy from laughing so much. Parker had a humorous side she hadn't expected, and he seemed as content to be with her as she was to be with him. As though they belonged together. She scarcely noticed anyone around them. Only when talking about his youth was he hesitant with information, and Caitlin wondered why. He seemed to adore his mother and talked about his father with respect. What had happened? She'd read in his file that both his father and brother had died in a car accident. Perhaps that was what was so painful.

Parker insisted on paying the bill, as she suspected, and finally there were no more excuses to stay. "Well, we'd better get going," she said. "I still need to pick up Amy." They walked out into the crisp night. The air was tingly cold and the dark sky so clear that she could see the stars. She sighed in appreciation.

"You should see the stars in my little valley," he said, smiling. "They stand out like you wouldn't believe."

"I believe it." She'd believe anything at that moment.

The drive to his apartment went all too quickly. "Thanks," he said, reaching for the door. "It was nice."

It had been more than nice. She hadn't enjoyed herself so much with a man for as long as she could remember, and she was loath to have it end. "What about checking out your apartment? You might need sheets or whatever."

"Oh, right." He dug in his coat pocket and took out a

paper. "Number 21-C. That means the second floor, I think."
He started walking, and Caitlin locked her car and followed.

The three-bedroom apartment was clean, if worn, and the
air inside hot and dry as though someone had turned up the
heat. One of the bedrooms was locked, but the others had no
sign of life. There was food in the fridge, labeled with the name
"Bob."

"Apparently I have a roommate named Bob," Parker said.

Caitlin would never under any circumstances rent a room
without knowing her roommates. Even in college she'd been
particular about that. "Could be short for Roberta."

Parker laughed. "I doubt it. I guess I pick either of these
rooms. Oh, wait. There's another key here. Maybe it fits one of
the other bedrooms." He shrugged off his coat and experi-
mented while Caitlin watched. He was wearing a flannel shirt,
open at the neck where it revealed a T-shirt. He wore the
clothes comfortably and with grace. She watched him move,
unable to take her eyes away.

"Ah, it fits this door."

She stepped closer to see that the narrow room sported a
bookshelf, a dresser, a small closet, and a single bed with
folded sheets and blankets at one end. That was it. Not much
bigger than a college dorm room.

He turned to leave and bumped into her. "Sorry. Didn't
realize you were there."

The connection sprang to life the instant he touched her.
They stared at each other without speaking. Caitlin willed him
to reach out to her, but he stood motionless, his hands at his
sides.

"Caitlin." His voice was low, almost a plea.

Everything was up to her. She could turn and lead him out

of the apartment, or she could reach out and touch him. She stepped forward.

He made a noise in his throat. "Last night you said . . ."

"Forget what I said." Her voice sounded as though she'd just awakened, and in a way she had. She liked Parker. She wanted to get to know him. She wanted to take a chance.

His lips were on hers in an instant, pulling her close. She shivered at his touch, afraid and exhilarated all at once. So different from her practiced kiss with Mace Keeley earlier that day.

She could feel the beating of his heart, pounding out a rhythm that matched her own.

Sally was right. Not that she needed to let herself become too involved or anything. They could simply date a while and then she'd have him out of her system. If that was possible. She'd never before met a man like Parker Hathaway.

He kissed her again, this time more tenderly, as though his lips never wanted to leave her skin. She loved the taste of him, and his smell, slightly tinged with sweat from his workday. The tremors his touch sent through her. She wondered what it would be like to see him every day, the possibility of having him become a real part of her life.

At that thought everything shifted, and the feelings became far too significant to be contained in a temporary dating situation. If she wasn't careful, she could lose herself in him entirely. Not a wise thing to do with a man who had someone else in his life. Someone innocent and small who had to come first.

This was a huge mistake.

She pulled away, struggling for breath, for composure. Parker gave her his lazy smile. "What's wrong?"

"This is." She turned her face away, blinking against threatening tears.

"Caity." He sounded confused, as she knew he had a right to be.

"I'm sorry. I shouldn't have . . ." She had been going to say, "led you on," but she hadn't really been leading him on. Only herself. What made her think dating him for a few weeks would free her? It would only make her more vulnerable.

His hand reached for her chin, drawing her face around to him. "It's okay," he said hoarsely. He kissed her once more, brushing her lips lightly, and then whispered in her ear, "Come on. We should go now." He took her hand, leading her toward the door.

Nodding, she went with him, feeling unsteady as though walking in a dream.

CHAPTER

17

Caitlin awoke in her bed alone on Thursday morning. Weak light filtered in through her blinds, making a pattern on her quilt. The angle of the light told her it was still early but time to get up. She stretched as thoughts of Parker and last night came rushing back, both the fun time they'd had at dinner and the encounter at the apartment. Everything had been so right, so natural—until the fear set in. After that, it had been a relief to escape alone to her car.

Oddly enough, she'd slept rather well—after reliving the scene only a half-dozen times.

Forcing herself from the bed, Caitlin readied for her day. She planned to get Parker in to see a family judge that day, or tomorrow at the latest. Then he'd get to see Madeline. Maybe that would give him the patience to trust in the system.

Her phone rang. "Hello?"

"Hey."

It was Kenny. "What's up?"

"Absolutely nothing. I'm sorry, Caitlin. Some of my contacts caught up with Ron Briggs's friends, but they claim they don't know Dakota Allen or anything about her drug use."

"What about the new boyfriend? Where'd he get that car?"

"A car dealership. He works there now."

Caitlin's heart plunged. "She had drugs at the house a few weeks ago. That doesn't just go away."

"I'm gonna find an excuse to go inside her house today. I have a uniform that looks like the gas—"

"I don't want to know details," Caitlin said hurriedly. She hoped he wasn't doing anything illegal.

"Well, I'll look around as much as possible, but the police covered it when the girl was missing, so I don't expect anything big. She'll be careful."

"There has to be someone who can connect her to the drugs."

"If there is, I haven't seen any sign of them. But it's early yet. I have more people to talk to. Unfortunately, that means more time."

"Whatever it takes. My case hinges on finding something. If not, my client could serve time." Not finding any sort of evidence hadn't been a thing she'd considered seriously before. People using drugs just weren't that smart.

"She'll mess up sooner or later," Kenny said, voicing her thoughts. "It's a matter of time."

Unless it was Parker who was lying. What if he'd made everything up to get off the charges? To evoke sympathy? He could be playing her even now. She didn't want to believe that, but even his tenderness at the apartment last night could have been a ploy.

"Keep trying. I'll talk to my friend at the police station later. Maybe they've had better luck."

"Later, then." Kenny disconnected the phone.

Caitlin stared at it and sighed. Where was Parker now? Already at work? Driving there? Was he thinking of her?

She flopped onto the bed, her arms outstretched, tears running down her face. Suddenly she hated her life. She hated being an attorney and working with criminals. She wanted to change her name and run away to a deserted island and lie in the sun all day, sipping something cool and fruity.

"Caitlin?" Amy was in the doorway, looking at her with concern, her shirt buttoned wrong and her hair standing up on one side.

For a minute Caitlin didn't move or speak. Amy came farther into the room, sitting down on the bed. "Are you sick?"

"No," Caitlin whispered. "Maybe." How could she tell her sister that she was falling in love with a man who might turn out to be a criminal? With a man who made her want to give up everything to be with him? One thing was sure, she was certainly crazy. She had to get a grip. On herself and on reality.

She forced herself to a seated position, wiping the tears away. "I'm fine. Just tired."

"I love you, Caitlin." Amy's worried face hadn't changed, so Caitlin knew she was still transparent. Time to put on her attorney mask—and maybe she could keep it on the next time she saw Parker.

Caitlin scooted over to Amy and began re-buttoning her blouse. "What do you want to eat today? We still have some of your favorite cereal." She hoped her sister wouldn't plead for warm oatmeal with raisins. It was nearly time to leave.

"Okay." Amy's smile was back, and the tension was leaving her body. "But there's a surprise in the kitchen. It's for you."

"What?"

"He brought them. But he didn't stay. You were in the shower."

Caitlin jumped to her feet and ran to the kitchen. Sitting on the table where Parker had eaten the other night was a vase filled with sunflowers. *Sunflowers in November,* she thought. There was a card, and she opened it hastily. In bold letters it read: *I can wait. Parker.*

Caitlin gripped the note tightly in her hand, partially crumpling it.

"What does it say?" Amy asked.

"Nothing important." Caitlin opened a drawer and threw the note inside.

•   •   •

Sally had nothing new to report, the judge couldn't review Parker's case until the next day, and Kenny called to say he had to take a few hours to work on another case. Caitlin began to worry.

Shortly before noon, Parker called. "Any news?"

"The judge will see us tomorrow." Caitlin tried to sound upbeat.

"That means I won't be able to see her tomorrow, doesn't it?"

She could imagine him raking a hand through his brown hair. "Most likely. They usually give the caregiver a day or so to work out arrangements."

"I can't stand this."

The fact that they had no leads or evidence on Dakota was more troubling to Caitlin, but she didn't want to make his day worse. "Look," she said, "can you name any more of Dakota's friends? Or people who might know what she's up to?"

"You haven't been able to find anything, have you?"

She shook her head, forgetting he couldn't see her. "We're still working on it. Don't worry too much."

"What about any news from CPS? Have they called?"

"No."

He was silent. "Caitlin, I'm worried. Madeline hasn't called again."

She started to say that Kenny was watching the house, but he wasn't at the moment, and come to think of it, he hadn't mentioned seeing Madeline that day.

"You want me to trust the system," Parker said. "But it's driving me crazy not knowing that Madeline's safe. What should I do? Can you go over there and check on her?"

"I don't have a reason."

"What about on some pretense as my attorney? Please, Caitlin."

She'd meant to thank him for the flowers, but now they seemed inconsequential. She swallowed hard. "I'll see what I can do."

"Thanks." He paused, and when he spoke again his voice was lower. "Will I see you today?"

"I don't know. Maybe." There was no real reason for them to meet, except that she wanted to see him.

She worked through lunch, and finally at four she loaded herself up with files, called it an early day, and went to pick up Amy. Instead of going home, she drove back to Salt Lake City, to the south side where Madeline and Dakota lived. She parked across the street, looking at the house. The neighborhood was old and run-down, though not nearly as bad as where many of her clients lived. The yard around Dakota's house in particular had been let go, and the weeds had choked out much of the grass. A battered car was in the driveway, so Dakota was probably home. By every account, she didn't appear to be working at the moment.

"Is this where the little girl lives?"

"Yes." Caitlin had told Amy the bare minimum about Madeline to stop her endless questions.

Amy opened the door. "Come on. I want to see her."

Caitlin felt a chill. What was she doing bringing Amy here? What if there was danger? Worse, what if there wasn't danger and Parker was obsessed? What if she was falling for a crazy man?

Falling.

She closed her eyes briefly, willing those thoughts to a far corner in her mind. She'd brought Amy as her excuse. With Amy, she hoped Dakota wouldn't simply slam the door in her face. They walked up the crumbling steps and knocked on the door. Amy hummed under her breath, unconcerned, but Caitlin's empty stomach churned with acid.

The door opened, and to Caitlin's relief, Madeline stood there. Her brown eyes lit up. "Caitlin! You remembered! Is this your sister?" She looked up at the towering Amy without fear. "She's big."

"She's tall, but she's only just a little older than you are. I came so you two could meet." Caitlin looked beyond the child, trying to sense if someone was in the room behind her.

"I like your dad," Amy said. "We had a tea party. I told him to hold out his pinky like this." She mimicked drinking tea.

"We could have a tea party," Madeline said eagerly, opening the door wider. She shivered in the shorts and T-shirt she was wearing. "Come in. It's cold out there."

Caitlin threw out an arm to stop Amy from rushing inside. "Is your mother here?"

"She's in the bedroom with my brother. I'll get her."

Caitlin allowed Amy to step inside far enough so they could close the door behind them. That gave them relief from the cold; it would also be harder for Dakota to kick them out. Caitlin surveyed the room. None of the furniture was new-looking or particularly clean, but the room didn't look neglected or abused. Her eyes went to the TV, which sat on a scratched wooden cart in the corner of the room. No small plastic bag of drugs. Had there ever been?

There was movement down the hall, and Madeline came back into sight, followed by Dakota, who carried a young toddler in her arms. She was wearing tight, low-riding jeans and an oversized sweatshirt. No shoes. Her roots had been redone, and her hair looked nice, if a bit too blonde for Caitlin's taste. She appeared younger and less sharp than she had at the police station. She must have been sleeping, which would explain the mascara beneath the heavy-lidded eyes, the messy hair, and the half-asleep child in her arms.

Why was she sleeping at this time of day? Was she sleeping off drugs? Was she pregnant? Or maybe she'd had a late night with her boyfriend.

The tentative smile on Dakota's face vanished when she saw Caitlin. "You're Parker's lawyer," she said without preamble.

"I'm his court-appointed representative," she said automatically. Sometimes those words helped because they made it clear that she wasn't being paid by the client himself, and that she hadn't solicited his business. Some might also assume she didn't have a choice in representing a client, though that wasn't quite true. She could walk away at any time, recusing herself from the case. Given her obsession with Parker, she probably should. "But he's not why I'm here," she added hurriedly. "Last Monday I told Madeline about my sister and promised I'd let them meet. Today seemed like a good opportunity to keep my promise."

"Caitlin picked me up early," Amy put in. "She's usually late. I hate it when she's late." She lowered her voice and added to Madeline, "She's always too tired to have tea."

"My tea set's in the kitchen." Madeline took a step in that direction, signaling for Amy to follow.

"Madeline!" her mother said sharply. "They aren't staying."

Madeline frowned. "But—"

"She's right," Caitlin interjected. "We only stopped by for a minute." Caitlin met Dakota's eyes. "Maybe we can get them together another day."

Dakota's lips pursed. "You're defending him," she hissed. "He took my baby."

Madeline's eyes grew wide, and she looked ready to cry. "Mommy," she whined. The little boy in Dakota's arms lifted his head to stare into his mother's face. After a few seconds of looking, he kicked to get down and then toddled over to his sister, who put her arm around him. He was a beautiful child, Caitlin saw, as beautiful as Madeline. Dakota certainly had good genes in that respect.

Caitlin's mind searched for a way to defuse the situation. "I'm sorry we came. I just thought the girls might like the company. I know what it's like being a single mother. Sort of. I have custody of Amy. She's a special girl and likes to play with girls her, uh, intellectual age."

Dakota's attention shifted to Amy, who was squatted now on the ground, talking to the little boy and giggling like a child. "Oh," Dakota said, the anger gone from her voice.

"Well, we should be going now." Caitlin motioned to her sister. "Come on, Amy."

229

Dakota narrowed her eyes. "You really didn't come to talk about the case?"

"No—unless there's something you want to say."

"I told the DA everything." Dakota's face brightened, and Caitlin wondered if she was thinking of Mace Keeley. Caitlin had barely thought of him since he'd kissed her the day before, but she could still remember when he had been on her mind almost constantly. Before she'd met Parker.

"You've talked with him?"

"Several times. Apparently he's brilliant. Never loses a case."

Caitlin wondered who had told her that. "He's very good in the courtroom. Has a certain flair." *Almost like an actor.*

Dakota relaxed further, her blue eyes gleaming. "If I wasn't getting married . . ." She lifted her brow suggestively.

"I know exactly what you mean." But Caitlin stifled the urge to laugh. How ludicrous to think Mace would ever consider a relationship with someone like Dakota Allen.

Yet what had Dakota been like when she and Parker had first met? It must have been about ten years ago, when they were barely out of their teens. They would have been full of youth and life, determined to enjoy themselves, doing what they saw as bucking the system. Parker was a different man now, or so the reports indicated. Something had caused him to change. Had it only been Madeline's birth? Maybe.

Yet perhaps there was something more, something she'd overlooked. She'd have to go through the reports again to see if they contained a hint of something more.

Did it really matter?

Yes. Because if something hadn't changed him, maybe he wasn't really changed. Maybe he'd simply become better at lying.

Blocking these thoughts, Caitlin forced her mind back to the conversation. "You're getting married?"

"Yes. As soon as all this is behind me." Dakota fluttered her hands, making sure Caitlin saw the small diamond ring on her finger.

"Do you plan to sue for full custody?"

"I have full custody now. But soon I'll be able to make sure Parker doesn't keep—" Dakota broke off as though suddenly becoming aware that the children were listening. "Go to the kitchen and show her the tea set," she told Madeline.

When they were gone, she continued, her voice lowered. "Anyway, it was an awful time. I was so afraid."

So afraid that according to Sally, she'd waited several hours before calling the police.

Caitlin chose her words carefully. "I've talked a lot in the past few days with your ex-husband, Ms. Allen. I know what he did, and that it was wrong, but oddly enough he seems dedicated to his daughter."

Tears sprang to Dakota's eyes. "Everybody believes him, but you don't know him like I do. I had to live with him. He's controlling. He forces you to do what he wants. I couldn't stay with him."

Caitlin thought of how Parker had acted last night at his apartment. She thought of the flowers and the note: *I can wait.* In her book, those weren't the words of a controlling man. But if Dakota had felt half the attraction for Parker that Caitlin felt, even a suggestion from Parker might have seemed that way. Yet hadn't it been Dakota who walked away from the relationship? Dakota who claimed Madeline wasn't Parker's child?

Dakota was watching her, but Caitlin couldn't tell if the gaze was calculating or honest. "I see," Caitlin said. "Well, we really should go."

"When this is all over, I wouldn't mind you coming by with your sister. Is she good with children?"

Caitlin had thought Dakota understood about Amy, but apparently she didn't. "Amy loves children," she said, not bothering to explain again.

On the way home, Amy was full of conversation about her "new friend and the cute little boy." Caitlin let the sounds roll over her. She should call Parker and let him know what happened. At least he'd know that for the moment, Madeline was fine.

She didn't want to call him. Despite all her blossoming doubts, she wanted to *see* him. Yet showing up at his apartment today wasn't practical or wise. Or attorney-like. Instead, she'd give him a call when she arrived home, using her best business voice. As though nothing personal existed between them.

In the end, there was no need for the call. When she pulled up at her house, Parker's blue truck was sitting in front. "You're late," he called cheerfully, lugging two grocery sacks up to the garage, where Amy ran to him excitedly.

"What are you doing here?" Amy asked.

"Bringing you dinner. I missed you last night, and you did say that those pizza pie things were your favorite food, didn't you? I hope I got the right kind."

Amy delved into the grocery bag he extended toward her. "Yay!" she shouted.

Caitlin reached his side more decorously, though her heart was skipping ahead. He grinned. "For us there's steak. Do you like steak?" He hesitated, furrowing one eyebrow. "Do you know how to make it?"

She laughed. "Slap it in a pan and turn on the stove. Actually, I have a barbecue out back, if you want to brave the cold."

"Now that's something I can do. This coat is impenetrable."

Amy was already inside the house, still giggling over her treat. Caitlin met Parker's eyes. "I just came from Dakota's."

He held very still, waiting, his eyes intense.

"She wasn't very happy to see me, but Madeline's fine."

"How did Dakota look?"

"Sleepy. I think I woke her up. I don't know who sleeps at this time of day. Maybe she got a new job we don't know about."

He shook his head. "She does that sometimes. Takes something in the morning and sleeps all afternoon."

"Something as in drugs?"

He nodded.

Caitlin felt his worry; it poured off him as strongly as his desire for her the night before. "Well, Madeline's okay for now, and we're working on the rest. Come on. Let's go fire up the grill."

• • •

Out on Caitlin's tiny back deck, Parker stood before the barbecue grill, struggling to recapture the happiness he'd felt at being with Caitlin again. Yet after hearing about Dakota, his thoughts kept going to Madeline. Weekends were the best party times in Dakota's view. He'd usually taken Madeline during most weekends, though officially the agreement was every other week, so what would Dakota do with Madeline now?

He reached for the spatula and flipped over the steaks. His breath curled white into the cold air. "How're they coming?" Caitlin asked, slipping through the partially open glass door.

He smiled at her appearance. She'd changed from her customary suit to black pants and a snug cream-colored top. Her hair was down, and she looked so inviting that it was all he could do to remain moping at the grill. "Nearly there. Just a bit more on that first side again."

She looked out over her small backyard, which was still an expanse of dirt, the moonlight reflecting from her blue eyes. She was beautiful. But he realized he needed to keep his distance. After last night, he couldn't trust himself not to kiss her and scare her away. Every instinct told him they had something special, but his mind knew that was not the way it worked. If he wanted more with Caitlin, more than a few weeks of casual dating, he had to wait.

Wait until what? He wasn't exactly sure. Wait until she fell in love with him? Until she was sure? Until the case was over?

Although his decision to wait had seemed so simple—even noble—last night and even this morning when he'd bought the flowers, now he was no longer sure. His hopes of proving to the world that Madeline was in danger were swiftly being shot down, and that brought him closer to acting. He must save Madeline one way or another, and for the moment that meant not letting things go too far with Caitlin. He didn't want to hurt her. She wasn't just a beautiful face anymore, but a woman whose every word thrilled him. A woman who tenderly took care of her sister, a woman who ferociously went after what she believed to be right. A woman with dreams that seemed as unattainable as his own. That was why he'd pulled back last night when she'd hesitated, and why he wouldn't touch her now. She deserved more, but he couldn't allow his growing feelings for her make him unwilling to do what might be necessary to save his daughter. He knew Dakota, and he knew what had happened in the past.

"Penny for your thoughts." Caitlin's arm brushed against him.

That if I kiss you again, I'll never be able to leave you. He forced a grin. "My thoughts are worth way more than that. Actually, I was thinking about your lawn. I know a guy who delivers sod. Gather a few neighbors and in an afternoon next summer, you'll have yourself a nice place for Amy to play."

"I'll ask you for his name then. Next summer."

It wasn't a question, not quite, but he wished more than anything that he could promise to be there to help, to arrange it all. He could lay the sod himself in a few hours. Instead he only said, "I think the meat is ready."

"Great. Let's go in."

His thoughts were jumbled. This scene—a man, a woman, and Amy acting the child—was so . . . right, and yet wrong because Madeline wasn't there. He ate quickly, wondering what he could do to get himself away. He'd been wrong to come here, wrong to assume he could pursue a normal relationship with a woman as classy and beautiful as Caitlin. There were too many consequences for both of them. He raked a hand through his hair.

"You're going to pull all your hair out." Amy grinned at him, much in the way that Madeline would have. His heart ached.

"Your phone," Caitlin said. "Isn't that your phone?"

He grabbed it quickly. "Hello?"

"Daddy?"

"Hi, baby. Are you okay?"

"Reese is crying and crying and Mommy's in the bedroom. She won't answer the door."

"Okay, sweetheart, don't worry. It'll be okay. Just stay on the phone." He covered the receiver. "It's Madeline. Says her brother's crying, and she can't get Dakota to the phone."

235

"You can't go over there. We'll have to call the police."
Caitlin reached for her phone. "Or at least Sally."

Madeline was speaking again, and Parker tried to focus on
what she was saying, but her words were abruptly cut off.
There was a brief flurry of noise, the phone dropping to the
floor, and then a terse woman's voice. "Parker, is that you? I
told you not to call here. You have no right!"

Parker thought quickly. He didn't want to give Madeline
away by admitting that she'd been the one to dial his number.
"I wanted to talk to you," he lied. "But Madeline said her
brother was crying and that you weren't around."

"I was right here," Dakota snapped. "What did you want?"

"To let you know there's going to be a hearing tomorrow,
about visitation."

"I know, and I'm going to fight you on it."

"Please, Dakota. I just want to see her. That's all."

"Leave us alone." She hung up.

Parker stared at the phone a few seconds before shoving it
back into his pocket.

"I'm sorry," Caitlin said.

He shrugged. "It's okay." He looked at his nearly empty
plate. "Look, Caitlin, thanks for letting me barge in, but I've got
to go now." He pushed back his chair and stood up quickly.

"You don't have to go." She stood with him, too close, driving his thoughts away from Madeline.

"Yes, I do." He looked back and forth between Caitlin and
Amy, who watched him with her wide green eyes. For a
moment he wanted to weep for the woman Amy might have
become. Or was it for himself and Caitlin? Definitely for
Madeline. She was paying for his poor choices. If only he
hadn't been a rebellious idiot growing up. If only he'd been
more like his big brother.

He shut his eyes briefly and then strode toward the door.

Caitlin hurried after him. "Parker, you can't do anything about this. You can't go over there. If you're still worried, I'll call Sally and have her send someone, but you have to remember the restraining order. If you have any hope of gaining visitation rights tomorrow, you must not violate that. I'm speaking as your attorney, and as your friend."

"Friend?" He smiled, hoping that would take off some of the mockery he'd injected into the word.

"Yes," she said softly. ·

They stood staring at each other for a long moment. Parker wanted to lose himself in her. He wanted a normal life.

He forced himself to look away, to open the door. "I'll see you tomorrow." His voice was gruff. Glancing back, he saw her nod, her lips slightly parted, her tongue wetting her bottom lip. She didn't look at all like his lawyer. With a groan, he reversed his step, coming so close to her that they were almost touching. He kissed her, cutting off the kiss before she had time to respond properly. Knowing that if he held the contact a second longer, he wouldn't be able to remember that he was first and foremost a father. Within seconds he was out the door and jogging to his truck, feeling Caitlin's gaze following him.

He drove to Salt Lake and parked two blocks south of Dakota's house, going on foot from yard to yard. The overgrown shrubbery with dead leaves still attached and the many evergreen trees lent themselves to subterfuge. Soon he was in the backyard, careful to keep to the far side and to not make any noise that would alert the dog next door. From his vantage point, he could look into the large kitchen window, glowing with warmth in the dark night. Madeline was at the table eating something. Her brother was in a high chair nearby. Dakota wasn't in view, but he sensed movement off to the side.

The air was so cold it bit into his lungs, but that wasn't what brought the tears to his eyes. He slumped against the huge trunk of a bare tree, weak with relief. *She's okay.*

The sound of a car interrupted his thoughts. Probably the boyfriend. Sure enough, the new car Caitlin had told him about turned into the driveway, pulling to the side of the house where the garage should have been, if the owner had built one. He watched as the big man walked to the side door that led into the kitchen. It hurt to know that another man could be with his daughter when Parker officially couldn't even talk to her.

In minutes he was back in his truck, but he didn't start the engine. Looking out at the dirty remains of the snow, he cried.

18

Parker smiled at Caitlin, wondering why he felt so nervous to see his daughter when it was all he'd been fighting for. The judge, after talking to Madeline and the child advocate, Mr. Reeve, had agreed to allow Parker three supervised visits a week with Madeline. "No time like the present," the judge added at Caitlin's question about when the visits could begin. Then he'd assigned Caitlin to be the supervisor for the first visit that would take place immediately in a room down the hall, though normal visits would occur at a different location with a regular facilitator, the cost of both to be paid by Parker.

As Madeline entered the room, Parker could hear Dakota shrieking in the hall. "He steals my baby and now he gets to—" The closing door cut off her remaining words.

Madeline ran to him. "Daddy!"

He'd never seen her smile so bright. "Madeline." He held her close for a long moment, her little arms wrapping tightly around his neck. He drew her back to kiss her cheeks, then held her again more tightly, blinking furiously to stop the tears. He met Caitlin's gaze over Madeline's shoulder. She smiled and he nodded gratefully. She was right; this was better than nothing.

Madeline was talking and talking, telling him about her dream last night, about the new car she'd ridden in, and getting pulled over by the policeman for not being in a car seat. "Mommy was so mad," she confided. "But the policeman was nice to me." Then there was Reese and how he was finally learning how to hold a cup instead of his bottle. Her voice lowered. "But most of the time, he spills it on the floor."

Parker let it roll over him, content to hear her voice, and understanding that the meaning wasn't nearly so important as their being together. At the same time he was aware of Caitlin watching them and the fact that Dakota was outside the door, seething in fury. Well, privacy shouldn't be as important to him, either. Not now.

He hadn't counted on Madeline's boredom. After ten minutes of nonstop talking, she asked, "Can we go see Grandma?"

"No, honey. We have to stay here at the courthouse today. Maybe next time we can work out something better. Maybe we could go sledding." He shouldn't have said that because the judge had been clear that he could see her only inside and closely supervised. Today Caitlin was responsible for making sure they didn't take off, and even if she let them slip away, there was still Dakota standing guard at the door. He could see her angry face periodically in the tiny rectangular window next to the door.

Well, maybe his mother could supervise the next visit. She'd be far more lenient.

Staying in the room was a little like being in prison, and it made him feel guilty, as though he'd done something so terrible that Madeline was forced to pay the price of visiting him. They played with his phone, told stories, and looked out the window. The minutes ticked by slowly, and though Madeline started to cry when it was time to go, Parker could also sense her relief at finally being able to *do* something. For her, an hour of forced confinement in one small room with few distractions was torture. He'd have to come better prepared the next time he was allowed to see his daughter. If they didn't put him in a real prison first.

He hugged Madeline close, wiping her tears. "Look, sweetie, don't be sad. There's something more. A secret."

"What?"

Parker looked up to make sure Caitlin was out of earshot. "I might come to see you soon. If I do, I'll throw a little rock at your window, and you can look out and wave. Okay? Don't open the window or anything, unless you see it's really me."

Madeline's smile returned. "Okay," she whispered. "And then we'll go see Grandma."

He let her think that. "Don't tell anyone."

"I won't."

"It's time to go now."

"I love you, Daddy."

"I love you, too, Madeline. You're my best girl. Forever."

He motioned to Caitlin and she came over. "Go with Ms. McLoughlin, okay?"

"Her name is Caitlin, Daddy." Madeline looked up at Caitlin. "Am I going to see your sister again?"

"I wish, but we can't today. I'm sorry. Come on." Caitlin held out her hand and Madeline took it. Parker watched as they vanished through the door, feeling a sadness that sat in his stomach like a ball of lead.

Caitlin returned within minutes, walking slowly across the room and sat beside him. "She's so adorable. Gave me a big hug before she left."

"She likes you."

"I like her, too." She placed a hand on his arm, obviously sensing his distress. "It'll be better somewhere else. They have toys and things. Yards, too. Or so I hear."

"It's cold outside. She wouldn't last long." He let his head drop to his hands, trying not to feel anything. "I need to have unsupervised visitation."

There was silence for long seconds and then, "If you were allowed unsupervised visits, can you honestly tell me you wouldn't disappear?"

"Are you asking for her or because of us?"

She looked away and said quietly, "Does it matter?"

He thought a moment and then shook his head once, sharply. "I guess it doesn't. But it's a fair question. She's still in danger, and leaving might be the only way to save her life. Unless you've found something we can use. Have you?" The question was tinged with hope. She'd been talking on the phone for most of this bittersweet hour. Maybe she had good news.

She shook her head. "I'm sorry. The private investigator is still coming up dry. Dakota must have really gone out of her way to clear any tracks. But don't worry, he's not giving up. Not yet. Of course this does make our case a lot more difficult. The more time passes, the harder this is going to be to prove—especially if she really is clean."

A chill crept down his back. "She isn't. Is there a way to make her take a drug test?"

"I'll certainly try, but the motion will likely be denied without any other proof factors."

"Are you telling me I'm going to go to prison?"

"No!" She stood, moving to stand in front of him. "I will find something on Dakota. I believe you."

The way she said it, he knew she'd begun to have doubts. He wasn't prepared for how much that hurt him. Why should he care? A week ago, he didn't even know her name. So what if she felt right, if they felt right together? So what if she no longer believed? None of it mattered in the face of Madeline's safety.

He rubbed a hand across his face. "I'd better get to work." He stood, looking past her, not wanting to see that truth in her eyes.

"Parker."

He hesitated. "Yes?"

"I'm doing my best."

He met her gaze directly. "What if your best isn't good enough?"

She bit her lip, making him vividly recall the softness there. "It will be."

He nodded and took a step.

"Parker."

He stopped again.

"When did you change? You rebelled all your teenage years. You were living with Dakota, going along with that sort of life, and then everything changed. You said once before it was because Madeline was born, but that wasn't all, was it?"

He shook his head. "I had a brother. He was the perfect one. Always compliant, the obedient, favorite son, while I bucked against every rule my father set down. I used to time how fast I could made my father angry. Five seconds was my record." The thought made him sick now. "I was determined to be everything my brother wasn't. He earned scholarships, he could fix almost anything, he was brilliant. I was nothing compared to him. And then one day they were in a car and there was an accident, and they died. Madeline had been born just before that, and I already had regrets, but suddenly all the regrets in the world didn't matter." Tears blurred her face and he looked away. "I could never tell my dad I was sorry. I could never tell my brother how proud I was of him. I'd let all the opportunities slide by. There was only my mother, and I was all she had left. I knew it was time to grow up. So I did."

She took a tentative step toward him. "For the record, I think you turned out great."

Still, he knew she didn't trust him. Not yet. Maybe not ever. He'd been a fool to think she could. Nodding in her direction, he started again for the door.

"Call me if you need anything. I'll be home tonight." It was an invitation, one he couldn't afford to accept because he'd already made a choice.

"I'll be working late," he said. "To make up for this morning." She nodded. Was that disappointment in her eyes? It was all he could do not to stride to her and take her in his arms.

He walked down the hall, stopping once to look back in her direction. She was in the hallway now, talking to that pretty-faced DA, the one who wanted to put him in prison. She was smiling. The man put a hand on her back, leaning forward as though concentrating on what she was saying. Touching her.

This was a man from Caitlin's world, the kind of man who wore suits and who worked out in a gym where there was always water and soap nearby. A man who spoke the language of depositions and briefs and arraignments.

Yet she had kissed Parker.

Stop.

It was over. After tonight there wouldn't be any reason to worry about Caitlin.

• • •

"Well, I don't know," Caitlin said to Mace, aware of how close he was. With difficulty she forced her mind from Parker and the disappointing visit with Madeline. "Tonight is hard."

"You have to work?"

"No," she said, and then immediately wished she'd lied. In a lower voice she added, "It's my sister."

"Your sister?"

He leaned forward to better hear her reply, placing a warm hand on her waist. As she stiffened with surprise at this public display, she spied Parker at the end of the hall, heading out of the courthouse. Their gazes met briefly and then he was gone.

It's not what you think, she wanted to yell. But wasn't it? Last week she'd been dreaming of being somewhere romantic with Mace.

So what did she really want?

Two young attorneys she didn't recognize walked by, their conversation abruptly ceasing. They nodded as they passed, both ogling Caitlin and giving knowing smiles to Mace. She could have sworn one winked.

Men.

"So what if we made it short?" Mace said. "I really have to be at that meeting with the Salt Lake DA tomorrow evening. I hate changing our date, but it's sort of an emergency thing."

"I heard she'll be picking another assistant soon. Is that true?"

"Actually, yes."

So Mace was angling for the job. She couldn't see the purpose. Who'd want to spend more time managing than actually being in the courtroom?

"I could pick you up right at five tonight. We can have a

quick dinner and talk. There's something important we have to discuss."

Caitlin was tempted to agree, but what if Parker showed up at her house and she wasn't there? He needed her. Or was she fooling herself? "Why don't we discuss whatever it is right now? I can make time."

Mace looked momentarily flustered, his eyes darting around as though looking for some way out. "All right. I know where there's an empty room."

"Why don't we use this one? No one's here at the moment." Caitlin went inside, feeling vaguely uneasy. If she'd thought the room small when it contained a rambunctious four-year-old and her frustrated father, now it seem microscopic.

Mace closed the door behind them, locking it. "So we're not disturbed." He came toward her, reaching out and pulling her over to the side so they couldn't be seen through the small oblong window next to the door.

"Mace, what are you doing?"

"Finally we're alone." He lowered his head and began to kiss her. "This was a great idea," he whispered against her lips. "I've been dreaming of doing this all day."

Caitlin turned her face away. "Look, Mace. Not here."

He stopped kissing her, but his arms tightened around her. "I know you like me, and I feel the same way." His hand began to slide up her back.

"Mace! This wasn't what I intended when I invited you in here. You said we needed to talk. This isn't the time or place for . . . this. Let me go!"

"Why?"

"Because I want you to." She took a breath. "Look, I'm sorry, but there's someone else. I didn't know myself until last night. I didn't mean it to happen. I can't go out with you."

His eyes hardened. "I know you aren't what you seem. I know you were responsible for the conviction against Chet Belstead, particularly how the police found the murder weapon. I can't prove it yet, but I think there's enough circumstantial evidence that would destroy your career."

She held her body rigid. "What are you saying?"

"I'm saying I know what you did."

"Is this how you're getting dates these days?"

"Are you denying it?"

She lifted her chin until their faces were inches apart. "Chet Belstead raped that girl. He stabbed her with a knife so many times she almost died. That's what's important. Any evidence the police found has no connection to me. Now take your hands off me!"

"I've decided I'll stay quiet. You don't have to worry. I like you." His face bent toward hers again. "All you have to do is be nice to me."

Fury burst to life in her heart, fanned by the degradation she felt. She wanted to kill him. She wanted to smash him into a bloody pulp and bury his remains in an unmarked grave. Better yet, she wanted him to experience the fear and humiliation Belstead's girlfriend had felt the night she'd been attacked. "Oh," she said with false sweetness, "but wouldn't my confession help you win the appointment with the DA?"

His hold on her relaxed slightly. "That was my plan at first, but I don't care about that now. You can't deny the attraction between us. Everyone knows how you feel about me."

His utter assurance disgusted her. Had she really been so obvious? "Whatever I felt for you walked out that door the moment you brought me in here," she retorted. "Frankly, I'd rather be disbarred than spend another minute with you."

Shock filled his face, and she took advantage of his surprise to break free and start walking to the door. A second later he grabbed her, his fingers digging cruelly into her upper arm. Fear abruptly sliced through her anger. "Let me go!" she demanded.

He hesitated, apparently still confused. "I said let me go!" she repeated, accentuating each word. "Or are you another Chet Belstead?"

His expression went from angry to furious. "So that's the way you want to play. Well, you've made yourself very clear. You're going to regret this. Mark my words." His lips curled. "Frankly, I don't know what I ever saw in you." He relaxed his hold just as a key turned in the lock. Wyman Russell appeared in the doorway with the two young attorneys that had passed them earlier. Wyman looked concerned, the others eager.

Mace tried to fake a confident smile, despite the flush of anger still covering his good-looking face. Caitlin laughed, walking toward the door. When she passed the young attorneys, she said, loud enough for everyone to hear, "Sorry to disappoint you guys, but he's definitely not my type." She turned on her heel, leaving them gaping after her.

She was nearly out of the building when Wyman caught up with her. "You took him down a notch or two," he said, chuckling.

Her anger was dissipating. "I shouldn't have done that. He says he's going to try to get me disbarred, and if he does, how will I support my sister?"

"I can think of a way."

"What, go out with you?"

"I didn't mean that." His face flushed. "I meant working for my new law firm. Look, it's going to be okay. There were three witnesses to what just happened, and if he goes after you about the Belstead case, there won't be a judge or attorney in town who won't know he's doing it because you burned him." He laughed. "I mean, what a shock! He hasn't lost a bet in three years."

"He had a bet about me?"

"Well, it's sort of understood. He hits on all the single attorneys eventually. Like I said before, you can't trust him. That's what I meant. I knew he was angling for you. I also know he's still stringing along that woman in California."

She sighed internally. "Thanks for coming when you did. Things might have taken a turn for the worse."

"I saw you go in there with him and rounded up a key right away."

That was sweet. Why couldn't she fall for a man like Wyman? He might not be as hot as Mace or Parker, but he was a nice guy. A nice married guy.

"How's your wife?"

He shrugged. "We're meeting this weekend to talk."

"Good luck."

"I meant what I said about working with me."

She flashed him a smile. "If Mace gets me fired, maybe I can be your assistant."

"You mean one of our attorneys."

"Not if he manages to get me disbarred."

"Then he's actually got something on you?"

"I didn't do anything I wouldn't do again."

"Then I'll trust you and hope you'll only be fired, not disbarred."

She couldn't help but smile. "Thanks, Wyman." She turned and walked out into the cold streets, wrapping her arms around herself for warmth. Exhaustion fell heavily on her shoulders. She wished she could go home. She wished she could see Parker.

Where was he at that moment? Was he thinking about her? How odd that in this past week he'd become so large a part of her thoughts. Seeing him stuck in that small room with Madeline had torn her apart, but nothing she did for his case seemed to make any difference. As it stood, he was headed toward prison, leaving Madeline to be raised by a woman who might be on drugs, and there was nothing she could do about it.

She'd told him to trust her, but what if she couldn't deliver?

Taking out her phone, she dialed Kenny once more. "Sorry," he said without greeting. "I just don't have anything except my gut that tells me she's hiding something. This woman is not good for those children, but I can't prove it."

"Yet, you mean."

"I'm looking into the boyfriend now. That might be where I get the break. He appears to have a nice job and car, but there's something odd about him."

"Thanks, Kenny." Caitlin tried to keep her disappointment from her voice. "Call me if you hear anything."

"Of course. Bye now."

In Parker's place, she might just take Madeline and run. And that, she knew, was exactly what he planned to do.

Unless she stopped him.

CHAPTER

19

Caitlin reached her car, opening the doors with a click of her remote and sliding inside. She dialed Sally's number and plugged in her earphone before starting the car. "Anything new?" she asked hopefully when Sally answered.

"Sorry. We did a small drug bust at a party in that circle—friends of Dakota's friends—but they claim Dakota has no connection to them."

"Lying?"

"Maybe. People like that lie about everything, even when they don't have to lie. It's an addiction. Most don't even know the truth anymore."

Caitlin was all too familiar with the type. "Look, Sally, I have another favor to ask."

"Anything."

"Could you take Amy home with you again? There's something I have to do tonight."

251

"Does this involve Parker?"

"It's just that—Sally, I'm afraid he's going to run."

"Do you know that, or are you guessing? Because if you think it's true, I have to act."

"No, you don't. I'm telling you this as a friend, not in your capacity as a police detective."

Sally was silent a moment. "Fine. But think about this: maybe we've both been wrong about Parker Hathaway. Maybe he's the one lying."

"You think I haven't considered that?"

"What exactly is happening between you two?"

"I don't know. I've never felt this way before. It's like . . ." *If he doesn't kiss me I'll shrivel up and die.* But that was silly. She'd only known him five days.

"Like what?" Sally was still waiting for her to finish.

"I only met him on Monday, but it feels like much longer."

"You're falling for him, that's what's happening. I could see it coming the moment I saw you together Wednesday morning. I take it that means gorgeous DA is out of the picture?"

"You got that right."

"What happened?"

Caitlin wanted to tell her friend the whole story so they could commiserate together over what a total jerk Mace was, but she couldn't explain without incriminating herself. Sally was a loyal friend, but she was a stickler for the letter of the law and wouldn't look kindly upon any interference in the Belstead case.

"Look, I'll fill you in on that later. Just take my word for it. The man's a total moron. I don't know what I ever saw in him."

"Well, he's good-looking."

"I don't care how good-looking he might be. He's an idiot.

Look, I just wanted to know if you've found anything and if you'll watch Amy for a bit. I understand if you have plans."

"No, no. That's fine. Tony's got a bowling tournament tonight, and I was going to meet him there but not until later— just to get in on the celebration part. Bowling's boring for onlookers." She paused. "Unless it's in the summer and they take their shirts off."

Caitlin rolled her eyes. "Right. Thanks, Sally."

"You let me know if you need anything."

"I will."

Caitlin drove home first and changed into her red silk dress that took inches off her waist, making the most of her figure. Never would she have worn the outfit to work or out with someone like Wyman. She would have worn it with Mace on Saturday, though she knew now that would have been a mistake.

Now to find Parker before it was too late.

•   •   •

Parker surveyed the array of items on his bed: clothing for several days for both him and Madeline, food supply, toiletries, all the cash he had in the bank, and the ten thousand he'd gotten from his mother's card. She'd put more in, she said, and he could use the card again later if necessary. It would take him years to pay her back, but he'd do it and gladly. He was a hard worker and could make good money when he put his mind to it. Maybe he'd finally start that business he'd always been thinking about. First, he had to get through the next few weeks without getting caught.

He'd signed the deed to his truck over to his mother so she could sell it, and she'd paid a friend for a junky old car with the title to be transferred later. Or more like never, as he'd abandon it in Vegas. Somehow he'd have to get new ID, a new life. Until he did that, he'd be living in hiding.

A life on the run. Was it really necessary?

He slumped to the bed, thoughts of Caitlin nearly overcoming his determination. Slowly he took out his phone and dialed Dakota. Maybe she'd be reasonable. Maybe she'd give him a glimmer of hope so that he could stay.

"Hello?" She sounded pleasant, not at all her normal self. He stiffened.

"Hi, Dakota. It's Parker."

"Sorry, Parker's not home. We're divorced anyway, you know."

Wasted.

"Dakota, this is Parker. Are you alone?"

"Parker? You can't call the police. I'm not home. And no, I'm not alone. I'm with my fiancé. That's right. We're getting married and leaving this stupid state. How's that? You may be better-looking, but he gives me what I need."

"Dakota, where's Madeline?"

"She's fine. Now leave me alone." She started calling him dirty, vicious names, her voice still sweet and slurring. The incongruence almost made him want to laugh.

"Where's Madeline?" he asked again, but another, deeper voice came on the phone.

"Bug off. She's mine now." *Click.*

The boyfriend, the one who had more muscles than he had hair—or sense, apparently.

If they were together somewhere, then where was his daughter? He began shoving things into the extra suitcase he'd bought. When he was finished, he filled his smaller suitcase as well and then set them by the door. Finished. There was nothing more to do. He grabbed his keys.

Was there time to stop and see Caitlin? But if he did that, would he have the courage to leave? Shaking his head, he opened his door, hefted the suitcases, and crossed the shared living room. His roommate still didn't appear to be home, and in fact Parker hadn't seen him once.

He opened the door and there she was, Caitlin, standing with one hand up to ring the bell. Her hand lowered, and her black coat fell open to reveal a shimmering red dress. She'd never looked lovelier, and he had difficulty forcing himself to ask, "Is there news?"

"No, but we need to talk."

"I can't."

She glanced down at the suitcase in his hand and at the other on the floor where he'd set it to open the door. "Going somewhere?" He didn't answer as she stepped into the room. "Parker, you can't leave."

"Are you going to stop me?" He set down the other suitcase.

"No." She was so beautiful. The copper hair cascaded down her back, over her shoulders. His breath failed him, and for a moment he could do nothing but stare.

Her coat slid to the floor, and they were in each other's arms. Nothing in his life had ever felt so right. "It'd be better if you left now," he whispered.

"I'm not leaving until we talk this out."

He wanted to talk about it, to establish a base where they could go forward into the future. But they couldn't have a future, and living only for the moment was what had trapped him with Dakota, what had given Madeline such a raw deal. He wouldn't do that again. He couldn't promise her what wasn't his to give.

Or maybe he was putting too much stock in her words, in her kiss. Caitlin had shown no surprise that he was leaving. She'd known. So maybe she was simply here to say good-bye. At least he'd have this last glimpse of her to warm him over the next lonely months as he struggled to create a new life with his daughter.

Then a thought struck him. Maybe Caitlin wasn't there to say good-bye but to convince him to stay. Perhaps that was what he could see in her blue eyes.

"Kiss me," she said in a soft voice, not even loud enough to be called a whisper.

That was his undoing. He didn't know how or why, but somewhere along the line he'd fallen in love with her, and kissing her had suddenly become as necessary as breathing. He kissed her deeply, relishing the feel of her in his arms. Every emotion felt new and more powerful than he'd ever experienced.

Yet there was so much separating them, especially the fact that she'd come to convince him to stay. More than anything, he didn't want to leave. He wanted to stay and see where these emotions would take them in the next days and months and years. Knowing the impossibility of this desire was every bit as painful as the joy of kissing her now.

"Excuse me?" A male voice came from the doorway of the apartment.

Both he and Caitlin froze as a short, stocky man with a full beard came the rest of the way into the room, pocketing keys he'd apparently used to open the door. In one hand he carried a large paper grocery bag. His brown eyes surveyed them.

"You must be Bob," Parker said, slowly moving away from Caitlin.

"And you must be my new roommate."

"Parker Hathaway."

"Nice to meet you." Bob offered Parker his hand. "Can I speak to you in the kitchen a minute?"

Parker glanced at Caitlin, whose pale skin was slightly flushed. "Uh, yeah." Hopefully Bob was the relatively normal guy he appeared to be and not recently released from prison. "I'll just be a minute," Parker said to Caitlin.

Bob led him to small kitchen where he began unpacking the paper grocery bag. "Uh, we need to have some ground rules about having women over."

The guy had to be kidding. "It wasn't like we were . . . she just came to see me before I left."

"You're moving out already?"

"Yeah, something came up, so I'm heading out of town." Parker thought he should shut up now. No doubt the police would be interviewing good old Bob after he disappeared. "Mexico," he added to confuse potential investigators.

"She's classy. Where'd you pick her up?"

"I didn't pick her up. She's my law—we've been working together on something. What you saw when you walked in sort of took us by surprise."

"I don't know why. It's a wonder the room wasn't in flames with all the sparks between you. I'd been standing there for quite some time before you noticed me."

Parker watched an ant march across the countertop. Bob certainly had a point. There was a connection between him and Caitlin, and it was just as well the man had come in when he had. Parker had to remember to be more careful. The last thing he wanted was to hurt Caitlin—and that meant he needed to keep her at arm's length.

Bob wrote his name on a jar of mayonnaise and shut the refrigerator. He yawned. "Well, if you're moving out, I guess we don't need to talk. I've worked forty hours in the past three days and I'm beat. I'm going to sit down on the couch and watch a bit of TV. You two are welcome to join me if you want." He looked so smug that Parker wanted to bash his face.

"Uh, no thanks." Even if he were staying in Utah, his idea of a good evening wouldn't be staring at a TV with Bob. No, he would rather be alone with Caitlin, with a promise of many more days to come.

Except that they didn't have more days. Or even this one. Now that his mind had cleared, Parker had begun worrying again about Madeline. Was she safe? Dakota had obviously been partying when he'd called.

"Nice to meet you, Bob." Parker nodded and returned to the main room where Caitlin was standing by the couch. He pulled her into his arms and traced the freckles on her face with his fingertip, stopping on her bottom lip. So much for arm's length.

She kissed his finger before saying, "Let's go to my place. I'll cook dinner."

He kissed her again, long and deep, loving the way her eyes closed. "You're so beautiful, Caity." He took her hand, their fingers intertwining. "You go ahead. I'll deal with my suitcases and be right there. But don't worry about dinner. I'll take you out somewhere nice."

"Okay," she whispered. Her eyes went beyond him, and Parker knew Bob had come into the room.

He walked Caitlin out into the hall, pulling her to him again and holding her far too long.

Then he did the only thing he could do. He gave her a final kiss, stepped back, and let her go.

He waited exactly three minutes before hefting his suitcases and taking them down to the car he'd hidden down the block.

Caitlin's car was nowhere to be seen, and he was both grateful and disappointed. He forced himself to start the ignition and drive not to Caitlin's house but in the opposite direction.

Because there was Madeline. There would always be Madeline, and even if it meant closing a door, walking out on Caitlin, there was no other choice. He wouldn't ask her to share a life on the run. He wouldn't come to her empty-handed. Though every nerve in his body protested the separation, he set his jaw in determination. He was the only one who could protect Madeline.

He drove past the house he'd rented for Dakota. The place was dark, as he hoped it would be. Walking stealthily, Parker made his way to the window. In the next few minutes, he would end up in jail or on his way to Vegas with Madeline. He threw the tiny rock at the window. Would she be awake? Would she look out or run to her mother in terror? It was already dark but not yet ten o'clock, so she might not be in bed.

A face appeared in the window. Fear pounded through him, but it was only Madeline. The window opened. "Daddy?"

"Shhh."

Her voice lowered to a whisper. "Did you come to get me?"

"Yes."

"Wait. I have a chair. I got it from the kitchen. I have to put it on my bed."

She vanished but reappeared within seconds, tall enough to climb onto the windowsill. There was no screen, so soon she was in his arms, and he was folding her under his coat. "What about Reese?" she asked as he reached up to shut the window.

"He'll be all right."

"But he was sick tonight. We were over at Lyn's for dinner, and he was crying. He threw up."

"Is he sleeping?"

"Yes."

"I bet he'll be better in the morning."

They made it to the car without being seen. At least he hoped. Now if everything went well, he might have as many as fourteen hours to put space between them and Salt Lake City before the alarms went off.

"Where's the truck?" Madeline asked.

"I traded it for this."

"Why?"

"Well, partly because it gets better gas mileage. You and I are going on a long trip."

Her eyes sparkled. "Goody! I love trips."

Parker tried to enjoy her enthusiasm, but his mind kept returning to Caitlin. What would she think of him when she realized he wasn't coming? Would she feel used and betrayed, or had he just barely salvaged a chance to be with her after all this was over?

If it was ever over.

There was also the strong possibility that Caitlin would realize what he had done before he was safely away and call Sally. Parker stepped harder on the gas pedal. The more miles between him and Salt Lake City, the better.

20

Every part of Caitlin's body felt alive. Her senses were acute. She noticed the homemade wooden turkey sitting on a neighbor's front porch, the way the melting snow sparkled in her headlights, how the stars seemed bright and the night darker. Each of her heartbeats was an individual thing, like a beat on a drum that was so big it filled the entire world.

That didn't stop the worry from setting in as she pulled into her garage. Was she doing the right thing by convincing Parker to stay? There was no pretense that he was attracted to her, but beyond that she really knew nothing. And the suitcases. He'd been going to leave.

Well, what of it? She'd do the same thing herself, wouldn't she?

He had to trust her a bit longer. She would find the information. She'd go over to Dakota's every day to check on Madeline, if that's what it took.

And if he still left?

She climbed from the car, slamming the door a little too hard. She wasn't going to dwell on that thought. No, she was going inside, freshen her makeup, fix her hair.

Bong! went another beat of her heart.

Sometime later, when the house smelled thoroughly of baked sugar cookies, her favorite candle aroma, she began to worry. Where was Parker? Even if his roommate had insisted on talking some more, he should have been here by now.

The headiness of the air made her feel almost drunk. Walking to her bedroom, she looked in her closet for something better to wear, but the red dress was the best she had.

To think that she'd been going to wear it on a date with Mace. A sick feeling churned in her stomach. How could she have been so very wrong about him?

Don't think about Mace, she ordered herself.

Her thoughts returned easily to Parker, to the way he'd looked at her, the huskiness in his voice when he'd said she was beautiful, the connection she felt at his touch.

She sat down on the sofa and flipped on the TV. There was nothing interesting on, not that she could have paid attention anyway. Her nerves hummed, and every sense seemed tuned to waiting. Waiting for the sound of his truck. Impatient, she went into the kitchen for a glass of water, taking it back to the couch. The glass clinked on the coffee table, making a sound that brought back memories of family holidays, her first boyfriend, outings with Sally.

Yawning, she pulled a blanket over her, the red dress too thin to offer much protection against the increasing night cold. Worry began gnawing in her belly. Was she doing the right thing going out with Parker?

He'd leave. She was sure of it.

No, she could get him to trust her. There was something between them. Something powerful. He would stay.

She closed her eyes and saw herself wrapped in Parker's arms on a warm, sandy beach, Amy and Madeline playing together nearby. She stretched slowly, languorously, her body soaking up the sun and Parker's nearness.

A rush of wetness caused her eyes to blink open, and she was startled to realize that she'd been sleeping. Her glass lay empty on her lap, a dark stain marking where the last bit of the water had run out, soaking her leg underneath the blanket. Her mouth felt like peach fuzz and tasted considerably worse.

Her eyes went to the clock, and for a moment she stared at it, unable to comprehend. It was after two. That she'd fallen asleep while waiting for Parker didn't concern her—she was always so exhausted that at any moment of inaction her body threatened to shut down—but that he wasn't there did worry her. Had he come while she was asleep?

No, she would have heard the door.

Then she knew, without really knowing how, that he was gone. That last moment in the hall, when he'd clung to her, had been a good-bye. Not a proper one, in her view.

I'm such an idiot. He'd gone without explanation. He'd left her here waiting. How he must have laughed at the idea of her waiting for him to come. Blood flooded to her face. She tried to work up anger or indifference, but she was too wounded to feel either. Tears wet her face as she hugged her arms to her stomach.

After the initial hurt faded, she told herself she needed to get up and call Sally. She had to let her know he was running. There was the slimmest chance that he was still in Utah, but Caitlin would bet her whole career that he wasn't.

Not that she cared in the least about her career.

She'd been such a fool. She'd thought she could convince him to stay, to trust in her. But in the end he hadn't believed in her abilities.

And maybe he was right.

She pulled the blanket around her and let the tears—and sleep—come.

•   •   •

An insistent buzzing flitted around Caitlin's head, waking her from a cold and uncomfortable dream. She blinked, looking around. She was lying curled up on her couch under a single blanket. She could hear the heat on, which meant it was morning, though still early by the dim light she saw through the blinds.

She came to an unsteady seated position, her head weighted by a dullness that she knew had come from too little sleep. The buzzing came again, and she traced it to the cell phone on the side table where she'd put it the night before. The thought that it might be Parker made her grab for it. "Hello?"

"Finally!" It was Sally. "Where have you been? I put the girls to bed last night when you didn't come to get Amy."

Amy. "Oh, I'm so sorry! I completely forgot."

"That must have been one long date."

Caitlin flushed, not even wanting to consider what Sally would say if she knew how Caitlin had ended up alone. "Yeah, sort of."

"Caitlin? Are you okay? You sound funny."

"Nothing. Now stop yelling in my ear. Look, there's something I have to tell you. It's important."

"Is this about Parker?"

Caitlin's heart plunged to her stomach, and she wished she

could go back to sleep and forget everything that had happened this week. "Sally, I think we might have been wrong about him."

"He's gone, isn't he?"

"Yes." The word came out a strangled whisper.

"I'm sorry." Then Sally's voice became crisp and businesslike. "I'll put out the word. We'll find him."

Caitlin sank to the bed. "You should go to Madeline's first. I might be wrong." Yet she knew she wasn't.

"I'll call her mother."

"Let me know."

"I will."

The phone went dead, and Caitlin let it slip to her lap. She'd done her best to convince him to stay, to trust in her, but in the end everything between them had been false. To tell the truth, she wasn't sure she even believed him anymore. When the police caught up with Parker this time, he'd go to jail for certain, and Caitlin wouldn't represent him. No way. She didn't even want to see him again. Ever.

She put on her coat and checked her pockets for her keys, then drove to Sally's in a haze. When she came inside, Amy managed to tear her eyes from the Saturday morning cartoons long enough to give her a hug. "I didn't have any pajamas," she said. "So Sally let me use her pants. And this is Tony's shirt." The blue material dwarfed even Amy, drooping on her tall frame, but she spun around as though modeling the most beautiful dress.

Sally hid her smile as Amy plopped again onto the couch, already absorbed with the cartoons. "No answer at Madeline's house. Her mother isn't picking up her phone."

Caitlin checked her watch. Nine-thirty already. "She's probably still sleeping."

"I called the precinct. I was reminded that there has been no crime committed yet, but I sent a uniform over anyway."

"He's gone," Caitlin said with surety.

"How do you know?"

Caitlin lowered her voice, though Amy and Sally's daughter were oblivious to anything but the TV. "I saw him at his place last night. I went home when his roommate showed up, but he was going to come and get me. To go out."

"Did something happen at his apartment?" Sally looked pointedly at her rumpled dress.

Caitlin pulled her coat tighter around her, knowing her face was a bright red. "Nothing happened. He kissed me, that's all. Look, I don't want to talk about it. He's just gone."

"Oh, honey. I'm so sorry." Sally hugged her.

For a suffocating moment Caitlin couldn't swallow the lump in her throat. "Please, I need to go home." She made her voice louder. "Come on, Amy. We have to go."

Sally watched them leave, her eyes glittering with curiosity. "Go find Madeline!" Caitlin wanted to yell at her, but she knew Sally was already doing everything in her power. In minutes, Madeline's disappearance would be all over the news.

But it was already too late.

"Is something wrong?" Amy asked. "You look mad."

"I'm just a little sad." More like desperately and horribly sad. Why had she allowed herself to be so caught up by him? It had felt almost as though he was a puzzle piece that fit the missing part of her. She closed her eyes for a moment, willing the hurt to leave. Everything would be okay. She would go on. She always went on. Besides, Amy needed her.

Sally was already calling her cell phone as Caitlin pulled into her driveway. "You're right," she said. "Madeline's gone. There's a chair on her bed, and the window latch wasn't engaged, like it'd been shut from the outside. No fingerprints yet, except Madeline's. Whoever she's with, she seemed to have gone willingly."

"Parker."

"Probably. The officers tell me Dakota's raging mad."

"Did she let them in right away?"

"Yes."

"And?"

"Nothing. It's the same as before. Clean. I've got officers looking for fingerprints now."

"And Parker?"

"He hasn't shown up at his apartment. The landlady said he only paid a week in advance."

"What about his mother?"

Sally heaved a sigh. "Parker gave her his truck, and she's selling it to a neighbor. Rumor has it she's selling the house, too, though there's no sign up."

"So she knew he was going."

"I think so. But that only means she might be the one who'll lead us to him. We're getting a warrant to flag her accounts now, in case he's using her credit cards."

That sounded logical, but it made Caitlin feel even worse. The woman was probably as duped by her son as Caitlin had been. "How could I have been so wrong?" She didn't realize the words were out until Sally responded.

"I'm the one who asked you to represent him. He fooled me, too."

Sally, of course, didn't know the whole of it—that Caitlin had liked him so much that nothing else seemed to matter at the time.

Stupid.

"We'll find him." Sally's voice was grim.

"He's not going to hurt her."

"Who's to say? If he's actually been dreaming up everything about the drugs, what might he dream up next?"

A shiver of fear shot up Caitlin's spine, but she shoved it aside. "No," she insisted. "He loves Madeline."

"I hope you're right. I'll talk to you later."

"Thanks." Caitlin stared at the phone for a long minute after Sally hung up. She was still sitting in the car behind the wheel, though Amy had long since bolted from the car and was inside, probably in front of the TV. Caitlin couldn't bring herself to care. Why shouldn't Amy watch as much TV as she wanted? It wasn't as though it would ruin her chances of a good future.

I've done it this time, she thought, letting the tears roll down her cheeks. *Done it big.* She had broken her rule about getting involved, and now her heart would have to pay.

21

Parker stopped before exiting the Las Vegas hotel. He was sure he hadn't been followed from Utah, but he always checked to make sure no one was openly watching the outside of the hotel. They'd been here a week, registered under false names, and Parker knew they'd have to move on soon. Nevada was too close to Utah, and how many fathers were visiting with only their young daughters for company?

Madeline was the darling of the hotel. Both the guests and the employees loved her, and twice she'd gotten a stomachache from so many people giving her too many candies. She didn't look much like the fair-headed, light-skinned child she had been. Her hair was cut short and dyed black, and her skin was a deep bronze—mostly thanks to a bottled tan, though some of it was real as they spent hours each day walking under the thin sun through the city. She was loving their life, especially being with him so much.

But Parker found that Vegas held nothing for him. Half of

him, it seemed, had been left in Utah. He'd felt broken in this way once before, when Dakota had told him Madeline wasn't his child, but this was even worse somehow. There was no going back, no chance of remaking the past. At night he dreamed of Caitlin, and he regretted not showing up at her house at least to say a real good-bye. Then Caitlin could have moved on without him under her skin. Without the memories to stop her from letting go. Without the hurt that could cripple her chance of forming another attachment. Like with that pretty-boy attorney.

He felt a rage of jealousy at the thought. *I should have stayed with her.*

Yet he'd made the only choice he felt he could as a father, and now he had to live with it. Live for Madeline. And that meant making hard decisions about the future. No, the hard decision had been made before they'd left Utah. Now the decisions were just more decisions, something he had to do to create a stable, normal life for his daughter.

An elderly man and his gray-haired wife emerged from the elevator—Shane and Orla O'Doherty. Madeline pulled her hand away from Parker's and ran to them. This couple was a particular favorite of hers because Mr. O'Doherty always carried gum in his pocket, and Orla saved Madeline the umbrellas from her drinks. Madeline had quite the collection by now. Mr. O'Doherty was an investment banker in Chicago, and the couple was obviously well-off since they were staying in one of the expensive suites on the top floor. The tan they sported was definitely not from a bottle but from vacations to exotic places.

With a last look at the street, Parker waited for the O'Dohertys to reach him. Madeline was already saying her thanks for the treat and twirling her newest drink umbrella between her fingers. As usual, she was talking up a storm, and he listened to make sure she wasn't saying anything that might be seen as suspicious. He'd reminded her time and time again to refrain from talking about personal things and to say they were from California if anyone asked. So far she'd remembered pretty well, but Parker was careful not to leave her alone with anyone for more than a few moments in case she slipped and began talking about her real life. They'd been lucky so far.

"A sweet lass there," Mr. O'Doherty said, as he did every day. The fact that he'd lived in Ireland as a young boy was apparent in his speech.

"Thank you. She is a good girl."

"They're leaving tomorrow, Daddy!" Madeline's mouth curled downward in a frown.

"That we are." Mrs. O'Doherty set a brown hand on Madeline's head. "We'll be able to see our granddaughters. We'll tell them all about you, little one."

"I like your voice," Madeline said. "You sound like Caitlin. She's my friend's sister."

Parker tensed when Madeline mentioned Caitlin, but when she didn't elaborate, he relaxed. "Her parents were Irish," Parker volunteered.

Madeline's head bobbed up and down. "She's got long red hair. It's curly. And blue eyes. She's so pretty, and nice, too." She laughed and added. "My dad kissed her! My friend Amy told me."

Parker knew Amy had been to Madeline's house, but according to Caitlin they'd only been alone in the kitchen for a short time. Apparently, it had been long enough.

"An Irish gal, eh?" Mr. O'Doherty's eyes were knowing. "You won't ever get her out of your blood. It isn't possible, I tell you. I tried many times with Orla."

His wife punched his arm playfully. "Oh, did you now? Silly man. I would never have let you get away."

Parker had a glimpse of his mother and father joking around in a similar manner when he was very young. What would his father be like now if he'd lived? What would he say about Parker's life? Would he have mellowed enough to see the good in him? Well, that was something Parker would never know. But he did know that he had to make a plan for his future—and fast—especially if he wanted to take care of his mother in the way his father would have. He still hoped it wouldn't be necessary for her to sell her house and go into hiding with him. Any day now Caitlin might find the needed proof. But was she even looking anymore? Maybe not.

He took a deep breath, making a rapid decision to risk asking Mr. O'Doherty about job possibilities in Chicago. "I've been thinking about going to Chicago myself. You wouldn't know anyone in the construction business, would you? Someone who might need a hand?"

Mr. O'Doherty's left eyebrow rose. "Maybe. But what about your work in California?"

For an instant Parker had forgotten the fake life he'd created for himself—that he was a joint owner in a construction business in California—and he searched his mind for something plausible to say. "We're about finished with our current projects, and business is slowing because of the poor real estate market. My partner can take care of the few other projects we have coming down the pipeline, so I've been thinking about trying something new. My girlfriend was born in Chicago and has always wanted to go back."

Mr. O'Doherty exchanged a look with Mrs. O'Doherty. "I knew a woman would be behind the idea. There is always a woman behind crazy ideas."

"And a good thing," Mrs. O'Doherty said. "Our friend here is too handsome to be alone for long. He needs a woman."

"You might as well give your girlfriend what she wants." Mr. O'Doherty clasped a hand on Parker's shoulder. "I can't make guarantees, but if you decide to come to Chicago, I'll introduce you around." He handed Parker his card. "It won't be easy starting over."

"I work hard." Parker looked pointedly at Madeline. "I have a lot of reasons to want to succeed."

"You do at that. I'll look forward to hearing from you."

Parker watched them go. Until this very moment, he'd been undecided about where to start. He'd known from almost the first day that they couldn't stay in Vegas. But where would be the best state to lose themselves in? He'd met people from at least a dozen states. He'd even met a family from Iowa who actually owned a construction business, and their adult daughter had made no secret of the fact that she liked Parker. She'd hinted he would be welcome there, probably so he could marry her. She had been so friendly that Madeline had actually started avoiding her. Parker was relieved because he didn't know how much longer he could stave off her advances. Not that she wasn't attractive. She simply wasn't Caitlin.

Now the idea of Chicago was like a fresh breeze, blowing away the confusion. Maybe it was foolish to think he could go and make a new life there, but he was young and hardworking. His determination would take him far. He told himself he chose Chicago because it was far from Utah, but ultimately he knew it was because of Caitlin.

What would she think of him in Chicago? He smiled at the thought before realizing it was a strong possibility she would never even know.

Madeline tugged on his hand. "Aren't we going for a walk?"

"Actually, I think we're going to find out about going to Chicago."

Her eyes widened. "Can we go on a plane? A big one?"

"I think we'll drive."

"In that old car? But it was hot."

"No. Not that one. Remember? I already gave that car away. We'll rent a new one. It'll be really nice." Renting a car seemed safer than an airplane, though he couldn't use his own ID at either place, but he was working on that angle already.

"Can I take chips and candy?"

"Of course. And your DVD player." Investing in that portable machine had been the best thing he'd done since arriving in Vegas. "I'll buy you a new DVD, too."

She gave him a hug. "You're the best daddy in the whole world!"

After that she was silent for a long while as they walked out of the hotel and aimlessly down the street. Then she said, "I wish we could tell Caitlin and Amy about Chicago."

"I do, too."

"Then why don't we? Maybe they'd want to come with us. Amy and I could play tea party." A mischievous glint came to her brown eyes. "And you could kiss Caitlin."

Parker knew she said it to make him laugh, but instead the comment seemed to cut into the part of him that still hoped. He stopped walking and looked down at his daughter. How could he tell her that Caitlin would probably never forgive him for his choice? It was possible she didn't even believe that Madeline had been in danger. He'd seen the doubt in her eyes.

"I'm sorry," he said slowly, "but I don't think that's going to happen."

That afternoon, he took Madeline to a park where he could sit on a bench and watch her play. The day was cool and she wore a jacket, but the temperature was nowhere near Utah's freezing weather.

A dark-haired man in a leather jacket and black jeans came to sit beside him. "Nice day," he commented. He was young, not more than twenty-five, and good-looking in a way that likely attracted women. His build was on the thin side, but there was steel in the set of his jaw.

"Good for moving on," Parker said. "Do you have them?"

The man laid a folder on the bench between them. In the week they'd been in Vegas, Parker had cautiously checked into buying a new identity and had finally found this man. He charged far more than people selling stolen social security numbers and badly forged licenses, but he guaranteed that no one would ever become suspicious because of the documents. Parker assumed that meant he'd used the name of a child who had died, perhaps even a fictitious child. He didn't know and didn't care to know.

He took an envelope from his coat pocket and set it on top of the folder. It contained twenty-five hundred dollars, the second half of his initial payment. He'd pay two more installments later, after he was settled. He hoped that was where it would end.

The younger man slipped the envelope into the folder and pulled out the documents, leaving them on the park bench. He picked up his folder. "Good luck."

Parker watched him leave and then slowly scanned the park to see if they'd attracted any attention. There were two women talking on a far bench, and an amorous pair of teenagers on another, but none seemed interested in what Parker was doing. He moved the documents onto his lap. Two social security cards, two birth certificates, and one driver's license.

They left for Chicago that night. No use in hanging around any longer. He'd followed Utah news as best he could from the hotel, and though the features on Madeline weren't appearing as often as they had in the beginning, he knew Sally and others would still be searching. No doubt the Feds had been called in. Traveling under his own name would have been a huge mistake. At least now he'd be able to earn a living.

He was really going to do it. Go to a city he'd never been to before and start a new life. Wild and spontaneous had been his calling card in the old days, but for the past four years, he'd lived a different sort of existence altogether. Steady, reliable, and if the truth be told, a little boring. A man who wanted to suffer for the sins of his past. Now the adventurous man that still lived inside him was coming awake, filled with excitement at what the future might hold. No, he wasn't the youthful Parker, who hadn't let himself care about even those who loved him most, but a blend of the new and old. A blend of fun and fatherhood, adventure and duty, love and responsibility.

His heart still ached, but that wasn't unfamiliar to any of his incarnations. Yet even there he felt a change—not significant enough to be called real hope, but perhaps if there was any chance of winning Caitlin back in the future, Chicago just might show him how.

CHAPTER

22

S orry, Caitlin," Kenny said. "Nothing yet. Do you still want me to continue?"

Caitlin thought for a moment. An entire two weeks and weekends had passed since Parker had vanished. Kenny's search seemed pointless now—and had for weeks. Only her own stubbornness had kept him on the job, though reduced to part-time. "I guess not. There's no reason now that he's gone." No one cared if Dakota was doing drugs anymore; they only cared that Parker had kidnapped his daughter.

"Well, there's my gut."

"Your gut?"

"For what it's worth, honey, I think this Dakota character is as guilty as sin. The kid's better off away from her."

She hated the pity in his voice. Pity for her loss. Kenny hadn't been fooled by the facade she wore these days. "It's all been a lie, Kenny. There's no proof. Besides, it doesn't matter. He's gone."

"Whatever you say. It's your dime."

"Send me a bill."

"I will. Call me if you change your mind."

Caitlin hung up, feeling weary. She looked numbly at the stack of papers on her desk. More briefs to write, more criminals to move along in the system. Mechanically, she began to type out the words she knew so well. The brief didn't really need passion or brilliance. Just another knife attack and a man destined for prison.

A knock at the door interrupted her distracted thoughts. "Come in."

Caitlin stiffened when Norma Hathaway stepped into the room. She had never met Parker's mother, though she'd seen a picture in the file Sally had put together. She was a short, sturdy woman with shoulder-length hair dyed a medium brown that did not quite match the myriad of wrinkles on her pale face. Wrinkles that seemed to have come before their time. Her brown eyes were tired, but they looked just like Parker's. Only where his exuded vitality and confidence, this woman's seemed unsure and frightened.

"I hope it's okay." She moved into the room with unmistakable grace.

"Please, sit down." Caitlin had stood as she entered and remained standing until Mrs. Hathaway had settled in one of the seats in front of her desk.

"It's about my son."

"There's nothing I can do," Caitlin said quickly. "By leaving, he's broken the conditions of his bail, and when they find him he'll be in jail until the trial."

"They told me. That's not why I'm here. Before he left, Parker told me you were researching about Dakota. He had great hopes of you finding something that would help him and keep Madeline safe."

Poor deluded woman. "We didn't find anything. I'm sorry, Mrs. Hathaway, but we're beginning to think the drugs were figments of Parker's imagination."

"No!" Mrs. Hathaway's face came alive, and Caitlin could see where Parker got his looks, if not his height. "I heard them talking. I go with him to drop Madeline off sometimes, and Dakota didn't deny anything when he accused her. She as much said she'd do it again, that she could do anything she wanted, and there was nothing he could do about it. They had an awful fight. You've got to believe me. Madeline was in danger—I absolutely know that! Do you think I'd sell stocks and clean out my savings if I didn't know for sure?"

Caitlin didn't point out that most of the mothers of her clients did that every day. "You cleaned out your savings?"

"A loan. He's good for it. With all the work he's done at my house the past years, I owe it to him anyway. And I know he'll always take care of me. That's the sort of son he is. Besides, I have other money in stocks and the house."

Caitlin wondered if she should mention that she knew Mrs. Hathaway planned to sell her house. In fact, it was entirely possible the woman knew where Parker was. Could she get him a message? If so, what would Caitlin say? The hurt in her chest was so big there was no room for anything else.

Mrs. Hathaway leaned forward, her eyes holding Caitlin's. "Look, I know he had a rough beginning in his life, but he was always good inside. Never teased or tormented kids or animals when he was little, always respectful of me and other women. He just couldn't live up to his dad's expectations, and his brother . . . Well, Parker and I have never talked about it, but his brother was awful to him. He enjoyed having his daddy all to himself, enjoyed being the successful one. He lorded it over Parker far too much. I should have stepped in earlier, but then it was too late and Parker was gone. Yet despite all that, he found his way back to me."

Caitlin pulled a few tissues from the box on her desk and handed them to Mrs. Hathaway.

"Thanks." She wiped tears from under her eyes. "I know how all this looks, but I wanted to ask if you would please keep looking for proof against Madeline's mother. Something to free my boy if the police catch up to him. Like I said, I have money. I've cashed in some stocks, and I can cash in more. Parker and Madeline are all I've got, and I don't want to spend any more time away from them. This could drag on for years. I'll go where I have to—I need to be with them—but I'd rather bring them home. And there's still that other little boy, Madeline's brother. He's in danger, too."

Caitlin had a glimpse of Parker's eyes, only instead of being intense like his mother's they were shadowed with attraction for her as they had been that last night. The night she tried to convince him to stay.

The woman must have sensed a softening around her. "Please?"

Caitlin sighed. "I got to know Parker pretty well during the week I knew him. I asked him to trust me. He didn't."

"I'm not surprised. There's never been anyone he could really trust, not even me, and Madeline means the world to him."

"Did you know that he might not even be her father?"

"That's a lie! I see Parker in Madeline's face all the time. I know she's his."

"But you don't seem surprised that Dakota might claim he isn't the father."

"She's hinted at it before to me. But I know it's just one more way Dakota tried to control him."

Since Dakota hadn't brought the idea up to the police, Caitlin had to agree.

Norma Hathaway seemed to take her silence as permission to proceed. "Tell me, were you close to finding anything?"

"No. It was only a feeling."

She sat up straighter. "See? Then you know there's something. And also why he had to leave. He had to make sure Madeline would be safe."

Caitlin felt like crying on this woman's shoulder. She would understand what that last night had meant to her, and how crushed she'd been when Parker had walked out. Instead, she asked softly, "Has your son been involved since his relationship with Dakota?"

Her head turned slowly from side to side. "He said he'd never trust another woman again. I hoped that wouldn't last. He's a good man and deserves to be happy." She studied Caitlin for a long moment. "You're not telling me everything, are you? Was there something between you and my son?"

For an instant Caitlin was tempted to lie, tempted to put on her attorney deadpan and deny everything. But Norma Hathaway looked at her with a mixture of pain and hope, the same feelings Caitlin had tried fruitlessly to crush for the past weeks. "I liked Parker very much, Mrs. Hathaway. I tried everything I could to get him to stay, but he didn't."

Her eyes were shining now. "You're involved with him. I can see it in your face."

"There was attraction, that's all. It didn't matter. He left anyway. And he took Madeline."

"Did he tell you he was going?"

Caitlin bit back the inclination to tell her that was none of her business, but she shook her head. "We had a date the last night he was here. He didn't show up."

"Then he must really care about you. He probably realized that if he'd shown up, it would have been too hard to leave."

"He could have trusted me."

"He'll be back." Her voice lowered as though she suspected there were listening devices in the room. "He's coming back for me."

"Mrs. Hathaway, you shouldn't tell me that. Please don't tell me anything about Parker. I'm not your attorney, or his anymore, and I'll have to tell the police."

"I'm not telling you anything except that he doesn't make promises lightly. Now, please, will you keep looking into his exwife? I'll pay all that I can."

He doesn't make promises lightly. Problem was that he hadn't made Caitlin any promises at all except that he could wait. Well, he'd apparently mastered that. Only now the waiting was hers, and she hadn't signed up for it.

"Please?" Mrs. Hathaway asked again.

Caitlin hesitated a few more seconds before nodding slowly. "I guess I can do that." She waited for the woman to leave and when she didn't, Caitlin reached for the phone and dialed Kenny's number. "I changed my mind, Kenny. I want you to keep looking for a while."

"I knew you'd say that. Don't worry, I'm still following her. I got a feeling. How about if I follow up all my remaining leads and see what happens? If I don't find anything in another week, we can drop it. I don't mind pulling my best on this. After all, your client might have saved his daughter, but there's still another child at that house. Cute little thing, even if he does seem to be crying all the time. The mother can't seem to do anything with him."

"I think he used to spend most of the time with his father until recently." Caitlin found she was actually beginning to feel sorry for Dakota. Maybe there was more to the woman than she knew. Maybe she had reasons for becoming the woman she was now. Reasons that started and ended with Parker Hathaway. Look at how just five days with Parker had changed Caitlin's life.

"I'll keep you informed."

"Thanks." She flipped the phone shut.

"Thank you. I'll let you get back to work now." Mrs. Hathaway arose and took a few steps toward the door before pausing. "Look, I wanted to tell you that I heard something in my son's voice a few nights ago when he was talking about you. I think it was hope. That's the only reason I dared come today. I know everything's a mess and you have no reason to trust us, but maybe you can find it in your heart to wait a bit. Give him a chance."

I can wait. That was what his note had said, arriving in a bouquet of bright, beautiful sunflowers. They still stood on her kitchen counter, wilted now, though she could barely look at them.

Caitlin couldn't speak. The anger and hurt whirled around inside her, mixed up with memories of his kiss. Fortunately, Mrs. Hathaway didn't seem to expect an answer. She glided to the door with her strange grace and vanished.

Caitlin closed her eyes. A mistake because now the memories were back in full force. He'd kissed her, made her blood rush, all the while planning to leave her behind. That's what hurt the most, that he hadn't confided in her. They had been good together, and she knew from past experience that such a connection was hard—nearly impossible—to find, much less forget. Maybe it was even similar to what her parents had felt when they had been together. Maybe that's why her father had been unable to go on after her mother's death.

She let her head drop to her hands, her fingers splaying in her hair, palms pressing against her eyes. More than anything she wanted to forget. No, she wanted another try. She wanted Parker. To talk with him. To convince him to stay.

Or maybe so he could ask her to go with him.

"Caitlin?"

She looked up to see Jodi at the door. "Sorry for barging in. I knocked but there was no answer. Your phone went to messages. Boss man's looking for you."

"Thanks, Jodi."

Caitlin made her way to Mr. Tyson's office, wondering what new case he would assign her to now. Another rapist? Another man who killed his girlfriend's baby?

I'm so tired of this.

As she reached Mr. Tyson's office, she came face-to-face with Mace Keeley emerging from the office. "What are you doing here?" she rasped, not hiding her disgust.

Mace smiled pleasantly, looking relaxed and in control. "Just making a visit, that's all."

"Right." She pushed past him into the office, not believing him for a moment. Her being called into Mr. Tyson's office at the exact same time as Mace's visit couldn't be a coincidence.

"Ah, ·Caitlin, please have a seat." Mr. Tyson indicated a chair. Caitlin sat on the edge, back straight, willing her senses to stay alert.

Mr. Tyson shifted a few papers on his desk without looking at her. He was a trim man with white hair and eyebrows. His face was also pale, but his eyes were a bold blue, seemingly brighter for each year that sapped the color from the rest of him. Today he wore a white sport coat and tan slacks.

"Caitlin," he said, finally lifting his eyes. "I've had a disturbing report from the DA's office. I called you in to see what you have to say about it. I'd hoped to have them here at the time, but their representative had to leave."

"I passed Mace Keeley on the way in."

"I see." He studied her. "Caitlin, you're an excellent attorney, and you have done a magnificent job for us, but Mr. Keeley seems to think there are some irregularities in some of your cases."

Caitlin sat even straighter and opened her mouth, but Mr. Tyson shook his head. "I understand you will have a lot to say about that. It's why I brought you in here. I wouldn't even have bothered, but I have good information that says Mr. Keeley might just become second in command at the DA's office, and I want to be sure where we stand."

"Did Mace tell you that he both threatened and sexually harassed me several weeks ago at the courthouse? There were at least three witnesses. As for my cases, there is absolutely nothing wrong about them. I've worked hard to get every criminal on my list a fair shake, whether they deserved it or not."

A rueful smile played on his lips. "That's what I thought. Well, about the harassment anyway. I knew there had to be something else. Look, Caitlin, these are serious charges, both on your side and on his."

She shrugged. "I was willing to let it go. He's the one coming in here."

Mr. Tyson waited for a few minutes before speaking. "Caitlin, are you sure there's nothing else I should know about? I'll stand behind you one hundred percent because I believe in you, but if there's anything amiss I could be putting this whole department in jeopardy."

Caitlin's indignation faded. He had no plans to put her out

to the wolves, and suddenly she found that she couldn't keep up the pretense. "There was something. Something you should know."

He nodded, folding his hands atop his desk, waiting.

"That rape case I had a few weeks back. Chet Belstead."

"I remember."

"I sent Kenny Pratt to question the people on Belstead's route home. I gave him a different date, though, so it was totally unrelated to the case. Could have been any case. He found a boy who remembered hearing something and advised him to call the police. That's what led to finding the knife."

Mr. Tyson leaned back. "On the surface it seems you did nothing wrong. You weren't directly involved in the information."

"I hoped he'd find something." She didn't want to be excused so easily. It was a breach of ethics, and she knew it. "I knew about the knife in the jacket from my client. He mentioned it in one of our interviews as a sort of . . . well, twisted courtship, for lack of a better word."

"I know the type. I'm sorry that's something you've had to deal with."

Caitlin shrugged. They both knew it went with the territory. "Apparently Mace became suspicious at how the police were given the evidence and started sniffing around Kenny. As far as I know, Kenny's told him nothing about who he was working for. I think Mace wanted to use the information about my possible involvement to help him get promoted, even though Belstead was as guilty as they come. Then he changed his mind and decided I could do other things that would be more gratifying for him."

"I get the picture." He put a hand under his chin, supporting the elbow with his other arm that lay horizontally across his stomach. "So where do we go from here?"

She shrugged. "I don't know. I wish I could go back, but I can't."

"I think you've learned a valuable lesson. The real question is, would you do it again? In this business I can almost guarantee that you will face similar challenges in the future. Can you adhere to the standard we must maintain?"

She was silent a long moment before saying quietly, "That's just it. I don't know."

Mr. Tyson nodded. "Don't worry about Mace. I'll fix him. But I want the names of the witnesses you mentioned, just to be sure we have backup before I wade into the fray. And if anyone asks you questions about this, you refer them to me. As of this moment, I am your counsel on the matter."

Caitlin felt a huge relief. "Thank you."

"Meanwhile, I want you to take the rest of this week and get where you can either finish or hand off your cases. Then I want you to take two or three weeks off while we get this mess cleared away once and for all and decide if you really want to stay here. Don't get me wrong—I want you to. I think you're the best attorney working here at the moment, the best we've had in a long time. But if you're going to stay, you have to be able to answer negatively to that question I asked you. You know as well as I do the reasons we cannot pick and choose when it comes to the fine lines of the law. No one should have that kind of power. It's too dangerous."

She nodded, blushing furiously, her English cool abruptly deserting her. "Thank you," she repeated. She stood and made her way quickly to the door.

"Oh, and Caitlin?"

"Yes?"

Mr. Tyson smiled, looking more like a grandfather than a powerful attorney. "I know how tough this all is, and I want you to know that if you decide not to stay, I'll still write you a glowing recommendation. There are many firms that could use your skills to protect the innocent. And maybe you wouldn't face as many ethical dilemmas."

Caitlin felt like crying. "I'll keep that in mind."

"I don't blame you for what you did. Sometimes you have to go with your gut feeling."

How she found her way back to her office through the tears, she would never be sure. But something in her had changed. She felt as though a burden had been lifted from her shoulders, a heavy burden that had been weighing on her for a very long time.

CHAPTER

23

P arker rolled up the building plans and stored them with satisfaction before catching the bus that would take him home to Madeline. The plans were every bit as good as the architect had promised. If they could pull it off, the expansive high-rise would be an accomplishment of a lifetime. And he would be a part of it, a major part—not just a crane operator but one of the planners and foremen.

He and Madeline had visited Shane and Orla O'Doherty the same day they'd arrived in Chicago ten days ago. Ten very long and productive days. Mr. O'Doherty had underplayed his connections, and before he knew it, Parker had been rubbing elbows with local contractors who not only were willing to put him into the trenches with their regular crews but to give him a chance as a foreman. Parker had slept little in the past weeks, and every second he could spare from work or taking care of Madeline, he was visiting sites or studying construction plans. There were some notable differences in constructing such a large building, and there were many new city codes to learn, but the differences were not as many or as important as he'd expected. More vital to them were his organizational skills and the feel he had for the project.

He was going to make it. He would have to work himself nearly to death in these first months, but he would give Madeline the life she deserved. Of course that didn't mean everything was how he wanted it. He didn't even try to pretend that this life could make him completely happy. Despite his satisfaction at work, there was an emptiness inside that he couldn't overlook.

Mrs. O'Doherty had insisted that he use one of her household employees to look after Madeline until they were settled, and every day when he picked her up at their expensive downtown apartment, Mrs. O'Doherty would say in her slight Irish lilt, "So when is your girl coming? Madeline could use her company, and I daresay you could use the support, too."

She had no idea how true that was. "To tell the truth," he finally told her, "I don't know that she's coming after all."

"Well, it's hard to woo a woman properly when you're so far apart. You should go get her. Or tell her you're moving on. Maybe that'll spark a fire under her. At any rate, you can't go on this way. If she doesn't want you, I know a lot of ladies who will."

Parker gave her a smile. "Thank you for your faith in me." He reached out a hand for Madeline. "Come on, sweetheart. Time to go home."

Parker thought about Mrs. O'Doherty's comments as they walked half a block to where he'd parked the company truck the contractor had insisted he use while overseeing the job. He wanted to contact both his mother and Caitlin, but while he was sure of his mother's response, Caitlin was a complete wild card. What made him think she'd want him now? And if he felt guilt for ripping his mother from her comfortable life, how could he even begin to expect that Caitlin could leave her prestigious job as an attorney to accommodate his life on the run?

Yet Orla O'Doherty was right in a way. He could put off his decision regarding Caitlin for months, hoping for a miracle. Months where she might go on with some pretty-boy attorney and forget the fire between them.

He needed to act.

Or let go.

Maybe letting go was best for all of them. Utah already seemed like a distant dream, something no longer a part of him. Except at night he sometimes thought about his family's little valley and the stars shining brightly above in the sky. Would his mother sell the land? Selling would probably be a good decision since he had no idea how long he'd be in hiding, but he hoped she wouldn't.

For some reason, his dreams of the valley always included Caitlin, and in those dreams it was always summer, definitely not snowing. It had snowed most of the ten days they'd been in Chicago, and Parker had taken to carrying an umbrella to protect Madeline from the wet weather.

Logic said he should wait to do anything. He still hadn't figured out a safe way to contact his mother, much less Caitlin. The cell phone he'd given his mother had been noted by the police during her questioning, and likely they were monitoring it. She would be past anxious by now, and that knowledge weighed heavily on him. But leaving things the way he had with Caitlin was worse—almost as bad as it would have been leaving Madeline.

He had to know where they stood.

Even if it risked everything he'd worked for? She could just as easily turn him in to the police as fall into his arms. Her sense of justice was strong, and he'd given her little reason to trust him.

"Daddy?" Madeline tugged on his hand. He always made sure to hold her tightly as the traffic in this part of the city was thick in the evenings. Around them people walked briskly to their destinations, faces hidden and bodies rounded by layers to stave off the cold.

"What, sweetheart?"

"Can we have macaroni and cheese tonight?"

That would be a test of his limited cooking skills, given that he hadn't yet bought any boxes of mac and cheese. "We can try. We have macaroni, and we can grate some cheese. It might not taste the same."

"That's okay. I love cheese."

"I know you do." They had reached the truck, and he opened the door, swooping her into the air with a flair that made her giggle. Emotion caught in his throat at how incredibly precious she was. No matter that leaving had split him in two, he had to be careful never to forget or play down the fact that Madeline had been in danger every moment she'd stayed with Dakota.

Ten minutes later, as they rode up in the elevator in their apartment building, an idea occurred to him. An idea so intriguing that Caitlin might not be able to pass it up. At least not if she still held any feelings for him in her heart. And if he could just be with her, he knew he could convince her.

"Can I open the door with the key?"

"Sure, sweetheart."

If he was really careful, it might work. Madeline finally managed to open the door, and he went inside the furnished apartment to the drawer in the kitchen where they kept the phone book.

"Daddy, what about the macaroni?"

"This will only take a minute. Why don't you get out the cheese?"

The trick would be making sure nothing was traceable, not even to the credit cards obtained with his new identity. But maybe, just maybe, he had enough luck, or karma, or whatever they were calling it these days, to make his idea work. The rest would be up to Caitlin.

• • •

On Friday afternoon, Caitlin looked up to see Wyman Russell standing in her office doorway. She snapped shut her briefcase for what would be the last time in at least a few weeks and started toward him.

"So, you're really doing it."

"People do take vacations." Though it was really a forced leave of absence, she was trying to stay positive.

"Not people who are going to work with me." He stood aside to let her pass. "Seriously, I came to tell you I'm officially not a deputy DA anymore, and that I put in a good word for you with your boss about what happened with Mace."

"I knew you would." Caitlin reached out to touch his arm.

He put his hand over hers and for a moment they stood there in the doorway, not moving or speaking. Finally, Caitlin said, "Wyman, I really appreciate everything you've done. I just don't know what my plans are yet."

"I know that. But I also know you've been avoiding me."

"Your divorce isn't final."

"Yes, it is. That's what I came to tell you."

"Oh," she said. He was nice and she enjoyed his company, and she had every intention of going out with him again. Still, there was nothing driving her to him, no heat that made her desperate to have him near.

Truth was, she wanted what she had felt with Parker. *I am such a fool.*

"Who is he?" Wyman asked. "It's not Mace, is it?"

She snorted in an unladylike manner. "Not on your life. Really, Wyman, it's not anyone, or at least not anyone I can do anything about. I just need time to sort my life out. It's been a difficult few weeks."

They walked to the parking lot in a comfortable silence. The truth was she was thinking more and more about working with Wyman, and maybe eventually, when the memories of Parker had faded, there could be something more between them. She wanted a family, and Amy hadn't let up on the baby idea.

The hurt of that night with Parker did at times seem to be lessening. She'd begun telling herself the separation made everything seem bigger than it had been—especially the attraction between them. How could such power be real? But several times a day something would remind her of him and the feelings would rush back, taking her breath away with their forcefulness, every bit as painful as that morning when she'd awakened at her house and discovered he'd really gone.

Wyman opened her car door. He bent and kissed her, not on the cheek as he'd been doing these past weeks, but on the lips. He tasted warm and slightly of mint. Pleasant, comforting. Why couldn't she feel more? Not only did he seem to have a genuine affection for Amy but he would be an attentive boyfriend. For an instant, Caitlin had a wild urge to grab him and kiss him silly to get Parker out of her mind.

Ridiculous.

Gently, she pulled away. "I have to go. I told Amy I'd be early."

"I'll call you, then."

"Sounds good." She waved as she left the parking lot. He was still standing where she'd left him.

Snow lined the streets and there was ice on the road. Now that November was almost ended, and Thanksgiving decorations packed away, Christmas lights were beginning to appear. Amy would insist on putting up lights this year. Maybe Wyman would help. There was a comfort in not doing it alone.

Except why couldn't she seem to swallow that stupid lump in her throat?

She picked up Amy and had scarcely arrived home when a messenger appeared at the door. He was a red-haired, scrawny kid with the gangly awkwardness of the teen years he hadn't yet left behind. "Caitlin McLoughlin?" he asked, extending an envelope.

"That's me." For a frightening moment, she thought he carried a subpoena that would force her to testify about what she had done in the Belstead case. With clumsy hands she opened the envelope, but inside she saw only the edge of what looked like an airline ticket. Relief flooded her. Of course this child wasn't delivering a subpoena; he looked about the age to be delivering pizzas. Besides, her boss was taking control of the situation.

"What's this?" she asked. "An airline ticket? I don't understand."

He shrugged. "I'm just a courier, ma'am. I pick up and take what they tell me to. There should be a note or something. I'm sorry about it being so late. We tried to deliver it two nights ago, but no one was home, and yesterday the courier who was supposed to bring it came down with the flu. Now if you'll just sign here."

Caitlin signed, all the while her hands burning to investigate the full contents of the envelope. She turned from the boy as he ran out over the snowy yard, shutting the door with her hip. Slowly, she pulled out the ticket.

Chicago. For tomorrow morning.

Chicago?

There was no note, just the ticket. Who would have sent such a thing? She hadn't shared her dream of returning to Chicago with anyone. Except Parker.

A sudden dizziness made her reach out to the wall to steady herself. Her breath was caught in her throat. It had to be him. But why? What had he to gain? He couldn't expect that she would jump onto a plane at his whim. Yet even as she thought this, hope flared bright and strong, surprising her with its strength. She'd thought she was beyond that. Especially now.

Just as quickly another realization fell like a dead weight on her chest, crushing the hope from her. He'd sent her a ticket. A *single* ticket. What did he think—that she'd leave her career, her home, drop all her life to go on the run with him and Madeline? And what about Amy? Maybe her home and job could be replaced, but he had to know she would never desert Amy.

Of course he knew, so this obviously wasn't an invitation to enter his life. That it was a dated ticket hinted he would be waiting at the other end, but what would that mean anyway? She wanted a relationship, not a weekend fling.

More likely, and even more hurtful, was that he wouldn't even be there, and the ticket had been the cheapest available, a way of throwing the police off his trail in Las Vegas where they'd at last tracked him to a certain hotel. Sobs caught in her throat. All at once the three weeks since Parker had left seemed like three hours, and she was still waiting for him to come to her.

The ticket fluttered to the floor. Leaving it on the carpet, she stumbled into the kitchen. She could hear the TV blaring from her room where Amy was probably ensconced in the big bed, her eyes fixed on the screen.

Could Parker be in Chicago? What would make him go there? She wished desperately that she hadn't shared her dream. The single ticket was a mockery of her trust.

Worst was the knowledge that she wanted to hop on the plane and see if he was there waiting. What would it hurt? At the very least, she'd get a free trip to the city where she'd been born. The logical part of her mocked her, saying such an idea was ludicrous. You didn't fly hundreds of miles for a man who'd left without saying good-bye, for a man you'd known less than a week. Yet part of her yearned to do just that.

What was it her boss had said about going with her gut? What was her gut saying about Parker?

Yet it really didn't matter what her gut said. There was only one ticket, and that absolutely did not translate into a future together. Gut feeling or no gut feeling, she would never leave Amy to use his gift, not for any extended length of time. That was a fact, and the attorney in her would never let her forget it.

Exhaustion made her mind numb and her body slow. What she needed was a good night's sleep. Maybe she should start taking sleeping pills. Ha! Not as long as she was responsible for Amy. She tried to ignore the bitterness. Amy was her sister, and she loved her more than life. Parker was just a man. Soon she'd stop seeing him every time she shut her eyes. Soon she'd stop smelling him, remembering his kiss, how she'd laughed with him. Stop imagining lying in his arms and watching the stars in his little valley.

Caitlin dropped her head into her hands, tears leaking between her fingers, as she replayed the events of the past weeks. Could she have done something more to convince Parker to trust her? Had he only been using her all along, hoping she'd work harder on his case if her emotions were involved? The thought made Caitlin want to curl up into a ball and die. At this rate, never dating again was beginning to look attractive.

Amy wandered into the room. "Don't you want these?" she asked, holding something out. "They were on the floor. Can I draw on them?"

She was holding two tickets.

Two?

Caitlin grabbed them. Sure enough, there were two!

"I hope I didn't ruin them. They were stuck together. One's ripped a little. I didn't mean to rip it."

"That's okay." All at once choices stretched out before Caitlin, if not in endless combinations then at least more positively than before. He hadn't sent her a single ticket; he'd thought of Amy, and that said a lot.

There was still the chance he wouldn't be there, and the tickets really were a simple thank-you for her representation. Or more likely for the help with his case. Her stomach churned. If he wasn't there, it would mean there never had been anything real between them—anything besides the strongest attraction she'd ever experienced. There was also the increasing likelihood, given that Kenny hadn't been able to turn up proof, that Parker had been lying to her about Dakota and the drugs.

Still, Norma Hathaway had been pretty convincing.

Caitlin debated for several long seconds, but when it came right down to it, none of this mattered. She needed to see Parker, and if these tickets meant a chance of that, she was going. She would choose to take the risk.

"Amy," she said, her voice shaking with barely controlled excitement, "how would you like to go on a trip? We could go on a plane and everything."

"A real plane?" Amy's smile grew by the second. "I *do* want to go! Yes!"

"Then let's go pack."

She'd finished Amy's suitcase and was halfway finished with her own when she heard the phone ringing. Caitlin answered it, not glancing at the number.

"Hi, beautiful." Kenny's exuberance made her smile.

"You have something?"

"I found an old house owned by the boyfriend through some fake company. From what I observed of the comings and goings, it looks suspiciously like a meth lab."

"You think Dakota knows about it?"

"She was there last night. Not long. An hour maybe. The little boy was screaming for some reason. That's probably why they left so fast. This afternoon, I saw two known drug dealers leaving—people who were definitely involved with the suicide guy Dakota lived with at that other meth house. I've been following them for a couple hours, but I've lost their trail. Anyway, I'll text you the address of the house when we hang up."

"Thanks. I'll let Sally know."

Of course calling Sally meant the possibility of blabbing about the ticket, and Caitlin didn't want to tell her, even if it was best for Madeline. Then again, if the information Kenny had found led them to the proof they needed, Parker would have been right all along.

Quickly she dialed Sally's number. "Sally? Listen. Kenny called. He says he has something. Maybe we weren't wrong to trust Parker after all." She quickly outlined Kenny's suspicions. "I'm texting you the address he sent. Could you check it out?"

"Yes, but I want to call Kenny for the particulars and then do a bit of checking on the house's history. If I smell a rat, I'll drive by with some of the guys on my way home. I have nothing better to do." Sally spoke casually, though Caitlin could sense an underlying excitement in her voice. This case had nearly driven Sally crazy, especially when Parker's trail had dried up in Nevada.

"Thanks. And Sally, double check on the little boy while you're talking to Dakota. If this turns out to be real, he's not safe any more than Madeline was."

"I'll take care of it. But look, don't get your hopes up too high."

Too late for that. Caitlin was either headed for ecstasy or disaster. "Don't worry about me. I know what I'm doing."

"And what is that?"

For the first time in three weeks, Caitlin felt real joy. "I'm going on a little trip."

CHAPTER

24

The streets were already dark as Sally drove up to the house with five of her fellow officers. The house was small like those in the rest of the neighborhood but not in disrepair. In fact, it looked like an ordinary house on any ordinary street.

For a moment, Sally saw what looked like a glimmer of light coming from a basement window, partially hidden by a metal window well. But no, that was most likely the reflection of the street lights.

They had protective gear stashed in the cars against a possible need to shield themselves from toxic chemicals that might be lurking in the air. One whiff would signal the level of toxicity.

She crunched over the unshoveled walk, praying they wouldn't have to fire their weapons. You never knew how drug dealers would react. At least Kenny's observations at the house that day had been strong enough to give them reason to conduct a search. Good thing Caitlin had kept him on the job, never mind what it must have cost her both emotionally and in cold, hard cash.

She felt distracted as she considered her last conversation with Caitlin. Where was her friend going? It wasn't like her to go on a trip without notice. Something was going on, either at work or in her love life. Caitlin had refused to divulge more information, though Sally had at least exacted a promise that she would call later with details. Sally had a sneaking suspicion this sudden trip involved Parker, not so much because of the timing but because of the happiness she'd heard in her friend's voice, an aliveness that had been lacking the past three weeks. She'd been encouraging Caitlin for years to get out there and find a man, but if this really did have to do with Parker, Sally wasn't sure it was a good idea.

Maybe I should have her followed, Sally thought as they forced the front door open.

"Clear!" shouted first one officer and then another as they searched each room in the house. Besides random pieces of furniture and a box of old pizza, there was nothing to find.

"Do you smell smoke?" Sally asked.

Jim Clegg swore. "Where's the basement?"

They searched frantically for the door, hoping to save whatever evidence the basement might contain, but they barely made it down the steps before being overwhelmed by smoke. "No can do," Sally screamed. "Get out!" That explained the light she'd seen in the basement, and judging by the swiftness of the blaze in the unfinished basement, it had an efficient fuel. Her lack of concentration had seriously cost them.

By the time they made it outside to the snow-covered ground, they could see flames in the corner bedroom on the main floor, and the scream of the fire truck one of the officers had called was only blocks away.

"Nothing," Jim muttered, taking off his breathing mask, his face contorted with frustration. "From what I could see, the basement was empty. If there was anything here, they've moved it and torched the place to get rid of any evidence."

"They must have been warned."

"How? That PI was the only one who knew about this. You think he blabbed?"

Sally shook her head. "Not a chance."

"We might still be able to lift evidence if we can get that fire out soon."

"Maybe. But you're right; this doesn't add up. Let's take a drive." She signaled to the other officers that she was leaving and headed down the drive.

Jim jogged to keep up. "Where're we going?"

"To see Dakota Allen. And her boyfriend."

"You think they're going to 'fess up?" His upper lip curled slightly, but Sally didn't take offense. It was just a tick. She reminded herself to encourage him to wear a mustache. Many men with receding hairlines looked good with mustaches. Not as great as her Tony with his closely shaven head but good nonetheless.

"No. But we might catch them by surprise." Truth was, something was eating at her. Something that first Caitlin and then Kenny had mentioned on the phone. But what had it been?

She revved the car as Jim slid into the passenger seat. "Hey, watch it." He gestured to the growing crowd of people in front of the house. "We have company. Don't want to be a bad example."

She gave Jim a flat grin. "Whatever. You're just mad because I'm driving."

The firemen had arrived and were doing their thing, and the blaze would be under control in minutes. More officers were arriving to help with the crowd. Sally knew they would evacuate the nearest houses, and normally she'd stick around to help, but her mind was still gnawing on the thought she'd had earlier. It was something Caitlin had said when she'd called with the address of the meth house. But what?

Fishing out her cell, she dialed Caitlin's number.

"Hello?" Caitlin sounded out of breath.

"Is something wrong?"

"Just leaving the store parking lot. I needed some things for my trip. I have to be at the airport really early in the morning. What's going on?"

"The house was torched just before we got there. Fire started in the basement. Someone was on to us."

"But no one knew." Pause. "No, Amy, you can't take the gerbils. Mrs. Burnside's going to watch them."

"What?"

"Sorry. Talking to Amy."

Sally knew if they were taking the gerbils to neighbors, that meant a trip of more than a few days.

"So what about Dakota?" Caitlin asked. "What does she have to say?"

"I don't know. I'm heading there now."

"No one could have tipped her off. I mean, they might have seen Kenny, but that's unlikely. He's the best."

Sally had been in the business too long not to recognize trouble. "Something else must have happened—something that might have led to the meth house. So they torched it."

"But what? Her house was clean. You've been over it."

"I know."

Caitlin drew a swift breath of air. "The child. He was at that meth house last night with Dakota. Kenny said he was crying."

Something clicked in Sally's brain. That was it—the thought that first Caitlin and then Kenny had mentioned. The child. "Kids always cry."

"Not kids with neglectful parents. Not as much anyway. They know there's no use. I'm probably wrong, but make sure you check him. Please."

Sally swore under her breath. "I'm at her street now. I'll let you know."

A sense of urgency mushroomed in Sally's chest. In the years she'd known Caitlin, her hunches were as good as the proof most people offered. It was one thing they had in common—Sally also had good hunches. That was why she'd been so angry when Parker had disappeared. She couldn't understand how she'd been so wrong about him.

Maybe she hadn't been wrong.

Why had the meth house been torched? Sally would trust each of the officers there with her life; there was no leak. That meant another connection.

Under the blanket of snow, Dakota's run-down neighborhood looked better somehow, the unkempt lawns and refuse covered with white snow. The street wasn't busy. In fact, for a Friday night it was far too still.

Sally was racing through the snow the moment she pulled the car to a stop, her hand reaching to ring the bell several times in rapid succession. Nothing. She rang again. Finally, Dakota appeared. She looked exhausted or hung over, her blonde hair hanging straight and limp against her face.

"What do you want?" Her hand fluttered to eyes that were puffy from sleep. Or was it from tears? "Did you find

Madeline?" The question came as a slow afterthought, telling Sally that it hadn't been first on her mind.

"No. We may have some leads, though." Calling Caitlin's sudden decision to go on a trip wasn't exactly a lead, but it might be. "I'd like to take another look at her room."

"You've already been through it."

"It'll only take a minute."

There was a noticeable hesitation. "My son's asleep in there. He's not feeling well."

"Oh? What does he have?"

Dakota shrugged. "He threw up last night. Now he's just sleepy."

All of Sally's senses kicked into high gear. She noticed the deepening lines in Dakota's face, the eyes that seemed to be near panic, the way she kept glancing over her shoulder. Looking for someone. The boyfriend? He was here. Sally had seen his car outside, though there was no sign of the man at present. But the fear emanating from Dakota hadn't been caused solely by this supposedly friendly visit from the local police.

"Where is your son?" Sally took a step inside the house.

"You can't come in. Go away."

"Is someone here threatening you?" Sally asked softly. "I can help."

Dakota stared at her dully for a few seconds. "There's nothing wrong. I just want to you to get out of here so I can take care of my son!"

Sally met Jim's eyes. She gave the slightest shake of her head and pushed past Dakota.

"You can't do this!" Dakota screamed.

Sally strode down the hall, hand ready on her weapon, knowing Jim would be ready, too. She flung open the door to

306

the children's room. Lyn, the boyfriend, was kneeling by the twin bed where little Reese lay, his bald head close to the boy's chest. One of Reese's small hands was outstretched, hanging partially off the bed. Unmoving.

Lyn jerked to his feet. "What are you doing here?"

Sally drew her gun. "Step away from the child." If she was wrong, she could be severely reprimanded, maybe even lose her job, but she'd trusted her instincts far too long to begin questioning them now.

"He's fine!"

"He doesn't look fine." In fact, he was pale and barely breathing.

"He was just sick last night. We're going to wait a few hours and if he doesn't get better, we'll take him to the doctor."

Sally nodded at Jim to signal that he was to cover Lyn and Dakota. She holstered her own gun and knelt beside the bed. She felt for the child's pulse and found it at last, barely a flutter. *Dear Lord*, she prayed, *let him be okay.*

"Reese," she said, gently patting the child's face. "Reese?" No response. She looked back at Dakota, who was standing across the small room near the crib, her fingers laced tightly in the bars. "How long has he been like this?"

"He was like this when we woke up this morning."

Fury raged through Sally. "He's been like this all day? Why didn't you take him to the emergency room?" She pulled out her cell and dialed 911.

"I've sat by him all day!" Dakota came to the bed now, kneeling and taking her son's hand. "Please wake up, Reese. Please."

"Why didn't you take him in earlier?"

Dakota glanced at Lyn quickly and then away.

"Did he tell you not to? Why is that?"

"Don't tell 'em anything," Lyn shouted.

Dakota buried her face in her hands and shook her head.

"Get him out of here," Sally growled.

Jim grabbed Lyn's arm, but the heftier man shrugged him off. "I'm not leaving."

Jim pointed his gun at Lyn's chest. "Yes, you are. We'll wait for the ambulance outside." Lyn eyed the gun, as though calculating his chances. Sally stood up, her own gun back in her hand.

Suddenly Lyn dived for the door at a run. Jim was after him in an instant, and Sally knew she'd have to trust him to his job. She turned back to Dakota. "What happened? Did he do something to your son?" Her voice was remarkably calm.

Dakota shook her head and sobbed. "I was going to take him in, I promise. He's going to be okay. He's got to be."

"Sally? Are you here?"

Sally stiffened at the voice coming from the hallway. What was Caitlin doing here? "In the bedroom," she called.

Caitlin came in, her coat askew and her eyes anxious. "Is he okay?"

Sally shook her head.

"Oh, no." Caitlin went to the bed, kneeling next to Dakota, her eyes fixed on Reese's tiny, pale face. "I'm so sorry, Dakota. What happened?" Pause. "It was the drugs, wasn't it?" Her voice was sympathetic, not accusatory. Sally had seen Caitlin break witnesses on the stand with that tone, but tonight her sorrow was real.

Dakota's cries became louder. "Last night. He . . . drank some . . . of the water at the house," she sobbed. "The water for the meth."

Caitlin made a soft, despairing noise in her throat, her hand reaching out to stroke the child's face.

Sally tore her eyes from Caitlin, focusing back on Dakota. She wanted to strangle the woman. "You should have taken him in last night!"

"He cried and threw up. Then he went to sleep. Lyn said it was all out."

"That's what you wanted to believe. But you knew better—I can see that you did. Mothers are supposed to take care of their children. They aren't supposed to put them in danger. You stupid, stupid woman!" Without volition, Sally's hands came up to strike Dakota, but Caitlin's voice stopped her.

"The ambulance. It's here."

"You disgust me!" With that parting shot at Dakota, Sally went outside to tell the rescue workers what they were up against. She'd have to call the hospital, too. Maybe Reese could be saved.

More police officers had arrived at the scene, and Sally spotted Lyn in handcuffs. She'd let the officers deal with Dakota, too. If she didn't stay away from the woman, she might kill her with her bare hands. In Caitlin's car parked across the street, Amy was peering curiously out the window. The backseat was stuffed with luggage.

"Sally." Caitlin was at her side. "You couldn't have known."

"I did know." Hurt filled Sally's chest. "I knew Parker was telling the truth from the beginning. I *felt* it. That's why I asked you to help him. But I failed to find the proof we needed in time. I let both those kids down."

"I failed, too. But Madeline's alive because Parker didn't give up. Thank heaven."

Sally turned. "It's him you're going to see, isn't it?"

Caitlin didn't answer, but a soft smile came to her lips, accompanied by a blush that made her radiant. A woman in love. Did she know it herself?

"Tell him I'm sorry," Sally said.

"I hope it's not too late."

Sally gripped her shoulder. "Don't let it be. Let this all be worth something." She pushed at Caitlin. "Go get ready for your trip. You're going to Nevada, aren't you? I'll bet he's still there."

"He could be anywhere. But I'm hoping he's in Chicago."

CHAPTER

25

The plane was dark, and Caitlin tried futilely to read. Beside her, dressed in bright pink cords and a pink and orange sweater, Amy was snoring, her mouth open wide. Amy had been remarkably content during their time at the airport and on the plane. She'd watched planes take off, eaten everything offered to her by Caitlin or the flight attendants, slept when she needed to, and had taken up conversations with at least a dozen perfect strangers.

Caitlin, on the other hand, had been so nervous she hadn't been able to sleep at all, not the night before or on the plane. Would Parker be waiting at the airport? Or were these tickets his way of telling her thank you?

Or good-bye?

There was a bitter taste in her mouth as she wavered between a surety that he would be there and the certainty that he wouldn't. One moment she was feverish with hope and the next filled with despair at what she had lost. She understood now that Parker wasn't just any man. So what if he wasn't a high-powered, intellectual attorney? He was a smart and caring man, and hardworking to boot. Willing to do what he knew was right, despite the consequences.

Caitlin pictured the limp form of Madeline's little brother as she'd last seen him lying on Madeline's bed. He'd died shortly after making it to the hospital, and the knowledge was unbearable to Caitlin. If Madeline had been at the house that night, she might have also drunk the contaminated water. She might now be fighting for her life, instead of safe with her daddy.

"The saddest thing is," Sally had told her before her flight that morning, "the doctor said he would have lived if they'd taken him in right after he drank the water. Instead, they waited, and then when they realized they'd have to take him to the emergency room, they waited even longer so they could cover their butts by torching the house."

When she shut her eyes, Caitlin could see the still little figure. So tiny and helpless, his mother sobbing at his side. She loved him, of that Caitlin was certain, but not enough. Dakota had never loved anyone more than she loved herself.

But Madeline was safe! It always came down to that. Parker had been telling the truth all along. Of course if he wasn't waiting for her in Chicago, he might never know, or at least not for a long time. He wouldn't know that he could return home.

Then again, maybe even if he did know, he wouldn't want to come home.

Please, Caitlin prayed. *Please, come back to me.*

• • •

Parker knew the plane would be landing in less than an hour. Would Caitlin be on it? He had no way of knowing. Only after sending the tickets had he realized that he couldn't meet her openly at the airport as he'd planned. The risk to his daughter was simply too great. Yet he would be at the airport all the same.

Just a look, he promised himself. *To see if she actually came.* With his new black dress coat and dark sunglasses, she might walk right past him without noticing. Maybe he'd be able to tell somehow that she hadn't told Sally about the tickets, that she'd come only because she loved him.

The daydream fell apart every time at that point, because how could he know her that well after only five days? And he couldn't risk his daughter. Maybe he could follow Caitlin and contact her later during her stay. After he was certain. Maybe.

Regardless, he would be at that airport today. Waiting.

"Rosie is my best friend," Madeline said as he slipped her shirt over her head.

"Well, you be a good girl. Don't boss her around." He was leaving her with the neighbor for the morning because taking her to watch for Caitlin wasn't a good option.

He dragged a brush through her hair without finesse. "Ow," she said. "Give it to me. I can do it myself."

Minutes later they knocked on the neighbor's door and the mother answered. "Oh," she said, looking surprised. "I forgot you were coming. I'm sorry, but I have bad news. Rosie's been sick all night, throwing up everywhere. She's sleeping now, but she still has a fever. You'll have to play another day."

This was something Parker hadn't planned for. He'd under-played the importance of his appointment to both Madeline and Rosie's mother, so he couldn't exactly push now. Besides, he didn't want Madeline sick. "Thanks anyway," he said with a forced smile.

They went back to their apartment for Madeline's coat. "I'm

going with you?" Her sadness at not staying with her friend vanished instantly.

"Sure. I have to stop by a place for a few minutes, and then we'll go somewhere to eat."

She hugged him. "I love you, Daddy. When we go home, I'm going to tell Reese and Grandma all about Chicago."

Parker didn't have the heart to explain the full ramifications of their flight, but it did soothe him that she had barely mentioned Dakota, though she talked constantly about her grandmother and Reese.

Outside it was snowing. Not just snowing but snowing as though someone was dropping huge bucketfuls of snow directly on top of the city. Madeline giggled and made to step out into the snow, but he caught her arm and opened the umbrella. "No, sweetheart. You'll be the one throwing up next if you go out in that."

He could barely see through the windshield as he drove to the airport, following the directions he'd printed the day before at work. There was plenty of time left to make it to the airport, even in this snow. But why was he even going? Caitlin wouldn't be there. He knew she wouldn't . . . and yet how could she not? There was something between them, something that could last more than a dozen lifetimes. Did she even understand that the message was from him? For all he knew, she had many grateful clients who knew she wanted to go to Chicago. There was also the strong possibility that she was out with that pretty-boy attorney or had work that wouldn't allow her to leave town.

He raked a hand through his hair, studying the traffic as he guided his truck through the streets. The car in front of him slowed to a crawl, and soon he was almost at a standstill. "What's going on?" Parker asked aloud, craning his neck to see through the whiteness battering the windshield.

"Why are we stopped, Daddy?"

"Probably an accident. People drive too fast. Is your seat belt tight?"

She tugged on the belt crossing her booster seat. "It's tight."

Parker stared out into the white world, unable to believe his rotten luck. He wasn't going to make it. He wouldn't be at the airport to see if Caitlin still cared. Panic filled him. He studied the map and saw that they were about a mile from the airport. A piece of cake on foot in normal weather—and without Madeline. He waited twenty more precious minutes.

They were coming closer to the airport, but they might as well have been in another state. He definitely wasn't going to make it in time.

"Okay, let's walk." He eased the truck over to the side of the road. "You hold the umbrella," he said to Madeline. "I'll carry you on my shoulders."

Madeline giggled as he ran past the line of unmoving vehicles. The airport wasn't too far away now, but the snow was still coming down hard, and in a few minutes Parker was wet from the chest down. His feet were freezing. Cars were still backed up as far as he could see behind him, and ahead there was an accident involving a bus and a delivery van.

Snow pelted him as he ran past the accident and on to the airport. He let Madeline down outside the airport doors, and fortunately she was nearly dry. His watch said nearly noon, and the plane was to have arrived at eleven-forty. He shut his eyes a moment before opening the door. If the flight hadn't been early, she might still be at the airport, maybe collecting her luggage.

Or she could be long gone.

He checked the luggage carousels and then waited outside the security gates, looking at each passenger as they came from the gate area. No Caitlin. The probability of finding her was growing slimmer by the second.

"Daddy, can I get a drink?"

"Sure." He took her over to a machine and bought her an orange soda pop. She sat on the bench next to the machine, sipping contentedly.

"Why are we here?"

"I'm just looking for someone. It'll only take a few minutes." In fact, they could probably leave now. If Caitlin had been on the flight, she wasn't here any longer.

Someone passed by him, bumping into his arm. "Excuse me," said a tall woman with graying hair.

"No problem."

She nodded and turned back to her companion. "I'm not surprised the flight was delayed with all this snow."

Hope flooded him, and he searched the room for the huge screens that gave updated flight information. Why hadn't he thought of that before? That he hadn't said a lot about his state of mind. "Stay right here, Madeline. I'm just walking over to that TV there. I want you here where I can see you."

"'Kay." She took another sip of her drink, swinging her legs.

His soggy shoes creaked as he crossed the room and began comparing flight numbers to the one on the damp, crumpled paper in his pocket. The flight from Salt Lake City was delayed and only now arriving. He hadn't missed her! Returning to the bench with Madeline, he sat back and waited. They were partially obscured by the drink machine, but he had a clear enough view.

There! His heart nearly stopped beating. She was coming through the security gate, Amy behind, her large body looking ridiculous in her bright pink and orange clothes. Caitlin was loaded down with two carry-on bags and a huge rolling suitcase. Amy pulled an identical suitcase and carried a green jacket over her shoulder. Caitlin laughed and said something to Amy. She was more beautiful than he remembered. Her copper hair was freed from its usual clasp, curling around her face. Her eyes were bright, her freckled skin perfect.

He studied the other passengers also coming through the security gate. No Detective Crumb or other official-looking person. Had she really come alone?

After passing the gate, Caitlin stopped and scanned the large room slowly. Her tongue slowly wet her lips. Parker pulled his head back momentarily as she glanced his way, glad that Madeline was standing on the bench now, near the drink machine where she couldn't be seen.

Caitlin's bright smile faltered and died, as though turned off by a switch. She stood there for a minute more as though considering her options. Finally, she took a determined breath and reached for Amy's hand, the happiness on her face replaced with resolution. She turned and began walking away.

Was he going to let her go? If only he could be sure she hadn't told anyone.

"Madeline, stay here again," he said in a low voice. "Over here on the end where I can see you."

He stood and followed Caitlin.

• • •

He wasn't there.

Her disappointment was so all-encompassing that it took every ounce of pride in her to keep walking. Even when he learned that he was in the clear and could come home, it would make no difference to their relationship. It was over.

"We'll get a taxi to a hotel I read about on the Internet

yesterday," she told Amy brightly. "You'll love it there. It's really homey. At least it looked that way on the computer." She had addresses of her parents' friends to look up later, but for now, she desperately needed a hot bath and some sleep. Her hope must have been what had kept her going this long, because suddenly her exhaustion felt like an impossible weight.

"I'm hungry." Amy changed hands on her suitcase handle.

"They have wonderful food here. You're going to love it."

He wasn't here. She had been a fool to have hoped. Yet why did she *feel* him? Why was her heart reaching out and finding . . . something?

She stopped walking. Amy continued ahead several paces before she turned and looked curiously at Caitlin. "Why did you stop?"

Caitlin didn't answer. She released her suitcase, dropping one flight bag to her side and then the other. Slowly she turned.

He was standing behind her, about twenty-five feet away. He looked different. His hair was longer and his face more tanned—probably from his time in Nevada. She'd been there in the winter before, and some of the days had been sunny. He wore black dress pants and a long black coat instead of his usual jeans and bulky work coat. Dark glasses covered his eyes.

One thing hadn't changed. The connection between them instantly leapt to life—no, it had already burned with life. Now the link revived and strengthened as their eyes met. He took a step and then stopped, a question on his face. But she knew the answer. She ran to him, threw herself into his arms. He hugged her tightly. There was no need for words. He kissed her, his fingers tangling in her hair. For a long moment there was no one else in the huge room. People streamed past, miraculously parting around them.

Magic.

"Is there some reason you're sopping?" she asked, when she could finally bring herself to speak. She was wide awake now, her every nerve alive with his nearness.

He grinned. "There was a traffic jam. I jumped out of the truck and ran here."

"I see." Her eyes flicked to the huge windows where, sure enough, snow still fell at a steady rate. "Ever hear of an umbrella?"

"Madeline had—" He broke off and glanced away. She followed his gaze to an empty bench by a soda pop machine. She felt his body tense, his head jerking around, as he searched anxiously.

"Daddy, are you finished kissing? Amy's hungry, and we want to have a tea party."

Caitlin turned to see Madeline standing next to Amy, a wide smile covering her little face.

Parker stared at her for barely a second. "No. I am definitely not through kissing Caitlin. Amy, make sure Madeline doesn't run off." With that, he turned Caitlin's head and kissed her again. "I hope you came to stay," he said against her lips. "And that you didn't bring the police." This last was said only half jokingly.

She allowed herself another long kiss before replying. "No. To both questions."

"To both questions?" Hurt registered in his voice. "You won't stay?"

She took pity on him. "I've come to take you home."

"I can't. You know that. Please stay, Caity. It won't be as hard starting over as you might think. I've got good prospects here. We could have a family."

Her heart thundered in her chest. "Parker Hathaway, are

you proposing?" For a moment she wished she didn't have to tell him he was free from running, that she could agree to stay here with him for a few years—or forever—hiding away from the world.

"I'm doing more than proposing." The brown eyes staring into hers were serious. "I'm offering you my whole life, Caity. I love you. I know it's a sacrifice leaving everything behind, but I promise I'll make it up to you. I'm miserable without you."

His whole life—that's what he was offering. No small thing. She wanted to accept his gift, but first she had to tell him everything. "There's something you need to know. I was packing to come here when Sally found the proof we've been looking for."

She thought he'd ask about the proof, but instead he said, "You came even though you weren't sure I was telling the truth?"

"The proof was in here." She put her hand to her heart.

His eyes told her what that meant to him. "What did Sally find?"

Glancing at the girls to make sure they couldn't hear, she said quietly, "Dakota's in jail. Reese ended up drinking water contaminated with meth chemicals. If you hadn't taken Madeline away, there's no telling what might have happened."

"The boy?"

"He didn't make it." She winced at the pain in his face and at her own memory of that pale, still little body. "I'm so sorry. The good news is there's not a prosecutor anywhere who would try to make kidnapping charges stick now. You'll have to jump through a few hoops when you get home, but I'm confident you will be completely exonerated."

"How am I going to tell her?" He glanced over her shoulder

at Madeline. She was sitting on Amy's suitcase, showing Amy her umbrella.

"Maybe don't say anything for a while. Just love her. It'll be all right." Caitlin drew Parker's head down and kissed him again, wanting more than anything to take away his hurt. Though their mood had turned somber, the connection between them was as strong as ever.

Some time later he drew away long enough to say, "Might be better for Madeline—for all of us—to stay here for a few years. If it's still your dream. That's why I chose Chicago."

All at once her confusion about the future faded away. No need to choose between jobs in Utah when she had everything she wanted right here. "We'll stay, then. For now. But we'll have to go back to clear things up."

"Of course."

He kissed her again, and she could feel the warmth flowing between them, evoking the promise of their future together.

"I was so afraid you wouldn't come," he whispered in her ear.

"I was so afraid you wouldn't be waiting."

He made a noise in his throat. "As long as there's any chance you want me, Caity, I'll always be waiting. Always." He kissed her one last time before drawing away and putting his arm possessively around her. "Come on, girls. Let's go home."

Discussion Guide

1. When Parker first took Madeline from her mother's house, her younger brother, Reese, was also in the room. Given the outcome of the novel, was Parker's decision not to take the boy, either at that time or later in the story, a correct choice? Discuss how a split-second decision can change an entire future.

2. How did Parker's relationship with his father and brother influence the person he later becomes? What about his relationship with his mother? What major events in Parker's life caused the changes in his early lifestyle?

3. How do you think Parker's mother felt in wanting to protect and defend her son and granddaughter and yet not wanting to break the law? What do you think she should have done? Why?

4. Discuss Caitlin's mixed feelings about her sister. How has her choice to care for Amy affected her life?

5. Is Caitlin happy in her career? What do you think might make her happier?

6. Discuss the different men in Caitlin's life. What are their strengths and weaknesses? Do you think Wyman would have been a good choice for a relationship? What about Parker? Do you feel he is permanently reformed? Why or why not?

7. Did Caitlin make the right choice in passing along evidence to the police? What about her duty to her client? What about her duty to society? Do you think she should be disbarred for her actions? What about Mace Keeley? Should action be taken against him for his treatment of Caitlin?

8. Although Parker's actions in taking Madeline were against the law, do you feel the end justifies the means in this story? What mistakes do you feel Parker made? What did he do right? What parallels do you find between Parker's taking Madeline and Caitlin's choosing to pass information to the police about her client?

Author's Note

Several years ago, shock radiated throughout Utah when an infant was found dead after ingesting methamphetamines she had found in a plastic bag on the floor of her home. What made this tragic circumstance even more notable and horrific is that weeks earlier her father had forcibly taken her from her mother and transported the baby across state lines, hoping to protect her from her mother's substance abuse. Authorities found the little girl, placed her back with her mother, and sent the father to jail for assault and burglary. A little more than a week later the baby was dead, and the mother was charged with desecration of a corpse for moving the baby's body to cover up her own drug abuse. All charges against the father were eventually dropped.

Sadly, this is not the only story of a child becoming the victim of a parent's drug use. In Tulsa, a young boy grabbed a drink of what he thought was water but which was actually lye used in making meth. He survived, but his esophagus was burned away, and he will never be the same. Other children who have ingested similar chemicals were not so fortunate.

One mother, heavily doped up on drugs, accidentally rolled over and smothered her child as they napped together on the couch. A six-year-old boy showed law enforcement officers in detail how his daddy made drugs. In meth homes throughout the country, baby bottles share sinks and refrigerators with meth containers, and the drug is often made in the same kitchen where food is prepared. Poison is only inches away from dinner plates and glasses of milk. Law enforcement officers wear protective gear when dismantling these meth labs, but the children who live there are unprotected from the toxic fumes that saturate their bodies, clothing, and toys—if they are lucky to have such things. Often these houses have no food, no toilet paper, and no sheets on the beds. The children are completely neglected, and the houses are filthy. Many of these children show developmental delays, organ injuries from the fumes, heart problems, seizures, and violent behavior.

Chief Deputy C. Philip Byers from the Rutherford County Sheriff's Office in North Carolina writes: "In 2004, over 2700 children were found in methamphetamine labs seized by law enforcement officials nationwide. Children were present in 34 percent of the total lab seizures in the United States."[1]

Some of those children were injured or killed when the labs were seized. As shocking as that is, however, experts estimate that only a small proportion of meth labs are ever found.

States seem to be losing the battle against methamphetamine addiction. Child welfare, law enforcement, substance abuse, and treatment systems are overloaded. Some estimate that more than 8.3 million children in the United States live with a parent who has a substance abuse issue. Nearly 2 million child abuse cases each year are investigated, and half a million of those have enough evidence to act on. Some 200,000 children are removed from their homes each year.[2]

But what about the cases that aren't proven? What about the children who fall through the cracks but are still at risk? To what lengths might a noncustodial parent be compelled to go to protect a child from danger?

These were the questions I thought about as I began writing *Saving Madeline*. I wanted to show one man's dilemma in balancing his need to protect his daughter against his duty to obey the law, and to depict his struggle in an overloaded system where there are no second chances for the innocent victims.

Please keep in mind that though the idea for this novel was inspired by the numerous true stories I researched, the plot, characters, and resolution in *Saving Madeline* are completely fictional. No actual experiences or interviews of real people were used in the text itself.

Neither does this story in any way reflect the life of the sweet Madeline to whom I dedicated this book. Though challenged with muscular dystrophy, that Madeline has the great good fortune to have been born to loving and responsible parents.

Could a story such as that in *Saving Madeline* actually happen?

I believe so. The outcome for my make-believe Madeline is what I wish could happen for similar little children caught in real-life tragedies. At the same time, the story is a heartfelt dedication to all those children who, like Madeline's brother, Reese, have no one to fight for them and who do not survive.

NOTES

1. http://www.sheriffs.org/userfiles/file/CongressionalTestimony/
   Deputy_Philip_Myers_Testimony_on_Fight_Against_Meth.pdf
2. http://www.gu.org/documents/A0/Impact_Meth_Abuse_on_ Children_
   and_Families.pdf

About the Author

Rachel Ann Nunes (pronounced noon-esh) learned to read when she was four, beginning a lifelong fascination with the written word. She began writing in the seventh grade and is now the author of more than two dozen published books, including the popular *Ariana* series and the award-winning picture book *Daughter of a King*.

Rachel and her husband, TJ, have six children. She loves camping with her family, traveling, meeting new people, and, of course, writing. She writes Monday through Friday in her home office, often with a child on her lap, taking frequent breaks to build Lego towers, practice phonics, or jump on the trampoline with the kids.

Rachel loves hearing from her readers. You can write to her at Rachel@RachelAnnNunes.com. To enjoy her monthly newsletter or to sign up to hear about new releases, visit her Web site, www.RachelAnnNunes.com.

Movers and Shakers

African Dynamics

VOLUME 8

Movers and Shakers

Social Movements in Africa

Edited by

Stephen Ellis
Ineke van Kessel

BRILL

LEIDEN • BOSTON
2009

This book is printed on acid-free paper.

Library of Congress Cataloging-in-Publication Data

Movers and shakers : social movements in Africa / edited by Stephen Ellis, Ineke van Kessel.
   p. cm. — (African dynamics ; 8)
   Includes bibliographical references.
   ISBN 978-90-04-18013-0 (pbk. : alk. paper)
   1. Social movements—Africa—History—20th century. I. Ellis, Stephen, 1953-
II. Kessel, Ineke van.

   HM881.M674 2009
   303.48'40960904—dc22

                                                          2009033244

ISSN   1568-1777
ISBN   978 90 04 18013 0

PRINTED IN THE NETHERLANDS

Contents

Acknowledgements

We would like to thank all those who have helped in the production of this book. This includes not only the authors of the various chapters, but all those staff members of the Afrika Studie Centrum, Leiden, who helped in the organization of the workshop and conference where the first drafts of the chapters were presented. In particular, we would like to thank our colleagues who have helped with the work of editing and preparation of the text of this volume, and especially Ann Reeves, Kiky van Oostrum and Mieke Zwart. Finally, we are most grateful to the Koninklijke Nederlandse Akademie van Wetenschappen (KNAW, the Royal Dutch Academy of Sciences) for its financial contribution to this project.

Stephen Ellis
Ineke van Kessel
Leiden, July 2009

Introduction:
African social movements
or social movements in Africa?

Stephen Ellis & Ineke van Kessel

This volume is the outcome of a workshop and conference held in Leiden on 23-24 October 2008 and features the papers that were presented then, but were revised prior to publication. There were lively and highly focused discussions in the workshop on the first day of the proceedings and this introduction draws heavily on those debates and insights from all the participants.

It is appropriate to begin with an explanation of the thinking behind this project and to list some of the tentative conclusions that can be drawn. We began this venture with an open mind as to whether it concerned social movements as global phenomena that, in the present case, happen to be situated on the African continent or whether, on the other hand, we are dealing with social phenomena of a sort unique to Africa and which are therefore difficult to analyze in a comparative perspective. At the outset, we were unsure of the degree to which the theoretical work that has been done on social movements in general would be relevant to the study of African societies. We deliberately avoided beginning with a definition of a social movement drawn from the existing literature, which is largely based on studies of Europe, North America and Latin America, because that would risk excluding movements in Africa that might take a different form. We kept in mind the possibility that some social movements in Africa might be largely driven by outside stimuli in the form of inducements from aid donors. However, we also had to realize that if African movements are seen from the outset as *sui generis,* then not only does comparison with movements elsewhere become difficult, it also risks perpetuating the view that everything that occurs in Africa has its own special rationale, dictated by a context so radically different as to stand beyond global comparison. It would be better, we thought, first to assemble studies of at least some movements in Africa that could conceivably be described as social movements and only then to compare them with the existing literature.

To make this task possible, the first two chapters in this volume attempt a summary of the extensive literature that already exists on the subject of social movements. The first of these, by Jacquelien van Stekelenburg and Bert Klandermans, presents an overview of the development of social movement theory over several decades. They describe how early writers on the issue tended to view public protest as arising from impatience with more orthodox forms of interaction. When people took to the streets, this was stated or implied to be a sign of an irrational element inherent in mass action. Over time, this classic paradigm became increasingly unsatisfactory and was supplemented or replaced by analyses of the structure of social movements by writers who emphasized its political element. Social constructionist theories posed a series of questions about how individuals and groups perceive and interpret socio-political conditions, focusing on the cognitive, affective and ideational roots of contention. These theories tend to view social movements not only as a rational form of response but even as a necessary element of democracy. Many social movement theorists are themselves activists or former activists and they tend to emphasize the rational element in protest action. Some of the authors in the present volume have also played an activist role in the movement they describe, or in other social movements. Africa is quite familiar with the phenomenon of the scholar-activist, as is illustrated in the examples of Mahmood Mamdani, Jacques Delpechin and many others from all parts of the continent. In this respect at least, Africa fits quite well into the global landscape of social movements. Most recently, analysts have tended to observe the changing forms and goals of social movements in the light of globalization and the rise of information technology, which have created new possibilities for networking far beyond local neighbourhoods or even the national context.

A second theoretical chapter has been contributed by Adam Habib and Paul Opoku-Mensah and deals with the literature on contemporary social movements in South Africa and in Africa more generally, questioning how data from Africa relate to the debates that have emerged in the global academy. Habib notes that two assertions have been widely made in the literature on social movements: first, that the fulcrum of social struggles for a human development agenda has shifted from the arena of production to that of consumption, and second, that struggles concerning identity are replacing ones overtly oriented towards material issues, especially in post-industrial societies. Habib feels that a more nuanced interpretation is required, as assertions such as these are not fully satisfactory when applied to the evidence from Africa. It is true that social struggles, especially in South Africa, have expanded into the arena of consumption – perhaps unsurprisingly as South Africa, with Africa's largest economy by far, in some ways resembles the 'developed' countries of Europe and North America more closely than other parts of Africa do. However, not only have movements concerned with relations of production continued but they remain crucial to the sustainability of struggles concerning consumption. While identity movements and struggles are increasing, material issues are as relevant to these struggles as they were to earlier social movements. Habib argues that social movements are vital in many democratizing societies in providing the substantive uncertainty that is necessary to create accountability among political elites to their marginalized citizens, thereby advancing a more sustainable human-oriented development agenda. In effect, he maintains that social movements are vital for a functioning democracy, particularly in states with only one dominant party. But it does not necessarily follow that social movements themselves are inherently democratic.

After these general introductions to the literature, eight case studies are presented. These cover a wide – but not necessarily representative – range of social movements in Africa. They include the Islamic Courts Union in Somalia, Islamic social movements in southwest Nigeria, the legacy of liberation movements in South Africa, Catholic social movements in Malawi, the anti-slavery movement in Mauritania, the global campaign against blood diamonds, and women's movements in Liberia. There are also the so-called 'campus cults' in Nigeria that have emerged from the efforts by military governments to disrupt the student movement. These campus cults can thus be considered, quite literally, as an 'anti-social' movement.

We began this project, then, unwilling to apply a definition of social movements that is drawn from a literature strongly influenced by North Atlantic and Latin American data, and yet wanting to study a range of movements in Africa to see whether it was possible to discern any common threads among them. We decided that it was best to adopt a pragmatic approach that, at least at the start, was open-minded. In other words, we would bear in mind some of the provisional conclusions drawn from the literature on social movements and make use of the instruments of social movement theory, while remaining open to the possibility that not all aspects of the relevant African phenomena would necessarily fit into these theories.

Clearly certain questions of a universal nature can be asked about movements all over the world, and some crucial questions can usefully be posed regardless of geographical setting. For a long time, scholars have explored questions such as why people rebel or, perhaps more importantly, why they do not rebel.

In view of the diversity of the movements discussed in this volume, we asked our contributors to address the following issues:

- What are the historical origins of the social movement being analyzed?
- How does it mobilize support? Who are the people likely to participate?
- In what ways does the social movement under scrutiny frame its message?
- How does it relate to other social movements?
- Is it still in existence? Has it ceased to exist? If so, how and why?

In the discussions that ensued during the workshop and conference in Leiden, participants heartily endorsed our approach of not starting with an orthodox theory and subsequently examining the extent to which African cases fitted it. It became apparent that many movements in Africa that could be called social movements inasmuch as they are rooted in social networks rather than in state policy and insofar as they are concerned with broad social issues, are of a rather hybrid nature when considered with reference to conventional social-science categories. They often display social, political and religious characteristics that overlap one another.

The international context

It became clear at an early stage in the discussion among the authors repre- sented in this volume that, more than elsewhere, the international context in which social movements operate is of considerable significance. African states in general are particularly vulnerable to external pressures of various sorts in Africa. When considering the flow of different sorts of resources – financial, moral and political – in the constitution of African social movements, we should take care not to limit our vision to exchanges between Africa and the West. The Middle East, India, China and other Asian powers are fast becoming more im- portant in this regard. By the same token, South Africa is assuming a significant role by offering funds and moral leadership to the rest of the continent, some- times providing an entry point to Africa for international networks or organiza- tions seeking to expand their activities.

The international human-rights discourse has provided inspiration and moral legitimation for a range of causes, including the campaign against slavery in Mauritania and that against blood diamonds in Sierra Leone. Furthermore, social movements in Africa frequently have a pan-African dimension. Thus, the president of SOS Esclaves in Mauritania drew inspiration from attending a meeting in Switzerland as well as from the World Conference against Racism, Racial Discrimination, Xenophobia and Related Intolerance that was held in Durban in 2001, while relying heavily on his alliance with an anti-slavery movement in Niger. Similarly, the campaign against blood diamonds in Sierra Leone served as a model for comparable movements in Angola and the Demo- cratic Republic of Congo (DRC). Activists in Uganda campaigning against a proposed change in the constitution to allow yet another term for President

Museveni sought advice from activists who had conducted a successful campaign in Malawi against a third term for their country's president. In South Africa, the international dimension was vital to the struggle against apartheid. International alliances gave access to weapons, money and ideas ranging from Marxism-Leninism to a liberal discourse on human rights, gender rights and gay rights. And the African-American connection in the United States was crucial in organizing sanctions.

This international connection to social activism in Africa is not only ideological in nature but also contains an important financial and logistical aspect. Many social movements in Africa are dependent on funding from external donors. However, there are also exceptions, as Ben Soares shows in his study of the NASFAT movement in Nigeria. Foreign funds may come either directly or through locally based non-governmental organizations (NGOs). Although donor dependency obviously has an effect on the form assumed by social movements in Africa, it would be a fundamental mistake to see these movements as no more than an extension of Western NGOs. Even when Africans are in receipt of funds, they are not passive, and relations with donors do not consist solely of a one-way flow of resources. Organic intellectuals in Africa have learned how to play the system to their own advantage, in a local variation of the well-known pattern of interaction between the local and the global spheres. If we take a longer-term historical perspective on this point, we can appreciate that an initial pattern of ideas flowing into Africa can become a reverse current in a later phase. A good example is the Christian missionary movement in Africa, which for many years was indeed one-way traffic, but in recent decades African Christian churches have reversed the flow by reaching out to other parts of the world. It is interesting to note that Europe, the continent that historically initiated the modern Christian evangelization of Africa, is now seen by many African Christians as a godless continent in need of spiritual reawakening.

Even when money and other resources are clearly flowing from the rich world to Africa, there may still be reciprocal elements to the relationship. In solidarity networks, the providers of money may need approval bestowed by their African counterparts. Without this blessing, the providers lack credibility and legitimacy. During the struggle against apartheid, many anti-apartheid movements in the West allowed the African National Congress (ANC) to set the agenda and define priorities. The ANC's blessing was itself a precious resource, as illustrated by the intricate distinctions assumed by the ANC's leadership in exile, which made subtle distinctions in addressing its Dutch allies: members of the Anti-Apartheids Beweging Nederland (AABN) were classed as 'comrades', while the activists of the Komitee Zuidelijk Afrika (KZA) were considered merely as 'friends'.[1] Similarly, in the Sierra Leonean case described in this volume, Canadian activists, including some senior politicians, were legitimized in their campaign against blood diamonds by the support of African NGOs.

In a relationship where an external donor brings money and other resources and an African movement may bestow legitimacy, it is common practice to present different facets of a movement to different partners in different settings. Thus, the ANC in exile was wont to use a human-rights discourse in Western capitals, while using the vocabulary of anti-imperialism in conversations with its socialist allies. Fundraisers for the United Democratic Front (UDF) became particularly agile at playing the donors, using a human-rights discourse to finance a struggle that increasingly took on socially radical features in South Africa itself. Funds for the UDF-aligned media were sought by appeals to the universal principle of press freedom, while media activists inside South Africa saw their social-movement media as a weapon of political struggle, and had little patience with liberal notions of plurality. It is instructive to read Ineke van Kessel's chapter on how former activists now consider their activities of twenty years ago. But then again, the profile designed by the leadership of a movement may differ radically from the understanding of the same movement at grassroots level. In the case of the campaign against blood diamonds, which enjoyed great success at the beginning of this century, the international profile of the campaign organization closely resembled the standard format of Western NGO campaigns, but on the ground in Sierra Leone it functioned as part of local anti-war movements, as Lansana Gberie explains in his contribution in this volume.

The particular importance of the external dimension to African social movements can be placed within the context of a much wider set of relationships that could be termed 'extraversion'.[2] Jean-François Bayart has demonstrated that the accumulation of political power and social prestige in many parts of Africa has, sometimes over a period of centuries, been dependent on access to external resources. The latter have included money and imported consumer goods, but also less tangible benefits. In return, African entrepreneurs have supplied their foreign interlocutors with other assets. Until the twentieth century this notoriously included slaves but it could also include access to mineral resources or other commodities required by international traders. In the industrial age, Africa has itself not been a significant producer of manufactured goods. The import of capital and goods from outside has been balanced by the provision of other services including political support required by donor countries for diplomatic pur-

---

[1]   Sietse Bosgra, 'From Jan van Riebeeck to solidarity with the struggle: The Netherlands, South Africa and Apartheid', in SADET (South African Democracy Trust), *The Road to Democracy in South Africa*, 3, part I, p. 556.

[2]   Jean-François Bayart, 'Africa in the world: A history of extraversion', *African Affairs*, 99, 395 (2000), pp. 217-267.

poses, and various forms of moral legitimation. This form of exchange has historically taken many different forms from the age of mercantilism through to the age of the Millennium Development Goals, but a notable element of dependency has been the main characteristic of the relationship. This was seen many decades ago and incorporated into a formal theory, first elaborated by scholars of Latin America and subsequently adopted by Africanists, that was very influential in the last few decades of the twentieth century.[3] Dependency theory, closely associated with Marxist scholarship, postulated that a core group of developed countries had historically used their power to construct a world system in which peripheral territories were kept in a permanent state of dependency, were needed for their raw materials and other assets but were prevented from developing the degree of industrialization or economic sophistication that would enable them to break out of their peripheral status. Dependency theory was largely superseded in Western academies of learning in the 1980s[4] but it has remained influential among African intellectuals.

As Bayart hints,[5] many aspects of development theory actually remain more relevant and cogent than may appear at first sight, provided it is recognized that Africa's dependency is the historical consequence of action by various parties. It has not simply been imposed on Africa but has been historically formed by complex interactions. Dependency is a political resource that has been of considerable benefit to some of those Africans who have contributed to its elaboration. It is helpful to consider the relationship between African social movements and external funders in this regard. It is not just the imposition of a political project by the rich but an interactive relationship that has complex moral, political and financial elements. As Veronika Fuest points out in her study of the highly dynamic Liberian women's movement, which played an important role in bringing peace to that troubled country and whose success was crowned by the election of Africa's first elected female head of state to the applause of much of the world, it is also a movement that has been dominated by women from some of the country's elite. Families that have made their fortune over generations from their success in situating themselves at the juncture of Liberian society and its external links, most notably with the US, may in a sociological sense be carrying on a family tradition more than they are articulating a 'new' social movement.

---

3   See notably Walter Rodney, *How Europe Underdeveloped Africa* (Bogle-L'Ouverture Publications, London, 1972).
4   Cf. Colin Leys, *The Rise and Fall of Development Theory* (James Currey, Oxford, 1996).
5   Bayart, 'Africa in the world', pp. 219-220.

Diasporas

Related but distinct is the relationship between social movements in Africa and African diaspora communities in the rest of the world. In recent decades, the number of Africans living permanently or semi-permanently outside their continent of origin has increased enormously. African communities are now a permanent feature in many parts of Europe, North America and the Middle East, and increasingly in Asia as well. Many diaspora communities retain a close interest in their countries of origin, sending remittances home for the upkeep of their families, making trips home whenever possible to supervise the construction of a house, and often contributing money to help finance the building of churches or mosques. Many people living abroad naturally retain a close interest in news from home, discussing matters with friends, perhaps reading the press online and keeping in touch by phone.

Contacts with people living in the diaspora can have an important effect on social movements in Africa itself, and indeed this is one of the most prominent elements of numerous African social movements. Yet in our survey of the theoretical literature on social movements and in the expert summaries contained in the first two chapters of this book, we find little or nothing about the role of diaspora communities in the dynamics of social movements. Similarly, political scientists have generally not devoted much attention to the notion of diaspora states such as Eritrea and Somalia, societies that are kept afloat largely by migrant remittances and where even the state may be heavily reliant on funding or other contributions from the diaspora. The latter is a source not only of money but may also provide remittances of a social and moral nature. From Islamic clerics to Marxist students and from gender activists to campaigns for global justice, African diaspora communities play a vital role in the flow of ideas. Decades ago, when diaspora communities were less numerous, the flow of ideas was on a relatively small scale but with the advent of the Internet, fax and cell phones it has developed the potential to become an instant tidal wave. The potential for global mobilization has become greater than ever before. The types of people who live in diaspora communities may vary from one context to another, making it important to identify the social profiles of people who move out of the country as well as where they move to. As Boniface Dulani notes, it tends to be critics of the regime in place who leave a country. This might not be for political reasons in the first instance but residence abroad may cause them to become more critical of their home government. Moreover, diasporas are to be found not only in the rich world but also in Africa itself. In the case of Malawi, many exiles in the time of Life President Dr Hastings Kamuzu Banda went to live in Zambia and Tanzania, from where they could play an active part in the 1990s democratization campaign that eventually succeeded in removing him from office. But, as Dulani points out, actions by exiles can only be effective if there is also an internal challenge to the regime.

The relationship between internal and external components of African social movements can draw on many other examples. Thus, the ANC mission-in-exile for three decades conducted both armed insurgency and a diplomatic campaign against apartheid but its activities only became really effective in the 1980s when the movement's exiled leadership was able to link up with internal movements, notably the rapidly growing trade-union movement and the United Democratic Front. Another example is provided in this volume by Lansana Gberie, who describes the role played by the Liberian and the Sierra Leonean diasporas in the blood-diamonds campaign, which was also taken up as a foreign-policy instrument by countries in Europe and North America. Conversely, in the case of Mauritania's anti-slavery movement, Ould Zekeria attaches little importance to the Mauritanian diaspora, pointing out that Mauritanians abroad tend to be overwhelmingly from families of the country's slave-owning elite rather than descendants of slaves or ex-slave families. Moreover, most of the Mauritanian diaspora is located in the Arab world where anti-slavery agitation is little known. In fact, Mauritania's slave-owners use Islam as a discourse to legitimate practices of slavery. This, too, strengthens the argument not only for considering the role of diaspora populations in Africa's social movements but also for appreciating the social nature of a particular diaspora population. There are very few Mauritanian Arabic speakers in Europe and North America. The non-Arabic-speaking diaspora in those areas is larger, however, and has a significant impact on the internal politics of racism and ethnic conflict, while keeping slavery alive as an issue in the foreign media.

State and non-state

A further specificity of social movements in Africa is that they often exist in countries where the state is much weaker than it is in Europe or North America, or where it barely even exists at all in the sense of hosting a bureaucracy that is able to implement synchronized activity in fields such as policing, justice or other functions that would normally be regarded as essential to any state. The most extreme example in Africa today is Somalia, and Jon Abbink's chapter on the Islamic Courts Union in Somalia raises the interesting question of whether it is actually permissible to speak of social movements in the effective absence of a state. So much of the literature produced on the basis of case studies from other continents implies, at the very least, that social movements are in some sense the natural adversary of the state since they frequently formulate demands for state action or, alternatively, protest against such action. By the same token, social movements are often considered to articulate a vision of an alternative social order, realistic or otherwise. But here again, we can find examples in Africa of social movements that develop a pragmatic partnership with the state or that identify other adversaries. An example is the Treatment Action Campaign (TAC) in South Africa, one of that country's most effective civil-society coalitions since the end of the apartheid era, that initially targeted the pharmaceutical industry in its efforts to provide access to generic anti-retroviral drugs for HIV/AIDS patients. Only in a later phase did the South African government become the TAC's main opponent, as the activist movement campaigned to make anti-retrovirals widely available to people living with AIDS. Ultimately, the TAC won its most significant battle in the courtroom, an organ of the state itself, even though it took years before the government effectively implemented the court's verdict. Recourse to the courts is a route sometimes taken by environmental movements and gender activists but also by movements seeking broader goals, such as the UDF in South Africa. For labour movements in Africa and elsewhere, capital is usually the primary opponent but they may eventually direct their campaigns at the state with demands to initiate or enforce legislation on labour conditions such as a minimum wage, safety standards and/or social benefits.

Another instrument associated with states but that can be mobilized by social movements to advance their cause is diplomacy. Of the cases analyzed in this volume, the one that relied on this technique most heavily was the campaign against blood diamonds that was primarily initiated by a Canadian NGO with an African connection and supported by the Canadian government. Thereafter, the blood-diamonds campaign came to receive the support of other governments and even the United Nations, which applied legal sanctions on diamonds emanating from some war zones. At first sight, one might suppose that the blood-diamonds campaign, which was remarkably successful in pricking the conscience of consumers in the rich world and initiating international action, was actually non-African in almost everything but its effects. However as Lansana Gberie shows, the campaign was supported by local activists in Sierra Leone who were able to use this powerful international campaign to further their own agendas. It is one of many examples of where social activists in an African country are able to leverage their influence by recourse to various forms of state action, in this case overwhelming on the part of states external to the region.

From Nouakchott to Johannesburg, shaming a government can be quite an effective tactic in realizing social goals. The Mauritanian anti-slavery group SOS Esclaves has used this strategy to particularly good effect, and each time Mauritania is exposed as one of the world's last outposts of slavery, its government feels humiliated. Since slavery has already been legally abolished in Mauritania, the government often simply resorts to the politics of denial.

There is an embedded religious element associated with many social movements in Africa. In North America, Europe and other locations where social movements have been extensively studied, churches or other religious groups, considering themselves to have a special moral role as guardians of society's ethics, may initiate a social campaign, for example in opposition to abortion in the US, that employs many of the classic tactics of social movements in general. In the case of the anti-abortion movement, this is largely aimed at overturning a Supreme Court ruling on the legality of abortion. In other instances, a social movement with a broad social base may enlist particular support from churches or other religious groups if they perceive it to have a particularly moral aspect, such as the Campaign for Nuclear Disarmament in the UK. In an earlier period, religion was central to the campaign to abolish the slave trade founded in Britain in the eighteenth century, and this is often seen as the first modern social movement. In the US, religious institutions contributed powerfully to the US civil-rights movement that had such an enormous effect not only on US politics and society but also on the way social movements were perceived by academic writers. In Africa however, entire social movements may appear to be preoccupied with religious issues to the apparent exclusion of more conventional forms of social action. A highly controversial case is the student Pentecostal movement in Nigeria, which can be viewed simply as a religious movement operating outside the purview of the state or of political demands but is more persuasively seen as a movement for the renewal of the social contract binding society and state that takes a distinctive form.[6] The 'campus cults' described in Stephen Ellis's chapter can be seen as youth gangs with innocuous origins as student clubs that, over two or three decades, were manipulated by Nigerian military governments to break the power of the country's student movement, which was so feared by the military on account of its potential for mobilizing force. What is of particular interest in this regard is that the Pentecostal movement that emerged on Nigerian campuses in the 1970s was also vying for the allegiance of students, and identified the campus gangs not merely as anti-social elements but as Satanic, implying a very particular theological character. This attitude is best understood not merely as a reaction to the violent nature of Nigeria's campus cults but as a reflection of a long history of initiation societies in which social power is deemed to be derived from contact with the invisible world.

Much of the academic literature on religious movements in Africa bases itself on a materialist analysis. It departs from the supposition that religious ideas and practices do not have any substance in and of themselves, viewing them as clues to the nature of the forces that truly shape society, assumed by

---

[6]   Cf. Ruth A. Marshall, *Political Spiritualities: The explosion of Pentecostalism in Nigeria* (Chicago University Press, Chicago and London, 2009).

many social scientists and historians to be those related to physical resources and material reality. However, if we think of religion in terms of spiritual power, and religious practice as access to that power,[7] its political dimensions become fully apparent. The NASFAT movement in southwestern Nigeria does not articulate any demands that might be considered political by reference to conventional state politics. However in a Nigerian context where religion is generally considered in terms of spiritual power and where state politics are notoriously empty of moral content, a religious movement acquires a political connotation that it might not have in another context. This is even more evident in the case of the Islamic Courts Union in Somalia presented by Jon Abbink. In Somalia, where a functioning state barely exists, such a religious movement assumes a very obvious political role.

For the rest, social movements in Africa can and do make use of the gamut of methods that are commonly associated with social movements the world over. These include demonstrations, the use of the mass media to broadcast a message to a wider audience and tactics of civil disobedience designed to attract public attention and frustrate the state with a view to causing it to pay attention to activists' demands.

Framing

One of the most interesting aspects of social movements is the issue of their 'framing' or, in other words, the general context in which any given action or repertoire of actions is presented or interpreted. In many of the best-known cases, a relatively simple and localized set of activities may be presented by skilled leaders as something much larger. An example is when the sabotage of an oil pipeline in southern Nigeria, perhaps even by a group that is situated half-way between a social group and a money-making venture, is presented as an attack on the collaboration between oil companies and the Nigerian state. Nor is it only local leaders who sometimes present their movements in these broad terms. As research on social movements is currently fashionable in the acada-mic world, researchers are apt to spot social movements in every corner of the world.

The point of this last remark is not to suggest that there were no social movements before social scientists arrived to describe and analyze them in terms of a sophisticated theory. Similar movements surely existed prior to this but were labelled differently. This seems to be a particularly important point with regard to Africa where a great deal of writing in both academic journals and the press has been based on the supposition that societies steeped in tradi-

---

[7]   Argued in Stephen Ellis & Gerrie ter Haar, *Worlds of Power: Religious thought and political practice in Africa* (C. Hurst & Co., London, 2004).

tion have been making their way into the modern world. It is quite easy to find examples of many movements intent on dealing with matters of widespread concern within a given society or community but that have been classified as anti-witchcraft movements or messianic movements or otherwise relegated to various categories of traditionalism. In retrospect, one may also wonder whether the mass mobilization of societies in the final years of colonial rule, which in most of Africa was in the 1950s, that was generally analyzed by historians and political scientists in terms of nationalist movements may not also be usefully seen as an example of social movements. Our purpose in saying this is not to argue that the people who demonstrated in favour of independence fifty years ago were not real nationalists but to argue that a recurring theme in African history is the mobilization of significant numbers of people around issues that preoccupy or interest them. These are socially rooted and often have a religious aspect but may also be articulated by leaders in terms of precise political demands. The form that the latter take is strongly influenced by the nature of the state in any particular case. In the heyday of nationalism, it made sense to 'frame' social struggles in the national context, just as in the struggle against apartheid it made sense to do the same with concerns about rent increases and electricity supply problems, presenting them as secondary consequences of the core problem. When a state does not effectively exist, as in Somalia today, struggles for social issues will be presented differently.

This point of view finds an echo in some of the existing literature on social movements in Africa. In his critique of the state-centrist and society-centrist perspectives prevailing among Africanists in the West, Mahmood Mamdani questions the universalist pretensions of a civil-society-governed perspective. He wonders whether the civil-society discourse is no more than a restatement of an earlier perspective, that of modernization theory, with its notion of the 'traditional' as the problem and the 'modern' as its salvation. In his view, the concept of civil society allows almost no room for the 'traditional'. The same might be said about social movement theory. Ifi Amadiume, one of the contributors to the volume on social movements edited by Mamdani and Ernest Wamba-dia-Wamba,[8] argues that the idea that social movements are seeking social or political change is too limited. She proposes instead an example of anti-power movements that simply seek to defend and maintain their own autonomy, and identifies this trait as the central characteristic of indigenous women's movements in Africa. These movements, she argues, may be considered

---

[8]   Mahmood Mamdani & Ernest Wamba-dia-Wamba (eds), *African Studies in Social Movements and Democracy* (Codesria, Dakar, 1995).

'traditional', but they are not 'pre-modern'.[9] Another relevant example mentioned in the same volume is the case of labour unions in Zimbabwe. These, it is argued, grew out of burial societies formed by workers and small traders or entrepreneurs. In the Eurocentric perspective on labour history, this type of community organization is situated on the lower levels of an evolutionary scale that culminates in full-blown class-conscious labour unions as the most mature stage. Such a perspective blinds us to the real dynamics of African labour movements and of a repertoire of protest and resistance that is much broader and more diverse than strikes and boycotts alone.[10]

We consider this a valid perspective and the absence of case studies of 'traditional' movements in this volume does not imply that we see social movements as an exclusively modern phenomenon. While we have hardly explored the realm of the 'traditional', other perhaps than in passing in the case of the Nigerian 'campus cults' that bear such a close resemblance to traditional initiation societies, we have attempted to situate the study of social movements in Africa in the broader context of social movement theory.

Chronology: Generations of social movements?

By the 1990s, it had become received wisdom in social movement theory that an earlier generation of social movements had been succeeded by a generation of so-called 'new social movements'. Thus, the first edition of the authoritative book by Donatella della Porta and Mario Diani[11] strongly endorsed the paradigm of 'new social movements', that is movements that had developed since the late 1960s relating to issues such as women's rights, gender relations, environmental protection, ethnicity and migration, peace and international solidarity. These new movements were perceived as having a distinctly middle-class basis. Sporting the label 'new', the movements were clearly differentiated from the models of working-class or nationalist collective action that had historically preceded them. However, in the second edition of their book, which was published in 2006, these authors question the neat transition from working-class to middle-class activism that they had earlier espoused. The reason for their doubts was the sustained challenge mounted by broad coalitions of very heterogeneous actors against neoliberal globalization. The 'Battle of Seattle', when

---

[9] Ifi Amadiume, 'Gender, political systems and social movements: A West African experience', in: Mamdani & Wamba-dia-Wamba (eds), *African Studies in Social Movements*, pp. 35-68.

[10] Introduction to Mamdani & Wamba-dia-Wamba, *African Studies in Social Movements*, p. 12.

[11] Donatella della Porta & Mario Diani, *Social Movements: An introduction* (Blackwell, Oxford, 1999).

large numbers of demonstrators gathered to protest during a World Trade Organization ministerial conference in 1999, was seen as the beginning of a new phase. It showed the ability of demonstrators from all over the world and a great variety of backgrounds to express their views in a context where neo-liberalism was no longer regarded as the only viable path to development but was highly contested. The global financial crisis that began unfolding in 2008 has served to further undermine the dogmas of the so-called Washington Consensus, giving new impetus to campaigns for sustainable development and global justice as well as new legitimacy to local struggles against privatization and commercialization. In the preface to their 2006 edition, Della Porta and Diani remark that there are surely continuities between the generation of 'new social movements' and the contemporary wave of global justice campaigns. However in addition to continuities, they also perceive new patterns of collective action that are significantly different from the familiar characteristics of largely middle-class-based movements. Working-class action, they observe, seems to be back with a vengeance.

This shift in paradigm helps to narrow the gap between social movement theory and the African experience. Movements in Africa never did fit into the sketch of a neat chronological succession from working-class to middle-class activism or, in Habib's phrase, from the arena of production to the arena of consumption. Labour struggles in Africa have not come 'back with a vengeance', as they have always been an integral part of a wide range of social movements, even if the study of working-class action became less fashionable in the era when so many academic researchers were preoccupied with postmodernity. Recent examples include Zimbabwe, where the trade-union movement has been instrumental in building the opposition coalition assembled under the umbrella of the Movement for Democratic Change. In South Africa, the labour movement constituted a vital part of a broader anti-apartheid coalition. Even the struggle against hereditary slave labour is not over in Africa, as Zekeria Ould Ahmed Salem's chapter on SOS Esclaves in Mauritania shows.

At the end of this exercise, we are left with the impression that social movements abound in Africa and that they inevitably adopt particular features as a result of the social and political context in which they operate. When a significant part of a country's population lives abroad, the diaspora may take on an important role in framing debates or interpreting them for the outside world. Religious debates that might sometimes appear almost other-worldly can assume a distinct social and even political colour in a situation where the state itself is seen as being morally void, or is hardly present at all. Traditional and new forms may be inextricably mixed. If this gives food for thought for theoreticians of social movements, then this volume has served a dual purpose:

documenting a few examples from the great diversity of social movements in Africa as well as contributing to more inclusive social movement theories.

Social movement theory:
Past, present and prospects

Jacquelien van Stekelenburg & Bert Klandermans

When and why do people protest? And who is likely to parti-cipate in public protests? Around 1900, influential sociologists regarded all street protest as deviant behaviour. The classic paradigms held that (relative) deprivation, shared grievances and generalized beliefs were determinants of protest. The early scholars of contentious politics depicted protest as the politics of the impatient, maintaining that protest had an irrational element to it. As dissatisfaction with these classic paradigms grew, new ones emerged: structural paradigms such as re-source mobilization and political process. While resource mobilization theory focuses on organization as a resource, political process theory emphasizes the political element of protest. Simultaneous with the rise of the structural paradigms was the emergence of social-constructivistic paradigms that concentrate on how individuals and groups perceive and interpret socio-political conditions. They focus on the role of cognitive, affective and ideational roots of contention and are broadly organized around three concepts: framing, identity and emotions. This chapter discusses these concepts as well as the social-psychology approach to social movements. The socio-political context of contentious politics is changing due to processes such as globalization and liberalization, and it is argued that these changes influence the rise and fall of social movements and their collective actions. Most social movement scholars assume that mutual integration of the structural and constructivistic paradigms can yield satisfactory explanations.

Social movements and collective action

The reason why people protest has occupied social scientists for a long time. The French psychologist Le Bon, a founding father of collective action studies, regarded all street protest as a form of deviant behaviour and developed his theory on crowds during a period of great social unrest in France in the 1890s. He believed that the destruction of religious, political and social beliefs in combination with the creation of new conditions of existence and thought as a result of the modern scientific and industrial discoveries of the time were the basis for a process of transformation of mankind's thought. Ideas from the past, although half shattered, were still very powerful he believed, while the ideas that were to replace them were in a process of formation. The consequence, in his analysis, was a period of transition and anarchy. Le Bon's ideas were reflected in classic breakdown theories that regarded participation in collective action as an unconventional, irrational type of behaviour.[1] The classic paradigm held that (relative) deprivation, shared grievances and generalized beliefs were determinants of participation. In fact, early students of the subject depicted contentious politics as the politics of the impatient and maintained that protest had an irrational element to it.[2]

Times changed and so did both contentious politics and theoretical approaches to contentious politics. The late 1960s saw a huge growth in social movement activity: the student movement, the civil-rights movement, the peace movement, the women's movement and the environmental movement all flourished. Interpretations of major forms of collective action changed from being viewed as spontaneous 'irrational' outbursts to movement activities with concrete goals, articulated general values and interests, and rational calculations of strategies. Breakdown theories clearly fell short as explanations of this proliferation of social movement activity, all the more so because it seemed to be preceded by *growing* rather than *declining* welfare. This, combined with changing forms of collective action, required new theoretical approaches, and several developed in the 1970s.

These new theoretical approaches can be categorized as structural and social constructivistic paradigms. Resource mobilization and political process are examples of structural approaches. While resource mobilization places an emphasis on organizational aspects and resources, the political process approach emphasizes the political aspects of collective action. The social constructivistic perspective, on the other hand, concentrates on how individuals and groups perceive and interpret these conditions and focuses on the role of the cognitive,

---

[1]   B. Klandermans, *The Social Psychology of Protest* (Blackwell Publishers, Oxford 1997).

[2]   N.J. Smelser, *Theory of Collective Behavior* (The Free Press, London, 1962).

affective and ideational roots of contention. It is broadly organized around three concepts: framing, identity and emotions (culture is also referred to but is not elaborated on in this chapter). These terms are also key concepts in social-psychology approaches to protest. Social psychologists maintain that people live in a perceived world and respond to the world as they observe and interpret it. To understand why people protest, it is necessary to know how they see and interpret their world, and social psychology focuses on subjective variables. Social-psychology approaches are, therefore, prototypical to social constructivistic approaches.

Obviously, the past and the present of social movement theory reveal different paradigms stressing various aspects of social movements and the actions they stage. They provide different answers to questions about why people protest, who protests and the forms of protest that protesters are involved in. Table 1 provides an overview of the answers provided to these questions by the different approaches to social movements.

Since the 1990s the context of contentious politics has changed significantly. Inseparably intertwined processes such as globalization, the development of the network society and the information society have given the world a new look. Networks are becoming the prime mode of organization, with formal networks embodied by organizations giving way to less formal networks rooted in the personal life world of individuals and to more diffuse group belongings.[3] Moreover, the rise of new communication technologies (the Internet, email, cell phones) is intensifying change and its pace.

Fundamental changes in society can affect contentious politics. After all, the spread of information and networks are essential elements of mobilization and one assumes that such fundamental changes are having a profound impact on the dynamics of contention. Indeed, scholars of social movements argue that recent social and cultural changes have lead to a 'normalization of protest'[4] and have created a social movement society.[5] This has posed new challenges to social movement theory. Are dynamics of contentious politics? In the final section of this chapter we will elaborate on what we see as the prospects of social movement theory and relate them to developments on the African continent. This is a precarious undertaking, especially considering the rapid pace of change.

---

[3]   J.W. Duyvendak & M. Hurenkamp (eds), *Kiezen voor de Kudde. Lichte gemeenschappen en de nieuwe meerderheid* (Van Gennep, Amsterdam, 2004).

[4]   P. Norris, S. Walgrave & P. van Aelst, 'Who demonstrates? Anti-state rebels, conventional participants, or everyone?', *Comparative Politics*, 37, 2 (2005), pp. 189-205.

[5]   D. Meyer & S. Tarrow (eds), *Towards a Movement Society? Contentious politics for a new century* (Rowman and Littlefield, Boulder, CO, 1998).

Table 1   Theories on participation and the emergence of social movements

	Classical approaches	Contemporary approaches		
	Mass society collective behaviour	*Resource mobilization*	*Political process approach*	*Social con- structivistic approaches*
Why people protest	Grievances, discontent, anomie, class conflict	Resources, opportunities, social networks efficacy	Political opportunities (cognitive liberation)	Social con- struction of reality: - (meaning) construction - identity - emotions - motivation
Who protests	Alienated, frustrated, disintegrated, manipulated, marginalized people	Well- organized, professional, resourceful social networks; embeddedness	Coalitions between challengers / political elites; embeddedness	Countercultural groups, identity groups; embeddedness
Forms of protest	Spontaneous, irrational, expressive, violent (panics, fashions, mobs, crime)	Rational, planned, instrumental (institutional politics, lobbying, interest groups)	Rational, instrumental, polity-oriented (elite contention lobbying, indigenous minorities disruption i.e. sit-ins, strikes)	Ideological, expressive, identity-oriented (cultural and religious organizations, self-help groups, alternative lifestyles)

First however, we discuss the past and the present of social movement theory and sketch our subject of interest, namely social movements and collective action. There are numerous definitions of what a 'social movement' is. In this chapter a few definitions will be given, all departing from different theoretical angles and emphasizing different aspects of the phenomenon. A working defi- nition of what we see as social movements and (their) collective actions is as follows: social movements are interlocking networks of groups, social networks and individuals, and the connection between them is a shared collective identity that tries to prevent or promote societal change by non-institutionalized tactics.[6]

Breakdown and marginalization: The past

Classical approaches, for example collective behaviour theory, mass society theory and relative deprivation, rely on the same general causal sequence moving from 'some form of structural strain (be it industrialization, urbanization, unemployment) [that] produces subjective tension and therefore the psychological disposition to engage in extreme behaviours such as panics, mobs etc. to escape from these tensions'.[7] The various versions of classical approaches agree on this basic sequence and differ only in their conceptualization. To appreciate the similarities underlying these various formulations, let us briefly review a number of them.

Le Bon, as mentioned earlier, can be seen as the founding father of collective action studies and his ideas are reflected in several subsequent theories. He did not conceive of contentious politics in a very positive manner, perceiving crowds as primitive and irrational. He believed that individual members of a crowd become submerged in the masses, assuming a sense of anonymity and losing their sense of responsibility. Today, however, it is felt that Le Bon exaggerated the violent and irrational character of crowds.

Smelser[8] and Blumer[9] are viewed as breakdown theorists. Both held that political protest had its inception in tension and societal transition as a result of industrialization, urbanization and unemployment, and that it derived its motivational power from dissatisfaction with current forms of life. For Blumer, the motivating forces for collective action were, in addition to dissatisfaction and subsequent agitation, 'wishes' and 'hope' for a new scheme or system of living. In this way he dissociated himself from the notion that contentious politics were irrational acts rooted solely in agitation and frustration. Implicitly, in emotional terms, he depicted a rational, efficacious side to contentious politics. This perceived probability of making a difference was later described as 'cognitive liberation'.[10]

---

[6]   D. della Porta & M. Diani (eds), *Social Movements: An introduction* (Basil Blackwell, Oxford, 1999).

[7]   D. McAdam, *Political Process and the Development of Black Insurgency, 1930-1970* (University of Chicago Press, Chicago, 1982), p. 7.

[8]   Smelser, *Theory of Collective Behavior*.

[9]   H.G. Blumer, 'Collective behavior', in A. McClung Lee (ed.), *Principles of Sociology* (Barnes and Noble Books, New York, 1969).

[10]   McAdam, *Political Process and the Development of Black Insurgency*.

Kornhauser[11] popularized the notion that people were vulnerable to the appeals of dictatorship because of a lack of restraining social networks. He argued that Nazism developed in Germany because Hitler was able to appeal directly to the people due to their alienation and anomie. This conforms to Putnam's more recent discussions of the alleged decline of social capital[12] but stands in contrast to social movement studies that consistently show that it is people who are firmly embedded, rather than those who are alienated, who are politically active.[13] Indeed, 'very little participation [is found] in either ordinary political activity or revolutionary outbursts by misfits, outcasts, nomads, the truly marginal, the desperate poor'.[14]

Gurr[15] argued that when changing social conditions cause people to experience 'relative deprivation', the likelihood of protest and rebellion significantly increases. Feelings of relative deprivation result from comparisons of one's situation with some standard be it in one's own past or in someone else's situation, or some cognitive standard.[16] If one concludes that one is not receiving the rewards or recognition one deserves, the feelings that accompany this assessment are referred to as relative deprivation. If people assess their personal situation, this is egoistic or individual deprivation; if they assess the situation of their group, it is called fraternalistic or group deprivation. It was assumed that fraternalistic relative deprivation was especially relevant in the context of movement participation.[17]

In conclusion, classical approaches tend to describe contentious politics as spontaneous, irrational, expressive and often violent outbursts of collective action in reaction to felt grievances, discontent and anomie. Protesters, according to classical approaches, are stressed, alienated, frustrated, deprived, disintegrated and marginalized individuals affected by economic crises, an unfair distribution of welfare, social rights, and normative breakdown.

---

[11]   W. Kornhauser, *The Politics of Mass Society* (The Free Press, London, 1995).

[12]   R. Putnam, *Making Democracy Work: Civic traditions in modern Italy* (Princeton University Press, Princeton, NJ, 1993).

[13]   McAdam, *Political Process and the Development of Black Insurgency*; B. Klandermans, J. van der Toorn & J. van Stekelenburg, 'Embeddedness and grievances: Collective action participation among immigrants', *American Sociological Review*, 73 (2008), pp. 992-1012.

[14]   C. Tilly, *The Contentious French* (The Belknap Press of Harvard University Press, Cambridge, MA, 1986).

[15]   T. Gurr, *Why Men Rebel* (Princeton University Press, Princeton, NJ, 1970).

[16]   W.G. Runciman, *Relative Deprivation and Social Justice* (Routledge, London, 1966).

[17]   *Ibid.*

Resources, opportunities and meaning: The present

With the growth in social movement activity on both sides of the Atlantic in the late 1960s, protest started to be perceived as positive and a way of improving politics. It was even seen as essential in a mature political system, rather than as threatening or undermining democracies.[18] Social movement scholars of the 1970s and 1980s, who often happened to be activists themselves, were not persuaded by theories that labelled them as alienated, frustrated and disintegrated and their protest behaviour as irrational. They felt that the psychological make-up attributed to movement participants by the classical approaches did not fit them and argued that, if anything, movement participants were integrated rather than isolated.[19] Clearly, the classical approaches failed to account for this outburst of social movement activity being seen as positive rational politics and preceded by a *growth* rather than a decline in welfare.

The changing perspectives on contentious politics and the growth of social movement activity in prosperous times made researchers in the US and Europe question where, if not from deprivation, social movement activity comes from. The answer was sought in different directions. In the US, structural approaches shifted attention from deprivation to the availability of resources, political opportunities and mobilizing structures to explain the rise of social movements, while in Europe, the social constructivistic 'New Social Movement' (NSM) approach focused attention on the growth of new protest potential, with grievances and aspirations resulting from the developing post-industrial society.[20] While the structural approaches in the US tend to pay a great deal of attention to the *how* of collective action, the social constructivistic approaches in Europe attempt to explain *why* individuals are inclined to such actions.[21] We will explore these approaches in turn.

Structural approaches

Structural approaches investigate how characteristics of social and political context determine the opportunities or constraints for protest. These approaches reject grievances and ideology as the explanation for the rise and decline of movements. Structural approaches have always taken as their point of departure the fact that grievances are ubiquitous and that the key question in movement participation research is not so much why people are aggrieved, as why aggrieved people participate. Two main paradigms emphasize, firstly, the distri-

---

[18] *Ibid.*

[19] McAdam, *Political Process and the Development of Black Insurgency.*

[20] B. Klandermans, H. Kriesi & S. Tarrow (eds), *From Structure to Action: Comparing social movement research across cultures,* Vol. 1 (JAI Press, Greenwich, CT, 1988).

[21] *Ibid.*

bution of resources and the organizational characteristics of social movements ('resource mobilization') and, secondly, contextual factors such as the political and institutional environment ('political process').

Resource mobilization theorists wanted to move away from strong assumptions about the centrality of deprivation and grievances to a view that sees grievances as being a component – sometimes a secondary one – in the generation of social movements.[22] Assigning grievances a subordinate position in theories explaining the rise and fall of social movements leads directly to an emphasis on mobilization processes or the dynamics and tactics of social movement growth, decline and change.

> The resource mobilization approach examines the variety of resources that must be mobilized, the linkages of social movements to other groups, the dependence of movements upon external support for success, and the tactics used by authorities to control or incorporate movements.[23]

Resources can mean anything from material resources – jobs, income, savings and the right to specific goods and services – to non-tangible resources, such as authority, leadership, moral commitment, trust, friendship, skills and habits of industry. The reasoning goes that group conflict in its dynamic aspects can be conceptualized from the point of view of the mobilization of resources. Mobilization refers to the processes by which a discontented group assembles and invests resources for the pursuit of group goals. Conflict and change can be analyzed from the point of view of how resources are managed and allocated and the manner in which these resources can be redirected in the pursuit of group goals.

Resource mobilization scholars view social movements as a set of opinions and beliefs in a population that represents preferences for promoting or preventing social change.[24] To predict the likelihood of preferences being translated into protest, the mobilization perspective focuses on pre-existing organization and the integration of those parts of a population that share the preferences. Social movements whose related populations are highly organized internally are more likely than others to spawn organized forms of protest. Resource mobilization theorists focus explicitly on the organizational component of activity. They argue that resources (money, labour, legitimacy, etc.) must be mobilized for action to be possible. The degree of activity directed towards the accomplishment of goals is perceived by resource mobilization theorists as a function of the resources controlled by an organization. In summary, people

---

[22] J.D. McCarthy & M.N. Zald, 'Resource mobilization and social movements: A partial theory', *American Journal of Sociology*, 82, 6 (1977), pp. 1212-1241.
[23] *Ibid.*, p. 1212.
[24] *Ibid.*

protest from a resource mobilization perspective because they are able to mobilize resources and feel politically successful. Prototypical protesters are rational, well-organized, professional and resourceful people who undertake well-planned collective action with the goal of solving social problems.

Resource mobilization theory has not escaped criticism. It borrows its concept from the vocabulary of economics (the flow of resources, costs and benefits, supply and demand, organization, movement entrepreneurs, movement industries) and is particularly suited to the depiction of social movements such as rational entities weighing up the costs and benefits of their action.[25] However, expressions such as 'costs and benefits' may make activists and scholars of social movements feel uncomfortable, as they convey notions of cold calculation being applied to social action which instead is often inspired by ideals and passion. But this is exactly the notion that resource mobilization theorists want to convey, namely that the ebb and flow of social movement activity results from the ability to mobilize resources and the perceived chances of success rather than from rising or declining grievance levels. In addition, it has been argued that resource mobilization theorists fail to acknowledge the strength of indigenous resources. For instance, McAdam shows that the growth of the black insurgency movement in America in the 1960s was related to 'injected' resources from elites but that indigenous resources such as informal networks providing solidarity, trust and leadership were important as well.[26] Finally, 'resource mobilization theorists are to be faulted for their failure to acknowledge the power inherent in disruptive tactics'.[27] Piven and Cloward have argued that opportunities for protest occur when broad social changes and the restructuring of institutional life take place. Under such circumstances, the poor will take the opportunity to use the only power resource they have, namely protest. However, these 'extraordinary occurrences' that are 'required to transform the poor from apathy to hope, from quiescence to indignation'[28] are limited in number. In normal circumstances, the struggle to survive takes up all the time and energy poor people have, and only when daily life severely breaks down does protest emerge.

While resource mobilization theorists explain the rise and fall of social movements by features internal to the movements themselves, such as the availability of resources and organizational aspects, political process theorists focus on external features, like changes or differences in the political and institutional environment of social movements. They argue that political environments vary

---

[25] *Ibid.*

[26] McAdam, *Political Process and the Development of Black Insurgency.*

[27] *Ibid.*, p. 30.

[28] F.F. Piven & R.A. Cloward, *Poor Peoples' Movements: Why they succeed, how they fail* (Random House, New York, 1977), p. 14.

over time and between areas. The paradigm proposes changes in or differences between political structures as the main explanation for the rise and fall of social movements and that differences from one country or era to another stem from the process by which a national political system shapes, checks and absorbs the challenges confronting it.[29]

Three ideas are central to the political process approach: first, a social movement is a political rather than a psychological phenomenon; second, a social movement represents a continuous *process* from its creation to its decline rather than a discrete series of developmental stages; and third, different forms of action ('repertoires of contentions') are associated with different spatial and temporal locations.[30] For Tilly, one of the leading theorists of the political process approach, action repertoires are specific actions such as riots, demonstrations, strikes, sit-ins, petitioning or lobbying that are carried out by collective actors over a specific period of time. Tarrow expands this concept and suggests that 'actions are not only what people do when they are engaged in conflict with others, it is what they know how to do and what others expect them to do'.[31] The form of action chosen by social movements depends on factors including the structure of the political system (e.g. democratic institutions, the existence and structure of political parties, and possibilities for direct participation), the level of repression, and cultural traditions. The actions of social actors are, therefore, not purely random. Instead, action repertoires are shaped by structural variables and the cultural context in which they originate.

By studying the changing action repertoires in France over the last four centuries, Tilly[32] demonstrated that social movements draw on action repertoires that develop over long periods and change in conformity in an evolving context. If a prevailing repertoire of contention changes significantly at some point, the change is a symptom of a substantial alteration in the structure of power. An expansion of the state in nineteenth-century France, including a nationalization of politics, was, for instance, accompanied by a major change in the repertoire of collective action. The more spontaneous tax rebellions and bread riots aimed at the local authorities more or less disappeared and were replaced by more coherent forms of contention. The centralization of the state played an essential part in the creation of modern social movements with a

---

[29]   C. Tilly, 'Social movements and national politics', in: C. Bright & S. Hardine (eds), *Statemaking and Social Movements: Essays in history and theory* (University of Michigan Press, Ann Arbor, MI, 1984).

[30]   Tilly, *The Contentious French*.

[31]   S. Tarrow, *Power in Movement: Collective action, social movements and politics* (Cambridge University Press, Cambridge, 1994), p. 31.

[32]   Tilly, *The Contentious French*.

repertoire that is still present today: the strike, the demonstration, and the protest meeting.

Tarrow[33] studied the cycle of protest that swept across Italy from the late 1960s through the early 1970s and showed how protest spread from students' and workers' movements to virtually every sector of Italian society and gave rise to extra-parliamentary groups, violence and, finally, a return to traditional political patterns. In other words, by utilizing the political opportunities offered by the system, social movements create an ideologically and socially favourable environment for new social groups to mobilize.

Political structures have also explained differences in protest activity *between* countries.[34] For instance, the protest repertoire of social movements in Switzerland that were struggling within a direct democracy appeared to be more moderate than the radical repertoire employed by French social movements fighting their cause in a closed democracy.[35] To strengthen the case for the argument that direct democratic procedures have a moderating effect on the action repertoires of social movements, Kriesi and Wisler[36] showed that within one country, the Swiss federal state, differences between Swiss cantons regarding direct democratic procedures had an impact on the action repertoires employed within these cantons. The German-speaking cantons were more open than the Latin ones and, not surprisingly, social movements based in the German cantons employed a less radical action repertoire than their Latin counterparts.

McAdam is a political process theorist who, while emphasizing structural aspects of the environment, also focuses on subjectivity. He explained the rise and fall of the civil-rights movement in the United States between 1930 and 1970 with reference to political opportunities, political efficacy and institutions like black churches and black colleges.[37] While classical theorists saw a direct link between social instability and political insurgency, McAdam saw only an indirect relationship, as illustrated in Figure 1.

McAdam argues that two necessary conditions need to be in place to turn social instability into political insurgency: (i) available resources and open

[33] S. Tarrow, *Democracy and Disorder: Protest and politics in Italy 1965-1975* (Clarendon Press, Oxford, 1989).

[34] P. Eisinger, 'The conditions of protest behavior in American cities', *American Political Science Review*, 67 (1973), pp. 11-15.

[35] H. Kriesi, R. Koopmans, J.W. Duyvendak & M. Giugni, *New Social Movements in Western Europe* (University of Minnesota Press, Minneapolis, MN, 1995).

[36] H. Kriesi & D. Wisler, 'Direct democracy and social movements in Switzerland', *European Journal of Political Research*, 30 (1996), pp. 19-40.

[37] McAdam, *Political Process and the Development of Black Insurgency*, p. 7.

Figure 1 McAdam's 1982 political process model

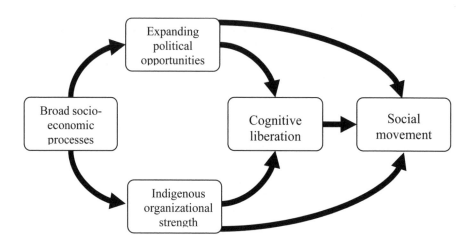

political opportunities, and (ii) cognitive liberation. Although the political process model builds upon the resource mobilization approach, in contrast to this approach, it also takes the indigenous organizational capabilities of aggrieved populations into account. The second condition, that of cognitive liberation, proposes that the subjectivity of actors makes resources usable and collective action viable, and helps actors and groups to frame their situation as unjust and liable to change.[38] Political opportunities and organization alone do not produce social movements. Mediating between political opportunities and organizational strength are people and their hopes and fears. In general, the political process approach argues that the ebb and flow of movement activity is related to the opening up and closure of political opportunities. Protesters are rational, instrumental, polity-oriented people who seize opportunities by lobbying and forming coalitions with political elites.

Several studies make a convincing case for the political process approach but some fail to explain political protest, and others show that the approach is more effective in one context than another. The lack of theory concerning the specific mechanisms that link political process to movement activity is identified as the fundamental problem in explaining these divergent results.[39] Moreover, incen-

---

[38] Piven & Cloward, *Poor Peoples' Movements*.
[39] R. Koopmans, 'The missing link between structure and agency. Outline of an evolutionary approach to social movements', *Mobilization*, 10 (2005), pp. 19-36.

tives and expectations necessarily involve interpretation, just like opportunities and constraints.[40] Indeed, if there were a perfect correlation between objective and subjective environments, there would be no need to distinguish between the two, whereas research suggests that this is often not the case.[41]

Social constructivistic approaches

The development of social movement activity in the prosperous times of the second half of the twentieth century shows differences between the US and Europe. While there was an emphasis in the US on structural aspects such as resources and political opportunities, answers were formulated in Europe in terms of new constituencies with new needs, values and aspirations arising from developing post-industrial societies, producing what were dubbed New Social Movements. This 'NSM approach' argued that processes of modernization created two groups of constituencies. The first were groups that had lagged behind due to marginalization processes related to industrial modernization (youth, women and the elderly were especially seen as groups threatened by the automation of productive work). The second were groups with a specific vulnerability resulting from modernization processes.[42] In particular, the post-war generation, whose material needs were satisfied, developed post-material values from which emerged such new needs and aspirations as self-actualization and participation.[43] This group came into conflict with a political and social system that was chiefly materialistic. The NSM approach was social constructivistic in emphasizing social changes in identity, lifestyle and culture. NSM scholars utilized identity as their core concept, with Melucci arguably being the most explicit.[44] He thought collective identity 'bridge[s] the gap between behavior and meaning, between "objective" conditions and "subjective" motives and orientation, between "structure" and "agency"'.[45]

However, social constructivistic approaches were not an exclusively European matter and the hegemony of structural approaches in the US began to be

[40] J. Goodwin & J.M. Jasper, 'Caught in a winding, snarling vine: The structural bias of political process theory', *Sociological Forum,* 14, 1 (1999), pp. 27-54.
[41] B. Boyd, G.G. Dess & A. Rasheed, 'Divergence between archival and perceptual measures of the environment: causes and consequences,' *Academy of Management Review,* 18, 2 (1993), pp. 204-226.
[42] Klandermans, Kriesi & Tarrow, *From Structure to Action.*
[43] R. Inglehart, *The Silent Revolution: Changing values and political styles among Western publics* (Princeton University Press, Princeton, NJ, 1977).
[44] A. Melucci, *Nomads of the Present: Social movement and identity needs in contemporary society* (Temple University Press, Philadelphia, PA, 1989).
[45] A. Melucci, *Challenging Code* (Cambridge University Press, Cambridge, 1996), p. 69.

challenged in the mid 1980s.[46] The social constructivistic perspective concentrates on questions of how individuals and groups perceive and interpret material and socio-political conditions. Social constructivists argue that if we want to understand why people protest, we need to know how they perceive and interpret their social-political context. A number of European and US social movement scholars with social-psychology backgrounds called for attention to be paid to meaning and its construction and identity. They referred to explanations founded in emotion, such as interpretation, symbolization and meaning, and to social-psychology expansions of structural approaches such as resource mobilization.[47] They argued that structural explanations are limited because individuals who are in the same structural position do not display identical behaviour. A shared position can never provide sufficient explanation of individual behaviour.[48] Even if people display identical behaviour, their motivational background and their accompanying emotions may still be different.[49]

This social constructivistic approach draws on past views but is not a return to the classical approaches of the 1950s. While both classical and social constructivistic approaches recognize that emotions and cognition are important to collective action, the classical approaches see them as pathological, whereas social constructivistic approaches perceive them as the normal, ubiquitous aspects of social and political life. Social constructivistic approaches try to understand why people who are seemingly in the same situation respond so differently. They question why some people feel ashamed of their situation, while others take pride in it; why some are aggrieved, while others are not; why some define their situation as unjust, while others do not; why some feel powerless, while others feel empowered; and why some are angry, while others are afraid. These are the issues that social constructivistic approaches to social movements seek to answer. We now turn to meaning (or construction), identity, and emotional and motivational explanations as examples of contemporary social constructivistic approaches.

---

[46] R. Benford, 'An insider's critique of the social movement framing perspective', *Sociological Inquiry*, 67, 4 (1997), pp. 409-430.

[47] B. Klandermans, 'Mobilization and participation: Social-psychological expansions of resource mobilization theory', *American Sociological Review*, 49, 5 (1984), pp. 583-600.

[48] D. Snow & P. Oliver, 'Social movements and collective behavior: Social psychological considerations and dimensions', in: K.S. Cook, G.A. Fine & J.S. House (eds), *Sociological Perspectives on Social Psychology* (Allyn and Bacon, Boston, MA, 1995).

[49] J. van Stekelenburg & B. Klandermans, 'Individuals in movements: A social psychology of contention', in: B. Klandermans & C.M. Roggeband (eds), *The Handbook of Social Movements Across Disciplines* (Springer, New York, 2007).

The first involves the meaning that people attach to their social environment. This is the direct or indirect subject of investigation by students of protest. Perceptions are not fixed but are susceptible to interpretation and thus play a role in the construction of meaning.[50] And participation in collective action thus depends not only on perceptions of structural strain, availability and the deployment of material resources, the opening up or closing of political opportunities or a cost-benefit calculation more generally but also on the way these variables are constructed and framed and the degree to which they resonate with targets of mobilization.[51]

Social movements play a significant role in the diffusion of ideas and values to the extent that some scholars see the construction of meaning as a movement's primary function.[52] Through processes such as consensus mobilization[53] or framing,[54] activists seek to disseminate their definition of a situation to the public at large. Participating because of common interests or ideologies requires a shared interpretation of who should act, and why and how. Movements affect such interpretations by the information they disseminate, a process known as 'framing'. Social movements do their utmost to communicate how they interpret a social, political or economic change (its diagnosis) and what should be done (the prognosis) as a reaction to perceived losses or unfulfilled aspirations.[55] The more individual orientations, values and beliefs become congruent with activities, goals and ideologies of social movement organizations, the greater the level of sharedness. Gerhards and Rucht's study[56] of flyers produced by the various groups and organizations involved in protests against the International Monetary Fund (IMF) and the World Bank in Berlin is an excellent example in this respect. The researchers showed how links were constructed between the ideological framework of the organizers of the demonstration and those of the participating organizations to create a shared definition of the situation.

With regard to social identity, the clearest definition that has been located in the social-psychology literature is presented by Tajfel and Turner. According to

---

[50] W.A. Gamson, *Talking Politics* (Cambridge University Press, Cambridge, 1992).

[51] D.A. Snow, E.B. Rochford, S.K. Worden & R.D. Benford, 'Frame alignment processes, micromobilization, and movement participation', *American Sociological Review*, 51 (1986), pp. 464-481.

[52] R. Eyerman & A. Jamison, *Social Movements: A cognitive approach* (Polity Press, Cambridge, 1991).

[53] Klandermans, Kriesi & Tarrow, *From Structure to Action*.

[54] Snow *et al.*, 'Frame alignment processes'.

[55] *Ibid.*

[56] J. Gerhards & D. Rucht, 'Mesomobilization: Organizing and framing in two protest campaigns in West Germany', *American Journal of Sociology*, 98, (1992), pp. 555–596.

them, identity is 'that *part* of an individual's self-concept which derives from his knowledge of his membership of a social group (or groups) together with the value and emotional significance attached to that membership'.[57] Hence a social identity makes people think, feel and act as members of that specific group. But people have many social identities. Why do some social identities become central to mobilization while others do not? Probably the most powerful factor that brings group membership to mind is conflict or rivalry between groups, and in times of inter-group conflict, people are inclined to take to the streets on behalf of their group.

Collective action is a group rather than an individual phenomenon but in the end it is individuals who decide whether or not to participate. This raises the question of what connects the individual to the collective. Identification with the group involved seems to be the answer. The influence of identification processes on protest participation refers to the circumstances in which people identify with the others involved. People participate not so much because of the outcome associated with participation but because they identify with the other participants. Group identification changes the focus from what 'I' want to what 'we' want. Collective action participation is seen as a way to show who 'we' are and what 'we' stand for, and people experience commitment and solidarity with other members of the group. In addition, group members have the idea that 'we' have much in common (by way of shared grievances, aims, values or goals). Group identification seems to be a powerful reason for participating in protest.[58]

Little is known about the influence of emotions on protest behaviour. Yet it is acknowledged that emotions permeate all the stages in social movement participation: recruitment, staying in and dropping out. Emotions function as accelerators or amplifiers,[59] making things move more quickly or sound louder. In the world of protest, 'accelerating' means that one's motives for joining, staying in or leaving a social movement translate into action more quickly due to emotions, while 'amplifying' means that these motives become stronger. Few researchers have focused on the complex emotional processes that channel fear and anger into moral indignation and political activity. Those of us who have been part of protest events or have watched reports on protest events in the media may find this hard to believe. However partly as a reaction to the classi-

---

[57]   H. Tajfel & J.C. Turner, 'An integrative theory of intergroup conflict', in S. Worchel and W.G. Austin (eds), *The Social Psychology of Intergroup Relations* (Brooks/ Cole, Monterey, CA, 1979), p. 63.

[58]   For overviews, see S. Stryker, T.J. Owens & R.W. White (eds), *Self, Identity, and Social Movements* (Minnesota Press, Minneapolis, MN, 2000) and N. Ellemers, R. Spears & B. Doosje (eds), *Social Identity: Context, commitment, content* (Blackwell Publishers, Oxford, 1999).

[59]   Van Stekelenburg & Klandermans, 'Individuals in movements'.

cal approaches that stressed the irrational character of movement participation and partly because they are complicated phenomena, emotions have not featured prominently in the social movement literature. Even 'affective' phenomena such as moral shocks[60] or suddenly imposed grievances[61] have been primarily approached from a cognitive point of view. But all demands for change begin with discontent. Emotions warn people of threats and challenges and propel behaviour. Moreover, affective measures, such as affective commitment[62] and injustice,[63] have the biggest impact on behaviour. Thus if one wants to understand engagement in collective action, one must understand the workings of emotions.

Goodwin, Jasper and Polletta argue that emotions are socially constructed but that 'some emotions are more [socially] constructed than others, involving more cognitive processes'.[64] In their view, emotions that are politically relevant are at the social construction end of the scale. For these emotions, cultural and historical factors play an important role in the interpretation (i.e. perception) of the state of affairs by which they are generated. Obviously, emotions can be manipulated. Activists work hard to create moral outrage and anger and to provide a target against which these can be vented. They have to weave a moral, cognitive and emotional blanket of attitudes. Framing theory has provided a way to link ideas and the social construction of ideas with organizational and political process factors. These studies, however, deal almost entirely with the cognitive components of frames and neglect any emotional components. Powerful frames might, however, be related to the values and emotions that they contain and it might be argued that frames not only resonate cognitively but also emotionally.

These issues are all related to questions of motivation. Demands for change are rooted in a notion of belonging (identity) and experienced grievances (constructed meaning) in combination with emotions related to a specific grievance. Although, typically, many members of disadvantaged groups are dissatisfied with their collective situation and strongly sympathize with the goals of collective actions, often only a small proportion actually participate in protest to

---

[60] J.M. Jasper, *The Art of Moral Protest* (University of Chicago Press, Chicago, IL, 1997).

[61] E.J. Walsh, 'Resource mobilization and citizen protest in communities around Three Mile Island', *Social Problems*, 29, 1 (1981), pp. 1-21.

[62] Ellemers *et al.*, *Social Identity*.

[63] T.R. Tyler & H.J. Smith, 'Social justice and social movements', in D.T. Gilbert & S.T. Fiske (eds), *Handbook of Social Psychology*, 4th ed. (McGraw-Hill, Oxford, 1998).

[64] J. Goodwin, J.M. Jasper & F. Polletta, *Passionate Politics: Emotions and social movements* (The University of Chicago Press, Chicago, IL, 2001), p. 13.

achieve these goals.[65] In collective action research therefore, the motives underlying participation have become a key issue.[66]

Over the last two decades, social psychologists have investigated the motives behind participation and demonstrated that instrumental reasoning, identification, emotions and ideological factors form a motivational constellation in response to the question about why people participate in contentious politics.[67] Interestingly though, this motivational constellation seems to be context dependent: Van Stekelenburg, Klandermans and van Dijk ,[68] for instance, showed that, in demonstrations organized by a labour movement, people tend to be instrumentally motivated whereas demonstrators against neoliberalism are more ideologically motivated. In more general terms, people are inclined to take the instrumental path if a conflict is framed in terms of material interests and the ideological path if it is framed in terms of conflicting principles.

In conclusion, social constructivistic approaches argue that protesters live in a perceived reality and that threats and opportunities are socially constructed and/or framed by social movements and other social and political actors. Group identification plays a key role in what protesters think, feel and do and protesting is as rational or irrational as all social behaviour. People participate therefore not only in collective action for instrumental reasons but also because they identify with others involved or because they want to express their anger and indignation at a target if they believe that their values have been violated. Social constructivistic approaches investigate how perceptions, emotions and identities shape a person's motivation to take part in contentious politics. There appears to be a great deal of merit in utilizing social constructivistic approaches alongside structural approaches when studying contentious politics. However, social constructivistic approaches are characterized by their variety. They have four key themes – the construction of meaning, identity, emotions and motivation – but a common framework to allow the integration of these variables is clearly missing. Social constructivistic studies tend to consist of single case-studies that inevitably have little to say about contextual variation. However, one needs to understand the characteristics of the socio-political and mobilizing context to make sense of the findings in a specific country or period of time. This requires comparative studies rather than single case-studies.

[65] G. Marwell & P. Oliver, *The Critical Mass in Collective Action: A micro-social theory* (Cambridge University Press, Cambridge, 1993); Klandermans, *The Social Psychology of Protest*.

[66] *Ibid.*

[67] *Ibid.*

[68] J. van Stekelenburg, B. Klandermans & W.W. van Dijk, 'Context matters: Explaining why and how mobilizing context influences motivational dynamics', *Journal of Social Issues* (forthcoming, 2009).

The social constructivistic approach thus runs the risk of fragmentation and decontextualization. In an attempt to bridge the gap between the objective existence of the opportunities and resources in the environment, as opposed to the protesters' subjective perception, social constructivistic approaches clearly need a common framework that integrates key themes and takes the socio-political context into account.

Contextualized contestation: The prospects

In the rapidly globalizing world of the network society and the information society,[69] streams of migration are creating diasporas in which flows of ideas and resources are influencing contentious politics in both their homelands and in their host countries. At the same time, globalization has resulted in more transnational and supranational political institutions such as the European Union, the United Nations and the IMF that are having an ever-increasing impact on people's daily lives. Some scholars believe they can detect the emergence of a new social fabric, which they have baptized the 'network society',[70] arguing that networks have become the prime mode of organization and structure of society. Formal organizations have turned into networks of networks, which in turn are intersected with informal networks rooted in personal life worlds and more diffuse interpersonal group settings. The logic of the network society pervades all spheres of social, economic and cultural life.[71] In addition, new communication technologies are giving rise to the information society,[72] as new technologies intensify societal change and pace. As Held puts it:

> … what is new about the modern global system is the chronic intensification of patterns of interconnectedness mediated by such phenomena as the modern communication industry and new information technology and the spread of globalization in and through new dimensions of interconnectedness.[73]

It should be noted that Held made his statement at a time when the real communication revolution was still to come.

---

[69] M. Castells, *The Rise of the Network Society* (Blackwell Publishers, Oxford, 1996); H. Rheingold, *Smart Mobs: The next social revolution* (Perseus, Cambridge, MA, 2002); B. Wellman, 'The network community', in B. Wellman (ed.), *Networks in the Global Village* (Westview, Boulder, CO, 1999), pp. 1-48; R.K. Garrett, 'Protest in an information society: A review of literature on social movements and new ICTs', *Information, Communication, and Society*, 9, 2 (2006), pp. 202-224.

[70] Castells, *The Rise of the Network Society.*

[71] *Ibid.*

[72] Garrett, 'Protest in an information society'.

[73] D. Held, 'Democracy, the nation-state and the global system', in David Held (ed.), *Political Theory Today* (Polity Press, Cambridge, 1991), p. 145.

Societies are changing fundamentally and this affects contentious politics. After all, information and networks are essential elements of mobilization and one could assume that such profound changes must be having an impact on the dynamics of contention. And as a result of these transformations, the field of contentious politics has changed significantly.[74] Protest as a political tactic has diffused across a range of constituencies and claims. Contributing to and resulting from such diffusion is an increased tolerance for protest so that engaging in political protest is no longer stigmatized. Moreover, protest in Western democracies has generally been an effective tool for politically disadvantaged groups both on the left and the right.[75] This conveys the message that the tactic is not only legitimate but also effective. Simply because more citizens have protested more frequently and on more diverse issues, more experienced protesters are available for subsequent protest calls.[76] The legitimacy of protest, its proven efficacy and the ample experience of protest among citizens will all influence the dynamics of contention.

Changing society, changing paradigms?

Perhaps more than in any other sector of comparative politics, the study of contention is sensitive to developments in the real world.[77] We therefore assume that, just as in the 1960s, contemporary changes in society will give rise to new approaches. Contentious politics is a multi-faceted phenomenon with socio-political, organizational and social-psychology roots. To investigate who rebels and on what issues requires inclusive models. Yet the connection between structures that canalize grievances into contentious politics is a thorny but relatively underexposed issue in the protest literature.

This observation is not new. In 1988 Klandermans, Kriesi and Tarrow suggested a research agenda with the emphasis on comparative research and the integration of structural, cultural and motivational factors.[78] Their book was the first tangible outcome of a prolonged exchange between representatives of the

---

[74]   D. della Porta & S. Tarrow (eds), *Transnational Protest and Global Activism* (Rowman and Littlefield, Lanham, MD, 2005).

[75]   W.A. Gamson, *Strategy of Social Protest* (Wadsworth Publishing, Belmont, CA, 1990).

[76]   V. Taylor, 'Mobilizing for change in a social movement society', *Contemporary Sociology*, 29, 1 (2000), pp. 219-230; Meyer & Tarrow, *Towards a Movement Society?*

[77]   D. McAdam, S. Tarrow & C. Tilly, 'Comparative perspectives on contentious politics', in: M. Lichbach & A. Zuckerman (eds), *Ideas, Interests and Institutions: Advancing theory in comparative politics* (Cambridge University Press, Cambridge, 2007).

[78]   Klandermans, Kriesi & Tarrow, *From Structure to Action.*

American and European approaches and this resulted in an increasingly closely knit network of contacts across the Atlantic that was instrumental in organizing a series of conferences and edited volumes. In 1996 a book edited by McAdam, McCarthy and Zald[79] was released with a widely shared synthesis of three broad sets of factors to analyze the emergence and development of social movements: the structure of political opportunities and constraints confronting the movement; mobilizing structures; and framing processes. Two additional synthesizing efforts came in 1999 from Della Porta and Diani[80] and in 2004 from Snow, Soule and Kriesi,[81] all of whom drew together political opportunity, movement framing and the social network theory. So although social constructivistic approaches are usually framed as being opposed to structuralist accounts, the contemporary research agenda calls for an integration of structural, political and sociological theories of movements with social constructivistic approaches rooted in social psychology and cultural sociology. Yet research agendas focusing on comparative research and theoretical syntheses of structure and agency are as relevant today as they ever were. To be sure, theories of contentious politics are currently more sophisticated than previously but many questions remain unresolved, such as how the political and mobilizing context 'translates' into contentious politics. These questions require interdisciplinary and comparative studies. Such studies have not featured prominently in the social movement literature, perhaps because truly interdisciplinary and comparative studies are so complex. Therefore, the question as to how characteristics of socio-political structure might translate into action is as relevant now as it was in 1988 when Klandermans, Kriesi and Tarrow first drew attention to it.

An explanatory framework, which we developed in collaboration with Stefaan Walgrave, might be useful here because it highlights precisely the interaction between structure and action as its point of departure. It crosses interdisciplinary boundaries that connect the micro level of individual protesters with the meso level of social movements, and the macro level of national political systems and supranational processes. We started from the notion that the answer to questions such as who protests, why people protest (i.e. the issues) and the forms of contention (e.g. grassroots activity, civil war) lies in the interaction of supranational processes, political processes at the national level and the mobilizing context (see Figure 2).

What follows elaborates on contextual variation. Given that this is a chapter in a book on social movements in Africa, the framework will be discussed

[79] D. McAdam, J.D. McCarthy & M.N. Zald (eds), *Political Opportunities, Mobilizing Structures, and Cultural Framings* (Cambridge University Press, New York, 1996).
[80] Della Porta & Diani, *Social Movements*.
[81] D.A. Snow, S.A. Soule & H. Kriesi (eds), *The Blackwell Companion to Social Movements* (Blackwell Publishing, Oxford, 2004).

against the background of the continent's (contextualized) contestation. Conflict in Africa is still widespread and tenacious and is often rooted in material poverty, scarcity, ecological decline and inequality. Inter-group conflicts are partly related to historical and current international engagements in Africa but also emanate from local tensions and the workings of unequal and corrupt socio-political systems. These international, national and local conflicts translate into and shape daily life and have long-term effects that fuel conflict in new forms. Indeed, if anything, Africa is *the* continent in which to observe contextualized contestation.

Figure 2 Contextualized contestation

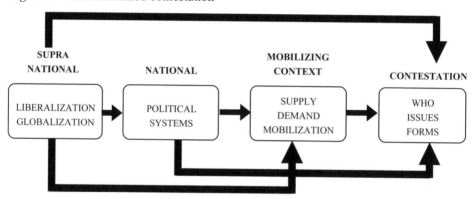

Supranational processes. It is increasingly important these days to take the international dimensions of contestation into account and this is certainly true in Africa. First, political and economic liberalization processes have had a profound impact and perhaps even a certain causative influence on the emergence of new social movements or the transformation of existing ones. Second, socio-political changes, shaped by donor-country pressure, global regimes of development policies or ideals and democratization, human-rights discourses and religious expansion appear to have a crucial impact on contestation in Africa. And third, streams of migration have created diasporas in which flows of ideas and resources such as money and organizational experience, but also education, influence the mobilizing structure and thus contentious politics in migrants' home countries. These wider processes of liberalization and globalization (both in terms of influx and outflux) have influenced national political systems, shaped mobilizing structures and had an impact on contentious politics in Africa in ways that remain largely unclear.

In the social movement literature, it is increasingly acknowledged that social movement activity is evolving in response to processes of globalization,[82] and how contention is moving from the national to the transnational level is being examined.[83] Scholars have identified, for instance, the mechanisms and paths along which this scale shift is occurring,[84] the close relationship between global governance institutions, nation states and transnational social movements,[85] and the multilayered opportunity structures in which movements operate nowadays.[86] Briefly, all these studies show that the socio-political context in which movements operate to spread their aims and ideas is not simply national or only supranational but there is a mix of supranational, national and local influences.

National processes. Countries vary in terms of the circumstances they create for contentious politics. The political opportunity structure, the openness of the political system for challengers, the access points available for people to defend their interests and express their opinions and the temporal political configuration have all been identified as determinants of the incidence and type of protest in democratic polities.[87] With regard to Africa, states are often said to be failing, levels of democratization tend to be low and many are being led by corrupt dictators. Apart from pervasive misgovernance and gross abuses of state power, the nature and role of 'ungoverned political spaces' across the continent is poorly understood: how do they enhance conflict and translate it into contentious politics? Although the social movement literature is quite elaborate as far as the effects of repression are concerned, little is yet known about the influence of supranational processes on contention within a state. How do, for instance in Zimbabwe which is arguably one of the world's most repressive states, international lobbies, boycotts, the absence of food and medical care or resources provided by diasporas create chances for social movements to prevent or promote social change? While misgovernance or non-governance, failing states, repression and corruption are not unique to Africa, their direct political impact is probably greater than elsewhere, inhibiting institution-building, development and the fair distribution of resources. Again it remains a question of how the

---

[82]   D. della Porta, H. Kriesi & D. Rucht (eds), *Social Movement in a Globalizing World* (Macmillan, London, 1999); Della Porta & Tarrow, *Transnational Protest and Global Activism.*

[83]   S. Tarrow & D. McAdam, 'Scale shift in transnational contention', in: Della Porta & Tarrow, *Transnational Protest and Global Activism.*

[84]   *Ibid.*

[85]   M. Keck & K. Sikkink, *Activists beyond Borders: Advocacy networks in international politics* (Cornell University Press, Ithaca, NY, 1998).

[86]   *Ibid.*

[87]   R. Koopmans, 'Political. Opportunity. Structure. Some splitting to balance the lumping', *Sociological Forum*, 14 (1999), pp. 93-105; Tarrow, *Democracy and Disorder: Protest and politics in Italy.*

sphere of governance, politics, power and the state in specific countries influences the mobilizing context and the quality and extent of contentious politics.

Mobilizing context. The mobilizing context in a country can be described in terms of supply, demand and mobilization.[88] While the demand side of protest refers to the protesters' potential in a society; the supply side refers to the characteristics of the social movement sector in a society. Mobilization refers to the techniques and mechanisms that link supply and demand. We will consider these factors one by one.

A demand for protest begins with levels of grievance in a society.[89] The deep insecurities of life in many African countries – ecological, material, social, political and health-related (notably due to AIDS) – may have a direct impact on perceived grievances and thus on conflict behaviour. New religious identities are also developing in some forms and settings, resulting in radical contentious politics. In addition, it seems plausible that a demand for change is defined by the diasporas as well. How these grievances are shaped by the (supra)national context and translated into demand for protest is an interesting but so far unanswered question. Even less is known about the role of the mobilizing context as translator, facilitator and organizer of ethnic conflict, religious confrontations and resource-related conflicts. Why do certain grievances end up in contentious politics that originate in conflicting principles while others end up in contentious politics originating in conflicting material interests?

With regard to the supply side of contentious politics, this concerns the characteristics of the social movement sector in a society, its strength, diversity and contentiousness. Traditionally, the social movement sector is conceived of as a conglomerate of movement organizations, such as trade unions, associations, liberation movements or civil-society organizations,[90] that provide the more or less formalized infrastructure from which contentious politics is built.[91] Increasingly however, we are seeing protest participation rooted in every-day networks of participants and social movement actors involved in diffuse and decentral-

---

[88] B. Klandermans, 'The demand and supply of participation: Social-psychological correlates of participation in social movements', in Snow *et al.*, *The Blackwell companion to social movements* (Blackwell Publishing, Oxford, 2004).

[89] Klandermans, *The Social Psychology of Protest*.

[90] McAdam *et al.*, *Political Opportunities, Mobilizing Structures, and Cultural Framings*.

[91] M. Diani & D. McAdam (eds), *Social Movement Analysis: The network perspective* (Oxford University Press, New York, 2003); D. McAdam, *Freedom Summer* (Oxford University Press, New York, 1988); McCarthy & Zald, 'Resource mobilization and social movements'.

ized networks.[92] How does the political system (repressive or otherwise) shape the supply side? Is it because of repression and/or bans on open mobilization that organizations go underground and turn into loose networks? Egypt and Yemen, where inclusive informal social networks (rather than formal organizations) are an essential mechanism for spreading Islamist ideas,[93] offer examples. Does religious identification influence the political arena in divided countries with a failing political system (e.g. Nigeria) as religious community leaders create alternative routes for mobilization? What do activists and political actors of a previous generation do after their 'projects' have ended in success or failure? Examples here are the evolution of the former leaders and membership of anti-apartheid movements in South Africa and their changing careers. These political actors emanated from social movements and have transformed them.[94] How do social movements and actors evolve in current post-colonial African conditions shaped by liberalization and globalization? How do, for instance, large resourceful organizations, like the UN, with their influential global justice, human rights and democratization framework shape and influence the supply side? Globalization in Africa also entails the rapidly growing role of China (and other Asian countries) on the continent and often evokes counter-responses by Africans.

Finally, processes of mobilization bring demands for protest together with a supply of protest opportunities. Globalization and the development of the network society and the information society have radically changed mobilization techniques. New information and communication technologies have altered the ways in which activists communicate and mobilize. Is typical grassroots mobilization changing as a result of the use of these new communication technologies? How are social actors mobilizing for change in a repressive political system and who is being addressed in a situation of non-governance or misgovernance? How does the spread of innovative ideas and practices, which is playing a central role in the shift of scale,[95] influence the mobilization techniques employed by activists? At a general level, supply, demand and mobilization are supposedly shaped by the supranational and national context. At a certain level, the mobilizing context is further coloured by characteristics of contestation, most notably the specific issue concerned. Little is known about

---

[92] Duyvendak & Hurenkamp, *Kiezen voor de Kudde. Lichte gemeenschappen en de nieuwe meerderheid*; Melucci, *Challenging Codes*; V. Taylor, 'Mobilizing for change in a social movement society', pp. 219-230.

[93] Q. Wiktorowitz, 'Introduction: Islamic activism and social movement theory', in Q. Wiktorowicz (ed.), *Islamic Activism: A social movement approach* (Indiana University Press, Bloomington, IN, 2004).

[94] See van Kessel's chapter in this volume.

[95] Tarrow & McAdam, 'Scale shift in transnational contention'.

the way mobilizing contexts vary, how such variation is determined or how it impacts on the characteristics of contestation.

In short, we could ask a series of questions concerning contestation with regard to Africa: Who participates in protest? What are their socio-demographic characteristics? Are they the elite or ordinary people? Why are they protesting (i.e. on which issues)? What forms of protest are being employed (i.e. demonstrations, sit-ins, lobbying, riots)? How are they being mobilized?

First, let us look at who the participants are. Some scholars argue that new information and communication technologies are helping to fabricate new connections among people from diverse backgrounds, resulting in mobilizing structures that might be more diverse and inclusive on gender, race and ethnicity, and nationality.[96] Indeed, protest participation has gradually normalized and all sorts of people are resorting to protest to demand change.[97] But it is not clear whether this is the case in Africa too. Are the most deprived people taking to the streets or is it only the elite? Moreover, the question remains as to whether new information and communication technologies are as influential in Africa as they appear to be in the Western world.

The question of *what* people are protesting for focuses on issues and motivation. Issues may have different origins, in the form of conflicting principles or conflicting material interests. For extremely deprived people, the struggle to survive takes up all their time and energy. Does this imply that mainstream African protest has its origin in material interests and that instrumental motivations push people on to the streets?

Concerning forms of protest, the action repertoire is influenced by the (supra)national and mobilizing context. This may have an effect on whether activists organize large mass-based organizations, whether they lobby and organize petitions, or whether discontent turns into bread riots. Obviously, all these forms of contestation have their own motivational dynamics and appeal to different people.

Conclusion

This chapter has discussed how developments in the real world have influenced the study of contention. It started with classical approaches, such as mass society and collective behaviour theories, that tried to explain large movements before the Second World War like Nazism and Communism. The growth of social movement activity with a goal-oriented and rational focus in the 1960s called for more structural and rational approaches such as the political process

---

[96]   Taylor, 'Mobilizing for change in a social movement society'.

[97]   Meyer & Tarrow, *Towards a Movement Society?*; see also Norris *et al.*, 'Who demonstrates?'

and resource-mobilization approach and for more social constructivistic approaches derived from cultural sociology and social psychology. Since the 1990s, activists mobilizing for social change have been operating in a dramatically changing social-political context. Social movement scholars have reacted with arguments about synergy, making the case for synergizing structural and social constructivistic approaches. The final sections therefore presented an explanatory framework for contextualized contentious politics in which we can integrate influences from supra(national) and mobilizing contexts within a particular country. Obviously, a comprehensive master framework that brings these elements together is still to be built. The most important challenge is probably the integration of the concepts proposed. In this regard, moving from static to more dynamic explanations of contentious politics is important. The recent conceptual shift, proposed by McAdam, Tarrow and Tilly,[98] to look for mechanisms and processes that occur in many different kinds of movements and that lead to different outcomes depending on the specific contexts within which they occur may be a useful direction. Indeed, studying contentious politics in a more dynamic way would do justice to the theoretical and empirical richness of the concepts and could be crucial for gaining better insight into the processes at hand. The study of contentious politics is now much richer, more sophisticated and more synergized than it was sixty years ago. The 'war on paradigms'[99] of the 1980s and 1990s seems to have been replaced by a new decade of 'synergy'.

The 'roadmap' presented here has tried to exemplify the approaches used in the study of social movements over the last sixty years and it is hoped that the explanatory framework will be useful to social movement scholars all over the globe, but especially in Africa. Social movements have been well studied in the European and Latin American contexts but only sporadically in Africa, and then mainly in South Africa. Current developments across African societies might invite social movement scholars to try and explain these dynamics of contention by applying insights from the social movement literature as developed in non-African contexts.

---

[98] D. McAdam, S. Tarrow & C. Tilly, *Dynamics of Contention* (Cambridge University Press, New York, 2001); McAdam *et al.*, 'Comparative perspectives on contentious politics'.

[99] S. Tarrow, 'Bridging the quantitative-qualitative divide', in: H.E. Brady & D. Collier (eds), *Rethinking Social Inquiry: Diverse tools, shared standards* (Rowman and Littlefield, Lanham, MD, 2004).

Speaking to global debates through a national and continental lens: South African and African social movements in comparative perspective[1]

Adam Habib & Paul Opoku-Mensah

This chapter reflects on the empirical cases of contemporary social movements in South Africa and Africa in relation to the debates that have emerged in the global academy. In particular it responds to two assertions that have become common in this debate; first, that the fulcrum of social struggles for a human development agenda has shifted from the arena of production to consumption, and second, that identity movements and struggles are replacing the overtly material ones, especially in post-industrial societies. Studies of social movements in South Africa and Africa, however, suggest that both these assertions are too simplistic, and that in reality a more nuanced interpretation is required. While the scale of social struggles has expanded in the arena of consumption, the South African and African case studies suggest that movements in the arena of production not only continue to retain vibrancy, but also are crucial to the sustainability of struggles of consumption. Moreover these same case studies suggest that while identity movements and struggles are indeed on the increase, material issues are as relevant to these struggles as they have been to the earlier social movements. Finally the chapter concludes with the argument that these movements are crucial in many of the democratizing societies for creating the substantive uncertainty that is necessary for facilitating the accountability of political elites to their mar-

---

[1] This chapter is in part based on the concluding chapter of R. Ballard, A. Habib & I. Valodia (eds), *Voices of Protest: Social Movements in Post-Apartheid South Africa* (University of KwaZulu-Natal Press, Pietermaritzburg, 2006).

ginalized citizens so that a more sustainable human-oriented development agenda is realized.

Introduction

The study of social movements has undergone something of a revival in recent years, partly due to the resumption of social struggles on the international plane. The most prominent is of course the anti-globalization movement that first made its public presence felt on the streets of Seattle but has since mobilized in almost every city where any of the international financial agencies have held their meetings. Indeed, this explosion of global struggle has spawned an unprecedented number of transnational organizations, the vast majority of which are directed at reforming some element of the global order.[2]

Social struggles have not only increased on the international plane or in OECD countries but have also become a prominent feature of the political scene in many of the countries of the South. This is especially so in the Third Wave of democracies where a decade or two of market-oriented economic reforms have eroded the popular support and legitimacy of newly established democratic regimes.[3] One of the most prominent cases of national struggle is the Chiapas rebellion in Mexico but similar popular revolts have manifested themselves in many parts of the developing world and have even toppled governments.

Where social struggles emerge, academics and scholars often follow. The explosion of global and national struggles has provoked a plethora of studies on global and national social movements[4] but there was also an independent impetus for these social movement studies. An earlier generation of studies polarized into three distinct blocs inspired by resource mobilization, political opportunity and identity-oriented theories. In recent years however, there have been a number of initiatives to bridge the divides and develop a comprehensive explanation of the rise, operations and decline of social movements.[5]

[2] H. Anheier, M. Glasius & M. Kaldor, 'Introducing global civil society', in H. Anheier, M. Glasius & M. Kaldor (eds), *Global Civil Society* (Oxford University Press, Oxford, 2001).
[3] A. Przeworski, *Sustainable Democracy* (Cambridge University Press, Cambridge, 1997).
[4] J. Clark, *Global Civic Engagement* (Earthscan, London, 2003); J. Keane, *Global Civil Society?* (Cambridge University Press, Cambridge, 2003); R. Taylor, *Creating a Better World: Interpreting global civil society* (Kumarian Press, Bloomfield, 2005).
[5] D. della Porta & M. Diana, *Social Movements: An introduction* (Blackwell Publishers, MA, 1999); D. McAdam, S. Tarrow & C. Tilly, *Dynamics of Contention* (Cambridge University Press, New York, 2001).

Contemporary social movement theories are not only distinguished by the way they resort to a multiplicity of explanatory variables but also to the rise of new popular orthodoxies. Two of the most prominent of these are that identity movements and struggles are replacing the previously overtly material ones, and that the fulcrum of social struggles for a human-development agenda has shifted from the arena of production to consumption, both of which are seen to expressly manifest themselves in post-industrial societies. This chapter speaks to these two assertions in the global academy but from the perspective of the African experience.

The empirical foundation of the analysis is the first comprehensive national study of contemporary social movements in South Africa, which was convened by the Centre for Civil Society and the School of Development Studies at the University of KwaZulu-Natal, and was funded by Atlantic Philanthropies and the Ford Foundation. It represented the collaborative engagement of over twenty academics and researchers and studies of seventeen social movements, struggles or organizations were undertaken over a two-year period. Similar research questions on the character, leadership, operations and significance of the movements were addressed in each of the studies and resulted in a level of generalization about South African social movements.[6] The case studies are supplemented by an ever-growing body of empirical analyses of contemporary social movements across Africa, a collection that constitutes a unique conceptual lens through which the assumptions of and the debates in the global academy can be tested and reflected upon respectively.

Is the African experience an appropriate reference point for engaging the debates in the global academy? African societies are, of course, not post-industrial societies and so it may seem unfair to respond to the theoretical assertions on social movements from a context that is so socio-economically different. But is it intellectually sustainable for the global academy to develop a theory of social movements – with universal ambitions – on the narrow experiences of post-industrial societies? Even if it were, one African experience – the South African one – would still be relevant as the country represents an interesting hybrid, reflecting the post-industrial and developing worlds. And it is also a transitional society in constant evolution and a state of flux, with elements of both the past and the present. This makes it a useful social laboratory within which social scientists can investigate collective expressions of protest, state response and societal evolution.

This chapter thus addresses the debates on social movements in the global academy from the perspective of the African continent's, and in particular South Africa's, contemporary social struggles. It begins by summarizing the

---

[6]   Ballard, Habib & Valodia (eds), *Voices of Protest*.

debates in the social movement literature on the relevance of identity and material struggles, and the arenas in which they can be mobilized. This is followed by an analysis of the South African and African case studies and how they speak to the global debates. The chapter then considers the relevance of these movements for democracy and a human-oriented development trajectory, with the conclusion drawing together the major threads of the analysis.

New-found dogmas in contemporary social movement theory

Current explanations of social movements are built on three foundational elements: the political structure that defines opportunities and constraints,[7] the human and financial resources that enable a movement's mobilization and operations,[8] and the identities that provide the impetus for actors to become involved and provide legitimacy for the movement. Of course these three distinct elements were, as indicated earlier, the explanatory variables that were advanced by three distinct schools in social movement theory. Yet it is the third, which focuses on the central role of identity, that has been particularly influential in contemporary explanations of social movements. This identity-oriented paradigm insists that the identity, status and the values of actors are what make the ultimate difference in the mobilization of collectives.[9] These subjective elements, they argue, create what Melucci[10] terms systems of reference that enable the shared feelings of grievance or outrage that prompt people to form collectives and actively enter the political arena.

It is important to remember the context in which this theory originated. Largely developed to explain the rise and influence of so-called 'identity-based' movements – racial or religiously constructed, women's, gay rights and even environmental collectives – in economically developed western democracies, it challenged Marxist interpretations that placed distributional issues at the centre of explanations of social movements. Yet this paradigm, while initially popular within the academy, nevertheless lost its shine as it was subjected to a barrage of criticism in the 1990s. However the explanations once again came into vogue

---

[7] S. Tarrow, *Power in Movement: Social movements, collective action and politics* (Cambridge University Press, New York, 1994).

[8] J. McCarthy & M.N. Zald, *The Trend of Social Movements in America: Professionalization and resource mobilization* (General Learning Corporation, Morristown, NJ, 1973); C. Tilly, *From Mobilisation to Revolution* (Addison-Wesley, Reading, MA, 1978).

[9] A. Touraine, *The Voice and the Eye: An analysis of social movements* (Cambridge University Press, Cambridge, 1981); A. Melucci, *Nomads of the Present: Social movement and identity needs in contemporary society* (Temple University Press, Philadelphia, PA, 1989).

[10] Melucci, *Nomads of the Present*.

with the explosion of transnational organizations and mobilizational collectives, many of which questioned and challenged the neoliberal tenets of official globalization initiatives.

The point to note is that this explanatory paradigm's popularity returned among not only its earlier advocates but also among many of its earlier critics within the academy and the movements themselves. The well-known sociologist Michael Buroway[11] makes the case for why an identity-based explanatory paradigm is more useful for understanding the myriad of social struggles against the various elements of official globalization. In his view, globalization as it is defined and advanced by its political, policy, and corporate architects has enabled the expansion of the market in hitherto uncharted territory. The net effect is that its consequences have begun to impact on a far wider set of stakeholders than in earlier epochs. He thus concludes that in this 'post communist era progressive struggles have moved away from distributional politics to focus on identity politics or what Nancy Fraser calls a politics of recognition'.[12]

A related but distinct assertion in the contemporary explanation of social movements and struggles is the increasingly widely held belief among both scholars and activists that the fulcrum of mobilization and anti-hegemonic political activity is shifting from the realm of production to that of consumption. Again, Buroway's article makes this assertion explicit. Drawing on Polanyi,[13] he suggests that counter-hegemonic potential lies not only in the realm of production, as classically understood, but also in the domain of consumption and the market:

> Everyone suffers from the market in as much as unrestrained it leads to the destruction of the environment, global warming, toxic wastes, the colonization of free time, and so forth. ... Whereas alienated and degraded labour may excite a limited alternative, it does not have the universalism of the market that touches everyone in multiple ways. It is the market, therefore, that offers possible grounds for counter hegemony. We see this everywhere but especially in the amalgam of movements against the many guises of globalization.[14]

And he is not the only one with this view in the academy. David Harvey[15] in *The New Imperialism* arrives at a similar conclusion on the basis of his analysis of neo-liberalism, which he argues is Capital's response to the problems of over-accumulation that emerged in the last three decades of the twentieth century. His analysis holds that the dominant logic of capital accumulation in the

---

[11]   See M. Burawoy, 'For a sociological Marxism: the complementary convergence of Antonio Gramsci and Karl Polanyi', in *Politics and Society*, 31, 2 (2003).
[12]   Burawoy, 'For a sociological Marxism', p. 242.
[13]   K. Polanyi, *The Great Transformation* (Beacon Press, Boston, 1957).
[14]   Burawoy, 'For a sociological Marxism', p. 231.
[15]   D. Harvey, *The New Imperialism* (Oxford University Press, Oxford, 2003).

contemporary period is what he calls, following Rosa Luxemburg, 'accumulation by dispossession' which forces 'the costs of devaluations of surplus capitals upon the weakest and most vulnerable territories and populations'.[16] The result is an explosion of struggles outside the arena of production around the privatization of basic services and the displacement of the poor and marginalized. Harvey concludes that greater attention needs to be paid to the struggles occasioned by accumulation through dispossession and that links need to be forged between these and proletarian struggles at the point of production.

While there is not much that can be disputed in Harvey's carefully constructed and nuanced conclusion, the more extreme readings of these processes both within the academy and among social-movement activists must be questioned. In the case of the latter, a growing perception has been that unions have lost their potential to serve as institutional agents for counter-hegemonic struggle, and the only hope now remains in a range of radical social movements located in the arena of reproduction. Ashwin Desai has explicitly expressed this view, as has Richard Pithouse who asserts that:

> ... the idea of the multitude has freed many from both the fetish of the proletariat as the only viable agent of challenge to capital and the fetish of the nation as defender against capital. Given the reality that most resistances in contemporary South Africa are at the point of consumption (basic services, housing, health care, education etc) rather than production, and are largely community rather than union driven, as well as the complete immersion of the South African elite into the trans-national elite, these are very welcome releases.[17]

How then do these two assertions, which have effectively become the dominant orthodoxies not only within the social-movement literature but also among progressive social-movement activists themselves, stand up to the South African and wider continental case studies? It is this question that the next section considers.

Reflections on the South African and continental case studies

It may be useful to begin this reflection on social movements in contemporary Africa by focusing on South Africa and with the obvious and perhaps banal remark that these institutions are essentially the products of the post-apartheid moment. However this is not to suggest that they are emerging from a vacuum.

---

[16]   Harvey, *The New Imperialism*, p. 184-185.
[17]   Richard Pithouse, 'Solidarity, co-option and assimilation: The necessity, promises and pitfalls of global linkages for South African movements', in *Development Update*, 5, 2 (2004), p. 182; see also M. Hardt & A. Negri, *Empire* (Harvard University Press, Cambridge, MA, 2000).

Clearly their strategies, activities and orientations draw on the experiences, repertoires and other rich heritage of struggle in South Africa. Nevertheless, the post-apartheid moment has imparted a particular character to them. Whether it is the economic crisis of the post-apartheid South Africa as is manifested in its unemployment and poverty rates, the cost recovery initiatives of the local state, made mandatory by the policy choices of post-1994 state elites or the demo-cratic and essentially liberalized political environment of this period, all crucial-ly influenced the genesis of these movements, their evolution and their strate-gies and tactics. But this is where their similarity ends.

This is important to note because in the emotive atmosphere within which political debate occurs these movements are often implicitly projected by both state elites and public officials, and social-movement activists themselves as a coherent homogenous entity. Some political leaders and public officials have intimated that these movements undermine democracy because of their engage-ment in extra-institutional action. And some social-movement activists and in-tellectuals, on the other hand, portray the movements in romanticized terms, describing them as arenas of free democratic debate and participation epito-mized in a 'principled internationalism, a socialist vision, and an independent mass-based mobilisation and struggle as an ideological and organisational alter-native to the capitalist ANC'.[18]

The South African and continental case studies of social movements both challenge the assumption of homogeneity underlying these views, for not only do they speak to a somewhat hypothetical ideal rather than to the current reality of social movements but they also generalize the respective ideal as charac-teristic of all within the social-movement universe. As a way of reminding our-selves of the heterogeneity of grassroots activism, it is useful to undertake a typology of what it is that social movements in South Africa and the wider con-tinent oppose.

First, a large swathe of activism in South Africa is directed against govern-ment policy on distributional issues, particularly with regard to the inability of many poor South Africans to access basic services. Privatization and cost re-covery are perceived as the key elements debilitating delivery. Movements that reflect such campaigns include, among others, the Soweto Electricity Crisis

---

[18]   D. McKinley, 'The rise of social movements in South Africa', in *Debate: Voices from the South African left*, May 2004, p. 17-21. See also P. Bond, 'Strategies for social justice movements from Southern Africa to the United States', *Foreign Policy in Focus (FPIF)*, January 2005; Gudrun Lachenmann, 'Civil society and social movements in Africa: The case of the peasant movement in Senegal', *The European Journal of Development Research*, 5, 2 (1993), pp. 68-100.

Committee,[19] the Anti-Privatisation Forum,[20] the former Concerned Citizens Forum,[21] the now-divided Western Cape Anti-Eviction Campaign,[22] and the Treatment Action Campaign.[23]

Similarly, the emergence of social movements on the African continent has taken place within the context of deprivation, rights denial and injustice. This context is characterized by a lack of access to basic services like water, medicine, housing and electricity. It is the various claims to and demands on governments for these rights that have shaped the logic and coherence of the various movements that have emerged on the continent. These include but are not limited to the Ghanaian, Zambian and Zimbabwean Anti-Privatisation Forums that are similar to the one operating in South Africa.[24]

Second, some movements oppose the state, banks and private landlords through opposition to eviction and attempts to secure land tenure. Movements in South Africa that have taken up these struggles are the Landless People's Movement,[25] the Concerned Citizens Group,[26] and the Western Cape Anti-Eviction Campaign.[27] Social movements in other parts of Africa have mobilized in response to similar issues, including the land question. This includes, for instance, the San people in Botswana who achieved global visibility in December 2006 following a court decision that affirmed their right to their ancestral lands in the Kalahari Desert, a right that had been usurped by the Botswana government.[28] In Kenya too there is an emerging land movement that is often

---

[19] A. Egan & A. Wafer, 'Dynamics of a 'mini mass movement': Origins, identity and ideological pluralism in the Soweto electricity crisis committee', in Ballard, Habib & Valodia (eds), *Voices of Protest.*

[20] S. Buhlungu, 'Upstarts or bearers of tradition? The anti-privatisation forum of Gauteng', in Ballard, Habib & Valodia (eds), *Voices of Protest.*

[21] P. Dwyer, 'The concerned citizens forum: A fight within a fight', in Ballard, Habib & Valodia (eds), *Voices of Protest.*

[22] S. Oldfield & K. Stokke, 'Building unity in diversity: Social movement activism in the Western Cape anti-eviction campaign', in Ballard, Habib & Valodia (eds), *Voices of Protest.*

[23] S. Friedman & S. Mottiar, 'Seeking the high ground: The treatment action campaign and the politics of morality', in Ballard, Habib & Valodia (eds), *Voices of Protest.*

[24] M.C. Brill, 'Exploring the emerging social movements in Africa at the third African social forum', *Africa Action,* January, 2005; Bond, 'Strategies for social justice movements'; P. Bond, *Fanon's Warning: A civil society reader on the new partnership for Africa's development* (Africa World Press, Trenton, NJ, 2005).

[25] S. Greenberg, 'The landless people's movement and the failure of post-apartheid land reform', in Ballard, Habib & Valodia (eds), *Voices of Protest.*

[26] Dwyer, 'The concerned citizens forum'.

[27] Oldfield & Stokke, 'Building unity in diversity'.

[28] Brill, 'Exploring the emerging social movements in Africa'.

associated with the organization commonly known as the Kenyan Land Alliance.[29]

Third, there is a base of familiar unions in post-apartheid South Africa that are targeting government policy on employment conditions as well as labour practices in the private sector. Most of these unions are housed within COSATU which, although in alliance with the current government, has nevertheless continued to engage in adversarial mass action.[30] The limitation of these formal-sector unions has, however, been their inability to deal with the changing nature of work and the growing layers of informal workers. This challenge has been taken up by nascent campaigns like the Self-Employed Women's Union (SEWU) that target the local state on accommodating workers and traders rather than challenging their bosses about conditions of service. Notwithstanding the SEWU's demise in 2004, its agenda is continuing to impact on mainstream unions.[31]

Although African trade unions have lost their traditional dominance as they now have to share their political space with other actors, they still remain central to employment issues. Across the continent, they have been at the forefront of mass demonstrations to change standards of employment[32] and in fact remain one of the few organizations that have continuously had continental reach through the Organization of African Trade Union Unity (OATUU). Other organizations, like the Kenya Human Rights Commission (KHRC), have also worked in this area to highlight the plight of workers in export-processing zones (EPZ) and those working on flower farms.[33] Moreover, oil workers on several of the delta platforms have similarly pressed vigorously not only for higher wages but also for broader community demands through their movements in Nigeria's delta region.[34] This 'social movement unionism'[35] is typical of trade-union activity across the continent, including South Africa, and has most

---

[29] Onyango Oloo, 'Social movements set to assert their presence at WSF Nairobi 2007', *Pambazuka News* (http://pambazuka.org/en/category/comment/38952, December 21, 2006).

[30] A. Habib & I. Valodia, 'Reconstructing a social movement in an era of globalisation: A case study of the Congress of South African Trade Unions (COSATU)', in Ballard, Habib & Valodia (eds), *Voices of Protest.*

[31] A. Devenish & C. Skinner, 'Collective action in the informal economy: The case of the self employed women's union, 1994-2004', in Ballard, Habib & Valodia (eds), *Voices of Protest.*

[32] Oloo, 'Social movements set to assert their presence at WSF Nairobi 2007'.

[33] *Ibid.*

[34] Bond, 'Strategies for social justice movements'.

[35] E. Webster & K. Von Holdt, 'Towards a socialist theory of radical reform: From resistance to reconstruction in the labour movement', paper delivered to the Ruth First Memorial Symposium (University of the Western Cape, 1992).

recently been demonstrated in the Zimbabwean Congress of Trade Union's (ZCTU) participation in the democratic struggle in Zimbabwe.

Fourth, significant activism is being directed against corporations and the government on issues of pollution and the environment. One such action in South Africa that has been sustained over a long period of time is community action in South Durban. In addition, the Environmental Justice Networking Forum represents a group of organizations that have been instrumental in shifting popular environmental consciousness from green conservation issues to brown issues that emphasize social justice.[36] The environment also provides a target for social-movement mobilization in the rest of Africa. Two of the more visible movements at the forefront of such mobilization include Kenya's Green Belt movement founded by the 2004 Nobel Peace Prize winner Wangari Maathai[37] and the environmental movements in the Niger Delta whose strategies have included sit-ins at the local offices of multinational companies and, increasingly, more radical and violent actions involving the kidnapping of foreign workers.[38]

Fifth, some organizations in South Africa have sought to counter social prejudice against refuges,[39] sexual minorities[40] and women,[41] especially through reforms of government policy infrastructure. The HIV/AIDS crisis provides a natural target for social-movement mobilization against the policy and service-delivery infrastructure in Africa. While it is a stand-alone movement in some regions, in others it is part of the economic justice movement and/or the women's movement.[42] The core of the movement is predominantly women, although its leadership tends to be primarily male. It is fighting against the

---

[36] J. Cock, 'Connecting the red, brown and green: The environmental justice movement in South Africa', in Ballard, Habib & Valodia (eds), *Voices of Protest*.

[37] C. Obi, 'Environmental movements in sub-Saharan Africa: A political ecology of power and conflict, civil society and social movements. United Nations Research Institute for Social Development. Programme Paper 15, January 2005; M. Salih, *Environmental Politics and Liberation in Contemporary Africa* (Kluwer Academic Publishers, London, 1999).

[38] Obi, 'Environmental movements in sub-Saharan Africa'; Bond, 'Strategies for social justice movements'.

[39] B. Amisi & R. Ballard, 'In the absence of citizenship: Congolese refugee struggle and organisation in South Africa', in Ballard, Habib & Valodia (eds), *Voices of Protest*.

[40] T. Dirsuweit, 'The problem of identities: The lesbian, gay, bisexual, transgender and intersex social movement in South Africa', in Ballard, Habib & Valodia (eds), *Voices of Protest*.

[41] S. Hassim, 'The challenges of inclusion and transformation: The women's movement in democratic South Africa', in Ballard, Habib & Valodia (eds), *Voices of Protest*.

[42] Brill, 'Exploring the Emerging Social Movements in Africa'.

prejudice and stigma associated with HIV/AIDS as well as for permanent treatment for HIV/AIDS patients. It thus involves diverse actors ranging from healthcare and/or home-based care providers, people living with HIV/AIDS, educators, professionals, the gay, lesbian and bisexual communities, trade unions and some faith-based communities. Examples include the Pan African Treatment Access Movement (PATAM); Gays and Lesbians of Zimbabwe (GALZ); Zimbabwean Activists on HIV/AIDS (ZAHA) and the Kenyan Network of Women with AIDS/HIV (KENWA). These movements all frame the HIV/AIDS challenge within the context of human rights and economic justice, with the objective of achieving universal, accessible and comprehensive treatment and care for all those living with HIV/AIDS. For instance KENWA, with its more than 3000 members, has focused its mobilization on issues of human rights (especially women's rights), treatment access, stigma, reproductive rights and access to credit, insurance and mortgages.[43]

Finally, movements in Africa that oppose multilateral organizations and transnational corporations (TNC's) because of their links with broader global movements like the Jubilee campaigns.[44] The most notable of these is Jubilee South Africa, which opposes multilateral organizations and foreign corporations in relation to debts that cannot be paid or in terms of claiming compensation from businesses that operated in South Africa during apartheid.[45] It has also lobbied the current South African government to take a stronger social-justice approach, particularly regarding reparations for victims identified through the Truth and Reconciliation Commission. Other African examples include the Third World Network (TWN), the Zimbabwe Coalition on Debt and Development (ZIMCODD), the Uganda Debt Network, the Third World Forum, the West African Social Forum, the Forum of African Alternatives and the Senegal-based Environment and Development Action-Third World (ENDA).[46] In ad-

---

[43] *Ibid.*

[44] Bond, 'Strategies for Social Justice Movements'; Alingué, Madeleine Andebeng L., 'African Transatlantic Resistance and Movements', in Atilio Boron & A. Gladys Lechini (eds), *Politics and Social Movements in an Hegemonic World: Lessons from Africa, Asia and Latin America* (Consejo Latinoamericano de Ciencias Sociales (CLACSO), Buenos Aires, 2005), pp. 245-258; Joan Baxter, "Another Africa is possible': Social movements organize to challenge dominant economic policies', *From Africa Recovery*, 16, 1 (April 2002).

[45] C. Rustomjee, 'From economic debt to moral debt: The campaigns of jubilee South Africa', in Ballard, Habib & Valodia (eds), *Voices of Protest*.

[46] Ebrima Sall, 'Social movements in the renegotiation of the bases for citizenship in West Africa', *Current Sociology*, 52, 4 (2004), pp. 595-614 (http://csi.sagepub.com/cgi/content/abstract/52/4/595); Bond, 'Strategies for social justice movements'; Brill, 'Exploring the emerging social movements in Africa'; Kehinde Olayode, 'Pro-democracy movements, democratisation and conflicts in Africa: Nigeria, 1990–

dition to working primarily on debt cancellation, trade and foreign aid, the Jubilee Campaigns and debt and development groups like AFRODAD are also engaged in the interconnected issues of access to services. Trade unions, other forms of organized labour, political parties and think tanks – many of them anti-capitalist in orientation – also engage with this movement at varying levels.[47]

In summary, social movement mobilization in Africa and South Africa is a product of, and responds to, a concrete context of deprivation, rights denial and injustice. The continent's social-movement landscape is incredibly heterogeneous but for analytical purposes it is possible to categorize African movements as follows: Anti-Corporate Globalization/Economic Justice; Democracy and Transparency; Environmental; HIV/AIDS; and Women and Youth.[48]

This heterogeneity is exhibited not simply in terms of activities or issues. Increasingly, it is being reflected in the strategies adopted by social movements in Africa too. Even movements that operate under the rubric of anti-globalization adopt different strategies against multilateral organizations like the IMF, the World Bank, the World Trade Organization (WTO) and governmental bodies like the African Union. While some movements are willing to collaborate with these institutions, others are adopting a more confrontational approach. The willingness to collaborate and engage seems to vary by region, with movements in Southern Africa, particularly in South Africa, preferring non-engagement. West Africans, by contrast, appear to have the largest number of organizations willing to engage with the African Union and the international financial institutions. Overall, a radicalization and militarization of Africa's social movements would seem to be under way, with the use of violence by the movements in the Niger Delta providing the best example of this phenomenon.[49]

This typology of social movements and the thematic concerns they are mobilizing around suggest that distributional issues are still central in Africa. Indeed, a good proportion of the movements in categories one, two, three and six, have emerged as a response to the economic crisis and its manifestations,

---

1999', *African Journal of International Affairs*, 10, 1-2 (2007), pp. 127-146; Baxter, 'Another Africa is possible'.

[47] Brill, 'Exploring the emerging social movements in Africa'.

[48] Sall, 'Social Movements in the renegotiation of the bases for citizenship'; Bond, 'Strategies for social justice movements'; Brill, 'Exploring the emerging social movements in Africa'; Olayode, 'Pro-democracy movements, democratisation and conflicts in Africa'.

[49] Brill, 'Exploring the emerging social movements in Africa'; Bond, 'Strategies for social justice movements', and Patrick Bond, *Fanon's Warning: A civil society reader on the new partnership for Africa's development* (Africa World Press, Trenton, NJ, 2005).

and were deliberately founded to effect a redistribution of scarce resources in favour of marginalized communities. It is only categories four and five, those addressing environmental concerns and prejudices directed against specific communities respectively, that are not overtly organized to speak directly to distributional deficits.

Even in these explicitly identity-based movements however, distributional issues colour their politics. The case studies in South Africa of the gay,[50] environmental,[51] women's[52] and refugee[53] movements show that even while identity is an important driver within these movements, distributional questions have by no means been marginalized. In fact, these case studies demonstrate that a huge contestation exists within these movements around distributional issues. As Dirsuweit[54] points out, the gay movement is divided over the questions of distribution that are raised by the poverty of a significant proportion of its members. The same is true of the environmental movement, which is increasingly being forced to take on 'brown' rather than 'green' issues, thus addressing the socio-economic concerns of marginalized communities and highlighting the principle of environmental justice.[55] Similarly a study of two prominent environmental movements in Sub-Saharan Africa, the Movement for the Survival of Ogoni People of Nigeria's Niger Delta and the Green Belt Movement of Kenya, demonstrates that they operate within a transformative logic in which struggles for power over environmental resources connect with broader popular social struggles for empowerment and democracy. Many environmental conflicts in Africa are driven by a challenge to dominant power relations that continue to benefit the 'few' and threaten the survival of the majority.[56]

These case studies suggest that identity-based social movements in Africa, typical of those in the developing world, are being driven by an intricate mix of identity and distributional pressures. And there is no reason to assume that this is a peculiarly African phenomenon. Indeed, Teresa Dirsuweit[57] suggests that a similar mix of pressures defines movements in the industrialized world too.

---

[50] Dirsuweit, 'The problem of identities'.
[51] Cock, 'Connecting the red, brown and green'.
[52] Hassim, 'The challenges of inclusion and transformation'.
[53] Amisi & Ballard, 'In the absence of citizenship".
[54] Dirsuweit, 'The problem of identities'.
[55] Cock, 'Connecting the red, brown and green'.
[56] Obi, 'Environmental movements in sub-Saharan Africa'. See also Salih, *Environmental Politics and Liberation in Contemporary Africa*.
[57] Reflecting on the writings of I.M. Young, *Justice and the Politics of Difference* (Princeton University Press, Princeton, 1990) and *Inclusion and Democracy* (Oxford University Press, Oxford, 2000); and N. Fraser, *Justice Interruptus: Critical Reflections on the 'postsocialist' condition* (Routledge, New York, 1997).

After all, there is growing evidence that inequalities and poverty are increasing in industrialized countries. This, together with the fact that a large part of the world where social movements are active are developing contexts, suggests that distributional issues need to be an explicit component of the theory-building agenda of social-movement scholars.

What of the second assertion that the arena of production is no longer as relevant for organizing counter-hegemonic struggles? Implicit in this view is the suggestion of union impotence in the face of a resurgent community activism to represent the interests of marginalized communities. But the South African case studies suggest that this is too easy a read of contemporary developments. After all, even in the pre-1994 era, community struggles accounted for a significant number, if not the majority, of the struggles against the apartheid state from as far back as the 1950s.[58] Even more important is the fact that the union movement today is a vibrant component of the social-movement universe, notwithstanding its alliance with the ruling party. COSATU may not phrase its agenda and activities in counter-hegemonic terms but this has not completely disarmed the federation.

This is the central message of Habib and Valodia's [59]analysis of COSATU's evolution, operations and politics in the contemporary era. They argue that a political disjuncture with the dominant element in the ANC leadership has emerged following the government's adoption of the Growth, Employment and Redistribution (GEAR) Strategy in 1996. Indeed they maintain that this has translated into a progressively more adversarial stance on the part of COSATU vis-à-vis the government and the ANC leadership.

This has manifested itself in general strikes and struggles against GEAR, AIDS and Zimbabwe in recent times. Some social movements, like TAC, have of course recognized this and explicitly entered into an alliance with this social movement in the realm of production. It needs to be noted that in pure membership terms, COSATU, which had a registered membership of 1.8 million in 2003, dwarfs almost all the other social movements combined.[60]

The problem of course is the impression created by the union federation's alliance with the ANC, an alliance that has at times placed the federation on the defensive, forcing it to conduct some struggles within the institutional parameters of the Tripartite Alliance. But the movement's combativeness resurfaces from time to time. The most recent examples are COSATU's vociferous attacks on Mbeki's leadership and his presidency: he was accused of sliding the country

---

[58] M. Mamdani, *Citizen and Subject: Contemporary Africa and the legacy of late colonialism* (Princeton University Press, Princeton, NJ, 1996).
[59] Habib & Valodia, 'Reconstructing a social movement in an era of globalisation'.
[60] *Ibid.*

towards a dictatorship[61] and supporting Jacob Zuma's bid for the leadership of the party and the country. These developments, together with COSATU's social-movement orientation, suggest that the unions are still alive and very relevant to the struggle to represent marginalized communities. Again this suggests, if only because South Africa's socio-economic context is so similar to those in the rest of the developing world, that the realm of production cannot be ignored as an arena of mobilization and organization of counter-hegemonic struggle and that, as a result, unions must be retained as one of the institutional agencies as they are capable of conducting and leading such struggles. The South African case studies imply that the arena of production is as relevant as that of consumption in hosting organizations for the counter-hegemonic struggle prompted by the multiple manifestations of globalization.

This is also true for other parts of Africa, both at the national and continental levels. In the latter arena, OATUU still remains a visible player in institutional politics[62] but perhaps the role of the trade unions is most visible in the democratic movements that have challenged and overthrown dictatorships in a number of African countries. In Zambia, for instance, the Chiluba-led opposition that challenged and eventually defeated the entrenched rule of Kaunda's United Independence Party was the product of the Congress of Trades Unions. Similarly, opposition in Zimbabwe to Mugabe's dictatorial regime has been facilitated by the National Constitutional Assembly (NCA), a pro-democracy network whose membership comprises the main civil-society organizations in Zimbabwe including the Zimbabwe Council of Churches, the Zimbabwe National Students' Union, and the Zimbabwe Congress of Trade Unions (ZCTU). The main opposition party, the Movement for Democratic Change (MDC), is itself a product of the NCA, having been formed by the Zimbabwe Congress of Trade Unions in 1999.[63] Across the continent, with weakened opposition parties and legislatures, trade unions still remain the vanguard of the democratic movement.

The African case studies, including the South African one, strongly contest two of the orthodoxies evident in the contemporary global literature on social movements. At best, they recommend a more nuanced reading, one that stresses the relevance of distributional concerns and their ability to mobilize collectives, and the importance of the sphere of production as a site for counter-hegemonic activity. Of course it is recognized that these orthodoxies speak to some aspects of current realities, but only partially. More detailed and extensive descriptions

[61]   *Business Day*, 2 June 2006.
[62]   Brill, 'Exploring the emerging social movements in Africa'.
[63]   A. Habib & P. Opoku-Mensah, 'Mobilizing across Africa: Civil society and democratisation', in *South African Yearbook of International Affairs 2002/03* (South Africa Institute for International Affairs, 2003).

of social-movement realities would recognize the equal relevance of identity and distributional concerns, as they would the simultaneous importance for contemporary social movement struggle of the arenas of both production and consumption. This experience is not necessarily peculiar to Africa. In fact given the bifurcated economic realities of contemporary South Africa and the increasing inequalities around the world, these African case studies could speak to the full realities of social-movement activity across the industrialized and developing worlds.

Social movements, development and democracy in (South) Africa

What is the impact of these movements on the development trajectory and the consolidation of democracy in South Africa and the rest of Africa? As indicated earlier, some have argued that these movements undermine the democratic project by explicitly challenging, through extra-institutional action, legitimate and democratically elected governments. The essential problem with these interpretations is that they conflate and confuse the stated aims of social movements with their immediate systemic effect. Whatever the ultimate distant goals of these movements may be, their impact needs to be assessed in relation to their immediate systemic effects. And the most obvious tangible effect of social movements on the political landscape of this continent is that they represent the interests of the poor and marginalized, and put pressure on governments to pay greater attention to the welfare of these groups. Social movements are thus an avenue for marginalized people and those concerned about their possibility to impact on material distribution and social exclusion and to claim a certain degree of influence and power over the state itself. In contexts where formal political systems have failed to produce significant political parties to directly champion the cause of the poor, social movements contribute to the restoration of plurality in the political system.

This then raises the more significant contribution of contemporary social movements in Africa. The fundamental purpose of a democracy is to make state elites accountable to the citizenry. This is the only way to effect not only public participation but to guarantee a development trajectory in the interests of all the citizenry, including its most marginalized and dispossessed.[64] Such accountability is founded on the emergence of substantive uncertainty in the political system, and political uncertainty is of course the essence of democracy. It takes one of two distinct forms; institutional or substantive. Institutional uncertainty – uncertainty about the *rules* of the game – implies a vulnerability of the democratic system to anti-democratic forces. Substantive uncertainty – uncertainty

---

[64] A. Habib, 'South Africa: conceptualizing a politics of human-oriented development', *Social Dynamics*, 34, 1 (2008).

about the *outcome* of the game – is about the perceptions of ruling political elites in a democratic system and whether they will be returned to office.[65]The former – institutional uncertainty – is bad for democracy as it raises the prospect of a return to authoritarianism in the Third Wave of democracies. The latter – substantive uncertainty – is good for democracy because it keeps politicians on their toes and makes them responsive to their citizenry.

There has been a great deal of investigation into and reflection on institutional uncertainty[66] but little work has been done on substantive uncertainty. This should not be surprising given that researchers and activists concerned with democratization have been preoccupied with the business of transcending authoritarian regimes and institutionalizing democratic ones. Nevertheless, the lack of attention to substantive uncertainty has significant political costs and indeed the weakness of many contemporary democracies lies precisely in this arena. Despite the presence of institutional mechanisms to promote substantive uncertainty – legislative elections, the separation of powers, civil liberties, opposition political parties, an independent press – this goal still eludes much of what Huntington[67] has called the 'Third Wave' of democracies. One reason for this is the shift in power from the legislature to the executive of governments around the globe over the last two decades. Another emanates from the inclination of democratizers and democratization scholars not to rock the boat in societies undergoing democratic transition. Fearful of the very real danger of a reversion to authoritarianism, these actors have focused on procedural aspects of democratization and made significant political and institutional concessions to the state and economic elites of the authoritarian order. Finally, it can be explained by the honeymoon phenomenon during which citizens are reluctant to vote against liberation parties that were responsible for coordinating popular rebellions that brought down authoritarian regimes.[68]

As a result of these developments and peculiar contextual factors, such as the racialized or ethnic character of South Africa's principal opposition parties – the Democratic Alliance (DA), the Inkatha Freedom Party (IFP) and the New

---

[65] A. Schedler, 'Taking uncertainty seriously: the blurred boundaries of democratic transition and consolidation', *Democratization*, 8, 4 (2001), p. 19.

[66] G. O'Donnell & P. Schmitter, *Transitions From Authoritarian Rule: Tentative conclusions about uncertain democracies*, 4 (John Hopkins University Press, Baltimore, 1986); G. O' Donnell, 'On the state, democratization and some conceptual problems: A Latin American view with glances at some Post-Communist countries', *World Development* 21, 8 (1993); S. Huntington, *The Third Wave: Democratization in the late twentieth century* (University of Oklahoma Press, Oklahoma, 1991).

[67] *Ibid.*

[68] F. Fanon, *The Wretched of the Earth* (Penguin Books, Harmondsworth, 1967), p. 137; Mamdani, *Citizen and Subject*, p. 21; A. Mbembe, *On the Postcolony* (University of California Press, Berkeley/LA, 2001), p. 104.

National Party (NNP) – the ANC has not been seriously threatened at the polls. This lack of substantive uncertainty has eroded the citizenry's leverage *vis-à-vis* state elites. The ANC, as the dominant party in the liberation movement, came to office with an overwhelming electoral mandate but, despite this, its policy concessions over the last decade have been largely to foreign investors and domestic capital (both black and white) because it was able to take its citizens' votes for granted. Policy concessions in favour of capital are most graphically reflected in the abandonment of the Reconstruction and Development Programme (RDP) and the adoption of GEAR. The net effect has been a transition that has de-racialized the apex of the class structure and economically favoured the upper echelons and strata of South African society.[69]

An antidote to this state of affairs is the reintroduction of substantive uncertainty into the political system. Of course there may be much debate on the precise institutional mechanisms that could facilitate substantive uncertainty. Some might maintain that it need only involve electoral reform and the emergence of social movements[70] while others suggest that it would require the former coupled with the break-up of the tripartite alliance and the abandonment of corporatist institutions.[71] All of this could facilitate uncertainty, which is necessary to loosen the existing configuration of power in South African society. What it is important to note in this debate, however, is that none of the other elements *except* the presence of social movements exists or is likely to emerge in the foreseeable future. For now at least, social movements are the only hope for introducing substantive uncertainty and thereby facilitating the accountability of state elites to the citizenry.

It is instructive to note that the South African government's recent shift to a more state interventionist and expansive economic policy with a more welfarist orientation coincided with the emergence and heightened activity of social movements in South Africa. While it would be difficult to establish direct causality between the shift in state policy and the emergence of social movements, very few observers of the South African scene would deny that social movements contributed to the emergence of a political climate that encouraged state elites to become more responsive to the country's most marginalized

---

[69]   A. Whiteford & D.E. Van Seventer, 'South Africa's changing income distribution in the 1990s', *Studies in Economics and Econometrics*, 24, 3 (2000), pp. 7-30.

[70]   R. Mattes & R. Southall, 'Popular attitudes toward the South African electoral system', *Democratization*, 11, 1 (2004); Ballard, Habib & Valodia (eds), *Voices of Protest*.

[71]   A. Habib & R. Taylor, 'Political alliances and parliamentary opposition in post-apartheid South Africa', *Democratization*, 8, 1 (2001); A. Desai & A. Habib, 'Labour relations in transition: The rise of corporatism in South Africa's automobile industry', *Journal of Modern African Studies*, 35, 3 (1997).

citizenry. This shift in state policy is naturally not without problems and has as yet not gone far enough.[72] It could also be argued that such shifts are the enlightened twin of the strategy of repression. For Harvey, drawing on Gramsci, '[t]he power of the hegemon ... is fashioned out of and expressed through an ever-shifting balance between coercion and consensus'.[73] Realizing that it has opened the door for others to gain support through more explicitly worded anti-poverty manifestos, the ANC government shifted to recapture ground in the build-up to the 2004 election.

South Africa is again not unique in Africa in this regard. The one-party regimes of the post-colonial era were not very responsive to the interests of their citizens, corruption and patronage flowered, and elite interests predominated. These only came under sustained attack and political elites became more open to citizens when civil society coalesced in opposition or when violence erupted in society. The most recent demonstration of this is Zimbabwe. It was when the MDC emerged, itself a product of the NCA, that the Mugabe regime started to talk about the socio-economic rights of rural peasants. Of course ZANU-PF also resorted to violence, which spiralled the economy into crisis. Nevertheless, it is the challenge to one-party dominance as a result of social mobilization that has conditioned Zimbabwean political elites to be more socially responsive.

This pattern repeats itself time and time again across the continent: Zambia, Kenya, Nigeria, South Africa, Zimbabwe and many others are all examples of this political process. Recognition of it enables us to conclude that the effective operation of social movements is a necessary, if not a sufficient political condition to prompt a sustainable shift in state policy in the interests of South Africa's poor and marginalized. A more human-centred development trajectory and the consolidation of democracy require, in part, the systemic presence and effective functioning of contemporary social movements in South Africa.

---

[72] A. Habib, 'The politics of economic policy-making: Substantive uncertainty, political leverage, and human development', *Transformation*, 56 (2004).

[73] Harvey, *The New Imperialism*, pp. 37-38.

4

African civil society, 'blood diamonds' and the Kimberley process

Lansana Gberie

'People are very angry. They want to say, 'God, why did diamonds be, you know...? Why did you let diamonds be put in Sierra Leone?' We do not know how come ... Sierra Leone with such a wealth can be, you know, in such a global mess.'

Abu Brima, National Coordinator, Network Movement for Justice and Development, Freetown, Sierra Leone; Interview with Voice of America (VOA), 13 January 2000.

The campaign against 'conflict' diamonds – those defined as having been illegally mined and sold by rebel armies to fund wars in Africa – was a singular phenomenon of NGO/civil-society activism in Africa. Beginning inauspiciously with research by little-known and poorly funded groups, the campaign quickly attracted the attention of dozens of governments and the diamond industry and came to dominate discussions on the civil wars in Sierra Leone, Angola and elsewhere in Africa. It provided material and background for books, journal articles and academic dissertations, development programmes; an award-winning song by the American rapper Kenye West; a major Hollywood blockbuster and several documentaries and films (including a Nigerian one). In both its intensity and effect, the 'conflict diamonds' campaign qualifies as a highly successful social movement – a campaign which, though loosely organized and coordinated, was sustained over a significant period of time and was geared towards specific social goals, namely economic and social justice and peace.

This chapter examines how the campaign started, the role of African civil-society groups in sustaining it and why it was so successful and led to sanctions against rebels in Sierra Leone and the Liberian government (thereby no doubt significantly

helping the peace process in both countries). It was also in-
volved in the introduction of the Kimberley Process Certifi-
cation Scheme (KPCS) – a global, UN Security Council-
endorsed system requiring the tamper-proof certification of all
rough diamonds traded (worth annually at the time about US$
7 billion).

[The] high influx of foreign mining companies and the lack of pro-poor mining policies coupled with inadequate implementation mechanisms reinforce the power-lessness of the people and undermine their livelihood goals. Artisanal [diamond] mining is largely uncontrolled and uncoordinated resulting to [sic] high rate of smuggling, environmental hazards and poor living/working conditions. The government is largely promoting the economic agenda of the International Financial Institutions to the extent that the real livelihood needs of the poor are compromised in favour of foreign mining companies/investment. [Our] programme seeks to promote good corporate governance, environmental protection, community beneficiation and strict adherence to international standards.

Statement by the Just Mining Campaign, Freetown, 2001

The 'conflict' or 'blood' diamonds campaign effectively lasted for a little over three years, probably a shorter lifespan than any other comparable campaign in history. Largely because of its short duration, the highly successful social movement it generated as a global human-rights campaign was rather inchoate. Many observers and some of its leading participants primarily experienced its international dimension. As a movement, it was mainly driven by Western activists and NGOs and it led to the Kimberley Process Certification Scheme (KPCS), the international system of control for the movement of rough diamonds. From this vantage point, the campaign was of a largely intellectual nature, driven by well-researched reports, manipulation of media reporting, and high-level lobbying by NGOs and liberal Western politicians. What has been almost completely ignored in the assessment of the phenomenal success of the campaign is the great impetus that it enjoyed from the very beginning by the involvement of African NGOs operating in such troubled spots as Sierra Leone and Congo,[1] two countries where resource-driven warfare came to attract massive international attention. In these two countries, the issue fed into important local concerns about social justice and economic development, and became a rallying ground for civil-society activists spearheading peace movements. As a

---

[1]   Following Crawford Young, I refrain from using the official designation 'Democratic Republic of Congo'. As Young writes, the 'democratic' title remains 'a grotesque misrepresentation of political practice,' making the designation 'Congo-Kinshasa' or simply 'Congo' the most appropriate in the circumstances. See Crawford Young, 'Contextualizing Congo conflicts,' in: John F. Clark (ed.), *The African Stakes in the Congo War* (Fountain Publishers, Kampala, 2002), p. 29.

result, it gained enormous traction within a very short period, overtaking other rights-related international campaigns like those against residual forms of slavery in Sudan and the somewhat narcissistic campaign against the fur trade. It moved swiftly from accusations and denials to concrete steps taken by over 42 governments around the world and the UN Security Council to effectively address the problem, namely that diamonds mined illegally and traded internationally by anti-government or insurgent groups in Africa were being used to fund their violent campaigns. The steps introduced included sanctions against groups and countries held to be culpable and, more creatively, the launch of the Kimberley Process Certification Scheme (KPCS). The campaign was undoubtedly also the strongest influence in the indictment and subsequent trial for crimes against humanity and other offences, by the UN-backed Special Court for Sierra Leone, of Liberia's President Charles Taylor, the first African head of state to face such a judicial process.

In both its intensity and effect, the 'conflict diamonds' campaign clearly qualifies as a highly successful social movement, a campaign which, though loosely organized and coordinated, was sustained over a significant period of time and was geared towards the specific social goals of economic and social justice, and peace.

This chapter examines how the campaign started, the role of African civil-society groups in sustaining it, and why it was so successful. It resulted in sanctions against rebels in Sierra Leone and the Liberian government (thereby no doubt significantly helping the peace process in both countries), and the KPCS, the global UN Security Council-endorsed system requiring the tamper-proof certification of all rough diamonds (worth annually about US$ 7 billion) before they are traded internationally.

How it started

The term 'conflict diamonds' has gained such currency and evokes such passion that it is hard to believe that the issue was first brought to public attention in late 1998 by Global Witness, a small British NGO operating from an untidy office in London. The group's chief campaigner was a young London former disc jockey with a taste for designer suits – Miami Vice rather than Savile Row. The group had been investigating the illegal timber trade in Cambodia – from which the murderous Khmer Rouge guerrillas were making US$ 20 million a month at its height in the early 1990s – but in 1998 it turned its attention to Angola, a state ravaged by decades of bloody warfare. In a report entitled 'A Rough Trade'[2] that was released in December 1998, Global Witness reported that the

---

[2]   Global Witness, 'A Rough Trade: The role of companies and governments in the Angolan conflict',

National Union for the Total Independence of Angola (UNITA), a rebel group with a reputation for psychotic brutality that then controlled over 60% of Angola's rich diamond reserves, had generated US$ 3.7 billion between 1992 and 1998 to underwrite its war effort, effectively making it one of the most profitable business enterprises in Africa.[3]

The disclosure was significant in more ways than one. The Angolan war had started as a war of liberation in the late 1960s and, after independence in 1975, morphed into a full-scale 'ideological' war with important Cold War implications. With the end of the Cold War and with it the loss of American and later South African support, UNITA, led by ex-Maoist Jonas Savimbi, seemed to have lost political justification and support for continued warfare. UNITA's campaigns effectively devolved into banditry, and Global Witness's findings made it clear that diamonds had become the main explanation for the continuing violence in Angola, as the principal source of funding for UNITA. Pillage rather than politics had become a goal of warfare. This violence had led to the deaths of nearly one million Angolans, the displacement of millions more, and had rendered a potentially wealthy country into one of the most miserable, not to say dangerous, in the world.[4]

At the time that Global Witness published its report, the South African-based De Beers, which controlled about 80% of the global rough diamond trade, had been boasting about its ability to mop up diamond supplies from even unstable areas like Angola, and continued to buy offices in Guinea, the Democratic Republic of the Congo (DRC) and elsewhere in Africa. This meant that technically it could not deny buying diamonds from a group like UNITA. Global Wit-

---

(http://www.globalwitness.org/media_library_detail.php/90/en/a_rough_trade, December 1, 1998).

[3]   The US$ 3.7 billion figure is, of course, a guesstimate, but a reasonable one. Christopher Cramer, who has attempted to present a more nuanced picture of the reasons for the continuation of the Angolan war (rather unsuccessfully, in my view) suggests that the cumulative revenue from diamonds traded by UNITA from 1989 to 1998 was 'probably US$ 2-3.5 billion'. To put this figure into perspective, Cramer notes that the Reagan-era US aid to UNITA 'peaked around US$ 40-60 million a year between 1989 and 1991'. Though critical of the overly economistic interpretation of the war, Cramer notes that even Angolan army officers (technically at war with UNITA) and 'running supply businesses in the Lundas would trade openly with UNITA diamond bosses, selling and exchanging goods across a river that was also a frontline'. See Cramer, *Civil War is not a Stupid Thing: Accounting for violence in developing countries* (Hurst and Co, London, 2006), p. 155.

[4]   On the devastating impact of the Angolan war, see Inge Brinkman, 'Angolan civilians in wartime, 1961-2002,' in John Laband (ed.), *Daily Lives of Civilians in Wartime Africa: From slavery days to the Rwandan genocide* (Greenwood Press, London, 2007), pp. 169-194.

ness was unequivocal about the purpose of its publication. Its intention, it stated, was 'to stimulate debate and action on a well known and much reported issue: the key role that diamonds have played in the Angolan conflict in the last ten years'. It added that:

> [there] is a dangerous acceptance amongst the international community that the mechanics of the trade in diamonds, particularly from UNITA controlled areas, are beyond any real controls. Global Witness investigations show that governments flout the United Nations Security Council (UNSC) embargo on unofficial Angolan diamonds (those not sold under the control of the Angolan government diamond parastatal, Endiama).[5]

Global Witness's report quickly elicited denials and prevarications and, because the Angolan war had complex origins, the objection that diamonds were only incidental appeared reasonable to some.[6] The issue was, however, taken up by others and the focus was then on a war where criminality was easy to establish: the Revolutionary United Front's (RUF) war in Sierra Leone. This chapter focuses on this particular conflict and how it shaped (and was in turn shaped by) the 'conflict' diamonds campaign.

The heart of the matter

From 1991 Sierra Leone suffered devastating attacks by the Revolutionary United Front (RUF), a uniquely brutal rebel group that used terror tactics, like amputations, to force the mass displacement of people and the occupation of productive areas of the country for the sole purpose of pillage. The country's rich alluvial diamond reserves were among its early targets. By 1998, the RUF's

---

[5]   Global Witness, 'A Rough Trade'. The Global Witness report was supported by a UN Panel of Experts report on Angola less than two years later. Headed by Canadian diplomat Robert Fowler, the panel documented UNITA's extensive network of support and collaboration with shady business people and some African governments. The report, released in March 2001, estimated UNITA's diamond trade as being worth between US$ 3 billion and US$ 4 billion between 1992 and 1998. The report noted that diamonds played 'a uniquely important role within UNITA's political and military economy'. See Section 111 (1) 77 "The Significance of Diamonds for UNITA" (http://www.un.org/News/dh/latest/angolareport_eng.htm, September 22, 2008).

[6]   *Ibid.* The Fowler Report noted three reasons why diamonds were so important to UNITA's ability to continue its deadly operations: 'First, UNITA's ongoing ability to sell rough diamonds for cash and to exchange rough diamonds for weapons provide the means for it to sustain its political and military activities. Second, diamonds have been and continue to be an important component of UNITA's strategy for acquiring friends and maintaining external support. Third, rough diamond caches rather than cash or bank deposits constitute the primary and the preferred means of stockpiling wealth for UNITA'.

campaign had caused the death of upwards of 50,000 people, displaced two-thirds of Sierra Leone's population of about 5 million and destroyed over half of the country's already limited infrastructure. Yet little was known of this war in the wider world. Throughout the 1990s the RUF was a mysterious, deadly force and its leader, a cashiered army corporal called Foday Saybanah Sankoh, only a disembodied and inarticulate voice that was occasionally heard on the BBC African Service. Areas under its control were inaccessible to outsiders, including journalists. Consequently, RUF violence was simply dismissed as 'senseless' and, therefore, incomprehensible.

After a particularly devastating attack on Freetown in 1999 by the RUF and its allies of renegade soldiers from the Sierra Leonean Army, Partnership Africa Canada (PAC) decided to do a study of the war for the purpose of policy advocacy. The group's three researchers adopted the methodology used by Global Witness to understand the Angolan conflict and focused on the RUF's looting of Sierra Leone's vast alluvial diamond fields. The reasoning behind this was that the rebel group had not articulated any coherent political platform, was completely devoid of ethnic or regional support, and appeared viable only because it had access to significant resources – as yet not fully determined – with which it was underwriting its campaign.

The result was 'The Heart of the Matter: Sierra Leone, Diamonds and Human Security',[7] which was launched simultaneously in Ottawa (Canada) and Freetown (Sierra Leone) in January 2000. The launch was the result of an ingenious strategy that came to sustain the campaign and make it so effective: it involved active collaboration between the Canadian-based group and an influential Sierra Leonean-based NGO called the Network Movement for Justice and Development (NMJD). NMJD had been established in 1998 with the aim of 'promoting justice and sustainable development at all levels in society' and was coordinated by Abu Brima, an outspoken, not to say militant, long-term activist who hailed from Kono, Sierra Leone's main diamond district, and a place despoiled by largely unregulated mining activity. Collaboration between his group and the Canadian-based PAC was forged during the research, and continued throughout the campaign and beyond. The Canadian-based authors participated by telephone during the launch of the report in Freetown in a live radio discussion of the report and its recommendations. This was organized by NMJD

---

[7]   Ian Smillie, Lansana Gberie & Ralph Hazleton, *The Heart of the Matter: Sierra Leone, diamonds and human security* (Partnership Africa Canada, Ottawa, 2000). The title is borrowed from the novel by Graham Greene, who was a British secret service agent posted in Sierra Leone during the Second World War. Greene investigated suspicions that diamonds from the then-British colony were being smuggled to Germany through Vichy French territory (neighbouring Guinea).

and is an indication of the crucial role that the mass media can play in such campaigns.

The PAC report was an attempt to understand the war, not the diamond industry itself. However by examining the role of diamonds in the political economy of Sierra Leone in the context of the war, the report was able to trace the long and slow corruption of Sierra Leone's diamond industry since the stones were first commercially exploited in the country in the 1930s. It showed that mainly through illicit mining and smuggling, in which Sierra Leone's successive leaders from the British colonial overlords to the country's post-independence leaders colluded, diamond exports dropped from a peak of two million carats a year in the 1960s to less than 50,000 carats by 1988. Sierra Leone's populist president during most of this period, a former trade-union leader named Siaka Stevens, tacitly encouraged illicit mining and he himself became involved in criminal or near-criminal activities. The RUF's rebel war began in 1991 and, from the outset, Charles Taylor, the Liberian warlord and later president who helped train and launch the rebel group, acted as a supplier of weapons, diplomatic supporter, banker, trainer and mentor to the RUF.

The report claimed that the rich alluvial diamond fields of Kono District and Tongo Field were among the RUF's earliest and most prized targets and argued that diamonds were a key part of Taylor's calculation. 'The Heart of the Matter' concluded that:

> ... only the economic opportunity presented by the breakdown of law and order could sustain violence at levels that have plagued Sierra Leone since 1991 ... it is ironic that enormous profits have been made from diamonds throughout the conflict, but the only effect on the citizens of the country where they are mined has been terror, murder, dismemberment and poverty.

The PAC report showed conclusively that there was virtually no oversight of the international movement of diamonds and that, during the 1990s, billions of dollars worth of diamonds were imported into Belgium from Liberia, even though Liberia produces very few diamonds itself. Big companies and small were colluding in the laundering of stolen diamonds. The same was true of Congo Brazzaville, which is conveniently adjacent to Congo Kinshasa, and which also mysteriously became a major diamond producer. UNITA too, as Global Witness had noticed, financed much of its war in Angola through the sale of diamonds and traded with impunity throughout Africa and Europe.

The report's key argument was that diamonds had, in the course of the long war, become indispensable for the RUF: the gems in Sierra Leone were mainly of an alluvial nature which meant that they were widespread and easily mined. Their trade was highly unregulated internationally. Lacking political support and a motivating ideology, the RUF was able to enhance its power and political significance by criminally expropriating these valuable resources to acquire weapons and hire mercenaries.

By laying bare the political economy of Sierra Leone's decade-long war, the PAC report found an explanation for the dynamics of the conflict and the reasons for its intensity, apparent 'senselessness' and almost intractable nature. The explanation helped to shift discussion of the war, in academic, journalistic and policy-related circles, away from complacent and somewhat racialist explanations evoking notions of mindless African savagery and nihilism to more easily grasped and appreciated preoccupations: resource exploitation, criminal appropriation and power.

NMJD and CENADEP

While the international dimension of the trade was the galvanizing element for Western NGOs and researchers, the more immediately important and tangible issue for Brima's NMJD was related to internal governance: official corruption, the lack of proper regulatory mechanisms in Sierra Leone, and the tendency for local politicians to protect foreign companies or mining interests at the expense of the long-suffering indigenous population. NMJD declared its position on internal governance in Sierra Leone in these searing terms:

> Corruption is endemic in Sierra Leonean society; all sectors ranging from the central government right down to local communities have been affected by high levels of corruption. This is manifested in mismanagement of national resources, weak capacity of service providers and lack of monitoring and punitive mechanisms to discourage perpetrators of corrupt practices. This has led to a culture of impunity. There is also an apparent lack of responsiveness of successive governments to the needs and aspirations of the populace (irresponsible leadership).[8]

In September 2000 and working through its Just Mining Campaign that had been launched immediately after the release of 'The Heart of the Matter', NMJD convened a National Consultative Conference on diamond mining in Sierra Leone. It brought together hundreds of civil-society activists from all over the country but particularly from the diamond-mining areas, dozens of artisanal miners, chiefs, journalists and some politicians. The main topics on the agenda were: security ('rebel control of major mining areas and how to gain control of those areas'); the role of the government in diamond mining; the impact of mining on the environment; the generation and distribution of revenue from mining; the role of civil society in framing mining policy; the cultural dimension of diamond mining; and, lastly, the international dimension of diamond mining (with 'a healthy international environment favourable to peace

---

[8]   Position paper issued by NMJD in 2000, shortly after the launch of 'The Heart of the Matter' (in this author's possession).

and development'). Among the key resolutions was a ban on diamond mining for five years until all mining areas had been liberated from rebel control and proper regulations had been put in place; the declaration of a UN trusteeship over diamond-mining areas; the removal of all foreigners from mining areas and a new definition of citizenship for those who were to have access to diamond-mining areas restricted 'by birth and not by ownership of Sierra Leonean passport'; and, the allocation of 10% of government royalties on diamonds to mining communities for 'community development programmes'. Civil society, led by the Just Mining Campaign, was to play an active role in shaping government policy towards mining.[9]

Brima explained what followed:

> [Our] aim was ensuring that the Sierra Leone diamond industry operates legally, openly, and for the benefit of Sierra Leoneans – diamonds must become an asset, rather than a detriment, to peaceful long-term development. [We demand] that the country and the [diamond] industry adopt a human rights framework in mining policy formulation and implementation. In the past, mining was the preserve of government and a few individuals, mainly foreign nationals. The [Just Mining] Campaign had to develop new ways to incorporate civil society. This entailed innovative strategizing. To empower the people and make them owners and beneficiaries of their resources, we formed alliances with numerous sectors of civil society, educated the public, and confronted those with a vested interest in maintaining the status quo.
>
> The first step was to establish task force coalitions of civil society groups all over the country. After significant outreach, task forces comprised of human rights groups, environmental organizations, academic institutions, the Bar Association, student and trade unions, community development organizations, individual activists, theatre groups, youth, nurses, and women's groups began to develop. The establishment of task forces – at the national, provincial, and ... district levels – allows for participatory structures for education, mobilization, and action on mining issues. The rights of the people to participate fully in policies and decisions affecting their lives are essential to establishing accountability and social responsibility in the mining industry and to curtailing the abundance of weapons of war bought with the proceeds from minerals.[10]

In this effort, 'expanding and strengthening strategic alliances with international organizations was essential,' Brima wrote. 'The task force coalitions worked in close collaboration with international groups such as Partnership Africa Canada, Global Witness, International Peace Information Service, Action Aid, Oxfam, and Amnesty International. This collaboration focused international attention on the issue of conflict diamonds and elevated the struggle to an

---

[9]   See (http://www.sierra-leone.org/nmjd093000.html, January 2009).

[10]   Abu Brima, 'Mining for the People', *Human Rights Dialogue*, (http://www.cceia.org/resources/publications/dialogue/2_09/articles/945.html, February 9, 2003)

international level.' Brima's account is a welcome corrective because the global coverage of the 'blood diamonds' issue – for example, the Hollywood production *Blood Diamond* featuring Leonardo DiCaprio, Djimon Hounsou and Jennifer Connelly – tended to portray the campaign as entirely Western-driven, with Africans appearing simply as props. As a result of the Just Mining Campaign, the Sierra Leone government established the Diamond Area Community Development Fund, assigning part of the proceeds from the export tax on diamonds to the development of mining communities, and legislated to streamline the cumbersome process for obtaining mining licenses and make the industry more transparent.

Thousands of miles away from Sierra Leone, in Central Africa, the *Centre National d'Appui au Développement et à la Participation Populaire* (CENADEP) was trying to grapple with the effects of the far more complicated and tragic conflict in Congo (Kinshasa). It was inspired by the work of PAC and NMJD to become the focal point for a civil-society Natural Resources Network. The group began in 2002 by monitoring the exploitation of natural resources, in particular diamonds, in Congo as well as investigating issues of transparency and (human) security in the extractive economy.[11] The programme was financially supported by Partnership Africa Canada and aimed to contribute to 'the search for a lasting peace and the development of the Congo by combating illegal and criminal practices in sectors that have been at the root of conflicts in the country: extractive mining and the exploitation of natural resources'. Within two years, CENADEP was able to establish focal points in every province in the vast and logistically challenging Congo. It also developed an advocacy campaign at national and international levels. By 2003, it was undertaking activities, such as conferences, debates and roundtable discussions, with the government on issues relating to the management of natural resources. It was also leading missions to various provinces for research and the dissemination of information, as well as producing a documentary on diamond dealers in Kinshasa.[12] In January 2009, when this author visited Hamuli in CENADEP's offices in Kinshasa, the group was still working on the issue of resource management and maintaining programmes around artisanal mining in two provinces in Congo. However in such a vast and complicated country, progress like that achieved in Sierra Leone by NMJD appeared to be elusive and parts of the country, in particular the diamond-rich eastern regions, were still enmeshed in war. Issues of governance appeared to be secondary to the more urgent task of ending the fighting, disarming tens of thousands of combatants and unifying the country.

---

[11]   Interview with Baudouin K. Hamuli, Director-General of CENADEP, Kinshasa, January 2009.
[12]   See Partnership Africa Canada's *Year in Review 2002-2003* (www.pacweb.org, January 2009).

Britain, Canada and the UN

The impact of 'The Heart of the Matter', mainly due to the widespread and compelling publicity it received in the international media, was especially dramatic in some Western capitals. Canadian Foreign Minister Lloyd Axworthy, who had made human security the linchpin of his policy, welcomed the report and used it in his extensive advocacy on behalf of Sierra Leone in the UN Security Council and elsewhere. In quick order, his department organized a one-day seminar on the economic dimensions of civil war, to which he invited the authors of 'The Heart of the Matter' (this author was the rapporteur) and leading scholars interested in the issue, and appointed David Pratt, an MP (and subsequently Defence Minister), as Special Envoy for Sierra Leone. This was a role that allowed the Canadian government to become more actively involved in the Sierra Leone peace process and play a central role in the debate about reforming the corrupt international diamond industry.

The British government, Sierra Leone's most important foreign ally and biggest aid donor, took the report equally seriously. Shortly after it was launched, British Foreign Office Minister Peter Hain visited Sierra Leone, where he referred to the report in a stirring speech to parliamentarians and civil-society activists:

> I am determined to look for ways to stamp out the theft of Sierra Leone's diamonds, and the way they have been used to fund conflict. [...] Why is it that the government of Sierra Leone derives almost no revenue from diamond sales? And why am I being told that the Liberian annual diamond exports are beyond its diamond mining capacity?

In London a week later, Hain told UK government officials that the RUF's access to the diamond fields was the key reason for the lack of progress in the Sierra Leone peace process and called for an aggressive UN military deployment in those areas:

> I want to see the United Nations peacekeepers, in particular the Indian contingent which I saw camped at the main airport outside Freetown, deployed across the country where they ought to be, which is the eastern side of the country where the RUF rebel combatants have been, and are still in large numbers, where the diamonds are and where a lot of trouble has occurred.[13]

The first attempt by a UN contingent to deploy in the areas was botched a few months later, leading to the capture of hundreds of UN troops by the RUF. A UN Panel of Experts was appointed by the Security Council shortly after this debacle to investigate 'the link between trade in diamonds and trade in arms and

---

[13] Quoted in Lansana Gberie, *A Dirty War in West Africa: The RUF and the destruction of Sierra Leone* (Hurst and Co., London, 2005), p. 186. Part of this section is drawn from Chapter 8 of this book.

related materiel' that was helping to sustain the RUF war effort. It found conclusively that diamonds constituted 'a major and primary source of income for RUF' in 'sustaining and advancing its military ambitions'. The panel released its report in December 2000 stating that the 'bulk of the RUF diamonds leave Sierra Leone through Liberia', whose president, Charles Taylor, sold them to dubious contacts, pocketed most of the proceeds and arranged weapons and other deals (including drug purchases) for the RUF. The United Nations estimated the RUF's diamonds exports as being 'from as little as US$ 25 million per annum to as much as US$ 125 million per annum'.[14]

The UN report was solid amplification of the PAC findings, and after its release, the UN General Assembly immediately adopted the resolution with the aim of breaking the link between rough diamonds and conflict in Africa. The Security Council soon imposed targeted sanctions on Liberia and the RUF, and similar sanctions were also imposed on Sierra Leone's diamonds until a UN-monitored certification system was introduced in September 2000. Perhaps the most interesting finding in the PAC report, from the point of African activists and Western NGOs, was that there was virtually no oversight on the international movement of diamonds: the diamond business was shrouded in total secrecy that suggested massive levels of corruption. A previous report by a UN Panel of Experts on Angola – the Fowler Commission's report that was issued in March 2000 – had drawn similar conclusions. It noted that the diamond industry:

> ... [had] failed to establish an effective import identification regime with respect to diamonds. Nor has any effective effort been made to monitor the activities of suspect brokers, dealers and traders – virtually all of whom appear to be able to travel freely and operate without hindrance...
>
> The unwillingness or inability of the diamond industry, particularly in Antwerp, to police its own ranks is a matter of special concern to the Panel. Persons known within the industry to be dealing in UNITA diamonds have as a general rule neither been exposed by the industry, nor subjected to any sanction by the industry ... Lax controls in some producing countries may enable UNITA diamonds to be passed off as diamonds of different origin, and a number of countries that do not produce any diamonds still export rough diamonds as originating from their territory. Moreover, diamonds on the open market have traditionally been handled without controls as to the origin, and it has been sufficient merely to record provenance, i.e. where the diamonds have been shipped from as they arrive at the markets. It can sometimes be difficult for the countries of destination to differentiate between the countries of provenance and origin.[15]

Liberia was one of the most glaring examples of a place where this kind of laundering was happening, but other countries were also apparently complicit.

---

[14]   *Ibid.*, p. 186.
[15]   http://www.un.org/News/dh/latest/angolareport_eng.htm, March 10, 2000.

The Gambia, for example, was found by the UN panel on Sierra Leone to have been the source of diamonds worth US$ 500 million traded on the Antwerp markets over the years, even though the country produces no diamonds whatsoever. Clearly a great deal of diamond laundering was going on. This finding, as suggested by the Fowler Report, triggered interesting arguments about the 'origin' and 'provenance' of diamonds, an issue settled only by the Kimberley Process Certification Scheme (KPCS), a system that significantly helped to curtail the flow of money to rebel and associated groups in the region and beyond, thereby helping to end the war.

Primary resources and conflict

It is important at this point to underline the intellectual context in which the 'conflict' diamonds campaign thrived. At the end of the 1990s, an interesting debate on the economic dimensions of violent conflict in Africa gained huge momentum. Perhaps the most influential product was 'Greed and Grievance: Economic Agendas in Civil Wars'[16] and a World Bank report[17] that was a somewhat more detailed and dramatic illustration of the key points of 'Greed and Grievance' and argued that:

> While objective grievances do not generate violent conflict, violent conflict generates subjective grievances. This is not just a by-product of conflict, but an essential activity of a rebel organization ... The task in post-conflict societies is partly, as in pre-conflict societies, to reduce the objective risk factors. However, post-conflict societies are much more at risk than implied by the inherited risk factors, because of this legacy of induced polarizing grievance. Either boundaries must be re-established between the political contest and violence, or the political contest must be resolved. Neither of these is easy, which is why, once a civil war has occurred, the chances of further conflict are so high.

Perhaps in no other conflict in Africa could Collier's depressing analysis better apply than to the bloody rebel war in Sierra Leone. Beginning as armed incursions from Liberia, the conflict devolved into a savage civil war in which the RUF, backed by Taylor, wreaked havoc primarily on civilians in the countryside and gained control of the alluvial diamond-rich regions of eastern and southern Sierra Leone. Understanding the predatory nature of the Sierra Leone war took some time but once this had happened, efforts to end it, including UN

---

[16]   Mats Berdal & David Malone (eds) & International Peace Academy (IPA), *Greed and Grievance: Economic Agendas in Civil Wars* (2000).

[17]   Paul Collier, 'Economic causes of civil conflict and their implications for policy', World Bank (www.worldbank.org/research/conflict/papers/civilconflict.htm). Collier has published a more nuanced version in *The Bottom Billion: Why the poorest countries are failing and what can be done about it* (Oxford University Press, Oxford, 2007).

sanctions on diamonds and timber, accelerated. Thousands of UN troops had to be deployed to disarm the militia factions, help the state restore normative order and curb the widespread criminality the war had helped trigger.

William Reno was probably the first scholar to emphasize the economic motives of insurgents spearheading the war in Sierra Leone, which he correctly saw as being intimately linked to Charles Taylor's insurgency (preferring the term 'warlordism') in Liberia. He argued that the key driver of the conflicts was Taylor's continued looting of Liberia's hardwood timber, and his access to Sierra Leone's diamond reserves. Warfare in this view was simply profitable theft: pillage rather than politics was the key driver of the conflict.[18]

A number of salient issues tended to support this view. Firstly, although the corruption and irregularities of Sierra Leone clearly helped set the stage for its unravelling in the 1990s, the violent RUF was certainly not motivated by any evident desire for social justice or a wish to reconfigure the country in ways that would make it more responsive to its overall citizenry. In other words, governance and democracy were not the issues. The spread of violence and its perpetuation undoubtedly had more to do with the weaknesses and failure of the state the insurgents took on than with any mass appeal or intrinsic strength enjoyed by the RUF. The grievances of the majority of the people against the estranged elites in the capital city were real but there is no evidence that the insurgents represented those grievances in any meaningful sense.

Secondly, the RUF, as mentioned earlier, was desperate from the start to latch on to and exploit the diamonds, Sierra Leone's primary resource, that were abundant in the country's vast alluvial fields. This desperation became an obsession. In the end, whatever high ideals some of the insurgents might have held, the control and exploitation of diamonds became their primary motivation. According to the UN, the RUF made millions of dollars from the illegal exploitation of diamonds, money that served mainly to enrich the rebel leaders.

Perhaps most importantly, the RUF targeted mainly civilians, rather than any armed opponents, and there was little or no attempt to win over the general populace. There was no systematic political programme that would appeal to the general citizenry, nor any coherent ideology that might serve to provide insight into what the insurgents would do once they gained power. When they temporarily took power at the invitation of rogue soldiers in 1997, the result was continued pillage, violence and destruction, and a total inability to set up any stabilized form of governance. Indeed the behaviour of the RUF in power was so wanton and destructive that hundreds of thousands of Sierra Leoneans fled the country and there were mass protests and nationwide anti-government

---

[18]   William Reno, *Warlord Politics and African States* (Lynne Rienner Publishers, Boulder, CO, 1998).

demonstrations. The regime was ostracized by the international community, with no country at all opting to recognize it. This gave Nigeria, as the regional power, the impetus to work with a growing civil defence group in February 1998 to oust the junta – the Armed Forces Ruling Council (AFRC) – of which the RUF was an integral part. Once out of power, the rebels regrouped and, aided by the capture of the diamond-rich Kono district, re-armed and launched a devastating attack on Freetown in January 1999. The attacks led to another round of negotiations with the government that were brokered by the UN and the US and led to the Lomé Peace Agreement in July 1999. This agreement instantly became notorious for granting general and unconditional amnesty to the RUF as well as, even more outrageously, control of the country's diamond mining to its leader, Foday Sankoh.

The Kimberley Process

The 'blood diamonds' campaign quickly came to include a wide and diverse cast of characters – academic researchers associated with Western NGOs and think tanks; freelance writers and journalists; traditional human-rights groups and Western NGOs and advocacy groups like Partnership Africa Canada (PAC), Global Witness, Amnesty International, Human Rights Watch, Oxfam, World Vision and Action Aid; African civil-society groups like NMJD and CENADEP; politicians and diplomats; and, later, movie stars and award-winning musicians. The stakes, at least from the point of view of the campaign-ers and many others, were very high and involved the lives of millions of Afri-cans. Ian Smillie, a Canadian development specialist who was research coordi-nator for Partnership Africa Canada, put it in these dramatic terms:

> Conflict diamonds have contributed to the deaths of hundreds of thousands of people over the past decade. They have fuelled wars; they have led to massive civilian dis-placement and the destruction of entire countries. They have capitalized on the much larger traffic in illicit diamonds that are used for money laundering and tax evasion, or are simply stolen from their rightful owners. While conflict diamonds represent a small proportion of the diamond trade, illicit diamonds represent as much as 20 per cent of the annual world total ... This level of illegality created the opportunity and the space for conflict diamonds, and regardless of how current conflicts unfold, it will continue to present a threat to peace and stability in Africa. Conflict diamonds are a major human security problem, and illicit diamonds are their spawning ground.[19]

The sense of urgency that the campaign represented was captured even in the sedate language of the United Nations. At the height of the 'blood' diamonds

---

[19] Ian Smillie, *The Kimberley Process: The case for proper monitoring* (Partnership Africa Canada, Ottawa, Occasional Paper 5), 2002.

campaign, in December 2000, the United Nations General Assembly unanimously adopted Resolution 55/56 on the role of diamonds in fuelling armed
conflict in Africa with a view to 'breaking the link between the illicit transac-
tion of rough diamonds and armed conflict, as a contribution to prevention and
settlement of conflicts'. It noted that the General Assembly:

> recognize[s] that conflict diamonds are a crucial factor in prolonging brutal wars in
> parts of Africa, and underscored that legitimate diamonds contribute to prosperity
> and development elsewhere on the continent. In Angola and Sierra Leone, conflict
> diamonds continue to fund the rebel groups, the National Union for the Total Inde-
> pendence of Angola (UNITA) and the Revolutionary United Front (RUF), both of
> which are acting in contravention of the international community's objectives of
> restoring peace in the two countries.[20]

The UN defined 'conflict diamonds' as 'diamonds that originate from areas
controlled by forces or factions opposed to legitimate and internationally recognized governments, and are used to fund military action in opposition to those
governments, or in contravention of the decisions of the Security Council'.[21]
Estimates of 'conflict diamonds' were put at between 4% and 15% of the
world's total at different times. In purely financial terms, this was clearly important because even the low figure represented a significant volume of cash in
impoverished Africa when set against the US$ 7.5 billion annual trade in rough
diamonds. In fact, it was estimated that as much as 20% of the world's rough
diamond trade was illicit in nature and characterized by theft, tax evasion and
money laundering.[22]

Meetings leading to the KPCS began in May 2000 when South Africa's
Minister of Minerals and Energy, concerned about the threat to the legitimate
industry posed by growing media and NGO publicity around 'blood' diamonds,
convened a conference of interested parties, including De Beers, other diamond
consortia, governments and NGOs, in Kimberley, the home of South Africa's
first diamond mines. A month before the meeting, Minister Phumzile Mlambo-
Ngcuka (who later became Thabo Mbeki's deputy president) visited Canada
and requested a meeting with the authors of 'The Heart of the Matter'. This
author had an hour-long meeting with her and members of South Africa's powerful trade unions at the South African consulate in Toronto. The Minister, the
embodiment of charm itself, stressed that her government was very concerned
about the role that diamonds were playing in conflicts in parts of Africa but
insisted that diamonds were playing a far more positive role in South Africa and
Botswana. She mentioned that the livelihood of tens, if not hundreds, of thousands of people in her country and elsewhere depended on the diamond industry

[20]   http://www.un.org/peace/africa/Diamond.html, September 22, 2008.
[21]   Ibid.
[22]   Smillie, The Kimberley Process: The case for proper monitoring.

(a point stressed by the trade-union representatives) and that, as a result of these two considerations, South Africa was spearheading a process to try and put an end to the 'conflict' diamond business and make the industry clean. 'Let's try this process first,' she urged, 'and if it doesn't work, you can then, as we say in South Africa, "go into the bush".'[23] The PAC report had, in fact, suggested this kind of engagement but raised the spectre of a consumer campaign, and *not* a boycott. This implicit threat appeared to be enough: an opening for engagement with governments and the industry had been sedulously created and it was now being taken up by a powerful player in the diamond industry.

PAC (as well as Global Witness) duly received an official invitation from the South African government to the May 2000 meetings in Kimberley. Negotiations were held with governments, the diamond industry and NGOs on the creation of a global certification and monitoring system. The Kimberley meeting was followed by another in Luanda (Angola) in June and a third in London in July. Although the NGO presence at these early meetings was at first limited to PAC and Global Witness, other far more powerful groups, like Amnesty International, Oxfam International, a European 'Fatal Transactions' consortium and representatives of a coalition of 80 American NGOs, including all the major US church organizations and led by World Vision and Physicians for Human Rights, began to attend the meetings of the Kimberley Process (as it came to be known).

In the year the process started, the international diamond industry produced more than 120 million carats of rough diamonds with a market value of US$ 7.5 billion. At the end of the diamond chain this would be converted into 70 million pieces of jewellery worth close to US$ 58 billion. The big South African company De Beers purchased by far the majority of the rough diamonds, and could more or less set the price. But other important players were emerging which made the process of regulation more urgent. In fact, it would emerge that countries engaged in cutting, polishing and trading polished (not just rough) diamonds needed to be brought on board as well. In 2000, for example, Israel exported US$ 5.3 billion in polished diamonds to the US, India US$ 2.5 billion and Belgium US$ 2.4 billion.[24]

A month after the first Kimberley Process meeting, an iconoclastic diamond trader and publisher of an influential journal on diamonds, Martin Rapaport, visited Sierra Leone. A mercurial and flamboyant American with diamond

---

[23] The expression was widely used during the struggle against apartheid to refer to guerrilla or violent conflict or insurgency, and the minister was alluding to threats by some NGOs – emphatically not including PAC – to mount a campaign for a consumer boycott of diamonds.

[24] Ian Smillie & Lansana Gberie, 'Dirty Diamonds and Civil Society' (paper written for *Civicus*, 2001).

interests in Israel, Antwerp and elsewhere, Rapaport published a feisty and
widely circulated article entitled 'Guilt Trip' on his return in which he cursed
'the bastards [who are] not just stealing [Sierra Leone's] diamonds' but are also
'trading them for guns'. The real challenge facing Sierra Leone and the world
diamond trade, he wrote, 'is how to stop this horrific murderous cycle of illegal
diamond activity'.[25] Rapaport posted 'The Heart of the Matter' report on his
website in its entirety.

It was in this overheated climate that the RUF made the disastrous error, in
May 2000, of attacking and capturing over 500 UN peacekeeping troops, killing
some in the process. Civil-society groups in Sierra Leone, many of whom were
now active in the campaign against the conflict and who had long been inflamed
by the foolishness of the 1999 Lomé Peace Agreement that had given control of
the diamond industry as a bribe to Foday Sankoh to encourage his participation
in the peace process, mounted a massive demonstration in front of Foday
Sankoh's villa. Sankoh's bodyguards responded by firing live bullets at the
unarmed crowd, killing 19 people including a journalist. The world's media
descended on Sierra Leone after this outrage and the forgotten war quickly
dominated newspaper front pages and news broadcasts around the world. The
events were almost unanimously described as 'The Diamond War'.

Pressure was also emerging from other powerful and influential sources.
After a visit to Sierra Leone in December 1999, US Congressmen Tony Hall
and Frank Wolf – a Democrat and a Republican respectively – introduced a bill
in the House of Representatives aimed at preventing the flow of illicit or 'conflict' diamonds into the United States. And after the launch of the PAC report in
January 2000, Canadian Foreign Minister Lloyd Axworthy decided to use
Canada's position on the UN Security Council to expand the diamond discussion from a narrow focus on Angola to one that would embrace the issues in
Sierra Leone as part of his focus on human security. Axworthy would himself
make a well-publicized visit to Sierra Leone later.

Shortly after the Kimberley Process meetings started, a joint Belgian/UK/US
mission to Sierra Leone was undertaken to develop an experimental tamper-
proof certification system for rough diamonds, the details of which were approved by the UN Security Council in August 2000. Just prior this, the World
Diamond Congress was held in Antwerp from 17-19 July. Normally devoted to
the technical and commercial aspects of the industry, this Congress was almost
entirely given over to the issue of conflict diamonds. Representatives from
governments and NGOs, including PAC, participated and the industry agreed
on reforms that would represent the most fundamental set of changes it had ever
tried. It called, for example, for 'redline' legislation in all countries that im-

---

[25] *Ibid.*, p. 4.

ported diamonds as producers, manufacturers or dealers. Banks, insurance companies, shippers and others would be included in the system. A World Diamond Council was proposed and subsequently inaugurated to help move the process forward. The industry proposals were taken to government meetings in London in July 2002, the third in the Kimberley Process and, as before, NGOs were also present. The London meetings were followed by two days of hearings at the Security Council's Sierra Leone Sanctions Committee to explore the connection between diamonds and guns in the war. Of great significance was the fact that the hearings included testimony from governments, the diamond industry and individual experts. The Council refused to invite NGOs like PAC because some member nations objected to their presence but some of the strongest language up to that point on the issue of conflict diamonds was added to the record by 'individual experts' from PAC, Global Witness, Amnesty International and others. A noteworthy feature of the hearings was that, for the first time in the UN's history, a hearing of this nature was open to the public and was widely reported on.

About forty countries and dozens of NGOs continued to meet for a couple of years after the first meeting in Kimberley in 2000 but tensions between governments and NGOs became apparent at a meeting in Brussels in April 2001 when the NGOs expressed their frustration with delays in creating a global certification system in a widely circulated press release that noted disappointment over the 'lack of progress in efforts to end the trade in conflict diamonds'. The NGOs continued:

> Further stalling and inaction will damage the credibility and the viability of the diamond industry, and the jobs it provides for hundreds of thousands of people. More importantly, it will allow rebel armies in Angola, Sierra Leone and the Democratic Republic of Congo to continue their brutal wars against innocent men, women and children.[26]

Though the relationship between NGOs and governments had never been easy, it was the first time that such a rupture was made public. No one, least of all the NGOs, wanted conflict in the delicate process and soon afterwards the two parties were brought together.

Partnership Africa Canada and Global Witness continued to ratchet up interest in the issue by producing reports showing the various dimensions of the diamond trade: (i) on Guinea after RUF rebels and Taylor's mercenary army invaded the country in late 2000 and early 2001, striking at its rich alluvial fields in the forest regions;[27] (ii) on Southern Africa, putting a question mark

---

[26]   *Ibid.*, p. 6.
[27]   Lansana Gberie, *Destabilizing Guinea: Diamonds, Charles Taylor and the potential for wider humanitarian catastrophe* (Partnership Africa Canada, Ottawa, 2001).

against the overall economic benefits of diamonds;[28] (iii) the criminal nature of the diamond industry in Congo;[29] (iv) a study of the Kimberley Process itself, setting out a case for monitoring the rough diamond trade;[30] and (v) on Sierra Leone following the UN intervention in late 1999 and the implementation of a diamond-certification scheme, showing how RUF diamond-mining interests were hampering the peace process there.[31] Global Witness had earlier published a paper setting out the possibilities of identifying and certifying rough diamonds as an effective way of controlling the trade.[32]

A powerful impetus to the process came from a somewhat unexpected source. A major article in *The Washington Post* in November 2001 alleged that operatives from the Middle Eastern terrorist group, al Qaeda, had visited RUF-held diamond-mining areas several times and arranged to purchase diamonds in deals worth millions of dollars prior to the 9/11 attacks in the US, implying that diamonds might have helped fund the attacks. Correspondent Douglas Farah stated in his article that the al Qaeda network 'reaped millions of dollars in the past three years from the illicit sale of diamonds mined by [RUF] rebels in Sierra Leone' and that one of the RUF's senior officials, Ibrahim Bah, of Senegalese origin, acted as 'a conduit between senior RUF commanders and the buyers from both al Qaeda and Hizbollah, a Shi'ite Muslim organization linked to Lebanese activists who have kidnapped numerous Americans, hijacked airplanes and carried out bomb attacks on US installations in Beirut'. The West African Shi'ite Lebanese community had always been suspected of having sympathies for Hizbollah, an organization that is 'active in all these countries and [is] deeply involved in many businesses across the [West African] region'.[33] Interestingly, three months before 9/11 and five months before the *Washington Post* article appeared, the names of two of those associated with the alleged relationship, Ossailly and Nassour, were placed on a travel ban announced by the United Nations Security Council. A member state had supplied these names to the Security Council. The ban also affected senior Liberian government officials and 'other individuals providing financial and military support to armed

---

[28] Ralph Hazleton, *Diamonds Forever or For Good? The economic impact of diamonds in Southern Africa* (Partnership Africa Canada, Ottawa, 2002).

[29] Christian Dietrich, *Hard Currency: The criminalized diamond industry of the Democratic Republic of Congo and its neighbours* (Partnership Africa Canada, Ottawa, 2002).

[30] Smillie, *The Kimberley Process.*

[31] Lansana Gberie, *War and Peace in Sierra Leone: Diamonds, corruption and the Lebanese connection* (Partnership Africa Canada, Ottawa, 2002).

[32] Global Witness, *Possibilities for the Identification, Certification and Control of Diamonds* (London, 2000).

[33] Douglas Farah, 'Al-Qaeda cash tied to diamond trade: sale of gems from Sierra Leone rebels raised millions, sources say', *Washington Post*, 2 November 2001.

rebel groups in countries neighbouring Liberia, in particular the RUF in Sierra Leone'.[34] The 9/11 Commission, set up by the US government to investigate the forces behind the terrorist attacks in September 2001, would later play down any connection between the attackers and Sierra Leonean diamond interests.[35] However for a time, the disclosures in *The Washington Post* significantly boosted the argument for tighter controls of the international diamond trade and, by implication, support for the Kimberley Process where it mattered most, namely in the US, which is by far the biggest consumer of diamond products (accounting for over half of jewellery sales worldwide).

The pressure could no longer be resisted and agreement was reached in March 2002 on the principles and most of the details of a system that would be introduced in January 2003. Provisions for the regular independent monitoring of national control mechanisms were not, however, agreed and remained an issue of serious contention for the NGOs concerned about the system's credibility and effectiveness. A final agreement was drawn up in Interlaken, Switzerland, in November 2003 requiring participating countries to ensure that all rough diamonds for export carry a Kimberley Process certificate of origin. The UN Security Council endorsed the agreement, making it international law.

The Kimberley Process is now backed by national legislation in more than 70 countries and, under it, each agrees to issue a certificate to accompany any and all rough diamonds to be exported from its territory and clearly certifies that the diamonds are 'conflict-free'. Technically, it requires each country to track the diamonds being offered for export back to the place where they were mined or to the point of import – a solution to the issue of provenance and origins – and a set of standards for these internal controls must be met. All participating countries that import rough diamonds are bound by agreement not to allow any rough diamonds into their territory without an approved KP certificate. The Kimberley Process system requires the same levels of compliance in Belgium, the UK and Canada as it does in Sierra Leone, Guinea, China, Russia, Brazil and Congo, implying the same levels of technological and bureaucratic competence. This is probably its main flaw but in spite of this, however, Ian Smillie has suggested that the system has been a success:

> We believe that the Kimberley Process is a success. It is a success because although there are still pockets of conflict diamonds in Côte d'Ivoire, the worst of the wars fuelled by conflict diamonds have now ended. It is also a success because it has forced a huge volume of illicit diamonds to the surface and out of the trade...
>
> One of the reasons for the success of the KPCS, now acknowledged by everyone involved, is that it was a process, not a formula imposed from outside, and it was a

---

[34]   Lansana Gberie, *War and Peace in Sierra Leone*, pp. 14-22.

[35]   Farah has since continued to protest the truth of his claims. See *Blood from Stones: The secret financial network of terror* (Broadway Publishers, New York, 2004).

process that involved governments, industry and civil society organizations like PAC. That is the good news. The KPCS has helped to consolidate the peace in several African countries...[36]

As further examples of this success, Smillie rightly cited the boom in diamond exports since the Kimberley System was introduced in Sierra Leone and Congo, the latter registering its best exports since the discovery of diamonds in the country about a century ago. A Diamond Certification system, anticipating the Kimberley System, was instituted in Sierra Leone in September 2000, four months after the UN Security Council passed Resolution 1306 that placed a ban on diamond exports from Sierra Leone. It was primarily meant to deny the RUF a market, and was complemented by a ban on Liberian diamond exports several months later. The certification system was created with the assistance of the Belgian Diamond High Council, which had been criticized in the PAC report for ignoring the problem of conflict diamonds. In addition to a Sierra Leonean diamond valuer, an independent valuer was also appointed. Official exports of Sierra Leonean diamonds have increased dramatically. In 1999, the country officially exported only US$ 1.3 million worth of diamonds but in the 12 months after the certification system was introduced (i.e. between October 2000 and September 2001), legal exports jumped to US$ 25.9 million (210,675 carats). Exports for the year 2001 (January to December) totalled 222,500 carats, which were valued at US$ 26 million. This figure represented a monthly average export of US$ 2.17 million, which was extraordinarily high compared to the years prior to the introduction of the system. This trajectory has since continued, with exports rising almost every year. Diamond exports in 2003 were worth US$ 75 million, in 2004 the figure was US$ 126 million; and in 2005, it was US$ 142 million. The value of diamond exports dropped slightly in 2006 to US$ 125 million but rose again in 2007 to US$ 141 million.

Conclusion

Two US congressmen, Tony Hall (D-Ohio) and Frank Wolf (R-Va.), as well as Senator Patrick Leahy (D-Vt.), nominated PAC and Global Witness for the 2003 Nobel Prize. 'We are convinced that the goal of ending the scourge of conflict diamonds is achievable primarily because of the length to which Partnership Africa Canada and Global Witness have gone', the legislators wrote in their letter to the Nobel Committee of the Norwegian Parliament. They also noted that the groups:

---

[36] Ian Smillie, 'Diamonds, Kimberley Process, and the Development Diamond Initiative' (http://www.ccafrica.ca/nrc/Ian%20Smillie%20Speach.pdf, November 28, 2006).

succeeded because they have avoided polarizing campaign tactics that could have alienated the diamond industry and key governments, whose support is critical to a solution. They understood that, despite the shocking difference between the advertised image of diamonds and the often harsh reality of the trade, a boycott could result in a backlash against a product whose legitimate trade is the backbone of many economies.[37]

The groups were not awarded the Nobel Prize – it went to an Iranian female activist in 2003 – but the fact that they were nominated at all for this prestigious award just three years after the campaign started is testimony to how effective and timely the 'conflict' diamonds campaign was deemed to have been.

As so often happens, the work of groups like NMJD and CENADEP that added a great deal of moral gravitas and energy to the campaign sadly went unrecognized. But because they were based at the scene of the devastation that propelled the campaign and worked tirelessly to sustain it, they were the true heroes. Too often campaigns of this nature, spearheaded by Western NGOs, appear as narcissistic indulgence, and fringe radical groups too often substitute doctrine for knowledge, and irritation with their own political and economic systems out of concern for the world's truly disadvantaged. The result can then be confusion and harm to the people they profess to represent. The lesson to be learnt from the 'conflict diamonds' campaign is that for advocacy to be taken seriously it has to be well-informed and sensitive, and should take on board the interested parties, particularly representatives of the people the advocates profess to be concerned about.

As for the countries, Sierra Leone, Angola and Congo, that inspired the 'conflict diamond' campaign, there has been significant progress in peace consolidation and infrastructural development although there are naturally still problems. The former Minister for Mineral Resources in Sierra Leone, Mohamed Swaray-Deen, appeared very pleased with efforts made by his government to better govern the diamond sector but frankly admitted that problems remained. 'Without doubt,' he said, '[the key] problems are illegal mining and smuggling, but especially smuggling.'[38] And illegal mining and smuggling, as the minister well knew, have been the key problems in the industry since the commercial exploitation of diamonds started in Sierra Leone in the 1930s. Importantly, government revenue from the increased diamond production remains minimal. Diamond exporters pay an export tax of 3% of the value of the goods. In addition, there is income tax, which is calculated for companies at 30% of their

---

[37] Rob Bates, 'Conflict diamond NGOs nominated for Nobel Prize', *JCK Online.com*, see also
(http://www.professionaljeweler.com/archives/news/2002/040402story.html, April 4, 2002).

[38] Interview with Mohamed Swaray-Deen, Freetown, December 2005.

income after other applicable deductions. But where the holder of a mining lease has yet to make a profit, or where the chargeable income is below 7% of the investment, the company pays a flat 3.5% rate of income tax. There are also the license fees paid for mining (minimal), dealing (also fairly insignificant) and exporting (at US$ 500,000 annually, this is a significant sum). However all these taxes totalled less that US$ 10 million in 2007. Still, the government considered it necessary to grant special tax concessions to some mining companies. For example, it granted the biggest diamond-mining venture in the country, Koidu Holdings Limited, duty-free facilities for the equipment and other mining-related goods it imports into the country, along with waivers regarding residential permits for dozens of its foreign employees. Such concessions are not limited to diamond companies. An internal government review of the mining industry estimated in 2006 that accumulated revenue losses from several concessions granted to the titanium mining company, Sierra Leone Rutile, will amount to US$ 98 million from 2004 to 2016.

These concessions are part of the legacy of the war. Poor infrastructure and the image of a violent and unstable place have made the country unattractive to foreign investors and such concessions, the government argues, are needed to attract investments. The struggle continues in Sierra Leone.

5

The Islamic Courts Union:
The ebb and flow of a Somali
Islamist movement

Jon Abbink

The Islamic Courts Union (ICU) in Somalia was a social-religious movement with a political programme. This internally diverse movement emerged from local Islamic courts active in Mogadishu in the late 1990s. In the absence of state authority and public security in 2004, it responded to the social needs of local people and grew into a large militia force that, by late 2006, controlled much of southern Somalia. In December 2006 a military campaign by Ethiopia, in support of the Somali Transitional Federal Government, ousted the ICU. The movement subsequently declined, split and withdrew to transform itself into a new military grouping. Its socio-religious programme waned, its violent militant agenda re-emerged and it morphed into a new nationalist movement.

This chapter considers the ICU as a social movement and questions its precedents, its social-reformist agenda and ideology, and its mobilizational procedures. The reasons for the rapid rise of the ICU in 2006 within the unstable and militarized society of southern Somalia have to be understood against the background of Muslim movements that existed in the country in earlier decades and unsuccessful attempts to establish a national government. This is marked by a mixture of political segmentation determined by the Somali clan-family system, socio-religious innovation, economic competition and local political manoeuvring in the stateless environment of southern Somalia since 1991. While local political dynamics are very important, the analysis also relates ongoing conflicts in Somali society to global geopolitics and Islamist radicalism.

Introduction: Locating the Somali case in social movement theory

This chapter presents an interpretive case study of the Islamic Courts Union (*Midowga Maxkamadaha Islaamiga* in Somali) in southern Somalia, an Islamist movement that was active from c. 2004 to 2008 and had social and political aims reflecting both internal diversity (and division) and a new international positioning. A study of this movement reveals the crucial role of international contacts of all the actors on the Somali scene. This was not only evident in the persistent presence of neighbouring countries but also in the growing influence of transnational Islamic ideologies and networks, including that of Somali diaspora communities.[1] These external sources provided funding, new narratives of nationalism and religious identity, and foreign-trained cohorts that impacted on socio-religious practices and ideologies in Somalia. It can be argued that seemingly local developments, like clan-militia fighting, religiously motivated battles, piracy, looting, terrorist actions and the work of Islamic charities are inextricably linked to global flows and thus highly relevant to politics and security developments in the region as a whole.[2]

Somalia has been in the midst of major societal transformation since 1991, not only due to the destructive civil war and the internal struggle that wrecked the country (at least its southern part), but also the transformation of customary religious life and social structures. One part of the story is the emergence of radical forms of Islam and these, although representing a minority of Somalis, seem to have become entrenched in society and redefined people's social and religious identification. The ICU, originally known as the 'Supreme Council of Islamic Courts of Somalia', was founded in 2004[3] and is an intriguing example of a movement that emerged in extreme conditions of statelessness, civil war, humanitarian crisis and social disarray in southern Somalia.[4] It was characterized by mobilization and recruitment on the basis of (a specific form of) Muslim

---

[1]   One in every ten Somalis lives in the diaspora, mainly in the US, Western Europe, the Middle East (Gulf States, Saudi Arabia) and neighbouring countries in the Horn.

[2]   Cf. Said S. Samatar, 'Unhappy masses and the challenge of political Islam in the Horn of Africa', *Horn of Africa* 20, (2002), pp. 1-10. See also Andre Le Sage & Ken Menkhaus, 'The rise of Islamic charities in Somalia: An assessment of impact and agendas', Paper for the 45th Annual International Studies Association Convention, Montreal, 17-20 March 2004.

[3]   In Somali: Golaha Sare ee Makhamaddaha Islaamiga ee Soomaaliya.

[4]   I do not discuss Somaliland here as it is a quite different story. See Seth Kaplan, 'The remarkable story of Somaliland', *Journal of Democracy*, 19, 3 (2008), pp. 143-157, and Mark Abley, 'Successful country doesn't exist', *Toronto Star,* 11 September 2007.

identity as expressed via local (clan-based) *shari'a* courts. In a comparative sense, the movement was challenging and perhaps puzzling to outsiders.

While social movements in Africa were present in the late-colonial and post-colonial era as nationalist insurgent groups, neo-traditional movements or in the more classic form of trade unions and civic organizations, variations based on a predominantly religious agenda have been rare[5] and little studied. Compared to other parts of the world, similar ideas on recruitment, ideology and socio-political agendas around grievances or political aims in Africa were always present but cultural commitments and value orientations of movements as well as their strategies differed markedly. In Africa, movements with an allegedly religious identity basis are growing in importance, often as their adherents see the classical social movements, such as trade unions, parties and civic associations, as ineffective or conservative.

This plethora of new socio-political movements in Africa has broken the framework of social movement paradigms that we know from the mainstream literature and that have been developed on the basis of mainly European and American cases.[6] New combinations of social, neo-ethnic, religious and criminal elements of collective self-definition have emerged and are taking shape in semi-collective, often opportunistic, alliances resonating with recent theories about 'low intensity conflicts' and 'new wars'. When studying these movements in Africa, the challenge is to explain their emergence, mobilization potential and evolving agendas as they unfold.

In much of the literature one comes across a conception of social movements as primarily grievance-based and democratically oriented collectivities of people or social groups, usually neglected by the state, that are striving for the public good. This idea of legitimate grievances and of democratic aspirations cannot, however, be part of the definition of social movements, as it would prejudge their nature. As the Somali case will illustrate, some movements are political groups aimed at imposing their agenda and exercising power in a coer-

---

[5]   The Kenyan Mungiki movement, which emerged in the 1990s, is another example of a complex, 'neo-ethnic' social movement based on a mixture of religious and socio-political elements. However subject to brutal government repression, it lost its leadership and has transformed into a movement where criminal and violent activities have undermined its socio-political agenda. See for a recent study, Awinda Atieno, 'Mungiki, 'Neo-Mau Mau' and the prospects for democracy in Kenya', *Review of African Political Economy*, 34, 13, 2007, pp. 526-531.

[6]   South Africa is the only country in Africa where social movements have occurred in significant measure and been studied in recent years. See for example, Richard Ballard, Adam Habib, Imraan Valodia & Elke Zuern, 'Globalization, marginalization and contemporary social movements in South Africa', *African Affairs*, 104, 417 (2005), pp. 615-634.

cive fashion, with social aims or issues as secondary. Others want to impose an exclusivist programme on society, merging the social and the political in a comprehensive religious cloak. The definition of social movements must, therefore, be more nominal and open, focusing on mobilization and public action towards an aim at variance with the state, other movements or forces in society. In this chapter I use the general definition offered by Olzak[7] and define a social movement in its broader sense as a purposive collective movement voicing demands for fundamental change in society, mobilizing around one or more public causes and following a strategy of change. A broad variety of issues can be addressed by a movement, ranging from state discrimination, neglect, socio-economic and political marginalization to perceived value differences.

In the case of the Islamic Courts Union (ICU), questions can be asked about whether it is, or was, a social movement and, if so, how it differs from those known from the literature. It was certainly a movement of people acting collectively with a social and political programme, claiming public causes and dressing their actions in a religious garb, sincere or otherwise. They addressed social problems that emerged in the vacuum of post-1991 Somalia and the collapse of its central state. However, according to sociologist Tilly,[8] the ICU would probably not qualify as a social movement because in his strict definition, based on Western European experience, it seems to lack the specific complex of defining elements (campaigns against target authorities; action repertoires, public displays).[9] However I claim that the ICU and its predecessors should be tested against historical examples and in this case it could be said to be a collective action movement adapted to the quite specific, *stateless* environment of a clan-divided society. It is of prime importance here to look at the emergence and actions of movement *elites*.

A challenge when studying African cases is how to address cultural frameworks[10] and the – often disruptive – religious factor in social movement re-

---

[7]   See Susan Olzak, 'Ethnic and nationalist social movements', in: David A. Snow, Sarah A. Soule & Hanspeter Kriesi (eds), *The Blackwell Companion to Social Movements* (Blackwell/Malden, Oxford/Carlton, 2004, p. 666.

[8]   Charles Tilly, *Social Movements, 1768-2004* (Paradigm Publishers, London/Boulder, 2004), pp. 3-4, 7.

[9]   His definition of a social movement in his essay 'From interactions to outcomes in social movements' (in: M. Giugni *et al.* (eds), *How Social Movements Matter*, p. 257) is equally restrictive and although perhaps applicable to Europe may not be so for many other societies.

[10]   See Stephen Hart, 'The cultural dimension of social movements: A theoretical reassessment and literature review', *Sociology of Religion*, 57, 1 (1996), pp. 87-100.

search.[11] Cultural-religious factors are quite different and probably more important for social movements in Africa than elsewhere. A movement that observers may see as religious or social is often at the same time inherently political (or vice versa) because the domains are fused and drawn upon opportunistically. This is certainly true in the Somali case. It could be contended that religion was the 'master frame'[12] of the ICU for their view of Somali society and their course of action but it should not be forgotten that Somali clan-group thinking (i.e. social organization based on the segmentary patrilineal principle, or *tol* in Somali) interacted with this. I refrain here from fully answering the question about whether the ICU was really a social movement and instead aim to explain the movement with the help of insights from social movement theory (cf. van Stekelenburg's chapter in this volume). Within the various theoretical traditions of social movement research, a 'political process approach'[13] seems promising in explaining the ICU, although a more comprehensive social-constructivist point of view would also be helpful in view of the strong identity aspects in the movement (Islamist ideology) that gave it additional mobilizing capacity.

The Somali civil conflict is fully connected to transnational global politics and can no longer be explained solely as a part of the country's socio-political crisis and its divisive clan system: the ICU was not only responding to a domestic agenda of social grievances. Somali actors have placed themselves in alliance with transnational flows of funds, organizational forms and ideologies. Indeed both the current Somali Transitional Federal Government (TFG) and the ICU were decisively influenced by foreign connections, with the ICU opting exclusively for those in the Muslim world.

The Somali arena today:
Fragmentation, insecurity, persistent violence

Somalia has been bad headline news in recent years: political disorder, persistent civil strife,[14] terrorist actions, military abuse, a catastrophic humanitarian

---

[11] Cf. Christian Smith, 'Correcting a curious neglect, or bringing religion back in', in: Christian Smith (ed.), *Disruptive Religion. The Force of Faith in Social Movement Activism* (Routledge, London/New York, 1996), pp. 1-25. The role of the symbolic-cultural dimension in social movement is treated well in: Donatella della Porta & Marco Diani, *Social Movements: an Introduction* (Blackwell/Malden, Oxford/Carlton, 2nd edition, 2006), but they do not touch on the role of religious elements.

[12] Cf. Della Porta & Diani, *Social Movements*, p. 79.

[13] *Ibid.*, pp. 16-18.

[14] See Hussein Adam, *From Tyranny to Anarchy: The Somali experience* (Red Sea Press, Trenton, NJ/Asmara, 2008).

situation for 30-40% of the population,[15] extortion, the kidnapping and killing
of aid workers, and a piracy-infested coastline unsafe for international ship-
ping.[16] While there are huge numbers of studies and reports on Somali and a
good general understanding of the underlying problems of state failure, social
(dis-)organization and economic life in the literature, the country's politics are
exceedingly complex.

Although two parts of the former state of Somalia – self-declared independent Somaliland and the less-successful but fairly stable Puntland[17] – are enjoying relative calm, southern Somalia and notably the capital Mogadishu and its
environs have remained locked in insecurity and political fragmentation, first
under warlords and clan militias (1991-2005) and since 2006 in devastating
violence between parts of the ICU and TFG troops supported by Ethiopian
forces that have been in the country since December that year. At least 10,000
people, about 60% of them civilians, have been killed since the December 2006
war, many more have been wounded and hundreds of thousands have become
internally displaced persons (IDPs).

Since the collapse of the central state in Somalia, the various insurgent
movements have not succeeded in forging a new state and have plunged the
country into civil war and a predatory economy. The history of the ensuing civil
conflict and war is too complex to cover here.[18] However, communal conflicts
and population movements have created deep antagonisms between various clan
and sub-clan groups, opportunistic alliances for economic gain and massive
victimization of minorities and non-clan Somalis.[19] For example, in the wake of
the expansion of the then-powerful USC militia of General Mohammed Farah
'Aydeed', Mogadishu was flooded with many Hawiye clan people (notably the
Habr-Gedir sub-clans of Murosade, Suleimaan and 'Ayr) who replaced or

---

[15]   See the alarming report by the Food Security & Nutrition Analysis Unit Somalia,
       Quarterly Brief (Nairobi, issued 12 September 2008. Online at:
       www.fsausomali.org, accessed on 1 September 2008.
[16]   Piracy along the Somali coast was already being recorded in 1998. A major action
       was the capture on 4 January 1999 of the MV Sea Johana by units of the radical
       Islamist *Al Ittihad Al Islami* group. See S. Coffen-Snout, 'Pirates, warlords and
       rogue fishing vessels in Somalia's unruly seas'.
       (www.chebucto.ns.ca/~ar120/somalia.html, June 1, 1999); R. Middleton, *Piracy in
       Somalia*. London: Chatham House, Briefing Paper, October 2008.
[17]   Their armed border conflict in 2007, however, shows that one cannot speak of
       stability here either.
[18]   See Hussein Adam, *From Tyranny to Anarchy*, p. 81f.
[19]   The popular perception of Somalia as a homogeneous country is not true. There are
       significant minorities and groups falling outside the clan system (with its five major
       clan-families of Dir, Darod, Hawiye, Rahanweyn and Isaaq).

chased out non-Hawiye inhabitants, a lot of whom were from the Darod clan. Similar displacement happened in the countryside, for example in the Rahanweyn agricultural areas. The many unresolved conflicts of interest and illegal appropriations constitute an important sub-text surrounding the perennial conflicts in Somalia today.

Heavily hit by repression and war in the final years of the rule of President Mohammed Siyad Barre who was in power from 1969-1991, Somaliland declared independence in 1991 and disassociated itself from the idea of a pan-Somali state. Puntland followed in 1998 by declaring autonomy but not independence. Southern Somalia has remained divided and stateless. In spite of the absence of a central state since 1991, not all has been chaos and mayhem. While Somali society fell back on clan territories, the rule of clan elders, local NGO activity and Islamic organizations, local self-governing units emerged and to a large extent stabilized the rural areas. In the cities, predatory militias and warlords were dominant and insecurity, especially in the large towns like Mogadishu, remained rampant. But even there, efforts at community regulation emerged, although largely within same-clan units.

Paradoxically, the Somali economy has had a mixed record over the past years. While poverty is deep-rooted, state services non-existent and the agro-pastoral sector in serious crisis, there is a free, mostly unregulated economy with a booming trade and telecom sector[20] as well as a transnational criminal/racketeering sector that brings in money. And in the last two years millions of dollars have also come from piracy off the coast. The qualified economic success of the entrepreneurial sector has allowed Somali businessmen and movements to tune in to global economic networks and forge new political-ideological connections. Not only are hundreds of millions of dollars being transferred from the Somali diaspora[21] each year (flowing to all parties in the conflict but especially to the Islamic Courts movement) but religious funding and arms flows from Middle Eastern countries and Eritrea are also relatively easily arranged.[22] The informal, trust-based and highly effective *hawala* money

---

[20] See Bob Feldman, 'Somalia: amidst the rubble, a vibrant telecommunications infrastructure', *Review of African Political Economy*, 113 (2007), pp. 565-572.

[21] A recent World Bank report mentions the very high amount of $ 1 bn annually, or 71.4% of GNP. See Samuel M. Maimbo (ed.), *Remittances and Economic Development in Somalia. An overview* (World Bank, Washington, DC, 2006), p. 5. The UNDP in 2007 estimated half this sum.

[22] Well-documented in the reports of the UN Monitoring Group on Somalia. See for instance the amazingly detailed report of November 2006 (www.fas.org/asmp/resources/govern/109th/S2006913.pdf, November 21, 2006). Eritrea's support was also admitted by the former ICU leader back in 2006, see

transfer systems have undoubtedly contributed to the funding of militants and terrorists[23] in Somalia as well,[24] and economic interests are an important driver of the conflict.[25]

Over the past eighteen years, various efforts have been made to rebuild a nation state, often at the instigation of outsiders such as the UN. These efforts were perhaps premature and unduly top-down because they sidetracked the then-ongoing 'building blocks' approach to Somali political reconstitution, which was widely seen as the best way forward.[26] The external state-building effort gave rise to the Transitional National Government (TNG) in 2000 which was constituted at a conference in Arta, Djibouti. After its collapse, it became a somewhat more representative Transitional Federal Government in 2004, with a five-year mandate. It was based on difficult negotiations in Mbagathi, Kenya, offering a compromise between clan-families on representation and the division of power. The TFG, led by the former Puntland president and veteran Somali politician/warlord Colonel Abdullahi Yusuf Ahmed (of the Omar Mahmud/-Majerteen/Harti/Darod clan), was recognition, to an extent, that a future Somalia should be significantly federal in structure.[27] However it soon ran into trouble and was not able to relocate to Mogadishu due to the insecurity and lack of authority there. One problem was that Abdullahi Yusuf, although experienced and strong, was controversial due to his authoritarian style and his close relationship with Ethiopia. He was not a conciliatory president.

The other forces providing alternative sources of survival and social order were Islamic movements, notably the Islamic Courts in Mogadishu. Before they appeared on the scene as an organized movement in early 2006, they had been building a constituency based on a range of service-oriented Islamic associa-

---

'Somalia: Islamists refuse talks, acknowledge Eritrea', Reuters news message, 26 July 2006.

[23] Terrorism is defined in this chapter as unpredictable violent action against non-combatants and innocent people with the intent to kill and destroy, create existential fear and subvert the public order, usually with a stated political aim.

[24] Robert Feldman, 'Fund transfers-African terrorists blend old and new: *hawala* and satellite telecommunications', *Small Wars and Insurgencies*, 17, 3 (2006), pp. 356-366.

[25] Cf. Sabine Grosse-Kettler, *External Actors in Stateless Somalia. A war economy and it promoters* (Bonn International Center for Conversion, Bonn, BICC paper 39, 2004).

[26] Cf. Matt Bryden, 'No quick fixes: coming to terms with terrorism, Islam and statelessness in Somalia', *Journal of Conflict Studies*, 23, 2 (2003), pp. 24-56.

[27] Incidentally, its Charter also recognized Islam as the state religion and *shari'a* as an important source of national law.

tions and charities that had existed in the country for decades (founded on the Muslim duty of *zakāt*).

Earlier Muslim movements in Somalia: A religious infrastructure

Somalia has been a Muslim country since at least the thirteenth century and has known a wide range of (mostly Sufi)[28] Islamic associations with their important mystical orders and holy men as mediators and models of piety. Virtually all Somalis are nominally members of a Sufi order, the most important being the Qadiriyya, the Idrisiyya and the Salihiyya. Women are also members. These orders are usually non-political but can be used as organizational vehicles for resistance when faced with external enemies, as in the rebellion by Mohammed Abdulleh Hassan against colonial rule in 1900-1920. While Islam is a core element in the identity of Somalis, they also recognize clan affiliation and customary or contract law (*heer*) as defining elements in their heritage. The rise of the ICU was due to the long, organized presence of Islam in Somalia. A number of the organizations are mainstream Muslim associations of a social, educational and/or religious nature, and some are militant, with a programme of coercive or violent expansion and international connections and ambitions. Among the indigenous Somali organizations the most important are:

- *Harakat al Islah* (Movement for Revival) This movement was founded in 1978 with the aim of reconciling Islam and the modern world. It did not openly operate under the Siyad Barre regime but was more of a network of educated urban professionals and students. It ran social, humanitarian and educational activities and was said to opt for 'Islamic democracy'. Their programme rejects Salafism and the use of force, and the organization is known to be open to contact with foreign organizations, also those in the West.[29]
- *Ahl As-Sunna wal Jama'a* (People of the Sunna and the Community) This was set up in 1991 and has its basis in Somali Sufism, to which it claims to provide national leadership. It is a movement with branches elsewhere, is opposed to militant/reformist Islam and claims to represent traditional, main-

---

[28]   See Lee V. Cassanelli, *The Shaping of Somali Society: Reconstructing the history of a pastoral people, 1600-1900* (University of Pennsylvania Press, Philadelphia, 1982); Ioan M. Lewis, *A Modern History of Somalia: Nation and state in the Horn of Africa* (Westview Press, Boulder, CO, 1988).

[29]   International Crisis Group, *Somalia's Islamists* (ICG, Brussels, 2005, Africa Report no. 100), p. 14. A longer study of *Al Islah* is contained in Andre Le Sage, *Somalia and the War on Terrorism. Political Islamic movements and US counter-terrorism efforts* (Cambridge University Press, Cambridge, 2004, unpublished PhD thesis), pp. 159-184.

stream Muslims in Somalia.[30] They specifically tried to counter Salafist-Wahhabist versions of Islam, and thus inevitably became involved in politics. The group played a role in the peace negotiations in Mbagathi (Kenya) that led to the TFG in 2004. Its efforts to mediate between politics, radical Islam and Somali Muslim traditions have often placed it in a difficult position. In late 2008 it started to form militias to counter the *al Shabaab* insurgents.

- *Al Ittihad al Islami* (Islamic Unity) This movement was founded in 1984, bringing together the two earlier Islamic groups of *al Takfir al Wahda* (also called *Wahda al-Shabaab al-Islaami*) and the Somali branch of the Salafi *Ikhwan al Muslimiin* (Muslim Brotherhood) that were both formed in the 1960s but suppressed by former President Mohamed Siyad Barre. *Al Ittihad al Islami* was first led by the Somaliland *sheikh* Ali Warsame, a Saudi-educated Wahhabist cleric still active today.[31] While *al Ittihad* had a social component, it was primarily a political Islamist movement of militants, aiming to islamize Somali society, install an Islamic state in Somalia and agitate among Somali Muslims in Ethiopia. It became embroiled in violent disputes and battles with a variety of opponents in and outside Somalia and had a record of imposing its Islamist agenda (see below).

- There are also Islamic missionary groups like the *Jama'at al-Tabligh*, the *Ansar as-Sunna*[32] and an association of Somali *'ulema*s called *Majma' 'Ulimadda Islaamka ee Soomaaliya*. While these have no social or charitable programmes, their ideological influence is significant and impacts on traditional forms of Somali Islam.

These various groups are best considered as religious rather than *social* movements with a clear programme and agenda of social protest. They were primarily organizations bent on fostering Somalia's Islamic identity and furthering the interests of Somalis in a state where political opposition was impossible. The exception is perhaps *Al Ittihad al Islami*. Since the early 1980s it has been a constant presence in Somalia in various forms, both as a social movement with its own services and propagandist-educational activities and as a religiously motivated militant movement.[33] It formed various opportunistic alliances with some of the Somali Muslim civil-society associations outlined above. It has a record of terrorist attacks within Ethiopia that were part of its attempt to stir up unrest among Ethiopian Somali Muslims. Its bases in the

---

[30]   Matt Bryden, 'No quick fixes', p. 34.

[31]   He is a member of the Somaliland Habr-Ja'elo/Isaaq clan.

[32]   International Crisis Group, *Somalia's Islamists,* pp. 16-18.

[33]   For a detailed account by an Ethiopian academic, see Medhane Tadesse, *Al-Ittihad: Political Islam and Black Economy in Somalia* (Mega Printing, Addis Ababa, 2002).

Gedo region just across the Ethiopian border provoked a campaign by the Ethiopians in 1996-1997 that dislodged them and killed many of their leaders.

After this defeat, *Al Ittihad Al Islami* abandoned its international ambitions and developed a domestic agenda aimed at creating a semi-legal social network within Somali society, which was reminiscent of the National Islamic Front in Sudan before the 1989 coup. Though never renouncing its international links, it went into social projects, education and organizational activities to win a grass-roots constituency and gain adherence for its views on Islam and society among the general population.[34] It built up a network of sympathetic clerics, most of whom had trained in other Muslim countries and were asserting their views of 'proper Islam' as opposed to Somali variations, i.e. a rejection of saints and Sufism. *Al Ittihad Al Islami* became active not only in southern Somalia but also in Somaliland and Puntland, trying to gain a public presence by calling for stricter Islamic morality in the public sphere in the two countries. The assassination of various foreign humanitarian workers, teachers and civil-society figures were also attributed to the movement. Their actions were controversial and generated unrest,[35] but they had a following. After the TNG's formation in 2000 they were close to the new government[36] and are still around today although they have lost some of their momentum in the wider society.

Filling the state vacuum: From *Al Ittihad al Islami* to the ICU

The Islamic Courts Union, later called the Supreme Islamic Courts Council, emerged as an organized force in 2004 and, with a military wing, in early 2006. This marked their arrival on the political scene. The ICU's rapid rise and decline in the unstable and militarized society of southern Somalia are intriguing. The organization was led by several former *Al Ittihad Al Islami* figures, most importantly by former army colonel and *al Ittihad* leader Hassan Dahir 'Aweys', (of the Ayanle/'Ayr/Haber-Gidir/Hawiye clan) who became chairman of its *Shura* or Advisory Council. Sheikh Sharif Sheikh Ahmed (of the Agon-yare/Abgal/Hawiye clan), a former teacher and an *Ahlu as Sunna wal Jama'a* member, has been its Executive Council head since 2004 and has always been presented as a moderate leader. When it was set up, the ICU was internally

---

[34] Cf. Andre Le Sage, 'Prospects for *Al Itihad* and Islamist radicalism in Somalia,' *Review of African Political Economy*, 28, 89 (2001), p. 475.

[35] See Somali journalist Bashir Goth's interesting article, 'Thwarting the menace of Islamism in the Horn of Africa', on the Somaliland website (www.awdalnews.com/wmview.php?ArtID=4146, November 8, 2004).

[36] According to Medhane Tadesse, (*Al Ittihad*, pp. 113 and 126), the TNG was dominated by *al Ittihad* people.

diverse and had radicals, (ex-)terrorists, Salafists and mainstream Muslims within its ranks. Islamist clerics like *Sheikh* Fuad Mohamed Qalaf were its ideologues.[37] As stated above, the ICU emerged from a number of *shari'a* courts in the Mogadishu region and its predominant clan base was Hawiye/-Habr-Gidir. In the course of late 2005-2006 it evolved into a movement with a large militia force with its own 'technicals' (pick-up trucks with machine guns mounted in the back) and other weaponry. It acted as another armed force, rejecting the TFG and planning its military downfall. The ICU could thus in many respects be compared with the warlord/clan militia forces, pursuing a similar armed struggle to power but in this case in the name of Islam.

Their significance can be explained by the practical concerns of ordinary Somalis and business people with improving public safety and eliminating the predatory warlords and loose militias. While many ordinary people had cooper-ated with and profited from warlord or militia activities (if they were of the same clan), the general perception was that the warlords and militias had over-played their hand by holding with impunity the city of Mogadishu in a strangle-hold of violence, abuse and extortion. The Islamic Courts responded to an increasingly felt need among Somalis for public order and an end to the whole-sale insecurity that had become a serious impediment for business and progress. To consider the ICU *from its start* as a front for radical Islam is, therefore, a mistake.

New modes of national governance and judicial structures in the clan-ordered anarchy of Somalia had constantly been sought since 1991, with at least a dozen attempts to constitute a national government. It should not be forgotten though that in the meanwhile many local solutions to the problems of instability and state absence were also developed. Indeed before the formation of both the TNG in 2000 and the TFG in 2004, Somalia had already gone a long way to creating working local/regional units based on a combination of clan-elder rule, deep-rooted customary law (*heer*), Islamic law and NGO activity (mainly those of Somali women). This was the so-called 'building blocks' approach.[38] How-ever, the hotspot of Mogadishu remained violent. In the socio-political and legal vacuum of the city – and several other towns like Beledweyn and Kismayo – the Islamic Courts emerged as the only force with authority, providing a prag-matic regulation of disputes, combating street crime and protecting business deals. In the urban context, clan elders and customary law had lost much of their relevance as sources of judicial regulation.

---

[37] Remarkably, he had worked in Sweden for 12 year as the imam of a Stockholm (Rinkeby) mosque before returning to Somalia in 2004.

[38] Cf. Patrick Gilkes, 'Briefing: Somalia', *African Affairs*, 98, 1999, p. 577.

The courts were originally regular *shari'a* courts, like those found all over the Muslim world. The first phase of the courts' movement began just after the collapse of the state in 1991 when the Islamic group *Al Ansar as-Sunna* set up the first court in the Madina neighbourhood of northern Mogadishu, and was active within the Abgal sub-clan of Hawiye. Others followed, in Mogadishu and elsewhere, like the Hawadle clan court in Beledweyn, but this first wave of courts declined in the late 1990s due in large part to intra-Abgal clan competition, radical elements trying to take them over and a growing resentment to harsh *shari'a* punishments like the amputation of limbs. After a few years, a second wave of courts emerged in Mogadishu and Merca, and in 2000 they formed a *shari'a* Implementation Council, on which Hassan Dahir 'Aweys' reappeared. He was chairman of the Ifka Halane court (predominantly of the 'Ayr sub-clan), which was founded in 1998 and was known to be a hard-line court.

At the Arta peace conference in Djibouti in 2000, the Islamic Courts were represented as a movement.[39] In the next few years, eleven courts appeared in Mogadishu: ten from Hawiye sub-clans and one from the Jareer-Bantu people. They tried to transcend clan interests and appeal to wider principles of conflict regulation and justice 'on the basis of Islam', and partly succeeded. Their spokesmen often drew explicit parallels with the time of the Prophet Mohammed who, when establishing Islam as the dominant religion, had agitated against Arab clan divisions. The courts forged an alliance, thus increasing their relevance as an incipient social movement, and the ICU found support among a growing number of local businessmen, some of whom became the movement's core financiers. Members of the individual courts were Muslim clerics but also business people and clan elders and they became popular by creating order, cleaning up the streets and finding solutions to the problems of crime and insecurity caused by the warlords and criminal bands. That an Islamic message was part of the deal was accepted for the time being. As Ken Menkhaus noted, 'Though many Somalis were deeply uneasy with the radical and reckless direction the ICU leadership gradually took, they were willing to tolerate almost anything in return for public safety'.[40] This was realized by mediation in intra-clan dispute resolution, a furthering of inter-clan cooperation, the imposition of fines and compensation payments, and the enforcement of judgements and agreements, for which militia were used. Most of the courts, interestingly, took

---

[39]   See 'Interview with Islamic Courts chairman Hassan Sheikh Mohamed Abdi', in the In-Depth IRIN report 'Somali National Peace Conference' (www.irinnews.org/InDepthMain.aspx?InDepthId=54&ReportId=72096&country=yes, July 2000).

[40]   Ken Menkhaus, 'Who broke Mogadishu?', *The Guardian*, 17 January 2007.

care not to go against the principles of Somali customary law (*heer*), certainly not before their takeover of power in Mogadishu. They were usually supported in local communities and received voluntary financial contributions from both businessmen and the general population.

The ICU was formed in 2004 and sought an extension of the authority of the courts that morphed into a social movement with a more structured leadership and wider socio-political aims derived, in part, from Islamic charities and movements that existed before the Courts' movement emerged. They tried to bring the entire country under their influence, stabilize it and form a new structure of (religious) authority to replace the state.

This success, having responded to social needs and built up momentum, attracted Islamist militants, activists and former *Al Ittihad* leaders who saw in the Islamic identity and popular acceptance of the courts a way to move forward with their agenda of islamization, denying the relevance of Somali customary law and other sources of legislation. In addition, they saw the chance to subvert their main opponent, namely the TFG and its strongly anti-*al Ittihad* president Abdullahi Yusuf (who had prevented an *Al Ittihad* coup in Puntland in 1992).[41] At this juncture and fuelled by former *Al Ittihad* members, the expansion of the courts, by taking on militias as their executive arm and enforcing their rule, went beyond its regular jurisdiction and brought them to the threshold of politics. It was a crucial moment in recent Somali history when a potentially positive social movement turned into a political force, but one jeopardizing the chances of its own success by embarking on expansion using violent means. This was also a development that most Somalis did not appear to approve of, although it was indicative of the fundamental changes in Somali society and Somali Islam.

ICU rule: June-December 2006

The ICU was a heterogeneous alliance of Islamic groups, Islamic courts and radical-Islamists in opposition to the TFG. As noted, it had its roots in the earlier *Al Ittihad al Islami* that was formed in 1984,[42] which explains why parts of the ICU were already geared to a radical Islamist agenda. The ICU took over power in Mogadishu in June 2006 after it chased out a coalition of clan-militia leaders and warlords from Mogadishu. These warlords had divided southern Somalia and Mogadishu into personal business fiefs and were responsible for the road blocks, arbitrary rules, the extortions and most of the violence against

---

[41] For a good survey, see International Crisis Group, *Somalia's Islamists*, pp. 5-6.

[42] See Matt Bryden, 'No quick fixes', p. 28, and Sunguta West, 'Somalia's ICU and its roots in *al-Ittihad al-Islami*', *Terrorism Monitor*, 4, 15, 27 July 2006.

civilians. Some of them had loosely declared their allegiance to the TFG but did not submit to its authority.[43] In a notoriously ill-judged policy, the US government, concerned about terrorist *al Qa'eda* operatives in Somalia, had been supporting an alliance of such warlords with logistics and funds since early 2006.[44] Surrealistically called the Alliance for the Restoration of Peace and Counter-Terrorism (ARPCT), the US believed them to be a bulwark against terrorist elements within the ICU.[45]

After the ICU defeated the ARPCT in June 2006, it reigned in Mogadishu for six months and extended its rule to most of southern Somalia, bringing increased security and public order. Road blocks were removed, garbage was collected and many criminal gangs were taken off the streets. Its ideology had, however, become clearer in its leaders' pronouncements[46] and was unambiguous. As the Islamic Courts' first vice-chairperson Abdelrahman M. Jinikow said in September 2006: 'We will only approve a constitution based on theology because an Islamic constitution is the only one that serves all of us justly'. He added that the TFG government's current 'man-written constitution has nothing to do with Islam' and that '[a] secular constitution, whether it is democratic or any other, is never fair and right, and Muslims have only one constitution which is entirely based on Allah's Koran that will avail all Muslims in the world now and Hereafter'.[47] They tried to impose strict *shari'a*-based rule, which soon evoked resentment. The idea that the ICU was a benign and fully accepted regime has to be dismissed in view of the violence they inflicted[48] and the un-

---

[43] Many warlords, notably in the countryside and the smaller cities, remained outside the ARPCT. An example is the notorious Yusuf Mohammed Siyad 'Indha'adde (Hawiye, 'Ayr sub-clan), who had established himself in Merca and appropriated plantations and other property there. In 2006 he joined the ICU and became one of its most uncompromising spokesmen.

[44] See 'U.S. secretly backing warlords in Somalia', *Washington Post*, 17 May 2006.

[45] See also Matt Bryden, 'Washington's self-defeating Somalia policy', CSIS, Africa Policy Forum comment (http://forums.csis.org/africa/?p=18, December 6, 2006).

[46] See for example an interview with Hassan Dahir 'Aweys' in Rod Norland, 'Heroes, terrorists and Osama', *Newsweek*, 22 July 2006, and also 'Militia leader calls for Islamic rule in Somalia' (AP news message, 13 October 2005). An interesting confidential document on their programme is a letter by Hassan Dahir 'Aweys' (http://wikileaks.org/wiki/Category:series/Inside_Somalia_and_the_Union_of_Islamic-_Courts , November 9, 2005).

[47] See 'Somalia: we accept no constitution other than Islamic – Islamic courts', Shabelle News Media message (www.benadir-watch.com/2006%20News/0906_Islamic_courts.pdf, September 6, 2006).

[48] A few examples: after they took over they had women without veils publicly lashed, they introduced *shari'a* law punishments literally, like amputations and stonings,

popular measures they took.[49] The independent media and women's NGOs were threatened as well and is evidence of how the ICU quickly marginalized the role of civil society.

With inflammatory rhetoric, the ICU set out its wider political ambitions in the region: 'uniting all Somalis in the Horn of Africa',[50] '[the] installation of a *shari'a*-based Islamic state' and '*jihad* against Ethiopia'.[51] This reflected the ICU's immaturity as a movement.

An important result of the ICU victory was its takeover and appropriation of many of Somalia's economic activities. Some of the ICU's major financial backers were indeed important businessmen, like Ahmed Nur Jim'ale, former chairman of the telecom/remittance company *Al Barakat*, and trader Abukar Omar Adani who had his own militia.[52] In fact, the start of the ICU offensive in 2006 may have been sparked by a conflict over the control of the profitable El Ma'an port (30 km north of Mogadishu) between Adani, calling in ICU militias, and militia leader Bashir Raghe.[53] In addition, in late 2006 many of the thousands of former warlord militia members of the defeated ARPCT, the *moryaan* (marauding armed youths), turned up in ICU militias, perhaps less out of religious conviction than because of perceived economic prospects (a fixed salary of US$ 70 to US$ 150 per month).

---

they shot and killed people watching television, and in one incident they dragged wounded, loyal TFG supporters in Bu'ale from their hospital beds and killed them (cf. United Nations Joint Logistics Center, NGO-SPAS, 'Somalia – security update, report no. 44/06', 26 Oct. – 01 Nov. 2006). The *Al-Shabaab* militia, the main perpetrator, had already built up a record of abuse and violence in previous years, including targeted abductions, the assassination of aid workers and civil-society activists, and other grave desecrations. This fits with the record of terrorist actions of its predecessor *Al-Ittihad al-Islami.*

[49] This led Somali researcher Said S. Samatar to note that if Somalia were to be left to sort itself out alone, the movement would be absorbed by clan-based politics and lose its prominence and radicalism. See his 'Why Somalia is no territory for Islamic terrorists' (http://wardheernews.com/Articles_06/August_06/15_somalia_no_territory_for_terr orists_samatar.html, August 16, 2006).

[50] For example, they also threatened Somaliland and made pronouncements against its budding democracy and relative stability.

[51] For example, 'Somali militia declares jihad against Ethiopia', *International Herald Tribune*, 9 October 2006, and 'Somali hardliner calls for foreign jihadists', *The Observer*, 24 December 2006.

[52] See: Report of the Monitoring Group on Somalia pursuant to Security Council resolution 1676 (2006), UN document S/2006/913, p. 10.

[53] Both men were members of the Warsangeli/Abgal/Hawiye sub-clan.

In the six months up to December 2006 there were half-hearted negotiations between the ICU and the TFG on power-sharing. When in December that year the ICU threatened to conquer Baidoa, the town where the weak but internationally recognized TFG of Somalia was entrenched, the Ethiopians, who were fearful of an Islamist government on their doorstep and committed to the IGAD peace process,[54] moved in 'at the request of the TFG' with thousands of soldiers and defended the TFG. A quick push towards Mogadishu ousted the ICU from the capital, forced them to disperse and go back to their (mainly Hawiye) clan territories where they were reproached by clan elders for having provoked the Ethiopian intervention with their armed campaigns.

International dimensions: Impact of the Ethiopian intervention

Before 2006 Ethiopia had followed developments in Somalia with an apprehensive eye, wary of the ICU's Islamist element. Ethiopia sees itself as having legitimate security concerns regarding Somalia in view of two previous wars and a possible radicalization of its own Muslim population (ca. 38% of the total). While its role has not always been positive, Ethiopia appears to be working for a stable and manageable Somalia. Its relations with Somaliland and Puntland are good but the South is a problem. The Addis Ababa government also fears ethno-nationalist sentiments among the Ogaden Somalis, some of whom had links with *Al Ittihad al Islami* in the 1990s and have been waging an armed rebellion against the Ethiopian administration in Somali Region 5, which intensified in 2007 with a terrorist attack by the ONLF (Ogaden National Liberation Front founded in 1984) on an oil exploration site in eastern Ethiopia in which 65 people were killed.

Ethiopia has consistently supported the Somali Salvation Democratic Front (SSDF) of the current TFG president Abdullahi Yusuf and various non-Islamist groups among the Digil-Rahanweyn in the Bay-Bakool regions bordering Ethiopia. It rejected the previous transitional national government that emerged from the 2000 'Arta Process' in Djibouti and gave rise to an even weaker government with less legitimacy than the current TFG.

Within the IGAD framework, Ethiopia supported Abdullahi Yusuf's bid for the presidency in 2004 and made itself 'guarantor' for the newly constituted TFG. The seat of this government in Baidoa was protected in part by Ethiopian troops, as was the case when the ICU forces, having refused meaningful nego-

---

[54] This process of negotiations under the auspices of the IGAD (International Governmental Authority on Development, an organization of states in the region) in Kenya in 2002-2004 involving Somalia's various clan factions led to the Mbagathi agreement to establish the TFG in October 2004.

tiations with the TFG, advanced on Baidoa in December 2006 with the intention of conquering it. Their ultimatum to the TFG and the Ethiopians, made in the same reckless manner as most of their other actions, was met with a rapid offensive by the TFG and the Ethiopians that militarily cleared out the ICU from Mogadishu, destroyed much of their militia and infrastructure, and allowed the TFG (but not Parliament) to enter Mogadishu.

Ethiopia was aware of the (still ongoing) support that Eritrea was providing to those opposed to the TFG and their own forces, including *al Shabaab* and other militant groups. The UN Somalia Monitoring Group reports of 2006 and 2007 documented the arms flows and other foreign assistance in remarkable detail.[55] A proxy war is thus still being fought out, preventing easy domestic resolution of the conflict.

The impact of the Ethiopian intervention on the domestic scene since early 2007 has been substantial. It has led to the ICU dividing into at least three sections, reflecting the various social bases and ideological currents of Somali Islam, as well as different responses to the military defeat and offers by the TFG to negotiate.

ICU defeat and transformation

In addition to the military campaign by the TFG and the allied Ethiopian armed forces, there are also underlying societal reasons for the ICU's fragmentation, like centrifugal political segmentation (determined by the complex and ever-present Somali clan-family system), problems resulting from economic competition (land grabs, extortion and control over export products), local political manoeuvring in the stateless environment, and ideological differences rooted in ambivalent Somali nationalism and cultural identities.

While the ICU as such has been dissolved since its defeat, some remnants centred on the militias have slowly reconstituted themselves in the countryside with foreign and local support. And as the ICG noted in 2007, the 'grassroots network of mosques, schools and private enterprises' that was part of the ICU movement and had spread 'the Salafist teachings and their extremist variants remains in place and continues to expand'.[56] This includes Somaliland where

[55] Report of the Monitoring Group on Somalia pursuant to Security Council resolution 1676 (2006), UN document S/2006/913, pp. 11-17; Report of the Monitoring Group on Somalia pursuant to Security Council resolution 1676 (2006), UN document S/2007/436; Report of the Monitoring Group on Somalia pursuant to Security Council resolution 1766 (2007), UN document S/2008/274, pp. 20-21.
[56] International Crisis Group, *Somalia: The tough part is ahead* (ICG, Brussels, 2007, Africa Briefing no. 45), pp. 1, 9.

several of the *Al Ittihad* and ICU leaders came from[57] and where Islamists have been working underground to disrupt the prevailing political system.

In January 2007, core remnants of the ICU militias renamed themselves the Popular Resistance Movement in the Land of the Two Migrations (PRM). Two other names also surfaced: the Brigades of *Tawhid* and the Jihad in the Land of Somalia. They were committed to armed resistance by every possible means and, in the meantime, also developed their commitment to a radical, though not well-elaborated Islamist ideology.

On the political front, the ICU leadership, including what the media always calls the 'moderates', reorganized in Asmara, Eritrea, and formed the Alliance for the Re-Liberation of Somalia (ARS). After being released from Kenyan custody and debriefed by the Americans in early 2007, former ICU head Sheikh Sharif Sheikh Ahmed became the leader, but with Hassan Dahir 'Aweys' still in the background. Initially supporting any kind of armed action against the TFG forces, government officials and the Ethiopians, including shellings, ambushes, targeted killings and suicide attacks, they later chose to negotiate. On 9 June 2008 a deal was struck at a conference in Djibouti by the TFG and the ARS. They agreed to end all violence (on condition that there was a timetable for the departure of Ethiopian troops) and work towards power-sharing and reconciliation.[58] But this approach lacked significance among the radicalized militias.

The ICU's legacy was notably claimed by a radical sub-group led by the *Al Ittihad Al Islami* veteran Hassan Dahir 'Aweys', and younger activists like Afghanistan veterans Aden Hashi Farah 'Ayro'[59] (of the Ayanle/'Ayr/Habr-Gidir/Hawiye clan), Mukhtar Robow (Leysan/Sideed/Mirifle/Rahanweyn clan) and Mukhtar Abdirahman (probably a Habr-Ja'elo/Isaaq). The latter three were leaders of a militant group known by the name of *Harakat al-Shabaab* (or *Mujahidiinta/Hizb al-Shabaab*, i.e. Fighters/Party of the Youth). This group engaged in systematic attacks on Ethiopian troops and Somalis loyal to the TFG. A campaign of classic urban terrorism was unleashed, resulting in hundreds of civilian victims. *al Shabaab* was in many respects a continuation of the *Al*

---

57   When working on this chapter in late 2008, news was received of a fivefold suicide bombing by *Al Shabaab*-affiliated militants in Somaliland that had left 28 civilians dead and dozens wounded. See 'Suicide bombers kill at least 28 in Somalia' (www.africanews.com/site/Suicide_bombers_kill_28_in_Somaliland/list_messages/21336).

58   See 'Agreement between Transitional Federal Government and the Alliance for Re-liberation of Somalia (www.iss.co.za/dynamic/administration/file_manager/file_links/SOMALIPAX9JUN08.PDF?link_id=29&slink_id=6044&link_type=12&slink_type=13&tmpl_id=3, June 9, 2008).

59   He was killed in an American air strike on 1 May 2008.

Ittihaad Al Islami movement, and had originally been a militia allied to two radical Islamic courts in Mogadishu (Sherkoolo and Ifka Halane). After defeat in December 2006 it turned to a violent, non-compromising insurrection, led by the figures mentioned above as well as other Islamists. Former warlord Yusuf Mohammed 'Indha'adde' and jihadist Hassan Hersi 'al Turki' followed the same path, although they are not formally part of *al Shabaab*. They were able to draw support from a network of radical Somali Salafist clerics known for their jihadist pronouncements and statements against westerners, non-Muslims and dissidents.[60]

Al Shabaab-affiliated leaders in the 1990s undoubtedly served as contact men and protectors of (non-Somali) *al Qa'eda* operatives,[61] amongst whom were the three involved in the 1998 and 2002 bomb attacks in Kenya.[62] *Al Shabaab* thrives on foreign funding from Arab countries and a radicalized/-nationalist Somali diaspora.[63] They thus flout the domestic Somali constituency and feel accountability to no one except Allah.[64]

Despite the pounding the ICU and its militias received from the Ethiopians and the TFG and the unpopularity of their violent political agenda among large sections of the Somali public, including many of the (divided) Hawiye clan-family, the presence of a radical Islamist social movement in Somalia has now been established. This is in no small part due to support from foreign players, such as Eritrea and some Middle-Eastern Muslim countries, and will be a feature of the Somali political scene for years to come. In the process of their

---

[60] See, for instance, the statements of *sheikh* Nur Barud Gurhan, chairman of the Kulanka Culimaada, a Salafist group in Mogadishu, in 'Western aid workers accused of conversion', Reuters news message, 22 April 2004.

[61] For *al Qa'eda*'s presence in East Africa, see Andre Le Sage, *Somalia and the War on Terrorism*, Chapter 3.

[62] Fazul A. Muhammed (who narrowly escaped arrest in Kenya in September 2008), Saleh Ali Saleh Nabhan, and Tariq Abdullah (Abu Talha 'al-Sudani'). Other *al-Qa'eda* men include Ali Swedhan, Samir Said Salim Ba'amir, Mohamed Mwakuza Kuza, Issa Osman Issa and (probably) the Somali Ahmed Abdi Godane. Cf. International Crisis Group, *Somalia: Countering terrorism in a failed state* (ICG, Brussels, 2002). See also a report on Gouled Hassan Dourad, a Somali detainee in Guantanamo (www.dni.gov/announcements/content/DetaineeBiographies.pdf, September 15, 2008). See also Roland Marchal, 'Islamic political dynamics in the Somali civil war', in A. de Waal (ed.), *Islamism and its Enemies in the Horn of Africa* (C. Hurst & Co., London, 2004), p. 139.

[63] Cf. Stig Jarle Hansen, 'Misspent youth – Somalia's Shabab insurgents', in *Jane's Intelligence Review* (http://jir.janes.com/public/jir/terrorism.shtml, September 1, 2008).

[64] Cf. Robert Walker, 'Meeting Somalia's Islamist insurgents', BBC news item, (http://news.bbc.co.uk/2/hi/africa/7365047.stm, April 28, 2008).

(re-)emergence, the social agenda of Muslim movements, including that of the Islamic Courts, has been pushed aside in favour of a religious-political one that is bent on exclusive power and the coercive institution of a new 'moral regime', subverting the civic dynamics of Somali social forces and the agency of established grassroots interest groups.

The ICU and its associates have thus been militarized and transformed by a radical Islamist section that has defeated the aims of the social movement that established it. No doubt the brazen Ethiopian campaign and US anti-terrorism actions like air strikes on militants have contributed to this. But it is also a sign of the fundamental transformations that Somali Islam and its social infrastructure have been going through in the last decade: the decline of authority structures based on clan law and elders, the fragmentation of clans, the emergence of new independent economic power bases, and the rise of a new generation of foreign-funded and supported activists and religious men combating Somali culture, customary law and mainstream Islam dominated by Sufi orders. Apart from the subversion of customary law and the clan elders' influence, this development has marked the weakening of other social forces like traditional socio-religious associations and locally rooted Muslim movements, such as *Al Islah* and the *Ahl as-Sunna wal Jama'a*, that recognized the traditional dual nature of power in Somalia[65] and rejected an exclusivist, politicized Islam, as well as a decline in the fortunes of local NGOs, notably women's groups.

ICU fragmentation and the growth of the jihadist movement

The dominant insurgent force today is again the *al Shabaab* which, despite showing some internal diversity, is committed to an *al-Qa'eda*-type ideology. It has been the most important movement on the ground (up to mid-2009) and has done most of the fighting. It is organized in regional, relatively autonomous units and is becoming rooted in local communities that contribute funds and supplies, either on a forced or voluntary basis. *Al Shabaab* is trying to fuse Somali nationalism, which appeals to many (provoked by the presence of Ethiopian forces in the country), and radical Islamism conceived in global terms. In 2007, in a script well-known in global jihadist discourse, the PRM started showing suicide-bomber videos online. And in September 2008, some *al*

---

[65] See Ioan M. Lewis, 'Dualism in Somali notions of power', *Journal of the Royal Anthropological Institute*, 93 (1963), pp. 109-116. While religious leaders could become involved in (armed) struggle against a perceived external threat, within Somalia this duality was respected and reflected the socio-political organization of society, and political power was not translated or validated in religious terms (*Ibid.*, p. 115).

Shabaab spokesmen publicly admitted their affinity to *al-Qa'eda* ideology and were clearly set on the road to terrorism.[66] Their subsequent shelling of Mogadishu airport and the Ugandan and Burundian AMISOM forces, in which many civilians were killed, confirmed the trend.

Global militant-jihadist discourse has taken root among Somalis and is being spread by foreign-educated clerics and activists (in Saudi Arabia, Sudan, Egypt and the Gulf States), leading many of these groups to propagate a 'pure Islam' and an anti-clan and anti-Somali policy. Several Muslim countries and private individuals are providing funds for Islamic charities, mosques, *madrasa*s and private universities, not to mention other material support including arms and supplies (from Iran, Libya and Syria).[67] Predictably, the above-mentioned Islamist fighting groups, following the global discourse of jihadist Islamism, started propagandist Internet sites[68] calling for jihad and the 'liberation' of Somalia.

The deal made by the ARS with the TFG in June 2008 is evidence of a careful road to rapprochement, but the chance that the radicalized past of the ICU will accept it is slim. It appears to be too late because militant armed elements, such as *al Shabaab* and related Islamist militias that follow a narrow and uncompromising agenda, are likely to fight on using terror tactics.[69] They have faced criticism from many of their own clan members, with parts of the Hawiye and Rahanweyn clan-families (where key leaders of *al Shahaab* come from) disavowing their violent tactics.[70] In response, *al Shabaab* activists have targeted those who speak out and assassinated several of them, including clan elders. This development shows that clan dynamics are again impinging on the Islamist agenda and may limit its appeal. Despite this, radical Islamist opposi-

---

[66] Cf. one of the most notorious *al Shabaab* leaders, Mukhtar Robow, cited in Ed Sanders, 'Conditions may be ripe for *Al Qaeda* in Somalia', *Los Angeles Times*, 25 August 2008.

[67] See the report cited in footnote 38, pp. 21-26.

[68] See (www.qaadisiya.com), announcing the PRM's formation on 19 January 2007. It soon appeared they were *al-Shabaab* and were regrouping. Other websites were: www.kataaib.net (the official *Al Shabaab* site until 23-01-2009, when it was closed down) and www.abushabaab.worldpress.com (in English), also closed down in early 2009.

[69] In March 2007 they summarily executed and mutilated several captured TFG soldiers. See 'Somalia, Events of 2007', in *Human Rights Watch Report 2008* (Human Rights Watch, Washington, DC, 2008). (http://hrw.org/englishwr2k8/docs/2008/01/31/somali17757.htm, 2008).

[70] See for instance, 'Somalia - Mogadishu community leaders appeal to *al Shabaab*', a news message (www.garoweonline.com/artman2/publish/Somalia_27/Somalia_Mogadishu_community_leaders_appeal_to_al_Shabaab.shtml, October 7, 2008).

tion forces have been regaining the upper hand on the battlefield as a result of their international connections with other Muslim countries and networks in terms of funds and other support. In late 2008 they occupied the major city of Kismayo and installed an Islamist regime there, including *shari'a* criminal law.[71] In December 2008 the announced withdrawal of Ethiopian troops materialized and in early 2009 *al Shabaab* forces took Baidoa as well. The reluctance of the Ethiopians to perpetually buttress the TFG is explained by the fact that the TFG did not meet their expectations of forming a government, and without the promised support from the AU and the international community, they with drew. The TFG did not succumb to the pressure but saw the resignation of Abdullahi Yusuf and, in a surprise move, the election by an extended Somali parliament of Sheikh Sharif Sheikh Ahmed of the ARS-Djibouti as the new Somali president. His more moderate and conciliatory tone has invited support from Somalis and undermined the support base of the radicals. But the TFG will remain vulnerable, if not succumb, at some point,[72] and there may still be an Islamist regime in Mogadishu. In March 2009 the new president declared that *shari'a* would be the main law of Somalia, giving in to another demand by the Islamist radicals. But *al Shabaab* showed themselves to be rejectionist by not accepting the new TFG under the leadership of their erstwhile ally. Hassan Dahir 'Aweys' of the ARS-Asmara initially rejected the new TFG but in April 2009 announced his intention to return to Mogadishu and conditionally work with the new TFG. However, when he had returned in May, he denounced contacts with the Sheikh Sharif government and called for its removal. As leader of the *Hizbul Islam* coalition of four smaller radical-Islamist factions, he clearly aimed to become government leader himself. Violence fuelled by *al Shabaab* and *Hizbul Islam* actions has continued. It also provoked the formation of militias under the banner of the mainstream Sufist-oriented *Ahl as-Sunna wal Jama'a* who in early 2009 chased *al Shabaab* out of several towns in central Somalia. Thus a new round of fighting began, indicating that *al Shabaab* had reconfigured itself as a militant movement superseding the ICU and was aiming

---

[71] On 28 October 2008 it was reported that they had started to stone Somali women for committing adultery. BBC news message, 'Somali woman executed by stoning' (http://news.bbc.co.uk/2/hi/africa/7694397.stm, October 28, 2008) and 'Rape victim, 13, stoned to death in Somalia', *The Guardian*, 2 November 2008, (www.guardian.co.uk/world/2008/nov/03/somalia-rape-amnesty, November 2, 2008).

[72] See Steve Bloomfield, 'Troop pull-out leaves government on brink', *Sunday Herald*, 11 October 2008. The ongoing offensive of the *al Shabaab*, supported by terror attacks, brought this moment near in June 2009.

to achieve its goals (of gaining power and installing a theocratic state) through violent means rather than a broad social programme.

Conclusion: The transformation of a social movement

The ICU and its constituent parts undoubtedly had traits of a grassroots social movement by being involved in dispute resolution and exercises in social justice and attempts to restore some degree of social order. It certainly was, to cite Olzak's definition, 'a purposive collective movement voicing demands for fundamental changes in society, mobilizing around one or more public causes and following a strategy of change'. ICU activities could be claimed to have been beneficial to an urban constituency and came to stake claims for fundamental change in a wider national arena, although they were not al all democratic. The fact that in 2006 this movement quickly went on to take economic and political functions and violently claim exclusive socio-political space was because the state in Somalia had not only collapsed but had effectively dissolved so that the movement – and its religious currents – had no political structures or powerful state adversary to confront, unlike social movements in Europe, Latin America or South Africa. The ICU had to fill a vacuum to not only provide services but also create new narratives of legitimacy and authority. It decided to seek a basis in Islam, offered as an encompassing, absolutist ideology claiming to fill civic space and ground people's social identity. But any social movement, as an invented institution, is prone to change and metamorphosis, as Tilly noted.[73] That the ICU allowed itself – perhaps having no choice on a playing field dominated by violent competition for power and allegiance and no other 'unifying' discourse than Islam available – to be taken over and dominated by radical Islamists as to leadership and political ideology was a result of its inexperience and its unclear, perhaps underdeveloped, socio-political programme. It was likely also a reflection of the basic impossibility of developing a real political Islam. Many in Somalia feel this to be a contradiction in terms, notably in view of the deeply engrained duality of notions of power in Somali culture – the religious people (*wadaad*) versus the politicians or warriors (*waranle*).[74] Political power is, furthermore, usually seen as corrupting religious values, and perhaps vice versa. It is the old problem that beset *Sayyid* Mohammed Abdulleh Hassan back in the early 1900s.[75]

---

[73] Tilly, *Social Movements,* p. 14.
[74] Cf. Lewis, 'Dualism in Somali notions of power', p. 114.
[75] Cf. J. Abbink, 'Dervishes, *moryaan* and freedom fighters: cycles of rebellion and the fragmentation of Somali society, 1900-2000' in J. Abbink *et al.* (eds), *Rethinking*

The social movement of the ICU has fragmented and lost direction. The broader-based ARS has taken its place since 2007 as a political opposition force but as such was not present in Somalia. The courts could regain legitimacy and make an impact by refocusing on what they do best, namely dispensing justice in local social and other disputes, seeking reconciliation and accommodation between different groups and clan units, and refraining from politicizing their role. In these domains they can still do more than the perennially weak, erratic and unreliable TFG, which has not been able either to institutionalize itself or gain sufficient loyalty[76] and work towards national inclusiveness. It has the character of a phantom government without a social presence and with its various units like the army, police or security forces often operating fully on their own and not responding to the cabinet ministers who are nominally in charge. Its record of abuse and the bad name its Ethiopian allies have inevitably received in Somalia due to the ongoing violence are preventing progress. A compromise formula between the two – the TFG and the ARS – is inevitable but realities on the ground have so far prevented this.

The ICU movement yielded various moderate as well as militant/violent parts in 2008, with the latter subverting anything good that the ICU had achieved when in power in Mogadishu. Among them, *al Shabaab* turned in fact into an 'anti-social movement', targeting its own people and predictably rigidi-fying its policies with, as the core issue, the unconditional withdrawal of the Ethiopians (thereby hoping that an implosion of the TFG would follow) and the coercive establishment of *shari'a* rule in a theocratic state. Beyond this, no specific political ideas have been voiced. For them, all means to these ends are justified. The following incident is characteristic:

> On 7 October 2008 the chairman of a traditional elders' council in the Hiraan region, Mr Da'ar Hersi Hoshow, was shot and killed. Hundreds of protesters took to the streets in Beletwein, the capital of Hiran, following the assassination. The protest turned violent with demonstrators throwing rocks at Islamic Courts fighters, who effectively control Beletwein and the surrounding regions after Ethiopian troops withdrew last month [September 2008]. No group claimed responsibility for the murder, but the assassination came a day after he publicly renounced the *al Shabaab* insurgents' threats against the aid agencies CARE International and International

---

Resistance: Revolt and Violence in African History (Brill, Leiden, 2003), pp. 328-365; and Hussein, *From Tyranny to Anarchy*, p. 76, 221.

[76] Although it probably commands the nominal allegiance of the majority of southern Somalis: the Darod and Rahanweyn clan-families, the larger part of the Abgal-Hawiye clan, and many minority groups.

Medical Corps. He had also suggested that *al Shabaab*'s threat was intended to 'starve' the local people.[77]

This killing, not the first to be directed against a legitimate social current in Somali society, namely the clan elders who represent legitimacy and authority in the local context, confirms that Islamist radicals have taken over the struggle and annexed the social-movement element in Somali insurgency. Clan-family divisions and competition for power and resources of any kind (money, guns, land, water and women) have come to dominate the struggle in southern Somalia based on earlier struggles in the 1990s and are not easily resolved.[78] This is reminiscent of the deep divisions and violence left by *Sayyid* Mohammed Abdulle Hassan, the anti-colonial militant and proto-nationalist of the early twentieth century.[79] It took decades to overcome the damage done by his Islamist armed movement and the current antagonisms in Somalia may indeed have revived the conflict and memories of the divisions he generated.

The present conflict shows that the ICU, which originally emerged as a partial solution to the challenges of social disorder and the problems of degenerated clan mediation mechanisms and failing social support systems in Somalia, has been overtaken by a radical Islamist ideology based on foreign models. This ideology is carried by certain clan groups and elites within those clan groups more than by others. The clan system is not, as often alleged, inherently divisive (see the experiences in Somaliland and Puntland) but only becomes so when Islamist ideology is let loose on it. The Islamist politicization of the country's problems has subverted the courts' potential and their socially reconstitutive role. It has made a particular form of Islam dominant: the Salafist-jihadist version that fuses religion and politics in a violent narrative, presenting armed force and terror as the apocalyptic means to the goal of Islamist theocratic rule, and which is not popular among most Somalis. This has prevented authentic social movements from developing.

The result appears to be a Somali society more divided than ever and one burdened by a discourse of violence and revenge. There is a Somali saying that

---

[77] Based on the news story 'Somalia: chairman of elders' council assassinated in central Somalia' (http://allafrica.com/stories/200810080085.html, October 7, 2008). Since October 2008 and in a fully predictable scenario, there have been many other reports of the stoning of rape victims, the cutting off of thieves' hands and even the beheading of sheikhs by *Al Shabaab* forces. One example is Abdi Sheikh and Abdi Guled, 'Somali Islamists behead two sheikhs' group', *Reuters news message*, 20 March 2009.

[78] See Ken Menkhaus, *Somalia. A Country in Peril, a Policy Nightmare* (ENOUGH Project, Washington, DC, 2008) (www.enoughproject.org/files/reports/somalia_rep090308.pdf).

[79] See Abbink, 'Dervishes, *moryaan* and freedom fighters', p. 346.

goes as follows: *Nabar doogi ma haro* ('An old wound will not go away'). If this is true, the Somalia conundrum, which is following a historically familiar cyclical pattern of group rivalry and violence, will probably be with us for another generation at least.

6

Liberia's women acting for peace: Collective action in a war-affected country

Veronika Fuest

This chapter explores the historical and socio-political factors that have facilitated the emergence of the women's peace movement in Liberia, which has been credited with the election of the first female African head of state. It highlights specifics of the country's settler history, of autochthonous/indigenous constellations of gender relations, and precursors of women's collective action. On the one hand, shared experiences of the civil conflict have activated the potential for female modes of organization. On the other hand, 'identity work' by the leadership of the movement, which was instrumental and indispensable in bridging internal class, ethnic and other divides, has also been informed by international feminist discourse. Special attention is devoted to the role of the international community and the national government in shaping the structure of political opportunities, allowing for the emergence, maintenance and transformation of the movement.

Introduction

In 2005, Liberian voters chose a woman, Ellen Johnson-Sirleaf, to be their president. This has generated worldwide interest. The first-ever election of a female head of state in Africa can be seen as a sign of a wider social movement associated with peace. Indeed, a number of scholars have credited women's organizations with exceptional social inclusiveness and a concomitant potential for peace-building.

The fact that gender identities play an important role in determining levels of trust – with much higher levels of trust in women-dominated organizations than in those dominated by men – has important implications for the potential role of different organizations in rebuilding social capital …[1]

This chapter explores the factors that have facilitated the emergence of the women's peace movement in Liberia, including specifics of the country's history and processes of 'identity work',[2] and discusses some of the aspects of its social range and internal divisions. Special attention is devoted to the role of the international community and the national government in shaping the 'structure of political opportunities'[3] concerning the emergence, maintenance and transformation of the movement.

After the outbreak of civil war at the beginning of the 1990s, Liberia witnessed the formation of a number of women's organizations. These appear to have increased exponentially particularly since the end of the conflict in 2003. Various informal women's organizations at the local level have emerged in response to local problems and offer self-help in areas of, for example, joint production, reconstruction, marketing, security, 'trauma healing' and traditional skills training. To some extent, the flourishing of women's groups reflects entrepreneurial attempts to gain access to donor funding in general, and some of the local organizations have been established in response to aid agencies' frequent preference to channel funding to women's groups. In Monrovia and other cities in the centre and northwest during the war, women were highly visible 'as activists for peace and as agents of reconciliation'.[4] Leaders and members of these organizations worked across faction lines and acted as mediators, often at great personal risk. They organized marches, formulated petitions and attended national and international conferences.[5]

[1] C.O.N. Moser & F.C. Clark (eds), *Victims, Perpetrators or Actors? Gender, armed conflict and political violence* (Zed Books, London/New York, 2001), p. 10. Cf. also Swanee Hunt & Cristine Posa, 'Women waging peace', *Foreign Policy*, May/June (2001), pp. 38-47; and K.H. Karamé (ed.), *Gender and Peacebuilding in Africa* (Norsk Utenrikspolitisk Institutt, Oslo, 2004).

[2] David A. Snow & Doug McAdam, 'Identity work processes in the context of social movements: Clarifying the identity/movement nexus' in: Sheldon Stryker *et al.* (eds), *Self, Identity and Social Movements* (University of Minnesota Press, Minneapolis, 2000), pp. 41-67.

[3] Cf. Jacquelien van Stekelenburg & Bert Klandermans, 'Social movement theory: Past, presence and prospects', in this volume.

[4] Mary H. Moran & M. Anne Pitcher, 'The "basket case" and the "poster child": Explaining the end of civil conflicts in Liberia and Mozambique', *Third World Quarterly*, 25, 3 (2004), p. 506.

[5] Nadine Puechgirbal, 'Involving women in peace processes: Lessons learnt from four African countries (Burundi, DRC, Liberia and Sierra Leone)', in K. Karamé (ed.), *Gender and Peacebuilding in Africa*, pp. 47-66; African Women and Peace Support Group, *Liberian Women Peacemakers: Fighting for the right to be seen, heard, and counted* (World Press, Trenton, NJ, 2004).

When considering the emergence of Liberian women's groups, it can be seen that, according to Tilly, there are three main elements to a social movement: campaigns (a sustained, organized public effort making collective claims on target authorities); a repertoire (the employment of different forms of political action involving associations and coalitions, public meetings, processions, vigils, rallies, demonstrations, petition drives, statements to and in the public media, and/or pamphleteering); and the concerted public representation by participants of unity, numbers and commitment.[6] These elements were all operative in the organized actions of Liberian women during and after the civil war.[7] Various external observers have agreed that, compared to other countries, there has been an extraordinary degree of determination and militancy in the Liberian women's peace movement. And this was years before Ellen Johnson-Sirleaf was elected as Africa's first female head of state in 2005. For example, Moran reports that anthropologists in the 1990s were struck by the democratic nature of the gender dialogue and the 'empowered females'.[8] In a comparative article, Moran and Pitcher noted 'that there was far more peace-oriented activity by explicitly women's organisations going on in Liberia; furthermore, these organisations existed at all levels from the most powerful urban elites to illiterate villagers'.[9] More recently, the Liberian women's peace movement was given international recognition in the film entitled *Pray the Devil Back to Hell.*[10]

Research was undertaken in the capital, Monrovia, and in urban and rural locations in the northwest, centre and southeast of Liberia (in Bong and Lofa counties from 2005 to 2007, and in Grand Gedeh and Sinoe counties in 2008). Participant observation was used at village meetings, gender workshops and at a women's conference, and interviews were held with business women, male and female farmers, urban residents of all ages and key informants such as leaders of women's organizations, local and national politicians, development agencies and staff working for non-governmental organizations (NGOs).[11]

The results presented here acknowledge the complexities of the social differences and divisions in Liberian society. Firstly, the people living in Liberia's north, centre and west can be distinguished as being socio-politically, ecologically, agriculturally, linguistically and demographically different from the

---

6   C. Tilly, *Social Movements, 1768–2004* (Paradigm Publishers, Boulder, CO, 2004).
7   Cf. African Women and Peace Support Group, *Liberian Women Peacemakers.*
8   M.H. Moran, *Liberia. The Violence of democracy* (University of Pennsylvania Press, Philadelphia, 2006), p. 43.
9   Moran & Pitcher, 'The "basket case" and the "poster child"', p. 504.
10   Fork Films (http://www.praythedevilbacktohell.com/nonflash/about.htm, October 22, 2008).
11   The author is grateful to the Max Planck Institute for Social Anthropology, Halle/-Saale, Germany, and to the Welthungerhilfe for providing funding for field research.

population in the southeast.[12] Liberia's northwest and centre constitute the so-called Mande-speaking 'Poro complex' of secret societies, a region historically marked by a distinct socio-political system of ranked lineages with powerful elders or chiefs and gendered, mutually exclusive, secret societies, colloquially known as Poro (for the male society) and Sande (for the female society). By contrast, the Kruan-speaking groups in the southeast are characterized by acephalous communities, less important secret societies and the institutionalized participation of women in traditional government.[13]A second important dimension of socio-political variation is constituted by Liberia's history of 'black colonialism', which is considered unique in Africa. Descendants of freed slaves that were resettled from the US and elsewhere in the nineteenth century founded Africa's first republic in 1847 and, as a small minority, they dominated the country's political, social and economic life for more than 130 years. These so-called Americo-Liberians and 'Congos' (the name originally given to slaves intercepted while being illegally transported on the high seas, and put ashore in Liberia) fought, suppressed, exploited, traded and mixed with various African groups and constituted the country's ruling elite. A coup d'état in 1980 brought Afro-Liberians to power and the ensuing corrupt and repressive government, dominated by the president's ethnic group, was overthrown by 'rebel' forces that invaded Liberia under Charles Taylor in 1989 and ignited a civil war that would last for fourteen years.

Social and political antagonisms between Americo- and Afro-Liberians in the twentieth century were reflected in the social distinctions that emerged involving the label 'civilized', which is a notion loaded with religious and moral meanings and became an important identity marker of contextual claims to elite membership.[14] Thus historically, Liberia's women, and men for that matter, were both divided and united by a dichotomy juxtaposing educated/'civilized'/'Congo' (Americo-Liberian) with 'country'/'traditional'/'native' identities. Indigenous Africans had limited access to certain elite positions through formal education and assimilation into the Christian settler community, as a result of which they too could acquire a 'civilized' identity.

Thirdly, the war resulted in an emphasis on religious antagonisms between the Christian and Muslim sections of the population, and ethnic polarization.

---

12   For example, Warren L. d'Azevedo, 'Some historical problems in the delineation of a central west Atlantic region', *Annals New York Academy of Sciences*, 96 (1962), pp. 512-538.
13   Moran, *The Violence of Democracy*.
14   Elizabeth Tonkin, 'Model and ideology: Dimensions of being civilized in Liberia', in L. Holy & M. Stuchlik (eds), *The Structure of Folk Models* (Academic Press, London, 1981, ASA Monograph 20), pp. 307-330.

Two of the major warring factions were constituted by an ethnic group with a predominantly Muslim identity.

Concerns of women's organizations

Social movements offer an important vehicle for ordinary people's participation in public politics. In the sense of 'politics by other means', they may constitute the only means open for relatively powerless groups to challenge the dominant political structures or processes and the distribution of resources.[15] The distinction between the practical and strategic needs of women, first delineated by Molyneux,[16] seems useful in capturing the heterogeneous currents and concerns of the movement under discussion here. 'Practical needs' addressed by the self-help organizations (and many NGOs) include the most pressing basic needs for safe shelter, adequate nutrition, health care, clean water etc. By contrast, strategic needs address women's institutional opportunities and status in society, such as legal protection, access to education, employment and land rights, and an end to gender violence. By extension, they include the end of fighting in times of war. The organizations devoted to peace activism and later to political advocacy have been the motors of the women's peace movement. The following sections illustrate the scope and activities of the movement.

The Association of Female Lawyers in Liberia (AFELL), the Mano River Union Women Peace Network (MARWOPNET), and the Women in Peace Building Network (WIPNET) are among the most influential and visible organizations.[17] AFELL was established in 1994 to offer legal assistance to women and children who had suffered from violence and has effected the passing of two laws: the Act to Govern the Devolution of Estates and Establish the Rights of Inheritance for Spouses of Both Statutory and Customary Marriages (2003), in short the 'inheritance law' that aims to regulate women's marriage rights, rights to property and access to their children after divorce or the death of their spouse, and the 'rape law' (2006), which has turned rape into an non-bailable offence. MARWOPNET was established in 2000 by women peace activists from Guinea, Sierra Leone and Liberia on the occasion of a conference in Conakry of the regional economic grouping, the Economic Community of West

---

[15]   Cf. the contribution by Habib & Opoku-Mensah in this volume.
[16]   M. Molyneux, 'Mobilization without emancipation? Women's interests, the state, and revolution in Nicaragua', *Feminist Studies*, 11, 2 (1985), pp. 227-254.
[17]   Other organizations are the Liberian Women's Initiative (LWI), the Women of Liberia Peace Network (WOLPNET), Concerned Women for Liberia (CWO), Women in Action for Good Will, the Muslim Women's Federation, the United Muslim Women's Advocacy and Empowerment Organization (UMWAEO), the Muslim Women's Association for Peace and Social Justice, and the Coalition of Women of Political Parties in Liberia (CWPPL).

African States (ECOWAS). Internationally, it has been the most visible of Liberia's women's organizations as it was given considerable attention by the media and international agencies, and was awarded the United Nations Prize in the Field of Human Rights.[18] Without invitation, this organization produced a declaration during the peace negotiations in Accra in 2003. The women demanded inclusion in peace negotiations in line with the Resolution on Women, Peace and Security (SC Resolution 1325) adopted by the UN Security Council in 2000, which formally recognizes women's particular vulnerability in wartime and calls for their equal participation and full involvement in peace-making. WIPNET was founded in 2002 under the auspices of the West African Network for Peacebuilding (WANEP) and has been Liberia's most comprehensive women's organization with over 5,000 members in all of the counties involved in it. WIPNET's strategic goals have dominated from the start and its activists are acutely aware that external aid projects differ in their objectives or in the strategies they employ to achieve improvements in women's lives. They question well-meaning training programmes for women that pass on traditionally Western female skills and occupations.

WIPNET and MARWOPNET are umbrella organizations that have both made a special effort to embrace women from all ethnic and socioeconomic backgrounds to expand their basis for mass action, especially at the famous peace demonstrations in April and May 2003. Some activists have taken steps to narrow the social gap, for example by discouraging the use of 'big English' at meetings, workshops and conferences, which the 'civilized' habitually use to distinguish themselves from the 'country people'. Representatives of rural women have been consciously included, facilitation methods have been adapted to the needs of illiterate participants and interpreters provided for those lacking a good command of English. MARWOPNET's leaders determinedly took illiterate rural women to the Mano River Union conference in Conakry in 2001, to the astonishment of representatives from other countries, and WIPNET has also pointedly included women of different religious denominations in its organization in an attempt to reduce the dominance of Christian activists in NGOs. In practical terms, for example, Muslim women leaders have frequently been asked to deliver the opening and/or closing prayers at workshops and conferences.

The movement has commanded a range of symbolic resources on which the existence of shared identities depends.[19] In addition to slogans and songs, the women wear white T-shirts and white head-ties as symbols of their unity during their peace campaigns. Liberia's 'women in white' or 'white women' have been

---

[18]   Puechgirbal, 'Involving women in peace processes'.
[19]   Snow & McAdam, 'Identity work processes in the context of social movements'.

active conflict mediators in the years since the war and are widely recognized beyond national boundaries. At the WIPNET conference in May 2006, the founder of WANEP, a key speaker, stressed that whenever he travelled outside Liberia, he felt 'proud of being recognized by the white T-shirt women and the football star George Weah'. On International Women's Day in March 2007 and in 2008 the white T-shirts could still be seen at marches in Monrovia and in the distant coastal city of Greenville.

After the 2003 peace agreement, the main goal of the movement shifted to demands for the institutionalized political and economic participation of wo-men, and the radical stance taken by organizations such as WIPNET in favour of strategic needs seems to have been accepted by the Ministry of Gender and Development (MGD). Women activists have lobbied for legislative reforms to reserve at least 33 per cent of all seats in local and national elections for women. They have demanded balanced employment, law enforcement, access to and ownership of land, and training for legal staff such as land commis-sioners. They advocate special leadership training programmes for women and girls and are encouraging more female candidates to contest local elections that are scheduled for 2009. An emergent class of business women, which formed in the entrepreneurial vacuum during the war,[20] seems to be accommodating its interests within the movement too. Credit programmes and training to advance female entrepreneurship are also being called for. Pointing specifically at the constraints women face in the lucrative cross-border trade, a recent policy paper addressed the harassment women face from customs and immigration officers and demanded that gender-sensitive training manuals be developed for all offi-cials working at border posts.[21]

Formative and supporting factors

The formation of novel gender stereotypes, the maintenance of a collective female identity and the organization of activities have been nurtured by factors including internal identity politics and external markets. An obvious example is that the pattern, speed and spread of a movement depend on a functioning communications network. Communication has been vastly facilitated by the

---

[20]   V. Fuest, '"This is the time to get in front". Changing roles and opportunities for women in Liberia', *African Affairs*, 107, 427 (2008), pp. 201-224.

[21]   WANEP & WIPNET, *Women's National Agenda for Peace, Security and Develop-ment in Post-War Liberia*. Adopted 30 March 2006, presented to the Government of the Republic of Liberia (Women in Peacebuilding Network, Monrovia, Liberia); Ministry of Gender and Development and the United Nations, *National Women's Conference Report: Advancing women in peacebuilding, recovery and development in Liberia* (Monrovia, 5-9 May 2008).

exponential spread of mobile phones since the end of the war. Social networking in general has been dramatically transformed by this technology and is an area of study that merits further investigation. However, as a social category, women have had reasons for relating to the war in particular ways. The following sections differentiate for heuristic purposes three domains that intersect both conceptually and in (social) practice and that have contributed to the forming and maintaining of the movement.

The socioeconomic and political roles of Liberian women vary in many ways, the most obvious dimensions being generation, lineage status in the northwest, age-group identity in the southeast, and ethnic belonging including the Americo-Liberian sub-sections of society. However, images and practices central to the movement – of women as leaders and female collective action – have been built on traditionally cultural and social capital. As many scholars have demonstrated,[22] social movements typically emerge out of existing organizations and associational networks.

Firstly, Liberian society has always conceived women's agency and their collective action as being essentially separate from the realm of men. Moran stressed the importance of the traditional 'dual-sex' organization in Liberia, and for that matter in West African societies:

> Women simply do not view men as capable of representing them and their interests. At one level, this conviction may stem from the highly segregated nature of women's and men's productive activities in West African farming systems. Although complementary, these separate tasks may bring women and men into competition for such resources as land and labor. More important, however, may be the cultural constructions of women and men as radically different kinds of beings, manifest in such structures as the dual-sex political system, which underlies the belief that men cannot adequately represent women and vice versa.[23]

This dual organization of the sexes has not prevented women's organizations from the time-consuming consultation of powerful and knowledgeable senior males in times of need either in the past or the present. (Leaders of the women's secret society have also been accountable to male seniors of the Poro.) The fact that one of WIPNET's founders is male can be attributed to his network connections within West Africa, which have been useful in eliciting support from the West African Network for Peacebuilding (WANEP).

Secondly, Liberian women historically organized a wide range of collective activities in different contexts. The most influential traditional organization, which involved trans-ethnic inclusive activities, was the Sande in the country's northwest. In southeastern Liberia women organized themselves traditionally

---

[22] Cf. Snow *et al.*, 'Identity work processes in the context of social movements'.
[23] Moran, 'Collective action and the "representation" of African women: A Liberian case study', *Feminist Studies*, 15, 3 (1989), p. 444.

and supported their women's chief and councils of female elders, which are parallel institutions to the male-dominated structures in local politics.

Thirdly, notwithstanding ideologies of male dominance and corresponding institutions of social control, Liberian history has encompassed powerful women in both 'traditional' and 'modern' settings. Looking at the historicity of the status of women in other African countries, it could be suggested that the colonial 'disempowerment' that women suffered in other countries was not present in Liberia.

Female power in local public realms has, therefore, been a traditional feature in Liberia, notwithstanding women's structural constraints within a traditional system that has generally been labelled 'wealth-in-people' in a generalizing perspective inspired by political economy. Where labour has been a crucial political and economic resource in environments with a relative abundance of land, powerful men have accumulated women, the major workforce, and controlled and redistributed women's sexual and reproductive services to establish political alliances and win clients. Accordingly in Afro-Liberian societies, women's reproductive capacities and labour have been controlled by their lineage elders and their husbands' lineages.[24]

Women in the southeast of Liberia tend to perceive men and women as different and complementary instead of the latter being inferior. The 'cultural ideal woman is the hardworking wife and mother, the provider for her household. The ideal husband is generous and is expected to provide his wife or wives with gifts ...'.[25] In the southeast, parallel political structures for men and women in village governance have existed and survived,[26] involving institutions like 'women's chiefs' and councils of female elders with a deliberative role and the power of veto over certain decisions made by male councils. (For example, over-enthusiastic warriors in the past could reportedly be checked by the women's council.)[27] Such institutions have been absent in the more hierarchically organized societies of the north and west. Evidence suggests that among the Kpelle, for example, women have always been considered inferior to men. The dominant ideology of male superiority has centred on the male role of protection, support for women and provision for their children.[28]

---

[24] C.N. Bledsoe, *Women and Marriage in Kpelle Society* (Stanford University Press, Stanford, 1980).
[25] Moran, 'Collective action and the "representation" of African women', p. 453.
[26] V. Fuest, *Contexts of Conflict in Southeast Liberia. A study report* (Welthungerhilfe, Bonn, 2008).
[27] Moran, *The Violence of Democracy*, pp. 40-48, 147-148.
[28] S. David, '"You become one in marriage": Domestic budgeting among Kpelle of Liberia', *Canadian Journal of African Studies*, 30, 2 (1996), pp. 157-182.

In the northwest, traditionally gender-specific codes of behaviour have been transmitted by the secret societies. Boys' and girls' initiation, involving circumcision, was compulsory, with seclusion in so-called 'bush schools' that were separated by gender and originally lasted for several years. Sande and Poro leaders cast themselves as brokers and exclusive ritual managers between the realms of male and female and between the supernatural and daily life. Marriage and reproduction were mediated by the elder female leaders of secret societies who claimed to be in spiritual control of the well-being and reproductive capacities of initiated girls. Sande leaders and important members, such as midwives, could extract considerable fees and labour services from senior relatives of the initiates and their prospective husbands. Such entitlements were based on claims to command esoteric skills and knowledge enabling them to control a girl's fertility and health.[29] Although women as a class could not adopt any public political roles, individuals and particularly those belonging to ruling lineages could command space for socio-political manoeuvring. They could, for instance, generate considerable power by playing 'the male game' of controlling male and female junior dependents and securing male labour and allegiance.[30]

The traditional principles of hierarchical organization – gerontocracy, lineage status, patriarchy – became increasingly negotiable as they were crosscut by other principles evolving from the differentiation of Liberian society in the course of the twentieth century, such as formal education, employment in the public sector and access to the higher echelons of Liberian networks of patronage. Notwithstanding the dominant patriarchal ideology in Liberia, there was a comparatively large population of educated, professional women when the war broke out. Probably due to the heritage of matrifocality in the (former) slave families from the United States, Liberia's settler women enjoyed social and economic privileges/rights unheard of in the Western world of the nineteenth century. And since the middle of the twentieth century Liberia has revealed a striking representation of women in public office.[31] From the 1950s onwards, President Tubman carefully cultivated a new constituency among women, extended suffrage to women and appointed some to positions of authority,[32] and his supporters organized a women's political and social movement.

There have been precedents for collective female action as well as inclusive organizations. The historical experience of female pressure groups concerned with the good of the community can be seen as being grounded in a tradition of

[29] C.N. Bledsoe, 'Stratification and Sande politics', *Ethnologische Zeitschrift Zürich*, 1 (1980), pp. 143-150.

[30] Bledsoe, *Women and Marriage*.

[31] For details cf. Fuest, '"This is the time to get in front"'.

[32] A. Sawyer, *The Emergence of Autocracy in Liberia. Tragedy and challenge* (Institute for Contemporary Studies, San Francisco, 1992), pp. 280, 371.

women's collective action/mass protest in Liberia's southeast since pre-war times. The position of women chiefs has required support from collective female action; having a voice but not an equal voice requires women to act collectively to counteract the power of a political hierarchy in which they are junior partners.[33]

The Sande seem to have fostered an ideology of solidarity among women and female strength in the face of male harassment, inasmuch as certain skills for manipulating men were passed on at initiation and consolidated action was mobilized against men who transgressed society's rules. Initiated peers (of the same status) are reported to have practised mutual help in times of need. However, it is doubtful that the Sande asserted anything like local 'women's rights' in any institutional sense. Occasional enactments of solidarity seem to have been counterbalanced by the hierarchical cleavages within society and the interests of the leaders in enriching themselves, including the fabrication of charges of wrongdoing against men to create occasions for fines.[34]

Women's organizations with their various tasks in the agricultural cycle have existed since time immemorial. All over Liberia there are seasonal work cooperatives, for which the Kpelle term *kúú* has become a generic designation in Liberian English. Women's associations have long been a traditional feature of urban social life and women's savings and marketing cooperatives have been recorded since the middle of the twentieth century. In particular, church-based women's organizations of different denominations have provided an important site of cross-class, interethnic contact and collaboration. In Liberia's southeast, voluntary associations have generally been of greater significance than in the northwest. Beyond savings and loan cooperatives (*susu*), women's clubs also meet to save for entertainment, funerals and social insurance.[35] Evangelical and independent churches engaging in charitable and self-help activities multiplied in the 1980s as a result of increasing poverty and social polarization, with the majority of members being recruited from among the increasing numbers of urban women in the informal sector.[36]

---

[33] Moran, *The Violence of Democracy*, p. 48.
[34] C. Bledsoe, 'The political use of Sande ideology and symbolism', *American Ethnologist*, 11 (1984), pp. 455-467.
[35] Hans D. Seibel & Andreas Massing, *Traditional Organizations and Economic Development. Studies in indigenous cooperatives in Liberia* (Praeger Publishers, New York, 1974).
[36] Paul Gifford, *Christianity and Politics in Doe's Liberia* (Cambridge University Press, Cambridge, 1993), pp. 288-291.

Shared experiences of the war:
Identity enhancement and identity politics

Experiences of gender-specific violence have become a collective concern requiring measures to mobilize mutual help and external support. Different sources agree that about 70 per cent of women and girls experienced sexual violence during the war.[37] The peculiar paradox that increasing numbers of incidences of rape may correlate with a growth in women's organizations and women's status has been noted by Ibeanu with respect to Nigeria. In her study, many Ogoni men and women (61% and 82% of respondents) felt that a violent crisis raised the profile of women and their confidence to deal with problems confronting them and their community, and generally enhanced respect for women who are praised for their positive contributions. As a result, a number of traditional stereotypes about women have been challenged, such as their weakness and submissiveness.[38]

Liberian women's self-confidence seems to have increased too, challenging the traditional ideology of male superiority.[39] Urban as well as rural women stress that the experience of war made them realize that they were 'in the dark' before and are now 'waking up to the issue of leadership'. Many women are conscious, if not proud, of having coped during the war with crises without male support. They assumed responsibility for tasks previously performed only by men and they learned new skills such as brick making, building and roofing houses, and clearing farms. The war opened up new spaces for collective action. Local narratives refer to women who organized themselves to ensure their community's survival, mediated conflicts involving local (war) leaders, and/or calmed trigger-happy fighters. Women appear to have developed special negotiating powers with commanders, who could have perceived them as less threatening than men. Women were certainly able to organize crossing the lines of fighting more easily than men. And most significantly, an increase in women's political ambitions and in the legitimacy of women's political participation at national and local level seems to have been increasingly accepted by the male sector of the population. In view of what has been perceived (and constructed) as overwhelming evidence of men's multiple failures during the

---

[37] See, for example, Simone Lindorfer, *Assessment Report Liberia. Sexual and gender-based violence in Grand Gedeh, River Gee and Sinoe* (Medica Mondiale, Monrovia, 2005).

[38] Okechukwu Ibeanu, 'Healing and changing: The changing identity of women in the aftermath of the Ogoni crisis in Nigeria', in Sheila Meintjes *et al.* (eds), *The Aftermath. Women in post-conflict transformation* (Zed Books, London, 2001), pp. 189-209.

[39] Cf. also F. Olonisakin, 'Women and the Liberian civil war', *African Woman*, March-September (1995), pp. 19-24.

conflict, women's social and economic achievements and their impressive contributions to the common good during the war are discursively being emphasized. Female refugees were exposed to novel practices and ideas during their time in exile in other West African countries.[40] As an essay in informed speculation, I suggest that the sheer spatial extension and intensity of the Liberian civil war as well as the long-term displacement of at least half of the population resulted in particularly extensive experiences in new female roles.

As with social movements elsewhere, Liberia's women's movement is constituted by a bundle of narratives. Positive, binding functions demand audiences to concur and respond emotionally and produce comparable stories. Shared experiences are traditionalized through discourse grounded in moral expression. The recognition of a set of shared, repeated and meaningful references results in a collective identity that facilitates collective action.[41] Discourses around the experience of rape have contributed to the conceptualization of women as victims and as a group in need of special assistance. This aspect of humanitarian aid and solidarity (involving the formation of victim-perpetrator dichotomies) has been nurtured by support from the churches and by international NGOs since the early 1990s. Other references include stories of mutually achieved success as single providers for their families, and constructions from the past and present in terms of power structures characterized by gendered suppression. Women are not only the victims of rape: Liberian women are, retrospectively, also construed to have been mere objects of exploitation by men and treated like chattels in traditional society.[42] Their capabilities as (better) leaders surfaced during the war. (Women activists rarely mention particularistic interests or divisive practices such as the suppression and exploitation of young women by female elders.) In principle, groups and individuals can be seen to be drawing on a repertoire of positions and arguments. The traditional image of the modest, pious, unthreatening woman, the role of the peaceful mother and the caring household provider may be discursively emphasized in certain public situations, and the image of women as political animals with legitimate claims to power

---

[40]   V. Fuest, *Fruits of war? Refigurations and Contestations of Female Identities in Liberia*. Working Paper of the Max Planck Institute for Social Anthropology (Max Planck Institute for Social Anthropology, Halle/Saale, forthcoming); Fuest, "'This is the time to get in front'".

[41]   Gary A. Fine, 'Public narration and group culture: Discerning discourse in social movements', in H. Johnston & B. Klandermans (eds), *Social Movements and Culture* (University of Minnesota Press, Minneapolis, 1995), pp. 127-143.

[42]   Cf. Government of Liberia, Act to Govern the Devolution of Estates and Establish the Rights of Inheritance for Spouses of Both Statutory and Customary Marriages (Monrovia, 2003).

(based on human rights) in others. Most of these images resonate with those of the 'civilized' woman, which have been analyzed by Moran.[43]

The point of departure of the women in the peace movement was the realization that 'men were at the root of the war'.[44] The Minister of Gender and Development argued at a conference in June 2005 that:

> ... evidence has shown that women's participation in political decision-making bodies improves the quality of governance. Studies have also shown a positive correlation between increased women's participation in public life and a reduction in the level of corruption.[45]

The image of peaceful women-in-leadership – which is also essentializing in substance – is being activated to support claims to political leadership: women are needed as leaders to secure enduring peace and good governance. MARWOPNET, like other actors in this arena, tends to stress the propensity of mothers as 'natural' experts in the reintegration of child soldiers, not threatening the traditional patterns of gender dominance but capitalizing on an essentializing image of women as providers/caring mothers. A prominent member of AFELL stated that:

> Women are ... a bedrock of any society whether educated or uneducated. ... The women artfully cross all lines of the various warring factions in search of food, water and medical services for their families as well as others who could not make it, and to earn an income to support the families. ... In war torn societies and out of war torn societies, it is the women who keep the society going...

At another conference in 2006, it was stressed that 'the challenge that we must face is to realise that women in other parts of the world happen to be far ahead from where we are'.[46] In the words of a prominent activist:

> ... for us, the task is far from over. This is only the beginning..... The women's movement must continue to be the watchdogs for the government and must continue to work towards the attainment of gender equality and women's empowerment at all levels and all areas ... and strategise on how to promote women's leadership in post-conflict peacebuilding in Liberia....

---

[43] M.H. Moran, *Civilized Women: Gender and prestige in Southeastern Liberia* (Cornell University Press, Ithaka, NY, 1990).

[44] Interview at the Ministry of Gender and Development, Monrovia, March 2007.

[45] Varbah Gayflor quoted in: European Commission and Konrad Adenauer Foundation, *Gender Awareness and Gender Equity in Liberia. The Gbarnga Conference 2005* (European Commission/Konrad Adenauer Foundation, Monrovia, 2005).

[46] This and the following quote are from WANET and WIPNET, *Women's National Agenda for Peace, Security and Development*, adopted 30 March 2006 (Women in Peace Network, Monrovia, 2006).

Support from international agencies

Studies of women's movements have often omitted the role of foreign actors, notably multilateral and bilateral aid and peace-building agencies. Reports on Liberia's 'women in peace' movement have usually stressed the indigenous agency of Liberian women. While I do not wish to diminish the important role and intrinsic motivation of the committed women who have participated in the movement, the possibility that without external support the women might not have been mobilized to such an extent should not be overlooked. Since the civil conflict, international support for women's organizations has gained momentum, particularly in those parts of Liberia that have constituted the major catchment areas of national and international aid, namely the urban centres and the counties or districts that are relatively easy to access by road from the capital. The peace movement was reportedly initiated in 1994 by a group of women who had been trained extensively in peace-building processes by international NGOs. A UN organization facilitated the participation of a comprehensive delegation of Liberian women at the Fourth Women's World Conference in Beijing in 1994, with this international experience working as a trigger in the unfolding of the Liberian women's movement. The endeavours of AFELL and other female activists in the field of legislation concerning women's rights have been supported by international consultants, organizations in the US and the UN Human Rights Office in Liberia. MARWOPNET's foundation was supported by the international NGO *Femmes Africa Solidarité*. Multilateral agencies have continued engaging women's organizations in demobilization, disarmament, reconstruction and rehabilitation programmes, and in the civic education projects preceding the 2005 national elections.

International agencies have provided, on the one hand, symbolic and material resources for the movement and, on the other, fora of communication which are essential to any kind of social movement. The most pertinent social spaces in the women's movement have been the leagues of conferences and workshops supported by the UN offices in charge of gender affairs in Liberia and international NGOs. Many of the recent policies pursued by the UN resonate with the measures proposed by Hunt and Posa within a policy framework of 'inclusive security'.[47] The so-called international community has been a particularly forceful factor and seems to dictate the direction that the movement is taking.

As elsewhere, the peace-building policies of the international community in Liberia include efforts at restructuring social relationships. International actors have been heavily engaged not only in areas of practical need – an estimated

---

[47]   Hunt & Posa, 'Women waging peace'.

180 foreign charities are said to be active in Liberia today[48] – but also in gender mainstreaming activities either directly or indirectly by sponsoring local NGOs. Concepts of gender equality and women's human rights have been transferred to Liberia from a variety of external sources. In recent years, UNIFEM, the United Nations Development Programme (UNDP) and other international agencies have provided funding for projects to integrate gender concerns into the government's national reconstruction and peace-building programmes. Aid is often only meted out to so-called 'community-based organizations' that can prove they have support from 50 per cent of the female representation in their leadership. Male and female staff in local NGOs employed by UN agencies or international NGOs have been exposed to gender mainstreaming workshops. Male and female Liberians have been trained as facilitators in peace-building, usually in other African countries (but sometimes in Europe) since the beginning of the 1990s. Such courses invariably involve gender issues, in particular the topics of leadership and gender-based violence, the concomitant discourse that contributes to polarizing the roles of perpetrator and victim according to gender. Members of local women's organizations, including those from rural communities, have been trained in the subject matter by different NGOs. Civic-education projects funded by international agencies have emphasized women's potential for leadership,[49] and workshops have been backed up by corresponding messages in media broadcasts with regional or nationwide coverage, in particular by UNMIL Radio and county-based radio stations sponsored by international organizations. With external support, WIPNET, for example, has run a *Voices of Women* radio programme in three counties for a number of years and the messages put across are reinforced by interactive theatre performances in some regions. Slogans and songs about gender equality and women's empowerment seem to be activated, often teasingly, as a kind of 'folk' wisdom in semi-urban contexts even in the country's interior. Not surprisingly since the election of the female president, gender issues have become an even more pervasive topic in the media, and various government affirmative action programmes are targeting girls and women directly. WIPNET, supported by UNDP, continues to be very involved, moving from women in peace building and women in leadership to civic education on women's human rights.

US-based agencies in particular support the strategic needs of Liberian women and President Johnson Sirleaf even received an award from the National Democratic Institute (NDI) for her work in promoting democracy in Liberia.

---

48 'Liberia. With a little help from her friends', *The Economist*, 23 August 2008, p. 34.

49 For example, in November 2007, a programme was launched by UNDP and the MGD to conduct leadership training for 300 women leaders in all counties; 'Liberia: LIPA, Gender Ministry Sign Agreement', *The Inquirer* (Monrovia), 6 November 2007.

The encouragement of gender equality has been linked discursively to the 'building of democratic strength in your nation for years to come' by the Speaker of the US House of Representatives.[50] Liberian women have reportedly participated in training programmes run by the Women and Politics Institute at the American University to learn the tricks of the trade from top political leaders. However Liberia's women do not need to leave their home country to receive training. For example, the NDI and Women's Campaign International train women in how to become more politically empowered in their own countries.[51] Women in rural Liberia are being encouraged to actively fight for their rights with support from the National Endowment for Democracy, an American organization, in a project that seeks to strengthen the advocacy capacity of rural women and sensitize them in their participation in local and national politics.[52] The UN mission in Liberia, UNMIL, is working closely with the Women's NGO Secretariat, the MGD and AFELL to disseminate the laws and policies for the protection and promotion of women and girls' rights in the country.

Constraints and divisions

As with any type of collective identity, gender identities do not constitute stable entities. They are flexible, subject to intra-group variation and intersect with ethnic, religious, class and other shared identities. Depending on the context, any one of these differences may be attenuated by groups or individuals.[53] In war-affected societies one may want to distinguish women analytically according to their differential access to economic resources, information, wealth and status, old from young women, women in remote rural areas and women in urban centres, but also according to new or recently emphasized roles (combatants, women who did not take up arms, 'bush wives', refugees, internally displaced people etc.), widows from married women, women intent on lasting change in gender relations and those who want to return to what they perceive as the stability of their pre-war arrangements. To complicate matters, the relative values and importance of those identities may be relevant only at certain stages in any woman's life. In addition to the ethnic, religious and class divides, the unity within the women's movement is jeopardized by yet further lines of

---

[50]   Courtney Hess, Washington, DC, 'West Africa: U.S. group honors women leaders' (www.allAfrica.com, October 27, 2007).

[51]   Nancy Bocskor, 'The changing global face of politics: training tomorrow's female leaders'. Women's Democracy Network
(http://www.wdn.org/Newscenter/Detail.aspx?ID=6, January, 2007).

[52]   See, for example, 'Rural women fighting for their rights' (www.allAfrica.com, June 16, 2008).

[53]   Henrietta Moore, 'The differences within and the differences between', in T. del Valle (ed.), *Gendered Anthropology* (Routledge, London, 1993), pp. 193-219.

division. As Hebert[54] has argued, feminist scholars have usefully offered explanations as to why women's social movements emerge but rarely have they explored why the goals of these movements remain out of reach. Many theorists acknowledge that the formation and functioning of social movements inevitably entail exclusionary practices concerning the collective identity that is identified as underlying these movements. Hebert has demonstrated that multiple lines of inclusion and exclusion associated with women's movements have occurred most notably along lines of ethnicity/race, class and gender. In addition, she mentions competitiveness among movement activists. Anecdotal evidence does indeed attest to problems within the movement under consideration that are arising from conflicts among the leaders of the various organizations and from the fact that the women's movement is run by members of the social elite.

Questions are also emerging about the inclusive range of the movement. Women certainly do not benefit from the gender discourse and affirmative actions if they do not have access to workshops, do not listen to the radio and/or do not understand English and live in an area where there are few programmes in local languages. In the remote southeastern border towns or the northwest of the country, discourse on gender equality is perceived as being 'something of the city', as respondents in the distant villages in Lofa and Grand Gedeh counties put it.

Here I want to focus on the religious/civilized identity which also includes aspects of a class and urban-rural divide in Liberia. It appears to entail not only the exclusion of Muslim women, notwithstanding efforts like those mentioned above to involve them, at least symbolically, but also implies conflict with uneducated women, in particular those non-Christian 'native' women with a stake in Sande society. In a variety of contexts both Americo- and Afro-Liberian women have been able to claim status as social seniors. In particular, the prestige of civilized status was enhanced by the Christian churches and their affiliated women's clubs and organizations that are open only to civilized women.[55] Significantly, Americo-Liberian women, women raised by Americo-Liberian families or by Christian missionaries have been crucial functionaries in the movement. Since before the war, Christian NGOs have played a major role in educating girls and given women leadership positions in their organizations, for example in the Christian Health Association of Liberia. A report on the movement states:

---

[54] Laura Hebert, 'Women's social movements, territorialism and gender transformation: A case study of South Africa', Paper presented at the annual meeting of the American Political Science Association, Marriott Wardman Park, Omni Shoreham, Washington Hilton, Washington, DC, 1 September 2005 (http://www.allacademic.com/meta/p41242_index.html, September 5, 2008).

[55] Moran, *The Violence of Democracy*, p. 83.

... religious beliefs, reflected in extremely high levels of affiliation to churches and mosques, are the foundation of many Liberian women's commitments to peace-making and their conviction that peace must start with the individual. As threats to survival grew and the need for personal peace intensified, *non-traditional spiritual movements* [emphasis mine, VF] became stronger and were often led by powerful women whose followers crossed ethnic and class lines. That these leaders were 'persons of God, who can be trusted' was an additional basis for solidarity among women.[56]

Women were particularly mobilized in the cities and funds were raised by establishing or employing international connections. (More than ever today, literacy is a crucial leadership skill, even in the rural areas. The leaders of the new Muslim women's organizations are literate because they have attended government schools in addition to their Qur'anic education.) Although rural and uneducated urban women have been impressively active members of the peace movement, there appear to have been serious 'class' divisions among them. In a sense the social and cultural capital that the movement was been built on and the religious identity of the majority of activists are harbouring seeds of dissention.

Since 1994 when educated women activists founded the network, there has reportedly been major conflict between the uneducated/'country' and educated/'Congo' women. It would seem that the uneducated have to some extent been instrumentalized by their leaders. It was not the elite women who were reported to have been seen 'sitting on the airfield', in other words performing the tedious task of daily peace demonstrations and praying in the rain and sun for hours, but rather 'the common women' in their white T-shirts. Educated members of the movement may also indirectly associate being 'civilized' with claims of being 'emancipated' or 'empowered'. 'We have seen the light' is one of many religious idioms used to express a new feminist consciousness in public discourse. What may be called a maternalistic attitude is surfacing concerning the agency of change, which is reminiscent of the historical commitment to the old 'civilizing mission' as an important dimension of the settlers' identity. In public contexts, 'civilized' activists may emphasize the necessity to 'lift up' their uneducated sisters who 'are still in darkness'. Rural women are construed to be in dire need of education and sensitization about 'their' women's rights in order to be delivered from male suppression. Christian women tend to stress their religiosity and perform as respectable members of society (perhaps to neutralize fears of the conservative men in power). The support of church leaders is being sought to build legitimacy. WIPNET women, after their march through the city

---

[56]   African Women and Peace Support Group, *Liberian Women Peacemakers*, pp. 34-35. There may be a connection between the movement and the mushrooming of Pentecostal churches in the wake of the war.

of Monrovia following their May 2006 conference, presented a peace torch to the President of Liberia, announcing that it had previously been blessed by the Catholic Church's archbishop. Even though WIPNET has made special efforts to be inclusive as a network, the traditional Christian-Muslim divide is maintained in practice for political expediency.

Many, if not all, leaders have capitalized on the training they have received in workshops and on the cultural and social capital they have gained as participants at international conferences. Women qualified in this way constitute a small minority of the well-educated who have become the coveted experts, trainers and managers employed by the international agencies that are constantly in search of female project partners (for reasons of political correctness). A decline in commitment to the women's collective cause has been observed among the elite women who are said to have found new pastures in government or in positions with international agencies. This appears to have weakened the movement. This process of concentration may even have reinforced class distinctions within the movement.

It should be mentioned that, ironically, the policies related to the law on rape whereby an increasing number of rape cases have been taken to court (albeit with dubious outcomes) throughout the country in the last two years and the ensuing debates may turn out to be a possible divider. First, women disagree about the reason for the increase in rape cases. The young urban women may be blamed by more traditionally minded female elders for their provocative ways of dressing and lack of morals. Secondly, women's concepts of female personhood differ. In the traditional rural context, rape tends to be perceived as a violation of property (of the family or the husband), which is shameful in principle and is therefore glossed over, particularly if the perpetrator is a relative. Or it is treated as a family affair, involving indemnification fees to the family concerned. Such practices do not match the conceptions of urban female human-rights activists who put the physical and psychological damage of the victim centre stage. Ideological debates about this issue can be heard even in the country's remotest villages.

Unwittingly, the international community seems to be contributing to divisions in the movement in yet another direction. The centralized organization of Sande society, which, like the Poro, had been courted and to some degree incorporated in Liberian government since the time of President Tubman,[57] served to organize self-help activities (meeting 'practical needs') for thousands of Li-

---

[57]   S. Ellis, 'The mutual assimilation of elites: The development of secret societies in twentieth-century Liberian politics', paper presented at the conference 'The Powerful Presence of the Past' (Halle/Saale, Max Planck Institute for Social Anthropology, October 2006).

berian women during the war.[58] The society was mobilized to join the peace marches but in a wider societal context, the Sande appears to have suffered a crisis of legitimacy in the wake of the war. Its activities were disrupted in many regions and a significant group of women in Liberia's north and west no longer consider membership of the Sande as being important in their lives (like men with respect to the Poro). In this domain, Liberian society has become divided down to the family level. Many urban girls – and the great majority of the urban population is female[59] – would not consider being initiated. Mothers refuse to send their daughters to the 'Sande bush' (often opposing the wishes of elder rural kin). Before the war such challenges were only heard of in the context of isolated incidents of Christian fundamentalism in missionary contexts.[60]

The fact that traditional institutions, in particular the Sande and Poro societies, have been weakened or even dissolved is discursively linked by elders, both male and female, to the perceived lack of respect and loss of discipline in young women, especially in the urban areas of the interior. ('The war has turned their minds.') Elders and leaders returning from exile have lobbied for the revival of initiations camps (bush schools) and praised the virtues of the secret societies regarding their (purported) regulatory and stabilizing functions but this spiritual vocation may of course be linked with the motivation of generating income from initiates' families. In many parts of the northwest, the secret societies are reported to have resumed their activities, sometimes with external support from NGOs in a (perhaps misconceived) effort to promote indigenous authorities that are assumed to hold legitimate offices in conflict regulation. It is worth mentioning that the re-legitimization of the Sande in Liberian society has been fostered by the current president, Ellen Johnson-Sirleaf, who courted the Sande network as one of her constituencies in the run-up to the elections in 2005. In this context, it is significant that one of the outcomes of a women's conference in May 2008 has been an appeal to the donor community to support the Ministry of Education and to schools and community leaders 'to develop innovative strategies … to harmonize traditional and academic schools schedules to encourage girls (*sic*) retention in schools'.[61] This indicates that 'bush

---

[58]   Interview with Mama Tumah Sieh, Executive Director for Women Affairs of the Ministry of Internal Affairs for twenty-five years and national representative of the Sande society (also in the Truth and Reconciliation Committee) in her 'village' near Monrovia, March 2007.

[59]   Government of Liberia, *2008 National Population and Housing Census: Preliminary results* (Liberia Institute of Statistics and Geo-Information Services (LISGIS), Monrovia, 2008).

[60]   Ellis, 'The mutual assimilation of elites'.

[61]   Ministry of Gender and Development and United Nations, *National Women's Conference Report.*

school' sessions have been resumed on a large scale because, as before the war, the sessions compete with the annual cycle of schooling times and parents often take their children out of school to have them initiated.

As an example of disjointed measures of donor support, other NGOs have tried to raise awareness about the damage caused by female genital mutilation (FGM) which is an integral part of initiation into the Sande. Apparently under pressure from the international community, the Ministry of Internal Affairs is working towards banning the practice but Sande leaders reportedly walk out of meetings whenever the issue of FGM is raised; considering it outrageous to discuss it with men or non-members. The oath they took obliges them to keep secret the circumstances surrounding the circumcision ritual and it prevents them from discussing the topic with non-members. Even though some Sande leaders are said to be very aware of the consequences of FGM, they cannot apparently stop the practice. They fear the punishment that will befall them if they do not fulfil their duty, as the penalty expected from the spirits is death, disgrace or life-long suffering. I cannot even begin to judge whether this is their personal/social 'truth' or whether it is a spiritual discourse employed to defend the order that privileges them. For the women's movement, it is politically expedient to embrace the Sande leaders as representatives of both traditional leaders and rural women at any public performance, such as a conference. Backstage, however, 'enlightened' (urban) women leaders are very critical of the revitalization of 'bush schools': they reject the transmission of traditionally submissive female roles and the practice of FGM.

Moving where? Conclusion and prospects

African women's participation in national politics has often been based in women's movements, even in the wake of civil conflict.[62] Liberia's women's movement, which is clearly a child of the civil war, contributed significantly to the election of Ellen Johnson-Sirleaf, and the movement has certainly enhanced the self-confidence of many women. While educated women cultivate new identities as agents of change, peace makers and professional or political leaders, the movement also appears to have brought about non-adherent potential beneficiaries in many sectors. School girls and illiterate women struggling to survive in the fields, streets and markets have expressed pride in the achievements of visibly powerful women, particularly the president.

However, the women's movement in Liberia seems to be crumbling. It has never been a united network of heterogeneous groups of actors united to serve

---

[62] Gretchen Bauer & Hannah E. Britton, 'Women in African parliaments: A continental shift?' in G. Bauer *et al.* (eds), *Women in African Parliaments* (Lynne Rienner Publications, Boulder, Col., 2006), pp. 1-30.

the cause of peace. Since 2003 the differences in interests among its members have become ever more important and, having been promoted by the international community since the early 1990s, the movement appears to have turned into a branch of the peace-building and development business. Many of its leaders are using their skills to engage in politics, international trade and business, and/or they are acting as 'development brokers' on behalf of their communities.

The movement has been led by women from national and local social elites who have successfully mobilized a range of women's organizations for peace activism, and subsequently for individual political participation. International agencies have offered massive support to institutionalize women's human rights. The big Monrovia-based organizations are still riding on the ticket of 'inclusive security' as promoted by the international community, particularly in the context of activities surrounding the 'rape law' and the pending local elections. Another crucial strategic need has recently been addressed by AFELL and the UN: women's rights to land. Local organizations, however, continue to be concerned with practical needs, where possible using the movement's network to mobilize external funding.

The perceived benefits of the women's movement seem to be recognized by many Liberian men, albeit selectively. As a force promoting security, peace, moral communities and conflict regulation, the movement is considered as a common good. In public discourse, the fact taken for granted in pre-war Liberian society that women were the sole providers for their families is generating more explicit respect today. Women's new opportunities for access to international resources are welcomed as assets for households, families and their communities. However, the emergence of new public domains of female activities, women's rights and women's direct competition for political resources is disconcerting for male asset-holders. The women's movement has also provided symbolic resources for girls and women striving to escape the control of their social seniors. In the cities, they are following well-established pre-war strategies of multiple partnerships;[63] and novel gender discourses are adding a new dimension to conflicts with the authority of the elders. They refuse to be told what to do by rhetorically referring to their rights. (To what extent this development is related to the observed dramatic increase in domestic violence is an issue still to be investigated.)

The movement's future continuity will depend on coherence between institutional reform, practical experience and the narratives and ideologies in place.

---

[63] V. Fuest, *'A Job, a Shop, and Loving Business'. Lebensweisen gebildeter Frauen in Liberia* (LIT Verlag, Münster, 1996); Olonisakin, 'Women and the Liberian Civil war'.

The efforts of committed women activists and affirmative action, represented by the Liberian president as well as the policies, resources and discourses offered by the international community and US-based organizations in particular, will contribute to upholding the women's movement.

7

Nurtured from the pulpit: The emergence and growth of Malawi's democracy movement

Boniface Dulani

Most accounts of the wave of democratization that swept across the African continent in the early to mid-1990s point to the pivotal role played by movements that successfully forced authoritarian regimes to embrace democracy. But how did these movements emerge in an environment where the political space was closed or severely limited? Drawing on Malawi's transition from authoritarian to democratic rule in the early 1990s, this chapter discusses how democracy movements in Africa came about through a process of regime rupturing after the intervention of exogenous actors in the political arena. In the case of Malawi, the Catholic Church was such an actor when, in 1992, it intervened in the political arena by issuing a highly critical pastoral letter that challenged the legitimacy of the thirty-year dictatorship of the then president-for-life, Hastings Kamuzu Banda.

Social movements and the democratization process in Africa

The history of post-independence African politics can be divided into two periods. The first, coming immediately after independence, was dominated by authoritarian forms of government that ranged from military to civilian dictatorships while the second is the era of democratization that started in the last decade of the twentieth century.

During the authoritarian era, African leaders devoted a great deal of energy to suppressing political dissent at both group and individual levels. Political parties were often completely outlawed, which was common practice in military dictatorships, and opposition parties were banned in one-party states.[1] Individuals who expressed even the mildest forms of dissent were imprisoned, frequently without trial. Some were assassinated or murdered by state security agents while the (few) lucky ones managed to escape and live in exile. In other instances, the business interests of individuals who were perceived to hold critical views were frustrated, in some cases, being expropriated by the state.[2]

The disbursement of patronage to supporters and opponents of the regime served as another instrument for the ruling elites to entrench power. As Medard notes, 'through patronage, the leaders [were able to] co-opt potential opponents and regulate the recruitment of the ruling class'.[3] Patronage networks thus served to undercut civil society by blocking opportunities for the emergence of strong and well-organized pro-democracy groups. Popular associations and organized groups, such as trade unions, that were considered to be hotbeds of dissent and to pose a potential challenge to the ruling elites were subsequently eradicated or emasculated. The only civic structures that were spared during the authoritarian era were those headed by hand-picked loyalists and that therefore posed no significant threat to the ruling elite As a result, political opposition was either wholly undermined and/or so weakened that the continent's authoritarian rulers were able to enjoy long years of unchallenged authority. Notable African leaders in this category include Malawi's Hastings Banda, Ivory Coast's Felix Houphouët-Boigny, Omar Bongo of Gabon, Paul Biya of Cameroon, Kenneth Kaunda in Zambia, Daniel arap Moi in Kenya and Robert Mugabe in Zimbabwe, to name but a few.

By its very nature, authoritarian rule created a lot of losers. Individuals who fell foul of the regime were either sent to prison, went into exile or were allowed to operate but in a severely restricted environment. These groups, together with other sympathizers, served as a latent opposition even if they faced significant obstacles to organizing and operating publicly.

The 1990s marked a new era in African politics that was characterized by the introduction of democratic politics. Between 1990 and 1993 for example, 27 of the continent's 53 countries made the transition from a one-party system or a military dictatorship to a multi-party democratic system. By 1994, single-party

---

[1]   See R. Jackson & C. Rosberg, *Personal Rule in Black Africa: Prince, autocrat, prophet and tyrant* (University of California Press, Berkeley, CA, 1982).

[2]   B. Muluzi, Y. Juwayeyi, M. Makhambera & D. Phiri, *Democracy with a Price: The history of Malawi since 1900* (Jhango Heinemann, Blantyre, 1999).

[3]   J-F. Medard, 'The underdeveloped state in tropical Africa: Political clientelism or neo-patrimonialism?', in C. Clapham (ed), *Private Patronage and Public Power: Political clientelism in the modern state* (Frances Pinter, London, 1982), p. 167.

authoritarianism had been formally abolished and replaced by multi-party democracy throughout almost the entire Sub-Saharan African region.[4]

The democratic transitions of the 1990s were, in most cases, contested events. On the one hand, the long-serving political elites resisted the introduction of democratic politics and used a variety of strategies to suppress any challenge to their hold on power. On the other hand however, there were the democracy movements – loose coalitions of groups that were united in their opposition to authoritarian rule – that emerged to play a decisive role in forcing the continent's numerous authoritarian regimes to democratize.[5]

As a social force, Africa's democracy movements were coalitions of groups united in their shared antipathy towards authoritarianism. They included women's movements, trade unions, university student groups, farmers' associations, university staff, civil servants, political exiles, underground opposition groups, business and lawyers' associations and other professional groups.[6] While the interests and backgrounds of these groups differed, they had a common denominator in seeking democratic change.

The potency of the democracy movements across Africa in forcing a transition to democratic forms of governance is demonstrated by Bratton and Van de Walle, who point out that out of the 21 cases of democratic transition that took place between November 1989 and 1991, sixteen (representing 76% of the total) were initiated by pro-democracy protest groups.[7] The critical role played

---

[4]   M. Bratton & N. van de Walle, *Democratic Experiments in Africa: Regime transitions in comparative perspective* (Cambridge University Press, Cambridge, 1997).

[5]   D. McAdam, J. McCarthy & M. Zald, *Comparative Perspectives on Social Movements* (Cambridge University Press, Cambridge, 1996); D. McAdam, S. Tarrow & C. Tilly, *Dynamics of Contention* (Cambridge University Press, Cambridge, 2001); L. Diamond, 'Beyond autocracy: Prospects for democracy in Africa', in Working Papers for the Inaugural Seminar of the Governance in Africa Program (The Carter Centre of Emory University, Atlanta, GA, 1989); K. Mengisteab & C. Daddieh, *State Building and Democratization in Africa: Faith, hope, and realities* (Praeger, London, 1999); Earl Conteh-Morgan, *Democratization in Africa: The theory and dynamics of political transitions* (Praeger, London, 1997); G. Nzogola-Ntalaja, 'Citizenship, political violence and democratization in Africa', *Global Governance*, 10 (2004), pp. 403-409; R. Joseph, *State, Conflict and Democracy in Africa* (Praeger, London, 1999); R. Press, *Peaceful Resistance: Advancing human rights and democratic freedoms* (Ashgate, Aldershot, 2006); A. Ngoma-Leslie, *Social Movements and Democracy in Africa* (Routledge, New York, 2006).

[6]   Ngoma-Leslie, *Social Movements and Democracy in Africa*; Press, *Peaceful Resistance*; Bratton and Van de Walle, *Democratic Experiments*.

[7]   M. Bratton & N. van de Walle, 'Neopatrimonial regimes and political transitions in Africa', *MSU Working Papers on Political Reform in Africa,* Working Paper No. 1 (Department of Political Science East Lansing: MI, 1993); See also Press, *Peaceful Resistance*.

by the democracy movements in forcing regime change in Africa suggests that the wave of democratization in Africa in the 1990s was a bottom-up process that was forced upon reluctant elites by social movements united in their demands for political change.

This bottom-up process of democratization challenges some of the leading theories that try to explain how regime change occurs and how social movements emerge. With regards to the literature on regime change, studies of democratization in Latin America and Eastern Europe have tended to emphasize the role of the ruling elites in initiating the process of change. In their groundbreaking work on democratic transition in the Americas, O'Donnell and Schmitter argued that regime change occurs through a process of elite fracturing. They went on to assert that 'there is no transition whose beginning is not the consequence – direct or indirect – of important divisions within the authoritarian regime itself'.[8] The African cases, however, fail to fit into this 'elite fracturing' model of democratization. Instead, the social-movement-driven process suggested a process of system rupturing from below, with the elites being compelled to introduce institutional change without any internal divisions.

Meanwhile the literature on social movements tends to locate their emergence within the framework of political opportunity structures, which emerge from institutional changes by the ruling elites that open up the political space to other actors. McAdam, for instance, argues that the emergence of widespread protest activities is the result of 'a combination of expanding opportunities and indigenous organization, as mediated through a process of collective organization'.[9] This position is shared by Tarrow who contends that opportunities for collective action against contentious politics emerge 'when institutional access opens, rifts appear within elites, allies become available and state capacity for repression declines'.[10] In more recent work, Ngoma-Leslie also embraces this institutional perspective, arguing that the emergence of the women's movement

---

[8]   G. O'Donnell, Ph. Schmitter & L. Whitehead (eds), *Transitions from Authoritarian Rule: Tentative conclusions about uncertain democracies* (John Hopkins University Press, Baltimore, 1986), p. 19.

[9]   D. McAdam, *Political Process and the Development of Black Insurgency, 1930-1970* (University of Chicago Press, Chicago, 1982), p. 20; see also P. Eisinger, 'The conditions of protest behavior in American cities', *American Political Science Review*, 67 (1973), pp. 11-28; McAdam, *Political Process and the Development of Black Insurgency*; C. Tilly, *From Mobilization to Revolution* (Addison-Wesley, Reading, 1978); J. Gusfield, *Protest, Reform and Revolt: A reader in social movements* (John Wiley, New York, 1970).

[10] S. Tarrow, *Power in Movement: Social movements and contentious politics* (Cambridge University Press, Cambridge, 1998), p. 71.

in Botswana politics was 'dependent on the receptivity of the political process'.[11]

While structural accounts offer a powerful framework for understanding the rise of democracy movements, they do not give sufficient information as to why the ruling elites would consent to introducing those structural changes in the first place, especially since they undermine their ability to remain in power. It is precisely because those who are entrusted with the responsibility to initiate any institutional changes are also often those with the most to lose that the North contends that, once created, institutions become sticky and only change incrementally.[12] The introduction of the institutional changes that enabled democratic movements to emerge and effectively challenge authoritarian regimes in Africa poses a major puzzle that I seek to address in this chapter. Why would authoritarian regimes make changes that create opportunities for the emergence of organized movements that threaten their own political survival? The discussion that follows attempts to unravel this by examining the emergence of the democracy movement in Malawi and the role played by the Catholic Church there in the process. I demonstrate that the origins of the democracy movements lay not in a process of wilful concessions by the ruling elites but instead were a result of the rupturing of the state apparatus that happened after the intervention of an exogenous actor in the political arena. In the case of Malawi, the rupturing resulted from a pivotal decision by the Catholic Church's hierarchy to intervene in the political arena by challenging the legitimacy of the one-party authoritarian regime in a way that served as a catalyst for the emergence of a democracy movement that subsequently went on to force the authoritarian regime to accept the introduction of institutional changes that led to the introduction of democracy.

'Living our Faith' and the birth of the democracy movement in Malawi

The period between Malawi's independence in 1964 and 1992 was characterized by tight control of the political space by the ruling elites. Under the 1966 Constitution, the Malawi Congress Party (MCP) was designated as Malawi's only legal political party, thus closing off any avenues for organized political opposition. The designation of Malawi as a constitutional one-party state was followed by a constitutional amendment in 1971 that conferred the status of President for Life on President Hastings Banda.

---

[11] Ngoma-Leslie, *Social Movements and Democracy in Africa*, p. 29.
[12] D. North, *Institutions, Institutional Change and Economic Performance* (Cambridge University Press, New York, 1990).

In the ensuing years, Banda embarked on a systematic and sustained process of consolidation of his hold on power by ruthlessly suppressing opposition voices. Membership of the MCP was made compulsory and was enforced by the party machinery. Meanwhile, the state's coercive institutions, the army and the police were frequently used to silence critical voices, detaining, torturing and sometimes even murdering individuals thought to hold anti-government views. Sindima, for example, captures the extent to which the Banda regime dealt with any opposition when he pointed out that:

> those who crossed paths with Dr. Banda and his MCP ... suffered untold physical and emotional pain inflicted on them and their family members ... a good number of political detainees spent many years in prison ... and some were never again heard of after they had been picked by the [Police] Special Branch or the Malawi Young Pioneers.[13]

In addition to the harsh treatment that was meted out on critics, the Banda regime had tight control of the media as part of its broader strategy of ensuring that the public would only have access to government-controlled propaganda. Private media sources were banned, while the censorship board became very active in restricting access to publications perceived as having contaminating political content. Meanwhile the trade unions, which had supported the Banda-led nationalist movement in the struggle for independence, were either legis-lated out of existence or brought under MCP control. Within six months of gaining independence, fourteen trade unions had been deregistered and all the civil-service unions were banned. At the same time, a number of the more fire-brand union leaders were co-opted and offered positions in government.[14]

It was within this tightly controlled political space that the country's Catho-lic bishops issued their historic pastoral letter entitled 'Living Our Faith'[15] on 8 March 1992. Although ostensibly addressed to the Catholic faithful, the pastoral letter clearly targeted a wider audience and was written in a language designed to provoke public action for political change. A total of 16,000 copies of the letter were distributed nationwide. In a bid to reach the largest possible audi-ence, 10,000 were printed in Malawi's national language, Chichewa, which is spoken by more than 65% of the country's population, a further 5,000 were

---

[13] H. Sindima, *Malawi's First Republic: An economic and political analysis* (University Press of America, New York, 2002). See also J. Lwanda, *Kamuzu Banda of Malawi: A study in promise, power, and paralysis* (Dudu Nsomba Publications, Glasgow, 1993); Muluzi *et al.*, *Democracy with a Price.*

[14] See L. Dzimbiri, 'The State and Labour Control in Malawi: Continuities and dis-continuities between one-party and multiparty Systems', *Africa Development,* XXX, 4 (2005), pp. 53–85.

[15] Episcopal Conference of Malawi (ECM), *Living our Faith: Lenten letter of the Catholic bishops to their faithful* (Montfort Media, Balaka, 1992).

printed in Tumbuka which is the main language spoken in northern Malawi, and the other thousand copies were printed in English. The pastoral letter was read out in all the Catholic churches across the country, with members being encouraged to get copies for discussion in their communities and villages.[16] All this combined to ensure that the message of political change advocated in the letter reached a significant proportion of the country's citizens.

Through references to Biblical texts and a language of freedom and justice, 'Living our Faith' identified some of the key weaknesses and failings of one-party, one-man rule. Specifically addressing what were considered the key socio-economic and political failings of authoritarian rule, the letter highlighted Malawi's need to move beyond one-man rule by making allusions to traditional proverbs that emphasized the benefits of shared leadership:

> [The strength] of African society ... resides in recognizing the gifts of all and in allowing these gifts to flourish and be used for the building of the community. '*Mutu umodzi susenza denga*' – no one person can claim to have monopoly of truth and wisdom. No individual – or group of individuals – can pretend to have all the resources needed to guarantee the progress of a nation ... the contribution of the most humble members is often necessary for the good running of a group.[17]

It is noteworthy that the pastoral letter's language did not portray the bishops or the Church as the agents of change. Instead, 'Living our Faith' was framed as a call for action, requiring Malawians to rise up and 'respond to this state of affairs and work towards a change of climate ... participation in the life of the country is not only a right; it is also a duty that each Christian should be proud of'.[18] 'Living our Faith' was a critique of authoritarian rule and a call for the emergence of a democracy movement to challenge the status quo.

Suffice to say, 'Living our Faith' marked the first time that the Banda regime had faced a domestic challenge of any magnitude. The atmosphere of fearful and silent acquiescence that had limited Malawian political discourse for three decades had been challenged, not by a small circle of activists and political exiles but from the pulpits in churches in every district in the country. 'Living our Faith' was subsequently seen as an invitation for bottom-up mobilization for regime change. In the words of Chirwa *et al.*, the pastoral letter:

> ... served as ferment, challenging various groups, especially the workers to organize and go on strike ... while at the same time, the exiled opposition felt emboldened

[16] P. O'Maille, *Living Dangerously: A memoir of political change in Malawi* (Dudu Nsomba, Glasgow, 1999).
[17] ECM, *Living our Faith*, p. 3.
[18] *Ibid.*, p. 6.

and saw the Letter as offering much needed moral support for their agitation for political change.'[19]

The 1992 pastoral letter almost instantaneously emboldened the anti-authoritarian movement in Malawi. As Lwanda puts it, 'Living our Faith' served as 'a spark that ignited Malawi's democracy revolution'.[20] The letter's ability to elicit such public response was due in large part to the fact that its overall message of change touched on issues that most of the public identified with and had longed for someone to voice. Within a week, students from the University of Malawi issued their own letter of solidarity, observing that the bishops had become the 'mouthpiece for the voiceless and powerless … [and that] the people of Malawi needed more than just political freedom at independence, they also needed a social and economic emancipation'.[21] This was followed by a march by university students to the residence of the Catholic Bishop of Zomba Diocese to demonstrate their solidarity. When the government responded to this demonstration by closing Chancellor College campus in Zomba, students from two other constituent colleges of the University of Malawi in Blantyre and Lilongwe staged their own street demonstrations in support of the bishops and their fellow students and called for the introduction of democracy.[22]

Other leading churches also weighed in embracing the message of 'Living our Faith' and echoing calls for urgent political reform. Among the churches that supported the Catholic prelates were the Church of Central Africa Presbyterian (CCAP) Blantyre and Livingstonia Synods, which issued their own statement on 4 June 1992 reiterating calls for social, political and judicial reform.[23] The decision by these two CCAP synods to show solidarity with the Catholic Church and the pro-democracy movement magnified the potency of

---

[19] W. Chirwa, N. Patel & F. Kanyongolo, 'Malawi: Democracy factfile' (Research report to the Southern African Research and Documentation Centre, SARDC, mimeo, 1998), p. 2; see also L. Mitchell, 'Living our Faith: The Lenten letter of the bishops of Malawi and the shift to multi party democracy, 1992-1993', *Journal for the Scientific Study of Religion*, 41, 1 (2002), pp. 5-18; J. Newell, 'A moment of truth? The Church and political change in Malawi', *Journal of Modern African Studies*, 33, 2 (1995), pp. 243-262; M. Nzunda & K. Ross, *Church, Law and Political Transformation in Malawi, 1992-1994* (Mambo Press, Gweru, 1995).

[20] J. Lwanda, *Promises, Politics and Poverty: Democratic transition in Malawi* (Dudu Nsomba Publications, Glasgow, 1996), p. 104.

[21] University of Malawi Catholic Studies Association, letter of 13 March 1992.

[22] O'Maille, *Living Dangerously,* offers a personal account of how university students and faculty embraced the pastoral letter and brought its contents to the attention of the international community.

[23] Nkhoma Synod, one of the three CCAP synods, did not support this statement. Banda himself and some of the senior MCP members belonged to the Nkhoma Synod.

the demands for political change because these church groups together accounted for more than half of Malawi's entire population.

For their part, private- and public-sector workers seized the opening created
by the pastoral letter and staged a series of unprecedented wild-cat strikes that
began in April 1992 and continued into the following year.[24] As with the university students, the strikers referenced their actions on the Catholic bishops'
calls for the equitable distribution of the benefits of development through improved wages and better working conditions. Elsewhere, democracy activists,
who until then had been operating underground, emerged and formed pressure
groups that began to campaign openly for the introduction of democracy. These
included the United Democratic Front (UDF) that had been formed in October
1991 as an underground group of influential Malawians who were disillusioned
with authoritarian rule. The extent to which the 1992 pastoral letter provided the
opportunity for the UDF to surface was captured by one of the group's founding
members, Aleke Banda, who pointed out that the pastoral letter 'was a source of
great strength to the pressure group and probably brought forward its existence
by at least ten years'.[25]

The immediate aftermath of 'Living our Faith' saw the creation of new civil-
society groups that aimed to promote and advance a democracy agenda. One of
the most influential civil-society organizations to emerge during this period was
the Public Affairs Committee (PAC), in September 1992, with its primary objective of taking a strategic lead in socio-political initiatives in the country.[26]
Operating as an umbrella organization for the nascent pro-democracy groups,
PAC drew its membership from the major religious groups in Malawi including
the Catholics, the CCAP, the Anglican Church, the Muslim Association of Malawi and the Christian Council of Malawi. Other members included the two
leading political pressure groups, the UDF and the Alliance for Democracy
(Aford), which was formed in Zambia by a group of Malawian political exiles
and intellectuals at the end of March 1992. Influential professional groups, such
as the Associated Chambers of Commerce and Industry and the Malawi Law
Society, were also among PAC's founder members. Elsewhere, non-governmental organizations focusing on issues of governance began to emerge as key
players in the democracy movement. Notable in this period were the Civil

---

[24]   K. College, *Trade Unions and the Struggle for Quality Services in Malawi* (PSI,
Johannesburg, 2004).

[25]   T. Cullen, *Malawi: A Turning Point* (Pentland Press, Durham, 1994), p. 58.

[26]   K. Ross, 'The Transformation of Power in Malawi, 1992-94: The role of the Christian churches,' in K. Ross (ed.), *God, People and Power in Malawi: Democratization
in theological perspective* (CLAIM, Blantyre, 1996).

Liberties Committee (CILIC), the Human Rights Consultative Committee and the CCAP 'Church and Society' programmes, to mention but a few.[27]

In addition to rousing and energizing domestic opposition to one-party rule, 'Living our Faith' made another important contribution by bringing together for the first time domestic and exiled political opposition groups to work as one united front. Although the exiled opposition had long been in existence, it had failed to establish a domestic presence within Malawi, which had allowed Banda to dismiss it as an isolated group of disaffected individuals that had no domestic support. However the 1992 pastoral letter gave the opposition in exile a measure of credibility as well as a moral rallying point for regime change.[28] Long years of political activism meant that they had the experience to give the fledgling democracy movement a big lift once domestic opposition surfaced. They brought with them new ideas for political organization that helped reshape and re-energize the democracy movement.

The extent to which the 1992 pastoral letter helped to galvanize the exiled opposition was demonstrated by the formation of Aford in Zambia towards the end of March 1992 by a group of Malawian exiles who were responding to the reformist message of 'Living our Faith'. Aford's objectives included campaigning for human rights and democracy in Malawi and the group chose Chakufwa Chihana, a former secretary-general of the Southern African Trade Union Coordinating Council, as its chairman. Capitalizing on the weakness of the one-party state that had resulted from the stinging criticism in 'Living our Faith', Chihana returned to Malawi on 6 April 1992 and immediately used the pastoral letter as the moral justification for political reform.[29]

The rupturing effect of the 1992 letter was further reflected in the emergence of a new and critical media. A total of sixteen newspapers were launched onto the market between March 1992 and early 1993, with the majority supporting the nascent democracy movement. Among the most vocal to emerge were the *Malawi Democrat, Michiru Sun*, the *Monitor* and the *Nation*. In addition to these new newspapers, pro-democracy groups used shortwave radio to broadcast messages from outside the country to the Malawian public via the South

---

[27] W. Chirwa, 'Civil society in Malawi's democratic politics', in M. Ott, K. Phiri & N. Patel (eds), *Malawi's Second Democratic Elections: Process, problems and prospects* (Kachere, Zomba, 2000).

[28] See J. Chakanza, 'The pro-democracy movement in Malawi: The Catholic church's contribution', in Nzunda & Ross (eds), *Church, Law and Political Transition in Malawi, 1992-1994* (Mambo Press, Gweru, 1995).

[29] K. Ross, 'The Transformation of power in Malawi'.

African Broadcasting Corporation (SABC), the BBC and Voice of America.[30] These new media forms offered Malawians a more critical perspective of their country's politics for the first time.

Although the Banda regime tried to fight a rearguard battle to discredit the Catholic hierarchy and the now resurgent democracy movement, it was unable to contain the mounting pressure for change that was being unleashed by 'Living our Faith'. The democracy movement continued to gather momentum and became increasingly independent of its religious origins. As a last act, the Banda government called for a referendum in June 1993 to decide whether Malawi should maintain the one-party system or adopt multi-party democracy. The mere fact that the authoritarian regime was forced to take this measure demonstrated that President Banda and the MCP no longer enjoyed the absolute power that had characterized Malawian politics for the previous three decades.

The democracy movement's ultimate victory came in June 1993 when the electorate voted by a margin of two to one in favour of multi-party democracy. Faced with this result, the government was finally forced to open up the political space by legalizing opposition party politics as well as relaxing the rules that had been used to silence dissenting voices. The 1993 referendum was followed by democratic elections on 20 May 1994. In a further repudiation of Banda, the UDF's Bakili Muluzi won a majority share of the presidential vote to become the country's first democratically elected president while his party scooped a majority of the seats in the new National Assembly.[31] Within two years of the release of 'Living our Faith', Malawi had abandoned authoritarian rule and embraced democratic politics, sweeping the old guard out of power.

From the preceding discussion it is clear why the democratization process in Malawi can be considered a three-actor game. The first player, the authoritarian regime, employed strategies to maintain its hold on power. Through its historic intervention, the Catholic Church became the second major player in the game, challenging the authority and legitimacy of one-party rule in a way that created opportunities for the emergence of the democracy movement. Combined, the Church and the democracy movement were able to compel the ruling elites to open up the political space, which culminated in the 1993/1994 transition to democracy. The sequence is illustrated in Figure 1.

---

[30]   N. Patel, 'Media in Malawi's democratic transition', in M. Ott, K. Phiri & N. Patel (eds), *Malawi's Second Democratic Elections: Process, problems and prospects* (Kachere Series, Zomba, 2000).

[31]   For a discussion of the 1994 election results, see L. Dzimbiri, 'Democracy and chameleon like leaders', in Kings Phiri *et al.* (eds), *Democratisation in Malawi: A stocktaking* (CLAIM, Blantyre, 1998).

Figure 1   Model of the transition to democracy in Malawi

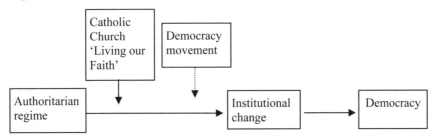

Without the Catholic Church's intervention, it would have been very diffi-cult for the democracy movement to organize against Malawi's authoritarian regime. The Church's challenge to authoritarian rule played a critical role in preparing the way for the emergence of the democracy movement, which then pressurized the authoritarian regime to embark on a process of institutional change. This eventually led to the transition to democratic rule. Unlike the predictions in the literature that social movements are preceded by institutional change that leads to their creation, the Malawian case suggests that the process of institutional change only came about after the new democracy movement had already emerged.

Beyond 'Living our Faith':
The Catholic Church and the democracy movement after 1992

In addition to its pointed criticism of the legacy of authoritarian rule, a central message in the 1992 pastoral letter was self-admonition by the Catholic clergy of their silence during the thirty years of one-party rule. The bishops described this silence during Banda's dictatorial rule as 'a failure on the Church's spiritual mission as proponents of the common good and that … it is no longer "pastoral" to sit back and pretend not to see problems in our society'.[32] The Church's silence during one of Malawi's darkest political periods was, there-fore, portrayed as a sign of acquiescence on the part of the Church to the dicta-torship and human-rights abuses that characterized this time.

As well as offering a moral impetus for the emergence of the democracy movement, 'Living our Faith' signalled a new direction for the Catholic Church, shifting from an entity that focused exclusively on the spiritual realm to a new mission that sought an active role in the political arena. This new interventionist mission has been demonstrated by the issuance of pastoral letters that comment

---

[32]   ECM, *Living our Faith*, p. 2, 12.

on current socio-political affairs. Between 1992 and 2008, Malawian prelates issued a total of eighteen pastoral letters, most of which offered some sort of political content. The most frequently recurring themes involved urging the Malawian public to exercise their right to vote, reducing corruption; advocacy for equitable development; information about the meaning of freedom and democracy; and criticism of anti-democratic traits in government.

To demonstrate that the Catholic Church's political engagement after 1992 had taken on a more permanent form, it established a number of bodies that would play an active role in the socio-political arena. These included the Catholic Commission for Justice and Peace (CCJP), which was established in the second half of 1992 to contribute 'to the common effort of the Episcopal conference and the whole Catholic Church ... in the creation of a just and peaceful Malawian society that promotes integral development and lasting peace'.[33] With branches in every Catholic parish across the country, the CCJP provides the Catholic Church with a grassroots network that can be easily mobilized to promote democratic governance. The significance of this grassroots network was arguably best illustrated between 2001 and 2003 when the ruling UDF party attempted to remove the constitutional provision that limits any sitting president to serving a maximum of two five-year terms. While the Catholic bishops expressed their opposition to the proposal in their 2001 and 2002 pastoral letters, the CCJP took the matter further by taking the lead in a public debate against the proposal and claiming that it would 'bring Malawi back to the dark age of dictatorship'.[34] As part of the campaign, the CCJP mobilized other pro-democracy actors under the common banner of the Church-NGO Consortium that went on to run a series of public demonstrations and lobbied MPs to vote against the proposals. The sustained lobbying and public demonstrations eventually contributed to the defeat of the proposal when it came before Parliament in July 2002.[35]

The Malawi Catholic Church's quest to identify with the democracy movement was also demonstrated through the establishment of media 'houses' that offer a faith-based perspective on contemporary socio-political issues. These include three radio stations and a printing press that specializes in publishing newspapers, magazines, books and political literature. One of these is the

---

[33] ECM, *Walking Together in Faith, Hope and Love* (Montfort Media, Balaka, 1999).

[34] CCJP, 'Statement of the CCJP in Malawi and the third term debate', *The Nation*, 6 April 2002.

[35] For a discussion of the third-term debates, see B. Dulani & J. K. van Donge, 'A decade of legislature-executive squabble in Malawi (1994 – 2004)', in M. Salih (ed), *African Parliaments: Between governments and governance* (Palgrave Macmillan, London, 2005).

Lamp,[36] a monthly magazine that publishes semi-academic articles on Malawi's democratic process, as well as pamphlets on themes such as 'building the country under democracy' and 'lessons on democracy.'[37] The overall impact of these contributions is difficult to quantify but they have undoubtedly had a positive effect in nurturing democracy in Malawi.

While this socio-political engagement continues to offer Malawians important lessons about democracy, the Catholic Church's engagement since 'Living our Faith' has not elicited the same level of public action as its 1992 pastoral letter did, with the possible exception of the interventions during the third-term proposals. This is perhaps not entirely surprising. After nearly three decades of sustained and unrelenting suppression of critical voices, the Church was uniquely placed in 1992 as one of the few platforms from which criticism of the one-party regime could be made without being silenced. Much of the power of the 1992 pastoral letter, therefore, lay in the fact that it voiced what everyone knew but few dared to say. Given the nature of democracy as a public good,[38] it was not surprising that very few people were prepared to risk the wrath of the authoritarian regime by organizing for political change. The Catholic Church's institutional autonomy from the one-party state, on the other hand, provided an enabling context for it to challenge the hitherto invulnerable face of authoritarian rule and create opportunities for the emergence of a strong democracy movement. Although the clergy continue to occupy a respected place in Malawian politics, they are now just one of many actors in the liberalized political arena. The fact that the interventions by the Malawi Catholic Church after 1992 did not elicit the same level of response as 'Living our Faith' can be attributed to the success of the original intervention. Having created the space for the democracy movement to emerge, the Church was able to take more of a back seat in the democratic arena.

Explaining the Malawi Catholic Church's shift from a passive to an active political mission

While the important role the Catholic Church played in the emergence of the democracy movement in Malawi has been demonstrated, the question still remains as to why, given the long years of authoritarianism, the bishops only intervened in 1992 to spark off the process that led to the eventual rupturing of authoritarian rule. In taking on the might of the Banda regime, the Catholic

---

[36] *Lamp* takes its title from the symbol of democracy proponents during the 1993 referendum.
[37] See http://www.montfortmedia.org/, June 28, 2009.
[38] Once available, democracy can be enjoyed by all citizens, including those who did not participate in its introduction.

bishops obviously put themselves at significant risk. As Chakanza and Mitchell observed, the ruling party's initial response to the 1992 pastoral letter was one of defiance.[39] The bishops were immediately arrested by the state police and placed under house arrest and an emergency session of the ruling MCP suggested that the bishops be killed and the Catholic Church banned.

Various circumstances, I would argue, combined to enable the Church to step in and challenge the Banda regime in 1992 in a way that had not been possible before. The first point to note is that the Catholic Church's intervention in the Malawian political arena in 1992 was partly a reflection of new theological developments within the Catholic Church worldwide: the Church was starting to embrace political engagement as part of its overall mission. Tracing its origins to the events of Vatican II, this new theology represented a transformation of the Church's understanding of its role in politics, shifting from a largely passive political entity to one of engagement in the quest for the promotion of the common good.[40] Rejecting the notion that the Church should restrict its actions only to the religious field, Vatican II advocated 'acts of resistance when the rule of law is to be defended against abuses perpetrated by those who exercise public authority'.[41] In the 1980s, this position was reiterated by Pope John Paul II, who urged the clergy to advocate for the 'reform of unjust structures – in particular their political institutions', and to 'replace corrupt, dictatorial and authoritarian forms of government by democratic and participatory ones'.[42] In the Malawian case, the Catholic clergy were similarly called upon by John Paul II to stand up against 'injustice and oppression' when the pontiff visited the country in May 1989.[43]

Embracing this new political activism, Catholic clergy in various parts of the world played a central role in nurturing movements that helped to bring down dictatorial regimes. In Latin America, for example, Catholic 'liberation theology' was influential in the democracy movements that ousted the military re-

---

[39]   Chakanza, 'The pro-democracy movement in Malawi'; Mitchell, 'Living our Faith'.

[40]   A. Gill, 'Rendering unto Caesar? Religious competition and Catholic political strategy in Latin America, 1962-79', *American Journal of Political Science*, 38, 2 (1994), pp. 403-425; see also S. Bate, 'One mission, two Churches: the Catholic Church in southern Africa, 1947-1997', in J. Brain & P. Denis (eds), *The Catholic Church in Contemporary South Africa* (Cluster, Pietermaritzburg, 1999), pp. 5-36.

[41]   Pope Paul VI, *Gaudium et Spes: Pastoral constitution of the Church in the modern world,* Encyclical, (www.vatican.va/archive/hist_council/documents/vat-ii_cons_19651207_gaudium-et-spes_en.html, July 12,1965).

[42]   John Paul II, *Sollicitudo Rei Socialis*, Encyclical, (http://www.vatican.va/holy_father/john_paul_ii/encyclicals/documents/hf_jp-ii_enc_30121987_sollicitudo-rei-socialis_en.html, December 30, 1987).

[43]   Chakanza, 'The pro-democracy movement in Malawi'.

gimes in the region.[44] On the African continent, Catholic clergy played similar roles in challenging authoritarianism in countries such as Zambia, Ivory Coast, the former Zaire, Congo Brazzaville, Togo and Mali, to mention but a few examples.[45] Criticism of authoritarian rule by the Catholic prelates in Malawi in the early 1990s was therefore part of a global activism by the Catholic Church, whose strength and influence had already been demonstrated in other parts of the world, as well as elsewhere in Africa.

While these developments were taking place within the Catholic Church, events on the international stage, particularly the end of the Cold War, combined to further weaken authoritarian rule in Africa and in the developing world in general. In the post-Cold-War era, authoritarian regimes could no longer be supported for simply favouring one side in the Cold War. Western aid donors made the introduction of democratic reforms a condition for the continued receipt of aid. In the case of Malawi, the Paris Donor Club's meeting of 11-13 May 1992, exactly two months after the release of 'Living our Faith', decided to withhold all budgetary aid pending the introduction of political reform and a greater respect for human rights.[46] This suspension of aid weakened the authoritarian regime still further and increased opportunities for democracy groups to mobilize for institutional change. While it could be argued that the suspension of aid alone could have precipitated the emergence of a democracy movement, the sequencing of events in Malawi, where the suspension of aid came after the clergy had already intervened, meant that the donors' decision could only buttress a process that had been initiated by the Catholic prelates.

The importance of the Church in acting as the initiator of political change has to be understood within the context of authoritarian rule itself. While the authoritarian regime went to great lengths to insulate itself by eliminating independent centres of power, the Church, especially the Catholic Church, remained one of the few independent centres left. Indeed, in the run-up to the 1961 elections when the majority black population were allowed to vote for the first time, the Catholic Church did not side with the MCP, the then main nationalist movement, preferring instead to support the Christian Democratic Party (CDP) whose leader, Chester Katsonga, was himself a practising Catholic.[47] Although it would be simplistic to suggest that the Catholic Church always had a fractious relationship with the Banda regime, it nonetheless enjoyed a

---

[44] See P. Gifford (ed), *The Christian Churches and Democratization in Africa* (Brill, Leiden, 1995).

[45] See J. Haynes, 'Religion and democratization in Africa', *Democratization*, 11, 4 (2004), pp. 66-89.

[46] Muluzi *et al.*, *Democracy with a Price.*

[47] C. Baker, *Revolt of the Ministers: The Malawi cabinet crisis, 1964-1965* (I.B. Taurus, London, 2001).

higher level of autonomy from the state than other mainstream churches did in this period. For example, the CCAP Church, to which Banda and some of his senior lieutenants belonged, was more supportive of Banda as a person and of his government.[48] The power of the Catholic Church as a key player in the political arena was buoyed by the growth in its membership over time. Although the Catholics were not the first Christian missionaries to arrive in what is present-day Malawi, the Catholic Church's membership has grown to three million out of a total population of about thirteen million, making it the country's single largest Christian denomination.[49]

The relative autonomy and independence of Malawi's Catholic Church as a countervailing force to authoritarianism was bolstered by its international character. The sense of belonging and accountability within a wider community of faith gave it an enhanced sense of independence within the highly totalitarian social and political structures prevailing in Malawi at the time. The significance of this international support was well demonstrated in the aftermath of 'Living our Faith' when messages of support for the bishops came from sister churches and interest groups in Malawi, Africa as a whole, the Vatican, the UK, the US, Canada and Europe.[50] Not only did these messages express solidarity with Malawi's bishops, they also implored Banda to desist from using the draconian methods that he had relied on for so long to eliminate his opponents.

The downside of the Catholic Church's political activism

While the Catholic Church's socio-political activism initially contributed a great deal to the process of democratization in Malawi, its high-profile presence in the political arena since 1992 seems to have exacted some costs, particularly regarding developments in the democracy movement. A number of the key pro-democracy actors always now appear to wait and to take their cue from the Church before initiating any meaningful political action of their own because the Church, in the past, was seen to be at the heart of the movement. So dominant was the role of the Catholic Church in the political arena that Immink and Chigona suggest that 'it has become accepted that the participation [of the Catholic Church] is almost essential to the process of consolidating democracy in Malawi'.[51] This over-reliance on the Church was demonstrated, for example,

---

[48] See M. Kansilanga, 'Church and politics in Malawi today' (Address to the CCAP General Synod Human Rights Workshop, Chongoni, 8 November 1995, mimeo).

[49] World Council of Churches, (http://www.oikoumene.org/en/member-churches/regions/africa/malawi.html).

[50] Chakanza, 'The pro-democracy movement'.

[51] B. Immink & G. Chigona, 'Between Apathy and Participation: The role of civil society and faith communities', in M. Ott, B. Immink, B. Mhango & C. Peters-

during the third-term debates between 2001 and 2003. Although the discussion on a possible third term for Muluzi started way back in 2000, civil-society organizations only began to seriously mobilize against the proposal after the Catholic prelates issued their 2001 pastoral letter criticizing the proposed constitutional amendments. And where the Catholic Church has remained silent on controversial political issues, such as the constitutional violations by Bingu wa Mutharika (President Muluzi's successor and a practising Catholic himself), the rest of the democracy movement has been equally silent.

Conclusion

This chapter has attempted to demonstrate how the Catholic Church served as an important stakeholder in precipitating the events that led to the emergence of the democracy movement in Malawi in 1992. While it would be a gross over-simplification to attribute the entire transition to democracy and its survival solely to the Catholic Church's political engagement between 1992 and 2008, no account of the process of democratization can ignore the significance of the Catholic Church's interventions, which began with the release of the historic 1992 'Living our Faith' pastoral letter. In a tightly controlled political system where political opposition was likely to result in a violent death, the pulpit became a powerful platform for criticism of authoritarian rule.

This chapter has also discussed the concept of 'path dependence' in the sense that if a democracy movement has received support from the pulpit, the men of robes remain central in nurturing it despite claims that the Church is apolitical and regardless of the emergence of new civil-society players, including political parties. Democratic progress in Malawi continues to be closely linked to the Catholic Church and the key challenge for the Catholic prelates remains when to let go and allow the democracy movement to wean itself from its spiritual origins. While the Church remains an active participant in the political arena, its participation is stunting the growth and maturity of democracy in Malawi.

Berries (eds), *The Power of the Vote: Malawi's 2004 parliamentary and presidential elections* (Kachere, Zomba, 2005), p. 139.

8

Bare-foot activists:
Transformations in the Haratine
movement in Mauritania*

Zekeria Ould Ahmed Salem

Slavery was a widespread phenomenon in much of pre-colonial Africa but Mauritania stands out as one of the few African countries where it persisted as an entrenched institution even in post-colonial times. Mauritania also offers a rare example of an emancipation movement founded and run by slaves, ex-slaves and descendants of slaves.[1] This pioneering social movement enabled people of servile origins to carve out a place for their protest actions in the public sphere. Previously, there had been isolated cases of slave revolts but El-Hor, an organization founded in March 1978 by activists of slave descent, developed into a social and political movement that ultimately entered the corridors of political power. El-Hor ('freeman' or 'emancipated' in Arabic) aimed to further the 'liberation and emancipation' of the 'heirs of slavery'.[2]

This chapter does not intend to primarily document the history of this struggle as such, even though it is not widely known. Instead, it analyzes the transformations undergone by the Haratine movement since its first actions in 1980. To this end, I describe the trajectory of the collective action as it developed at the interface between society, politics and the struggle for civil

---

*   Article translated from French by Noal Mellott (CNRS, Paris).

[1]   Roger Botte, 'De l'esclavage et du daltonisme dans les sciences sociales. Avant-propos', *Journal des Africanistes*, 70, 1-2 (2000), p. 13; Éric Komlavi Hahonou, 'Cultures politiques, esclavage et décentralisation. La revanche politique des descendants d'esclaves au Bénin et au Niger', *Politique africaine*, 111 (2008), pp. 169-186.

[2]   A. Daddah, 'Les héritiers de l'esclavage. La longue marche des Haratines', *Le Monde Diplomatique*, November 1998.

and human rights. The focus is on the movement's origins and
the successive changes in its form of organization, types of
actions and the outcome of its activism.

Context and origins

Located between the Western Sahara to the north and the Senegal River to the
south, the Islamic Republic of Mauritania has a population of about three
million.[3] Its geographical position between the Arab world of North Africa and
Black Africa explains some of the ambiguities in Mauritania's complex national
identity: Arab or/and African? Mauritanians are divided along lines of race and
ethnicity as well as social status. In terms of race, the main division is between
Black African Mauritanians or Afro-Mauritanians and so-called 'White' Arab-
Berbers or Moors. Given the lack of official up-to-date statistics, it is assumed
that nearly 30% are ethnic Black Africans (in particular, Haalpulaar, Soninke
and Wolof). Arab-Berber Moors make up the majority of the population and
refer to themselves as *bidhân* ('Whites') even though more than half of them
are, in fact, Black Moors.

In terms of social status, the legacy of slavery is still a crucial factor in the
social hierarchy of Mauritanian society today. Among both the Afro-Mauritanians and the Moors, there is a clear divide between the masters and the slaves
or people of slave descent. Although this social division is often expressed in
racial terms – white masters and black slaves – race and class do not fully
coincide. More than half of the Moors are Black Moors or Haratine, a group
primarily made up of slaves (*âbid*; singular: *'âbd*) and of persons freed from
slavery (*hratîn*, singular: *hartâni*) and their descendants. In Afro-Mauritanian
society, masters and slaves have the same skin colour and servitude is less
visible than in Moorish society. Activists claim that more than half of the total
population is of servile origins, but this remains disputed.

Moorish society has always practised 'chattel slavery',[4] usually based on
racial differences (Black slaves with Arab-Berber masters) and covered by a
conservative interpretation of Islamic law. The considerable number of former
slaves is evidence that slavery prevailed on a large scale and for a long time.
This chapter focuses on the emancipation movement among the Haratine. Moor
slaves and ex-slaves have no common cause with the Afro-Mauritanian slaves
and although they share the stigma of servile status, they are divided by language and historical experience. Among Afro-Mauritanians, slavery is less

---

[3]   Zekeria Ould Ahmed Salem, 'Mauritania, a Saharan frontier state', *Journal of North*
African Studies, 10, 3/4 (2005), pp. 491-506.
[4]   Joel Quirk, *Unfinished Business: A comparative survey of historical and contempo-*
rary slavery (UNESCO, Paris, 2008), pp. 105-107.

visible and the main features of servitude have been more or less successfully challenged by the authorities since the colonial period. Being of slave status carries a social and cultural stigma but it is not formally entrenched in the same way as in Moorish society. Paradoxically, this makes it more difficult for Afro-Mauritanians to organize in an emancipatory movement. The Haratine not only had the advantage of carrying more demographic weight but also had a more tangible cause as their subordinate status was an overt, undeniable fact.

Slavery past and present

In the traditional nomadic environment, slaves were ineluctably assigned the hardest tasks.[5] They experienced 'social death'[6] and total economic exploitation and in terms of Islamic law were considered legal minors.[7] Questioning the legitimacy of slavery has often been considered going against the national religion. Under Islamic law, slaves are not free to marry, cannot own goods in their own name or inherit property. Nor can they dispose of their own children or bear testimony before a court of law. Freedom and emancipation are valid only if duly granted by the master. The sale or conveyance of slaves as well as *jus primae noctis* were practised until recently. Slaves laboured under a kinship system that was all the more fictive since they belonged – in both senses of the word – to their master's family.[8]

Slaves and former slaves do not exist in the Arab-Berber group alone. Servitude was solidly rooted in the rigid social hierarchy of all groups in Mauritanian society regardless of ethnic origin.[9] The stigma of enslavement represented a widespread symbolic form of violence. When asked about this, El-Hor's historic leader, Messaoud Ould Boulkhier, declared:

[5]   Abdel Wedoud Ould Cheikh, *Nomadisme, islam et pouvoir dans la société maure précoloniale (XIe-XIXe siècles). Essai sur quelques aspects du tribalisme* (University of Paris V, Paris, PhD dissertation, 1985), p. 453.

[6]   Orlando Patterson, *Slavery and Social Death* (Harvard University Press, Cambridge, MA, 1982).

[7]   Meskerem Brhane, *Narratives of the Past, Politics of the Present: Identity, subordination and the Haratines of Mauritania* (University of Chicago, Chicago, PhD Dissertation in Political Science, 1997).

[8]   Benjamin Acloque, *Identité et statut de dépendant en Mauritanie. L'exemple de l'identité sociale des Hratin dans le système segmentaire et hiérarchique Bidan* (University of Paris X-Nanterre, Paris, Masters thesis, 1995), p. 41.

[9]   Ousmane Kamara, 'Les divisions statutaires des descendants d'esclaves au Fuuta Tooro mauritanien', *Journal des Africanistes*, 70, 1-2 (2000), pp. 265-289; Yaya Sy, 'L'esclavage chez les Soninkés: du village Paris', *Journal des Africanistes*, 70, 1-2 (2000), pp. 43-69; and Olivier Leservoisier, '"Nous voulons notre part!" Les ambivalences du mouvement d'émancipation des Saafaalbe Hormankoobe de Djéol (Mauritanie)', *Cahiers d'études africaines*, 179-180 (2005), pp. 987-1014.

Slavery also exists among Black Africans [...] I prefer my condition to theirs. The Black African slave, in his society and mind, is forced to die a slave; and his children too. Whereas I, a Haratine, am fighting to break out of this condition, they prefer presenting it as a specifically Moorish case and refuse to talk about what is happening among themselves.[10]

The country's successive governments have never addressed the issue of slavery as such regardless of the ethnic groups involved. The colonial administration widely tolerated such practices[11] and traditional slavery survived for a long time in post-colonial Mauritania. The public authorities have always adopted an ambiguous stance, combining denial, embarrassment and *laisser-faire*.[12]

Year after year, organizations involved in the fight against slavery are still reporting dozens of cases, although they usually refrain from estimating the number of victims. Mauritania is presented as an extreme case when it comes to slavery[13] and sometimes, in a simplified manner,[14] as an absolute counter example.[15] The aspiration to freedom still encounters barriers in odd situations in a country where, despite laws on abolition, the Constitution's preamble recognizes Sharia law as the main legal system. As applied by the customary courts, the pro-slavery interpretation of a not very codified Islamic law has led to litigation and disputes, sometimes inextricably in matters of inheritance, marriage, child custody, land ownership and salaries.[16]

The sizeable community that is descended from slaves still forms the country's most underprivileged social category.[17] The Haratine experience inferior economic, social and political conditions and if they are free, their freedom is

---

[10] Interview with Messaoud Ould Boulkhier in *L'Autre Afrique*, 57, 6 August 1997, p. 26.

[11] El Kehel Ould Mohamed El Abd, *Colonisation française et mutations sociales en Mauritanie: Cas de l'esclavage en milieu maure, 1900-1960* (University of Nouakchott, Nouakchott, Master's thesis in History, 1987).

[12] Mohamed Lemine Ould Ahmed, *L'abolition de l'esclavage en Mauritanie* (University of Dakar, Dakar, Master's thesis in International Relations, 1983), pp. 5-6.

[13] Amnesty International, *Mauritania: A future free from slavery?* (Amnesty International, London, 2002).

[14] Thierry Desjardins, 'Mauritanie: 700.000 esclaves qui veulent le rester', *Le Figaro*, 8 December 1995; Samuel Coton, *Silent Terror: A journey into contemporary African slavery* (Harlem River Press, New York, 1998).

[15] Kevin Bales, *Disposable People: New slavery in the global economy* (University of California Press, Berkeley, CA, 1999).

[16] Zekeria Ould Ahmed Salem, 'Droit du statut personnel et équivalence citoyenne en République Islamique de Mauritanie. Le cas du mariage', *La Pensée*, 336 (2003), pp. 37-53.

[17] E. Ann McDougall, 'Living the legacy of slavery: between discourse and reality', *Cahiers d'études africaines*, 179-180 (2005), pp. 957-986.

usually meaningless owing to their low economic status since they have subaltern jobs in urban or rural areas. Strongly marked by current and past slavery, their emancipation is limited due to the poverty in which most of them still live. Since political or legal emancipation has never been fully enforced, other factors have rekindled the debate about the abolition of slavery and bringing the Haratine issue to public attention.[18] The Haratine community has been politically shaped through struggles that have developed out of social, political and even ecological changes that need to be studied.[19]

An unlikely cause?

It is usually, and rightly, claimed that several factors have contributed to the emergence of the Haratine cause. Severe droughts in the 1970s undermined the conditions underlying both slavery and the agro-pastoral economy that corresponded to the traditional way of life.[20] By forcing most of the nomads to move to urban areas, this environmental catastrophe left many slaves destitute. Then the war in the Sahara, in which Mauritania was involved from 1975 to 1978, levied a large number of troops from among the Haratine who, in turn, gained a degree of collective emancipation. Finally but to a lesser degree, several young Haratine graduates decisively increased their group's social visibility. It was no accident that El-Hor came into being in 1978, the year in which all these processes came to a head.

Collective demands on behalf of both slaves and former slaves were voiced in a society used to the liberation of individual slaves as they were manumitted or ran away. Apart from a few isolated and sporadic revolts, an organized challenge had never been mounted to the institution of slavery. It had barely figured on the leftist agenda advanced by young political activists during the period of unrest between 1968 and 1974; and the arguments used by local Marxist groups usually omitted it. Preferring the classical dichotomy bourgeoisie/proletariat, the major underground movements at the time – the *Parti des Kadihines* (PKM) and *Mouvement national démocratique* (MND) – mainly sought to provoke the neo-colonial authorities. However, the few people with

---

[18] Zekeria Ould Ahmed Salem (ed.), *Les trajectoires d'un État-frontière. Espaces, évolutions politiques et transformations sociales en Mauritanie* (Codesria, Dakar, 2004).

[19] Abdel Wedoud Ould Cheikh, 'L'évolution de l'esclavage dans la société maure', in E. Bernus & P. Boilley (eds), *Nomades et commandants. Administration et sociétés nomades dans l'ancienne AOF* (Karthala, Paris, 1994), pp. 181-193.

[20] Urs Peter Ruf, *Ending Slavery: Hierarchy, dependency and gender in central Mauritania* (Transcript Verlag, Bielefeld, 1999).

slave origins who became involved in these movements gained basic training in methods of collective organization.

The educated members of the Haratine elite established El-Hor on 5 March 1978. Among its best-known leaders were Messaoud Ould Boulkheir (a civil servant), Boubacar Ould Messaoud (an architect), Mohamed Ould Haimer (a primary-school teacher), Boydiel Ould Houmeid and Achour Ould Samba (who would later be civil servants) and Mohamed Lemine Ould Ahmed and El Kehel Ould Mohamed El Abd (who would become academics). The movement also received support from several school teachers and students.

Before examining the organization's initial actions and transformations, let us take a look at its founding charter that formulated a sense of identity and set a political agenda.

Haratine nationalism: El-Hor's charter

El-Hor's charter (a preamble and three articles) was circulated clandestinely, like many other political tracts at that time. In addition to demands concerning the abolition of slavery, it offered a genuine plan for an infranational 'imagined community'[21] founded on a 'moral ethnicity'.[22] According to the preamble, 'the Haratine of Mauritania are still subject to forms of domination, oppression and exploitation' in spite of national and international legal measures. There was therefore the 'necessity of their collective consciousness and unified struggle'. This moral ethnicity did not aim to include all Mauritanians of slave descent, only those who shared a common Moorish ethnicity as well as a knowledge of Arabic. The key to liberation was to develop awareness among the Haratine: cognitive liberation was a precondition for social action.

After the first article stating the movement's name, the two other articles were devoted respectively to 'general political orientations' and 'objectives'. In proclaiming their movement's absolute autonomy – 'El-Hor does not identify itself with any other organization or movement' – the authors claimed that their actions were 'national, non-racial, anti-segregationist and anti-chauvinistic'. El-Hor called upon 'all persons of goodwill, individual, collective, national, foreign and international, for support in the just struggle to uphold inalienable human rights' (II-3). Article III states the reasons underlying the movement's existence:

---

[21] B. Anderson, *Imagined Communities: Reflections on the origin and spread of nationalism* (Verso, London, 1983).

[22] J. Lonsdale, 'Moral ethnicity and political tribalism', in P. Kaarsholm & J. Hultin (eds), *Inventions and Boundaries: Historical and anthropological approaches to the study of ethnicity and nationalism* (Roskilde University, Institute of Development Studies, Roskilde, Occasional Paper 11, 1994), pp. 131-150.

Fundamentally inspired by religion, exacerbated by an abusive interpretation of this religion by the privileged social strata, and maintained owing to the ambiguity or even the nearly complete silence in the country's legislation, the inequalities from which the Haratine suffer are not just economic, social, political and religious. They are also, and above all, inherent in a mentality with deep roots due to centuries of psychological conditioning. Fighting against all that is El-Hor's *raison d'être*.

Regarding the system of land tenure, the manifesto calls for reform so that those who work the land (i.e. the Haratine) own it themselves. Secondly, El-Hor announced its intention to fight slavery and all forms of unpaid labour, promising to focus on combating discrimination in education, which was especially important for the Haratine, and in particular those in rural slave ghettos (*adwaba*, singular: *adabay*). Blaming the government for its 'policy of obstruction' that kept the Haratine out of decision making, El-Hor demanded an 'actual participation in the exercise of power at all levels', starting with the (then single) party, the civil service and elective offices.

What stands out in this charter is the rejection of an Islam that endorsed slavery and justified the inferiority of the Haratine. It thus asked the Haratine to categorically oppose this religious conception. El-Hor demanded the abolition of slavery and devoted its efforts to modernizing Islamic law and jurisprudence. It asked the government to 'remove all the contradictions that exist between Muslim and modern law, in particular those having to do with the slave status, namely: the problems related to the incapacitation of slaves (property rights, testimony, inheritance) and to matrimony (marriage, concubinage)'. This represented ultimately a twofold form of subversion. The movement not only claimed to propose its own interpretation of Koranic law – one squarely opposed to the jurisprudence used in local Islamic circles – but did so from a social position – slave or freed slave – that was the least 'qualified' to make such an interpretation.

The charter's final article focused on the Haratine identity. The Haratine were 'insoluble' in any other ethnic group in Mauritania even though they belong, it is clearly stated, to the Moorish community. El-Hor opposed dividing the Haratine into sub-groups according to their degree of bondage or freedom, in particular the difference between those emancipated long ago (*khadhara*), recently (*hratîn*) and those who were still slaves (*âbid*). The nascent organization deliberately used general language in an effort to be inclusive and claimed to represent a homogeneous community that saw status differences as secondary in comparison to an identity labelled 'Haratine'. However this label was not chosen at random since it refers literally to emancipated slaves. In fact, the charter uses the word 'slavery' only once, to categorically reject slavery. After explaining how the Haratine identity set this group apart from other Mauritanians, it concluded by proclaiming the cultural and historical specificity of the

Haratine. It was El-Hor's duty, through its programme, to consolidate this specificity and obtain recognition for it.[23]

El-Hor intended less to overturn Mauritania's power structure or society than to become a full-fledged active part of it. The Haratine movement did not develop a radical or revolutionary vision. In later texts, El-Hor glorified fraternity with the Haratine, stating that it did not intend to seize power, even though its demands upset traditional and established holders of power.[24]

The charter galvanized Mauritanian society. Having successfully carved out a place for itself in the public sphere, El-Hor advanced its cause in the field through actions. It diffused its slogans in areas traditionally settled with slaves (*adwaba*) and on the impoverished margins of the urban areas where the Haratine were concentrated. It organized demonstrations and, by setting up 'cells', built up a territorial network through its work of conscientization (wake-up campaigns). Meanwhile, El-Hor was explaining the conditions of the Haratine to political organizations and officials although raising the taboo on talking about slavery met with circumspection and sometimes even hostility.

A subversive movement: El-Hor as seen by others

The *Mouvement de libération et d'émancipation des Haratines* was launched while a single party was in power. The *Parti du peuple mauritanian* had managed to incorporate nearly all protest movements since 1974 and given that the major political issue at the time was the country's involvement in the war in the Sahara, domestic politics were relatively calm. In this context, the public authorities wondered whether the time was ripe for a debate on the Haratine cause. However politicians were all baffled by, or even fearful of, an endogenous movement that was led by, and based on, an elite drawn exclusively from within the Haratine community. Small political groups saw the movement as serious competitor in a potential segment of the political market place.

What irritated people even more was the movement's claim that it had authentic roots in Mauritania, whereas most of the underground 'parties' (the MND as well as Black African or Arab-Mauritanian nationalists) embraced imported ideologies (proletarian internationalism, pan-Africanism, Nasserism, Baathism). El-Hor accused certain rivals of being ideological foreigners without any attachment to a genuinely national cause.

Another annoyance was that the Haratine wanted to assert themselves as a new autonomous national force in a context where political groups formed on an ethnic basis were vying for this community's support. The Moorish elite saw

---

[23] El-Hor, 'Charte constitutive' (Nouakchott, 5 March 1978) quoted in *L'Ouest saharien-Cahiers d'études pluridisciplinaires* 4 (L'Harmattan, Paris, 2004), pp. 183-188.

[24] Mouvement El Hor, *Hartani, mon Frère* (Akhukal Hartani), tract (1978).

El-Hor as a threat of discord within a purportedly unified community. In their view, the formation of a movement of Moors of servile descent undermined the automatic majority of the Arab-Berber group. They did not perceive the issue in terms of an oppressive ruling class and a subjected underclass campaigning for full civil and social rights. In this perspective, El-Hor disadvantageously complicated the situation given the delicate ethnic balance in a country where the only noteworthy cleavage in their eyes was between Moors and Black Mauritanians.[25] The Haratine movement arose at a time when Black Mauritanian nationalists were not very active, and the latter did not accept the creation of an organization for a group that they had hoped to rally so as to tip the population's racial balance in their favour. Their concern was even more justified since El-Hor was established during a war to acquire territory inhabited by White Moors in the Western Sahara. With the obvious demographic consequences, Black Africans were rightly fearful in case they definitively remained a minority in the country.

This generally hostile reception did not hinder the new movement. Due to the relative diversity of the Haratine, the utopia of a unified community had, of course, limited appeal and the majority of the people targeted were not particularly influenced by El-Hor's arguments. Through a window of opportunity, the organization managed to obtain results, sometimes because of its sweeping actions during the first years of its existence.

A successful movement: Time to act

The Haratine movement emerged as the regime of Moktar Ould Daddah, Mauritania's first president, was drawing to a close. The president was ousted by a coup on 10 July 1978, an event that overshadowed the slave revolts that were being quelled in various localities.[26] Like other small political groups, El-Hor organized a demonstration in favour of the new authorities and even signed, in the name of the Haratine community, a petition supporting them. It thus presented itself as a player on the national scene.

Meanwhile, El-Hor's activists were making themselves heard internationally. An awareness campaign was launched to reach out to the media and relevant NGOs, and it soon bore fruit. Anti-Slavery International, based in London,

---

[25] Philippe Marchesin, *Tribus, ethnies et pouvoirs en Mauritanie* (Karthala, Paris, 1992).
[26] Ould Ahmed, *L'abolition de l'esclavage en Mauritanie*, pp. 57-60.

started to work with El-Hor to assess the scope of slavery,[27] as can be seen in its report on Mauritania.[28]

However the real opportunity to go public came two years after the organization's creation, in July 1980, when the power of the state was shaken due to difficulties ending the country's involvement in the war in the Western Sahara. In April 1979, Colonel Mohamed Khouna Ould Haidalla had replaced colonels Moustapha Ould Mohamed Saleck and Mohamed Mahmoud Ould Mohamed Louly, the two successive heads of state since 1978. A specific event pushed El-Hor to organize protest demonstrations in several big towns including Nouakchott, Rosso and Nouadhibou after news broke of the sale of a slave named M'Barka in the town of Atar (Adrar) in February 1980. After activists were arrested, El-Hor were taken to court in Rosso in March 1980.

In this famous case and in line with argumentation frequently used afterwards, the Mauritanian authorities made it a crime to raise the issue of slavery. El-Hor's founding members (Boubacar Ould Messaoud, Boydiel Ould Houmeid, Achour Ould Samba and Samory Ould Beye as well as several other persons) were arrested, imprisoned, interrogated and finally arraigned before a military tribunal that held special hearings in Rosso. Most of the accused willingly admitted what they had done and that they had belonged to the movement.[29] They managed to turn the trial into a grandstand for their cause and it became an opportunity far beyond anything the anti-slavery activists could have hoped for and made a strong impact on the media. El-Hor's leaders received prison sentences of up to three months but the publicity surrounding around the trial would soon have spectacular effects both nationally and internationally.

The march towards abolition

The government of Ould Haidalla seemed to have decided to respond to Haratine demands and, in addition to the trial's impact and international support, the campaigns launched by El-Hor soon proved effective. In June 1980, the organization published a tract listing the major problems related to the continuation of slavery and asked the government to address these grievances.

As a result of international pressure and instability on the domestic front, the government responded rapidly and forcefully.[30] Hardly able to do otherwise, it

---

[27] *Ibid.*, p. 61.
[28] John Mercer, *Slavery in Mauritania today* (Anti-Slavery International, London, 1981).
[29] I would like to thank R. Botte for providing me with copies of the proceedings of this trial.
[30] Interview with Mohamed Khouna Ould Haidallah in *Espaces Calame*, 3, March 1994, p. 6.

was moving towards the formal abolition of slavery. It started by consulting *ulemas*. Their approval was less than outright and their *fatwas* were reserved. None proclaimed that slavery was illegal under Islam, but neither did any go so far as to advise against the proposed measure. Given the ambiguity of the doctors of Sharia law, the Home Office issued a statement on 3 June 1980 that instructed the regional authorities to combat an 'anachronistic practice'. On 5 June 1980, the *Comité militaire de salut national*, the governing body at the time, adopted a declaration abolishing slavery. The government newspaper enthusiastically explained the measure by borrowing from El-Hor: 'Since all Muslims are equal before Allah, there is no reason some of them should be enslaved by others'.[31]

Activists criticized all these efforts as being legally worthless and the authorities were forced, sixteen months later, to go a step farther and issue a decree abolishing slavery on 9 November 1981.[32] Its four short articles were ambiguous, oddly providing for state compensation for the 'persons entitled', i.e. the masters. Nonetheless, this order clearly signalled a victory for El-Hor. The law recognized that there were still slaves being treated like someone else's personal property since their owners were to be compensated for their losses.[33]

Later, Ould Haidallah's government issued its famous order for land reform in June 1983. Since land was to be held by individuals, the tribal authorities' traditional property rights were to be abolished. This law was supposed to allow slaves to own the land they worked[34] and was one of President Haidalla's last political acts before he was ousted by Colonel Mâaouya Ould Sid'Ahmed Taya on 12 December 1984. Taking into account the momentum gathered by the movement in the Haratine community, the new head of state appointed Messaoud Ould Boulkhier as Minister of Rural Development. This founding member of El-Hor received, it was claimed, the symbolically important assignment of land reform because there was to be a new policy of improving the conditions of the Haratine at the local level.

Beyond its symbolism, this appointment marked a turning point. First of all, it opened up access to decision-making positions to the Haratine elite. Secondly, it was evidence of the determination to endorse at least some of the conclusions drawn up by El-Hor. And finally, it signalled government recognition of El-Hor as a legitimate representative and spokesman of the Haratine community. Since then, no government has been formed without including at least some persons

---

[31] *Chaab*, 7 July 1980.
[32] Ordonnance n. 81.234 of 9 November 1981.
[33] Mohamed Lemine Ould Ahmed, *L'abolition de l'esclavage en Mauritanie*, pp. 67 ff.
[34] Bernard Crousse, 'La réforme foncière mauritanienne de 1983, étatisation ou individualisation', *Politique africaine*, 21 (March 1986), pp. 63-76.

from this community,[35] preferably from among El-Hor's founding members. This involvement in government considerably affected the movement's institutionalization and political prospects during Mâaouya Ould Taya's long term in office (1984-2005) and even beyond.

'Slaves' in power, 'slaves' of power

A major objective of El-Hor's founding charter seemed to have been achieved: persons from among the Haratine were now holding top positions. The process of turning the Haratine leadership into 'officials' was seen literally and the movement's request to share the national pie among the country's ethnic, tribal and social constituents started to be realized.[36] Since then, nearly all of the movement's outstanding members have held important positions in government and the Haratine movement can lay claim to considerable political advances. During the experimental municipal elections organized by Ould Taya in late 1986, El-Hor was less successful but was able to measure the support it had in the country. By sponsoring candidates, it gained electoral experience that would prove useful later.[37] Beyond the pursuit of personal careers, what was important about this involvement in politics was the position that the Haratine were working out in the recurring debates on Mauritania's national identity.

The experience gained in management and political office-holding spawned rivalries for the control of a movement increasingly involved in politics in the second half of the 1980s when the racial divide between Arab-Berbers and Afro-Mauritanians resurfaced along with the related issues of power-sharing and national identity.

Identity politics and the Haratine cause

The *Forces de libération africaines de Mauritanie* (FLAM), formed in 1986, signalled a radicalization of the claims made by Black African nationalists. In its famous 'Manifesto of the Oppressed Negro-Mauritanian', this new group called for armed struggle against Ould Taya's regime. The resurgence of the question of Black African minorities and their hostility towards the government, which was accused of being racist and of being monopolized by the White

---

[35] Zekeria Ould Ahmed Salem, 'Sur la formation des élites politiques et la mobilité sociale en Mauritanie', *Nomadic Peoples*, 2, 1-2 (1998), pp. 253-276.

[36] Zekeria Ould Ahmed Salem, 'La Centralité de la mobilisation tribale dans l'action politique en Mauritanie: Une illusion bien fondée?', *L'Ouest Saharien*, 2 (1999), pp. 127-156.

[37] El Arby Ould Saleck, *Les Haratins. Le paysage politique mauritanien* (L'Harmattan, Paris, 2003).

Moors, took a decisive turn in October 1987 with the failed coup by Haalpulaar officers. The three major instigators were tried by a military tribunal, sentenced to death and executed shortly afterwards. Dozens of presumed accomplices were thrown into prison and the Black African peril was declared a 'menace to state security'.

During all this, the long-standing debate on the country's identity was still raging. Two radical groups – the Moors and the Black African Mauritanians – were trying to win the Haratine community's support. An Arab nationalism of many forms (Nasserism, Baathism, etc.) was thriving, even in the military, opposing the idea of an African identity for Mauritania. In this tense atmosphere, El-Hor tried to present itself as separate from these competing nationalisms that were trying to recuperate the Haratine movement. From its very foundation, the organization had, in principle, adopted a position on the question of identity that was reflected in its well-known slogan: 'Arab but Black, Black but Arab'. Nevertheless, a debate flared up within the organization. Among El-Hor's few official declarations on this question was one from Boubacar Ould Messaoud (who would later head SOS Esclaves) to a Senegalese newspaper:[38]

> My skin is not a political programme [...] They are trying to establish a link between the activism of a few persons who have proclaimed themselves the spokesmen of a Black Mauritanian pseudo-community and the problem of slavery [...] In 1980, the fight against slavery was [led by] El-Hor, not them.

This heated controversy took a new turn following the clash between Mauritania and Senegal in April 1989, as citizens from each county living in the other were targeted. During these so-called 'events', as was the case during similar riots in 1966, the Haratine were accused of taking part in acts of violence against Black Africans, Senegalese and Mauritanians. It was even claimed that some Haratine had joined in the riots because of the aggression in Dakar against Bilal Ould Werzeg, a diplomat at the embassy and a founding member of El-Hor.[39] Whatever the case, the expulsion of nearly 80,000 Black African Mauritanians to Senegal and Mali caused unprecedented humanitarian problems while shortly afterwards, in 1990/1991, about 300 Black African soldiers fell vicitm during a bloody purge when they were accused of being antinationalistic and of supporting FLAM's 'extremist' doctrines. The death toll continued to rise. Black African nationalists did not give up on recruiting the Haratine for their combat. In 1990 FLAM's newspaper was tellingly called *Bilaal* after the first

---

[38]   *Sud Magazine* 4, January 1987, p. 1.

[39]   Charles C. Stewart, 'Une interprétation du conflit sénégalo-mauritanien', *Revue du Monde Musulman et de la Méditerranée*, 54, 1 (1989), pp. 161-170.

slave to convert to Islam and who became a well-known follower of the Prophet.[40]

Contradictions were emerging within El-Hor at this time. Some of the leaders supported the regime while others did not want to have anything to do with the military. The movement was also suffering from rivalries based on regions (east vs. southwest), language education (Arabic vs. French) or even ideologies. The desertion in 1990 of some of the leaders to join a group of Baathist Moors was seen as a defeat by some Haratine activists who wanted to remain equidistant from both Arab and Black African nationalisms.

The Haratine leadership remained divided over the question of whether to carry forward the symbolic issue of slavery. Since its foundation, the movement had often discussed if it should have a political or a social calling and this question was emerging once again. A rift was opening between a so-called radical wing that advocated pursuing this struggle and a more moderate wing for whom the Haratine issue was no longer political but social and economic. Positions hardened as a political strategy was hammered out and regardless of whether or not most of the Haratine felt represented by El-Hor (a hard-to-answer question), the organization turned out to be less of a federating, unifying force when circumstances forced it to position itself in a new political arena.

El-Hor, power holder or democratic opposition?

Before democratic fever broke out in Africa, part of El-Hor was increasingly at odds with Ould Taya's regime. In late 1990, certain members of the radical wing demanded political pluralism, blaming the authorities for undermining El-Hor's ticket (led by Messaoud Ould Boulkheir) during the 1990 municipal elections in Nouakchott. While several founding members sided with the regime (Boydiel Ould Houmeid, Mohamed Lemine Ould Ahmed, Sghair Ould Mbareck and Mohamed Ould Haimer), an active minority (Messaoud Ould Boulkheir, Boubacar Ould Messaoud and Omar Ould Yali) did not. The latter were among the leaders who sent open letters ('from 50', then 'from 150') to the head of state asking him to open political doors. Boubacar Ould Messaoud, who was thought to be close to the authorities, paid the price for this and was immediately dismissed from the official position he held.

Under mounting pressure from within and outside the country, President Ould Taya declared a pluralistic democracy on 15 April 1991. After laws installing a multiparty system were passed, Ould Taya's opponents joined the *Front démocratique uni pour le changement* (FDUC) in July 1991. This party included most of the political forces that wanted to put an end to the military

---

[40]   Marianne Marty, 'Les multiples usages de l'Islam dans le champ politique mauritanien', in *L'Afrique politique 2002* (Karthala, Paris, 2003), p. 57.

regime and, once legalized under its new name of *Union des forces démocratiques* (UFD), the front became the principal opposition party. Created for the presidential and legislative elections in 1992, the UFD was co-directed by Messaoud Ould Boulkheir, which was undoubtedly the reason why the issue of slavery had a place on the party's platform and it condemned violations of the human rights of Black African Mauritanians, civilians and soldiers.

The UFD supported an independent candidate, Ahmed Ould Daddah, for the presidential election on 24 January 1992 since support for Ould Boulkheir's candidacy had not been unanimous. The UFD did not survive Ould Daddah's defeat in an election that was only just won by Ould Taya under tense and dubious conditions. A new party, *Union des forces démocratiques/Ère nouvelle* (UFD/EN), formed around Ould Daddah but the leaders of El-Hor felt cramped in this new organization and, in 1993, dissatisfied with the handling of the Haratine question, El-Hor published a long document recounting its fight and discussing its uncomfortable position inside the party.[41] However its representatives did not quit the UFD/EN until 1994 and they created *Action pour le changement* (AC) in August 1995 with Messaoud Ould Boulkheir as president.[42]

Autonomy in party politics and the rekindled debate on slavery

The Haratine movement was now deeply entrenched in party politics. Though founded by persons of different origins, the AC was the first party actually controlled by Haratine. Since it accepted forming an alliance with Black African nationalists who had previously been activists in the UFD, its creation was seen as a radicalization of El-Hor. The AC was the first party to present a platform that gave priority to the fight against slavery and the advancement of the Haratine. Given the context, the party's creation was hugely significant and as an authoritarian restoration was taking place, the regime was cleverly manoeuvring to 'pass the democratic test' and enhance its image outside the country. Above all, it was acquiring a reputation of stability in a region that was relatively less secure.[43] Mauritania established diplomatic relations with Israel, thus improving its relations with the United States and muting the frequent criticism directed at it from America.

El-Hor apparently realized that its cause had not only been watered down owing to its involvement in party politics inside the country but had also been

---

[41]   El-Hor, 'Les Haratines. Contribution à une compréhension juste de leur problématique', Nouakchott (5 March 1993), 28 typed pages.

[42]   El Arby Ould Saleck, 'Les Haratin comme enjeu pour les partis politiques en Mauritanie', *Journal des Africanistes*, 70, 1 (2000), pp. 255-263.

[43]   Zekeria Ould Ahmed Salem, 'La démocratisation en Mauritanie, une *illusion* postcoloniale?' *Politique africaine*, 75 (October 1999), pp. 131-146.

hijacked by political groups outside the country, in particular Black African Mauritanians in the USA.[44] The creation of the AC and, in the same year, of SOS Esclaves has to be understood in this context. The *Confédération libre des travailleurs de Mauritanie* (CLTM) was also set up under the leadership of Samory Ould Bèye, one of El-Hor's founding members.

These political changes were occurring while the terms of the debate about the Haratine problem and slavery were slowly shifting. Since democratization in 1991, two opposite positions on slavery had formed in the country's independent media. According to El-Hor activists in opposition, slavery still existed as a practice and as a system of values fostered by a lack of action by the authorities. According to the regime's supporters, slavery had vanished and any actions should be directed at its mainly economic and social after-effects. Mentioning the existence of slavery amounted to an attack on national unity. The activists who adopted the first position were accused of manufacturing a fake problem for political purposes. The El-Hor faction that had joined the regime was even assigned the task of confronting their brothers in arms about this question. A *Comité pour l'éradication des séquelles de l'esclavage en Mauritanie* (CRESEM) was formed for this purpose in the mid 1990s and in 1997 it received the public support of the head of state who, during a famous speech, criticized politicians' exploitation of slavery's after-effects, setting off a major national debate that reflected, once again, a hardening of positions on the issue.[45]

This tension eventually affected the AC's political prospects. Having won but a single seat (Kébé Abdoulaye) in the 1996 parliamentary elections, the party was not represented in the National Assembly by anyone from El-Hor. In the more legitimate 2001 legislative elections however, it won four seats in parliament, including that of the charismatic Messaoud Ould Boulkheir.

The UN conference in Durban on racism and xenophobia (August-September 2001) provided El-Hor activists with a platform for reaching the international media. Since the early 1990s, the issue of slavery in Mauritania had been monopolized by Afro-Mauritanian activists abroad who had presented the issue in black-and-white terms. In their simplified version, in which all Afro-Mauritanians were the slaves of the Arabs, there was obviously no role for El-Hor.[46] El-Hor activists used the Durban conference to censor the regime's

---

[44] Alice Bullard, 'From colonization to globalization: The vicissitudes of slavery in Mauritania', *Cahiers d'études africaines*, 179-180 (2005), pp. 751-769.

[45] Mohamed Lemine Ould Ahmed, *Mauritanie-Nouvelles*, 236, 28 January 1997, pp. 12-13.

[46] Interview with Messaoud Ould Boulkheir in *Le Calame* 351, 8 May 2002; Michele Stephenson, *Faces of Change*, a documentary (Firelight Media Production, New York, 2002), 22 min. http://www.firelightmedia.org.

authoritarian restoration in Mauritania and its treatment of 'bare-foot activists', as Messaoud Ould Boulkheir and his comrades referred to themselves.[47] Re-elected in 1997 for a new six-year term, Ould Taya spared his opponents no pity. The UFD/EN was outlawed in January 2001. The AC's turn came in January 2002 after Ould Boulkheir railed in parliament against the persistence of slavery and criticized the lack of development programmes targeting the Haratine population.

Feeling the brunt of the government's harsh decisions, party leaders began looking for a new framework for action. The creation of a new party, the *Convention pour le changement*, was refused and it was not until 2003 that the pro-Libyan Arab nationalists of the *Alliance populaire progressiste* (APP), an elitist party that was losing momentum, proposed that Messaoud Ould Boulkheir and his Haratine companions join it along with Black Africans. This improbable alliance of usually competing micronationalisms had two consequences. On the one hand, it enabled El-Hor to present itself as a bridge between all the political persuasions in Mauritania and, on the other, it allowed 'Arabists', who auto-matically became a minority in the party's leadership, to change their ideology and appeal. Messaoud Ould Boulkheir became the APP's president, and El-Hor its driving force.

From 2003 to 2005, the political climate in Mauritania deteriorated. Ould Taya was re-elected president in controversial conditions for a third term in November 2003. Several attempted coups were foiled between June 2003 and August 2004 and Ould Taya was not ousted until 3 August 2005 by Colonel Ely Ould Mohamed Vall and his *Comité militaire pour la justice et la démocratie.*

The democratic revival and El-Hor's prospects

After removing Ould Taya, Colonel Ely Ould Mohamed Vall managed an exemplary transition towards democracy by March 2007. A coalition headed by an elected president, Sidi Ould Cheikh Abdellahi, came to power. Messaoud Ould Boulkheir and his party, the APP, held a special place in this coalition. The APP had won only five seats in the 2006 parliamentary elections and did not score well in the presidential elections, winning only 7% of the votes. Nevertheless, Messaoud Ould Boulkheir unexpectedly decided to endorse Sidi Ould Cheikh Abdellahi during the run-off in the presidential election in exchange for a few ministerial positions for the APP and the speakership in the National Assembly for himself. He also demanded that parliament adopt as its very first text a law criminalizing slavery with sanctions against those guilty of it. In compliance with this pre-election deal, the new government passed a bill

---

[47]   Interview with Messaoud Ould Boulkheir, *Le Calame*, 351, 8 May 2002.

on 9 August 2007 that made slavery a crime.[48] The APP immediately held a meeting at which Ould Boulkheir declared, 'After this act, only someone who wants to be a slave will be!'

This controversial statement shocked the leaders of SOS Esclaves, who had actively lobbied for this law against slavery, but with little success. They had failed to amend it and so to allow NGOs to be party to lawsuits about slavery. In fact, during all this, the leadership of SOS Esclaves proved that it was technically competent and endowed with a fighting spirit that only a few of El-Hor's leaders could match. It became obvious that politicians from the Haratine community were no longer the driving force for progress on this hugely symbolic question.

The Haratine social movement was shifting away from politics and political parties and towards advocacy and activism. This remarkable shift mainly affected SOS Esclaves, as my current research on this NGO shows.

From politics to advocacy, the ultimate transformation?

The development of the activism characteristic of SOS Esclaves represents one of the most important transformations undergone by the Haratine movement. By dramatizing the issue of slavery, this humanitarian human-rights NGO took the campaign back to its roots. Absorbed by politics, El-Hor was no longer the sole standard-bearer of the Haratine cause. SOS Esclaves came into being in February 1995 when, as we have already seen, political protest was more or less stifled due to the vigorous authoritarian restoration. The same process led both to the creation of the AC and underlined the commitment of Boubacar Ould Messaoud, the founding president of SOS Esclaves, to the struggle for human rights in Mauritanian society.

With the support of Messaoud Ould Boulkheir (El-Hor's charismatic leader and moral authority), Boubacar Ould Messaoud, an architect by education and a key figure in the struggle against slavery, wanted to launch a fight distinct from El-Hor's. And with encouragement from various s political sources, he thought an NGO could best broaden the struggle against slavery beyond the category of the Haratine. SOS Esclaves was a suitable name because it expressed a sense of urgency and danger.[49] The issue of slavery had to be moved out of the constrained game of politics and the intention was to bring together the descendants of masters and of slaves and place the issue on the national agenda.

However this NGO's founding took place amid suspicion and prohibitions. Some of El-Hor's original leaders did not accept this new project, seeing it as a means whereby Boubacar Ould Messaoud would take control of an agenda that

---

[48]   Loi n. 2007–048 of 3 September 2007.
[49]   Interviews with Boubacar Ould Messaoud, May-September 2008, Nouakchott.

had been jointly drawn up, and orient it in a different direction. As for the government, it was opposed to the new NGO and SOS Esclaves's first press conference was banned.[50] The only genuinely positive response came from outside the country, where the defence of human rights and the 'actions of civil society' were current catch-phrases.

New methods in a new framework of action

From the start, SOS Esclaves wanted its actions to be different from the familiar forms of mobilization. A natural action was to update information about clear and indisputable cases of slavery, with the goal being to present names and faces to personify the Haratine problem. The organization helped victims, contacted lawyers to defend them and inveighed against the judicial system's 'complicity'. It undertook and supported court actions and awareness campaigns and, in 1995, it circulated a 'note of information on slavery in Mauritania', which prefigured its annual reports. As of 1996 every report mentioned between thirty and forty cases ranging from servile, unpaid labour to fugitive slaves, land seizures, undue influence in matters of inheritance and separated families whose members were divided among 'masters'. The reports even mentioned acts of kidnapping, illegal restraint, usurpation and physical violence. Some cases were settled through the organization's interventions but the government was usually blamed for its lack of determination to eradicate these phenomena, punish offenders or protect victims in compliance with the many, already enacted, laws and legal measures.

The reports also contained analyses and concrete proposals for eradicating slavery.[51] It is interesting that the arguments used by SOS Esclaves reformulate the fundamental issues at stake. For them, emancipation does not mean an end to servitude insofar as other sorts of bonds still chain freed slaves to their former masters. Officially freed slaves are even more enslaved if society provides no means of guaranteeing real economic, social and psychological emancipation.[52]

SOS Esclaves owes part of its audience to the suits that the authorities brought against it after French television (FR3) broadcast a documentary about slavery in Mauritania. Boubacar Ould Mesaaoud presented presumed slaves to the cameras and, as a result of this, was arrested, judged and, in early 1998, sentenced to thirteen months imprisonment for 'belonging to an unrecognized association' along with Fatimata Mbaye (a lawyer), Cheikh Saad Bouh Kamara

---

[50]   Interviews with Jemal Ould Yessa, September 2008, Dakar/Nouakchott.

[51]   S.O.S Esclaves (www.sosesclaves.org., March, 2004)

[52]   Boubacar Messaoud, 'Esclavage en Mauritanie: De l'idéologie du silence la mise en question', *Journal des Africanistes*, 70, 1 (2000), pp. 291-337.

(a teacher) and Ibrahim Ould Ebetty (a lawyer). Although the Court of Appeals upheld the sentence on 24 March 1998, the accused were granted remission following pressure from various international organizations. SOS Esclaves gained visibility in the international media.

International backing has in fact always been a strategic point in the organization's support and legitimacy. SOS Esclaves has benefited from its alliance with *Conscience et résistance*, an organization in exile whose founder and leader, Jemal Ould Yessa, headed the European chapter of SOS Esclaves for a long time. Born into an emir's family in Tagant in central Mauritania, Ould Yessa is very active on the international scene and his support has lent credibility to the organization as he is one of the very few descendants of the Moor nobility to become an activist in an anti-slavery organization.[53]

At the national level, very few Haratine activists have rallied around Boubacar Ould Messaoud, whose personality has strongly marked SOS Esclaves and spurred criticism. For the president of this NGO, activism seems to have become a life-time career and he has repeatedly emphasized that 'Slavery is not a hobby horse but a personal obsession'.[54] El-Hor's long-time activists seldom join SOS Esclaves, which they see as the business of a comrade who has turned commitment into a solitary fight. Nonetheless, criticism of Ould Messaoud's motivations or sincerity has not stopped the organization from obtaining recognition and registering successes.

Recognition

The national and international recognition now enjoyed by SOS Esclaves is out of proportion with El-Hor's. The latter has remained an informal organization that has splintered into sub-groups and is deeply involved in politics. It is no accident that, while on a trip to the US in March 2008, the president of SOS Esclaves was asked to speak in the prestigious Woodrow Wilson Center for International Scholars (Washington, DC) and the Open Society Institute (New York). The *Washington Post* devoted a whole page to him under the headline 'How one brave man helped end slavery in his country'.[55] In its 2007 report on trafficking in human beings, the US State Department presented Ould Messaoud as one of the world's seventeen 'heroes' working to put an end to modern forms of slavery.[56] This recognition came but a few weeks after SOS Esclaves was nominated for Anti-Slavery International's 2008 award.

---

[53]   Interviews with Jemal Ould Yessa, September/October 2008, Nouakchott/Dakar.
[54]   Interview with Boubacar Ould Messaoud, *Mauritanie-Nouvelles*, 235, 23 January 1997 and *La Tribune* 297, 16 March 2006.
[55]   *Washington Post*, 23 March 2008.
[56]   www.america.gov/st/hrenglish/2008/June/20080604163846ajesrom

Since 2003 requests from abroad for alternative human-rights reports to those coming from the government have led to SOS Esclaves becoming increasingly indispensable. Under pressure from different international sources, Ould Taya's government was forced to grant it authorization in May 2005 and, as we have seen, SOS Esclaves was, after the military putsch of 3 August 2005 that ousted Ould Taya, associated with policies to extend rights and freedom. Since 2007, its president and its secretary-general have been members of the *Commission nationale des Droits de l'Homme* (CNDH) that is funded by the government and reports to the prime minister. The CNDH has not only inveighed against the persistence of problems related to slavery but also helped settle several cases.[57] Ironically, this official commission is chaired by the well-known and respected Mohamed Said Ould Hamody, a journalist and former ambassador who is none other than the son of the famous Hamody Ould Mahmoud. The latter, who died in 1969, was one of the very few Haratine who made a fortune in the 1940s and 1950s and naturally – like any wealthy man of his day – owned several slaves.[58]

SOS Esclaves may not, however, be the final form of mobilization for the Haratine cause. Groups of this sort are now proliferating and claim to be reviving and radicalizing the cause. Internationally, there is Moctar Teyeb's hyperactivism in the United States.[59] Claiming to be from El-Hor, he has become associated, under ambiguous circumstances, with an organization called the American Antislavery Group, which is active in Sudan. He even held the title of outreach director in this NGO in 2000 before being heard by the US Senate's Committee on Foreign Relations.[60] He set up the Haratine Institute, and persons with similar claims have set up another institute of this sort in France. In Mauritania, young activists, some of them previously from El-Hor or SOS Esclaves, recently created small groups with names such as *Conscience haratine* or *IRA*. They are trying to adapt their message to trends in the country or, at least, to advance their personal careers in politics. It is too soon to say anything about their impact or prospects. However they are evidence of the resilience of the Haratine movement and its ability to innovate.

0.3565332.html, June 4, 2008.

[57] Commission Nationale des Droits de l'Homme, *Rapport Annuel 2007-2008* (CNDH, Nouakchott, June 2008), pp. 21-23.

[58] E. Ann McDougall, 'A topsy-turvy world: Slaves and freed slaves in the Mauritanian Adrar, 1910-1950', in S. Miers & R. Roberts (eds), *The End of Slavery in Africa* (University of Wisconsin Press, Madison, WI, 2005), pp. 362-390.

[59] See the interview with Moctar Teyeb, 'Slavery is a state of mind', *Middle East Quarterly*, December 1999.

[60] William Finnegan, 'A slave in New York: From Africa to the Bronx, one man's long journey to freedom', *The New Yorker*, 24 January 2000, pp. 50-61.

Conclusion

All things considered, the actions taken by the Haratine movement have finally placed the question of improving the situation of the social strata made up of slaves and their descendants on the national political agenda. The movement's itinerary has been deeply shaped over the years by a confluence of factors and shifts of positions in Mauritanian politics. Both El-Hor and SOS Esclaves have played a crucial role in increasing awareness of the cause they defend and have managed to obtain recognition for this social category in politics. Despite its institutional weakness as a result of its emergence as an underground movement, the Haratine movement has been institutionalized by labour unions, political parties and society in general.

Nowadays, there are doubts about whether the Haratine movement is a single cause since ever more diverse actors are now conveying its themes and messages. In addition, the diversified Haratine community has changed independently of the political struggles centred on it. As a consequence, and despite the prestige that El-Hor's founding members enjoy in national politics, it cannot be concluded that they have fully succeeded in creating a 'moral ethnicity' unified around an identity in the pursuit of a common cause. And in spite of the current promotion of the Haratine cause as an outstanding example of a human-rights struggle, these changes are not likely to depoliticize an issue that runs so deep in debates about Mauritania's identity, current situation and prospects.

9

An Islamic social movement in contemporary West Africa: NASFAT of Nigeria[1]

Benjamin Soares

Much recent scholarship about Islam among youth has tended to privilege so-called political Islam or Islamism and the radicalization of Muslim youth. In this chapter, I shift the focus away from such objects of study to consider a new Islamic organization in Nigeria called NASFAT (Nasr Allah al-Fatih Society of Nigeria) that exhibits some features of a social movement. NASFAT also clearly illustrates the influence of Pentecostalism on Muslim religious practice with some even referring to the organization as 'Islamic Pentecostalism'. NASFAT's founders intended the organization to be both non-sectarian and non-political. Like some other modern Islamic movements, NASFAT has focused on questions of piety and ethics and has been very active in social and economic activities. However, NASFAT's development of business activities, which it has sought to explicitly link with Islam, has been rather distinctive, helping to define it as an Islamic social movement. Given the limited attention to such contemporary Islamic organizations and social movements, which challenge some conventional terms and categories of analysis of Islam, Muslim youth and social movements, the chapter is a preliminary attempt to trace

[1] I am most grateful to Professor Amidu Sanni of Lagos State University for introducing me to members of the NASFAT leadership. I am also grateful to Lateef Oladimeji for introducing me to NASFAT members in Abuja and would like to thank Ruth Marshall for her insightful analyses of Pentecostalism and Nigeria that helped me develop some of the ideas discussed in this chapter. Amidu Sanni, Rosalind Hackett, Rüdiger Seesemann, and LaRay Denzer offered useful commentary on earlier drafts. I remain responsible for any deficiencies.

the history of NASFAT and set it within the larger social and historical context.

Young people – whether considered as a demographic group, a generation or a segment of consumer society – have captured the imagination and, not infrequently, the opprobrium of social and political commentators for several decades now. At least since the Iranian Revolution, there has also been considerable interest in Muslim youth in the world. From the time of the Palestinian *intifada* when young people were key actors to the events of September 11, 2001 when young Arab hijackers engaged in spectacular acts of terrorism, Islam and especially young Muslims have been key objects of attention and have faced heightened levels of scrutiny.[2] This degree of interest in young Muslims and their activities is unlikely to abate any time soon.

Given this excessive interest in young Muslims, it is not surprising that much recent scholarship about Islam among youth has tended to privilege so-called political Islam or Islamism and various trajectories of the radicalization of Muslim youth in volatile and unstable settings in the world.[3] This is not least the case for Nigeria, especially in the predominantly Muslim north of the country where, for several decades, Muslim youth have been prominent religious and political activists.[4] Since the 1980s, there have been waves of Muslim radicalism in Nigeria from the millenarian Maitatsine movement to the more recent self-styled Nigerian Taliban. Following the extension of *sharia* to cover criminal law in twelve northern states beginning in 1999, scholars and other commentators have focused with great intensity on Islam and Muslims in northern Nigeria.

In this chapter, I shift the focus away from such objects of study, which are, of course, not without interest or importance,[5] to consider a new Islamic orga-

---

[2] See Ted Swedenburg, 'Imagined youths', *Middle East Report*, 245 (http://www.merip.org/mer/mer245/swedenburg.html, 2007).

[3] See, for example, Olivier Roy, *Globalised Islam: The search for a new ummah* (Hurst, London, 2004); cf. Linda Herrera & Asef Bayat (eds), *Being Young and Muslim* (Oxford University Press, Oxford, forthcoming in 2010).

[4] See, e.g., Roman Loimeier, *Islamic Reform and Political Change in Northern Nigeria* (Northwestern University Press, Evanston, IL, 1997); Ousmane Kane, *Muslim Modernity in Postcolonial Nigeria: A study of the society for the removal of innovation and reinstatement of tradition* (Brill, Leiden, 2003); Murray Last, 'Towards a political history of youth in Muslim Northern Nigeria 1750-2000', in Jon Abbink & Ineke van Kessel (eds), *Vanguard or Vandals: Youth, politics and conflict in Africa* (Brill, Leiden, 2005), pp. 37-54; Conerly Casey, 'Marginal Muslims: Politics and the perceptual bounds of Islamic authenticity in northern Nigeria', *Africa Today*, 54, 3 (2008), pp. 67-92.

[5] See Jon Abbink's contribution in this volume.

nization in Nigeria called NASFAT that exhibits some features of a social movement. As sociologist Charles Kurzman has noted, social movement theorists have until recently largely ignored the Muslim world (with the possible exception of Iran) since social movements defined in relation to Islam generally 'appear to be, and [might even] claim to be, so different from the secular, Western, left-liberal norms that social movement theorists generally espouse'.[6] In turn, scholars of Islam and contemporary Muslim societies have almost completely ignored research on social movements.[7]

I suggest that the study of new Islamic movements and social movement theory could be brought together for mutual benefit. The founders of the new Islamic organization of NASFAT were involved in one of Nigeria's largest and oldest Islamic organizations, which has been an important conduit for Muslim activism and proselytizing as well as occasional radical trends. NASFAT's founders launched an Islamic organization that has become dynamic, influential and perhaps one of the largest in contemporary Nigeria. They intended NASFAT to be both non-sectarian and non-political. Over time and like some other modern Islamic movements, NASFAT has focused on questions of piety and ethics and has been deeply involved in social and economic activities. However, NASFAT's recent development of business activities, which it has sought to explicitly link with Islam, has been rather distinctive, helping to define it as an Islamic social movement. Given the limited attention to these kinds of Islamic organizations and social movements, which clearly challenge some conventional terms and categories of analysis of Islam, Muslim youth and social movements, the following is a preliminary attempt to trace the history of NASFAT and set it within the larger social and historical context.

The context for a new organization

Nigeria currently has a population estimated at more than 140 million, with many claiming that it is about evenly divided between Christians and Muslims. Some even aver that Muslims might constitute a slight majority. Commentators are nevertheless nearly unanimous in noting the importance of religion in contemporary Nigeria. Numerous reports of Muslim-Christian tensions and conflict

---

[6]   Charles Kurzman, 'Conclusion: Social movement theory and Islamic studies' in Quintan Wiktorowicz (ed.), *Islamic Activism: A social movement theory approach* (Indiana University Press, Bloomington, 2004), pp. 289-303.

[7]   For notable exceptions, see Quintan Wiktorowicz (ed.), *Islamic Activism: A social movement theory approach* (Indiana University Press, Bloomington, 2004). None of the contributors, however, considers Sub-Saharan Africa.

in various parts of the country notwithstanding,[8] Muslims and Christians have long lived side by side in many places in Nigeria and one can sometimes even find Muslims and Christians within the same family. Some Nigerians have tried to fuse Islam and Christianity, as the name of the religious group 'Chrislam' in the southwest of the country suggests. But such efforts towards religious fusion or synthesis seem to be rather exceptional and increasingly so. In many places, there has been intense competition and higher levels of tension within and between different confessional groups. Given the mutual demonization by certain Christians and Muslims in Nigeria in recent years, such competition and tensions contribute to what Murray Last has called 'an economy of panic' that has been rather volatile.[9]

The 1970s oil boom, the subsequent massive investments in education, the unprecedented spread of the mass media and increased urbanization have all had a profound effect on Nigerian society and the practice of religion in particular. Although political liberalization came relatively late to Nigeria in the late 1990s, Muslim and Christian associational life flourished under the long periods of repressive military rule. While there has been considerable research on recent Christian developments in the country and in the historically Muslim north, particularly in the major urban centre of Kano, there has been much less research on Muslims living outside northern Nigeria.[10]

The new Muslim organization founded in 1995 is known as NASFAT;[11] an acronym of the Arabic portion of the organization's full name, Nasr Allah al-Fatih Society of Nigeria. *Nasr Allah* means literally 'the help of God' and is a phrase that occurs several times in the Qur'an.[12] *Al-Fatih*, means 'the victorious'. The entire phrase in Arabic could be translated into English as 'the help of

---

[8]   See Toyin Falola, *Violence in Nigeria: The crisis of religious politics and secular ideologies* (University of Rochester Press, Rochester, NY, 1998); Rosalind I.J. Hackett, 'Managing or manipulating religious conflict in the Nigerian media', in Jolyon Mitchell & Sophia Marriage (eds), *Mediating Religion: Conversations in media, religion and culture* (T. & T. Clark, Edinburgh, 2003), pp. 47-64; Murray Last, 'Muslims and Christians in Nigeria: An economy of political panic', *The Round Table: The Commonwealth Journal of International Affairs*, 96, 392 (2007), pp. 605-616; Adam Higazi, 'Violence urbaine et politique à Jos (Nigeria), de la période coloniale aux élections de 2007', *Politique africaine*, 106 (2007), pp. 69-91.

[9]   Murray Last, 'Muslims and Christians in Nigeria'.

[10] There has also been little research on Muslim-Christian relations in Africa more generally. See Benjamin F. Soares (ed.), *Muslim-Christian encounters in Africa* (Brill, Leiden, 2006).

[11] See Amidu Sanni's brief discussion of NASFAT in Amidu Sanni, 'Challenges and realities in the healing and power accession custom of the Yoruba Muslims of Nigeria', *Journal of Oriental and African Studies*, 15 (2006), pp. 145-156.

[12] It occurs in sura 10 of the Quran, which most commentators agree refers to the surrender of Mecca to Muhammad.

God is victorious'. However, in NASFAT's print media it is translated as 'there is no help except from Allah'.

It is useful to think of this new Islamic organization as a social movement and a specifically Islamic social movement, which can only be understood within Nigeria's plural and complex religious landscape and in relation to some of the socio-economic changes over the past two decades. The organization-cum-social-movement NASFAT was founded away from the historically Muslim northern part of Nigeria in the religiously plural southwestern region of the country that today is called Yorubaland. Southwestern Nigeria is a region where Muslims, Christians and practitioners of African traditional religions have lived together since the nineteenth century with the rise of Christianity. During that period, Christianity and Islam spread simultaneously.[13] Over time, Muslims, Christians and practitioners of African traditional religion – so-called Yoruba religion in this particular setting – have borrowed and appropriated from each other in ways that have invited admiration or scorn depending on one's perspective. Although Yoruba religion[14] and Christianity are both well-developed fields of study, Islam among the Yoruba – half of whom are estimated to be Muslims – remains curiously understudied.[15]

While the boundaries between different religious groups in southwestern Nigeria have been shifting and unstable over time, there are several important developments in relation to which NASFAT's rise must be understood. First, given the religiously plural landscape of southwestern Nigeria, Muslims from elsewhere in the country along with some Yoruba Muslims have at times disparaged the practice of Islam in Yorubaland as less 'pure' than elsewhere, more prone to 'mixing' with non- or un-Islamic elements, and so forth. For example, Muslims in northern Nigeria make constant reference to the nineteenth century – the jihad led by Uthman dan Fodio with his allegedly unwavering commitment to extirpate the un-Islamic and the polity, the Sokoto Caliphate that ensued

---

[13] See J.D.Y. Peel, 'The pastor and the *babalawo*: The interaction of religions in nineteenth-century Yorubaland', *Africa*, 60, 3 (1990), pp. 338-369; *Ibid.*, *Religious Encounter and the Making of the Yoruba* (Indiana University Press, Bloomington, 2000).

[14] For some of the most recent studies of Yoruba religion, see Jacob K. Olupona & Terry Rey (eds), *Orisa Devotion as World Religion: The globalization of Yoruba religious culture* (University of Wisconsin Press, Madison, 2008).

[15] For exceptions, see T.G.O. Gbadamosi, *Growth of Islam among the Yoruba, 1841-1908* (Longman, London, 1978); Patrick J. Ryan, *Imale: Yoruba participation in the Muslim tradition, a study of clerical piety* (Scholars Press, Missoula, MT, 1978); and H.O. Danmole, 'Religious encounter in southwestern Nigeria: The domestication of Islam among the Yoruba', in Jacob K. Olupona & Terry Rey (eds), *Orisa Devotion as World Religion: The globalization of Yoruba religious culture* (University of Wisconsin Press, Madison, 2008), pp. 202-220.

– when they talk about Islam and being Muslim today. And many Nigerian Muslims think that Uthman dan Fodio and his legacy (however it may be interpreted) should be the model applied across the board, also in places such as Yorubaland. But Islam has been present for a very long time in southwestern Nigeria and many Muslims there, including many Yoruba, are proud and not infrequently defensive of their religious traditions. They are also sometimes resentful that Muslims from elsewhere would deign to impose a model on them or denigrate the way they practise Islam. Be that as it may, many Muslims in southwestern Nigeria have been at the forefront of efforts to change or 'reform' the practice of Islam from within their own communities. As Stefan Reichmuth has observed, 'many educated Yoruba Muslims have been striving [especially] since the seventies to establish distinctly Islamic patterns of personal and communal life'.[16] Many Yoruba Muslims have wanted to affirm Islam and being Muslim. In doing so, they have frequently sought to distance themselves from Yoruba 'traditional' religion, as well as the Christianity of Christian Yoruba, many of whose followers embraced and benefited from Western education much earlier than Muslims.

Second, in recent years the rapid rise and spread of Pentecostalism in Nigeria and its increased presence in the public sphere have fundamentally altered the country's religious landscape. As we know from the work of various scholars,[17] Pentecostalism has drawn many people in southwestern Nigeria away from the mainline Protestant churches, the Roman Catholic Church as well as from African independent churches. Muslims in southwestern Nigeria have been in constant contact with Pentecostalism, which now saturates public life. Many, particularly young Muslims, have been attracted to Pentecostal services and activities with their lively worship, leadership roles and the health and wealth gospel. The appeal of Pentecostalism makes quite a number of Nigerian Muslims uneasy. In some ways, one could speak about the pentecostalization of Christianity in Nigeria. Other Christian churches, including the Roman Catholic Church, have revitalized their own charismatic traditions and appropriated Pentecostal styles and techniques to various degrees. This is also the case for some Muslims in Nigeria. Many Nigerians – Muslims and Christians alike – actually

---

[16] See Stefan Reichmuth, 'Education and the growth of religious associations among Yoruba Muslims: the Ansar-Ud-Deen Society of Nigeria', *Journal of Religion in Africa*, 26, 4 (1996), pp. 365-405, quoted on p. 387.

[17] See Ruth Marshall-Fratani, 'Mediating the global and the local in Nigerian Pentecostalism', *Journal of Religion in Africa*, 28 (1998), pp. 278–315; Rosalind I.J. Hackett, 'Radical Christian revivalism in Nigeria and Ghana: Recent patterns of conflict and intolerance', in Abdullahi A. An-Na'im (ed.), *Proselytization and Communal Self-Determination in Africa* (Orbis Books, Maryknoll, NY, 1999), pp. 246-267.

refer to organizations like NASFAT (sometimes with derision) as 'Pentecostal Islam' or 'Islamic Pentecostalism' and its members as 'Born-Again Muslims', and NASFAT helps to illustrate quite clearly some of the influence of Pentecostalism on Muslims, their religious practices and organizations.

Beginnings and *raison d'être*

In 1995 a group of ten young Yoruba men founded NASFAT, which they had originally conceived of as a prayer group for Muslim men who regularly met to pray together. In the following year, they decided to incorporate NASFAT as a formal organization. It is important to note that only one of the original founders, Abdullah Akinbode (b. 1957), seems to have had any formal, advanced Islamic religious training, or what we might call Islamic scholarly credentials. He obtained a BA in Islamic Studies from the University of Lagos (UNILAG), the massive state university in Lagos, Nigeria's most important economic centre and possibly its largest city, and then subsequently went on to complete MA studies in international law and diplomacy there too. Like Akinbode, the other founders of NASFAT were also Yoruba Muslims and university graduates and were all professionals working in banking and other modern sectors of the economy.

It is striking how NASFAT's founders are sociologically quite similar to some of the other new Muslim intellectuals[18] elsewhere in Africa and further afield in the Muslim world whose educational training in modern subjects often sets them apart from existing Muslim scholars – the *'ulama* – whose classical training is frequently restricted to traditional religious subjects, curricula and methods.[19] However, unlike the *lumpenintelligentsia*, Olivier Roy's rather disparaging moniker for some of the new Muslim intellectuals in the world today, the group of Yoruba Muslims who founded NASFAT were either solidly mid-

---

[18]   On new Muslim intellectuals, see René Otayek, 'Introduction: des nouveaux intellectuels musulmans d'Afrique noire', in René Otayek (ed.), *Le radicalisme islamique au sud du Sahara: Da'wa, arabisation et critique de l'Occident* (Karthala, Paris, 1993), pp. 8-18; Olivier Roy, *The Failure of Political Islam*, Trans. C. Volk (Harvard University Press, Cambridge, MA, 1994).

[19]   There have been many important transformations in 'traditional' Islamic education in Nigeria that are beyond the scope of this chapter. See, for example, Stefan Reichmuth, 'The modernization of Islamic education: Islamic learning and its interaction with "Western" education in Ilorin, Nigeria', in Louis Brenner (ed.), *Muslim Identity and Social Change in Sub-Saharan Africa* (Indiana University Press, Bloomington, 1993), pp. 179-197; Muhammad Sani Umar, 'Education and Islamic trends in Northern Nigeria: 1970s-1990s', *Africa Today*, 48, 2 (2001), pp. 127-150; *Ibid.*, 'Profiles of new Islamic schools in Northern Nigeria', *The Maghreb Review*, 28, 2-3 (2003), pp. 145-169.

dle class or, like most Western-style educated Nigerians and regardless of their religious background, aspired to the kind of middle-class lifestyle for which their modern Western-style university education prepared them, and to which they usually felt entitled.

With the serious economic decline following the fall in oil prices in the 1980s, the failure of the developmentalist model of the state and the further economic downturn during the years of chaotic military rule in 1990s, many Nigerians yearned for some semblance of normality and prosperity. Ruth Marshall has argued that 'Pentecostalism and new Islamic movements ... [have] pose[d] one of the greatest threats ever to its [the Nigerian state's] goal of national unity and ideologies of development'.[20] Islamic movements such as NASFAT (like Pentecostalism) have certainly become much more visible in the Nigerian public sphere. As the state has cut back on or stopped providing certain services, some religious organizations have stepped in to provide key services in the areas of health, social welfare, education and even security.[21] Rather than posing any kind of threat to national unity or even to state-promulgated ideologies of development, NASFAT has not only assisted in providing some of the much-needed and desired social services (see below) but has also helped to nurture and sustain ideologies of development and promote ideals of national unity.

Abdullah Akinbode, the one founder with Islamic scholarly credentials, who now has the title of NASFAT's 'Chief Missioner' and is the general overseer of the organization's activities, has explained that he and his friends wanted to found a new organization that met their own needs after leaving university. While they were students, they had been active in the Muslim Students' Society (MSS) of Nigeria, the major Muslim students' group that Yoruba Muslims founded in the 1950s. It subsequently spread to university campuses throughout the country and, in the process, students helped to transform the MSS into a national Muslim students' association, thereby shedding any identification solely with the Yoruba. Various Muslim activist groups have emerged from the MSS, including the Muslim Brothers, a large group that sought inspiration from the Iranian Revolution to transform Nigerian society, as well as various other groups that have splintered from the Muslim Brothers.[22]

---

[20] See Marshall-Fratani, 'Mediating the global and the local in Nigerian Pentecostalism', p. 282.

[21] For case studies of such processes among Muslims in Africa, see Benjamin F. Soares & René Otayek (eds), *Islam and Muslim Politics in Africa* (Palgrave Macmillan, New York, 2007).

[22] On the MSS, see Stefan Reichmuth, *Islamische Bildung und soziale Integration in Ilorin (Nigeria) seit ca. 1800* (LIT Verlag, Münster, 1998). Although the history of

The founders of NASFAT have stated that they wanted to found a modern organization that specifically addressed the needs and interests of Muslim youth. In a recent interview with a Nigerian journalist, Akinbode explained:

> At a point, we realised that it is not always easy for young people to comfortably be with older people with their peculiar ideas. I for one, cannot be in the same group with somebody who is 60, 70 or even 80 years old and you want me to be saying no to certain things he wants to do. He is used to the old fashion. The best thing for me is to come out of those societies and form my own with people who share the same values as me so that I will not be disrespectful to the elders. I will have more affinity with people of like minds and without condemning what the elders are doing we can carry on with our own ways. It is more of a way of conforming to modernity without losing trend with the dictates of Islam.[23]

As this clearly indicates, Akinbode and his peers saw their elders as being out of step with modernity. They were actively seeking a way to reconcile Islam and being Muslim with the modern society – frenetic, urban southwestern Nigeria – in which they were living. In founding a new Islamic organization, they were actually following the well-trodden path taken by many Muslims in this part of the country. There are many existing Islamic organizations in Nigeria, including the large and diverse modernist Islamic educational institutions and organizations that usually promote Western education, which have been active in Yorubaland since the first half of the twentieth century. Such organizations include the modernist Ansar-Ud-Deen Society of Nigeria ('Helpers of the Religion' Society) founded in Lagos in the 1920s[24] and Anwar-Ul-Islam ('The Lights of Islam'), an organization for members of the Indian Ahmadiyya sect, which has been around in West Africa since the first decades of the twentieth century.[25] Like its predecessors, NASFAT was also a new organization that targeted, at least initially, Muslim youth who fashioned themselves as modern, aspiring to achieve what NASFAT considers 'conformity with modernity'. Unlike those Nigerians of a more uncompromising 'maximalist' or radical bent,[26] they aim not to be 'disrespectful' of their elders. In other words, they try not to

---

these other Islamic organizations in Nigeria remains to be written, see the references in note 4

[23] Ernest Omoarelojie, 'Why NASFAT is growing', *The News* (http://thenewsng.com/interview/why-nasfat-is-growing/2009/02, February 9, 2009).

[24] See Reichmuth, 'Education and the growth of religious associations among Yoruba Muslims'.

[25] Although the study of the Ahmadiyya in Africa remains to be written, see Humphrey Fisher, *The Ahmadiyya: A study in contemporary Islam on the West African coast* (Oxford University Press for the Nigerian Institute of Social and Economic Research, London, 1963).

[26] On 'maximalist' styles of religion, see Bruce Lincoln, *Holy Terrors: Thinking about religion after September 11* (University of Chicago Press, Chicago, 2003).

publicly condemn or malign elders whose views and practices they might not like. Moreover, unlike more radical Muslim (and also some Christian) individuals, groups and organizations, NASFAT does not expect its members to reject or anathematize fellow Muslims who do not share their views.[27] In fact, some of NASFAT's officially stated 'moral imperatives' and 'shared values' include 'being caring, humane and tolerant' towards others. NASFAT members are enjoined to 'protect human dignity, and maintain and uphold the human rights of all persons' and 'respect the diversity of all cultures and religions'.[28] Such ideas about tolerance, human rights and respect for cultural and religious diversity are clearly unlike some of the Pentecostal and Islamic discourse in Nigeria that displays a marked tendency to demonize the religious other as well as African traditional religion and its practitioners.

At the same time, NASFAT's founders have emphasized how they wanted to found an Islamic organization that was non-hierarchical in nature. Today, its leaders and publications note that they want to avoid practices such as 'hero-worship' and 'ostentation', which they claim 'can hinder the attainment of our collective aspirations'.[29] Given Nigeria's reputation – indeed notoriety – for its 'big men' with their great wealth (however amassed), lavish lifestyles and coterie of clients, not to mention rampant and often brazen corruption, it is perhaps not surprising to see members of a new religious organization such as NASFAT rejecting the 'worship' of such persons and their public ostentation, as well as warning of the dangers and temptations of corruption. This eschewing of ostentation (and, by extension, corruption) is not unlike the rejection of materialism associated with Pentecostalism in earlier periods in Nigeria.[30] One might also read it as an overt rejection of the ostentation associated with the so-called gospel of prosperity and public displays of excessive consumption that have recently spread among Pentecostals in Nigeria and elsewhere. As already noted, NASFAT was founded at a time when the Pentecostal presence in the public sphere was increasingly pronounced. Moreover, Pentecostals' extensive use of mass media and their organizational acumen have helped to infuse urban land-

---

[27] This is one reason why it would be not only imprecise but also misleading to call NASFAT 'fundamentalist' as some have. See, for example, Kate Meagher, 'Manufacturing disorder: Liberalization, informal enterprise and economic "ungovernance" in African small firm clusters', *Development and Change*, 38, 3 (2007), pp. 473-503.

[28] These themes are repeated in NASFAT's promotional materials. See also NASFAT's *Code of Conduct* (NASFAT Society, Lagos, 2005).

[29] I have heard NASFAT members and leaders make such statements. The quotations are from the webpage 'About NASFAT', on NASFAT Nigeria's website (http://www.nasfat.org/about.php). See also NASFAT's *Code of Conduct* (NASFAT Society, Lagos, 2005).

[30] See Marshall-Fratani, 'Mediating the global and the local in Nigerian Pentecostalism'.

scapes with their presence.[31] Many young Muslims have been exposed to and, without necessarily 'converting', have participated in the ostentatious activities of Pentecostals that have helped to index their success.

It is noteworthy, however, how NASFAT's stated aversion to ostentation and so-called hero-worship is also directed in part towards existing Islamic religious practices and Muslim religious leaders, some of whom have earned a reputation for ostentation and conspicuous consumption. In launching NASFAT, its founders were consciously seeking to distance their organization from the Sufi orders, which have long had a prominent place in Nigeria and in the southwestern part of the country in particular.[32] In general, Sufi orders are organizations that are premised on a hierarchy along with the notion that certain Muslims – often called saints – are closer or have special access to God and his favour. Ordinary Muslims frequently take the founder of a Sufi order or a branch of such an order, his descendants and/or deputies as potential intermediaries with God or as possessors of special, secret knowledge. Many Muslims treat Sufi leaders with great respect and accord them all sorts of privileges, including considerable material resources. Indeed, this is the case for the Tijaniyya, including the branch of the Tijaniyya in Africa propagated by Ibrahima Niasse (d. 1975), who hailed from Kaolack in Senegal. Ibrahima Niasse's branch of the Tijaniyya – variously called the Tijaniyya Niassène or the Ibrahimiyya – has been the most prominent branch of the Tijaniyya in Nigeria, including southwestern Nigeria, and in Africa more generally for decades. Critics of the Sufi orders and the Tijaniyya in particular frequently condemn those involved in Sufi orders of encouraging 'saint-worship', which they explicitly equate with 'hero-worship'. Such hero-worship is precisely what NASFAT states it would like to avoid in its modern version of Islam.

In contrast to Sufi-informed ideas about religious hierarchy, the presumed need to defer to others higher up in such a hierarchy, and the special training one ostensibly requires from a Sufi master to advance within the hierarchy, NASFAT's founders explicitly talk about the 'equality of all Muslims' or at least the potential equality of all Muslims.[33] This emphasis on the equality of all Muslims would seem to be an attempt to downplay potential differences between Muslims, whether linguistic, ethnic, regional or sectarian. Such differen-

---

[31]   See *Ibid.*; Hackett, 'Radical Christian revivalism in Nigeria and Ghana'.

[32]   See, for example, Abner Cohen's classic study of Hausa migrants in southwestern Nigeria. Abner Cohen, *Custom and Politics in Urban Africa: a study of Hausa migrants in Yoruba towns* (Routledge & Kegan Paul, London, 1969).

[33]   This theme recurs in much of the NASFAT literature and on the NASFAT Nigeria website. It is noteworthy that there is no explicit rejection of Sufism or Sufi orders in NASFAT's literature.

ces have sometimes been key factors in various intra-Muslim debates and conflicts that have played out in the country.[34]

Taken together, the challenge to existing religious hierarchies, the implicit rejection of Sufi orders, the assertion of the equality of all Muslims and the rejection of ostentation, along with its ideas about rights and respect, illustrate how NASFAT as an organization is advocating modernist and reformist views of Islam. Such views have become increasingly popular throughout the Muslim world, including elsewhere in Africa. However as Roman Loimeier has argued, local and regional contexts invariably influence modernist and reformist positions and their development over time.[35] Indeed, the form that such modernism and reformism has taken bears the imprint of the Nigerian context and southwestern Nigeria in particular. In many places in the contemporary world, modernist and reformist Muslims are vehemently opposed to celebrations of the *mawlid*, the birthday of the Prophet Muhammad. Reformists usually argue that such practices are not Islamic. In their way of thinking, they are unlawful innovations that diverge from correct Islamic practice (Arabic: *bid'a*). This is, for example, the perspective of the massive Nigerian reformist Islamic organization, the Society for the Removal of Innovation and Reinstatement of Tradition, better known as Izala, which has been particularly active in northern Nigeria. Interestingly, NASFAT, unlike other organizations such as Izala, is not explicitly opposed to celebrations of the *mawlid*. In fact, like Sufi orders in Nigeria and elsewhere, NASFAT actually organizes gatherings for communal prayer during the *mawlid* where speakers emphasize the Prophet Muhammad and his exemplary life, which, they claim, all Muslims should strive to emulate in their own lives.

Much like the Sufi orders and other modernist and reformist organizations, NASFAT places great emphasis on piety and the correct practice of Islam. In contrast to the Sufi orders, there are no special, secret practices for initiates. NASFAT considers all Muslims as equal and therefore potentially perfectible. Each individual NASFAT member is enjoined to adhere to 'the Holy Qur'an and the sunnah', that is, the traditions of Prophet Muhammad. Although this is stated to be a collective endeavour for the organization's members, in practice it is a form of personal piety that is incumbent upon individual members. Indeed, it takes the form of individual obligations to apply Islam in one's life and by extension to encourage those around one to do the same. Such Islamization

---

[34] This is an area that requires much more research. See, for example, Murray Last, 'Muslims and Christians in Nigeria: An economy of political panic'; Susan O'Brien, 'La charia contestée: Démocratie, débat et diversité; musulmane dans les "États charia" du Nigeria', *Politique africaine*, 106 (2007), pp. 46-68.

[35] Roman Loimeier, 'Patterns and peculiarities of Islamic reform in Africa', *Journal of Religion in Africa*, 33, 3 (2003), pp. 237-262.

'from below' contrasts sharply with efforts to impose Islam from above as, for example, in the so-called *sharia* states in northern Nigeria and other self-styled Islamic states around the world. Although the individual Muslim is a key focus of NASFAT, being a member of the organization is also important, an issue to which we now turn.

Membership and activities

Several commentators, including the NASFAT leadership, readily point out that NASFAT's membership is largely comprised of members of the elite, including well-educated Muslims who are professionals, business leaders, government officials, doctors, lawyers and engineers.[36] This might even be the impression one has if one attends, for example, NASFAT services in Abuja, the federal capital of Nigeria where one can encounter many middle-class professionals, businessmen, civil servants working in government ministries and educators in attendance. However, in other places where I have attended NASFAT meetings, for example in neighbourhoods of Lagos, members and attendees clearly come from a wider array of socio-economic backgrounds.

Today, NASFAT claims more than one million members in Nigeria in more than 180 chapters throughout the country but also abroad in such places as Atlanta, Houston, London, Seville and The Hague.[37] Since NASFAT's founding, dense networks of relations have developed between members of the organization. Although NASFAT has spread rapidly and widely since it was founded in the mid-1990s,[38] it remains very much a Yoruba Muslim organization, arguably even a form of Yoruba Muslim cultural nationalism. It can be found anywhere where there are large concentrations of Yoruba in Nigeria and in the diaspora, and most members seem to be Yoruba. The Yoruba focus of the NASFAT is evident in some of the organization's publications, for example, its official prayer book that contains prayers in Arabic, presented in Latin transliteration alongside Yoruba translations. No African languages other than Yoruba seem to be used in NASFAT's official publications.

In some ways, NASFAT has become a veritable social movement though perhaps not as conventionally understood in social movement theory. Given the secular and Western orientation of most social movements' theorizing, Islamic social movements with their anti-secular and sometimes outright illiberal goals

---

[36] See Ernest Omoarelojie, 'Why NASFAT is growing'.
[37] A list of chapters is available on the NASFAT website (www.nasfat.org).
[38] A splinter group, led by the organization's first chief missioner, broke away from NASFAT and founded Al-Fatih Ul-Quareeb Islamic Society of Nigeria, and another organization emerged in turn from that organization. Such developments are beyond the scope of this chapter.

have been difficult to incorporate into such theory and therefore have usually been ignored. While not espousing explicitly illiberal goals, NASFAT neverthe-less challenges the secular and Western biases of social movement theory with its restrictive understanding of what might constitute a social movement and the goals and objectives of group social action.

It is striking that NASFAT has goals and objectives that are at once modest and yet far-reaching. NASFAT's promotional materials repeatedly stress that the organization intends to be 'pace-setting'. Its stated mission is: 'To develop an enlightened Muslim Society nurtured by a true understanding of Islam for the spiritual upliftment and welfare of mankind'.[39] According to Nigerian ob-servers of NASFAT, the organization appears to have no distinct creed or doc-trine and, in fact, seems to advocate what Dale Eickelman has called a 'generic' Islam of universals – prayer, fasting, charity and so forth.[40] This generic Islam is compatible with modernity and living in a society in which there has been in-credible political, social and economic uncertainty over the past few decades. It almost seems to follow that the organization focuses considerable attention on promoting its code of conduct, ethics and lifestyle. In this way, NASFAT is in keeping with some wider trends in the Muslim world where many Muslims have been increasingly concerned with questions about ethics and piety.[41]

NASFAT is involved in activities that are ostensibly a means to reach the goal of 'an enlightened Muslim society'. These activities include *da'wa* (Ara-bic), that is, the call or invitation to Islam, including instruction in the basics of Islam (prayer, fasting during Ramadan, the paying of alms or tithing, etc.), Islamic educational and Arabic language classes for children and adults, and all-night prayer sessions (which are also associated with Sufi orders and Pentecos-talism). There is nothing particularly unusual about any of these religious activities for the promotion of a generic Islam of assumed universals, not least for a modern Islamic organization or Islamic movement beginning with the Muslim Brotherhood founded in Egypt in the 1920s. Indeed, such religious activities are a good illustration of Islamization 'from below'. It is also not out

---

[39] The quotes are from 'Profile' (n.p., n.d.), a glossy promotional flyer obtained from the NASFAT World Headquarters in Ilupeju, Ikeja in January 2008. On Yoruba conceptions of enlightenment and related ideas, see J.D.Y. Peel, '*Olaju*: A Yoruba concept of development', *The Journal of Development Studies*, 14 (1978), pp. 135-165.

[40] Dale F. Eickelman, 'National identity and religious discourse in contemporary Oman', *International Journal of Islamic and Arabic Studies*, 6, 1 (1989), pp. 1-20.

[41] Cf. Roy, *Globalised Islam*; René Otayek & Benjamin F. Soares, 'Introduction: Islam and Muslim politics in Africa', in Benjamin F. Soares & René Otayek (eds), *Islam and Muslim Politics in Africa* (Palgrave Macmillan, New York, 2007); Benjamin Soares & Filippo Osella, 'Islam, politics, anthropology', *Journal of the Royal An-thropological Institute* (N.S.), 15, S1 (2009), pp. 1-23.

of the ordinary that NASFAT's *da'wa* activities are on the whole specifically geared towards other Muslims. In other words, *da'wa* activities do not appear to target Christians but are undoubtedly aimed at those Muslims who might be interested in Pentecostalism and might even convert from Islam to Christianity. As mentioned earlier, some Yoruba Muslims worry about the exposure of fellow Muslims to Pentecostalism.

In addition to such religious activities with the ultimate goal of 'spiritual up-liftment and [the] welfare of mankind', in NASFAT's way of thinking *da'wa* is also felt to encompass economic empowerment. In fact, one of the organiza-tion's explicitly stated and oft-repeated 'strategic objectives' is 'to promote [the] economic empowerment of our members'.[42] Such economic objectives are somewhat unusual for an Islamic organization, and especially for an Islamic social movement in the Nigerian context. However, it is not unlike the trend towards what some have called 'market Islam' in places such as Indonesia where Muslims are enjoined to discipline themselves in accordance with the demands of the market in neoliberal capitalism.[43] In an official NASFAT pub-lication, 'economic empowerment' is actually listed second – after 'recitation of a prayer book' – in a list of *da'wa* activities. The *da'wa* activities around economic empowerment actually come in the list prior to 'usrah [Arabic: family] classes' where the 'basic fundamental of Islaam [sic] are discussed on a weekly basis'.[44] Commenting on Nigeria's economic problems, NASFAT indi-cated that 'Due to [the] high rate of joblessness among Muslims, our secretariat [NASFAT] took it upon itself to source for employment vacancies from various companies for members and Muslims in general'.[45] It seems that economic empowerment comes prior to and is imperative for spiritual 'upliftment' and general welfare. In this way, NASFAT explicitly links economics with ques-tions of ethics. Despite its reputation for having many well-connected and well-educated members with good, well-paid jobs, the vast majority of NASFAT's current members in Nigeria seem to be, like many Nigerians, facing daunting economic obstacles and high levels of insecurity. However, NASFAT seems to hold out the promise to its members that individual ethical reform and economic empowerment go hand in hand.

---

[42]   'Profile' (n.p., n.d.).

[43]   Cf. Daromir Rudnyckyj, 'Market Islam in Indonesia', *Journal of the Royal Anthro-pological Institute* (N.S.), 15, S1 (2009), pp. 182-200, and Patrick Haenni, *Islam de marché: L'autre révolution conservatrice* (Seuil, Paris, 2005).

[44]   'Profile of Nasrul-lahi-l-Fathi Society' (n.p., n.d.), a four-page document printed on NASFAT letterhead, obtained from the NASFAT World Headquarters in Ilupeju, Ikeja in January 2008.

[45]   *Ibid.*

What makes NASFAT somewhat atypical at least as an Islamic organization in the broader Nigerian context is its active involvement in social welfare and health-related activities. In addition to the free medical services that it provides its members, NASFAT also organizes regular health initiatives – for example, blood-pressure monitoring and diabetes tests – that its members need and want. NASFAT is also known as a venue for people to deal with 'spiritual afflictions', to use the Nigerian language for spiritual insecurity and crises, which might be as much socio-economic as individual. Members are cautioned against resorting to 'magical practices', 'occult knowledge', sorcery and charms. While this is similar to widespread Pentecostal discourse in Nigeria, NASFAT articulates such warnings less vehemently than Pentecostals, for whom these practices are a major preoccupation. Instead of using 'magical practices', members are encouraged to engage in prayer and modern health-seeking behaviour via the services NASFAT provides.[46] It also organizes vocational training for its members, as well as marriage counselling services. Like many other religious organizations in Nigeria, NASFAT is thus involved in realms – such as health, and social and economic welfare – that transcend the narrowly religious.

One feature that certainly distinguishes NASFAT from other Islamic organizations in Nigeria and other Islamic social movements is the active and serious business plan that its leaders and promotional materials frequently highlight. Such plans have evolved over time and the organization has recently started to engage in large-scale income-generating activities. According to Akinbode:

> But the bottom line is that we don't want to be stereotypical by doing things the old fashioned way. We don't want to go cap in hand as we did before for alms. The alms we are collecting could be invested and with the profit we make from it we can do certain other things. That is why we took the option of going into business.[47]

Here, Akinbode is pointing to the insufficiency of relying solely on the compulsory alms (Arabic: *zakat*) that Muslims are supposed to give and the need for active investments that generate profits for reinvestment in the organization. Massive numbers of Nigerian Muslims perform the *hajj* every year, and NASFAT has launched a travel agency, Tafsan (NASFAT spelled backwards), that arranges travel for the pilgrimage. Aside from providing such potentially profitable services that are specifically religious, NASFAT also produces and markets a non-alcoholic malt beverage, Nasmalt, the profits from which are destined for *da'wa*, which includes economic empowerment. In accordance with the ban in Islamic jurisprudence on charging interest on loans, NASFAT had a cooperative bank that was subsequently transformed into a community

---

[46] These references to magic and the occult come from NASFAT's *Code of Conduct* (NASFAT Society, Lagos, 2005).
[47] Ernest Omoarelojie, 'Why NASFAT is growing'.

bank, Tafsan. With more than 150,000 depositors, Tafsan Community Bank offers interest-free loans.[48] There is a potentially large and lucrative market among Muslims in Nigeria for such Islamic banking services. NASFAT has also recently founded its own university, Fountain University, a name that does not clearly index that it is Islamic. The university, just one of many in the burgeoning private educational sphere amid public-sector educational decline, is located in Osogbo in Osun State and has recently received accreditation from the Nigerian government.

Central to all of NASFAT's business plans has been a sophisticated marketing plan that has helped to turn NASFAT into a known brand, recognizable in the crowded religious and media landscapes in southwestern Nigeria. Over the past few years, the branding and extensive marketing that NASFAT has developed has been a key element in its success in gaining public recognition. The branding of NASFAT includes a stylized logo with the NASFAT acronym in black typeface and the Islamic star and crescent motif in green. This appears on nearly everything NASFAT produces, distributes and sells. The NASFAT logo is becoming ubiquitous and is prominently placed on all media associated with the organization, as well as on all of the organization's promotional materials, signboards, posters, newspaper columns, bumper stickers, books, pamphlets, clothing, caps, key chains and handkerchiefs. Although the commercially marketed and profit-seeking venture Nasmalt beverage, Tafsan Tours & Travels and Fountain University do not feature the NASFAT logo, they often appear alongside the NASFAT logo in NASFAT promotional materials. The branding of NASFAT seems to be so important – and potentially profitable – that improper use of the brand and logo is clearly spelled out in NASFAT's 2005 *Code of Conduct*.

To accommodate the busy work schedules of most Nigerian Muslims and to compete with or offer an alternative to church services, NASFAT holds weekly meetings on Sundays. This is of course quite unusual for a Muslim group since most Muslims gather for communal prayers at midday on Fridays. Although there are other Muslim organizations in Nigeria (e.g. Al-Usrah based in Port Harcourt) that also hold Sunday-morning services, NASFAT seems to be the largest Muslim organization to do so. Like their Christian neighbours, NASFAT members also meet on Sunday mornings. The children learn the Qur'an while the adults listen to sermons and recite praise of the Prophet Muhammad, with their Sunday worship culminating in a communal prayer (*salat*). The weekly meetings also include prayer requests and testimonials, which are not ordinarily associated with Muslim religious activities and public worship in particular. After the communal prayer, people return home for Sunday lunch. NASFAT

---

[48] ' Profile of Nasrul-lahi-l-Fathi Society' (n.p., n.d.).

members are enjoined to wear white garments at the weekly services, something reminiscent of the *hajj* where people are required to wear white, showing that all Muslims are equal. However their white clothing looks similar to the 'white garment' worn by members of some African independent churches in Nigeria, and many Nigerians readily point this out. Those attending NASFAT services dressed all in white are, nevertheless, clearly distinct from many Nigerian Christians (men and women) who take great care to dress up in their finest clothes for church services at mainline Protestant, Pentecostal and Roman Catholic churches.

It is perhaps NASFAT's decision to hold its largest weekly gatherings on Sundays that has invited so much attention from non-members. As I noted earlier, many Muslims in Nigeria question Yoruba Muslims' ways of being Muslim. In fact, some non-Yoruba Nigeria Muslims look down on NASFAT, and its members are aware of this. The following remarks from a northern Nigerian Muslim intellectual are fairly typical. He told me that NASFAT is 'not very orthodox'. He claimed that NASFAT is essentially a Muslim Yoruba 'response to Christianity', whose members dress all in white, meet on Sundays and behave like Christians. In his view, NASFAT was too anchored in the Yoruba context and too mimetic of Christianity to be able to create and sustain universal appeal. In his view, NASFAT was destined to remain an exclusively Yoruba Muslim movement. Indeed, I have heard many Nigerians readily state that NASFAT is largely a Yoruba Muslim phenomenon and possibly even an atavistic form of 'Islamic Pentecostalism'.

Conclusion

NASFAT cannot be reduced to a 'response' to Christianity among the Yoruba or to trends in Pentecostalism. Its rise and rapid spread can only be understood within the recent social, political and economic context of Nigeria and the history of Yorubaland in particular. As I have shown, there is a very long tradition of Muslim youth founding new modern Islamic organizations in which they seek to distance themselves from their elders and partake in modernity and the opportunities it affords. Founded at a particular historical moment, NASFAT brought together Yoruba Muslims who sought to distinguish themselves from various others. These include fellow Yoruba who are Christians in all their denominational diversity but especially Pentecostals, other Muslims, Yoruba and non-Yoruba, including those who have called loudly for the implementation of *sharia*, and, last but not least, the ostentatious, that is, those social actors who are ubiquitous in contemporary Nigeria. Cognizant of the challenging circumstances most Nigerians face, NASFAT's leadership has devoted considerable attention to promoting ideas of unity, tolerance of one's fellow Muslims and non-Muslims, the provision of services the state has been unable or unwilling to provide, and an active engagement in business ventures with a view to facing the difficult economic conditions in the country, especially the chronic un- and underemployment of Nigeria's thwarted middle classes. NASFAT has been able to mobilize many people, combining individual attempts to reform the self ethically and advance economically. This particular case study illustrates how a new Islamic movement has been able to successfully organize and mobilize many Nigerian Muslims and seems to be helping them manage some of the serious social and economic challenges they face without necessarily leading to the kind of headline-grabbing social action that we have come to expect as evidence of a social movement and effective collective action. Given the paucity of interest on the part of social movement theorists in Islam, Muslim youth and Africa for that matter, such a case study of a new Islamic organization in Nigeria has much to teach these theorists about social movements in which religion is a key factor in social mobilization and action. At the same time, scholars of Islam and contemporary Muslim societies should accept the challenge to more actively engage with social movement theory from which they also stand to benefit, not least in the important endeavour of comparative reflection and theorizing.

10

The United Democratic Front's legacy in South Africa: Mission accomplished or vision betrayed?

Ineke van Kessel

The United Democratic Front, formed in South Africa in 1983 to coordinate protest against a new constitution that co-opted Coloureds and Indians but excluded Africans from political representation, has been lauded as a model of a successful social movement. The UDF served as an umbrella forum for hundreds of organisations, including student movements, youth, women, churches, trade unions as well as community based organisations. While the affiliates pursued their own agenda, the UDF infused these struggles with a broader meaning. The UDF's vision of a new society was not limited to 'one man, one vote' and legal equality: it aspired to an egalitarian, non-racial society in which participation would be more important than the political pluralism of liberal democracy.

South Africa's post-apartheid constitution has been praised worldwide as a state-of-the-art model of liberal democracy, but it is quite remote from the grassroots democracy envisaged in the 1980s. Inequality has increased post-1994, in spite of considerable accomplishments in sectors such as infrastructure, housing, water and electricity and social welfare. Did the leaders of the UDF and the ANC betray the goals of the liberation struggle when they joined the comfortable life of the middle class and the business elite? Or did South Africa realistically have no other options available amidst the triumphant neo-liberalism of a rapidly globalizing world? This chapter explores the legacy of the UDF: how do former activists make sense of present-day South African society?

Introduction

The United Democratic Front, formed in South Africa in 1983 to coordinate protest against a new constitution that co-opted Coloureds and Indians but excluded Africans from political representation, was the most inclusive social movement in South African history. The UDF served as an umbrella forum for hundreds of organizations involving youth, women, churches and trade unions, community-based organizations and student movements. These organizations each pursued their own agenda, ranging from free text books in schools to liberation theology and campaigns for lower rents and safer streets, but affiliation with the UDF infused these issues with a broader meaning. While tackling bread-and-butter matters, millions of South Africans felt themselves part of the liberation movement against apartheid. The UDF's vision of a just society was not limited to 'one man, one vote' and legal equality but aspired to a non-racial, egalitarian society in which participation and communalism would be the key values rather than the political pluralism and free-market principles of liberal democracy.

The UDF leadership emphasized that the Front was not a substitute for the banned liberation movements but it would hold the fort until the African National Congress could resume its rightful position. The ANC leadership in exile had given its blessing to the formation of the UDF as a broad front to coordinate the anti-apartheid struggle inside South Africa, while the ANC continued its underground activities as well as the armed struggle. However during the 1980s, the UDF developed its own distinct political culture. Its major goals were shared by all affiliates but modes of expression and political action varied considerably between affiliates as well as between the different geographical regions.

The ban on the African National Congress was lifted in 1990 and the UDF was disbanded in the following year. Its activists joined the scramble for positions within the ANC and subsequently in the government of the post-apartheid South Africa, at national, provincial and local level. While their primary goal – the abolition of apartheid – has been accomplished, post-apartheid South Africa is a far cry from the erstwhile ideal of an egalitarian non-racial society. The 1996 constitution has been praised worldwide as a state-of-the-art model of liberal democracy, but it is quite remote from the egalitarian grassroots democracy envisaged in the 1980s. Inequality has increased since 1994 in spite of considerable accomplishments in areas such as infrastructure, housing, water, electricity and social welfare.

Did the leaders of the UDF and the ANC betray the goals of the liberation struggle when they joined the comfortable life of the middle classes and the business elite? Or did South Africa realistically have no other options available amid the triumphant neo-liberalism of a rapidly globalizing world? This chapter explores the UDF's legacy and considers how former activists are making sense of present-day South African society. There is a burgeoning academic and popular literature on the subject ranging from political economy perspectives to cultural studies. The case for 'betrayal' is argued by Patrick Bond, John Saul and many others,[1] while authors like John and Jean Comaroff and Steven Robins take a different perspective and focus on the upsurge of identity politics in post-apartheid South Africa.[2]

I have opted here to focus on the perspectives and interpretations formulated by former UDF activists. The chapter is based on a research project in which I am revisiting the people and places that feature in my book on the United Democratic Front.[3] Interviews for the book were conducted in 1990-1991 with the national leadership of the UDF in Johannesburg and with local activists in three case studies in the Western Cape, Sekhukhuneland (then part of the Lebowa Bantustan and now a rural area in Limpopo Province) and Kagiso and Munsieville, twin African townships to the west of Johannesburg. The interviews in the follow-up project were conducted in the same locations between 2006 and 2008.

Mission accomplished or vision betrayed?

The 25th anniversary of the founding of the UDF on 20 August 2008 provided an excellent opportunity to gauge a range of opinions on the Front's legacy. Founding members profoundly disagreed on the crucial question about whether the UDF's mission had been accomplished or whether the ANC-in-government has betrayed their vision of a just society. Significantly, the commemorations were not only used to express nostalgia but also to voice a widely felt need for a new type of social movement, in the tradition of the UDF, to tackle current

---

[1]   John S. Saul, *The Next Liberation struggle: Capitalism, Socialism and Democracy in: Southern Africa* (University of KwaZulu-Natal Press, Scotsville, 2005); John S. Saul, 'The Strange Death of Liberated Southern Africa', paper presented at a seminar at the University of KwaZulu/Natal, 3 April 2007; Patrick Bond, *Elite Transition: From apartheid to neoliberalism in South Africa* (Pluto, London, 2000).

[2]   Steven L. Robins (ed.), *Limits to Liberation after Apartheid: Citizenship, Governance and Culture* (James Currey, Oxford, 2005); John Comaroff & Jean Comaroff, 'Reflections on liberalism, policulturalism & ID-ology: Citizenship & difference in South Africa', in Robins (ed.), pp. 33-56; Jean & John Comaroff, 'The struggle between the constitution and "things African"', in *The Wiser Review*, July 2004.

[3]   Ineke van Kessel, *'Beyond our Wildest Dreams': The United Democratic Front and the Transformation of South Africa* (University Press of Virginia, Charlottesville/ London, 2000).

concerns such as HIV/AIDS, xenophobia, poverty, housing, public safety, health care and the crisis in education.

On the day of the anniversary, the Rocklands Civic Centre in Mitchells Plain, a largely Coloured working-class town near Cape Town, filled with a nostalgic crowd that came to pay tribute to the ideals and values of the UDF. It was at exactly this place that some 12,000 people had gathered 25 years earlier for the UDF's launch under the slogan 'Apartheid divides, UDF unites'. The launch of the UDF was the largest political gathering since the 1950s. In the course of the 1980s the UDF would develop into a very inclusive movement accommodating a wide range of activists and activities from prayer services, militant marches, strikes and boycotts to attempts at an insurrectionary takeover of power.

Those who gathered at Rocklands in 1983 saw themselves as part of the liberation movement that would free South Africa from apartheid. By contrast, the 2008 gathering was organized by the provincial government of the Western Cape, which invited eminent speakers such as the Minister of Finance Trevor Manuel who had been prominent in the UDF leadership in the 1980s. Among the notable absentees was Dr Allan Boesak, a patron of the UDF, and in the 1980s one of its most eloquent spokesmen. In newspaper interviews, Boesak explained why he boycotted the anniversary celebrations:

> The celebrations (…) are not so much about the achievements of the UDF, since those achievements have all but disappeared from our political life, but more about campaigning for the next elections. I am uncomfortable with the thought that the same political party which moved with such unseemly haste to disband the UDF soon after the return of the exiles now celebrates the UDF as if it still existed.[4]

However another UDF founding member Minister of Defence Mosiuoa 'Terror' Lekota retorted that the UDF had achieved all of its goals. The UDF was launched to oppose the 1983 constitution and 'to appeal for the release of the prisoners, the return of the exiles and to start negotiations. There was nothing else that the UDF was supposed to achieve.'[5]

Allan Boesak chose his own platform to lambaste the ANC for its betrayal of the UDF's legacy. In his keynote address at the annual Ashley Kriel Memorial Youth Lecture at the University of the Western Cape, Boesak received rousing applause when he described South Africa's political situation as a 'real and ticking time bomb' fuelled by the anger and frustration of those who had become disillusioned by unfulfilled promises and the greed of 'drunk with power' politicians. He accused leading members of South Africa's new elite of aban-

---

[4]   *Cape Argus*, 21 August 2008.
[5]   *Die Burger*, 22 August 2008.

doning non-racialism 'for selfish politics and lust for power'.[6] A crowd of over 2,000 largely middle-aged former activists chanted the familiar 'Boesak, Boesak' when the cleric entered the hall. Allan Boesak has a longstanding love-hate relationship with the ANC that dates from his conviction on charges of fraud and theft. He served one year of his six-year sentence and was released on parole in May 2001. Boesak then returned to a career in the church. Questions and comments after his speech made it clear that there was considerable pressure on Boesak to take up a leadership position once again.[7] In a series of recent speeches and interviews, he spoke of a sense of alienation among Coloured people. While the UDF accommodated cultural diversity, thus providing a political home for African, Coloured, Indian and White South Africans, the ANC today is widely perceived as being a bastion of a more exclusive brand of African nationalism.

In his keynote speech at the official anniversary celebrations in Mitchells' Plain, Trevor Manuel also struck a critical note while painting a rather romantic picture of comradely solidarity and unity of purpose during the days of struggle in the 1980s. Manuel referred to the commitment, sacrifice and comradeship of the 1980s and regretted the demobilization of popular organizations in the 1990s. By relying excessively on the institutions of the state to deliver development, community organizations had 'sat back and allowed ourselves to be paralysed'. He criticized the lack of commitment in crucial sectors of the public service, notably education and health, and noted that 'the bulk of what we started remains incomplete'. Reminding his audience that revolutions are an ongoing process, he warned that 'revolutionary flames are extinguished by self-serving individuals and greed. We must know this and stop the hatred, bullying and personal enrichment.'

Manuel's speech was delivered during an episode of unprecedented factional quarrelling and backstabbing within the ANC, which in the following month (September 2008) would result in the ousting of President Thabo Mbeki and the ascent to power of Jacob Zuma's faction. It is perhaps against this background that his overly romantic notions of comradeship in the UDF can be explained:

> We were armed with an unbreakable trust in each other – the trust had a name – 'comradeship'. It allowed us to believe in each other and know that our backs would always be covered by those whom we called 'comrade'. Beyond that fundamental trust in each other, we were armed with self-belief – the path we were pursuing had never been walked.

---

[6] *Ibid.*
[7] Ryland Fisher, 'The rehabilitation of Allan Boesak' (http://www.thoughtleader.co.za/rylandfisher, July 7, 2008).

The phrase lauding the 'unbreakable trust' had other former UDF Western Cape activists sniggering. Although there is considerable nostalgia for the UDF days, activists acutely remember the factionalism and rivalry. Unlike Boesak, Manuel did not blame the ANC for disbanding the UDF but noted that UDF organizations had 'erred in giving up real power' after the exhilarating times of South Africa's first democratic elections in 1994.

> Organizations began to whither away. Our means, the street committees and the civics were replaced with a false belief that elected councils were sufficient, and that the legislation calling for participatory democracy would be adequate. (...) We must now realise that the dream of a developmental state cannot ever be attained merely by parliament – we need public servants as the agents for transformation. (...) Laws alone are insufficient. We must get the institutions of the people to work. We must change the relationship between the state and public servants from one shaped by industrial relations to one where the measure is transformation for development.

In conclusion, Manuel stressed that the power won through the ballot box 'needs to be supplemented by the means of organized communities acting with government. Our power will mean nothing if we fail to reignite the self-belief in our people.'[8]

Trevor Manuel and Johnny Issel were the two delegates from the Western Cape who travelled to Johannesburg in July 1983 to discuss the launch of the UDF with activists from Johannesburg and Durban. The factionalism in the UDF Western Cape is sometimes linked with their names: Isselites versus Trevorites. Tensions focused on the display of ANC symbols at public gatherings and later on recruitment in the armed struggle.[9] Issel insisted on the public display of ANC symbols, while Manuel wanted to proceed more cautiously. Similar disagreements occurred elsewhere about whether priority should be given to building strong grassroots organizations or flag waving and popularizing the ANC. If the UDF openly identified with the ANC, it ran the risk of being banned before it properly took off. Issel is clear about his priorities: 'I was building the ANC: nothing would stand in my way. I used whatever was available. (...) I was a commander.'[10]

While Trevor Manuel embarked on a highly successful career, serving in every cabinet after 1994, Johnny Issel could not find a place for himself in post-apartheid society. Issel, who describes himself as a professional activist, had expected the anti-apartheid struggle to culminate in an insurrection and not in

---

[8]   Trevor Manuel, 'Address to the 25th anniversary of the UDF', Rocklands Civic Centre, Mitchells Plain, 20 August 2008; *Cape Times*, 21 August 2008; *Cape Argus*, 21 August 2008.

[9]   Interview with Johnny Issel, 2003 (http://www.sahistory.org.za/pages/library-resources/interviews/2003_interview_jonny_issel.htm)

[10] Interview with Johnny Issel, 10 September 2008, Cape Town.

liberal democracy. He served for a while in the provincial legislature of the Western Cape but could not cope with party discipline. Subsequently he went into business but left South Africa in 2004 to spend a few years in Europe. 'I did not succeed in politics and neither in business. That challenged me to take stock of myself.' After suffering a couple of strokes and other health problems in London in 2006, he embarked on a 'spiritual journey that has given me calmness'.

At the time of my interview in Cape Town (September 2008), Johnny Issel, once a fiery activist steeped in Marx and Lenin, was into Buddhism. He had recovered sufficiently to be able to walk and suggested that I take him to Kirstenbosch Botanical Garden for the interview. Walking in these spectacularly beautiful gardens, we stopped to look at a framed photograph of Nelson Mandela. Stooping over the picture, Issel murmured: 'Is that not a pity that a man like Mandela is associated with the ANC?' I could not help laughing, and remarked that Mandela's entire life had been devoted to the ANC. He replied that he was not joking: 'It is a pity, what would Mandela think about the ANC today?' Johnny Issel, a lifelong professional activist, is no longer a member of the ANC and did not attend the UDF's 25th anniversary celebrations in Mitchells Plain: 'I was not invited, while I single-handedly organized the launch of the UDF'. He now believes that the UDF should have continued after 1990 as it was a 'wonderfully broad movement' and that the ANC forced the UDF to disband because the ANC leadership, on their return from exile, saw the internal mass movement as a threat.[11]

For a cabinet minister, Trevor Manuel was, and still is, unusually frank in acknowledging the shortcomings of the ANC-in-government and in criticizing the complacency, self-interest, corruption, greed and self-enrichment that have characterized much of the public sector and significant sections of the ANC leadership since 1994. A common element in Manuel and Boesak's speeches is the need for a reinvigoration of civil society. While some dream of a renewed United Democratic Front, many more former activists are discussing the need for new social movements that are not adversarial to the ANC government but generate sufficient popular pressure to keep the government on track while encouraging more initiatives from below.

The need for a new UDF type of social movement was discussed in more detail at yet another commemorative event. Speaking at Belgravia High School in Athlone, another largely Coloured suburb of Cape Town, Andrew Boraine, treasurer of the UDF Western Cape from 1983 to 1985, member of the UDF National Executive and underground ANC activist in the late 1980s, stressed the need for a new United Front. The UDF stood for inclusive politics, non-

---

[11]   *Ibid.*

racialism and alliances with all kinds of different partners who could further the anti-apartheid cause.

> Today, the situation is different. We have a more narrow, exclusive, racially-based politics. There is extreme intolerance for dissenting views. There is an acute hostility in the ANC towards civil society. The government is not focused on building non-racialism. There is a widespread sense of alienation, of exclusion from the political process. We are now living through the disaster of factional politics. People are chosen because they belong to the right camp, not on the basis of any merit. Nothing can be more dangerous for South Africa's future. The sense of accountability that characterized the UDF gave way to an attitude of arrogance towards communities. Honest criticism is deflected.

Summing up the conclusion of his speech, Boraine recalled how he stressed the need for a new United Front to unite forces against poverty, and for jobs and skills. He believed that the disbanding of the UDF in 1991 had been inevitable. In other parts of South Africa, the UDF had dissolved spontaneously as activists flocked to the ANC. It was only in the Western Cape that its disbanding had been contentious but maintaining the UDF Western Cape would have meant in practice that it would have become a Coloured wing of the ANC, which would have been irreconcilable with its principle of non-racialism.

> The problem was that civil society was disbanded. The ANC saw no need for an autonomous civil society, because it assumed that 'the ANC was the people', but that was true for only a short while.

In retrospect, Andrew Boraine believes that UDF activists made a fundamental mistake when they allowed the ANC to impose its hegemonic project and bring all organizations into line with the ANC.

> The internal movement gave in too easily to the exiles returning. And who were these people? Essop Pahad was for ten years the editor of the *Marxist Review* in Prague. We used to read it religiously, but it was rubbish of course. (…) But we were so much in awe of the ANC leadership that we did not question any of it.[12]

Boraine was not calling for a resurrection of the UDF but for new networks and a more inclusive and cooperative mentality. However, calls for a new type of United Front reverberated even after the commemorations were over. After the dramatic ousting of Thabo Mbeki from the presidency, rumours about initiatives to launch a new party or movement in the tradition of the UDF kept appearing in the media.[13] In October, a new party was indeed formed under the name Congress of the People (COPE), after the historic meeting in Kliptown where the Freedom Charter was adopted in 1955. Terror Lekota, UDF publicity secretary in the 1980s and Minister of Defence in Mbeki's cabinet, became the

---

[12]   Interview with Andrew Boraine, 15 September 2008, Cape Town.
[13]   *Mail & Guardian*, 26 Sept-2 Oct. 2008, p. 2.

chairman, while Allen Boesak agreed to campaign for COPE in the Western Cape. However, COPE does not seem to want to cast itself as the UDF's successor.

As is evident from the above, core UDF activists hold different perspectives about what constitutes the legacy of the UDF. While Johnny Issel was aiming for insurrection and a socialist revolution, Trevor Manuel and Andrew Boraine speak of the need to safeguard liberal democracy. Moreover, former UDF activists in the Western Cape are fairly unique in their nostalgia for the 1980s. The UDF Western Cape was dominated by Coloured and White activists, while Africans were not very prominent. In most other regions, the African activists in the UDF saw little or no distinction between the UDF and the ANC. For them, the UDF was founded as a temporary front for the banned ANC. Although I found widespread discontent about unfulfilled promises, there was little disagreement about the ANC's hegemonic project.

The different perspectives on the nature of the UDF can, in part, be explained by the demographics of the Western Cape. As a consequence of the Coloured Labour Preference policies, Africans formed a small minority in the Western Cape. In terms of apartheid policies, the Western Cape was to become an unofficial homeland for Coloured people: in 1980, Coloureds made up 54% of the population of the Western Cape, while Whites constituted 32%. The Coloured working class remained politically aloof, while Coloured intellectuals were more inclined towards Trotskyite organizations such as the Unity Movement. The ANC did have a presence in the African townships but the African population of the Western Cape formed a small minority of largely unskilled labour for a long time.

With the massive influx of Africans from the impoverished Eastern Cape, the Western Cape experienced a rapid Africanization, a process that continued at an accelerated pace in the 1990s and beyond. Stark changes in the demographic balance have no doubt contributed to a sense of alienation among Coloured people. This has been exacerbated by the ANC's affirmative action policies, which demand that the demographic profile be reflected in the employment profile in both the public and the private sector. In practice, this means that Coloured jobseekers in the Western Cape are now often bypassed in favour of African applicants.

The sense of frustration and alienation expressed by former UDF activists in the Western Cape has to be put into a wider perspective. The Western Cape is not representative of South Africa as a whole. Trevor Manuel, Allan Boesak and Johnny Issel were all classified as 'Coloureds' in apartheid terminology, while Andrew Boraine was a white student leader. My interviews with former UDF activists from Cape Town's African townships did not reveal similar levels of dissatisfaction. Although discontent is rife in other parts of South

Africa too, this is expressed in different ways. Before analyzing the different perspectives of the UDF's legacy in more detail, I will briefly sketch its history and adhere to a somewhat chronological order while specifically addressing the themes outlined in the introduction: (i) the UDF's historical origins; (ii) the way it mobilized support and its support base; (iii) how the Front framed its message; (iv) the way the UDF related to other social movements; and finally (v) why it ceased to exist.

What was the UDF?

Origins

After the banning of the African National Congress and the Pan Africanist Congress in 1960, the ANC leadership regrouped in exile. The armed struggle and campaigns to isolate apartheid South Africa through boycotts and sanctions dominated its strategy for the first two decades of its existence. In the 1980s however, the leadership in exile took the strategic decision to rebuild mass-based organizations inside the country. The UDF grew out of locally based initiatives but consultations were held with the leadership in exile as well as with the ANC underground.

During the 1970s, collective protest in South Africa was undertaken by two distinct social categories: black workers and black students. Their protest actions remained isolated phenomena rather than part of a coordinated rebellion. The 1980s however witnessed the growth of a broad-based social movement that mounted a sustained challenge to the apartheid state. From 1979 onwards, student activists actively sought to link up with community and workers' protests. School boycotts, rent and bus boycotts and the campaign against the imposed 'independence' of the Ciskei Bantustan all contributed to a new sense of optimism about the potential for mass mobilization and organization. Protest politics was shifting from uncompromising non-collaborationism to a more pragmatic result-oriented approach. By taking up the bread-and-butter issues that occupied people's minds at the local community level, activists succeeded in broadening popular organizations and involving a wide range of residents who would otherwise have been reluctant to become involved in overtly confrontational politics.

In the Western Cape, 1979 was a legendary turning point in popular politics. During a strike at a pasta factory, African and Coloured workers joined forces and linked up with community activists to organize a seven-month nationwide consumer boycott of the company's products. Students were drawn into the workers' struggle and workers became more politicized. This pattern of action, which brought victory for the unions, became a model for subsequent action, although another strike in 1980 in the meat industry ended in defeat for the unions. Elsewhere in South Africa, civic organizations began to emerge around 1980. 'Civics', as they came to be known, were local neighbourhood associations that took up residents' concerns about rents, electricity, transport, safety on the streets and education.

Around 1980 only the churches, the emerging independent trade unions and the (racially segregated) student organizations had a nationwide following. Student organizations proved important as recruiting and training grounds for activists. The Congress of South African Students (COSAS), formed in 1979, initially aimed to draw high-school students into community issues but after 1983 focused solely on school and student matters and limited its membership to high-school students. The now-excluded older and more experienced former students were instrumental in forming youth congresses, which took off in mid-1983 with the youth playing a crucial role in the rebellion of the 1980s.

From 1981-1982, many of these organizations became involved in discussions on the formation of a United Front to counter government plans for limited constitutional reforms. However, problems arose during these discussions regarding non-racial organizations that included white members, such as the South African Council of Churches (SACC) and the recently formed Federation of South African Trade Unions (FOSATU). The role of the white student organization NUSAS, a UDF affiliate, was also contentious.

Ultimately, it was a call by Allan Boesak in early 1983 that would be remembered as the impetus to form the United Democratic Front. The UDF was set up as an *ad hoc* alliance with the limited goal of countering the constitutional proposals of the governing National Party. The new constitution envisaged a tricameral parliament that would incorporate Indians and Coloureds in separate chambers, while whites would retain ultimate control. Africans would remain excluded from national politics: their separate ethnic 'national destinies' were to be pursued in the context of the Bantustans. As the government had come to accept the presence of Africans in urban areas as a permanent feature of a modern, industrialized state, urban Africans were to be given a very limited form of self-rule by elected town councils. These Black Local Authorities were responsible for raising their own revenue and the resulting rises in rents and service charges proved instrumental in igniting the township revolts of the mid 1980s.

FOSATU decided against affiliation with the UDF, wanting to maintain the autonomy of workers' organizations and to be able to take part in wider popular struggles on its own terms. The United Front formula posed the risk of workers being swamped by populist politics, as had happened to ANC-aligned unions in the 1950s. The smaller Council of Unions of South Africa (CUSA) affiliated to both the UDF and the Black Consciousness-oriented National Forum but ceased active participation in 1985, giving priority to merger negotiations with

FOSATU. Most community unions, which were organized along community rather than industry-sector lines, did however join the UDF.

The national launch of the UDF on 20 August 1983 in Mitchells Plain was attended by about a thousand delegates, representing some 575 community organizations, trade unions, sporting bodies and women's and youth organizations. As more organizations joined, UDF spokespersons measured the strength of the Front in a convenient shorthand: 600 organizations representing 2 million people. However, of the 575 organizations represented at the launch, 235 were branches of the Western Cape Inter Church Youth, a recently founded body of which not much was heard in subsequent years. The formula was eminently suitable for public-relations purposes and the UDF would stick in popular memory as a front representing some 600 organizations and 2 million people.

The UDF's first test of strength was the campaign for a boycott of the tricameral elections and the municipal elections for the Black Local Authorities. The boycotts were a resounding success. The state's efforts to co-opt Coloureds and Indians and a small elite of urban Africans had evidently failed. Widespread school boycotts accompanied the campaigns. Running parallel to the election boycotts and school protests, a third source of unrest was locally based community protest against increases in bus fares and rents. A series of township revolts began on 3 September 1984 with a two-day stay-away from work in the townships of the Vaal Triangle, a heavily industrialized region south of Johannesburg, in protest against rent increases. The Vaal uprising left 26 people dead and more than 300 injured. By the end of the 1980s the number of 'victims of the unrest' had exceeded 5,000.

These disparate strands of protest came together in a major stay-away from school and work in the Pretoria-Witwatersrand-Vereeniging area on 5 and 6 November 1984. Significantly, FOSATU and CUSA participated in an overtly political protest action for the first time. COSAS activists were instrumental in the preparations. This joint effort by students and workers provided the basis for optimistic strategizing about the emerging student-worker alliance. By the end of 1984 it was clear that South Africa had entered a phase of unrest that would be more serious than the Soweto Uprising of 1976.

After the successful boycott campaigns of the tricameral elections, the UDF transformed itself from being an *ad hoc* alliance into a more permanent movement that addressed a broad range of issues. It took the Front about six months to reorientate itself and develop a new agenda. Meanwhile, dozens of townships were the scene of escalating and sometimes violent protests against the Black Local Authorities and their attempts to raise revenue to cover their administrative costs. Local protest was mostly led by civic associations. Although most – but by no means all – civics were affiliated to the UDF, the Front had little control over local protest actions. From 1985 onwards however, the UDF leadership began to realize more clearly the mobilizing potential of bread-and-butter issues. Civics that dealt with everyday concerns could attract large numbers of not strongly politicized township residents. But political guidance was needed to infuse local struggles with a broader meaning. Through the UDF, disparate struggles regarding housing, transport, education and the cost of living could be seen as part of the fight against both apartheid and capitalism.

In July 1985, the funerals of three assassinated civic leaders from the small town of Cradock in the Eastern Cape drew a crowd of around 40,000 amid a massive display of ANC and SACP (South African Communist Party) flags. On 21 July 1985, the government declared a partial state of emergency and thousands of people were detained. In August, COSAS became the first UDF affiliate to be declared an unlawful organization. Two major treason trials ensured that a substantial part of the UDF leadership was taken out of circulation.

During the first two years, the Front was largely reactive but after 1985 the UDF no longer limited itself to reacting to and protesting against government policy. In numerous places, activists started undertaking a far more ambitious project: the construction of a new, egalitarian and morally just society. Civics were transformed into 'organs of people power'.

The first State of Emergency (July 1985 - March 1986) did not crush the rebellion but instead inspired new tactics. Consumer boycotts were introduced as a new political weapon, and with mass gatherings prohibited, street committees proliferated. Boycotts were hailed as an essentially peaceful Gandhian tactic of passive resistance but the enforcement of boycotts frequently entailed the use of physical force and harsh punishments. Successful boycott campaigns conducted by broad-based township organizations relying on participatory structures of decision-making served to reinforce the political and moral authority of the civics and other movements that stood for an alternative social order. Conversely, coercion, intimidation and abuse by undisciplined youth weakened support for boycotts. In several places, white-owned businesses proved ready to negotiate but local victories were necessarily limited without back-up from central or local government.

With school boycotts becoming a chronic rather than intermittent means of protest, the Soweto Parents' Crisis Committee was formed in September 1985 with the aim of encouraging high-school students back into school. Eventually, in December 1985, the ANC gave its blessing to the parents' initiative, which later widened into a nationwide campaign under the banner of the National Education Crisis Committee (NECC). The NECC supported the students' demands but transformed the slogan 'No Education before Liberation' into 'People's Education for People's Power'. Its efforts met with only partial success.

Boycotts gave ordinary people a sense of power. Many activists believed that a phase of 'dual power' had arrived and that a revolutionary takeover was imminent. But the pattern of resistance was uneven and coordination was lacking. It was not the UDF itself but local affiliates and people loosely associated with the UDF that wielded power in the townships. Officially, the UDF stuck to non-violent methods but the leadership was reluctant to condemn excesses such as the 'necklacing' (a car tyre doused with petrol) of suspected informers. On the one hand it feared alienating militant youth but on the other the leadership doubted its own capacity to exercise control over its unruly followers. When ANC President Oliver Tambo finally condemned necklace executions in 1986, his pronouncement had no visible impact inside South Africa.

More durable than the fledgling structures of people's power was the workers' power that manifested itself in a new giant federation of trade unions, the Congress of South African Trade Unions (COSATU). On 1 December 1985, over 10,000 people attended the launch of COSATU in Durban. In contrast to its predecessor FOSATU, the leadership of the 33 COSATU unions held that unions ought to be involved in community struggles and the wider political arena.

People's Power
The State of Emergency was lifted in March 1986. With rebellion spreading to remote corners of South Africa, boycotts flaring up intermittently, mounting international solidarity campaigns and increasing signs of nervousness among white businesses, the UDF felt confident that 'the people' would soon be empowered to shape their own destiny. 1986 marks the height of 'People's Power', of the belief that representatives of the people, even 'the people themselves', were marching to take control of 'liberated areas'. Liberated areas were defined in geographical terms and, as with townships, became no-go areas for the police. But the term could equally apply to spheres of life where 'the people' were taking over, such as schools, the community media or organs of popular justice. People's courts signified perhaps the most fundamental challenge to state authority as they exposed the lack of legitimacy of the apartheid state's criminal justice system. In some townships, people's courts were widely appreciated for their role in curbing crime, disciplining unruly youth and solving domestic conflicts. But elsewhere, these courts were resented for their harsh and arbitrary punishments and, if they were run by youth, they lacked legitimacy in the eyes of older residents.

The second State of Emergency, imposed nationwide on 12 June 1986 and lifted only in 1990, virtually amounted to military rule. Dozens of national and regional UDF leaders were detained, along with some 25,000 other South Africans, many under the age of 18. State repression was combined with a shady system of unofficial repression and activists became targets of faceless death squads and vigilantes. In October 1986, the UDF was declared an 'affected organization' and was thus prohibited from receiving overseas funds. Many affiliates and sympathetic organizations (churches, human-rights organizations, etc.) were, however, able to maintain access to foreign funding.

Although the UDF was badly hit, the State of Emergency did not bring township life back to 'normal'. Rent boycotts continued and provided a key rallying point for township activists. Street committees organized youth brigades to prevent the eviction of rent defaulters and where electricity had been cut off, volunteers moved in to reconnect township houses. Rent boycotts acquired their own momentum. Even without its political content, this tactic had obvious advantages as it augmented family income. Consumer and bus boycotts flared up intermittently but township residents began to show signs of exhaustion and a loss of patience with the 'rule of the comrades', young militants who often used heavy-handed and coercive methods. The fate of the UDF seemed sealed when it was effectively banned in February 1988. UDF leaders not in detention went into hiding. Youth organizations adapted to a semi-underground existence, but most civics ceased to function.

This period of despair and forced inactivity had a sobering effect on leading activists. When new political space opened up in 1989, they emerged from detention and hiding with a new realism. No longer intoxicated by views of imminent liberation and insurrectionary bids for power, they set out to rebuild organizations.

In the early months of 1989, the Mass Democratic Movement (MDM) asserted itself on the streets of the big cities. The main components of this flexible alliance were the UDF, COSATU and church leaders. The MDM and the remnants of the Black Consciousness Movement organized the Conference for a Democratic Future in December 1989, which called for a non-racial constituent assembly to draw up a new constitution. This year of transition from semi-legality to a fully legalized status for the ANC, SACP and the PAC was characterized by a new mood of pragmatism and a series of local negotiations prepared the way for talks on the central issue of state power.

Disbanding the UDF
After the lifting of the ban on the ANC in January 1990, the release of Nelson Mandela and his co-accused from prison and the return of the ANC leaders from exile, UDF activists deferred to the leadership of the historic liberation movement. In popular imagination, the ANC leaders in exile and those on Robben Island had acquired the status of larger-than-life heroes. Two sections of the UDF – youth congresses and women's' organizations – merged almost immediately with the ANC Women's League and the ANC Youth League. Within the UDF, three options were discussed: (i) disbanding; (ii) transforming itself into a coordinating structure for civil-society organizations; or (iii) waiting and making a decision later.

The argument for disbanding the UDF was that the Front had served its purpose and the ANC could now resume its rightful place. The UDF's continued existence would only cause duplication and confusion. The second option was to transform the UDF into a coordinating structure for civics, student organizations, religious bodies and those youth and women's organizations that decided against merging with the Women's' League and the Youth League. This position was favoured both by activists, who argued that an umbrella structure was needed to exercise hegemonic control, and by the proponents of an autonomous civil society. The wait-and-see option prevailed in 1990 but in 1991 the UDF decided to disband. Dissolution had become a foregone conclusion, as the UDF's most capable activists had been absorbed into the ANC. Paradoxically, the lifting of the ban on the ANC had a demobilizing effect: many people believed that they could now rely on the ANC to solve their problems. The UDF officially disbanded on 20 August 1991, exactly eight years after it had been launched. A dissenting voice came from Allen Boesak who believed that Coloured people in the Western Cape would be left without a political home as they saw the ANC as an African-dominated movement. The exiles and former prisoners who dominated the ANC Western Cape showed little understanding of local dynamics. His position that the UDF should be dissolved gradually as the need for it disappeared was not shared by other UDF activists.

Mobilizing a mass following: Methods and means
One of the characteristics of the UDF was its adroit use of a broad variety of media. Links with student organizations on campus and different resource centres offered access to facilities for printing, photocopying, printing T-shirts etc. The UDF and its affiliates produced vast numbers of posters, newsletters, community newspapers, ideological treatises, banners and T-shirts, which resulted in a high level of visibility.

The UDF leadership displayed a keen awareness of the importance of public relations. It was able to count on sympathetic coverage in many domestic publiccations and in the international press. Where the ANC had a mixed reception due to its commitment to armed struggle, the UDF gained nearly universal popularity in the world's media.

The use of low-threshold campaigns that focused on people's immediate daily concerns rather than on high-brow politics proved appropriate when organizing large numbers of township residents. In the second half of the 1980s, violent repression by the security forces angered many ordinary people who until then had not been particularly politicized. Feeling under threat from a vindictive police and faceless death squads, township residents developed a strong sense of community.

In the early years, the UDF was largely dependent on local donations but from 1985 foreign funding started flowing, transforming the UDF from a movement that relied on volunteers and spontaneity to a more bureaucratically run organization employing considerable numbers of organizers. Foreign funding paid for some of the members' transport and accommodation costs at national and regional conferences, and for telephone and fax bills. The availability of (overseas) funding was thus crucial to the project of building a nationwide political movement. According to Azhar Cachalia, the UDF's treasurer, 'a lot more than half' of the UDF's funding came from abroad.[14]

Inevitably, control over resources, notably funding, was a source of dispute between UDF regions and UDF Head Office, as well as between and within affiliates. Compared to trade unions or the ANC after the ban on it was lifted, the UDF was run on a very modest budget. In 1989-1990, the UDF had an income of about R.1.7 m, excluding grants for specific expenses such as the Conference for a Democratic Future. Numerous affiliates, like community newspapers, advisory offices and civic organizations, had their own sources of local and/or foreign funding, allowing them a considerable degree of autonomy.

Making sense: Framing the message
The UDF not only coordinated and directed internal resistance to apartheid but also provided a cultural framework that lent a wider meaning to a variety of local struggles. By participating in rent boycotts, stay-aways, boycotts of white-owned businesses and school protests, people not only addressed their immediate concerns but played their own part in the struggle for a new social, political and economic order.

The UDF's vision was for an egalitarian, non-racial society with a strong emphasis on grassroots participation. Participation was more important than pluralism. This vision of a just society also had a strong moral component and religious inspiration and legitimation were characteristics of many activities. UDF followers were not only engaged in a struggle against apartheid and capitalism but also against the forces of evil.

Although its leadership clearly identified with the banned ANC, they initially decided against adopting the Freedom Charter. Advocating the Freedom Charter would probably have invited state repression and limited the Front's possibilities of expanding beyond the known Charterist organizations. Only in August 1987 after COSATU had adopted the Freedom Charter did the UDF follow suit. Oliver Tambo's message on 8 January, broadcast on the anniversary of the founding of the ANC, provided a sense of direction to UDF activists who religiously tuned in for the latest guidelines. Affiliates and regions maintained

---

[14]   Interview with Azhar Cachalia, 25 January 1992, Rotterdam.

their own lines of communication with the ANC centres in exile. They all claimed to be toeing the line prescribed by the organization.

Alliances: Inclusion and exclusion

The UDF never had a constitution, only a set of Working Principles that stated that affiliates would retain their organizational autonomy. The UDF's umbrella formula proved eminently suitable for combining a broad range of organizations, from middle-class whites to rural African youth. The Front's formula enabled people to identify with the banned ANC but without exposing themselves to state repression. It allowed for organizational flexibility and accommodated a range of manifestations of protest and rebellion, from prayer services to militant youth actions. The UDF configured visions of an alternative social, political and economic order without imposing a political orthodoxy on its heterodox following.

Although the UDF as a multi-racial, multi-class alliance was undoubtedly the most inclusive movement in South African history, it could not claim to represent all the peoples of South Africa. In terms of race and ethnicity, it was truly inclusive. The main trade unions however opted to remain outside the UDF ambit, even though a fairly good working relationship developed in the second half of the 1980s. Liberal whites were reluctant to fully associate with this increasingly radical social movement but found a common platform on human-rights issues. Big business (which was, by definition, white business) could not be an ally in view of the UDF's anti-capitalist platform. However the Front did attempt, with some success, to lure business away from the apartheid government's disastrous policies.

Some sections of South African society were notably absent from both UDF structures and discussions on organizational strategy. The independent African churches, domestic workers, farm workers, migrant workers and squatters remained on the margins. The UDF's own principles excluded Bantustan-based structures, such as Inkatha. Some of the heirs of the Black Consciousness Movement, notably AZAPO (Azanian People's Organization) formed their own platform in the National Forum, but this never developed into a mass movement.

UDF legacies

From universalism to particularism: What happened to non-racialism?

The struggle against apartheid was framed in terms of universal values. The ANC-in-exile campaigned to have apartheid condemned as a crime against humanity. Nowadays ANC politicians make frequent recourse to the particularist values of Africanist ideologies, advocating 'African solutions for African problems' or invoking 'African traditions'. In the case of Zimbabwe, the call for 'African solutions' – meant to delegitimize policy interventions from the West – often comes from the very same politicians who once campaigned for sanctions and boycotts of apartheid South Africa.

A recent example is a statement by Cassel Mathale, the ANC's candidate for the Limpopo premiership. As the *Mail & Guardian* reported, Mathale is a director of at least ten companies in the mining, construction, farming and hospitality sectors, some of which have benefited from lucrative government contracts in Limpopo. 'This thing of conflict of interest is just a fabrication', Mathale said. 'As Africans we must not allow that. We should allow everyone to go into government. (...) The most important thing for us [as politicians] is to disclose our business interests to the public.'[15] In the 1980s, activists claimed their rights as South Africans and as fellow human beings. Now apparently, a prospective premier claims that 'as an African' he cannot be bothered with concerns about conflicts of interest.

African nationalism seems set to become the new hegemonic discourse. It may indeed provide the glue by securing the loyalty of the ANC's main constituency but in the process another cherished principle of the liberation struggle, non-racialism, is increasingly coming under pressure. Numerous Coloured, Indian and White UDF activists have become disillusioned with the exclusive brand of African nationalism that has succeeded Mandela's Rainbow Nation. Although they may be quite content with their careers and current status in society, they are no longer active members of the ANC. The UDF provided them with a political home but their initial enthusiasm for the ANC was dampened by a sense of non-belonging. In 2007, journalist Ryland Fisher, a former UDF activist in the Western Cape, published a book entitled *Race*. In the introduction, he argues that issues of race, racism and race-consciousness continue to pervade every corner of South African society. Like many Coloured students of his generation, Fisher adopted the identity of 'black', influenced by the writings of Steve Biko.

> Recently, however, I have noticed that people who used to accept me as black now refer to me as coloured and, by that action, exclude me and others who may or may not look like me from the majority of South Africans once again.[16]

Have the erstwhile ideals of a participatory, egalitarian society been betrayed? Whatever happened to socialism?
The participatory ethos is no longer as central as it was in the 1980s, although there are numerous interesting initiatives ranging from ward committees to PPP

---

[15]   *Mail & Guardian*, 29 July 2008.
[16]   Ryland Fisher, *Race* (Jacana Publishers, Johannesburg, 2007), p. 5.

(Public Participation and Petitions) units at provincial government level to the recently introduced community development workers. In many cases, however, these lines of communication amount to a top-down exercise in the management of public opinion.

As in the 1980s, I encountered a profound distrust of pluralism in my recent interviews in 2006-2008. ANC politicians in Sekhukhuneland tend to view opposition as illegitimate. It is acceptable to have the Democratic Alliance in Cape Town as that is something for whites, anyway. However, in one's own district, municipality or constituency, rival political parties such as the PAC and AZAPO ought to be silenced, sidelined or even 'crushed'. The distinct historical traditions in different parts of South Africa have produced different understandings of the concept of 'democracy'. The ANC has been deeply rooted in Sekhukhuneland for at least half a century. When I conducted my research in 1990-1991 into UDF affiliates such as the Sekhukhune Youth Organization (SEYO), I found that many activists had never heard of the UDF. Through their activities in youth movements, they belonged to 'the organization', and 'the organization' was the ANC.

Activists in Kagiso in the 1980s were organized in a civic association called the Krugersdorp Residents' Organization (KRO) that was affiliated to the UDF. Most township activists saw themselves as KRO activists. The Africanist tendency in Kagiso organized a rival civic association. The Western Cape lacks a strong ANC tradition but has a long history of fragmented political opposition as well as religious diversity. In the 1980s, UDF activists in the Western Cape were not inclined to accommodate political rivals in the anti-apartheid struggle but nowadays most former activists here view political pluralism as an essential characteristic of constitutional democracy.

About 1990, activists framed their aspirations in Marxist terms. When asked about his vision for South Africa, Maurice Nchabeleng, a youth leader in Sekhukhuneland, stated: 'I want the dictatorship of the proletariat'. Looking back, he now reformulates his ambitions at the time as: 'We wanted to go to the place of the whites'.[17]

Activists wanted a better life modelled on the comfortable lifestyle of white South Africans. This aspiration was framed in the dominant discourse of the liberation struggle at that time, i.e. a mix of Marxism and African nationalism. Marxism seemed to make eminent sense as an analysis of South African society and it also assured, with scientific certainty, that the class struggle would lead the workers to victory. Being versed in Marxism added to one's prestige as an 'advanced cadre'.

---

[17]   Interview with Maurice Nchabeleng, 10 March 2007, Apel.

Nowadays, becoming rich and focusing on individual advancement have become acceptable aspirations in ANC circles. Former activists frame their hopes in today's dominant terminology. But have the aspirations really changed? Or is it the mode of expression that has changed?

Egalitarian ideals are currently out of fashion. Among various former activists, Mrs Thatcher's TINA (There Is No Alternative – to the free market and liberal orthodoxy) has become received wisdom. Others do indeed speak of betrayal but more often than not they feel betrayed by former comrades rather than by more abstract ANC policies. Some critics of the neo-liberal order seem genuinely committed to their belief in a more just society but others just want a share of the riches. A former youth leader in Sekhukhuneland eloquently expressed his frustrations:

> Self-proclaimed communists have become capitalists. The ANC has become a bourgeois national democratic movement. Only people with money own the ANC. The SACP has become a forum for people who missed out on opportunities and positions. Some of them know nothing about communism.[18]

Still versed in Marxism, Moss Mabotha had a ready explanation: 'one's world outlook is determined by one's class position'. But in spite of all the articulate criticism, the bottom line of his resentment is that he wanted to be part of the good life. He admitted to being jealous: 'I also want to be rich'.

Although many former activists expressed a sense of dissatisfaction, their discontent was more often than not focused on former comrades in the struggle rather than on ANC policies *per se*. Youth leader Silas Mabotha, now a high-school principal in Sekhukhune, remarked that relations of trust among former comrades have been undermined: 'We cannot even advise former comrades because they suffer from paranoia. They think you are after their job.' Silas Mabotha, a respected militant and articulate youth activist, is no longer active in the ANC, 'just like most of us'. The ANC government, he complains, follows a capitalist agenda:

> The BEE (Black Economic Empowerment) is nothing else but building a black bourgeoisie. Unemployment is growing while some people become super rich. We see privatization, and casualization of labour. That is not what we fought for, privatization. They are trying to do away with government altogether.

However Silas Mabotha also wants to share in the fruits of liberation: 'We are worried that they will have run out of Mercedes before our turn has come'.[19]

Activists' networks in the 1980s were characterized by strong bonds of solidarity, and differences in socio-economic status between activists were generally quite modest. The stark increase in socio-economic differentiation since

---

[18]   Interview with Moss Mabotha, 15 March 2007, Polokwane.
[19]   Interview with Silas Mabotha, November 2006, Apel.

1994 has put considerable strain on comrades' networks. Can solidarity networks survive when members find themselves in vastly different positions? Is jealousy perhaps a means of keeping members in check and reminding them of their obligations towards group members?

Whatever happened to constitutionalism?
Why would the ANC want to undermine the very constitution that it fought for? In the political crisis that unfolded in the wake of ANC President Jacob Zuma's corruption trial, attacks on the courts by leading ANC personalities were fairly common place. Newspaper editorials and political analysts warned that the independence of the judiciary was at stake and wondered why the ANC would want to undermine the very constitution that it had fought for.[20] But this argument is based on incorrect assumptions.

The ANC accepted the constitution as part of the negotiated transfer of power but a liberal democratic constitution was not among the goals of the liberation struggle. Neither the ANC nor the UDF envisaged a system of liberal democracy. In the 1980s, 'liberal' was a term of abuse. The UDF's preferred mode of governance was popular democracy, modelled on that in Cuba, the German Democratic Republic or Frelimo's Mozambique.

The present South African constitution has been praised worldwide as a model of liberal democracy but liberal democracy was not what spurred on the masses who took to the streets in the 1980s. The clauses about gender equality, gay rights, the abolition of the death penalty and the legalization of abortion would in all likelihood not survive a referendum. However, the fundamental flaw in the view of many black South Africans is the property clause: a constitution that protects the ill-gotten gains of centuries of dispossession and apartheid lacks legitimacy. Did the Freedom Charter not promise that South Africa's national wealth, 'the heritage of all South Africans, shall be restored to the people'?

New social movements

While former activists met in late August 2008 to share nostalgic reminiscences of struggle solidarity, unity and clarity of purpose in UDF days, the ANC went through its worst crisis since 1994. In the aftermath of Thabo Mbeki's forced resignation as president on 20 September 2008, disgruntled ANC members discussed their options: to break away and found a new party or to attempt to recapture the ANC? Others spoke of the need for new social movements. One

---

[20]   For example in the *Mail & Guardian,* 11 July 2008.

such initiative, which aspires to operating in the tradition of the UDF, is the Coalition for Social Justice.

The Coalition for Social Justice was formally launched on 25 June 2008 in Saltriver, a suburb of Cape Town, in response to a series of xenophobic attacks on foreign nationals in the Western Cape. When the government's reaction to the refugee crisis was slow and haphazard, individuals and local organizations began providing humanitarian relief. As the announcement of the public launch of the Social Justice Coalition (SJC) stated:

> Lack of faith in the government, city, big business and even civil society has led us to respond individually and voluntarily. The Social Justice Coalition is an independent group that believes in freedom, equality, non-violence and [a] human rights framework that respects among others, the right of every person to life, dignity and access to health care. We commit ourselves to build a Social Justice Coalition that promotes a 'Marshall Plan' for development in South and Southern Africa based on prioritizing and meeting the needs of the poor and steadily and visibly reducing social inequality.

The core organization in this new coalition is the Treatment Action Campaign (TAC), itself a coalition of individuals and organizations that have successfully campaigned for adequate health care and access to anti-retrovirals for those with HIV. The TAC's campaign strategies were modelled on the UDF model of social activism, employing a broad range of tactics including mass protests, petitions, recourse to the courts, expert lobbies and international pressure on the South African government.

SJC meetings have attracted sizable crowds of young people as well as a number of prominent South Africans with good track records in human rights and anti-apartheid activism. Apart from the refugee crisis, the SJC has also highlighted the perceived laxity of the Mbeki government in addressing the crisis in Zimbabwe and the attacks on the judicial system following Jacob Zuma's court case.[21]

Media reports on the SJC often associate this new broad-based initiative with the legacy of the UDF. The SJC is of course not the only new social movement to spring up in post-apartheid South Africa. As described by Richard Ballard *et al.*, three overlapping but distinct types of struggle emerged when the honeymoon period of Mandela's presidency was over:[22]

---

[21]   Public Launch of the Social Justice Coalition (http://www.tac.org.za/community/node/2356, June 20, 2008); *Mail &Guardian* ,14 September 2008.

[22]   Richard Ballard, Adam Habib & Imraan Valodia (eds), *Voices of Protest: Social movements in post-apartheid South Africa* (University of Kwazulu-Natal Press, Scotsville, 2006), p. 2.

- Initiatives were directed against various government policies. The classic case here is the opposition by the Congress of South African Trade Unions (COSATU) to the Growth, Employment and Redistribution (GEAR) strategy that represented the post-apartheid government's decision to engage with trade liberalization and pursue economic growth as the mechanism for facilitating employment, and thereby promote redistribution.
- Other struggles focused on government failures to meet basic needs and address socio-economic rights. The most noted examples are the Landless People's Movement and the Treatment Action Campaign (TAC) that respectively address the slow pace of land redistribution and the government's failure to respond adequately to the HIV/AIDS crisis.
- Some struggles emerged to directly challenge the local enforcement of government policies and to resist government attempts at repression. The Soweto Electricity Crisis Committee, the Concerned Citizens Group and the Anti-Eviction Campaign are all attempts to organize poor and marginalized communities to resist local, provincial and national government attempts to cut off electricity and water, and evict residents.

In most cases however, these movements and organizations address a single issue. Attempts at building a broader platform that addresses a range of issues have been few and far between. Here the Social Justice Coalition may possibly provide an impetus towards a broader-based movement.

11

'Campus Cults' in Nigeria: The development of an anti-social movement

Stephen Ellis

Nigerians have become concerned by the problem of 'campus cults' – initiation societies rooted in the country's university and college campuses that are part-student club and part criminal gang. Some religious authorities regard certain of the campus cults as 'satanic' by reason of their activities and rituals. The anti-social aspects of these organizations are large-ly attributable to their manipulation by military governments as a counter to conventional student organizations. The campus cults are quite literally an example of an anti-social movement.

For the last decade or so, Nigerians have been concerned with the problem of 'campus cults'. This is the name given by the press to certain student organiza-tions that have proliferated on university campuses and that have become asso-ciated with a wide range of abuses and crimes, including murder. As time has gone by, people who joined such cults during their student years have graduated and advanced in their careers to the point that the existing campus groups are now connected to networks of cult members with senior positions in business or government. 'Campus cults', may, therefore, have their organizational centres in the nation's universities but their networks have spread through state and society.

Christian Pentecostal preachers in particular regard student cults, many of which bear ghoulish and gothic names, as manifestations of Satanism and call on cult members to break their links with them. Billboards on campuses warn about the dangers of such groups and urge students to shun them. Exactly how many distinct campus cults exist is impossible to say with precision but there would appear to be more than a hundred, with many thousands of members.

Membership appears to be overwhelmingly male but there are also organizations that are exclusively for women.

Cults of this nature can hardly be called social movements since they are closed rather than open, and serve private interests rather than aspiring to work for the common good. By most accounts, however, things were not always this way. The organizations called 'campus cults' today represent a perverse and destructive aspect of a student movement that is otherwise social in its orientation. 'Campus cults' have developed at the heart of the wider student movement. The nature of this relationship is such that it raises questions concerning the character of social action in Nigeria generally.

Nigeria's first university was established in Ibadan in 1948 and was originally known as University College, only later being renamed the University of Ibadan. After independence in 1960, the number of universities mushroomed, especially during the oil boom of the 1970s when the government founded universities in every part of the country. More recently, various individuals, corporations and religious bodies have established private universities, to the extent that there are now almost 100 universities recognized by the Nigerian Universities Commission, as well as 100 polytechnics and 150 technical colleges. Despite this growth, demand for one of the estimated 148,000 annual university places remains fierce and the expansion in the number of universities has, in fact, damaged students' job prospects, with graduate unemployment now estimated at about 60%.[1]

The Pyrates and its offspring

Nigeria's first main nationalist party, the National Council of Nigeria and the Cameroons (NCNC), recruited heavily among students.[2] It was in this context that in 1953 (or, in some accounts, 1952), University College Ibadan witnessed the foundation of a new type of student club conceived along the lines of an American student fraternity or a British university social club. Founded by seven undergraduates, it was known as the Pyrates Confraternity. According to a later analyst, who received an official appointment to investigate campus cults, the Pyrates originally aspired to 'a social liberating role', and represented 'an attempt to create a better society'.[3] It aimed to galvanize the fusty, Oxbridge-style atmosphere of what had been Nigeria's only university for some twelve years and to lobby for a more radical university politics generally. The

---

[1]   John Gill, 'UK looks set to benefit from Nigerian student boom', *Times Higher Education Supplement,* 11 December 2008.

[2]   Daniel A. Offiong, *Secret Cults in Nigerian Tertiary Institutions* (Fourth Dimension, Enugu, 2003), p. 1.

[3]   *Ibid.*, p. 3.

leader of the group was the young Wole Soyinka, who would later become a Nobel laureate. Embarrassed by what some student confraternities were to become, Soyinka has written a defence of the Pyrates in which he emphasizes the organization's youthful innocence.[4] As new universities were created, the Pyrates became popular on many of the new campuses, founding a branch, for example, at the University of Nigeria at Nsukka that was opened shortly after independence.

Nigerian student politics in the 1960s and 1970s, as in many other countries in Africa and indeed other parts of the world, were dominated by a rhetoric of radicalism. The most influential student leaders were stridently anti-colonialist. Marxism, pan-Africanism and opposition to apartheid in South Africa became favoured themes of student activists. The 1962 abrogation of the Anglo-Nigerian defence agreement, negotiated on the eve of independence, was attributed in part to pressure from student opinion.[5] As the number of students increased with the opening of new universities, the National Union of Nigerian Students (NUNS) became directly involved in national politics, being invited to join the 1977 Constituent Assembly that was discussing a new constitution that would accompany a return to civilian rule, replacing the military administrations that had run Nigeria since the country's first coup in 1966. However, the military government under General Olusegun Obasanjo, who led the country from 1977 to 1979, became so annoyed by the students' radicalism that it proscribed the NUNS and detained its president, Segun Okeowo. Radical university lecturers in Ibadan, Lagos, Calabar and at Ahmadou Bello University in Zaria were detained or fired.[6]

The Pyrates was generally in sympathy with the radical turn taken by student politics and remained an influential force within the student movement. Ben Oguntuase, a Pyrate in the early 1970s, later recalled that the confraternity was at that time the driving force in student politics at the University of Ibadan.[7] Another ex-member recalled the Pyrates in those days as offering 'an avenue to express strong feelings about the happenings in society',[8] still assuming the role of social gadfly that the organization had had at its inception. According to Oguntuase, by the early 1970s, members of the Pyrates wore uniforms for for-

[4] Wole Soyinka, *Cults: A people in denial* (Interventions III, Bookcraft, Ibadan, 2005), esp. pp. 58-74.

[5] cf. Gordon J. Idang, 'The politics of Nigerian foreign policy: The ratification and renunciation of the Anglo-Nigerian defence agreement', *African Studies Review*, 13, 2 (1970), p. 229.

[6] Reuben Abati, 'How Nigerian students murdered democracy', *The Guardian*, 11 December 2005.

[7] Interview in *Punch*, 8 August 1999.

[8] Femi Olugbile, 'Cult fever', *Vanguard*, 15 August 1999.

mal ceremonies and followed rules that were enforced by the society's officers, which could even include beatings. Initiation involved signing a pledge in red ink and drinking a Bloody Mary, a cocktail made with tomato juice. Some non-members are said to have believed that the drink was made with real human blood, perhaps an understandable misapprehension given the Pyrates's mock-piratical rituals and their reported use of violence for disciplinary purposes.[9]

During the 1970s, there was a growth in student confraternities that had a direct genealogical connection to the Pyrates. In 1971 or 1972 (sources vary on the date) an internal disagreement led to a dissident group leaving or being expelled from the Pyrates and founding a new confraternity known as the Buccaneers.[10] Thereafter, at a time when student numbers were increasing rapidly, there were further splits. Many of the new groups continued to show an ideological orientation, like the Black Axe, a group aligned with the fashionable philosophy of black consciousness.[11] The new confraternities, like their fore-bears, continued to regard themselves as fighters for justice.[12]

It was not only Nigerian campuses that were changing radically during these years, but society as a whole. The 1967-1970 civil war, successive military coups after 1966 and the development of an oil industry that had not existed when the Pyrates was established all contributed to a loss of the relative aura of innocence that had surrounded the Pyrates's early years. The rise of new student confraternities was part of a vogue for new civic and philosophical associations more generally. Many of the new associations and social clubs that were estab-lished in these years reflected people's attempts to address the problems of life in Nigeria's burgeoning cities, such as the burial societies and other mutual help societies that, in the absence of affordable commercial insurance, were a means of spreading risk.[13] Since many parts of Nigeria have the tradition of initiation societies, the plethora of new societies that came into existence in the 1970s no doubt owed something to people's general familiarity with the idea of social action through membership of a specific group. 'Social clubs', notes one writer, 'may be regarded as open and more practical versions' of the initiation societies that have such a long and important history.[14]

Sites of new forms of sociability and new ideologies, Nigeria's new univer-sity campuses also witnessed the rise of new religious groups. Most notable were the new Pentecostal churches that constituted autonomous spaces of reli-

---

[9]   Ben Oguntuase, interviewed in *Punch*, 8 August 1999.
[10] Offiong, *Secret Cults in Nigerian Tertiary Institutions*, p. 54.
[11] *Ibid.*, p. 69.
[12] *Ibid.*, pp. 56-59.
[13] Elechi Amadi, *Ethics in Nigerian Culture* (Heinemann Educational Books, Ibadan, 1982), p. 12.
[14] *Ibid.*, p. 13.

gious practice. Pentecostal student groups emerged as perhaps the most power-ful youth movement the country had seen since independence, to the extent that they soon eclipsed the secular student movement. The universities of Ibadan and Ile-Ife became 'hotbeds of Pentecostalism'.[15] On campuses with a signifi-cant presence of Muslim students, new Islamic movements became popular too, contesting the *sufi* brotherhoods that were closely connected to traditional forms of patronage and that young reformers criticized as inconsistent with correct forms of Islamic practice.

Changes in the associational life of millions of Nigerians in the 1970s were inseparable from the country's oil boom. The country's emergence from civil war was accompanied by a rapid growth in oil production. When the Organiza-tion of Petroleum Exporting Countries (OPEC) raised its prices fourfold in 1973, Nigeria also witnessed a massive and sudden increase in state revenues. Oil money flowed, generating a mania for wealth.[16] In the scramble for a part of the oil riches, which were distributed essentially across the state, Nigeria's tra-ditional agricultural staples suffered alarming falls in production. A US diplo-mat quoted a conversation he had had with Nigeria's top financial civil servant in December 1973, coincidentally the very month of the first OPEC price rise. The American reported his Nigerian interlocutor as acknowledging 'with dis-arming frankness' that the government 'knows perfectly well that its dev-elopment policies are contributing to an exacerbation of income disparities in Nigeria, but accepts this as part of the price of rapid development. The next generation [he added] will have to deal with the consequences.'[17] The writer Chinua Achebe, addressing an audience at Lagos University, had a dark fore-boding. 'God forbid', he said, 'that we should be the generation that had the opportunity to create Africa's first truly modern state but frittered away the chance in parochialism, inefficiency, corruption and cynicism.'[18]

The turn to violence

Even before oil had become king, Nigerian political parties were, in the words of the military leader Murtala Muhammed, 'in fact little more than armies organized for fighting elections'. Winning elections was 'a life and death strug-

---

[15] Ebenezer Obadare, 'White-collar fundamentalism: interrogating youth religiosity on Nigerian university campuses', *Journal of Modern African Studies*, 45, 4, 2007, p. 521.

[16] Andrew H. Apter, *The Pan-African Nation: Oil and the spectacle of culture in Nigeria* (Chicago University Press, Chicago, 2005), esp. chap. 1.

[17] National Archives of the United Kingdom, Kew, FCO 65/1529: draft dated 6 De-cember 1973.

[18] *Daily Times*, 20 January 1977, p. 25.

gle'.[19] The advent of expensive oil only heightened this effect. Control of the revenues was concentrated at the core of the state, which received the royalties and taxes from oil. The soldiers who controlled the state from 1966 to 1979, and the civilian 'super permanent secretaries' who were so influential in the Federal Military Government, decided who received what, when and how. When the country finally returned to civilian rule after the 1979 elections, there was a further expansion of the state patronage system that was based increasingly on oil wealth. A rapid fall in the price of oil in the early 1980s, for which the government had made no provisions, resulted in a political crisis. The inevitable military coup came on 31 December 1983.

It is generally agreed that the oil boom of the 1970s, followed by the sudden puncturing of the economic bubble created by high prices, transformed Nigerian society. A population whose ambitions had been stimulated by oil money was cruelly disappointed by its sudden disappearance. It was in this period that, by most accounts, Nigeria began to acquire an ugly reputation as the home of the international advance-fee frauds known as '419'.[20] A later head of Nigeria's anti-corruption agency, Nuhu Ribadu, was to state with regard to the civilian government of 1979-83:

> Let us call a spade a spade. This is the period when we started hearing about 419, it is the period we started having drug problems. It is a period when Majors (in the army) started buying property in London.[21]

This was also the period when there was a disturbing turn in the behaviour and reputation of the student confraternities that had flourished within the wider student movement in more optimistic times. Some of the new confraternities, like the Vikings, continued to give themselves names redolent of the original Pyrates and its offshoot, the Buccaneers. The latter spawned the Black Axe, soon joined by the Red Beret and many other newcomers. Holding their meetings at night and in secret, some of the new groups became associated with the rising number of violent attacks on university campuses. Their behaviour moved far beyond the light-hearted mock-sinister that had been the original style of the Pyrates. There were increasingly incidents of student clubs inflicting serious bodily harm on members as punishment or in the course of initiation ceremonies, fighting with rivals on campus, and being associated with violence generally. One ex-member of a student group recalled initiation as consisting of three weeks of what he called 'rigorous and heartbreaking activities', whose

---

[19]   Quoted in Richard A. Joseph, *Democracy and Prebendal Politics in Nigeria* (Cambridge University Press, Cambridge, 1987), p. 39.

[20]   cf. Harvey Glickman, 'The Nigerian "419" advance fee scams: Prank or peril?', *Canadian Journal of African Studies*, 39, 3 (2005), p. 472.

[21]   Speech delivered on 19 January 2006: *Punch*, 20 January 2006.

purpose was 'to toughen the heart of the otherwise innocent looking boy',[22] similar to basic military training or initiation into one of the traditional secret societies that have been powerful in Nigeria since pre-colonial times. During their induction ceremonies, many of the new confraternities made use of religious objects, universally referred to in Nigeria as *juju*, which further strengthened the resemblance with initiation into a traditional power society. So worrying did campus violence become that the Pyrates leadership announced its intention to withdraw from university campuses entirely and to relaunch the group as an adult society called the National Association of Sea Dogs. This it did, but in reality student Pyrates continued to operate on Nigerian campuses, disregarding its national leadership.

Nevertheless, there were people who took quite a positive view of what were now becoming called 'campus cults', recalling their origins in the idealism and social activism of an earlier generation. Philip Aghedo, a member of the Buccaneers for some fifteen years after being introduced by his uncle at the University of Benin in 1981, maintained that, in his day, candidate members of the Buccaneers were vetted for their intelligence and good behaviour before being invited to join. Aghedo stated with regard to the student confraternities:

> They train you to be useful to yourself and the society because the thinking governing conduct of the cult is that there must be somebody controlling the environment otherwise the environment will be controlling itself and there could be anarchy. If the cults fail to exercise some level of control in University, the lecturers and administrators can do whatever they like and get away with it.[23]

He attributed the violent clashes that occurred between rival groups to the fact that they were competing with each other in the unregulated social environment formed by students on campus.

In 1999, a single incident attracted the attention of the government and the media to just how serious the rivalries on university campuses had become. At Obafemi Awolowo University in Ile-Ife, a forty-strong war party from the Black Axe confraternity, some of them armed with machine-guns, attacked leaders of the student union who had complained to the university authorities about the cultists' activities. The five or more fatalities included the university's chief security officer. There were suspicions that the murderous activities of the Black Axe might have been associated with outside forces that had an interest in asserting control on the university campus. Groups like the Black Axe at Ile-Ife were recruiting local thugs to provide themselves with extra manpower to reinforce their presence in inter-group conflicts. They were also visiting herbalists

---

[22] 'Cultists confess at Fedpoly, Nekede', *Nigerian Tribune*, 14 September 1999.
[23] '5 million cultists on the loose', *Daily Times*, 18 July 1999.

in search of powerful amulets to protect themselves in fights, thus coming into contact with networks influential in a wider criminal and political underworld.[24] It was often said that the membership of campus cults was drawn disproportionately from children from elite families. The respected former vice-chancellor of Ibadan, Professor Ayo Banjo, noted that the leaders of confraternities or cults on campus – it is hard to know what to call them at this stage of their existence – systematically targeted first-year students from rich families, attempting to recruit them as part of a long-term strategy to strengthen their social networks. A common technique was for the leaders of a campus cult to invite a freshman to join an innocuous-sounding club. If the newcomer showed interest, he was subjected to increasing degrees of intimidation and blackmail, including kidnapping and physical violence, in an effort to coerce the recruit into full membership.[25]

Cults and student politics

The shocking Ile-Ife killings, occurring shortly after Nigeria's return to civilian government after an almost unbroken fifteen years of military rule, stimulated widespread public debate. Discussion soon spread from the campus cults themselves to the wider social environment in which they had arisen. It was generally recognized that the degeneration from student activism to murderous gangsterism was a reflection of the moral condition of the nation. Among those who have investigated campus cults, there is a consensus that the transformation from student activism to something less social and more violent was a development inseparable from wider tendencies in Nigerian society.

More specifically, the degeneration from confraternity to cult was a consequence of the policies adopted by some of the military governments that dominated Nigeria with only brief interruption from 1966 to 1999. General Obasanjo's banning of the National Union of Nigerian Students during his first period as head of state between 1976 and 1979 was the first of several attempts by the military to assert control over the universities. Even in secondary schools, there were cases of military governments drafting soldiers to work as teachers in an attempt to impose a military discipline on impressionable young minds. Former Buccaneer Philip Aghedo believed that the military, sent to institutions of learning in various capacities, 'unwittingly taught the youngsters the art of weapon handling and management'.[26] Professor Ayo Banjo has broadly agreed with this analysis, noting that many cultists 'admired the machismo of the tough military men, who ordered things to be done with immediate effect

---

[24]   Gabriel Osu, 'Stamping cults from our campuses', *Vanguard*, 30 August 1999.
[25]   Rotimi Oyedanmi, 'How to tackle cultism menace', *Guardian*, 6 January 2000.
[26]   '5 million cultists on the loose', *Daily Times*, 18 July 1999.

and brutally swept all obstacles out of their way'.[27] Still more damagingly, military governments sometimes gave covert support to campus groups as a means of destabilizing student unions, which were feared by the military men on account of their political radicalism.[28] In 1991, for example, during the rule of the Machiavellian General Ibrahim Babangida, student cults were used to destabilize student organizations on the Ile-Ife campus that had been agitating for improved bursaries.[29] University administrators, often appointed for their loyalty to the military government rather than for any academic or managerial qualifications, played one faction off against another among the students at their institutions. Secretive confraternities were instruments in the hands of vice-chancellors concerned primarily with political control of their campuses.

In these circumstances during the last two decades of the twentieth century when Nigeria was dominated by military governments with a general contempt for education combined with a fear of student radicalism, the campus confraternities were able to use violence and manipulation to become kingmakers in student politics. The rewards could be quite substantial for aspiring entrepreneurs of power and violence. Some youngsters became professional students, staying on campus year after year, collecting protection money and building up powerful personal followings. Once student associations had become not only politicized but also militarized, it was a short step to their being used for instrumental purposes in personal quarrels. Wole Soyinka notes the case of a university vice-chancellor who used one student confraternity or cult as a personal strong-arm squad to attack faculty members opposed to him.[30] By 2002, there were reports of former cult members being recruited by an incumbent state governor in the southeast, where shrines and secret societies play a key role in a particularly thuggish political system, as do goon-squads acting on behalf of politicians and even businesspeople.[31] Some cultists, having made connections with politicians and other powerbrokers during their time in student politics, have gone on to pursue careers in politics, government or the professions, while retaining their membership of their society. This means that some campus cults have developed into networks of influence that pervade wider sections of soci-

---

[27]   Oyedanmi, 'How to tackle cultism menace', *Guardian*, 6 January 2000.

[28]   See the round-table discussion published in *Vanguard*, 20-21 September 1999. On the anti-student politics of the military, Patrick Wilmot, *Nigeria: The nightmare scenario* (Interventions VI, Bookcraft and Farafina, Ibadan and Lagos, 2007).

[29]   Round-table discussion in *Vanguard*, 20-21 September 1999.

[30]   Soyinka, *Cults*, p. 30.

[31]   Nduka Nwosu, 'Assassination, a new culture in Igboland', *Guardian*, 2 November 2002. On the role of shrines in local business, politics and crime, Stephen Ellis, 'The Okija shrine: Death and life in Nigerian politics', *Journal of African History*, 49, 3, 2008, pp. 445-466.

ety. But they remain oriented to the interests of their members rather than to any wider social project. This is in contrast to the original Pyrates Confraternity, which aspired to pursue what its members perceived to be a progressive agenda for the improvement of society as a whole. Members of the Black Axe and no doubt some other groups are to be found as far away as the Netherlands, enmeshed in a small and often vulnerable Nigerian diaspora.

Perhaps the ultimate transformation of student confraternities into violent gangs has taken place in the Niger Delta, where a complex low-intensity war is involving dozens of armed factions. Researchers have identified over a hundred specific armed groups, many of them descended from university societies or modelled on them,[32] administering secret oaths of allegiance and relying heavily on violence. Alongside these – or perhaps intertwined with them, much as the original campus confraternities were intertwined with the official student unions – are militant groups that cultivate a more conventional guerrilla image, like the Niger Delta People's Volunteer Force (NDPVF) or the Movement for the Emancipation of the Niger Delta (MEND) that have conducted an armed campaign that has at times pitted them against the state and the oil companies. In the micropolitics of the federal and state government, the oil companies and local interest groups, shifting allegiances may cause some cults to become affiliated to larger groups, and even to work as enforcers for politicians, particularly during election campaigns.

In the convoluted and violent politics of the Niger Delta, the main distinction between the different types of organization is the quality of the individual allegiance prevailing within them. In the case of a cult, initiation is deemed to be for life and individuals seeking to renounce their allegiance may be subject to drastic punishment. Some of the cults operating in the Niger Delta are reported to have initiation rituals that can even include the murder of a member of the recruit's own family. Membership of such cults may range from a couple of dozen to several thousands. Some are pro-state or pro-government; some are anti-state, while others have no clear political objectives.[33] Individual organizations can be placed on a spectrum going from groups with political aims to purely criminal associations. At various times, their main occupations might be fighting each other for turf (necessary for access to oil-smuggling routes or other forms of enrichment), peddling the cocaine that is imported in bulk to pay for smuggled oil, and working for politicians as enforcers. Many of them make

---

[32]   Eghosa Osaghae, Augustine Ikelegbe, Omobolaji Olarinmoye and Steven Okhomina, 'Youth militias, self determination and resource control struggles in the Niger-Delta region of Nigeria', unpublished study, Consortium for Development Partnerships, 2007.

[33]   *Ibid.*

more or less explicit use of techniques of spiritual protection, such as bullet-proof charms and amulets.

In June 2004, the Nigerian government passed a law known as the Secret Cult and Similar Activities Prohibition Act that banned some one hundred named groups.[34] Others not named by the Act continued to exist and be involved in criminal activities. A former student cult member, looking back some years previously on his experiences, did not exaggerate when he noted: 'It has ceased to be play. It is war.'[35]

Society and anti-society

Initiation societies are a historically ingrained form of organization, particularly in southern Nigeria, and in pre-colonial times they played a key role in governance. In some circumstances these societies constituted a check on the power of the chiefs and kings and they often played a role in the administration of justice, and sometimes in commerce and trade. Under colonial rule, which was imposed in Nigeria during the twentieth century, the position of traditional initiation societies was distinctly ambiguous. At one and the same time, the logic of the British system of Indirect Rule was to reinforce institutions that played an established role in local government but also to treat these same institutions with a degree of hostility on account of their lack of transparency and their association with practices deemed by the colonial authorities to be unacceptable, including enslavement and various types of judicial killing. In fact, some traditional initiation societies continued to flourish during colonial times and played an important role in early nationalist politics.[36]

Since the 1950s, growing corruption in Nigerian politics, fuelled by vast oil wealth, has created an environment in which traditional or not-so-traditional secret societies have been able to flourish as lynch-pins of patrimonial politics in a complex system whereby the formal, legal dispositions of state power are intertwined with informal networks, some of them regulated in time-honoured fashion via the institutions of traditional religion.[37] Senior politicians and officials may, in addition to the public office they hold, also have a status within formal but nonetheless unpublicized organizations, ranging from traditional shrines to international networks such as the Freemasons or the Rosicrucians. Such networks are considered not only as a useful means of dispensing political patronage but, in many cases, also as channels for attaining esoteric power.

---

[34] See Annex.
[35] Olugbile, 'Cult fever', *Vanguard*, 15 August 1999.
[36] Cf. Tekena Tamuno & Robin Horton, 'The changing position of secret societies and cults in modern Nigeria', *African Notes*, 5, 2 (1969), pp. 36-62.
[37] Cf. Ellis, 'The Okija shrine'.

More than thirty years ago, the Nigerian government professed itself to be greatly perturbed by the existence of secret societies that were judged to be pervasive in places of public employment, including the civil service and the army. The army chief of staff was quoted as describing secret societies as 'a cancer which has eaten deep into all ranks of the Nigerian army'.[38] They were also said to have penetrated the ranks of High Court judges, the police, and even church leaders. In July 1977, the Federal Military Government issued a formal ban on public servants joining secret societies, concerned by evidence that members of secret societies protected one another and helped each other achieve positions of influence.[39] It was apparently as a consequence of this blanket ban on secret societies that the Pyrates was banned on some campuses: some fifteen students, for example, were arrested at the University of Calabar and the Calabar College of Technology in 1977 for being members of the Pyrates.[40] In general, however, the government's official hostility to secret societies at that time was not directed principally towards the universities where such bodies were in their infancy and not yet deemed to be a public nuisance, but towards the civil service and other branches of the state.

In view of this history, the story of Nigeria's campus cults needs to be understood in a broader social and political perspective. This includes an appreciation of how the country's political and civil society has been influenced by closed associations or initiation societies, and how these have been used or abused over a long period by politicians and others avid for power. As one journalist correctly observed, 'it is ... rather hypocritical that that society condones savage tendencies within itself while wishing the campuses to eradicate these same tendencies'.[41] Although certain key moments can be identified in this longer history of the coexistence of different forms of power, it has been, in retrospect, quite a steady process. While the colonial government banned certain traditional societies and shrines on the grounds of their association with such criminal practices as enslavement or the taking of human life, many such institutions in fact continued surreptitiously, existing within the bowels of Indirect Rule. Post-colonial governments in Nigeria, like their colonial forebears, sometimes declared themselves shocked to discover the degree to which institutions of state that had been conceived in the formal mode proper to a modern nation-state had in fact been infiltrated by networks of power with a different pedigree and no legal standing. From time to time, a scandal exposes this imbrication of different channels and practices of power to public view, and politicians duly call for the law to be enforced in all its majesty. But implementing

[38] Quoted in Tai Solarin, 'Belief in secret cults', *Nigerian Tribune*, 16 February 1976.
[39] Amadi, *Ethics in Nigerian Culture*, p. 8.
[40] *Daily Times*, 27 January 1977.
[41] Quasim Odunmbaku, 'A tale of two cults', *This Day*, 17 August 1999.

the law, even when appropriate, is extraordinarily difficult when it comes to dealing with secretive networks that have penetrated the state itself and that may be ruthless in their mode of operation.

The July 1977 ban on secret societies, announced at the height of Nigeria's first and most lethal oil boom, marked the point when government at its most senior level officially became concerned by the influence of secret societies. This was also the period when student confraternities were beginning to proliferate following the initial split of the Buccaneers from the Pyrates, the first of many organizations to be spawned in this way. Furthermore, it was the first period of spiritual awakening on the university campuses that had proliferated in the previous decade. The campuses became the mainspring of the Pentecostalist movement that has become so widespread and influential throughout Nigerian society. It was in the mid 1970s that Reverend Benson Idahosa, who was later to become the most famous of all Nigerian Pentecostalist preachers and the founder of a university that bears his name, first held services of cleansing for members of secret societies.[42] It is not just that the Pentecostalists and the cultists happened to be expanding their activities during the same period. Instead, there is an intimate connection between the two as they competed not only for the bodies but also the souls of students in their formative years, and the nation's future elite. In Pentecostal theology, the fight with the cultists is a battle with the forces of Satan and of darkness that threaten Nigeria. In the vocabulary of the social sciences, it is a struggle between a broad social movement on the country's university campuses that is oriented towards self-improvement and social action by means of both student unions and religious groups versus the activities of clandestine groups that have become dedicated to the narrow self-interest of their members and that are the very opposite of a social movement. The competition between these forces has been manipulated by powerful people, including military governments concerned with defending themselves against student radicalism and demobilizing social movements of many sorts, and also unscrupulous university administrators and even academic staff concerned with protecting their position within their institutions. Since Nigerians generally consider power not only in material terms but also in spiritual ones, the conflict between Pentecostalism and secret societies, even those with no apparently religious leaning, is couched in theological rhetoric. At stake are the hearts and minds of Nigeria's future ruling class.

The contests between rival networks of power and their religious, political and legal dimensions also reflect different visions and traditions of social action. Nigeria has a liberal constitution that provides for political expression through the conventional channels of party politics and parliamentary represen-

---

[42]   Yemi Folarin, 'Cults' secret out', *Daily Express*, 8 September 1977.

tation. At various times in the past, both under colonial rule and subsequently, large numbers of Nigerians have mobilized for political purposes in forms usual in liberal democracies, through trade unions, public-interest groups and so on. Military governments in particular often abhorred such activity, which could easily have threatened their own existence, and took steps to make social mobilization as difficult as possible. The closed and hidden groups of various sorts, ranging from simple personal networks to organized groups such as traditional initiation societies, religious networks and student confraternities, were sometimes used for this purpose. In passing, it should be remembered that the constitution explicitly bans secret societies.[43]

The fact that initiation societies have historically existed in southern Nigeria does not mean that the presence of quasi-traditional groups will always be felt. Such groups have been encouraged and instrumentalized for specific reasons, sometimes by the country's most powerful rulers. Nigeria is what it is today in the twenty-first century as a consequence of these actions, not simply because of the legacy of history.

It is interesting to note that most reports of student cults emanate from southern Nigeria, which is also the area where initiation societies were most powerful in pre-colonial times. However Wole Soyinka, in characteristically combative style, has attacked the notion that student cults are less rampant in the north than the south. He quotes the case of the Gamji cult, which is said to have been favoured by senior figures in Northern Nigeria, and manipulated by General Abacha in his bid to prolong his tenure of power in the 1990s.[44] He also points to the existence of the so-called 'Kaduna mafia',[45] the grouping of northern potentates often regarded as perhaps the most important enduring informal structure of power in Nigeria. However, while Soyinka's examples demonstrate that Northern powerbrokers are adept at forming discreet associations to further their collective interests, he does not demonstrate that universities in Northern Nigeria are as likely as Southern institutions to host student 'cults'. This apparent difference appears to reflect the distinctive historical trajectories of state formation in the North and South. Broadly speaking, the favoured strategy for two centuries of pursuing political hegemony in Northern Nigeria has been via the language and organizational structures associated with Islam, and this has served many Northern elites well. Since the establishment of Nigeria by British decree in 1914, Southern elites have generally found it more difficult to establish a hegemonic position. Individuals have often had recourse to unofficial power structures, such as secret societies, to advance their position. Although

---

[43] Section 38, sub-section 4 of the Constitution of the Federal Republic of Nigeria (1999). The full text is available at www.nigeria-law.org.

[44] Soyinka, *Cults,* p. 78.

[45] *Ibid.*

they have been generally successful in this undertaking at regional or local level, Southern Nigerian politicians have generally been unsuccessful in establishing a hegemonic position that would enable them to challenge the Northern grip on the power of the Nigerian state. Moreover, the imbrication of official and unofficial networks has resulted in enormous bureaucratic inefficiencies and has led to widespread demoralization. New religious movements in both North and South Nigeria represent campaigns not only of spiritual renewal but also the creation of spaces of autonomous action intended to be free from the moral complexities engendered by Nigeria's politics over the last fifty years.[46]

The analogy made by one journalist is very apt: 'Cultism is to the cultists what plotting is to the military [:] top secret'.[47] Particularly under General Ibrahim Babangida (1985-1993), Nigeria was subject to a style of rule whereby 'direct disbursals and administrative favours were increasingly supplanted by politically-influenced arbitrage in a variety of domestic markets', a process more simply described as 'zaïrianization'.[48] Nigeria's recent history has been one of social fragmentation that at times has been the deliberate strategy of elites insecure in their legitimacy. It has also been the instrument of less powerful citizens who have discovered that attachment to particular networks, including those in the form of a secret society, is an outstanding way of obtaining a slice of the national cake, which is the summit of Nigerian political activity. Far from being immune to this process, the universities, as a breeding ground of the national elite, have been important sites. It is small wonder that the movements with nationwide social aspirations that flourished in the first years of nationalism have been snuffed out, to be replaced by the factionalized and particularist politics of networks or by the religious language of renewal articulated by both Islamist and Christian reformers.

---

[46] Cf. Ruth Marshall, *Political Spiritualities: The explosion of Pentecostalism in Nigeria* (Chicago University Press, Chicago, forthcoming).

[47] Bayo Oguntunase, 'The problems of cultism in Nigeria (1)', *National Concord*, 29 June 1998.

[48] Peter Lewis, 'From prebendalism to predation: The political economy of decline in Nigeria', *Journal of Modern African Studies*, 34, 1, 1996, p. 97. The reference to 'zaïrianization' is on page 80.

Annex

List of groups banned under the Secret Cult and Similar Activities Prohibition Law 2004[49]

Agbaye	Eagle Club	Neo-Black Movement
Airwords	Egbe Dudu	Night Mates
Amazon	Eiye of Air Lords	Nite Hawks
Baccaneers (Sea Lords)	Fraternity	Nite Rovers
Barracuda	Elegemface	Odu Cofraternity
Bas	Executioners	Osiri
Bees International	Fangs	Ostrich Fraternity
Big 20	FF	Panama Pyrate
Black Axe	Fliers	Phoenix
Black Beret Fraternity	Frigates	Predators
Black Brasserie [sic]	Gentlemen's Club	Red Devils
Black Brothers	Green Berets Fraternity	Red Fishes
Black Cats	Hard Candies	Red Sea Horse
Black Cross	Hell's Angels	Royal House of Peace
Black Ladies	Hepos	Royal Queens
Black Ofals	Himalayas	Sailors
Black Scorpions	Icelanders	Scavengers
Black Sword	Jaggare Confederation	Scorpion
Blanchers	KGB	Scorpion
Black Bras	King Cobra	Scorpion Fraternity
Blood Suckers	KlamKonfraternity	Sea Vipers
Brotherhood of Blood	Klansman	Soiree Fraternity
Burkina Faso: Revolution	Ku Klux Klan	Soko
Fraternity	Knite Cade	Sunmen
Canary	Mafia Lords	Temple of Eden Fraternity
Cappa Vandetto	Mafioso Fraternity	Thomas Sankara Boys
Daughters of Jezebel	Malcolm X	Tikan Giants
Dey Gbam	Maphites /Maphlate	Trojan Horses Fraternity
Dey Well	Mgba Mgba Brothers	Truth Seekers
Dolphins	Mob Stab	Twin mate
Dragons	Musketeers Fraternity	Vikings
Dreaded Friends of	National Association of	Vipers
Friends	Adventurers	Vultures
Blood Hunters	National Association of	Walrus
	Sea Dogs	White Bishop

49 Osaghae *et al.*, 'Youth militias, self determination and resource control struggles in the Niger-Delta region of Nigeria'.

Bibliography

Abbink, J., 'Dervishes, *moryaan* and freedom fighters: Cycles of rebellion and the fragmentation of Somali society, 1900-2000', in J. Abbink *et al.* (eds), *Rethinking Resistance: Revolt and Violence in African History* (Brill, Leiden, 2003), pp. 328-365.

Adam, Hussein, *From Tyranny to Anarchy: The Somali experience* (Red Sea Press, Trenton, NJ/Asmara, 2008).

African Women and Peace Support Group, *Liberian Women Peacemakers: Fighting for the right to be seen, heard, and counted* (Africa World Press, Trenton, NJ, 2004).

Alingué, Madeleine Andebeng L., 'African Transatlantic Resistance and Movements', in Atilio Boron & A. Gladys Lechini (eds), *Politics and Social Movements in an Hegemonic World: Lessons from Africa, Asia and Latin America* (Consejo Latinoamericano de Ciencias Sociales (CLACSO), Buenos Aires, 2005), pp. 245-258.

Amadi, Elechi, *Ethics in Nigerian Culture* (Heinemann Educational Books, Ibadan, 1982).

Amadiume, Ifi, 'Gender, political systems and social movements: A West African experience', in Mamdani & Wamba-dia-Wamba (eds), *African Studies in Social Movements* (Codesria, Dakar, 1995), pp. 35-68.

Amisi, B. & R. Ballard, 'In the absence of citizenship: Congolese refugee struggle and organisation in South Africa', in Richard Ballard, Adam Habib & Imraan Valodia (eds), *Voices of Protest: Social movements in post-apartheid South Africa* (University of KwaZulu-Natal Press, Pietermaritzburg, 2006), pp. 397-412.

Amnesty International, *Mauritania: A future free from slavery?* (Amnesty International, London, 2002).

Anderson, B., *Imagined Communities: Reflections on the origin and spread of nationalism* (Verso, London, 1983).

Anheier, Helmut, Marlies Glasius & Mary Kaldor, 'Introducing global civil society', in H. Anheier, M. Glasius & M. Kaldor (eds), *Global Civil Society* (Oxford University Press, Oxford, 2001), pp. 3-22.

Apter, Andrew H., *The Pan-African Nation: Oil and the spectacle of culture in Nigeria* (Chicago University Press, Chicago, 2005).

Atieno, Awinda, 'Mungiki, 'neo-Mau Mau' and the prospects for democracy in Kenya', *Review of African Political Economy*, 34, 13 (2007), pp. 526-531.

Bales, Kevin, *Disposable People: New slavery in the global economy* (University of California Press, Berkeley, CA, 1999).

Ballard, Richard, Adam Habib, Imraan Valodia & Elke Zuern, 'Globalization, marginalization and contemporary social movements in South Africa', *African Affairs*, 104, 417 (2005), pp. 615-634.

Ballard, Richard, Adam Habib & ImraanValodia, 'Social Movements in South Africa: Promoting crisis or creating stability', in V. Padayachee (ed.), *The Development Decade* (HSRC Press, Cape Town, 2006), pp. 397-412.

Ballard, Richard, Adam Habib & Imraan Valodia (eds), *Voices of Protest: Social movements in post-apartheid South Africa* (University of Kwazulu-Natal Press, Pietermaritzburg, 2006).

Bate, S., 'One mission, two churches: the Catholic church in southern Africa, 1947-1997', in J .Brain & P. Denis (eds), *The Catholic Church in Contemporary Southern Africa* (Cluster, Pietermaritzburg, 1999), pp. 5-36.

Bauer, Gretchen & Hannah E. Britton, 'Women in African parliaments: a continental shift?', in G. Bauer & H.E. Britton (eds), *Women in African Parliaments* (Lynne Rienner Publications, Boulder, Col., 2006), pp. 1-30.

Bayart, Jean-François, 'Africa in the world: A history of extraversion', *African Affairs*, 99, 395 (2000), pp. 217-267.

Baxter, Joan, '"Another Africa is possible': Social movements organize to challenge dominant economic policies', *Africa Recovery*, 16, 1, (2002), p. 18.

Benford, R. 'An insider's critique of the social movement framing perspective', *Sociological Inquiry*, 67, 4 (1997), pp. 409-430.

Bledsoe, Caroline H., 'Stratification and Sande politics', *Ethnologische Zeitschrift Zürich*, 1 (1980), pp. 143-150.

Bledsoe, Caroline H., 'The political use of Sande ideology and symbolism', *American Ethnologist*, 11 (1984), pp. 455-467.

Bledsoe, Caroline H., *Women and Marriage in Kpelle Society* (Stanford University Press, Stanford, 1980).

Blumer, H.G., 'Collective behavior', in A. McClung Lee (ed), *Principles of Sociology* (Barnes and Noble Books, New York, 1969), pp. 67-121.

Bond, Patrick, *Elite Transition: From apartheid to neoliberalism in South Africa* (Pluto, London, 2000).

Bond, Patrick, 'Strategies for Social Justice Movements from Southern Africa to the United States', *Foreign Policy In Focus (FPIF)*, 20 January, 2005.

Bond, Patrick, *Fanon's Warning: A civil society reader on the new partnership for Africa's development* (Africa World Press, Trenton, NJ, 2005).

Bosgra, Sietse, 'From Jan van Riebeeck to solidarity with the struggle: The Netherlands, South Africa and apartheid', in SADET (South African Democracy Trust), *The Road to Democracy in South Africa*, vol. 3, part I, pp. 905-933.

Botte, Roger, 'De l'esclavage et du daltonisme dans les sciences sociales. Avant-propos', *Journal des Africanistes*, 70, 1-2 (2000), pp. 7-42.

Boyd, B., G.G. Dess & A. Rasheed, 'Divergence between archival and perceptual measures of the environment: causes and consequences,' *Academy of Management Review*, 18, 2 (1993), pp. 204-226.

Bratton, M. & N. van de Walle, 'Neopatrimonial regimes and political transitions in Africa', MSU Working Papers on Political Reform in Africa, Working Paper No. 1 (Department of Political Science, East Lansing, MI, 1993).

Bratton, M. & N. van de Walle, *Democratic Experiments in Africa: Regime transitions in comparative perspective* (Cambridge University Press, Cambridge, 1997).

Brinkman, Inge, 'Angolan civilians in wartime, 1961-2002', in John Laband (ed.), *Daily Lives of Civilians in Wartime Africa: From slavery days to the Rwandan genocide* (Greenwood Press, London, 2007), pp. 169-194.

Bryden, Matt, 'No quick fixes: coming to terms with terrorism, Islam and statelessness in Somalia', *Journal of Conflict Studies*, 23, 2 (2003), pp. 24-56.

Buhlungu, S., 'Upstarts or bearers of tradition? The anti-privatisation forum of Gauteng', in Richard Ballard, Adam Habib & Imraan Valodia (eds), *Voices of Protest: Social movements in post-apartheid South Africa* (University of KwaZulu-Natal Press, Pietermaritzburg, 2006), pp. 67-87.

Bullard, Alice, 'From colonization to globalization: the vicissitudes of slavery in Mauritania', *Cahiers d'études africaines*, 179-180 (2005), pp. 751-769.

Burawoy, M., 'For a sociological Marxism: The complementary convergence of Antonio Gramsci and Karl Polanyi', in *Politics and Society*, 31, 2 (2003), pp. 193-261.

Casey, Conerly, 'Marginal Muslims: Politics and the perceptual bounds of Islamic authenticity in northern Nigeria', *Africa Today*, 54, 3 (2008), pp. 67-92.

Cassanelli, Lee V., *The Shaping of Somali Society: Reconstructing the history of a pastoral people, 1600-1900* (University of Pennsylvania Press, Philadelphia, 1982).

Castells, M., *The Rise of the Network Society* (Blackwell Publishers, Oxford, 1996).

Chakanza, J., 'The pro-democracy movement in Malawi: The Catholic Church's contribution', in M. Nzunda & K. Ross (eds), *Church, Law and Political Transformation in Malawi, 1992-1994* (Mambo Press, Gweru, 1995), pp. 8-14.

Chirwa, W., 'Civil society in Malawi's democratic politics,' in M. Ott, K. Phiri & N. Patel (eds), *Malawi's Second Democratic Elections: Process, problems and prospects* (Kachere, Zomba, 2000), pp. 87-119.

Clark, J., *Global Civic Engagement* (Earthscan, London, 2003).

Cock, J., 'Connecting the red, brown and green: the environmental justice movement in South Africa', in Richard Ballard, Adam Habib & Imraan Valodia (eds), *Voices of Protest: Social movements in post-apartheid South Africa* (University of KwaZulu-Natal Press, Pietermaritzburg, 2006) pp. 203-224.

Cohen, Abner, *Custom and Politics in Urban Africa: A study of Hausa migrants in Yoruba towns* (Routledge & Kegan Paul, London, 1969).

College, K., *Trade Unions and the Struggle for Quality Services in Malawi* (PSI, Johannesburg, 2004).

Collier, Paul (ed.), 'Economic causes of civil conflict and their implications for policy', in *The Bottom Billion: Why the poorest countries are failing and what can be done about it* (Oxford University Press, Oxford, 2007).

Comaroff, Jean & John Comaroff, 'The struggle between the constitution and "things African"', in *The Wiser Review* (July 2004), pp. 6-7.

Comaroff, John & Jean Comaroff, 'Reflections on liberalism, policulturalism & ID-ology: Citizenship & difference in South Africa', in Steven Robins (ed.), *Limits to Liberation after Apartheid: Citizenship, governance and culture* (James Currey, Oxford, 2005), pp. 33-56.

Commission Nationale des Droits de l'Homme, *Rapport Annuel 2007-2008* (CNDH, Nouakchott, June 2008).

Conteh-Morgan, Earl, *Democratization in Africa: The theory and dynamics of political transitions* (Praeger, London, 1997).

Coton, Samuel, *Silent Terror: A journey into contemporary African slavery* (Harlem River Press, New York, 1998).

Cramer, Christopher, *Civil War is not a Stupid Thing: Accounting for violence in developing countries* (Hurst and Co., London, 2006).

Crousse, Bernard, 'La réforme foncière mauritanienne de 1983, étatisation ou individualisation', *Politique africaine*, 21 (March 1986), pp. 63-76.

Cullen, T., *Malawi: A Turning Point* (Pentland Press, Durham, 1994).

Danmole, H.O. 'Religious encounter in southwestern Nigeria: The domestication of Islam among the Yoruba', in Jacob K. Olupona & Terry Rey (eds), *Orisa Devotion as World Religion: The globalization of Yoruba religious culture* (University of Wisconsin Press, Madison, 2008), pp. 202-220.

David, Soniia, '"You become one in marriage": Domestic budgeting among the Kpelle of Liberia', *Canadian Journal of African Studies*, 30, 2 (1996), pp. 157-182.

D'Azevedo, Warren L., 'Some historical problems in the delineation of a central west Atlantic region', *Annals New York Academy of Sciences*, 96 (1962), pp. 512-538.

Della Porta, Donatella & Mario Diani (eds), *Social Movements: An introduction* (Basil Blackwell, Oxford, 1999).

Della Porta, Donatella & Mario Diani, *Social Movements: An introduction* (Blackwell, Malden/Oxford/Carlton, 2nd edition, 2006).

Della Porta, D. & S. Tarrow (eds), *Transnational Protest and Global Activism* (Rowman and Littlefield, Lanham, MD, 2005).

Della Porta, D., H. Kriesi & D. Rucht (eds), *Social Movement in a Globalizing World* (Macmillan Press, London, 1999).

Desai, A. & A. Habib, 'Labour relations in transition: the rise of corporatism in South Africa's automobile industry', *Journal of Modern African Studies*, 35, 3 (1997), pp. 495-515.

Devenish, A. & C. Skinner, 'Collective action in the informal economy: The case of the self employed women's union, 1994-2004', in Richard Ballard, Adam Habib & Imraan Valodia (eds), *Voices of Protest: Social movements in post-apartheid South Africa* (University of KwaZulu-Natal Press, Pietermaritzburg, 2006), pp. 255-277.

Diamond, L., 'Beyond autocracy: prospects for democracy in Africa', in Working Papers for the Inaugural Seminar of the Governance in Africa Program (The Carter Centre of Emory University, Atlanta, GA, 1989).

Diani, M. & D. McAdam (eds), *Social Movement Analysis: The network perspective* (Oxford University Press, Oxford/New York, 2003).

Dietrich, Christian, *Hard Currency: The criminalized diamond industry of the Democratic Republic of Congo and its neighbours* (Partnership Africa Canada, Ottawa, 2002).

Dirsuweit, T., 'The problem of identities: The lesbian, gay, bisexual, transgender and intersex social movement in South Africa', in Richard Ballard, Adam Habib & Imraan Valodia (eds), *Voices of Protest: Social movements in post-apartheid South Africa* (University of KwaZulu-Natal Press, Scottville, 2006), pp. 325-347.

Douglas, Farah, *Blood from Stones: The secret financial network of terror* (Broadway Publishers, New York, 2004).

Dulani, B. & J.K. van Donge, 'A decade of legislature-executive squabble in Malawi (1994-2004)', in M. Salih (ed.), *African Parliaments: Between Governments and Governance* (Palgrave Macmillan, London, 2005), pp. 201-224.

Duyvendak, J.W. & M. Hurenkamp (eds), *Kiezen voor de Kudde. Lichte gemeen-schappen en de nieuwe meerderheid* (Van Gennep, Amsterdam, 2004).

Dwyer, P., 'The concerned citizens forum: A fight within a fight', in Richard Ballard, Adam Habib & Imraan Valodia (eds), *Voices of Protest: Social movements in post-apartheid South Africa* (University of KwaZulu-Natal Press, Pietermaritzburg, 2006), pp. 89-110.

Dzimbiri, L.,'Democracy and chameleon like leaders', in Kings Phiri *et al.* (eds), *Democratisation in Malawi: A stocktaking* (CLAIM, Blantyre, 1998), pp. 87-101.

Egan, A. & A. Wafer, 'Dynamics of a 'mini mass movement': Origins, identity and ideological pluralism in the Soweto electricity crisis committee', in Richard Ballard,

Adam Habib & Imraan Valodia (eds), *Voices of Protest: Social movements in post-apartheid South Africa* (University of KwaZulu-Natal Press, Pietermaritzburg, 2006), pp. 45-65.

Eickelman, Dale F., 'National identity and religious discourse in contemporary Oman', *International Journal of Islamic and Arabic Studies*, 6, 1 (1989), pp. 1-20.

Eisinger, P. 'The conditions of protest behavior in American cities', *American Political Science Review*, 67 (1973), pp.11-28.

El-Hor, 'Charte constitutive' (Nouakchott, 5 March 1978) in *L'Ouest saharien-Cahiers d'études pluridisciplinaires*, 4 (L'Harmattan, Paris, 2004), pp. 183-188.

Ellemers, N., R. Spears & B. Doosje (eds), *Social Identity: Context, commitment, content* (Blackwell, Oxford, 1999).

Ellis, Stephen, 'The Okija shrine: Death and life in Nigerian politics', *Journal of African History*, 49, 3 (2008), pp. 445-466.

Ellis, Stephen & Gerrie ter Haar, *Worlds of Power: Religious thought and political practice in Africa* (C. Hurst & Co., London, 2004).

Episcopal Conference of Malawi (ECM), *Walking Together in Faith, Hope and Love* (Montfort Media, Balaka, 1999).

Episcopal Conference of Malawi (ECM), *Living our Faith: Lenten letter of the Catholic bishops to their faithful* (Montfort Media, Balaka, 1992).

Eyerman, R. & A. Jamison, *Social Movements: A cognitive approach* (Polity Press, Cambridge, 1991).

Falola, Toyin, *Violence in Nigeria: The crisis of religious politics and secular ideologies* (University of Rochester Press, Rochester, NY, 1998).

Fanon, F., *The Wretched of the Earth* (Penguin Books, Harmondsworth, 1967).

Feldman, Robert, 'Fund transfers-African terrorists blend old and new: Hawala and satellite telecommunications', *Small Wars and Insurgencies*, 17, 3 (2006), pp. 356-366.

Feldman, Robert, 'Somalia: Amidst the rubble, a vibrant telecommunications infrastructure', *Review of African Political Economy*, 113 (2007), pp. 565-572.

Fine, Gary A., 'Public narration and group culture: Discerning discourse in social movements', in H. Johnston & Bert Klandermans (eds), *Social Movements and Culture* (University of Minnesota Press, Minneapolis, 1995), pp. 127-143.

Fisher, Humphrey, *The Ahmadiyya: A study in contemporary Islam on the West African coast* (Oxford University Press for the Nigerian Institute of Social and Economic Research, London, 1963).

Fisher, Ryland, *Race* (Jacana Publishers, Johannesburg, 2007).

Fraser, Nancy, *Justice Interruptus: Critical reflections on the 'postsocialist' condition* (Routledge, New York, 1997).

Friedman, S. & S. Mottiar, 'Seeking the high ground: The Treatment Action Campaign and the politics of morality', in Richard Ballard, Adam Habib & Imraan Valodia (eds), *Voices of Protest: Social movements in post-apartheid South Africa* (University of KwaZulu-Natal Press, Pietermaritzburg, 2006), pp. 23-44.

Fuest, Veronika, *"A Job, a Shop, and Loving Business": Lebensweisen gebildeter Frauen in Liberia* (LIT Verlag, Münster, 1996).

Fuest, Veronika, *Contexts of Conflict in Southeast Liberia. A study report* (Welthungerhilfe, Bonn, 2008).

Fuest, Veronika, '"This is the time to get in front". Changing roles and opportunities for women in Liberia', *African Affairs*, 107, 427 (2008): pp. 201-224.

Fuest, Veronika, *Fruits of war? Refigurations and contestations of female identities in Liberia. Working Paper of the Max Planck Institute for Social Anthropology* (Max Planck Institute for Social Anthropology, Halle/Saale, forthcoming).

Gamson, W.A., *Strategy of Social Protest* (Wadsworth Publishing, Belmont, CA, 1990).

Gamson, W.A., *Talking Politics* (Cambridge University Press, Cambridge, 1992).

Garrett, R.K., 'Protest in an information society: A review of literature on social movements and new ICTs', *Information, Communication, and Society*, 9, 2 (2006), pp. 202-224.

Gbadamosi, T.G.O., *Growth of Islam among the Yoruba, 1841-1908* (Longman, London, 1978).

Gberie, Lansana, *Destabilizing Guinea: Diamonds, Charles Taylor and the potential for wider humanitarian catastrophe* (Partnership Africa Canada, Ottawa, 2001).

Gberie, Lansana, *War and Peace in Sierra Leone: Diamonds, corruption and the Lebanese connection* (Partnership Africa Canada, Ottawa, 2002).

Gberie, Lansana, *A Dirty War in West Africa: The RUF and the destruction of Sierra Leone* (Hurst and Co., London, 2005).

Gerhards, J. & D. Rucht, 'Mesomobilization: organizing and framing in two protest campaigns in West Germany', *American Journal of Sociology*, 98, (1992), pp. 555-596.

Gifford, Paul, *Christianity and Politics in Doe's Liberia* (Cambridge University Press, Cambridge, 1993).

Gifford, Paul (ed.), *The Christian Churches and Democratization in Africa* (Brill, Leiden, 1995).

Gilkes, Patrick, 'Briefing: Somalia', *African Affairs*, 98 (1999), pp. 571-577.

Gill, A., 'Rendering unto Caesar? Religious competition and Catholic political strategy in Latin America, 1962-79', *American Journal of Political Science*, 38, 2 (1994), pp. 403-425.

Glickman, Harvey, 'The Nigerian "419" advance fee scams: prank or peril?', *Canadian Journal of African Studies*, 39, 3 (2005), pp. 460-489.

Goodwin, J. & J.M. Jasper, 'Caught in a winding, snarling vine: The structural bias of political process theory', *Sociological Forum*, 14, 1 (1999), pp. 27-54.

Goodwin, J., J.M. Jasper & F. Polletta, *Passionate Politics: Emotions and social movements* (The University of Chicago Press, Chicago, IL, 2001).

Government of Liberia, *Act to Govern the Devolution of Estates and Establish the Rights of Inheritance for Spouses of Both Statutory and Customary Marriages* (Monrovia, 2003).

Greenberg, S., 'The landless people's movement and the failure of post-apartheid land reform', in Richard Ballard, Adam Habib & Imraan Valodia (eds), *Voices of Protest: Social movements in post-apartheid South Africa* (University of KwaZulu-Natal Press, Pietermaritzburg, 2006), pp. 133-153.

Grosse-Kettler, Sabine, *External Actors in Stateless Somalia. A war economy and it promoters*. BICC paper 39 (Bonn International Center for Conversion, Bonn, 2004).

Gurr, T., *Why Men Rebel* (Princeton University Press, Princeton, NJ, 1970).

Gusfield, J., *Protest, Reform and Revolt: A reader in social movements* (John Wiley, New York, 1970).

Habib, A. 'The politics of economic policy-making: Substantive uncertainty, political leverage, and human development', *Transformation*, 56 (2004), pp. 90-103.

Habib, A., 'South Africa: conceptualizing a politics of human-oriented development', *Social Dynamics*, 34, 1 (2008), pp. 46-61.

Habib, A. & R. Taylor, 'Political alliances and parliamentary opposition in post-apartheid South Africa', *Democratization*, 8, 1 (2001), pp. 207-226.

Habib, A. & P. Opoku-Mensah, 'Mobilizing across Africa: civil society and democratisation', in *South African Yearbook of International Affairs 2002/03* (South Africa Institute for International Affairs, 2003), pp. 267-274.

Habib, A. & I. Valodia, 'Reconstructing a social movement in an era of globalisation: A case study of the Congress of South African Trade Unions (COSATU)', in Richard Ballard, Adam Habib & Imraan Valodia (eds), *Voices of Protest: Social movements in post-apartheid South Africa* (University of KwaZulu-Natal Press, Pietermaritzburg, 2006), pp. 225-253.

Hackett, Rosalind I.J., 'Managing or manipulating religious conflict in the Nigerian media', in Jolyon Mitchell & Sophia Marriage (eds), *Mediating Religion: Conversations in media, religion and culture* (T. & T. Clark, Edinburgh, 2003), pp. 47-64.

Hackett, Rosalind I.J., 'Radical Christian revivalism in Nigeria and Ghana: Recent patterns of conflict and intolerance', in Abdullahi A. An-Na'im (ed.), *Proselytization and Communal Self-Determination in Africa* (Orbis Books, Maryknoll, NY, 1999), pp. 246-267.

Haenni, Patrick, *Islam de marché: L'autre révolution conservatrice* (Seuil, Paris, 2005).

Hahonou, Éric Komlavi, 'Cultures politiques, esclavage et décentralisation. La revanche politique des descendants d'esclaves au Bénin et au Niger', *Politique africaine*, 111 (2008), pp. 169-186.

Hardt, M. & A. Negri, *Empire* (Harvard University Press, Cambridge/Massachusetts, 2000).

Hart, Stephen, 'The cultural dimension of social movements: A theoretical reassessment and literature review', *Sociology of Religion*, 57, 1 (1996), pp. 87-100.

Harvey, D., *The New Imperialism* (Oxford University Press, Oxford, 2003).

Hassim, S., 'The challenges of inclusion and transformation: the women's movement in democratic South Africa', in Richard Ballard, Adam Habib & Imraan Valodia (eds), *Voices of Protest: Social movements in post-apartheid South Africa* (University of KwaZulu-Natal Press, Pietermaritzburg, 2006).

Haynes, J., 'Religion and democratization in Africa', *Democratization*, 11, 4 (2004), pp. 66-89.

Hazleton, Ralph, *Diamonds Forever or For Good? The economic impact of diamonds in Southern Africa* (Partnership Africa Canada, Ottawa, 2002).

Held, D., 'Democracy, the nation-state and the global system', in David Held (ed.) *Political Theory Today* (Polity Press, Cambridge, 1991), pp. 197-235.

Herrera, Linda & Asef Bayat (eds), *Being Young and Muslim* (Oxford University Press, Oxford, forthcoming in 2010).

Higazi, Adam, 'Violence urbaine et politique à Jos (Nigeria), de la période coloniale aux élections de 2007', *Politique africaine*, 106 (2007), pp. 69-91.

Hunt, Swanee & Cristine Posa, 'Women waging peace', *Foreign Policy*, May/June (2001), pp. 38-47.

Huntington, S., *The Third Wave: Democratization in the late twentieth century* (University of Oklahoma Press, Oklahoma, 1991).

Ibeanu, Okechukwu, 'Healing and changing: the changing identity of women in the aftermath of the Ogoni crisis in Nigeria', in Sheila Meintjes *et al.* (eds), *The Aftermath. Women in post-conflict transformation* (Zed Books, London, 2001), pp. 189-209.

Idang, Gordon J., 'The politics of Nigerian foreign policy: the ratification and renunciation of the Anglo-Nigerian defence agreement', *African Studies Review*, 13, 2 (1970), pp. 227-251.

Immink, B. & G. Chigona, 'Between apathy and participation: The role of civil society and faith communities', in M. Ott, B. Immink, B. Mhango & C. Peters-Berries (eds), *The Power of the Vote: Malawi's 2004 parliamentary and presidential elections* (Kachere, Zomba, 2005), pp. 139-158.

Inglehart, R., *The Silent Revolution: Changing values and political styles among Western publics* (Princeton University Press, Princeton, NJ, 1977).

International Crisis Group, *Somalia: Countering terrorism in a failed state* (ICG, Brussels, 2002).

International Crisis Group, *Somalia's Islamists* (ICG, Brussels, 2005, Africa Report no. 100).

International Crisis Group, *Somalia: The tough part is ahead* (ICG, Brussels, 2007, Africa Briefing no. 45).

International Peace Academy (IPA), Mats Berdal & David Malone (eds), *Greed and Grievance: Economic agendas in civil Wars* (Lynne Rienner, Boulder, CO/London, 2000).

Jackson, R. & C. Rosberg, *Personal Rule in Black Africa: Prince, autocrat, prophet and tyrant* (University of California Press, Berkeley, CA, 1982).

Jasper, J.M., *The Art of Moral Protest* (The University of Chicago Press, Chicago, IL, 1997).

Joseph, Richard A., *State, Conflict and Democracy in Africa* (Praeger, London, 1999).

Joseph, Richard A., *Democracy and Prebendal Politics in Nigeria* (Cambridge University Press, Cambridge, 1987).

Kamara, Ousmane, 'Les divisions statutaires des descendants d'esclaves au Fuuta Tooro mauritanien', *Journal des Africanistes,* 70, 1-2 (2000), pp. 265-289.

Kane, Ousmane, *Muslim Modernity in Postcolonial Nigeria: A study of the society for the removal of innovation and reinstatement of tradition* (Brill, Leiden, 2003).

Kaplan, Seth, 'The remarkable story of Somaliland', *Journal of Democracy*, 19, 3 (2008), pp. 143-157.

Karamé, Kari H., 'Gender mainstreaming the peace-building process', in Kari H. Karamé (ed.), *Gender and Peacebuilding in Africa* (Norsk Utenrikspolitisk Institutt, Oslo, 2004), pp. 11-26.

Karamé, Kari H. (ed.), *Gender and Peacebuilding in Africa* (Norsk Utenrikspolitisk Institutt, Oslo, 2004).

Keane, J., *Global Civil Society?* (Cambridge University Press, Cambridge, 2003).

Keck, M. & K. Sikkink, *Activists beyond Borders: Advocacy networks in international politics* (Cornell University Press, Ithaca, NY, 1998).

Klandermans, B., 'Mobilization and participation: social-psychological expansions of resource mobilization theory', *American Sociological Review*, 49, 5 (1984), pp. 583-600.

Klandermans, B., *The Social Psychology of Protest* (Blackwell, Oxford, 1997).

Klandermans, B., 'The demand and supply of participation: Social-psychological correlates of participation in social movements,' in D.A. Snow, S.A. Soule & H. Kriesi (eds), *The Blackwell Companion to Social Movements* (Blackwell, Oxford, 2004).

Klandermans, B., H. Kriesi & S. Tarrow (eds), *From Structure to Action: Comparing social movement research across cultures* (JAI Press, Greenwich, CT, 1988).

Klandermans, B., J. van der Toorn & J. van Stekelenburg, 'Embeddedness and grievances: Collective action participation among immigrants', *American Sociological Review*, 73 (2008), pp. 992-1012.

Koopmans, R., 'Political. Opportunity. Structure. Some splitting to balance the lumping', *Sociological Forum*, 14, (1999), pp. 93-105.

Koopmans, R., 'The missing link between structure and agency. Outline of an evolutionary approach to social movements', *Mobilization*, 10 (2005), pp. 19-36.

Kornhauser, W., *The Politics of Mass Society* (The Free Press, London, 1959).

Kriesi, H. & D. Wisler, 'Direct democracy and social movements in Switzerland', *European Journal of Political Research*, 30 (1996), pp. 19-40.

Kriesi, H., R. Koopmans, J.W. Duyvendak & M. Giugni, *New Social Movements in Western Europe* (University of Minnesota Press, Minneapolis, MN, 1995).

Kurzman, Charles, 'Conclusion: Social movement theory and Islamic studies', in Quintan Wiktorowicz (ed.), *Islamic Activism: A social movement theory approach* (Indiana University Press, Bloomington, 2004), pp. 289-303.

Lachenmann, Gudrun, 'Civil society and social movements in Africa: The case of the peasant movement in Senegal', *The European Journal of Development Research*, 5, 2, (1993), pp. 68-100.

Last, Murray, 'Towards a political history of youth in Muslim Northern Nigeria 1750-2000', in Jon Abbink & Ineke van Kessel (eds), *Vanguard or Vandals: Youth, politics and conflict in Africa* (Brill, Leiden, 2005), pp. 37-54.

Last, Murray, 'Muslims and Christians in Nigeria: An economy of political panic', *The Round Table: The Commonwealth Journal of International Affairs*, 96, 392 (2007), pp. 605-616.

Le Sage, Andre, 'Prospects for Al Itihad and Islamist radicalism in Somalia,' *Review of African Political Economy*, 28, 89 (2001), pp. 472-473.

Leservoisier, Olivier, '"Nous voulons notre part!" Les ambivalences du mouvement d'émancipation des Saafaalbe Hormankoobe de Djéol (Mauritanie)', *Cahiers d'études africaines*, 179-180 (2005), pp. 987-1014.

Lewis, Ioan M., 'Dualism in Somali notions of power', *Journal of the Royal Anthropological Institute*, 93 (1963), pp. 109-116.

Lewis, Ioan M., *A Modern History of Somalia: Nation and State in the Horn of Africa* (Westview Press, Boulder, 1988).

Lewis, Peter, 'From prebendalism to predation: The political economy of decline in Nigeria', *Journal of Modern African Studies*, 34, 1 (1996), pp. 79-103.

Leys, Colin, *The Rise and Fall of Development Theory* (James Currey, Oxford, 1996).

Lincoln, Bruce, *Holy Terrors: Thinking about religion after September 11* (University of Chicago Press, Chicago, 2003).

Lindorfer, Simone, *Assessment Report Liberia. Sexual and gender-based violence in Grand Gedeh, River Gee and Sinoe* (2 to 30 November 2005) (Medica mondiale, Monrovia, 2005).

Loimeier, Roman, *Islamic Reform and Political Change in Northern Nigeria* (Northwestern University Press, Evanston, IL, 1997).

Loimeier, Roman, 'Patterns and peculiarities of Islamic reform in Africa', *Journal of Religion in Africa*, 33, 3 (2003), pp. 237-262.

Lonsdale, J., 'Moral ethnicity and political tribalism', in P. Kaarsholm & J. Hultin (eds), *Inventions and Boundaries: Historical and anthropological approaches to the study of ethnicity and nationalism*, Institute of Development Studies, Occasional Paper 11 (Roskilde University, Roskilde, 1994), pp. 131-150.

Lwanda, J., *Kamuzu Banda of Malawi: A study in promise, power, and paralysis* (Dudu Nsomba Publications, Glasgow, 1993).

Lwanda, J., *Promises, Politics and Poverty: Democratic transition in Malawi* (Dudu Nsomba Publications, Glasgow, 1996).

Maimbo, Samuel M., (ed.), *Remittances and Economic Development in Somalia - An Overview* (World Bank, Washington, DC, 2006).

Mamdani, Mahmood, *Citizen and Subject: Contemporary Africa and the legacy of late colonialism* (Princeton University Press, Princeton, NJ, 1996).

Mamdani, Mahmood & Ernest Wamba-dia-Wamba (eds), *African Studies in Social Movements and Democracy* (Codesria, Dakar, 1995).

Marchal, Roland, 'Islamic political dynamics in the Somali civil war', in: A. de Waal (ed.), *Islamism and its Enemies in the Horn of Africa* (C. Hurst & Co., London, 2004), pp. 114-145.

Marchesin, Philippe, *Tribus, ethnies et pouvoirs en Mauritanie* (Karthala, Paris, 1992).

Marshall-Fratani, Ruth, 'Mediating the global and the local in Nigerian Pentecostalism', *Journal of Religion in Africa*, 28 (1998), pp. 278–315.

Marshall, Ruth A., *Political Spiritualities: The explosion of Pentecostalism in Nigeria* (Chicago University Press, Chicago/London, 2009).

Marty, Marianne, 'Les multiples usages de l'Islam dans le champ politique mauritanien', in Cédric Mayrargue (ed), *L'Afrique politique 2002. Islams d'Afrique: Entre le local et le global* (Karthala, Paris, 2003), pp. 51-68.

Marwell, G. & P. Oliver, *The Critical Mass in Collective Action: A micro-social theory* (Cambridge University Press, Cambridge, 1993).

Mattes, R. & R. Southall, 'Popular attitudes toward the South African electoral system', *Democratization*, 11, 1 (2004), pp. 51-76.

Mbembe, A., *On the Postcolony* (University of California Press, Berkeley/LA, 2001).

McAdam, D., *Political Process and the Development of Black Insurgency, 1930-1970* (The University of Chicago Press, Chicago, IL, 1982).

McAdam, D., *Freedom Summer* (Oxford University Press, New York, 1988).

McCarthy, J. & M.N. Zald, *The Trend of Social Movements in America: Professionalization and resource mobilization* (General Learning Corporation, Morristown, NJ, 1973).

McCarthy, J.D. & M.N. Zald, 'Resource mobilization and social movements: A partial theory', *American Journal of Sociology*, 82, 6 (1977), pp. 1212-1241.

McAdam, D., J. McCarthy & M.N.Zald, *Comparative Perspectives on Social Movements* (Cambridge University Press, Cambridge, 1996).

McAdam, D., J. McCarthy & M.N. Zald (eds), *Political Opportunities, Mobilizing Structures, and Cultural Framings* (Cambridge University Press, New York, 1996).

McAdam, D., S. Tarrow & C. Tilly, *Dynamics of Contention* (Cambridge University Press, Cambridge/New York, 2001).

McAdam, D., S. Tarrow & C. Tilly, 'Comparative perspectives on contentious politics', in M. Lichbach & A. Zuckerman (eds), *Ideas, Interests and Institutions: Advancing theory in comparative politics* (Cambridge University Press, Cambridge, 2007).

McDougall, E. Ann, 'A topsy-turvy world: Slaves and freed slaves in the Mauritanian Adrar, 1910-1950', in S. Miers & R. Roberts (eds), *The End of Slavery in Africa* (University of Wisconsin Press, Madison, WI, 2005), pp. 362-390.

McDougall, E. Ann, 'Living the legacy of slavery: between discourse and reality', *Cahiers d'études africaines*, 179-180 (2005), pp. 957-986.

McKinley, D., 'The rise of social movements in South Africa', in *Debate: Voices from the South African left*, May 2004, pp. 17-21.

McKinley, D. & P. Naidoo, 'New Social Movements in South Africa: A story in creation', *Development Update*, 5, 2 (2004), pp. 9-22.

Meagher, Kate, 'Manufacturing disorder: Liberalization, informal enterprise and economic governance in African small firm clusters', *Development and Change*, 38, 3 (2007), pp. 473-503.

Medard, J-F., 'The underdeveloped state in tropical Africa: Political clientelism or neo-patrimonialism?', in C. Clapham (ed), *Private Patronage and Public Power: Political clientelism in the modern state* (Frances Pinter, London, 1982), pp. 162-192.

Melucci, A., *Challenging Codes* (Cambridge University Press, Cambridge, 1996).

Melucci, A., *Nomads of the Present: Social movement and identity needs in contemporary society* (Temple University Press, Philadelphia, PA, 1989).

Mengisteab, K. & C. Daddieh, *State Building and Democratization in Africa: Faith, hope, and realities* (Praeger, London, 1999).

Mercer, John, *Slavery in Mauritania today* (Anti-Slavery International, London, 1981).

Messaoud, Boubacar, 'Esclavage en Mauritanie: De l'idéologie du silence la mise en question', *Journal des Africanistes*, 70, 1 (2000), pp. 291-337.

Meyer, D., and S. Tarrow (eds), *Towards a Movement Society? Contentious politics for a new century* (Rowman and Littlefield, Boulder, CO, 1998).

Mitchell, L., 'Living our Faith: The Lenten letter of the bishops of Malawi and the shift to multi party democracy, 1992-1993', *Journal for the Scientific Study of Religion*, 41, 1 (2002), pp. 5-18.

Molyneux, Maxine, 'Mobilization without emancipation? Women's interests, the state, and revolution in Nicaragua', *Feminist Studies*, 11, 2 (1985), pp. 227-254.

Moore, Henrietta, 'The differences within and the differences between', in T. del Valle (ed.), *Gendered Anthropology* (Routledge, London, 1993), pp. 193-219.

Moran, Mary H. 'Collective action and the "representation" of African women: A Liberian case study', *Feminist Studies*, 15, 3 (1989), pp. 443-460.

Moran, Mary H., *Civilized Women: Gender and prestige in southeastern Liberia* (Cornell University Press, Ithaca, N.Y., 1990)

Moran, Mary H., *Liberia. The violence of democracy* (University of Pennsylvania Press, Philadelphia, 2006).

Moran, Mary H. & Anne Pitcher, 'The "basket case" and the "poster child": Explaining the end of civil conflicts in Liberia and Mozambique', *Third World Quarterly*, 25, 3 (2004), pp. 501-519.

Moser, Caroline O.N. & Fiona C. Clark, *Victims, Perpetrators or Actors? Gender, armed conflict and political violence* (Zed Books, London/New York, 2001).

Muluzi, B., Y. Juwayeyi, M. Makhambera & D. Phiri, *Democracy with a Price: The history of Malawi since 1900* (Jhango Heinemann, Blantyre, 1999).

NASFAT, *Code of Conduct* (NASFAT Society, Lagos, 2005).

Newell, J., 'A moment of truth? The church and political change in Malawi', *Journal of Modern African Studies*, 33, 2 (1995), pp. 243-262.

Ngoma-Leslie, A., *Social Movements and Democracy in Africa* (Routledge, New York, 2006).

Norris, P., S. Walgrave & P. van Aelst, 'Who demonstrates? Anti-state rebels, conventional participants, or everyone?', *Comparative Politics*, 37, 2 (2005), pp. 189- 205.

North, D., *Institutions, Institutional Change and Economic Performance* (Cambridge University Press, New York, 1990).

Nzogola-Ntalaja, G., 'Citizenship, political violence and democratization in Africa', *Global Governance*, 10 (2004), pp. 403-409.

Nzunda, M. & K. Ross, *Church, Law and Political Transformation in Malawi, 1992-1994* (Mambo Press, Gweru, 1995).

O'Brien, Susan, 'La charia contestée: Démocratie, débat et diversité; musulmane dans les "États charia" du Nigeria', *Politique africaine*, 106 (2007), pp. 46-68.

O'Donnell, Guillermo, 'On the state, democratization and some conceptual problems: A Latin American view with glances at some Post-Communist countries', *World Development*, 21, 8 (1993), pp. 1355-1369.

O'Donnell, G. & P. Schmitter, *Transitions From Authoritarian Rule: Tentative conclusions about uncertain democracies* (John Hopkins University Press, Baltimore, 1986).

O'Maille, P., *Living Dangerously: A memoir of political change in Malawi* (Dudu Nsomba, Glasgow, 1999).

Obadare, Ebenezer, 'White-collar fundamentalism: Interrogating youth religiosity on Nigerian university campuses', *Journal of Modern African Studies*, 45, 4 (2007), pp. 517-537.

Obi, C., 'Environmental movements in sub-Saharan Africa: A political ecology of power and conflict, civil society and social movements. United Nations Research Institute for Social Development. Programme Paper 15, January 2005.

Offiong, Daniel A., *Secret Cults in Nigerian Tertiary Institutions* (Fourth Dimension, Enugu, 2003).

Olayode, Kehinde, 'Pro-democracy movements, democratisation and conflicts in Africa: Nigeria, 1990-1999', *African Journal of International Affairs*, 10, 1-2 (2007), pp. 127-146.

Oldfield, S. & K. Stokke, 'Building unity in diversity: Social movement activism in the Western Cape anti-eviction campaign', in Richard Ballard, Adam Habib & Imraan Valodia (eds), *Voices of Protest: Social movements in post-apartheid South Africa* (University of KwaZulu-Natal Press, Pietermaritzburg, 2006), pp. 111-132.

Olonisakin, Funmi, 'Women and the Liberian civil war', *African Woman*, March-September (1995), pp. 19-24.

Olupona, Jacob K. & Terry Rey (eds), *Orisa Devotion as World Religion: The globalization of Yoruba religious culture* (University of Wisconsin Press, Madison, 2008).

Olzak, Susan, 'Ethnic and nationalist social movements', in: David A. Snow, Sarah A. Soule & Hanspeter Kriesi (eds), *The Blackwell Companion to Social Movements* (Blackwell/Malden, Oxford/Carlton, 2004) pp. 666-693.

Otayek, René, 'Introduction: des nouveaux intellectuels musulmans d'Afrique noire', in René Otayek (ed.), *Le radicalisme islamique au sud du Sahara: Da'wa, arabisation et critique de l'Occident* (Karthala, Paris, 1993), pp. 8-18.

Otayek, René & Benjamin F. Soares, 'Introduction: Islam and Muslim politics in Africa', in Benjamin F. Soares & René Otayek (eds), *Islam and Muslim Politics in Africa* (Palgrave Macmillan, New York, 2007), pp. 1-24.

Ould Ahmed Salem, Zekeria, 'Sur la formation des élites politiques et la mobilité sociale en Mauritanie', *Nomadic Peoples*, 2, 1-2 (1998), pp. 253-276.

Ould Ahmed Salem, Zekeria, 'La Centralité de la mobilisation tribale dans l'action politique en Mauritanie: Une illusion bien fondée?', *L'Ouest Saharien*, 2 (1999), pp. 127-156.

Ould Ahmed Salem, Zekeria, 'La démocratisation en Mauritanie, une illusion postcoloniale?', *Politique africaine*, 75 (October 1999), pp. 131-146.

Ould Ahmed Salem, Zekeria, 'Droit du statut personnel et équivalence citoyenne en République Islamique de Mauritanie. Le cas du mariage', *La Pensée*, 336 (2003), pp. 37-53.

Ould Ahmed Salem, Zekeria (ed.), *Les trajectoires d'un État-frontière. Espaces, évolutions politiques et transformations sociales en Mauritanie* (Codesria, Dakar, 2004).

Ould Ahmed Salem, Zekeria, 'Mauritania, a Saharan frontier state', *Journal of North African Studies*, 10, 3-4 (2005), pp. 491-506.

Ould Cheikh, Abdel Wedoud, 'L'évolution de l'esclavage dans la société maure', in E. Bernus & P. Boilley (eds), *Nomades et commandants. Administration et sociétés nomades dans l'ancienne AOF* (Karthala, Paris, 1994), pp. 181-193.

Ould Saleck, El Arby, 'Les Haratin comme enjeu pour les partis politiques en Mauritanie', *Journal des Africanistes*, 70, 1 (2000), pp. 255-263.

Ould Saleck, El Arby, *Les Haratins. Le paysage politique mauritanien* (L'Harmattan, Paris, 2003).

Patel, N., 'Media in Malawi's democratic transition', in M. Ott, K. Phiri & N. Patel, (eds), *Malawi's Second Democratic Elections: Process, problems and prospects* (Kachere Series, Zomba, 2000), pp. 158-185.

Patterson, Orlando, *Slavery and social death* (Harvard University Press, Cambridge, MA, 1982).

Peel, J.D.Y., 'Olaju: A Yoruba concept of development', *The Journal of Development Studies*, 14 (1978), pp. 135-165.

Peel, J.D.Y., 'The pastor and the babalawo: The interaction of religions in nineteenth-century Yorubaland', *Africa*, 60, 3 (1990), pp. 338-369.

Peel, J.D.Y., *Religious Encounter and the Making of the Yoruba* (Indiana University Press, Bloomington, 2000).

Pithouse, Richard, 'Solidarity, co-option and assimilation: The necessity, promises and pitfalls of global linkages for South African movements', *Development Update*, 5, 2 (2004), pp. 169-199.

Piven, F.F. & R.A. Cloward, *Poor Peoples' Movements: Why they succeed, how they fail* (Random House, New York, NY, 1977).

Polanyi, K., *The Great Transformation* (Beacon Press, Boston, 1957).

Press, R., *Peaceful Resistance: Advancing human rights and democratic freedoms* (Ashgate, Aldershot, 2006).

Przeworski, A., *Sustainable Democracy* (Cambridge University Press, Cambridge, 1997).

Puechgirbal, Nadine, 'Involving women in peace processes: Lessons learnt from four African countries (Burundi, DRC, Liberia and Sierra Leone)', in Kari H. Karamé (ed.), *Gender and Peacebuilding in Africa* (Norsk Utenrikspolitisk Institutt, Oslo, 2004), pp. 47-66.

Putnam, R., *Making Democracy Work: Civic traditions in modern Italy* (Princeton University Press, Princeton, NJ, 1993).

Quirk, Joel, *Unfinished Business: A comparative survey of historical and contemporary slavery* (UNESCO, Paris, 2008).

Reichmuth, Stefan, 'The modernization of Islamic education: Islamic learning and its interaction with 'Western' education in Ilorin, Nigeria', in Louis Brenner (ed.), *Muslim Identity and Social Change in Sub-Saharan Africa* (Indiana University Press, Bloomington, 1993), pp. 179-197.

Reichmuth, Stefan, 'Education and the growth of religious associations among Yoruba Muslims: the Ansar-Ud-Deen Society of Nigeria', *Journal of Religion in Africa*, 26, 4 (1996), pp. 365-405.

Reichmuth, Stefan, *Islamische Bildung und soziale Integration in Ilorin (Nigeria) seit ca. 1800* (LIT Verlag, Münster, 1998).

Reno, William, *Warlord Politics and African States* (Lynne Rienner Publishers, Boulder, CO, 1998).

Report of the Monitoring Group on Somalia pursuant to Security Council resolution 1676 (2006), UN document S/2006/913.

Report of the Monitoring Group on Somalia pursuant to Security Council resolution 1676 (2006), UN document S/2007/436.

Report of the Monitoring Group on Somalia pursuant to Security Council resolution 1766(2007), UN document S/2008/274.

Rheingold, H., *Smart Mobs: The next social revolution* (Perseus, Cambridge, MA, 2002).

Robins, Steven L. (ed.), *Limits to Liberation after Apartheid: Citizenship, governance and culture* (James Currey, Oxford, 2005).

Rodney, Walter, *How Europe Underdeveloped Africa* (Bogle-L'Ouverture Publications, London, 1972).

Ross, K., 'The Transformation of Power in Malawi, 1992-94: The role of the Christian churches,' in Ross K. (ed.), *God, People and Power in Malawi: Democratization in theological perspective* (CLAIM, Blantyre, 1996).

Roy, Olivier, *The Failure of Political Islam* (Harvard University Press, Cambridge, MA, 1994).

Roy, Olivier, *Globalised Islam: The search for a new ummah* (Hurst, London, 2004).

Rudnyckyj, Daromir, 'Market Islam in Indonesia', *Journal of the Royal Anthropological Institute* (N.S.), 15, s1 (2009), pp. 182-200.

Ruf, Urs Peter, *Ending Slavery: Hierarchy, dependency and gender in central Mauritania* (Transcript Verlag, Bielefeld, 1999).

Runciman, W.G., *Relative Deprivation and Social Justice* (Routledge, London,1966).

Rustomjee, C., 'From economic debt to moral debt: The campaigns of jubilee South Africa', in Richard Ballard, Adam Habib & Imraan Valodia (eds), Voices of Protest:

Social movements in post-apartheid South Africa (University of KwaZulu-Natal Press, Pietermaritzburg, 2006) pp. 279-300.

Ryan, Patrick J., *Imale: Yoruba participation in the Muslim tradition, a study of clerical piety* (Scholars Press, Missoula, MT, 1978).

Salih, M., *Environmental Politics and Liberation in Contemporary Africa* (Kluwer Academic Publishers, London, 1999).

Sall, Ebrima, 'Social movements in the renegotiation of the bases for citizenship in West Africa', *Current Sociology*, 52, 4, (2004), pp. 595-614.

Samatar, Said S., 'Unhappy masses and the challenge of political Islam in the Horn of Africa', *Horn of Africa*, 20, (2002), pp. 1-10.

Sanni, Amidu, 'Challenges and realities in the healing and power accession custom of the Yoruba Muslims of Nigeria', *Journal of Oriental and African Studies*, 15 (2006), pp. 145-156.

Saul, John S., *The Next Liberation struggle: Capitalism, socialism and democracy in Southern Africa* (University of KwaZulu-Natal Press, Scotsville, 2005).

Sawyer, Amos, *The Emergence of Autocracy in Liberia. Tragedy and challenge* (Institute for Contemporary Studies, San Francisco, 1992).

Schedler, A., 'Taking uncertainty seriously: The blurred boundaries of democratic transition and consolidation', *Democratization*, 8, 4 (2001), pp. 1-22.

Seibel, Hans D. & Andreas Massing, *Traditional Organizations and Economic Development. Studies in indigenous cooperatives in Liberia* (Praeger Publishers, New York, 1974).

Sindima, H., *Malawi's First Republic: An economic and political analysis* (University Press of America, New York, 2002).

Smelser, N.L., *Theory of Collective Behavior* (The Free Press, London, 1962).

Smillie, Ian, 'The Kimberley Process: The case for proper monitoring'. Occasional Paper 5 (Partnership Africa Canada, Ottawa, 2002).

Smillie, Ian, Lansana Gberie & Ralph Hazleton, 'The Heart of the Matter: Sierra Leone, diamonds and human security' (Partnership Africa Canada, Ottawa, 2000).

Smith, Christian, 'Correcting a curious neglect, or bringing religion back in', in: C. Smith (ed.), *Disruptive Religion. The force of faith in social movement activism* (Routledge, New York, London, 1996), pp. 1-25.

Snow, D.A., E.B. Rochford, S.K. Worden & R.D. Benford, 'Frame alignment processes, micromobilization, and movement participation', *American Sociological Review*, 51 (1986), pp. 464-481.

Snow, D.A. & P. Oliver, 'Social movements and collective behavior: social psychological considerations and dimensions', in K.S. Cook, G.A. Fine & J.S. House (eds), *Sociological Perspectives on Social Psychology* (Allyn and Bacon, Boston, MA, 1995).

Snow, David A. & Doug McAdam, 'Identity Work Processes in the Context of Social Movements: Clarifying the identity/movement nexus', in S. Stryker, T. Owens & R.W. White (eds), *Self, Identity and Social Movements* (University of Minnesota Press, Minneapolis, 2000), pp. 41-67.

Snow, D.A., S.A. Soule & H. Kriesi (eds), *The Blackwell Companion to Social Movements* (Blackwell Publishing, Oxford, 2004).

Soares, Benjamin F. (ed.), *Muslim-Christian encounters in Africa* (Brill, Leiden, 2006).

Soares, Benjamin F. & René Otayek (eds), *Islam and Muslim Politics in Africa* (Palgrave Macmillan, New York, 2007).

Soares, Benjamin & Filippo Osella, 'Islam, politics, anthropology', *Journal of the Royal Anthropological Institute* (N.S.), 15, 1 (2009), pp. 1-23.

Soyinka, Wole, *Cults: A people in denial* (Interventions III, Bookcraft, Ibadan, 2005).

Stewart, Charles C., 'Une interprétation du conflit sénégalo-mauritanien', *Revue du Monde Musulman et de la Méditerranée*, 54, 1 (1989), pp. 161-170.

Stryker, S., T.J. Owens & R.W. White (eds), *Self, Identity, and Social Movements* (Minnesota Press, Minneapolis, MN, 2000).

Sy, Yaya, 'L'esclavage chez les Soninkés: du village Paris', *Journal des Africanistes*, 70, 1-2 (2000), pp. 43-69.

Tadesse, Medhane, *Al-Ittihad: Political Islam and Black Economy in Somalia* (Mega Printing, Addis Ababa, 2002).

Tajfel, H. & J.C. Turner, 'An integrative theory of intergroup conflict', in S. Worchel & W.G. Austin (eds), *The Social Psychology of Intergroup Relations* (Brooks/Cole, Monterey, CA, 1979), pp. 33-47.

Tamuno, Tekena & Robin Horton, 'The changing position of secret societies and cults in modern Nigeria', *African Notes*, 5, 2 (1969), pp. 36-62.

Tarrow, S., *Democracy and Disorder: Protest and politics in Italy 1965-1975* (Clarendon Press, Oxford, 1989).

Tarrow, S., *Power in Movement: Social movements, collective action and politics* (Cambridge Press, New York, 1994).

Tarrow, S., *Power in Movement: Social movements and contentious politics* (Cambridge University Press, Cambridge, 1998).

Tarrow, S., 'Bridging the quantitative-qualitative divide', in H. E. Brady and D. Collier (eds), *Rethinking Social Inquiry: Diverse tools, shared standards* (Rowman and Littlefield, Lanham, MD, 2004), pp. 171-180.

Tarrow, S. & D. McAdam, 'Scale shift in transnational contention', in D. della Porta & S. Tarrow (eds), *Transnational Protest and Global Activism* (Rowman and Littlefield, Lanham, MD, 2005).

Taylor, Rupert, *Creating a Better World: Interpreting global civil society* (Kumarian Press, Bloomfield, 2005).

Taylor, Verta, 'Mobilizing for change in a social movement society', *Contemporary Sociology*, 29, 1 (2000), pp. 219-230.

Tilly, Charles, *From Mobilization to Revolution* (Addison-Wesley, Reading, MA, 1978).

Tilly, Charles, 'Social movements and national politics', in C. Bright & S. Hardine (eds), *Statemaking and Social Movements: Essays in history and theory* (University of Michigan Press, Ann Arbor, MI, 1984).

Tilly, Charles, *The Contentious French* (The Belknap Press of Harvard University Press, Cambridge, MA, 1986).

Tilly, Charles, 'From interactions to outcomes in social movements', in: M. Giugni *et al.* (eds), *How Social Movements Matter* (University of Minnesota Press, Lanham, MD, 1999), pp. 253-270.

Tilly, Charles, *Social Movements, 1768–2004* (Paradigm Publishers, Boulder, CO/London, 2004).

Tonkin, Elizabeth, 'Model and ideology: dimensions of being "civilised" in Liberia', in L. Holy & M. Stuchlik (eds), *The Structure of Folk Models*. ASA Monograph 20 (Academic Press, London, 1981), pp. 307-330.

Touraine, A., *The Voice and the Eye: An analysis of social movements* (Cambridge University Press, Cambridge, 1981)

Tyler, T.R. & H.J. Smith, 'Social justice and social movements', in D.T. Gilbert & S.T. Fiske (eds), *Handbook of Social Psychology*, 4th ed. (McGraw-Hill, Oxford, 1998), pp. 595-629.

Umar, Muhammad Sani, 'Education and Islamic trends in Northern Nigeria: 1970s-1990s', *Africa Today*, 48, 2 (2001), pp. 127-150.

Umar, Muhammad Sani, 'Profiles of new Islamic schools in Northern Nigeria', *The Maghreb Review*, 28, 2-3 (2003), pp. 145-169.

United Nations Joint Logistics Center, NGO-SPAS, 'Somalia - security update, report no. 44/06', 26 Oct.-1 Nov. 2006).

UNRISD, *Transformative Social Policy Lessons from UNRISD Research*, UNRISD Research and Policy Brief 5 (2006).

Van Kessel, Ineke, *'Beyond our Wildest Dreams': The United Democratic Front and the transformation of South Africa* (University Press of Virginia, Charlottesville/London, 2000).

Van Stekelenburg, J. & B. Klandermans, 'Individuals in movements: A social psychology of contention', in B. Klandermans & C.M. Roggeband (eds), *The Handbook of Social Movements Across Disciplines* (Springer, New York, 2007), pp. 157-204.

Van Stekelenburg, J., B. Klandermans & W.W. van Dijk, 'Context matters: Explaining why and how mobilizing context influences motivational dynamics', *Journal of Social Issues* (forthcoming, 2009).

Walsh, E.J., 'Resource mobilization and citizen protest in communities around Three Mile Island', *Social Problems*, 29, 1 (1981), pp. 1-21.

WANEP & WIPNET, *Women's National Agenda for Peace, Security and Development in Post-War Liberia*. Adopted 30th March 2006 (Women in Peace Network, Monrovia, 2006).

Wellman, B., 'The network community', in B. Wellman (ed.), *Networks in the Global Village* (Westview, Boulder, CO, 1999), pp. 1-48.

Whiteford, A. & D.E. Van Seventer, 'South Africa's changing income distribution in the 1990s', *Studies in Economics and Econometrics*, 24, 3 (2000), pp. 7-30.

Wiktorowicz, Quintan (ed.), *Islamic Activism: A social movement theory approach* (Indiana University Press, Bloomington, IN, 2004).

Wiktorowicz, Quintan, 'Introduction: Islamic activism and social movement theory', in Q. Wiktorowicz (ed.), *Islamic Activism: A social movement approach* (Indiana University Press, Bloomington, IN, 2004), pp. 1-36.

Wilmot, Patrick, *Nigeria: The nightmare scenario* (Interventions VI, Bookcraft and Farafina, Ibadan and Lagos, 2007).

Young, Crawford, 'Contextualizing Congo conflicts', in John F. Clark (ed.), *The African Stakes in the Congo War* (Fountain Publishers, Kampala, 2002).

Young, I.M., *Justice and the Politics of Difference* (Princeton University Press, Princeton, 1990).

Young, I.M., *Inclusion and Democracy* (Oxford University Press, Oxford, 2000).

List of authors

Jon Abbink is a senior researcher at the African Studies Centre Leiden, where he heads the research group on 'Social Movements and Political Culture in Africa'. He is also Professor of African ethnic studies at the Department of Anthropology, VU University, Amsterdam. His research interests are political change and religious culture in Northeast Africa, ethnicity in Africa, and the anthropology and history of Ethiopia, subjects on which he published widely.
abbink@ascleiden.nl

Boniface Dulani is a Lecturer in Political Science at the University of Malawi, Chancellor College, Zomba. He has published on government and democracy in Africa, the role of civil society and faith based organizations in democracy, public sector reforms and elections. He is currently finishing his PhD in Comparative African Politics at Michigan State University on the topic of presidential term limits in Africa's new democracies.
ntwee2002@yahoo.co.uk

Stephen Ellis is a senior researcher at the African Studies Centre, Leiden, and Desmond Tutu professor in the Faculty of Social Sciences at the VU University, Amsterdam. He has published on a wide variety of African countries including Liberia, Madagascar, Nigeria and South Africa. His most recent book, co-authored with Solofo Randrianja, is *Madagascar: A Short History* (C. Hurst & Co., London).
ellis@ascleiden.nl

Veronika Fuest works as adviser for research development in the humanities and social sciences at the University of Göttingen, Germany. As a previous member of various research projects at different institutes she has published on a range of topics including various aspects of Liberian society, management of water resources in Ghana and practices of cooperative research. Her most recent work constitutes a continuation of her PhD research on women's social and economic strategies in pre-war Liberia.
V.Fuest@gmx.de

Lansana Gberie is an academic and writer, and is the author of *A Dirty War in West Africa: The RUF and the Destruction of Sierra Leone* (C. Hurst & Co., London, 2005). Gberie was a key researcher for Partnership Africa Canada's Human Security and International Diamond Trade project (PAC). He was co-author of *The Heart of the Matter: Sierra Leone, Diamonds and Human Security* (Ottawa, 2000). He has since authored many reports and studies for the

Project, and was editor of the Sierra Leone Annual Diamond Review published by PAC.
lagberie@yahoo.com

Adam Habib is Deputy Vice-Chancellor Research, Innovation and Advancement at the University of Johannesburg, South Africa. He has published extensively on the South African transition particularly in the thematic areas of democratisation, political economy, civil society and foreign policy. His recent co-edited books are *Voices of Protest: Social Movements in Post-Apartheid South Africa* (University of Natal Press, 2006), and *Racial Redress and Citizenship in Contemporary South Africa* (Cape Town, HSRC Press, 2008).
ahabib@uj.ac.za

Bert Klandermans is Professor in Applied Social Psychology at the VU University, Amsterdam. He has published extensively on the social psychology of participation in social movements and is the editor of Social Movements, Protest, and Contention, a book series published by the University of Minnesota Press. His publications include *Social Psychology of Protest* (Blackwell, 1997) and the co-edited volumes *Methods of Social Movement Research* (University of Minnesota Press, 2002), *Extreme Right Activists in Europe* (Routledge, 2006), and *Handbook of Social Movements Across Disciplines* (Springer, 2007).
PG.Klandermans@fsw.vu.nl

Paul Opoku-Mensah is an Associate Professor of Development and International Relations at Aalborg University, Denmark, and the Deputy Director of the Comparative Research Programme on NGOs, University of Bergen, Norway. His writings include "the State of Civil Society in sub-Saharan Africa" (in *Comparative Perspectives on Civil Society,* Kumarian, 2007); *Reconceptualising NGOs and their roles in Development (2007,* lead editor), and *NGOs and the Politics of African Development: The Ghanaian Experience* (VDM, 2009).
paulom@ihis.aau.dk

Zekeria Ould Ahmed Salem is Professor of Political Science at the University of Nouakchott, Mauritania. Recent publications include "Islam in Mauritania between Political Expansion and Globalization: Elites, Institutions, Knowledge, and Networks", in B. Soares and R. Otayek, eds., *Islam and Muslim Politics in Africa,* (Palgrave Macmillan, 2007); "Mauritania: A Saharan Frontier State", *The Journal of North African Studies*, Volume 10, Issue 3/4, September 2005, pp. 491–506. He is the editor of *Les trajectories d'un Etat-frontière – Espaces, evolution politique et transformations sociales en Mauritanie*, Dakar, Codesria, 2004.
zakariadenna@yahoo.fr

Benjamin Soares, an anthropologist, is a senior researcher at the African Studies Centre in Leiden. His publications include *Islam and the Prayer Economy* (Edinburgh University Press, 2005) and the co-edited volumes, *Islam, Politics, Anthropology* (Wiley-Blackwell, 2009) and *Islam and Muslim Politics in Africa* (Palgrave MacMillan, 2007).
bsoares@ascleiden.nl

Ineke van Kessel is a senior researcher with the African Studies Centre, Leiden. She has published extensively on anti-apartheid resistance in South Africa – notably *'Beyond our Wildest Dreams': The United Democratic Front and the Transformation of South Africa* (University of Virginia Press, 2000) – as well as on socio-political developments in post-apartheid South Africa.
kessel@ascleiden.nl

Jacquelien van Stekelenburg is a post-doc researcher at the Sociology Department of the VU University, Amsterdam. Her publications focus on the social psychological dynamics of moderate and radical protest participation with a special interest in group identification, emotions and ideologies as motivators for action. In 2006 she defended her PhD thesis entitled *Promoting or Preventing Social Change. Instrumentality, identity, ideology and groups-based anger as motives of protest participation.*
J.van.Stekelenburg@fsw.vu.nl

AFRICAN DYNAMICS

ISSN 1568-1777

1. Bruijn, M. de, R. van Dijk and D. Foeken (eds.). *Mobile Africa.* Changing Patterns of Movement in Africa and Beyond. 2001.
   ISBN 978 90 04 12072 6
2. Abbink, J., M. de Bruijn and K. van Walraven (eds.). *Rethinking Resistance.* Revolt and Violence in African History. 2003.
   ISBN 978 90 04 12624 4
3. Van Binsbergen, W. and R. van Dijk (eds.). *Situating Globality.* African Agency in the Appropriation of Global Culture. 2004.
   ISBN 978 90 04 13133 7
4. Abbink, J. and I. van Kessel (eds.). *Vanguard or Vandals.* Youth, Politics and Conflict in Africa. 2005. ISBN 978 90 04 14275 4
5. Konings, P. and D. Foeken (eds.). *Crisis and Creativity.* Exploring the Wealth of the African neighbourhood. 2006. ISBN 978 90 04 15004 8
6. Bruijn, M. de, R. van Dijk, and J-B. Gewald (eds.). *Strength beyond Structure.* Social and Historical Trajectories of Agency in Africa. 2007.
   ISBN 978 90 04 15696 8
7. Rutten, M., A. Leliveld and D. Foeken (eds.). *Inside Poverty and Development in Africa.* Critical Reflections on Pro-poor Policies. 2008.
   ISBN 978 90 04 15840 5
8. Ellis, S. and I. van Kessel (eds.). *Movers and Shakers.* Social Movements in Africa. 2009. ISBN 978 90 04 18013 0